The Dream Of Th

The Dream Of The Decade

Afshin Rattansi

The Dream of the Decade
The London Novels

The Dream of the Decade
Reproach
A Taste of Money
Good Morning, Britain

Copyright © 2005 Afshin Rattansi

Published in the United States of America in 2005

ISBN 1-4196-1686-2

Library of Congress Control Number: 2005909384

BookSurge, LLC
North Charleston, South Carolina

To order additional copies, please contact us.
BookSurge, LLC
www.booksurge.com
1-866-308-6235
orders@booksurge.com

"The crisis consists precisely in the fact that the old is dying and the new cannot be born; in this interregnum a great variety of morbid symptoms appears."

Antonio Gramsci, Prison Notebooks.

"I can still feel the force of it, as a passing gale."
ChristopherMacLehose, Collins Harvill.

"I admired it, particularly the pace and atmosphere." Christopher
Sinclair-Stevenson, Sinclair Stevenson Ltd.

"We enjoyed it." Maggie McKernan, Editorial Director, Jonathan
Cape Ltd.

"..enjoyed it.." Tim Binding, Penguin Books.

"He captures the atmosphere of the late 8os." Dan Franklin, Martin
Secker and Warburg.

"Interesting and involving." Laura Longrigg, William Heinemann
Ltd.

Picture Credits
Cover Photo by Shihab Rattansi
Plate 1 Calle, Tina Modotti, 1926
Plate 2 Pacific Marine Environmental Laboratory
Plate 3 London Hotel by Author
Plate 4 George Grosz, Blood Is the Best Sauce (The Communists
Fall, Inflation Rises), 1920
Plate 5 After Paul Strand

The Dream Of The Decade

For Zarin, Piyo and Shihab
But many others, too.

"...A society that has conjured up such gigantic means of production and of exchange, is like the sorcerer, who is no longer able to control the powers of the nether world whom he has called up by his spells."
Karl Marx and Friedrich Engels, 1888.

Kathleen's Prologue
Dhidhoofinolhu, South Ari Atoll, Republic of Maldives
Christmas Day, 2004

It's been two decades since he's been gone. I'd lie if I said that I'd been thinking about him every day.

There are the children to look after. There's been all the tooing and froing. After twenty years, it really does all seem a dream. London in the nineteen-eighties was revolutionary, charged up, constantly varying. I couldn't even show photos of myself to the children from way back then. To their eyes I would look artificial in those strange dresses and hairstyles. What happened to puffball skirts, anyway?

This has been hardly a rare separation from my husband, Alex. But there's something about being dumped with the children while he goes to even greater lengths making our life comfortable that makes me remember how I first met him. He's busy working on business projects in the Gulf and up to Iraq, of all places and it's all for me and the children. The Maldives beach huts here are any woman's fantasy of a desert island and spending Christmas 2004 with the kids will be a memory we shall share for ever. If only Alex was here with us!

I can walk from one side of South Ari Atoll to another in just thirty seconds. And the water is so shallow I don't even have to worry about the children. The food is irritating but I suppose I didn't come here for the food. The whole thing was Alex's idea. He's been doing business as far East as Indonesia and he said it would be better here than being cooped up in the flat, back home. Here we have our own island and the funny sounding name of Dhidhoofinolhu to laugh at.

Of course, I do worry about what Alex is up to. But he says things are much better in places like Baghdad than the television pictures would make us believe. I try and stop the children watching the satellite in our room, instead encouraging them to swim, sunbathe and play badminton.

I did ask to go to Baghdad with him. He said he was living in a gorgeous mansion. It's either safe or it isn't, after all. But he said he didn't want the children there. I love him but that didn't sound straight with me. Men never are straight with their wives in my experience, though.

I brought the following papers here with me on a sudden whim. We'd been tidying the loft and when I saw them in an old trunk, I put them together in a binder and felt unfaithful when I packed them in my son's suitcase.

Life, as you will see, was even more glamorous then. Alex was certainly doing much better. It was all before the nineties property crash that did for him and us. And then there were those dotcoms. Hopefully, the work in Iraq will get us up to speed—even to the levels we enjoyed back in 1986.

It's strange how I've lost touch with everyone in the story except for Alex. Or perhaps that's the same with everyone and their friends from 1986. I wonder what Julie is doing?

The two children are fighting with the Bangladeshi waiter over the food again. They are so fussy. My son is writing a school project about the environment and the erosion of coral reefs here. Right now, I turn my head and look at them. I can see them, my feet still in the glittering turquoise of the Indian Ocean. They are little people bathed in palm frond light and they have so much confidence, confidence that I gained later than them when I was careering around California working for weapons laboratories.

Nothing can touch us here. Not his dreams of decades or his interconnectedness obsessions.

"I'm just coming. Shut up, the both of you!" I holler before turning back to the glorious ripples and waves.

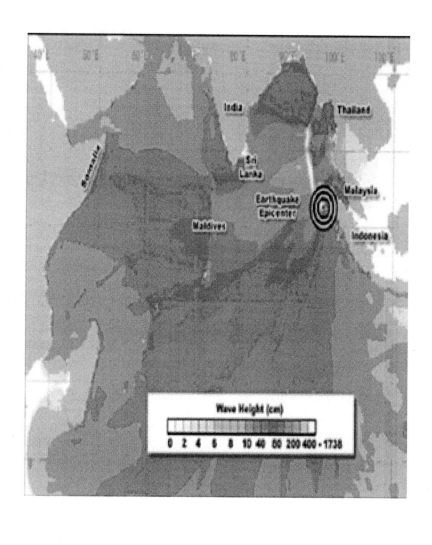

I
Los Angeles, California, U.S.A.
The Mid-Nineteen-Eighties.

Every time I use that brand of hairspray my hair becomes all sticky. Anyway, I get on with what I'm doing, staring into the mirror and puckering up my lips. I think I look pretty good. Yesterday I lay on the sun-bed for a couple of hours, then had a swim in Tony Pakula's pool—he lives up in Bel Air and is kind of cute looking, but everyone's after him—and then I played tennis with Marsha. She's supposed to be my best friend but last week she went off to see the latest Hockneys at the Getty with my boyfriend (well, kind of boyfriend) and the next I knew it she was jumping into the sack with him.

I don't really have many friends but then everyone else had a head start. They either picked up their cliques at USC or else found their friends at work. I only moved out here about eight years ago and being British I didn't really fit in. Sure, people liked me a lot, the boys seemed to think I was something different to the usual Californian blondes and sure I picked up the accent and even a little well worn Californian slang. But I missed England, or rather London, and yet I couldn't get up enough courage to leave. Los Angeles is like that, the heat, the luxury, the affluence trap you until you don't dare chuck it all up because of some longing to be back in the mother-country. Mind you, recently I've been picking up some of that courage; one of these days I'm returning, as the blues' song goes. I've learnt a lot here, a lot of useful things that I could use in London to my advantage. You see for all its affluence, LA is a very tough city. Once you've survived it, a wimp capital like London is a walk-over.

Some whacky artist is having an art-opening at The Stock Exchange III club tonight. The club's been re-launched quite a few times; the last opening party was great. I met a couple of English guys there and had them both before they left. 'Having' people is something everyone does over here. As long as you have the money or the looks (I have the latter) you can 'have' as many people as you so desire.

When I first came to LA everyone said I should try my luck at acting or modelling. I met a few producers that were interested but in the end it was me that decided that the starlight wasn't my cup of tea. I'm six feet tall, eyes of blue with a nose that my friends call retrouseé and long hazel-brown hair that has to be cut every three weeks. I drive a car called a Rabbit and every morning I work out at the gym opposite my apartment in Santa Monica. Santa Monica is where a lot of Brits settled and parts of it, like Ocean Avenue, look out onto the Pacific. When I first came to the city, the weather was cloudy (LA is often cloudy, something to do with all the smog that rises around its inhabitants, whether it be BO or Giorgio) and I thought, as I walked down Santa Monica pier, that this place was a little like Brighton. The pier has a run-down fair that has dilapidated bumper-cars and merry-go-rounds all staffed by Mexican losers trying to earn a living. The food's not the same as cockles, eels and fish 'n' chips but every time I felt a little homesick, I went down there, sitting on the wooden shafts and looking at the sun slowly set over the ocean.

After working out and having a shower I usually leave for work. The graphics design office I toil at is in a tower that's part of Century City. A lot of young successful executives work there but they're all really stuffy so I'm glad to leave at the end of the day. The work is interesting though. Back in England I used my artistic abilities on record covers and the layouts for underground newspapers; I was quite a rebel at the time. Now I use electronic gadgets like mice and graphic tablets to do really important things. At the moment, I'm working on an aesthetic design for missile nose-cones. After I finish with the project, designing the cone like a Michelangelo phallus, the scientists take it and see what small changes need to be made to put it into operation. And then, voila, out come 3,000 nuclear warheads with my name on them. Next week, we're beginning a really good project, related to the American Strategic Defence Initiative—that means a lot of money and very little work.

Anyway, back to tonight. It's pretty dark outside and I can see lots of Hopperesque hamburger and hot-dog joints raking lots of money. Most of LA seems to be office blocks now, apart from certain districts like Melrose, the equivalent, I suppose to Chelsea's King's Road. Driving in Downtown LA is something else entirely. Here the buildings are much taller than anywhere else but they lie between huge slums. I've never been down there but a friend of mine who was making an anti-drug commercial (which is funny in itself since he deals most of the coke that we take) said that it was terrible down there. He said that it was just thousands and thousands of Blacks and Mexicans sleeping in tents, if they were lucky, but more often than not just on the warm tarred streets. For me, the only danger is the five yard walk from the car park. I walk it uneasily, usually there's someone with me but tonight it's just me listening to the sound of my stilettos and a few car horns. There's a beggar on the street but he looks pretty harmless. I pass him and he shouts something I don't understand before I'm one of fifty or so people crowding around the door to the club. There are bright yellowy spotlights and a red carpet and two bouncers, one of whom I know really well. When I first came here I was pretty innocent and as I was trying to get into the Bamboozle Club (now closed down, which is a great pity), I thought I had to fuck the bouncer to get in. It wasn't a bad night either. He was looking after his boss's house in Palisades and we must have got through twenty bottles of Californian champagne. He was really fat, even for a bouncer. I can't remember his name now but I think I used to go for fat men back then, just for the sake of it.

"Hey it's me, Kathleen!" I shout not expecting to be heard above the din but, surprisingly, the guy looks straight at me and acknowledges my presence, making way for me in the crowd and kissing me on the cheek. His breath smells of peppermints which isn't a bad thing to smell of but as soon as I get on the red carpet I run upstairs, not wanting to get to close to the guy.

Upstairs, I look for the faces I know.

"Kathleen! It's me, Jonathan Alford the second," says a small man in turtle-shell glasses. I try to ignore him but he keeps pestering me for a dance. Thinking I should give some charity I say yes and lead him onto the huge dance-floor that's buzzing with bombshells and tall, dark handsome men. For a while I dance with John and then, seeing a blonde man with sparkling teeth I saunter towards him, edging closer and closer. He's wearing a Rolex but since Marsha never succeeded in teaching me how to tell a fake from the real thing I don't know he's rich. But then, as I establish eye-contact, I notice that his jacket seems to fan out as he dances—I can just make out the Armani label. It may not be a Brioni but it's good enough for me.

When the Prince track stops, he motions me to his table. Behind me, though I don't see her until I sit down, is an angry Californian babe. The man just smiles, apparently she's his sister and she's angry because she told her brother to bring some of the Gauloise Blondes that they got from Paris and he forgot them. He looks at me and smiles like he's saying "sorry, my sister had a bad childhood," (who didn't?) and then really says "what's your name?"

"Kathleen, what's yours?" I say, flickering my eyelashes and wanting this guy.

"My name's Andy, like Warhol," he says idiotically—I still want him. "Would you like some coke?"

"Sure," I reply before we get up and go to one of the outer bars where most people are cutting lines without any shame. When we sit down I'm not sure what to do, you see, I have a bit of a cold at the moment and my nose is clogged up with this gunge. Anyway, I sniff it all up and it seems to go OK. I'm dying to blow my nose, though, but I restrain myself.

Andy has disgusting hands, huge big ones like halibuts. I notice that his sister has to do most of the cutting and that she looks after the stuff. She's better looking than Andy too, but I couldn't stand the trouble tonight.

"It's good snow, ain't it?" he asks. I can hear his voice now, really tinny, like a young boy, even though he must be over thirty. I reply with a nod. "What do you do?"

"I'm from England, out on holiday," I always reply the same way so as to avoid saying I'm a graphic designer which might be construed as a little boring and I instead give the impression that I'm a one-night-stand-type-of-girl, free easy and just waiting helplessly for a holiday romance.

"Yeah? I knew a girl from England once. She ripped me off, stole some things from my apartment and...oh if I could get a hold of her," he flexed his halibuts.

"Terrible, I know English girls are a bit weird that way."

"You've got quite an American accent—how long have you been out here?" asks the sister, who's been eyeing up boys and chewing on a straw for the past few minutes.

"Not long, I guess I learn pretty quickly. What do you do, Andy?" I say turning back to Andy. The music is loud, the atmosphere sweaty, the girl sexily brushing off wisps of her blonde hair that momentarily cover up her facial features—but I won't go for her tonight.

"I'm a businessman, I work in computers mostly, buying and selling,"

There was an uneasy pause after his remark before I took the initiative and bent over and whispered into his ear: "Are you going to get rid of that sister of yours?" Suddenly, he got up and asked me to dance.

"Louisa, we're going to be quite a while, OK?" Andy said but Louisa had a far-away look in her eyes and nodded the same way she would have if Andy had said that he was ordering a large olive and anchovy pizza.

The DJ was only playing fast songs and so after a couple of tracks I edge closer to Andy and pull him towards me.

"Hey you English girls are pretty quick, aren't you?" he said.

"Come on, let's go."

I had him in the proverbial palm of my hand, leading him away like an idiot. On the way out I saw some of my friends but I ignored them. I just wanted to have Andy. There was no particular reason, he seemed a nice enough person—one couldn't tell anyway after only an hour or so of small talk—but as always Kathleen wanted a screw to pep her up. I told him I'd follow his car, a horrible old Chevy that he said he was borrowing while his Porsche was getting fixed. I didn't believe him but stared at his number-plate 'KICK' for about ten kilometres. Presumably, someone had already chosen 'KICKS' so he had to make do with a meaningless verb stuck on his fender instead.

We parked outside his apartment block and kissed on the pavement. I pulled away. I didn't want to kiss this guy, I wanted something other than his tongue inside me. I was even crying a little as I tried to make him understand. His apartment was on the top floor, a nice, cosy place with brilliant views of the constantly changing freeways dominating each room—it would have looked even better if he had the sense to call an interior decorator. Still, we were alone and there was a bedroom in the house so I sat down and waited for him to serve some wine. There's one piece of advice that I have to give any English people who come over here and that is not to touch the wine. Californian wine is by and large crap and most glasses I get I pour into the azaleas. Stick to the spirits or the wonderful choice of beers in this state. Anyway, by now I'm undressing him, pulling his trousers down as he escapes from his jacket. Once he's down to his boxers I push him onto the sofa.

"No," he says as my heart flutters but he only wants us to go to the bedroom. It's quite a nice room too, a promo poster from on of David Lynch's films on the wall and the strong scent of Ralph Lauren Polo aftershave in the air. I kiss him on the chest and lower him down on the bed, unbuttoning my 501s and pulling a flimsy T-shirt over my head. He smiles, he gapes looking like a complete moron as I pull down my panties and lay on him as I pull them off my ankles. I can feel him really big against me and from the corner of my eye I can see a pack of condoms on a table. He knows I've seen them too and thinks I probably want to use one.

"Come on," I say, relaxing him a bit, holding his thing as he enters me. I try to look away when we're pushing and pulling, I look around the room, at the furniture, the objects. I can see a matt black side-table adorned by some back-issues of Gentleman's Quarterly. He kneads my breasts with his big halibuts as I notice a couple of telephone directories. Digging my nails into his shoulders, I look out of the window at the thousands of reds and yellows that make up the freeway traffic. I try to focus on one of them, a light surrounded by darkness, a big lorry maybe. I follow it and just as it fades away I feel him come and then I climax too, like I always do.

2

London, England.

arly June has no boundaries." This is what I wrote, one night, looking over a city stooped in the lights of fast cars. It was an apartment, high above all the whoring and spitting lower down, all the way to street level. One in the morning and while high heeled shoes hit the pavement below all that occupied my mind was the temperature of the coffee I had forgotten about. It had lain on the window sill while my mind wandered and imagined, looking upwards from the dense black park and into a light orange sky. I ignored the merging lights of yellow and red, they sat in the corner of my eye. It was the black silhouettes of the trees against a wash that coloured the sky that seemed so much more calming. It's true that I hadn't forgotten the luxury of the fragrant leather seats that had brought me here but all I felt, as I looked over a city provoking so many cold emotions, was that I was alone. The green telephone behind me matched my eyes and seldom rang, only sitting as if it was a vase or a souvenir from a far-away place. I put my hand against the glass like a child, then took it away to see the imprint of the harsh lines that scarred the palm and the fingers. The old pencil and the white paper-pad lay on the stately brown rug below me. I thought, quite suddenly, of a walk I had taken in that park when I was ten or twelve. Then I was so much more fascinated by the setting sun and the immediate brightening of street illumination. I turned around, I remember, looking back towards the street and took great pleasure in the space that was left in the middle of such a complicated and crowded city. But that was a long time ago, then I had parents that could take me for walks and show me all the wonderful things that I now never see. Then, at least, I was interested—I remember the uninhibited emotion and the smiles that came from the heart. Then, there were no filters to my mind, only an ocean of trust that would never stir to the fact that these fantastic mazes of streets and lights, that these strange, tall buildings all waved such loneliness.

I was dressed in jeans and a blue jumper, walking and seeming so confident. I expected the love and I thought it would never end. And now, so long after those walks, I stare at what I think was my path and realise that those people, who showed me so much, have gone. It doesn't matter that they never saw my successes, that they couldn't even hope that one day I would be looking out from the top of one of the tall buildings getting all sentimental and upset. I wasn't upset, my face had none of those contortions, but I felt and I felt deeply and that's what matters now.

I took only a last glimpse, tightening my dressing gown, before pulling the string that closed and finished the image that never tired me. I reached behind the curtains briefly and pulled the cup of coffee carefully towards me before I drank the cold coffee in gulps, like medicine. Air-conditioned and smelling faintly of cologne, the room darkened with a switch and I went to sleep with the nearly silent murmur of traffic, so many storeys below. It was always there, every night, but it would never be a comfort that there were so many people all around me, travelling, sleeping, walking. That soft murmur was not the murmur of people, it was the murmur of a giant machine ticking away like the rails under a slow train. I left the coffee on the bed-side, unable to drink anymore, only feeling, as my head rested on the clean, hotel pillow, that I could cry from all this loneliness.

3

I was unaccustomed to sleepless nights and had recently taken to thinking about my past. This 'reviewing' of my life sometimes lulled me to sleep, at others it angered me.

I remember that house in which I was first brought into the world, 1960 it was, and with parents who were proud and relatively simple. My father, the accountant who came back from work full of stories about his small firm, would smoke cigarettes as if he wanted to leave this world as quickly as possible. I don't think he really loved my mother, more put up with her. He wanted to buy gadgets and technological fancies, wanted to buy useless antiques as she steadfastly held to the purse strings. My father and I felt like conspiratorial schoolboys, he buying me a chocolate bar and I feeling, as I ate it, that I was doing something secretive and not a little illegal.

All in all, it was a happy childhood. The cramped semi' in South London was strong enough not to crash down on us when there was a particularly heavy rain. I received lots of attention, too, what with being the only child. My mother was the one who influenced me more, however. She had great ambitions for her son. Though a little spoilt, I was always told of the value of hard work. My mother would act the devil as I was walked back from school. "Wouldn't you like that car?" or "Wouldn't you like that bike?" would be greeted with anxious nods before she said "well you're going to have to work extra hard at your studies."

Then, fuelled with ambition and optimism, everything collapsed. At the age of ten both my parents were killed in one of my father's second-hand cars. Possibly, my mind is playing tricks on me but I am sure that I can remember him fixing that old Ford Anglia for months on end. He'd come in, covered in grease, his armpits sweating through his shirt and my mother would raise her eyes as if in a kitchen sink drama, telling him that we would start without him if he didn't wash quickly.

The deaths, understandably, were a shock to me. The closeness in our family was to the exclusion of outsiders and with my only real relationships ended, I was to be looked after by an uncle that I had seldom met before. It was terrible at that house, he being a trendy liberal and not understanding life the way I was brought up to. He was a lecturer at the nearby polytechnic which marked him out as middle class. I survived those eight years, leaving school, bumming around, getting nowhere before making my greatest decision. I was going to work myself up from tea-boy to executive in two years.

The decision was a long time in the making. I had been learning to play the guitar, experimenting with the newly available drugs and even getting involved in radical politics — if nothing else than to make more friends. But this was a bad crowd, a group of middle class no-hopers that would have made my mother ashamed of me. Punk was happening in London and there was degree of excitement in the air and the little of my uncle's teaching that I was taken in by helped me to start work at an underground magazine. It was all adolescent stuff but out of all of it came someone special.

I haven't seen Kathleen for a long time. She very quickly realised the futility of the political games we played. I had known her a year when she left for Los Angeles.

She's a couple of years older than me and what I would call firmly upper class. When we first went out together I thought her accent was put on, up until I met her friend who also had this special kind of speech impediment. She was a little like one of the cars my mother tempted me with, something shiny, expensive. Something I could own if only I could afford it — if I worked hard enough. People, however, were more complicated than internal combustion engines and one day in autumn, she left.

She wasn't that rich, either — she didn't get on with her

parents and all the inheritance was going to her younger brother. She had a lot of contacts from her school and that together with hard work and charm got her places. I presume that she's not worrying about dimes and dollars in America.

As for me, I worked damn hard. The most wonderful thing about capitalism is that no matter how down you are, you can always get up again. All it takes is motivation, commitment and a little intelligence. I wanted the car and the luxury that went with it and I worked for it all. And now, I'm lying between silk sheets and wondering whether to have bacon and eggs or caviar and champagne for breakfast while my lazy fellow students at my grammar school are either claiming unemployment benefit or working themselves into early graves.

And yet, for all my successes, I am still not satisfied. I can't sleep at night, I'm lonely and I don't like the car much anymore. Perhaps, these are the symptoms of success or perhaps there is something wrong with me. Yes, I think there must be something wrong with me.

4

My mum used to tell me that the harder I work at present, the less I'll have to work in the future. She was right, of course. Working harder than everyone else in the past means that I have very little or no work to do in the present or future.

I have few friends but the ones I do have are very close. It's a mark of my friendships that even though I see them so often (we have more leisure time than most) we never argue or disagree. My best friend is Osman. He was at school with me, many years ago. I didn't know him very well back then but ever since we started working at the same firm we've become very close. Financially, he's not as secure as me but this doesn't affect our relationship—even though he started out with much more money. Osman is always confident, something he must have got from his family. He has never had to worry about a 'roof over his head' and had he not decided to work, would probably have made more money with a good stockbroker.

We go out a lot together. In the hotel suite, I have very little to do. I don't particularly like watching films or listening to music so the technological fancies that my father would have killed for lie idle. The only person that does use them is the maid, and of course Osman who chose the various electronic objects. But usually, we go out to bars and cafés, something that he loves more than anything else.

Osman takes great care over his appearance. His brown hair is meticulously slicked back and his complexion is cared for by a plethora of men's skincare products. He does all of this for a reason: girls in the bars we patronise love him for it. I've always found it surprising. For all his preening, his shoulders slope rather badly, his teeth are badly stained and his eyes are always the same dustbin-grey.

When Osman is busy, I usually sit in my room doing nothing. A year or two ago, I used to take a keen interest in the Stock Exchange, speculating on USM companies and sometimes winning a tidy profit. The hobby was time-consuming, a quality I required. But, once, I got severely burned on some bonds. That put me off the whole thing. Nowadays, I can sit for hours at a time in my room, looking out of the window, waiting for morning to come. The mornings are marginally happier for me. I work for three or four hours at the office, supervising and signing. It is during that time that I have a chance at forgetting my overriding unhappiness and my all-consuming sense of worthlessness.

5

It is morning and the green telephone rings at last. But it is only a short message, never telling me *why* I should wake up, only that I should. My mouth aches with the ashen flavours of fatigue, ready for orange juice; something, at least, to touch the emotions and work hard at the senses and finally wake me up. The chore of waking up, with its attendant shaving and brushing, done, I draw back the curtains to see the shocking grey sky and the dull colours now showing up against an image of a thousand cars. The thousand candles of the brake lights are insignificant in the light. Now, it seems no longer a vision evoking long-past experience but instead a motionless society living the losses of my dreams.

And, again, another intrusion. I feel cynical this morning; even though the intrusion is welcome I make myself hate it. The room-service trolley slides along the carpet, the boy's eyes glazed with indifference, waiting for tips and nothing else. It's no wonder that the sight of a man in a dressing gown prompts frowns — dressing gown pockets seldom carry change.

By the time I had felt sick and over eaten, sensing the grease of the frying pan, hundreds of feet below, I had seen the morning's troubles. 'The words of journalists seem so cold when you've just woken up,' I thought.

I left the room, confident and adorned by the cool fabrics and cuts of St. Laurent. The gentle cologne did nothing to pierce the air around me and I was glad to finally touch the pavement that I had thought so sordid the night before. The man in the silly hat, so quick to please, brought me my car. And all for a few more of those chunky coins.

I lean onto the seats that give little way, leather shined and comfy. The chauffeur knew where he was to go—it was my chauffeur. And all the while, as I sat watching streets and drivers and then trees, I felt so unfulfilled, so wasted. Sitting like a child again, my facial expressions rose from a still frantic amazement at the cold, desolate city around me. Hard stone outside, bricks that could make you bleed, broken glass that could kill you, and all so close to my protected car. When I leave the hotel I am always touched by fear. People don't respect individuals who have become successful though their hard work. I read about muggings and crime rates in the paper and fear holds me rooted. I fear even the short distances between myself and such a godforsaken society with such little respect. I try and smile, do they have anything to respect me for? I just exploited them all before they could exploit me. I rest my hand on the door hand-rest, still crouching and looking upwards. The windows are tinted, there is no need to avert my staring eyes because of the sharp sunlight that is breaking.

And what staring eyes! The city never fails to interest and amaze me. I am both terrified by it and drawn in by it. I see an old man selling newspapers. But again, I am wandering at a pace too far for my years. 'Age, the great divider and source of a lifetime of misapprehensions and indecisions.' I become scared again and miss a few views while I think about how unconfident I have become. The car stops and he opens the door for me and my entry into a great restaurant that is gilded by mirrors.

The doorman glances with recognition as I glide on a mattress of air, arriving at my table to meet my dining partner. Her blonde hair is flicked back and forth countless times over her scalp. The hair is bleached and I sit studying the menu, trying to evade her hardly precocious flirting. She has a sore throat and I, a fever.

"Hello, how are we today?" she asks, lighting a light cigarette, "you look rather pale." She says the word 'pale' softly; as if she was asking whether a person was for sale.' The mistake is ironic as it is her that is for sale, not me. She is one of a number of directors of a rival agency. Over the past few months, we have sat at this table discussing my company's take-over bid, with no apparent success.

"I didn't sleep that well," I reply, becoming conscious of the semi-classical muzak that's filtering in from hidden speakers, "I think I have a slight fever," I say, trying not to make it seem as if I am craving pity.

"It must be jet lag," she smiled as if it's funny and as if the fatigues caused by flight are a part of a status symbol, as if my tired eyes and my visa stamps are like a platinum card.

"Yes, that must be it," I say slowly, a trick I learnt. It gives one's partner the air of confidence in you, even if you agree to please.

I look around at the restaurant, a collection of tables and chairs set in a room anchored in one inch thick carpets and walls with vulgar paintings of the nineteenth century. Not even a leather-bound menu decorates the table, just stainless steel cutlery and white cotton napkins in tall glasses.

"You look so serious, why don't you relax sometimes? I know a great masseur, you should visit him. He's great for relieving stress. I think he has a sister who does it too," she says, touching my fingertips like they were Braille. She always makes the same caress before checking her affections and reflections in the sharp knife beside her.

"Yes, maybe I will. Look, I do feel rather ill, can we postpone today," I pause and think about what I say, "how about next week? I think I have to go and lie down," I was grateful to my mind and my mouth for their confidences. The bid will have to wait.

It's only when I get to the office that I begin to feel better.

Work was booming. My teams were fetching new multimillion clients at the rate of a couple per day. Companies yearned to change their image, their marketing, their public relations and their advertising campaigns. It was as if, exhausted of imagination, surface only could be the profit panacea.

Whilst the view from my office windows wasn't as deranged as from my room, my coffee breaks were still consumed by it. It was on just such a break, my eyes tired from looking at storyboards, accounts and due diligence forms from legal that I heard a commotion outside the door to my office. Three very tired looking black women, overweight and each of them in grey sweatpants and dour coloured baggy T-shirts had entered my space.

Susie, the temp who had been working exclusively as my PA bit her shoddily drawn lip. She was just a foot behind them. Over their shoulders, I could make out a certain office pause as three teams most directly in my line of vision stopped what they were doing to peer over at my open door and at each other.

"Sir," said one of the women. She was slightly fatter than the other two and had dyed her hair a muddy orange colour.

"It's fine," I said to Susie over the heads of them.

She smiled nervously. "Sorry about that," she squeaked, her petite frame and red V-neck, turning and receding as she went to her desk to finish her crossword.

"Hello sir," she was edgy, this woman with the muddy hair. The other two stood quietly to the left of her, looking about the room, eyes tracing an arc. "We are from the cleaning contractor company."

"You're coming in too early!" I laughed, sitting back behind my desk and leaning back on the chair's universal joint.

"Well, we had to come in now. We want you to help us. It's about the company."

I looked down at a board for our new orange juice account. A cartoon orange introduced himself in the first frame and in the second he was kicking a similar but pock-marked, flabby, greenish orange character, explaining that there was a purer, non-homogenized way to process juice.

"The cleaning contracts are in the hands of the freeholders of the building. There's nothing I can do about it, I'm afraid. It's out of my hands. We pay them and they pay you."

The other two shuffled half a yard from their spokeswoman. There was a silence that suggested there was more at stake here than when I was firing a thirty year old for not winning enough new work.

"They won't listen to us at all. You have to help."

"Look, mister, please. Just listen to me. They want to cut our rate. We each do three buildings."

"It's terrible what's happening."

I realised that I recognized one of the petitioners. I had often worked late before we moved to these new premises. I must have thrown an empty paper cup into one of her open rubbish bags. I remembered faces.

"What is your rate?" I asked, avoiding eye contact as I spoke, instead turning to the cartoon orange and wondering if the client sold lime juice, of how the green colour conflicted with the overall concept.

She revealed a figure far below any tax threshold.

"What do you want me to do?"

They began to open up, sometimes all three overlapping each other. They explained a predicament it took me some quarter-hours to understand. And I was interrupted by a couple of phone calls. Like everywhere in London, but more especially in the financial City, buildings were populated by different armies at night. Once the most ambitious office worker switched off the last functioning photocopies and left for a single pint or a half hour of evening television news, thousands of the poor flooded in for twelve hours work.

This impromptu meeting set me thinking. I hadn't registered the lives of our cleaners since the time I was working later and later nights, ascending the ladder by a quiet, subtle stealth. My head was full off the new accounts as they spoke of poor cleaning materials, harsh punishments for lateness and merciless understaffing policies. There was no sick pay, no paid overtime and no pension. I decided to help them.

We were anyway interested in purchasing more office space from the freeholder and the dozy non-executive board would never understand the reasons for dubious increase in cleaning costs.

I did get strange glances in the main open plan area of the office. I hadn't gone as far as backing unionisation but I had organised the doubling of the women's hourly rates. I'm sure that if I was an office junior and my boss had done such a thing I would have been vaguely motivated by the decision. But a new hardness had become the vogue.

I never, of course, saw the three supplicants again. I was gone from the office by the time they arrived. But in the mornings I sensed that my desk was tidier, the wall charts less dusty. The morning after the next salary day, a sorry-looking plant sat on my desk. With it was a huge thank you card with the signatures of one hundred women. It was nice. But it made me feverish.

Back to the car, back to the seats, back to telling the driver to move as fast and as far away as he can. My fever is raging and as the car picks up speed I see a succession of blurred images, restaurants, clothing shops, airline offices and crowds of people.

I remember the first time I had one of my 'mini-attacks'. It was during one of our raucous board meetings. Even when I was well, the participants seemed annoyed at being lectured to by a young upstart. Having to order people around who are twice your age is only one of the problems associated with early success. And then, when they see you spluttering and being carried out on a stretcher, you think that there's no point in this act. What's the point, you might as well face up to it—you're weak.

My driver knows that today is my weekly engagement with my analyst and drives me there accordingly

6

I've never respected my analyst and maybe that is the problem. Whenever I see him, I recall my doctor's advice. "See him, it'll do you good." After that, he launched into a long discourse about the misconceived notion of the social stigma attached to seeing a psychiatrist. He told me not to worry: "A psychiatrist checks the mental, a doctor checks the physical." And then, when I saw my one, this child of Freud, languishing in an expensive armchair, I noticed the similarity between him and my doctor. It turns out that they are brothers and in this way they enjoy an enormous extra income.

I walk into his hallway and upstairs into his sitting room, a room stifled by Englishness. The only un-English objects were to be found on the walls, drawings he called them. On my right is a meaningless scrawl having no conceivable tradition in any school of modern art; the other on my left is similar. They are freehand mind-diagrams, artwork penned by the doctor's patients. And now, as I descend into his ketchupy sofa, the classic stages of Freud begin to fill my mind, if not his mind. I look across his mahogany desk, on it are placed papers and ink-pots unused. Out of the window I see the neighbours, both rich, foreign banks.

"And how are we feeling today?" he asks, he always asks.

"Not too good, I'm afraid," I look to the floor. I am afraid of him more like.

"What's the problem—memories again?"

"Yes, memories," I say, emphasising my consonants, causing my speech to noticeably differ from his cool-cut public school accent, serene and emotionless.

"What memories?"

I become conscious of the different pronunciation again. My fever seems to have subsided though.

"My mother and father...again. I told you about it last time. I just have this great loss, that I wanted *them* to see my success, I wanted them to see I worked just as they told me to and now I have the things that they taught me to yearn for."

"What things?" he asks, picking up an amber pencil from his desk. I'm in his grip, now. He'll ask me about Oedipal relationships very soon.

"Cars, hi-fi, gadgets...things people like."

"But you said that they taught you to yearn for them."

"Well, maybe I would have wanted them anyway—everyone likes sports' cars."

"Yes," he replied, for a second following my gaze and looking out of the window. His Ferrari was parked outside on a forecourt.

The analyst provokes a little more. "Sometimes, I just think it's because I'm young, that I still need my parents."

"Yes, yes...everyone requires parents, a sense of belonging and all that," he's trying to look for signs, signs of complexes that are scattered across hundreds of volumes that line the room, "brandy?"

"No, thank you."

"You won't mind if I have one?" he asks before I motion for him to go ahead.

"So you're saying that your parents not so much as taught you but pointed you in the right direction," I nod, "and then you followed that direction," I nod, "and now you want to...er...you want *them* to see that you've made it."

Pause.

"Well, that's not too irrational a view. I myself wanted..." he stops. Psychiatrists aren't supposed to talk about themselves and this one prides himself on his privacy. "But, are you glad that you took this direction?" he finally asks.

"I'm not sure. I didn't only do it to show them, I did it to show myself...I think. Everyone aspires to luxury but I wanted to gain it, use it, profit by it."

"And how does one profit by luxury?" he asked, swirling his XO.

"The profit is, I suppose, time...time and freedom. I have much more time and the freedom, due to my wealth, which... allows me to decide how I spend that time."

"I want to tell you something: you know how they're shortening the working week or at least trying to? Well, in countries that have begun that change it has resulted in people not knowing what to do with their time. It takes a degree of intellectuality possibly, an interest in the probing of one's mind to really occupy one's time," he says, for the first time ever departing from the traditional Freud-speak (the problems and solutions are within you, I can only make you realise them).

"You mean, I should become a psychiatrist?"

"No, no...the probing of one's mind takes many forms: the arts, literature, music, the artistic sciences like mathematics."

"I have no interest in art. I've read a few books on it because people told me to, but I just don't think it's a good investment. All this talk about art-speculation, I'd rather...anyway, how does art-speculation relate to the state of one's mind, apart from the obvious worry of paying more than one should have for an object that clutters up the walls? As for music, I detest music...apart from maybe...well, cars. The sound of cars, of money changing hands, of newspaper-sellers. The city has a kind of music, I suppose. I like that."

"Good, good."

"But even that has begun to tire me."

"Oh. What about books?"

"I've read a few Jackie Collins'—when I'm on a plane for instance—but more out of boredom than anything else. Books are like camomile tea, really."

"I think we should do a hypnosis session today," the doctor advises after frowning a little. He gets up and takes a leather case from a shelf before setting it down. Hypnosis is something he's good at—he never fails to send me into a trance. Although the tape-recorded mutterings don't make any sense to me, I feel much better afterwards, as if an emotional burden has been temporarily lifted.

"I am young...just another forced feeling, my age. So much time, so much time, so much time. Beating the rest to show me, not anyone else. I needed something like I need now...yes...I need my mother and my father, the ones who held my hands as I stumbled over grass...yes, I *need* them."

Pause.

"Success...yes, I've reached it, I have seen from the summit. They were no roads to freedom that I met, though. No, these were roads to the decayed debris that is scattered over this wonderful city. The ones in ties without consciences. It leads to...the dream of the decade, that of the fast cars without reason and that sudden attack of odd-heroin-substitute at an age in the twenties.

"And it is only that asking...of what it is all for, those bounds without chains around a spinning wheel of disgrace. Disgrace is what I have stood for, with the chances I've had.

"I'm remembering moments, the ones that flit in the time it takes to blink an eye. The views from my bedroom windows... from disused buildings to romantic places. My first job.

"Yes, that was what I bought, sold, believed in, trusted in. That was what I made true for myself, not my dream but the dreams of millions, the dream of the decade."

7

Within an hour my brief fit of paid-up catharsis was over. I've wiped the tears that clean my cheeks each week and have endured my analyst's suspicious glances as I leave. I sleep in the car and leave without thanking the driver. And, once I have reached the top in a sterile lift I reach my room, the permanently rented one and relax with a drink, looking over my private indulgence, my view across the city, the river and her environs. It's a June evening, with the usual palest of blue skies. All this is my only indulgence. For a few hours I value my solitude, not looking forward to tomorrow's meetings. But, as I look out I fear crashing to the floor, keys in hand. I take a deep breath and take in the one-in-a-million time's gentle fragrance that wafts over the room. It seems to cure my uneasiness, but the view is now different; parts of the city have become obscured by haze.

As an antidote to my loneliness I call a girl I know and she tells me that she's busy—tomorrow's not OK either. I hang up and look at the hi-fi in the corner of the room. Beside it are records packaged in brightly coloured boxes. I remember asking the salesman how I should choose from so many pieces of music. He advised me that I should get box-sets, whole collections of disks from a particular genre. Unfortunately, all the genres I picked sound like the deathly warbles of a comatose patient. Osman likes them all, bands like Liar Fates and others are his favourite.

I rub the sofa that I'm sitting on, one of those leather ones dressed in shades that deserve to be run over by buses. Dejection always seems to breed cynicism in me.

I tire of channel-switching—even I know that de-regulated twenty-channel-television kills, so I stare at the telephone, filling myself with contempt. How those machines torment my life! But then it rings and it's Osman, come to rescue me from my plight and relieve the strains of his sweaty Jermyn Street shirt.

"Yes," I reply. I want to go out. Maybe I'll meet a model who's confused as I am. Model, because looks come top of the list as a qualification for an affair, after that it turns to money. But then, no-one ever seems to understand me, no-one has experienced what I have experienced and no Chelsea-girl who's dying slowly in a pearl necklace can help me. We discuss where to go and he decides. He once told me that I couldn't make decisions as well as I used to; it was just after I refused a 'high-performance' GTi, I think. Finally, we pick on a place and putting the phone down, the doses still melting in my head, I look at myself in the mirror. Spraying myself with inevitable cologne to the gratuitous flickerings of the television I should have never put on, I wonder why I do it. Possibly, girls need it like cars need petrol; no wonder they smile and frown like the radiators of high-speed cars. The girls I meet, none of them will ever watch the sun rise over this city. For them it's work in a few hours and they need all the sleep they can get.

I leave the room again and descend in the lift. Around me are the ever present men and women of the class I have such an interest in. The working class, of course, the class I was born into and the class that works. I have an interest in them, the hall-porter, the bus-boy and others because I want them to make it to the top too. Not out of any charity but rather to have people who come from backgrounds similar to my own. But things seem to have got harder now. Class is always a barrier but, for instance, look at all the German beer and how it's bottled. Even if you can afford it, you need a gloriously private education to open the thing. The doorman frowns as I leave the hotel but only because I'm saying the word 'Grolsch' like a mantra.

When I arrive at the bar I tell the driver to go home. He smiles—it's his four-year old son's birthday and he had wanted to go home all day. As I walk in, the deafening music floods my ears. I can already see Osman, recognising him by his arched nose and the double-breasted Prince-of-Wales check suit that I've seen him wear a few times. He's talking to a girl in a pink dress and he's laughing, his conspicuously sloping shoulders shaking wildly.

"Hi, Osman," I say it like it's a joke and then repeat it at a higher volume.

"Good to see you, my man, I thought it was about time for us to go out together," he says, smiling through a machined-tan. I stare at his glinting earring as he attracts the bar-maid's attention.

"I went to see that woman—what's her name?—today," I say, taking a stool.

"Yes, I know. I saw her this afternoon, she likes you," he smiles and I smile: different reasons, of course. I listen to the music and look around. "Yellows, pinks and light blues—not the eyes, but the blousons and slacks. They shine as decade-dreamers sip gin and cuddle. Osman's drinks arrive but they don't ease the situation, they only make me look for the gents'. Even though he's my best friend, I still feel uncomfortable with him. Secretly we both know we're very different from each other. We have different desires, different tastes and though Osman tries to educate me, I fail every time. "So what was wrong with you today? She said you acted very strangely."

"Just feeling down, the way everyone does," I smile, thinking about what she must have thought. But I'm being truthful, at least, even though the people next to me laugh. One of their friends, wearing a pair of pastel-hued shorts, has dropped a coin in the juke box and proceeds to dance around it. Girls watch on, impressed by the individual's taste—Dire Straits.

"Well, we'll have a great time tonight, I know it. I've bought a new car, you have to see it. It's the latest model," he says as if excited by his problem, "we can drive and talk. Hurry up and finish that drink."

They don't serve pints here, some bizarre decision on the manager's part to stop any pint-drinking nostalgia of the Hovis kind. All that 'working man' and 'community' crap is long over and no-one wants to re-kindle any old flames.

We're standing beside a red car designed in a way my father would have thought inconceivably ugly. My ears thank me for leaving the bar; one can still hear the music but it's very soft and the streets are, for the most part, silent and empty. Osman seems to collapse in a fit of 'ecstasy' as he demonstrates his in-car telephone. "Yes, that's wonderful," I say, my sentence trailing things like the car I'm soon in.

We drive until we reach a square in the middle of the city, a square of day-time ad-men and evening-time drinkers. At night it becomes empty except for homeless children. We catch glimpses, at least I do. And as I watch, I'm accompanied by a troop of sexist musicians trying to make the beauty of a guitar dull into slush. But then, I don't even like the guitar anymore. And doesn't the Armani suit touch the seat exquisitely? Don't you get that rush? Maybe I do...like the rush of a hungry child for his dinner.

He's talking about his contracts, his deals and his latest flames and all out of an unreasonable respect for me, a respect based, as with all these days, on the fatness of a wallet and whether you have a Rolex. I laugh about it sometimes. But just as he turned around that corner in Soho, the car gently thumped into a cardboard box, and you should have heard him scream. It was only one of those child wanderers, the ones we are told we have created, only a child in the cardboard box and only the blood Picasso-painted on the outside. Cardboard seems dull otherwise, the red makes it all exciting, enthralling. And then, as the engine switches off, an uneasy silence, an eerie, unforgettable silence. And then, after this, after all this, I promise the thought went through Osman's head, the thought of running away like a child, speeding off, hoping that there were no limbs pathetically clinging to the bumper. I didn't have the heart to joke that it was lucky he had chosen red for the colour of his car. But nor had the boy, because amongst the feelings of detachment, there was that famous sense of pain. Drawing on cursory first-aid knowledge I checked the cartoid pulse until I realised that there was no use. He was so thin! "Os! It's bad: get to the phone and call the ambulance!" I shout, serious to the point of fear and forgetting that there was a phone in the car. But as he listens with a usually applicable eighties' attachment, behind a half-plate of Golf-glass, electrically wound down, there was no feeling behind that made-up forehead. You could take the contents of the wild wine-bars I can hear in a silent torpor, you bring them out and put them in Osman's position—how many would do anything, how many when they realise that this boy is dead? How many when they realise that their peers will never accept it? He eases off the hand-brake and I think he's driving to a telephone booth. And I'm left wondering, blood, his blood, cooling my hand in the Soho breeze, watching the lights in front dim and the complexion of a boy I never knew, whiten.

8

He didn't come back, but you didn't expect him to. The accident concentrated my mind and I realised that he had to leave. It was a career decision from a Wayfarer-ridden warehouse-converter—in his position I might have acted the same way. And left alone that way, sensing that a bluebottle had arrived on my bare arm, thinking that insects only come out for the hell of it, I eventually stopped feeling too. A speckled black pair of trousers and a white rolled up shirt, displaying the gorgeous red colour of his blood I thought of silly things like my jacket was in his car. But these thoughts were filtered eventually and after efforts I left for the booth at the corner. A square always has corners, and though it was only a few feet ahead, well so was the car, I stumbled as if sorry for myself. Picking cold plastic to see the flashing display: "999 calls only," I pressed the number in quick succession, gazing back to see whether I could look at him. A car obscured it all. It's true—no one would notice him till morning.

I called and walked back, waiting in the breeze that seemed inexplicably colder. I brushed the hairs on my arms and leant on some metal bars as if I was at a photographic modelling session. I waited for a half-hour that took longer, minutes in which I didn't think of anything. My mind was classically blank, my inarticulacy betraying me. I had no chance to retreat. It arrived, and the officers, shining in glamorous black uniforms, the people that protected us from low-life squabbles, they came and asked me questions. The lights of an ambulance twirled, reflecting off the mirrored windows of buildings owned by my comrades, the ad-men. And I answered, hearing myself stutter and shiver, realising I had no identification, and realising that the tears running down my face were no evidence of innocence.

I was carried away in a car, less expensive than the one that had brought me there, wondering what I would say. I had no choice but to ignore the public school maxims and tell all. At least I was white, I've heard how the police treat people of another colour. I called the lawyer from a 'phone I should never have had to use and he arrived within ten minutes. The time was important to me and, for the first time, I felt that it was worth paying him. I waited in a room that lay like the one I thought I'd never see. It was like the pictures on *Panorama*, the dreaded DHSS and the quarters of musty dole-scroungers. But he cleared everything up, at least enough to let me sleep my next night outside a cell. Osman was gone, he couldn't be found. And the lawyer laughed, it all being so unusual for me. I always used to be careful about this, and wasn't the thought in his head that if Osman got away, couldn't I have? So we were both in trouble, because, and this was the most important point, the boy was dead. "Dead on arrival...not good...not good at all," he said. I remembered my first meeting with him, listening to him telling me that the best advice was the most expensive.

I declined the fat lawyer's offer of a lift home and took a shiny black taxi. He *did* give me some money and I was soon back in my elevator rattling spare keys and checking my face in the mirror. Checking it like nothing had happened, checking the stains like they were love-bites. I brushed the blonde hair back over my head, with wet hands, looking at how my white cheeks clashed with the blood on my wrist. The water stung my eyes making me rub at them more, until the whites turned slowly to red giving my green irises a tinge of yellow. My thin lips were still stained by a trace of blood.

I was tired, half-dead if the state exists, and the lawyer suggested I get some sleep. The joke of the day was from him: Sleep well this night because it might be my last. It was funny. And looking over to the city, through those clean, clear windows, back into darkness, it didn't look the same. Death does that, dried blood does that. I had disgustedly washed it off with a bar of designer soap hoping that the poor weren't all infected. I got into bed, lying against natural, almost Victorian sheets, trying to forget the horrible events, these excitements that I never wanted. Briefs that I should have looked at lie unread and I have to make myself dream, the dreams of another car, the dreams of a house on Malibu Beach, or the nightmares of a cold cell and the blonde-fancying homosexual inmates. The light goes out, and tomorrow the calls will start, the newspapers will start, the gossip will start and I, it would seem, shall end.

But I never drew the curtains, and I never slept. The sky, the same pale blue hue as yesterday, again winked at me as I slumped out of my bed, dying in the vapours of cologne and sucking at nicotine straws to wake me out of senseless depression. I called him, seven-thirty in the morning.

"Hello?" he asked, sounding gruff and disappointed.

"It's me. What am I going to do? They can't pin anything on me—can they?"

"I can see you slept on it," he laughs, the bastard, "well I have to see, we still don't know where Osman is. I know you're worried but couldn't you have waited longer?" he asks betraying his profession—hints of concern aren't the eighties' way.

"No, I couldn't. Look Osman's probably in Rio or somewhere by now."

"Oh, come on it's only an accident, most he could get is..." he said—I didn't listen.

"Well should I go to my meetings today?" I asked, trying to pull myself together again.

"Yes, of course. What did you think you were supposed to do, abandon everything?" he asked.

"You never said much last night," I said as if a humble character in a play.

"I know you're upset, things like what everyone else will think, but don't worry—you'll come out clean. "and then we said good-bye. I left to check the papers in front of me, again alone. I wasn't hungry, and now that plush scent, the sort you find in top department stores, was disgusting me. Dressed, though hardly a figure of fastidiousness, I left for the lobby. The lift with its usual orange glow, allowed me to watch the bags under my eyes as I wondered why I couldn't touch any of the work I had to do. It was all so simple, just some accounts to go over but I felt sick when I watched the figures total up magically, a calculator screen spewing out worthlessness. I walked out into an empty foyer, just the bus-boys and concierge to smile at. I walked through, changing my mind and entered the restaurant. "Black coffee, please." He nodded his head once I was seated in a *Louis* imitation, newspaper on table. Fiddling with the sugar spoon, nervous and feeling that I had lost the touch of an eighties' man, I saw a man and a whore walk in. It wasn't late at night and it was surprising to see how normal it seemed to foyer staff! The coffee came with all sorts of extra sugar and he wrote on his pad before walking away. And as I steamed up my face with a cup of espresso I saw the mistaken couple walk towards me. And with looks that meant they would never know embarrassment, they said hello. I knew him, met him at one of the office parties they hold in wine-bars. And her, well vulgarity knows no bounds.

"What are you doing down here, so early in the morning?" the man, whose name I can't remember, said.

"Oh nothing." I said, trying to convey that I'd appreciate them leaving. And they left soon afterwards, but only because he looked at his watch and acted the part of a busy man with appointments. I remembered who he was as I saw the birthmark on his wrist. His grey eyes shone during the smalltalk as if to warn me. But I was now talking to the concierge, telling him: "Room number 291," and walking out of the swivel doors, into that beautiful central London air. The air that's diluted by all those cars. The cars lie in wait for their accidents, as the people force their chins up spending hours trapped between others. It takes a tired ten minutes for me to cross the road before I walk, slowly, into the park.

A walk, one of those pleasures that are distinctively European. A walk that is made through the smog, a walk you can't take in LA And after a couple of minutes you begin to sense that famously diluted countryside—the leaves aren't drained and the fragrance of sap and dew reach out and call—words of wisdom, the wisdom of the ancients maybe. I have no Walkman and no stick to guide me and only a jogger could bump into me if I shut my eyes and let my feet carry me away, feeling the tarmac like a controlled car. My mind is blank again—each escapist blade of grass refreshes me. They allow me to mistakenly feel I'll make it through this day.

Children don't play here on weekdays so there is no love in their eyes to decipher and seize strength from. Children aren't meant to grow up playing here, even though health-fads have made a huge impression on Western civilisation. It's the muggings that deter the parents, but is it? Maybe we don't want them to see the natural remnants of the last age. The shrines of arcade games are there for them to meditate in. The light touch of a small, skinny finger on a button to the sound of a screeching bomb. Life and love are taught not to be respected, the divorces seem to teach the children without words—parents crouching in front of small children trying to explain their tears. There's no-one to watch kicking a ball, like I once did, oblivious as my ball and happy as no-one else.

An empty green park, with few flowers and all the summer breezes I could wish for but still I'm surrounded by a million cars and a thousand fake smiles, waiting to welcome you into the world of banality. Things tend to seem banal after a death, I remember how I felt after a couple of unimportant deaths that occurred on the way up. Unfrightened birds walk around with funny eyes and I feel it's such a pity we can't understand them because it always looks like they understand us. Why else do they run and fly away when you're in the country? Maybe because they don't want to impinge on our freedom; there's enough space for everyone in the country. And then why don't they care about our presence in the cities? because they know that we don't have the time to be free here and that under these tall buildings we are possibly only marking time before a fall of man.

When I reach a news-stand I notice that the newspapers don't have the story yet. I'm going to have to get onto PR in case they do. They should be able to dilute the story or even turn it around to my benefit. But then that department has never liked me. All of them won striped ties at public school and they've always resented *my* success.

9

I think about so many things as I sit at a particular bench, watching millions of people walk by a fence. With much effort, I tear myself away from the crouching position of *de rigor mortis* and walk through the city, past the shops of Oxford Street and along the pavements of Regent Street. And through Soho to Leicester Square, never pausing at the dramatic points of the night before. I ignore the stares, as one learns when one is born into a large city, or rather a cutting conurbation of social divide. Eventually, I make it to Covent Garden, the situation of my office, by now a late nine o'clock. Walking in, I see a reception-girl smile, a cute smile but a smile reeking of seeking promotion. Finally I reach *my* office, after walking past the secretaries with their questions that seem so unanswerable now. They follow me in, even though I thought I told them not to. I'm sitting in a room filled with the worst furniture nouveau, designed like they were in the worst art-gallery, but only because each curve of the jet-black *Le Corbusiers* now seems to symbolise the divide and strife of office politics. "Sir, you have a meeting at twelve-thirty with the accounts manager, and at one-thirty with the client from Laseri," she said in a voice without envelopes.

"Er, yes, can't I put them off?" I asked, completely at the mercy of the hooped-ear-rings, the pearl necklaces and the white blouses.

"You've already postponed those appointments Sir, and there are more in the afternoon sir..." she reeled the names of four people and their respective companies. Funny how I insisted on them calling me sir, right from the start—usually Garden executives pick blackberries in the piazza because they give their staff false states of security with the use of first-names—not that in Paris they use the impolite *tu*. It must have started in New York, we've heard of their 'friendliness'. But my thoughts are interrupted, by someone telling me I'm listless and having the nerve to ask whether I'm wearing myself out. I don't reply to that (I have worn myself out!). Then I'm left alone listening to the leather of my chair squeak under the strain, as I read the typed foolscap in front. The coffee comes in, moments later, so I couldn't start staining the papers with helpless tears. After another fake smile, I get up and look over at the rooves and through the windows, feeling as if I was about to fall at any moment. How long must I have stared at nothing in particular, feeling nothing in particular, because so much of my work is delegated? The accounts man enters, minutes later. "Mr. Saine, sir," the boy secretary announces. And soon after: "Hello," Mr. Saine says, mentioning my too personal first name. The indulgence of a real name is useless. In an office like this we all seem to be stereotypes!

"Hello, Mr. Saine. Everything's quite in order, I just checked over it all. What's the trouble?" I asked, loving the echo of a voice so confident and sure.

"Yes, everything's fine," he said, descriptions of the face useless since even if it wasn't blonde hair on top, the tan and the features were all regulation, "I was wondering whether you would be coming to Mr. Yup's party, he's leaving, sir."

Why do they keep calling me sir—I'm sure he's older than me. "Oh, yes, well I'll try and come, when is it? I'm always very busy but..."

"Next week, at that wine bar across the piazza," he said, pronouncing wine like wind—curious. "Here's an invitation," he handed me the piece of vulgarly painted card. Funny, I thought I'd sacked him, he always had his fingers in everywhere. He must have changed careers, maybe a concert pianist.

Saine left me to nervously chew at a tooth-pick, where had I got it from? Not more coffee, as she wheels it in and sets my table for a cigarette. *Marlboro* while I cough helplessly—again! White, the other executive comes in asking me whether I've heard the new compact disc from Liar Fates and Bean, (I miss-hear most things White says), I say 'no.' So he interrupts my musings for the awful, hideous sound of a dead guitar and a soul-less demon, churning out another record for my friend, White, to sleep to. "Look, I've got quite a bit of work..." I said about to be interrupted.

"Oh, yes, heard about the trouble," he said.

"What?" I asked

"Don't worry, it's quite alright. I'm not going to tell anybody."

"How do you know...what...what trouble?" I asked, shivering, somewhere in the bottom of a stomach that hadn't tasted junk for an hour.

"Osman and Eaglesbrook, that lawyer is something else," why does White use the preppy phrases borrowed from the high-school lawns of middle-America? "American isn't he?" he asks.

"Where did you meet Osman?" I asked.

"Oh, I didn't *meet* him, he called me, you know, wanted to know what's going on," he paused for a pathetic cigarette, unwrapping a packet of Camels, "Look, I know you're in trouble," serious expression, "and I know that I'm the only one that knows. I want something." His chapped lips curled on the last syllable before he thrust the cigarette into his long face and began lighting it.

How long must I endure the silent mannerisms of the whiz-kid double-crossers who believe, like me, that life's the dog-eat-dog game they learnt from Victor Kiam. They're second generation and have to answer to the first, and the first know all the tricks. White wants Christmas every day but doesn't realise that he was born in the wrong social position, born too far down to catch up and born just too late. "What do you want?" I asked replying with sad and what I think are surrendering eyes.

"I want a promotion, something better than what I'm doing now. I deserve it—don't I?"

He said it like he was asking whether I had seen a particular film in Leicester Square. And I replied, just as I would if he had—I pressed the intercom button and told Miss Josely to get rid of him. I was tired of these Dallas-clichés, they had become too common recently. Only last week, a man I had never seen had walked in telling me that he had photographs of myself in the Soviet Union. I pondered briefly on how he had got hold of photographs of myself changing planes in Moscow before I sent him on his way. He thought he could extort money from me for a harmless holiday snap! And in these days of *glasnost*, when Gorbachev's realising that capitalism is the ideal system anyway. This time the smiles of my busy workers were hardly fake. And a tiny entry on page five of the *Standard* greeted the commuters on their trains to much-written-about-suburbia. White had won a small skirmish, he had taken the revenge he had threatened. My friends had in turn left messages for me to pick up. The photograph was really quite flattering, as appealing as an ink-rag can make it. The important message, however, was scrawled by the hand of a concierge-clerk, under the *Hulton Tower Hotel* heading: "Call immediately—Don't worry, Eaglesbrook."

Don't worry! I called from the room, even the light of the sky had gone out. The hue of the view was like the dark greys of a puddle. "Hi, what's happening? Have you seen the paper?" I asked, sounding happy.

"Yes, yes, of course. It's not too bad. I've got friends there, that's why the story didn't damn you to the ground," he said, "the date's been arranged."

"Who gave the story?" I asked, at last annoyed.

"I don't know—probably Osman."

"I ran into White. He did it, he talked to you and he's talked to Osman," I said, stating the facts in the wrong order.

"Someone's just buzzed me, I'll call you back—we can discuss this more fully at another time. For the moment just lie low," he said, before I replied to a dialling tone. Buzz off is what he meant. The other executive, a trainee learning our rough, slippery ropes called and told me that we were receiving faxes from clients. That was all he had to say to tell me that my personal affairs were affecting the greater good of the company. He didn't need to say much more. "I'll call around tonight," I said putting the tired hand down. Alcohol for the hell of it, I watched for any crowds gathering outside. I wasn't famous enough for crowds—The secretive money-makers and wealth-creators are meant to be silent; liberally branded demolishers who bring house and hospital crashing down as they play with computers and telex machines. White wine, the foulest, the sort that your tongue recoils to. When things fall apart, and you wait in a room as glamorous as you can imagine, furnished in pinks and blues trying to be as tacky as the wine bars our leisure time is now spent in, when you know you're on bail, what do you do? Buy a Porsche, of course.

Telephone directories, cheques and test-drives—all so you can caress a leather-bound wheel and take glances out of a tinted window. Possessions—everyone buys the signs of success at the first opportunity. I'm not talking about company cars, I'm talking about one's very own. I should have bought one sooner: "Nice car," "Beautiful Car," "Where d'you get that car?" I answer them with a swish of a hand, even though the last question is aimed at the dock I'm sitting in.

10

As I sit in the dock I think about how I used to sit in my house, the house of my parents, watching the rain. The drops would coagulate, blending on the double glazing, scattering as on a car windscreen as the wind blew wildly. My parents were out somewhere that night, leaving me to glory in my freedom. I would turn on the television, listening to the grisly afternoon programmes behind the crush of inter-city trains nearby. I would watch the flickerings, loving my life in the house but also having a faint desire to emulate the glamour of those images. Even then, when life was sweet and simple, I needed more, hungered for more.

The court adjourned and I aimlessly walked out of the room, down some ornate staircases, out into the street and into a small café, the kind with a metal and glass case containing saveloy. As I sipped cautiously from the edge of a cup, fiddling with the solemn coffee spoon I wondered jovially about how long I would be free to sit at cafés like this. I was trembling, there were grains of sugar sprinkled over the plastic table, and my eyes darted about, looking from one object to another. All the while, as my actions seemed so steeped in senile disabilities, I asked: Why me? I have achieved what surely most have merely aspired to—I have achieved all of it. But the genie seems to have sinisterly escaped.

My verdict, though I have lost interest in it, is open. At least this is what Eaglesbrook has implied to me. He sat talking to me in a foolishly austere room, a ridiculous room with four walls painted a dirty white (Dulux colour 431, no doubt). "Now, you didn't murder him, did you?" he asked, laughing a little.

"You see, from the magistrate's or legal system's point of view you've made a success out of yourself. You've worked hard and got there," he wasn't laughing now and I was wondering where 'there' was, " but it now seems that you just broke under the strain of all that responsibility and success. You do have a lot of responsibilities, don't you?"

While he speaks I regret not getting involved in the politics of my profession. I met the magistrate at a party once, I haven't told Eaglesbrook. He had wanted some information about a company. I refused, of course. "Yes, I have a lot of responsibilities." Such a funny word, so long and cumbersome.

"Don't you feel it a burden?" he asked, his brow furrowing as his grey Eagle-eyes glared.

"If I felt it a burden, I'd give it up. I have the money. I have the money to pay your fat cheques every month, don't I?" I say getting angry and looking away.

"Yes, yes, of course, but this is what the prosecution will ask. The Crown needs facts but leaves space for conjecture. You are young, very young for what you do."

"I thought that that was an achievement, not a crime," I calmed suddenly, realising that I would have to appear sane for the magistrate.

"Of course," he used the phrase a lot, as if it was an advertisers' catchphrase, "but under so much pressure, don't you feel like..."

"Like murdering someone?" He wanted to sell me my innermost thoughts.

"What had you drunk last night?" he said, changing tactics.

"A brandy, I think, nothing much," I recall how brandy, cognac, was unaffordable in my youth. My parents never thought of drinking it, at least V.S.O.P.

"If they do win, if you have any doubts...it might be helpful if you were drunk, under the influence of a debilitating drug and all that, rather than appearing as if with the mind of a malicious murderer," he continued. "Anyway, did you have any strange experiences as a child, did you feel rivalled by other boys?" I couldn't understand his line of questioning, I didn't want to. "I mean, the boy was barely seventeen," he went on and on. I wonder if he knew I was seeing an analyst.

"No more..."

"I'm sorry, I mean...well, to rephrase it, did you have an unusually competitive instinct, a desire to beat your rivals down?" he interrupted.

"I felt rivalled, but the world is full of rivals, that's what drives us on," I replied confidently, "you can even look at my analyst's reports. I'm sane, truly sane and that's why I fight to overcome my rivals."

"Well, I don't think you had better say that in court, it's not good to mention an analyst. Why the hell are you seeing one anyway?" he laughed. "It all makes you sound like a man who loves the dog-eat-dog existence and that's something that a court of law will not admire. They love humility, even shame, not something that sounds faintly like greed," he said, his brow again tossing and turning as his eyebrows seemed to die and re-incarnate.

"But, no more than anyone else," I shouted. We are all taught to compete. Is my crime to have learnt well, to have stepped on too many faces to succeed?" You compete in your job, don't you? With other lawyers?" I said, feeling that my arguments were like the Winslow Boy.

"Yes, of course. But now that you've explained everything, the ins and outs of the plot as it were, I want to ask you...well, what puzzles me is why you didn't walk away. This friend of yours, Osmiro...something, you had known him a long time, he's the sort of person that walks away from a dying child, you must have shared enthusiasms, thought alike, why..."

He was staring intensely, hypnotised by the sound of his own voice. "Opposites attract," I foolishly interrupted. Why hadn't I walked away? Why, for that small spare moment hadn't I decided that my hard forged career was paramount, that the child was already dead, that there was a mistake, that I wasn't guilty and that there was no point in sacrificing my life?

This is what I reflected on as I sipped the dead coffee. The coffee was white, they had got the order wrong, and it tasted sour and creamy. I was too fatigued to argue and, instead, I thought about the dying child. The phrase was so emotive, and yet all it conjured up now was myself washing the last stains from my wrist and shirt, dousing the flame-red spots with water as I watched my reflection and smelled the soap.

Eyes a glaze, I continue to think about Eaglesbrook, accompanied by young acid house girls attired in the loud clothing of a few decades ago. They sit a couple of feet away and when one asks me for a light I see in her eyes a helpless and hazy glow. I cease to think about the case as I look at her short skirt and up to her brightly painted lips. A Cartier lighter later, I am in the street being asked by another of them whether it is my car.

"Yes," I reply, vaguely hearing a news-stand-man call out the latest drop in oil prices.

"Take us for a ride," she says in an upper-middle-class accent that reminds me of Osman's apartment.

"Sorry, maybe another time," I pause, about to advise them that they should work, follow careers so that one day they can have a big red car but decide not to. They're too old to take advice.

Ignoring the parking ticket, I feel somehow flattered that a group of ecstasy-minded girls should want to strike up a conversation with me. But there are plenty of people like me to spare. Chuckling, my car hadn't been clamped at least, I went into third, driving home and dreaming of the Latin Quarter and silly things like prison cells and headlines. I once spent a weekend in Paris with Kathleen.

At the hotel, my worries re-appeared, the messages of support not comforting me. The telexes of clients' withdrawals and the beautiful, shiny white envelope that had been kept from me were finally being bowled in. The latter was from above, a parent; a parent company ordering my wrenchingly climactic resignation.

That night, behind a sheet of chintz, I laughed like a sentenced man.

11

When friends gave me advice, I wondered what they were trying to prove. There's no love left in this world and I don't need anyone to tell me that tomorrow there's another day. Now, I long for a *Der fliegende Hollander* death with all the power it assumes. I need it. Nothing seems to be important, that's why I laugh from dawn to dusk.

I drive along a country lane, North of London, passing the Northern suburbs like they were dirt, ignoring the small gardens because the blossom of a tree and the flowering of a rose seem worthless. I put my cellular 'phone on hold because the calls, re-routed and revolting are flooding in. I stop at a petrol station to charge it, pick up a hitch-hiker with a black cat. One doesn't feel scared when one's a touch empty.

"Hi, that you?" a girl's voice asks—I switched the damn 'phone on.

"Who's this?" I sounded angry.

"It's Kathleen," she laughed in that sweet way, "I've been trying to get you all afternoon."

"The phone was off."

"Where are you?"

"Oh, just North of St. Albans, but I'm driving back to London now."

"You're driving?" she asks before I explained what I had bought.

"Sounds lovely," she was talking about my phone—she must have thought I was being vulgar.

"I've just got back from LA—for good."

"How come?"

"It wasn't what I wanted—LA isn't what they say it is."

"London isn't either," I replied dryly.

"You never wrote back," she said coyly, "things seemed to have changed. Where do you live? What are you doing? Look, let's meet." she said eventually.

"I'm not sure, I..."

"Come on, I haven't seen you for six years!"

"Okay."

"At that hotel we used to meet at—say seven?" I was happy to hear her voice, a voice that seemed pleasant, passionate. I imagined her eyes, glinting blue irises (coloured contact lenses, I think) that got her anywhere. She was clever too and after our love ended the way love does she cleverly jumped when the post-punk offer stumbled in. Under that made-up disguise, however, were a host of insecurities, occasionally surfacing in the form of tears and twitches. She had too many dreams, each one diverse and wholly different. Her trip abroad was her first step of independence, although I suspect it was funded more than a little by her reasonably-well-off parents. She had never got on with them although they were the ones always backing her up and dishing out to her whims. Five years ago I would never have imagined that she would return to London. The reason for it, I decided, was suspicious. But for all her secrecy and impulsiveness I had always missed her. Just seeing her walk down the street and smile, her hazel-brown hair tied back in establishment style and her bright eyes sparkling made my heart skip a beat and wish I had known her all my life.

There was more cologne on my body than usual that night. I still couldn't decide why she would return. It was going to be a shock for both of us. A week or so earlier, I could have told her of all my successes, all my fruitful dreams, that I was one of the youngest executives of this and that, and that I was a millionaire, status symbols that might be wasted on her; she never cared for them. Tonight though, I could only tell her that two days before she arrived I was accused of a callous hit-and-run and now my career had blown away in front of my eyes.

When I sat in my room, after putting my clothes on, I felt

fatigued. The driving had had the effects of a bad knock on the head. But ignoring the physiology I should have taken at university, I took the lift up to the final storey—the hotel I used to meet Kathleen at was this one, it was our 'in' joke to act like a rich, extravagant young couple, even though we sometimes had to think a while before we ordered dessert.

We kissed and went to our table, a sickly sweet perfume that reminded me of the past, the way fragrances tend to, lingered in the air. We were already embarrassed; we hardly looked at each other. We had both been wondering what the other's impression was going to be. Surveying each other's faces, in silence, she finally parted her lips. "You look just the same. In California all men have tans. I think I hate tans...you look god, striking," she paused at the vital word, I was looking awful after these past days. My face was what some people might call distinctive, what others called full of age, all I saw was a peeled tomato.

"You too," I smiled, "tell me about LA, I've been a couple of times, just never had the courage to call," I said, seeing that Kathleen looked prettier than before, and noticing that behind her attractive tan was a new confidence.

"I knew you were there, you really should have called," she said with an expression caused maybe by an unhappy memory. "LA's changed, it's...it's terrible. I told you about your tan, that's because over there the tan goes with an image, and everyone's concerned with image. I didn't have any real friends, well not really. They were all, I don't know, just obsessed. No-one realises there's a world out there. I missed London, too, I like Europe and New York's so expensive..." she went on, her eyes dipping and smiling as if noticing that apart from the tan I looked just as concerned with image as your average LA money-maker. Suit, tie, tan, wallet, apathy, so it goes on.

She had read the paper and knew a lot about my case. There had been no point to my vain attempt to cover it up. I explained the rest, and began to confide—something that had only recently become a hobby of mine. "This place is just the same," she said.

"No, they're all younger now."

"Yes — so it's the same over here, society cut in two," she laughed sarcastically.

"Yes," I said, remembering her graphic headlines in the underground paper *circa* 1978. "It was inevitable. Back then, we used to work on that paper and it was different. I think we've become more realistic, realised that we can't change the whole thing. We've matured."

"Exactly, we were younger then and we didn't know...the real world. So you've changed, too" she said.

"Yup. But why did you leave?"

"I was successful, the youngest this and that, I've still got the press cuttings, but I realised that the people around me... there was no culture," she explained, sipping the aperitif and not making the slightest bit of sense to me. I could never work out why we gave art subsidies to theatres with unsold tickets. "They don't have the time. You have to work if you want success and all this work, work, work thing. I don't know, it drains you, and the you end ups an emotional dead-head that's looking for something, always lost."

I listened to the American accent creep in.

"You're right, I know you're right, I haven't read a book, a real book, if that's any criteria, for ages. I haven't even picked up the new Collins, just can't be bothered, just can't summon up the effort. But when I was working I didn't have the time."

"You should try more. If you don't have the time then heaven help all of us. You were always the first with the latest Harold Robbins. Haven't you looked at that English guy, Jeffrey Archer?"

I shook my head.

"I just take it as it comes. In the end one has to look after oneself. But how do you feel?" she said unconnectedly.

"I feel a little ill," I looked down at the avocado vinaigrette, "it's just that I don't have anywhere to run to. I haven't been in LA, working for six years always having an option."

"Well, look at it this way, you've told me what's happened.

Now what are you going to do? Your career's finished," she said bluntly, she was only shy in other people's company.

"I'll start again," I was making myself confident by all this talk, I knew how to act in front of this person because she wasn't a person I could size up anymore.

"So who are your friends, who do you go around with?" she said interested after irradiated prawns. From her tone, I realised that she hadn't found success yet, she was too eager.

"I don't have anyone, if that's what you mean." I said.

"You're flattering yourself. I meant friends."

"No-one, you?" It seemed such an odd reply. "Do I really have no-one to go around with, anymore? Shall I be condemned to watch films amongst strangers?"

"I made a couple of friends, people are friendly out there. If you're lucky you make good friends. It was never the same as the years in London though," she said. The 'years in London' seemed like dreams, now. It seems we were ageing—the dreams now directed by an over-melodramatic *Selznick*.

"I know. But one has to change with the times, otherwise you get left behind. None of the punk era earned me any money and if I was still against this system I wouldn't have any friends, bar those trendy idiots with long hair. But then, I haven't found any real friends since throwing my lot with the system either," I said, "you can't protest and scream about the state all the time, you just do it while it's the thing to do. Attitudes to life are dictated by the state of the market, not by an esoteric state of heart and mind."

"Oh," she held my hand, reminding me of a lollipop-lady, "I'm going to have to talk to you, I'll be your friend," and I got the feeling she'd never said that to anyone else as confident, as sure and probably ill as me. "Let's get out of here," she whispered. I paid the bill, another charge, and we walked to the lift.

"Why not the lobby?" she said as I pressed the highest numbered lift button.

"Kathleen, I live here," and she burst out laughing.

12

A London night flickered behind, while the reminiscing and nostalgia seemed to consume my biography until I felt that I had failed. But, when I had woken up after a turbulent night of life, I remembered how it used to be (Kathleen's sexuality had been unimpaired by her sojourn in the States). This time, the city's awakening had no relevance, I felt detached and thin, at least until we had breakfast together. I *was* becoming thin, but this morning, when nothing could touch my heart, I could eat and eat. Today was the day I cleared my papers out of the desks, high above the piazza and street-bars. No-one needed to say anything as I streamed through the doors and piled up useless mail into dustbins. I ordered a lager in a bar, when I finished, a naïve gesture that made me frightened again.

"Didn't expect you here," said White.

"Go away," I said listlessly, realising that this was the chance to play up. Say I had a new job in the Middle-East or somewhere far away. But the reason I would never go away, why I wouldn't even settle in Esher or Elstree, driving cars into London and living a more stereotyped existence is that the city is part of me...Even a mews in one of those corners of Chelsea, where they're proud of the term 'Royal Borough', surely more appropriate for a young executive is too far removed from the bustle of the streets. I never yearned for a life in a tropical climate, in some kind of Eden. In that way I am different from my peers and if any economic collapse ever occurred, I would not be free to leave.

The existence that one realises in a hotel-room, for me, it's not the reason that a non-property-owning-lefty might make, it's the dream-like quality of it all. The lack of responsibility, the status value, the reasons that my peers might make, are not mine. For me it's the view from upstairs. He was talking.

As he spoke of my impending poverty I took comfort from the fact that my wonder-fall career was of little financial importance. With my much beloved accountants' help, I soon learnt how to manage my money so that the term 'overdraft' was unheard. But, as they say in the soaps every day, money can't buy you happiness. One misses the hideous office-parties and the horrible journey to work. But, no, I don't. Rather, what I miss is the security of life-style. Still, after the previous night, a certain type of vitality returned. When moment turned into month, an old friend gradually coming back into my life, I had to ask how long, but I restrained myself. For the first time, I didn't need solitude to be happy. She, in mysterious stripes, clutching my arms as she laughed would make the world a happier place. The inevitable roses, masses of water and gas, seemed all the more beautiful that summer.

I re-introduced myself to art with Kathleen. One night, she took me to one of those decrepit and over-subsidised theatres that they still have in London. Sitting high above the rest of the crowd in seats that seemed terribly expensive, we watched the scenes change, and the people fiddle with their thumbs. We, and they, yawn in unison, breathing in a cigarette-free atmosphere of drama without passion. Even Kathleen, so happy that tickets were so much cheaper than in America, realised that we had bought a diluted solution to boredom. When you have money, when you've bought all the designer etceteras, and when there's hardly anything you can't have, it's then that boredom crystallises, at least if your attitudes are inescapably caught in an eighties' groove. Even if they aren't, this was not Burton playing *Look Back In Anger*. We hadn't dressed up for the occasion, thank God, but our clothes were conspicuous. I'm sure (Kathleen didn't think so) that the leading actress was watching us as we made a hurried exit. If the ticket-prices weren't so high I'm sure that walking out of West End theatres midway through plays would be the norm. Into the foyer and we opened the doors to busy Sloane Square, looking for dinner. Every day fell into the pattern of continuous fun, busily searching for the antidote to boredom; the weeks and months flew by.

One night, after returning from an evening of tiring dancing, we couldn't get into the hotel. At first it was a minor event of vague disagreeableness. Kathleen looked closer and pulled her window down. "What's happening?" she asked a policeman who seemed a little lost. He said that it was a protest rally that had become violent. Both Kathleen and myself bent forwards and stared out. Petrol bombs and burning placards greeted an ill-looking government minister who was stumbling within a circle of riot-shielded policemen; he looked like an anaesthetised bull. I told Kathleen that I knew we should have given more attention to the news although I wasn't bothered about the scene. There wasn't much that I needed from the room. Even supposing the gigantic *Hulton Tower* should fall under a hail of sawn-off shotgun-fire, the only things special to me, that I would miss, would be things like an old moth-eaten photo of my mother and father, the sort of sentimental rubbish that one keeps. I call them sentimental because of the complex tapestry of affections woven by different young urban professionals. Most seem ashamed of their families. Usually, they are men and women who fail to understand the new tide of modern economics that characterises our age. Their only use is for gaining extra funds when a new share issue comes on the market.

Anyway, there we were sitting in a red, German car, windows, electrically wound down, the leather squeaking uneasily and as usual, watching the hundreds of lit-up projectiles hitting the carpeted foyer, when I commented to Kathleen that it was unusually warm. There was a pause as my eye followed an illuminated rock find its parabola and then we noticed the police firing into the crowd. Presumably, they were plastic bullets.

"I wish I had brought my camera," Kathleen said before

we returned to our silence, punctuated by the Doppler affected sounds of cars.

My mind was blank for those minutes and yet something of what I saw must have touched me in some way—my attention was distracted only by the ignition of Kathleen's *Cartier* lighter.

Slowly, I think Kathleen was reading a magazine by now, my face, my eyes began to show signs of dread; I had caught a glimpse of my reflection in the mirror. I pushed the window-button moments later, as the blaze at the front of the hotel became more fierce. I was brought up to have the utmost respect for property, private property. Kathleen gave an inexplicable chuckle as I thought. Maybe she was laughing because it wasn't her room that was burning.

Already, things were beginning to become difficult between us. Kathleen even seemed to have lost a little interest. She seemed to be obsessed, over-obsessed, with style and status and yet she wasn't just a star-struck girl with immature pretensions. There were things about her that seemed frightening, most of all her amoral positions. She had a little of the anarchist in her, I think.

Firemen, policemen, ambulance-men, they were all now at the scene, trying to cope as best they could as weary silhouettes descended fire-escapes and a megaphone from nowhere began to blast the command 'Evacuate the Area!' But behind the circle of a wheel, I could only revive a distant memory, a memory of a far-off moment.

It was only a moment; a couple of friends driving a cheap, old car. They were laughing and joking, we all were, as we glided from one party to the next. And there in the back of the car, so dark you could only see a face, Kathleen, a younger, less sophisticated, Kathleen, slapped me hard and square on the face. I can't remember whether that expression of amazement on her face came from her reaction to my look of surprise or a return-slap from my hand. The swish of my hand was hard, hitting her cheek before she smarted. If only I could still see her watery eyes glisten with surprise as I abandoned my inhibitions. The girl and the boy in the front didn't notice—just thought that the bottle of scotch had gone to my head. It had, and that's possibly why the moment was so memorable. It wasn't important, her telling me the smoke was disturbing her eyes, my dropping the cigarette on the seat and our dark, frantic search. Just her teenage pout, just a girl whose love-affairs were kisses with eyes closed, gladdened me. It was to be a long time afterward that we would meet again—that we would walk the Thames with embarrassment. She had already left when I next called her.

And in between, in those peculiar years that make up second adolescences, I met taxi-loads of scruple-less champagne-drinkers using their mouths the way their mums told them to. I never fitted in with their conversations, centring as they did on Henley Regatta or the party that Julian Hoggstrot pissed into a bottle of *Bollinger '65*. This was just experience overpowered by the alcoholic breath of rich kids, rehashed experience that summed up our world then. Only a toss of a champagne-glass away, the ground was crumbling beneath them—and so I thought at the time. But their crime, or contagious disease, was to do with oblivious minds, laughing in arrogance and yet touched by insults. Maybe I did become one of them, but now, as I sit firmly outside the ring, I realise that I was never like them. I had none of their flippant upbringings, life was always deadly serious for me. I remembered seeing their nostrils flare and their eyes widen when I told them, or just implied to them, that their actions were the actions of lost losers. After all, these were rich kids who were gradually losing their fortunes in an alcoholic haze. The facade of cute designer dresses, cut to perfect bop-beaten legs, that squirmed as they laughed, these were intriguing. But the curiosity wasn't important, the effect wasn't curious—it was devastating. All that fluffy hair, falling over beautiful faces—really beautiful—and those bright dewy eyes that drew you into them, surely it would have affected and attracted all of you out there. You cannot help falling for boys with such perfect Adonis-like features, shrouded in tans, blue eyes and short hair and no-one cannot fall for, girls who are so perfect, so seemingly inspired by a Louise Brooks or a

Marilyn as they talk and leave the gesticulation to their thighs and shoulders. The passion in their words may have matched my ideas of the conversational style of dead sheep, but they had different priorities, anyway. I had only one priority: to win. What attracted me was probably lust. But even lust was too obvious, it was something more obvious, it was something more subtle that touched my heart than just the visions of beauty promulgated in the mass media. For, why did I temporarily lose sense?

And that loss, that irresponsibility was my fault. We are all strong enough, and the nights on the bottle and the bed were my responsibility.

13

But responsibility was a strange way of living, for later we were be responsible to no-one except our group. It was a sudden change, the seventies-to-eighties manoeuvre. No-one could have guessed that spring '79 and how it would change the course of the eighties. We suddenly forgave the teenagers, proud soldiers of rebellion as they were, and they in turn 'grew up' and realised their responsibilities not to society but to themselves. Some pundits screamed about how our green and pleasant land was becoming both less green and less pleasant but as the decade wore on they became but croaky, sore larynxes in the wilderness. Before too long, they were totally ignored.

The act of analysing, of debating was, in itself, out of place now, not only in the country but even in my hotel-room. There wasn't going to be any Bastille-storming party of candles and misguided eyes — 'we don't have revolutions in this country,' and the small inconveniences nightly have little relevance. These troubles over energy and printers' ink, of raw materials and transport, of communication and health, these communities that are being shut down—what difference will it make? The train of progress runs fast and efficiency and freedom are not to be sacrificed for communities that are only a little more tight-knit then my sports-shirts.

"Let's go to my friend's house, she'll understand," said Kathleen after she had finished reading an article about the family of the chairman of the Federal Reserve Bank.

"Alright," I replied, smiling before Kathleen, meeting my eyes momentarily, turned away and spat out her cigarette with a flick of her tongue. As I rolled the windows up with the button I worried about my room and feared for its destruction. Then we left for South London and its suburban streets that I have loathed since leaving them. Again, I was doing things that I didn't want to; the clear awareness I have seems to be in confusing opposition to my actions. We drive and drive.

By the time we park, a light drizzle begins to attack and Kathleen and myself walk the ten yards to the house, listening to the rain and ignoring the water that falls on our clothes — 501s are probably waterproof. Two figures appear at the door, sleepy and tired-looking and swathed in smart clothes. They are wearing frowns and sad eyes...Kathleen smiles as we hear the loud oscillating bass and the voice singing of Music-Television and other audience-belittling trivialities. The guitars churn on as a dozen or so silhouettes dance in couples. "Party looks like just being over," someone in an Acid-House T-shirt says. Hired lights coloured in primary blues, reds and greens turn on and off, lighting the bookshelves in the front room; pine planks upon which lay neatly chronologically arranged copies of reflecting, glossy magazines. The kitchen is further behind, adorned with positioned empty bottles of wine and trays of sausage rolls. The perfume has all worn off and what is left is the stale atmosphere of a party you can find anywhere in this grey city on any Saturday night. Kathleen talked cordially with the hosts in her affectionate way and our place to sleep was secured. Worries over, I observed the people around me more closely. Everyone's eye-balls seemed motionless, nervous twitches about to begin as the DJ set up another track. It was almost amusing to be at a party of the sort I used to attend, back in different days. But at the back, further on from the kitchen, were not only the anxious rollers, squatting in all seriousness and silence as they licked Rizlas and burnt their tongues but also the ecstasy-heads searching for emotions. None of them dispensed with Hello's but all I wanted was a space on the floor. 'Crashing out,' I heard one of them laugh to someone on such a space.

Il me souviens de...another hypnotic session of monologues with my analyst. 'That café near the *Bois du Boulogne*, just outside

Paris, it was just like the one in that *Lemmon/Maclaine* film that's still on in the Latin Quarter in *version originale*. Where the extrovert reaches new heights and the brunette you do notice (and she notices you), looks silently on as the others flirt with your wallet. It's the party where the suits reek from the bulging upper-right-arm-pit but of course you're not interested. Or, rather, you are interested but not in the flaking hotel that you'd be brought to, instead it's the aniseed smell and the atmosphere of community that interests. But as the laughs change from sincerity to lies, and a party balloon slides on and off my head, I find that I'm not in that (some call it sleazy) un-erotic paradise. I've shut my eyes (where is Kathleen now?), and imagine another past scene. Where an enemy I despised without reason, because he slowed and half-ruined my successes, struck me and all went black. No vision, a dream knocked into consciousness and no chance to wake up. This wasn't the balloon, there was no outside affect like a dream of being stranded on an iceberg because the sheet fell off, this was death for no reason at all.'

At last, Kathleen's tongue, but how many hours was it? And behind my lips, the vein under my tongue throbs with pain. The street-lights are off and that palest of blue skies arrives once more. There was no smell of beechwood or sight of the morning Mercury to bring this night from the realms of a dreamy melodrama, but it didn't matter. Listlessness worked and ate its way in. Words became sighs, eyes became stings and passion became burnt toast. Even the customary drag and the squeaking of fragrant leather in the car didn't re-awaken me — what a pity this was to last for so long!

14

B reakfast?" I hear. And the question seems so useless
when everyone knows that the owners of this delightful
house have run out of Nescafé and the only milk is lying
in a bowl on the floor.

"Thank you so much for everything," I said, brushing dust
and cannabis off my jacket.

"It was a pleasure. It was such a pity that you were so tired,
it was one hell of a party," he says, one arm tucked around his
wife, and clichés undeniably tucked in his brain, "any friend
of Kathleen's is a friend of ours. Why don't we all go and have
some breakfast?"

"Yes, I'm afraid we're out of everything here," his wife says
turning to look at a desolate kitchen, "but there's a café around
the corner."

The husband is a plump looking creature with an
abundance of moles covering his neck and lower face. His
eyes are an uneducated yellow that divert one's attention to
his thinning strands of brown hair, just about covering his
scalp. He has shaved and doesn't seem to realise the emphatic
ridiculousness of his appearance. His wife, a tall, blondish
woman with grotesque features seems an altogether more
complicated person as can be seen from her observations on
the characters of some of last night's guests. Her breasts large
and conspicuous, sit firmly pointing outwards as she breathes
deeply from a well-rolled joint. Why does Kathleen know such
people, such obviously disfigured people? It turns out that (and
possibly I should have guessed from her horse-like movements)
she went to school with Kathleen and she is now a highly paid

public relations consultant. I have never heard of her but I *had* heard of her father, a millionaire cosmetics' manufacturer who seemed to have installed most of his anti-ageing creams in his wrinkled daughter's bathroom.

"C'mon we'll treat you, let's go into town." Kathleen says, giving me a jolt. She ignores me and rubs her eyes a little. I wondered momentarily whether the remains of the cash for the week should just be thrown away like this. It would take an hour to get to the West End, and we'd have to drop this couple back.

"That's great, but we'll take two cars, that way you don't have to take us all the way back. It's one of Harry's days off today." she says, making me wonder whether her husband usually works on Sundays. Kathleen drives my car and I sit with Harry in his Montego, I can't remember which car exactly. The girls are following us, presumably swapping gossip about what happened to the lesbians in Class 3a back at boarding school.

"What do you do Harry?" I say when we're in the car.

"First things first, where are we going?" he asks, smiling although all I can see is some unshaved goldish-stubble on one side of his face, clashing with his dyed-brown hair.

"My place—I hope everything's alright. We can have breakfast in my room, hopefully," I say, pointing in a direction. Suddenly, the accelerating force trespassed through my body. These cars are sickening. The car, added to Harry's obvious inability to judge distances, made me internally scream at each braking. The tiny roads of London, where parked cars are left littered around like bunkers for a lane-changing car, are not meant for people like Harry. My muscles tightened, every time we confronted a parked car at forty or fifty miles an hour. I looked over, a few times, and all I saw was his yellow eyes and a sheepish grin—this seemed to be all the excitement he got out of his life. And soon it was eighty to ninety miles an hour; Kathleen had disappeared behind us and Harry's glazed eyes only turned to me to watch which way my fingers pointed.

"I'm an accountant, management" he said.

"Really? Which firm?" I asked, presuming it wasn't a new firm and trying, very hard, to sound interested. I knew most of the firms but the farcical nature of the names of the partners in this company was amusing. He said the names as if bored by it all and told me that his life was his work.

"Yes, I've been there, ooh, five or six years," he said turning to me as I clung to my seat after we passed a red light. "Hope no-one saw us," he said laughing to himself. He pulled down the window and the wind blew straight into my face the rest of the way. Talking was impossible and my directions, as I battled with my lapels, were more and more timid. I have been in this position all too often, I expect that many others have too: moving at between eighty and ninety, changing lanes by the second and narrowly swerving around the cars in front. The traffic lights were the most painful, a sudden extraordinary force corresponding to Harry's ugly left shoe stamping on the brake pedal. It was, at least, accompanied by a pleasant lapse in the breeze. This allowed me to get my loosely gelled hair out of my face and see the scores of solitary drivers, each in their new cars, queuing behind us. It was around Hyde Park Corner that we finally hit into another car.

"You fucking idiot," said a dirtily-dressed man, leaving his Fiesta and knocking on my window. I embarrassedly pointed to Harry who was outside, inspecting the damage with great meticulousness.

"Terribly sorry about that, my mistake." Harry said with an uncharacteristic calmness. The damage, it seemed, was inconsequential and the cost would be minimal. The scowling Fiesta-man angrily exchanged numbers and letters with my friend and it was only quarter of an hour before we had driven off and huge clouds of black smoke began to rise out of the bonnet, stopping our journey once again.

"It's OK," I said, "That's my place. You can phone from there." Glad to be leaving the car, I dodged the traffic moving quickly to Marble Arch and climbed over various fences until both myself and Harry had made it into the air-conditioned foyer. It looked remarkably similar to the previous morning. Some areas of the lobby were cordoned off as were all but one of the main doors. Apart from this and the faint scent of white spirit there was nothing to remind me of the previous evening. "291," I said to the concierge, but he remembered me and Kathleen was already up there.

Harry was quiet in the lift, looking at the numbered buttons in the corner, seeming to mumble something. "My wife will kill me," I thought he said. I held my palm out to ask him to leave the lift first and we were soon inside my room joking about what happened. Harry and his wife, however, were not. "Hello, my car has broken down," he said nervously, over a telephone. Nervousness, I think, inevitably stretches from childhood— the candles blown out by the harsh breezes of the mouths of authority—and Harry showed too much confidence, too much sureness, a crack in the pavement or a loose step would near-kill him. He seemed to unravel in front of us, his true self shining. This was how he felt about his life, nervous, tense and sensing failure, not assured and confident. I pity him, of course. Any one would. And then I feel somehow responsible, I had employees like Harry and I treated them in a manner that maybe forced this sort of malaise upon them. It's a desolate feeling, knowing that my actions have been selfish and exploitative ones. It'll take something like the horrifying death of his wife and the fragrance of red roses melting over hearses to wake him up. Of course it's not worth it—the sacrifice of a horse-like, down-trodden, nicer woman for a realisation of sorts for dear old Harry.

I'm comfortable in analysing others. Myself is more difficult. Profound difficulties in business never prevented me from turning ideas into money. I had a talent for it but self-awareness and self-criticism, however, were not my strong points. No, they have always been sordidly painful.

Once Harry's off the 'phone, Kathleen orders breakfast and while Harry and his wife smile and talk I stare into their eyes with concentration. Harry talks as if confronting a policeman, adopting the most apologetic of tones, while his wife listens with impatience and gravity.

Kathleen turns on my TV set, one of those extra-technological ones that receive all manner of satellite broadcasts. Gently her long red finger-nails key BBC1. The images of royalty paying visits to hospitals are greeted by more smiles and it is only when I switch to ITV that the image darkens. The hotel we're sitting in is shrouded in orange light and the camera lowers, blurring the light on the film, to reveal stretchers being taken out and bloodstained victims with closed eyes entering lit-up ambulances. Surrounding the bodies of the injured is a mass of policemen, the paramilitary sort, and with their visors keeping their anonymities. It's strange, the understatement is useful, to watch your own home looking dark and ominous while you mess with croissants and squint because the sun is streaming into the room.

"Were you?...yes, of course you were here when the Brixton riots were on," I say as if talking about a long-forgotten Osborne-play. There's a pause—Harry and his wife keep talking.

"Seems it's been quite a night," says Harry obviously recovered after the TV report closes with the silhouettes of two policemen passing a burning car and driving off into Hyde Park.

"Everything's getting too close, it was alright when it was confined to South London," rejoins Kathleen.

"But..." I fail to even begin a sentence. I walk to the window and look down, it's too far below to see any burned out cars. I catch the rest of the conversation but I don't play any part in it.

"Are you alright?" Harry's wife was addressing me.

"He's always like this," Kathleen answers for me, for the first time ever in a conceited manner. All I wanted to do was to leave.

"Yes, I'm alright. It's just that we don't seem to have thought about what those rioters were thinking last night," I said, at last conjuring up a sentence, and becoming surprised at myself as it's uttered.

"Hoodlums," Harry mumbles, "They don't deserve our thoughts, they're just those people that go around mugging pensioners and..." on and on he went, just like I would have. Now, I'm no longer so sure and then, when the words become McCarthyist slogans, I intervene.

"That's not it at all, you've completely misjudged it all. You don't know what you're talking about." I promptly left the room, in that stupid movie-fashion, not knowing why I had said what I had said, and wondering whether it was my career that was making me feel down. Looking into the bathroom mirror, I had taken the wrong door, I looked at a dishevelled face, smelling faintly of dope and shadowed by stubble. I could hear what the others were thinking, yes HEAR what they were thinking. They were arriving at conclusion after conclusion all focusing on the themes of my immaturity, my nervous breakdown, my poor unemployed state and even my frustrated rioter-mentality.

Maybe they were even right.

15

When they had left, I rose from my bath and opened the door. "Oh, they've left," I said.

"Of course they've left. You really should use more tact, they did let us sleep the night there." Kathleen said as she leant onto the window-sill and flicked ash into a clear ashtray.

"I wanted a bath," I said and Kathleen turned away. I put a bath-robe on and walked towards her. "You're not angry, are you?" I asked. And I knew she wasn't because she smiled and kissed me. It's funny how none of those commuters below bother to look up at the windows, I never have to draw them for privacy only for darkness. But then I don't often look down.

We couldn't decide how to use our leisure—a picnic or a film? It never occurred to us that we should remember even a small part of the time spent watching a small world on the verge of collapse the previous night. Love transcends all—we were always taught it—and Kathleen meant more to me than anything else. What with her smiles and her glittering eyes, I felt the sweetness of that moment when a perfect face looks into your own and you feel that you could care for nothing else. That feeling of joyous finality when you feel, decide, that you want to live your life with this person and that without her it would mean nothing. But I seem to lie to myself when I write that I believe it. Experience teaches adults, corners them into a breeding ground for cynicism. Do I always have to be condemned into doubt? Is it a great stage of awareness that I have reached, when each moment is filled with unsureness? I blocked it out for the day, I made myself believe that all this would never end and that this was an unsurpassable, and stable, zenith.

But a reality forced by beads of sweat and satiation arrested the romance all too soon. Kathleen's sexual act consisted of innumerable contortions involving the most unusual twisting and writhing acrobatics I have ever encountered. Somehow, I could never admit to myself how strange and perturbing the actions were. The whole experience was, however, entirely pleasurable. Only afterwards did a type of virginal disgust seem to seat itself next to me and the reality of freedom being our downfall and glory set in. For me, freedom has begun to lose meaning. There is less and less that I am capable of, fewer and fewer chances to be had and little satisfaction. Just the presence of the room I sit in and the control it has over me seem to prove that I am far from free. The shades of colour that were designed to make the owner of the furniture feel pleased and happy are oppressive. The large pane of glass that gives me those brilliant vistas, allowing me the greatest use, the greatest realisation of the full physical potential of my eyes—this too has the opposite effect. Every move I make, whether to lean and flick ash or hold a glass to my mouth to drink, they all seem to be watched. A move out of turn seems to produce the most devastating and fantastic of fatalities. And in just a short time the love of a smile gives way to an all-to-real paranoia.

My career can be likened to a strongly shaken bottle of soda or a faulty-valved piston, and now as the cool dioxide and boiling water leaves, I discover that I'm empty and that my mind cannot be counselled into any state of security. It just didn't seem possible or even relevant anymore and the long, erroneous talks with Kathleen as we walked by the Serpentine had no effect, not even touching the depths of this moaning and stagnant torpor. I had lost the chance to use my abilities and employment, a conditioned predicament that we love, had been denied me...Days that were elliptically longer became shorter, the infamous day-to-day, schemeless life dragged on and on and I was only occasionally shaken into feeling pleasant by experiences that I assumed were false—art, sex and drugs.

Still, 'There's lots to live for,' I kept telling myself. But was there? Interests and leisure time had had to be forsaken for other duties. Leisure time had become boring or futile, driving fast and laughing aimlessly while propping up a bar in the West End and the like. But on one of the nights on which Kathleen had left for a hen-party with her friends I was to meet someone different. A bearded man, drawing on plain-paper while he sat drinking white coffee at a café. He had a face like the type you see in hackneyed photographic galleries, the classic pose of a bearded tramp sitting with his eyes looking at nothing and just symbolising pauperism. But he wasn't poor. After a long discussion during which he lingered over words like 'acid' or 'LSD', he invited me to his house. The house was in Islington, somehow fitting into the sprawling architecture and somehow comfortable with all its stuffiness and humidity. His friends were younger, but all older than me. They were artists who were taking time off from their mundane jobs to draw, talk, eat and sniff. A sense of senselessness seems a useless concept, but what sense was I using when my mind understood no fear, when my mouth tasted nothing and my ears only heard noise? The trip took all realities and burned them away for some hours. The dirty, grey walls had turned into bright blues and greens until slowly the hideousness of the 'real' world, as everyone calls it, seeped in and all I could feel was terrible. My upbringing, I presume it's my upbringing, allowed for no decisions as to whether the brief moments of ecstasy were worth the hours of post-high listlessness. (Rather, if it had been ecstasy, there wouldn't perhaps have been these post-high effects). The readings that this candle-lit community of mystics talked of afterwards were not ones I could readily discuss. But by the early hours of the next morning, finding myself sleeping on a hard wooden floor, cold and sweating, I wanted to go home. Home was a paradise that beckoned me and the taxi, a luxurious room on wheels led me away. Nightmarish hallucinations haunted my every inch, quietly. One just never forgets, I suppose.

I would tell Kathleen nothing about my experience and the small sachet, or doggie-bag of tablets that I had purchased would lay safely in my wallet. I didn't need the sachet but its potential as a fantastic television set, of a size smaller than anything technology will develop, was fascinating. 'The ultimate in leisure without background radiation and sitcoms.' It sat there, travelling in my inside pocket, while my blood-shot eyes, rheumy and close-set between long, interfering lashes, glared at the shameful streets of the dirtlands of North London. Enthusiasm had been revitalised on a foundation, of less than a handful, of dust.

But home *was* wonderful, I had regained a little lost passion about life. As I arrived at my door, fumbling with silicon keys, I was interrupted. A new neighbour had begun to chat about how he was staying at the hotel for a couple of months and that he had business in London. Understandably, in the state I was in, I was both lethargic and fascinated. What sort of businessman talked to a man who looked more like the tramp from so many storeys below? Possibly, he was worried about burglary and wished to create some form of 'neighbourliness' in the present climate of crime and punishment. But burglaries were a matter for the manager—so he must have been interested in *me*.

"Nice to meet you, I insist you have a cup of coffee with me," he said in an attractive American accent. I think that East Coast accents are somehow attractive, I remember when I was still copywriting and we decided to have a New Yorker enticing the viewer to indulge in a cup of carcinogenic decaffeinated granules.

"Er, no, really...it's," I said wondering why I couldn't just say 'No' and turn away.

"Come on," he said and he had persuaded me. I went to my room to quickly wash my face and seeing that Kathleen wasn't in (no doubt she slept over at a friend's house), I returned to Mr. Lewin, an American merchant banker who missed his wife terribly and loved his kids, back in the Big Core.

"It's not fair, all these business trips that upset the family core," he said as I thought hazily of the time I had spent in New York, my short business-trips, "at least I have some sorta relationship with my boss in that he only sends me out to the motherland when it's absolutely necessary," his posture was a slouch and in his golf trousers and white shirt he rubbed his stomach with his right hand.

"What do you do, mister?" he asked nicely.

"Various businesses. I was in advertising, but I retired a couple of weeks back. I realised that there were more important things than the board-room meetings and the fast-food lunches," I smiled as I invented more, "I wanted to live, you know what I mean?" The last words annoyed me.

"Yes, I sometimes like throwing in the whole thing, but what about the wife and kids? I suppose you're lucky, what with being' free and single and young. ," he said, smiling as only gentlemen of an earlier generation can. There was a pause before he went on. "I know we've only just met but...well, as an executive I've been trained in interpersonal relationships, back at business school, and well...you seem to be hiding something, just a little."

He seemed to imply that he was interrogating me as if I was his son playing truant from baseball-practice. "People as sensible as you don't give up a career that easily. I know when I was your age, just Thanksgiving holiday made me crave for the office. Maybe something better came along?"

"Not really," I began to wonder what, specifically, Kathleen was doing. "I can't really talk about it, Mr. Lewin," taken aback a little by his directness.

"OK...I'll stand easy. You know business is a tough life, someone said to me when I made my first loss — that was way back, before the corporation bought me over. I think it was my uncle, he'd seen everything, lived in Minneapolis during the depression, only as a kid, but he could feel it the way kids do. I mean he could sense it all approaching—my god, he could see it once '29 happened, all he had to look at was his dinner plate, if great Uncle Walter hadn't sold it off yet. Yeah, he saw the downturns—he was there in Detroit when the car industry wound down. I still remember when I was young, the neighbour, a really nice guy who ran the local hardware store, killed himself. No-one knew why, either. There were rumours,

of course, rumours that it was debts or something to do with
taxes but no-one believed them. He was doing fine in that
business, even expanding and then, one night, on goes the
oven, in goes the head and there he goes. Yeah, I remember
what my uncle said, God bless his soul, he said...well, you gotta
understand he said lots of things—he was always blaming the
niggers, their emancipation and all. That view may be a whole
deal unfashionable in Manhattan now, but it'll return, there
might just be some truth in the fact that blacks have smaller
brains. Anyways, the words of wisdom were: if you can't stand
the heat get out of the kitchen," he said between sips of the
vodka martini he had mixed and poured during the conversation.
I didn't touch mine and as he ended his monologue I thought
about identity and realised it was only class, not gender, race
or religion and that 'If you can't stand the heat, extinguish the
kitchen.'

"So you see, I know about troubles, I know about hardships,
maybe I can help you," he asked, his eyes, innocent for an
instant, turning up.

And in one big rush I told him everything, all the ins and
outs of these decrepit days. As I spoke of work, love and money
and freedom, he listened patiently, like, I suppose, a catholic
priest behind a screen.

And after my one and a half hours he said: "You're the one
in the news than? You're the exception to the rule."

"Sorry, what rule?" I said puzzled at this.

"You know, I may be from New York, but I still favour the
death penalty when it comes to murder. It's evil, evil, evil. We
gotta do God's business but you...you don't seem evil at all. This
must be what those lousy liberals are always talking about—the
one in a million innocent. ,

"Mr. Lewin, I didn't do anything wrong."

16

I gazed across his room, a room disturbingly similar to my own. Mr. Lewin detested it, while I had chosen to live this way. He had begun to talk about how important the agency was, the one I had worked for. He talked of corporate identity replacing individual souls and that it might end all wars. As he read the eulogy, I looked at the pride of place of the windows. The furniture was arranged so as to show it off, this dirty metropolis that sometimes came alive. From the corner of my eye I noticed a photo-frame surrounding a picture of a younger Mr. Lewin, with his pretty wife and two children. They seemed to be outside a church, its huge wooden doors in the background and, above, a shining cross of the Trinity made of small, shining metallic chips. Mr. Lewin's lips were slightly open, exposing a somewhat unfortunate pair of gap teeth. I didn't look much at the children or the wife.

As he went on, beginning a discourse on Gorbachev's evil designs, I took my jacket off and folded it onto my lap. Suddenly, I remembered the tablets, still tucked away in one of the pockets.

"...it's such a waste of time, here we are having to prevent these drug-crazed Commies from getting any grip on us when we should all be in church, celebrating life, the greatest...let me take your jacket."

"No...no, thank-you. Look, I think I'd better get back, I'm really tired but...we must meet again."

He seemed to look sad as I walked out, as if he needed, craved someone to talk to. It was an annoying, tedious trait that expected unwavering patience, a quality I lacked at the present

time. Besides, my shining, youthful image would have been
somewhat tarnished if drugs dropped from my pocket.

"We *will* meet again, won't we?" he asked at the door.

Back in my room, still without the passionate caresses of
Kathleen, I switched on the television, slowly sinking into the
sofa and one of those depressive malaises.

"...*economic growth in the United States has shown renewed
signs of slowing down and a spokesman for a leading merchant
bank, as reported in today's Financial Times, predicts that
without capital spending of any kind, whether it be for the
expansion of corporate production facilities or government
spending, the recession will loom ever nearer. Some say it
began a couple of months ago...Louis Ranzon reports...*"

I walked over to the window and leant on the sill, my head
against the pane. These past days of hideous vagrancy had taken
their toll and I realised that they were short term answers to
long term problems.

"...*the Gramm-Rudman legislation means that the budget
has to balance every year, so I don't think it's likely that
they'll be any more government spending. That added to
the fact that there looks like no burst in consumer spending
and no turnaround in our foreign trade position, means that
we've got problems coming...*"

Far below me, the hordes of lunch-time workers rushed to
and fro, inspiring only a hopelessness and a smile. Those people
out there had rejected me, the people that own, the people that
rule, the people that worked. They had thrown me away and
had gleefully watched as I writhed in my little ball of paper. To
make it worse I seemed to play up to my funeral well-wishers,
making conditioned responses such as taking tablets or drinking
myself from reality. I tried to think that this wasn't a funeral,
nor even an illness. Could it possibly be a resurrection? It was

too grandiose a theme for someone as small and insignificant as me.

"...and after Standing Oil's announcement that they are closing 200 petrol stations after their fierce take-over battle with Evans Oil, to finance annual financial charges we have a report on the over-leveraging of corporate America..."

I switched the set off and walked out, descending in the lift and out through the foyer and into the city, aiming to imitate a vagrant as well as I could. After an hour or so I wandered into a pub in a corner of one of those housing estates that someone decides to erect directly behind moneyed buildings. Council blocks always tend to be built against, or rather behind, the affluence so that there's only ever a five minute walk from a chic glamour to a grinding poverty.

I was sitting on an antique bench-like piece of furniture, lifting a pint glass to my lips and easing the beer mat off when I saw a girl sitting at the bar, crying. It wasn't that noticeable and the bar-tender, the only other person in the room, didn't see it. Maybe I was still recovering from my trip but, uncharacteristically, I walked towards her and asked her whether she would have a drink with me. She was holding a cigarette that she hadn't flicked for some minutes and the long tube of ash hung loosely to the burning filter. There was a pause before she lifted her eyes and smiled. She had large, slightly almond-shaped eyes, attended by hazel-coloured irises that seemed to shimmer. When I saw her face, her cupid-bowless lips, I thought of Kathleen. I didn't think of her because this unknown girl was like her, I just suddenly reflected on why I adored her so much. What qualities did Kathleen possess that I admired?

I looked away for a moment, at the tired looking mothers pushing prams and feeding their children bottles of *Coke*. I watched them trudge through the strata of rubbish outside on the pavement, holding their eyes to the ground.

"Yeah...can I have a spritzer?" Julie said, interrupting my

thoughts. She was smiling now but I was a little shocked—she spoke in the truest of eighties' cockney accents, a mixture of short and sharp East-end bursts punctuated by a minor-key drawl. The syllables bounced around, words brief and brusque, shooting from her beautiful mouth.

"Are you alright?" I ventured.

"Yeah, it's just that I'm doing a survey, hours are nearly over now and you look a nice sort of guy," she replied oddly.

I smiled, speaking to the bartender slowly. "What's the survey then? Did someone upset you by their remarks?"

"Oh no," she laughed, "I have to go to all these places, posh places and poor places, and check out how many people come up to me to ask me if I'm alright. See?" she said taking a small clear bottle of glycerine from her plastic handbag after quickly stubbing out her cigarette.

"So you rubbed it on your cheeks," I said, before she took my hand and touched her face with it.

"Yeah, it's all part of some social attitude survey, you know something about how uncaring a nation we've become. I can't see it myself, I've always thought it was uncaring, a part of British life. Anyway, what are you doing tonight?"

We talked for a long time, lubricating ourselves with liquor while I nervously sighed and covered my face with my hands, thinking of how different she was from the girls that traipsed through Sloane Street on weekdays. She demanded little attention and spoke so beautifully—that must have been why I liked her. She was generous, too, buying each alternate round from her plastic purse. She'd flick her short brown hair back through nervousness, at least sometimes, and it was then that, from certain angles, she bore a disconcerting resemblance to Kathleen. But Julie had an innocence, innocence that made her anxious to please. I invited her back to my place, explaining that I had walked into the pub mistakenly and that my car was back at home. I suggested taking a taxi but she wanted to walk. The moment her glycerined face looked up from the ground to my room was golden—until now she had been reluctant to go somewhere with a strange man and now, now that she had seen the financial-fashionables in the foyer, she was all for going back to her mother.

I persuaded her easily—the five or six hours in which we had talked made us feel we knew each other a little. Besides, she was generally up for anything. It was I , surprisingly, who was becoming tired. It occurred to me, as we walked in, that for each liberal idea that the other hotel guests had, there were a thousand prejudices. This girl would attract suspicious and thoughtful glances for all the time I knew her. Julie might be beautiful but anyone without the language of understatement was liable to bring out the upstairs-downstairs mentality in people. But then, maybe I was just exaggerating the problem, maybe it was I who had the hang-up about going out with a girl whose father didn't own a corporation.

In the end, however, it wasn't a cynical glance from Kathleen that I got, it was a laugh. After it, there was a shallow and pointless argument based on misunderstanding, allowing me to walk out with Julie on my arm. Kathleen had been watching television, munching on a plate of room-service asparagus. She had made me miserable and though Julie hugged me and attempted to cheer me up, I was thinking about Kathleen and her life, what she said at those gossiping, mews' parties and what she did. When Julie began asking questions about my relationship with Kathleen, I found Julie's flawless morality unapproachable.

She changed the subject, talking about the trials and tribulations of the Royals. She liked the topic just as she liked practising her French at the restaurant we were at. That day was one of the greatest days, even if I did sometimes patronise her to hell. Without a passion to change my circumstances, I required a passionate, all-consuming, selfish love. Whilst with others an embrace meant little, I was deeply moved when I was just *with* her. For quite a few weeks, I would not talk with Kathleen and, instead, see Julie, a girl five years my junior, a girl who was unemployed and actively seeking work in slum-like offices or sandwich bars or hair salons. Kathleen would never sleep in my room, instead Julie and I would spend days and nights of seemingly real-pleasure, talking, loving and eating. Through the shadows of pleasure to the days that Julie determinedly left for the job centre, I noticed that the evenings were already becoming fractionally longer, the days cooler.

It was months, not weeks that I continued like this, coming to the ground from my dream only when I met my neighbour, chance meetings in which I would notice his never-changing facial expressions and cuts of suit. When he saw Julie and myself, laughing and staggering from the lift, he proffered the same smile, a valuable smile. It was only that smile that gave me a sense of security and responsibility. Just the acquaintance of such an upright Christian citizen gave me that. It was only later that I realised that I had been ignoring his staggering and swaying beside the lift-portals.

And once I knew that he respected family life as much as he respected the Communist Party I knew that I had only Julie to rely on—for everything. We had a big disagreement when she got a job, I didn't want her to work as a clerk in an office block, it was unnecessary. I gave in and a typical ending to an all-consuming relationship ensued. The small, short arguments didn't seem important, we made up in minutes. But, all the while, my sensitivity and impulsiveness was ready to strike. You see, I was still very much alone.

17

When I first met Julie, her name evoked many images. These two syllables were somehow all-encompassing, embracing everything I thought, dreamt, felt and breathed. Now, however, it meant little, though now I knew what I should have known all along: no name has as beautiful ring to it as Kathleen.

For a while, Julie was wonderful. Especially, when I was coming to terms with Mr. Lewin. Mr. Lewin, apparently, had a blatant willingness to sleep with prostitutes. It disturbed me, not least because I was seeking a type of father-figure in him. After all, I had seen sex used as a boardroom tool, but never had I seen it used so expertly as a weapon against the family. He had seemed so sincere when he talked about his love for religion, family and country. I had been deceived. Those nights with Julie, while Kathleen scattered her clothes about this city, needed a justification, needed a being to redeem me and Mr. Lewin, albeit an American, gave me that justification. Simply knowing this man atoned for unfaithfulness; he seemed a 20th century holy man, an entrepreneur and family man, an entrepreneur and a family-man who would fight for his country and his God. I had even trusted him enough to confide in him.

I took an easy trip to the open space, Hyde Park, that lay forever in front of my window. This too yielded little satisfaction. Nothing seemed stable, there were always the uncertainties of the following day to face and the lights sparkling beneath a sun slowly setting over London neither pleased nor disgusted me. When I returned, Julie was looking out of the window, ready at last to persuade me to take me to 'her part' of town, somewhere she called home, a place to return to occasionally or regularly, but what is the point of these reconnaissance trips—I have never made any. Kathleen used to tell me that she loved certain parts of London, the lit up windows of Cadogan Square or the expensive facades on Sloane Street, even the smell of warm air in the underground. These things drew her to London more than just her vague ambition for success in the media over here.

Julie's part of town was quite far from the centre. The day I had met her, she had been visiting a friend who was fortunate to live in a council estate in the centre of London, others are not so lucky or so unlucky. Later, she explained that as well as glycerine, there were real tears on her cheeks. Her friend had had to fake a suicide attempt to be housed by the council three years ago. After getting it, she decided to buy it, fell behind on the mortgage payments and then really attempted suicide. Poor Julie and her friends!

Julie's home-town, set in the East of a capital swathed in variance was what I call city-suburbia. The members of this sad community wandered about badly designed concrete shopping-centres, minding their own business and only pausing to count their change or read the headline of a tabloid, generic cigarette poised between their chapped lips. Most of them were pensioners, walking slowly in outdated modes of dress, cold in the icy air and wondering how long their bones would take the chill. And amongst these crowds there was not a single smile. Eyes were an Orwellian-style blank, mouths were helplessly open or fixed straight, lying under discoloured nostrils. These were the people that despised the snobbishness and decadence of the West End of London—but for what? For a naive, hick mentality, the final evolutionary product of a Darwinian factory of lost dreams in which the conveyor belt probably squeaked. Their faces, their sadness made me cringe, these people seemed filthy in comparison to the beautifully washed and powdered faces of the West. Even their shoes, a true diviner of self-respect, were stained and encrusted in lost vegetables that had strayed from their stalls through rottenness and decay.

I thought about these people as we walked further through

the mazes of post-war council architecture, the manufactured street and road names of little worth, the smog-ridden tube stations burdened by their dull provinciality. Our search seemed a little pointless, it didn't matter who we saw here, they were all part of a subservient culture that had to be *made* interesting to stop it from seeming so uniform and grey.

"What's wrong?" she asked.

"I'm just tired, all this walking around," I said.

"It's all that smoking and worrying. Just loosen up when we meet my mates, OK?" she said before I nodded. We were going to see her friends, a meeting that I hadn't wanted even though I suppose it was fair that we should meet each other's cliques. The only irony was that my only friend, Osman, had disappeared from the mainland.

We eventually reached the small, semi-detached house in Northeast London, a vaguely reassuring sight for at least it wasn't in one of those estates. Then again, I along with the other estate-dwellers have an important affiliation—we both have rooms with views. Anyway, we opened the broken gate and I briefly looked at the badly kept green patch in front of the door. The sound was similar to that outside the front doors to my hotel: a rushing, crashing dual-carriageway lay in front of the house. Jack was holding a mug of tea when he opened the front door. After he had said hello in an off-hand manner that others would have thought nervous, he walked inside and left us to follow him. The first things I saw were the dangerous stairs and a doll-house-like table with an unplugged telephone lying on it. Above it, was a sheet of A4 paper and a list of the calls made this quarter; there weren't many.

The house was incredibly narrow and when I realised that Julie's friends merely rented one of the three flats that the house had been converted into I felt a measure of pity for them. However, I was fooling myself if I thought that I hadn't seen carpets as sheer, stairs as rickety or walls as bathed in dust. I had lived in a place like this, maybe only a little bigger, until the age of eleven.

We entered the living room and no-one got up. Planting

ourselves on an over-sized playgroup bean-bag, I smiled uneasily as I listened to Julie introduce me.

"Tea or coffee?" Jack asked me.

"Whatever you're drinking," I answered, staring at the crest on his blue track suit.

"What do you want?" Jack asked more insistently.

"Tea's fine thanks," I said, hoping that the sentence didn't sound like I didn't want it. He left the room whilst Julie talked to a boy sitting on the faded-print sofa. There was another boy at the other end and two girls sitting on chairs beside it. In pink synthetics, they seemed to be eyeing me up and down, but I could have been mistaken. Like an adolescent, I observed and wished to be observed. I looked around the room, at the framed Mona Lisa over the closed-off fireplace, the back-issues of Weapons' Monthly piled in a corner, the small framed and signed photograph of Margaret Thatcher, up on the bare mantelpiece.

"So what do you do?" Julie's friend asked me.

"Well, nothing really."

"Unemployed?"

"No, retired," I said, much to the merriment of the others. this was the extent of the conversation, leaving me to ponder on how little my accent had changed since my working-class upbringing. my attempts to converse, "what do you do?" left me unanswered and silent. Even "how do you know Julie" and "the weather forecast was wrong," didn't stir the silence. Jack interrupted my uneasiness with a Royal Wedding tray upon which was one cup of weak tea.

"Didn't you want anything?" I asked Julie.

"No thanks," she replied before turning away.

Jack sat himself between the two boys before Julie asked what they had all been up to.

"We went to the National last Saturday...met these really funny blokes," one of the girls was talking. the other was giggling. "We saw Bloat down there, but the music isn't as good anymore."

Another uneasy silence developed as Julie stunted her

social charm in favour of restraint. "So, what do you do?" asked Jack.

"We've been through all that," said the boy on the sofa, laughing, "we didn't really get an answer though. C'mon, let's go to the party then."

Soon we were leaving the house and walking down the suburban lane of small houses, each of us trying to fit into the width of the pavement. As we walked, I noticed the boy's and girl's (they were all younger than me) faces. In the house, they hadn't looked particularly pathetic. But now, now that they were again walking through the cold concrete mazes, they all assumed the likenesses of anaemic corpses. I, too, probably resembled them; we were of the same culture really.

After the estate, we crossed a couple of roads, stopping on the way to buy a few packs of beer which seemed to endear myself to the rest of the group. Then we reached a house that had a broken gate and a small green patch in front of the door. It looked so similar not only to the house that we had just been in but also to the rest of the houses on the street I thought we must have made a mistake. Julie was whispering in my ear: "You're alright, aren't you? I'm warning you, the party mightn't be good."

I smiled and put my arm around her, feeling the warmth of her woollen cardigan and brushing with her thick hair. She smiled back, showing dimples and the flashes of cold red on her cheeks.

Football; cricket; the girl next door; the postman's dog; the best radio DJs; the best clubs; imitations of last night's comedians; last week's visit to the flicks; car trouble if they were lucky to own one; the DHSS. These were all the elements of tonight's (and probably every night's) conversation. I sat listening, reacting to the vodka and 'h'orange. After an hour, through clouded eyes, I thought I recognised Bill Cates, a fellow student from my grammar school. he was looking at me too, sipping from a can of supermarket-beer. He looked much older, his hair was thinning and when he opened a wallet, that also looked familiar, to chip in for some more beer I could see a green coloured UB40 card skulking in one of the flaps.

Facial expressions began to blur and laughter resumed, possibly at me. But I had Julie to lean on while my thoughts spun to the latest white voice from New York and her taps-to-the-beat on my knee.

18

"Take me away from all of this," I didn't say to Julie. But I meant to, it seemed that I couldn't find my voice tonight. Bill Cates was still squatting on the carpet, now having picked up a newspaper through boredom: 'Police Acquitted in Cell-Death' it proclaimed.

In the lager-haze, I felt somehow in control. For all my neuroses, I didn't need Julie to sail me into calm seas of competence. And from that awareness rose pleasure, giving me the confidence to ask Julie whether she wanted to go. Wanting to please me, she agreed that the party was a little dull even though she had been talking all night and, let's face it, she loved these people. We said our goodbyes, mine being greeted by a gross indifference and walked out into the dark and frosty night. I put my jacket around Julie as we listened to the gravelly footsteps through the finely dusted street. The coincidences one comes to expect in a romance emerged in the form of a gleaming Byronic taxi, solitary and waiting for our fare.

"Taxi!" I shouted, waving my free arm.

We hugged each other tightly as we were driven home. As my head sat above Julie's shoulder, looking the opposite direction, I watched the lights speed by. Even in the taxi, it seemed cold and I felt glad that Julie was there with me, someone who could warm both my body and spirits. As we whizzed past Piccadilly Circus, I raised my eyes to the shimmering foreign adverts and lowered them to a police car, stationary and shining a screaming blue light from Eros to Shaftsbury Avenue. We had past into Piccadilly before we could see the faces of the angry black-and-white mob in handcuffs.

"You didn't like it, did you?" asked Julie tenderly as the Ritz flew past.

"It was alright," I replied, smiling, "You know that's where the MI5 offices are," I pointed to a building in Curzon Street underneath which a picket of some sort were staging a vigil. It seemed that the driver was taking us for the tourist-ride.

"MI6, sir, MI5 is near Westminster. That's the one that spies on foreign governments," said the driver before I shut the hatch.

"It is nice to be alone with you."

We walked arm-in-arm, crossing the foyer with a spring in our steps, whilst I tried to fit my billfold in my leather jacket. Like happy zombies, we waited for the lift, ascended with a silent thrust and arrived at the floor. Opening the front door and then, as Julie drank some water from the fridge in the kitchen, I opened the bedroom door. I must have left it ajar for a hundredth of a second, startled by the bed's lumpy fullness, its space-exhausting completeness, its two bodies lying in an embrace, the long hair hanging over the pillows like puppet strings.

"Come on, let's go to sleep, I'm tired out," Julie says once I've sat on the sofa. The bedroom door slowly swings open, interrupting the silence and a lethargic and night-gowned Kathleen enters the room, make-up less, contact-lens-less and underwear-less. Her eyes are an almost clear blue-grey.

"Hi, what have you two been doing then?" Kathleen says nicely, pinning her hair back into a ponytail with something like a rubber band. The sheer Stanislavskian professionalism makes me despise her. To retain her calmness in situations entirely unsuited to it is part of an education that I shall wonder about all my life.

"Some awful party—he'll tell you about it," Julie replies before affectionately jabbing me in the arm with her fingertips. There is nothing more to say and we fall into a silence, Julie biting or attempting to bite her nails and holding an uncharacteristically blank expression, Kathleen sleepily acting careless and myself folding my hands together, watching the moonshine like a light from a higher penthouse.

"So where are we all going to sleep?" asked Kathleen, yawning as if uninterested and then winking, smiling and showing off her sparkling teeth. Kathleen poured a few centilitres of sickly, blue curaçeo and sipped it from a crystal glass as the sleeping arrangements presumably weighed heavy on our minds. Julie then went up to the cocktail-cabinet and followed suit, pouring the blue syrupy drink and adapting to the newly-learnt customs of post-prandial, pre-sleep refreshments as if she was the daughter of an Onassis.

I seemed to react to the situation by craving the escape of sleep and didn't need so much as persuasion to spend the night on the sofa, somewhere inside devastated that I should not be allowed to sleep next to Julie. After Julie kissed me she turned out the light, smiling and telling me that there was nowhere Kathleen could go at this time. As she disappeared so Kathleen appeared from the kitchen looking concentrated and alert as she walked into the bedroom, turning to me before she slammed the door shut.

As the cars outside sped across Park Lane and beyond so they translated themselves into my dreams, me standing in the middle of a busy road, screaming as cars past through me.

And when I woke up, my back weary from being arched like a prostitute's, I saw the orange sun glow over streams of stationary cars, filled by single occupants breathing in lead, after so many days still not prepared for London's rush-hour. I walked away from the pane and into my bedroom as if automatically. I rubbed the stuff in my eyes and watching the bright light stream through my uncurtained bedroom, I looked down at my normally sparse bedroom, today littered by skirts, tops, tights and stray items of underwear, all cast aside in a manner suggesting they had been thrown. The girls were sleeping either side of the double bed, there was no third body, the one I had expected. I was tired again and wanted a bed to sleep in but it seemed that they were both out cold. I walked back out to the window and then back to the bedroom, trying to take a pair of pyjamas from the wardrobe without disturbing them. I heard my name being whispered.

"You must have been tired," Kathleen said, "you feel asleep in the middle of a conversation." I didn't remember any conversation. "I'm tired as hell—good night," she said after looking at me as I stood in a crumpled suit, my face unshaven and my fingers clutching the *Liberty*-print pyjamas. I crept out without answering, taking my clothes off in the bathroom and changing. Dressing-gowned, I left my apartment and knocked on Mr. Lewin's door.

"Good morning! What do you want, neighbour?" he asked, already dressed in suit and tie.

"Look, I'm sorry to barge in," I coughed, "but I don't seem to have a spare bed, can I sleep here?"

"Don't see why not. I guess I can trust you, I was going to tell you earlier but I've been so busy," he looked at his watch, "I'll be in Europe for a couple of days. The company hath spoken, wants me to see whether I can hunt down any successful companies. Anyway, can you just sort of look after the place?"

"I'm sure it'll be OK, there's a whole army of security staff after the siege last month."

"I know, but...well, you know what crime is like these days. There're so many people out there out of work and who want to cheat themselves into some money."

I nodded, my eyelids drooping as Mr. Lewin's white, crinkly face blurred. He put his hand on my shoulder, tossed a trilby on and left. I was soon sleeping in a comfy bed, as well made as the one in my room. I wondered why Mr. Lewin hadn't slept the previous night at the hotel, but I was too tired to explore the cause and effect.

It was about two hours later, deep in R.E.M., that I heard the electronic buzzer at the door. I walked to it, thinking about how Mr. Lewin couldn't be expecting a guest. All my muscles still ached and seemed abnormally tired. When I opened the door I squinted in the light, seeing high stilettos, small ankles and fat legs covered in fishnet stockings, a thin, very short pink dress beginning twelve inches above the knee and ending around a padded and conspicuous bra. Above this was a glinting, gold chain and a cross hanging around a slim neck and further still garishly painted lips, a bulbous nose and pale grey eyes, bloodshot and flickering behind pasted green eye shadow and false lashes. But even this coarse, ornament-like object, clashing with the hallway, didn't really wake me.

"What do you want?" I glanced at her curving, fleshy thigh and then at her face.

"Mr. Lewin asked for me," she said, leaning on the door-post, "Where is he?"

"Well, I think he's gone on a trip — he's going to be back in a few days, OK?" I said, gathering my dressing gown around my waist. She laughed.

"Is there anything I can do for you then? I've come a long way — aren't you going to give me some breakfast," she said softly, moving closer.

"As long as you're a friend of Mr. Lewin's," I said, moving backwards, "there're some things in the kitchen, I think, or you can phone up room service. Close the door behind you — you're sure you're a friend of Mr. Lewin's?"

"More than that," she said.

I walked back into the bedroom, hearing her shut the door as I took my gown off. About half an hour later the cover lifted and the girl, naked except for her stockings and a flimsy pair of zip-fastening panties tried to get in. "I'm tired too," she said.

"Go away," I said before turning over and returning to sleep, trying to ignore the new warmth and pushing her hands away from my midriff. Comatose for two hours, I was woken up by Julie and Kathleen briefly staring at me before leaving, this unknown girl sitting on the bed, her now bare legs crossed, her breast vulgarly falling into view.

"Sorry if I've got you into any trouble," she said, lighting a cigarette, "is it on Mr. Lewin's account."

'Account' I thought to myself before getting up, looking at the violet stain on the filter of her cigarette after she left. Julie opened the door.

"Who was that girl?" she said after a long time, angrily and sounding strange because of her tone.

"It was a call-girl..."

"What? No apology even?" she interrupted.

"A call-girl...it seems our neighbour hires her regularly... I've been caught in the cross-fire," I said wondering whether I had done the right thing in leaving her in Mr. Lewin's room and hating Mr. Lewin because of his lies.

"One of my friends does that," Julie said, "she spends the day sticking up labels in the telephone boxes...she earns a lot. She was clever, too," Julie seemed to grow pensive. "Anyway, I think Kathleen got the wrong impression, but I suppose neither of you care much anymore."

"Oh, I do care, Julie. If one partner doesn't trust the other than what's the point? You knew, you knew I hadn't done something stupid," I said, helping myself to the black coffee on the room-service trolley as Julie playfully touched my nose with her finger.

"I don't know...maybe you do go in for that kind of..." she was joking and I could get back to a little normality.

Summer was stopping. It even looked freezing out there. The leaves had begun to lose their green. I was looking out of the window, not liking the silence.

"We don't have to talk," said Julie, after I had made some hackneyed observations on the changing seasons in London. She was sitting next to me on the sofa as I looked puzzled, still shaken by everything that had happened. Julie had just had a shower and her towel had all but fallen off as she rested the side of her flushed face on my lap. "I like Kathleen. I think she's nice. I respect her. I can see what you saw in her, she's awful loveable," she was looking up at me but I was no longer paying much attention. "I mean, she has culture and all that, but she isn't snobbish about it all. She's confident and yet she has so much love, so much affection. Last night...oh, I love..."

I interrupted her, putting my hand over her lips, watching her smile as she buried her head deeper into my crotch. I thought about the two girls in bed together and smiled. I smiled, I'd once been told by one of Kathleen's school-friends, long ago, that she's once got off with a girl. It was this that created the tension with her parents. Poor Kathleen!" You sound as if you're really in love with her," I said suddenly.

"I think I probably am," she said, drawing away, "but what's up with you anyway? Why are you so tired? What did you do with that girl?" Again she was joking, loving her school-girlish sarcasm.

"Where did Kathleen go?" I asked but we lay together for a few minutes, kissing and feeling each other before the question became redundant but not answered.

"Hi, darling," said Kathleen, walking into the room. When she saw that I was there, her face became rigid and ugly with surprise, or maybe misunderstanding. Julie pulled her towel tightly around her and went to kiss her.

"What the hell are you?" asked Kathleen afterwards, "whoring bastard!"

Julie was quiet and I merely laughed, walking into the bathroom and waking myself up properly with a high-powered shower. Despite the height of the apartment, the spray is as pressurised as in the Alps. I remembered the instruction-guide which arrived when the hotel had it fitted. Physically, at least, I felt happier. Even the cologne was pleasant today. When I came out I saw them talking, whispering. As I watched them, animatedly communicating their thoughts and feelings, I wondered about how fast their friendship had crystallised. Two, seemingly different women, crossing class barriers that I had thought were impenetrable, had dropped all their inhibitions; so long as I wasn't there to spy on their affections. Their only common bond, it occurred to me, was their loneliness. Both had been cast aside by parents and relatives. Julie had once gone into great detail about her one very serious relationship and how her father had died. Actually, I hadn't paid much attention. I had given little importance to the story, instead selfishly and helplessly adoring her eyes and lips. But even this suddenly remembered event and another, Julie telling me that after her father's death she had stopped going around with boys, left me totally confused about the situation. It was quite normal for girls to demonstrate affections more physically than boys, but Julie and Kathleen seemed to embrace in a sensual, or rather erotic way. Not ever having been oversensitive about physical contact with others, or even able to diagnose sexual preference, I am sure that things were not what they seemed. Or rather, they were what they seemed.

"What's the ma..." Kathleen didn't finish her sentence as she too turned around to see me. Her tone was of disappointment and dashed expectation. But I stood there for only a few seconds before shutting the door behind me and getting dressed.

"Kathleen's inviting us to the Design Fair," Julie said as I left the bathroom.

"Oh," I replied, surprised and seeing the blatant reluctance in Kathleen's face and seeing Julie's towel rolled untidily into a ball on the thick carpet.

"Had you forgotten?" asked Kathleen snidely, "I invited you ages ago."

I took a tie from a bedroom cupboard and knotted it, listening to Kathleen explain what a design fair was to an eager Julie.

"Once there's was art," began Kathleen knowledgeably, "now there's design. It's the most wonderful concept...see this magazine, look at the graphics. The graphics, just the shapes and colours of the characters, not their order...look at that 'T'...they are responsible for the overall style and philosophy of the magazine. Now look at this advert...this too has a style and philosophy. You met Henry the other day, you know...that attractive boy."

"Yes, Kat, but..." Julie attempted to interrupt.

"Well, Henry works in philosophy—of a kind. He is given a brief...to design the overall identity of a company. It's fascinating..."

I was no longer pretending to straighten my tie but by now merely listening.

"Yes, but the advert and the magazine look pretty similar."

"Of course, that's the brilliance of design...it's now come of age and rules of signification have been drawn up. There are still differences between different sorts of product but only minor ones. It is basically the greatest form in which all the important facets of society at the moment manifest themselves."

"Gosh, it sounds really interesting."

"We should be there in an hour," said Kathleen, walking into the bathroom with Julie.

"Some people say that design is a virus making everything the same. But to you an me, artistic people, it's a great way of making money..."

I listened to Kathleen's confident words coming through the bathroom door. As I watched the cars and vans, I looked up at an electronic billboard, an advert for a recruitment agency, stark against the green mass behind it. 'FREEDOM' it proclaimed in a stylish script. The advert changed moments later. 'FROZEN PEAS' was the next message, again in the exactly the same script. I turned back to listen but there was now only the sound of running water. Returning to my view, I watched 'FREEDOM' return and smiled.

19

The journey to the large Victorian exhibition halls was uneventful and silent, leaving me to enjoy being sandwiched by two such schizophrenic, such engaging people. As we walked into the oppressively air-conditioned hall where countless trade-fairs had tired millions of people into buying and selling, Kathleen found two friends sporting slick-backed hair and grey suits. Their grey pallor and steady eyes matched, the latter moving slowly from Kathleen to Julie and then back again. In their strong looking hands sat sheaves of card and paper, decorated by colourful logos and accessible mottos. I looked at Kathleen's by-now azure eyes in the artificial mercury light and then around the hall, recognising faces and ties, submerged in my *milieu* of yesterday.

"Come on," snarled Kathleen, her black mini-skirt lifting over her slim thighs as she walked with the two men to where champagne was being distributed. The new privatised National Health Service logo was eye-catching, retaining the old letters, but now italicised and surrounded by blue ribbons and a gold stethoscope. One of Kathleen's friends knew the designer of the logo and Kathleen tried and failed to 'deconstruct' the meaning of it. Julie listened attentively, brushing her hair back and diverted only by one of the bikini-clad promotion girls that swung their waists past us as they handed out leaflets.

"Hello!" said someone behind me. I turned around and stared at the face of Mr. Saine, his description incommunicable. There was little that I could reply with, I thought of asking about a client that had been giving us a little trouble, or one of the secretaries who had been worried about the effects of

VDUs on her unborn child. In the end, I asked how he was and after a pause he shuffled away, lost in the crowds of businessmen, anxious to sell their products in new and imaginative ways.

I remember my first day at work, the sudden consciousness of the power of advertising and with it the eager-to-teach executives, proudly lending fifties' textbooks like 'The Hidden Persuaders' to a humble coffee-clerk. It seemed to me that as different accounts—soft drinks, high street banks to cars—were discussed, there was always something linking all of them: 'the mood of the moment.'

At the moment, the newly glamorised studio apartments in the East End, sparse and efficient, were the set for a whole variety of products. Advertisers attached their products to their agents' own dreams. Efficiency and uncluttered habitats where consumers threw out anything unnecessary were part of a dream for all society. We were not only chronicling passing trends but creating radical themes to embed in the public imagination. This activity itself had enthralled me only a few years ago, spurring me on and producing profound desires for success and power. But I was no longer one of them and whereas before I wouldn't attend exhibitions for fear of attracting people who were anxious for advice, now I was afraid of attracting scowls and frowns.

In the crowds around a graphic design company showing off their Computer Aided Design packages for defence contracts, Kathleen fell out of sight. Julie and myself, close together in the mêlée, what with all the audience participation, watched as if it were a Punch and Judy show, friendly-looking robots dancing around on a table, launching toy rockets and submarine torpedoes into the crowd.

Julie and myself left to have some lunch in the restaurant where well-designed, poor quality food was served to expense-account executives, out to impress. We presumed that Kathleen had left with some of her friends which I thought was a little impolite. It prompted only a sigh from Julie. She hardly ever opened her mouth, as if cast by a spell for which only Kathleen knew the antidote.

We walked out to the clamped car and then back into the foyer where we waited for an advertisement-covered black taxi. Julie's demeanour had affected me too and as we mounted the cab in the crisp West London air, I felt unsettled but also annoyed by Kathleen's disappearance. It had never occurred to me that there was anything sinister involved and the phonecall that we received, after hours of random channel switching of the television, was strangely ironic. Our hours had been spent watching violence and to be awoken by a threat of real violence could only summon up muted responses.

"Oh, Kathleen, no!" cried Julie, rather melodramatically, although I, too, was worried. I had always been suspicious about her effortless departure from Los Angeles—surely defence contracts were delicate matters and leaving a company on a whim would be highly irregular. Resignations took years to finalise in security-sensitive institutions, not days. Now, my suspicions had been realised. I was still not sure who 'had' her or for what motive, I only knew they wanted money and that Kathleen's friends were, by and large, a secretive lot.

At last, she was in some kind of danger; I hated myself for feeling so pleased about it all. I seemed to have temporarily lost some of my affection for her and Kathleen, so determined and untouchable, finally in danger, held myself nervously interested.

All of the details were over in a couple of damp and cloudy days in which the concrete landscapes I visited looked sharp and frightening and in which I had become a few thousands of pounds poorer. Kathleen had been little changed by her ordeal and rapidly returned to her usual self, relating the events of her adventure in an annoyingly proud and arrogant way. She had, possibly justifiably, reduced all my time-consuming conversations with Eaglesbrook about the complications of the case, to the direction of a gun barrel. The beautifully woven story, dyed in truth and fiction, was told with flourish to Julie, who sat on the floor biting her exquisite nails and waiting for Marlon Brando to appear.

After all the pressure and worry, we all needed a holiday

but what with my court proceedings approaching I was pretty tied down. I'm not sure how they persuaded me but, in the end, the girls left without me, hinting only subtly where their expeditions would take them, now that Kathleen's golden handcuffs were off.

Alone again, I slept late into the afternoon and watched television into the night. The hourly news bulletins went ignored, only sometimes a headline briefly catching my eye and taxing me; for an instant I thought about one of the thousands laid off in St. Louis, Detroit or Houston or one of the thousands killed in an earthquake many, many, miles away. Drinking began to play a part in my lethargy, but all of my hangovers were caused more by boredom than alcohol overdosing. And all those hours, shouting at the windows to escape from my life, waking and feeling dusty and tight, never knowing how to fill up my time, they were all pressed by guilt.

The curtains half-drawn, I would slump onto the sofa with a leg on a stool and begin to command the VCR to play and stop. I thought all of this would end soon, these hours in which I never had cause to dress, instead left to endure the burning apathy throbbing in my veins — day and night. I saw no-one but the room-service boy, an innocent-looking chap with pointed ears and large brown eyes and fidgeting hands, and a Far Eastern maid who smiled intermittently and never wore tights, even as winter approached. I worried about where Julie and Kathleen were. I had only given them money enough for a week and after that their non-appearance disturbed me.

Occasionally, in the bathroom, I would catch sight of my reflection in the mirror, my face looking thinner and thinner as I coughed up phlegm into the basin. I would madly spray perfume to get rid of the stale cigarette fumes and retire to the sofa again to view only grey skies above a cold and uninviting city, hardly changed but for a few uncompleted office developments and a couple of towering, steel cranes.

I was not sure about this 'guilt' and its cause and its remedy. But its symptoms I knew well. The pain from stomach to throat and the confusing current affairs that tempted me towards frustration and even anger. Newspapers piled up in a corner. There seemed little information in The Times, instead just ideologies clashing with events and rosy tinted half-truths about executives whose careers had fallen flat. This was not the time of insider dealers caught and sentenced as examples—this was a time of unexpectedly quiet corporate bankruptcies filling the financial pages with ambivalence and puzzlement. But then, reflecting on the city again, I realised that I still loved it. Instead of leaving for brighter prospects over the Atlantic or in the Far East, I had chosen to stay, risking only that I might seem like a Titanic band-leader. These weeks, I persuaded myself, were a time for thinking things out, a transition period in which I could weigh up my achievements to date. It was a marker that helpfully compartmentalised my life just as, I suppose, the time before a painter begins a new period.

I wondered one day, after deliberating upon the passage of time and my age, which of the maid and the room-service boy would be first to suggest a panacea that would reduce my obvious misery. It turned out to be the maid, who cautiously hinted that I might like to get some fresh air and stroll through the park. I thanked her and tipped her extra for her advice and left the hotel in a poorly-cleaned suit, realising almost immediately that the environment outside was much more irritating than that of my room. The lead-saturated air seemed much less fresh than that in my air-conditioned room. Nevertheless, I crossed the road, climbing over the knee-high fences, surveying the muddy grass with a broad grin on my face. As I walked past an ornate black-statue celebrating a historic battle that I had never heard of, I thought about Julie, this sketchy character who I knew only in a shallow way, this girl who I went about London with, both of us silent and paying optimistic attention to each other. She was impressionable and, for all her tough and hardened *milieu*, weak; weak not so much in her actions of self-improvement but also in her devotion to Kathleen, a spoiled girl with only a unique sparkle to highlight her against the thousands of others brought up in a similar fashion.

I walked for a couple of hours, walking by the Serpentine,

country-like but for the red streams of brake-light passing over a stone bridge. I walked past some large trees, their leaves transforming to ochre. And then, as I thought of Julie, I thought I saw both of them on a bench. I carried on, heedless of direction, instead transfixed upon red-anoraked Americans with cameras and arrogant swans and frightened swallows. Without knowing it I had begun to walk over paths already taken and only when I saw the badly dated Serpentine restaurant I calmed down. Inside, I ordered water and sat myself down in a setting conspicuously of another, greyer decade. I looked out towards boats and caught my reflection, my unintentionally sneering eyes, ringed in black and flecked by strands from the lump of blonde hair on my forehead. I looked like a blindly eyeliner-ed whore. I put my head in my hands, exhausted by my self-pity, as the waitress switched a radio on, before it announced the death-toll of "The Enterprise Culture", part of a fleet owned by a profit-making company. A passenger was speaking modestly of his part in the saving of lives and then, uncharacteristic of a hero, choked in anger, asking why the lessons of previous accidents hadn't been learnt. I stopped listening.

As I walked out I tried to remember where Julie and Kathleen had been going for their holiday. The name of the place was on the tip of my tongue and I stopped for a moment still not recalling which city, which country or even which continent they had chosen. I thought of them on a beach, lying next to each other and then tried to think of something else, only recognising that they must have gone South of the Mediterranean latitude. But then, just as I neared Knightsbridge Barracks, my walk was interrupted, by the sight of both of them. My eyes, half-closed in the bright grey light, shut and reopened before confirming their presence.

"Julie!" I shouted, waving my arm and watching them run away. Suddenly, I began to chase after them in a fatigued, last-joule-of-energy-run, before I foolishly let myself stumble and fall, later remembering only Julie's face as she looked over me, holding my hand, and then the screeching sirens of the ambulance that sped through the traffic to the hospital.

20

I don't think that I have ever spent a night in a hospital. All the health insurance forms had never meant anything to me. But this night I would spend, truly helpless, between starched sheets and surrounded by inelegant machines. There was no-one by my side when I woke up, and for a couple of minutes I just peered around the room like a spy. I could see the cars following their routes, far below and in the dark, the outlines of the branches of a tree just outside my window. I was too young for heart attacks or strokes, I thought.

I could clearly see the nurse as she talked to me about my accident but her words seemed jumbled and to blur into one another. 'Whatever my illness I would have to spend some weeks in convalescence' I thought.

"Was there anyone in to see me?" I asked, stuttering like a self-piteous cripple.

"There were two girls who brought you in. I think they left but I'm sure they'll be back tomorrow. It's time to sleep..." she said before stretching her uniform to draw the curtains, then smiling, and then turning out the light.

Possibly crying between the green blankets, my emotions were quelled by fatigue. The bed-pans and the smell of disinfectant made me feel the actual indignity of helplessness. I hoped that Kathleen and Julie wouldn't turn up—at least not until I had more control. Pride seemed to seep into my bones as I lay in the hospital bed. I'd have to ask for books the next morning although boredom in my hotel-room had never driven me to reading. I reached, with not a little pain, at the headphones and pressed the radio-station buttons. Uncomfortable as the ear-pieces were, I listened with subdued glee when I heard the midnight-news, telling of more oil-price decreases and Mexico's debt problem. Life, at least, was carrying on out there, and the next day inevitable visitors would bring me beauty and life. I thought about them both, bringing roses for me the next day, the nurse looking for a vase. But thoughts turned into sleep and then dreams—dreams in which the roses magically turned into funeral wreaths.

It seemed a long time waiting for the next morning but Julie appeared with some carnations and we talked. She must have had a long discussion with Kathleen the previous night. Her words didn't match her sad, hazel, eyes—she didn't want to upset me with half-truths. Even so, she had found time to apply her make-up, and this time I could tell that the style was Kathleen's. I didn't have the energy to express my doubts and we were soon speaking of superficialities.

"But it's a nice room, at least. You'll be out of here as soon as you start to love it," Julie said.

"One doesn't love hospital, Julie," I said morosely.

"You know what I mean," she smiled, "and then we'll sort out everything. But don't worry, otherwise you won't get better. And then there won't be anyone to keep an eye out on me and Kathleen," she winked.

"Yes, that's true. It's just I can't stand lying here. It's like I'm some old man being cared for," I said, finding myself more fluent than before. But Julie didn't reply, just the same strangely sad expression played on her face. How I hate pity!" So where are you going after this?"

"Back to the hotel-room. I'll probably see Kathleen, we'll just sit and watch TV."

"Good, I don't want you to do anything exciting," I said sarcastically.

"Well I better get back—I'll see you tomorrow."

"Thanks so much for the carnations, they've really brightened up the room," I said before she kissed me on the cheek, as if it were protocol, and left. The door with the little glass window banged shut before I saw her black outfit recede into the distance. Again, I was alone, this time I would have to endure the hours with no hope of another visit until tomorrow. She had brought a bag of books—quite a variety. Mailer, Len Deighton, Barbara Taylor Bradford, Jackie Collins, an inevitable nineteenth century Russian and even a Mary Renault. I looked at them for a few moments and began to read, waiting either for catharsis or escapist happiness. But I couldn't even bear the wait. I soon put the books back in their *Vuitton* bag and pushed the TV buttons at my bedside. Children's programmes were all I could see in the distance and the effort of calling the nurse to switch the video on was too much. All the while, I must have looked insane, a nervous twitch beginning in my left cheek. I asked whether she had a mirror and she had. My nurse began to take on the appearance of a saint after a day and a half in hospital, so keen to please and yet still not ideal. Nevertheless, compared to the National Health Service, this was paradise and what with their problems, I wondered why everyone didn't go private instead of sticking to a nationalised institution because of a romantically misplaced allegiance.

Weakly holding the light green plastic surround of the mirror, I twitched as I saw my reflection. My face looked thin, underneath the stubble. The complexion seemed drained and anaemic, the eyes circumfused by darkness, the pink and red lips bloodstained and chapped. Even the endearingly mischievous sparkle of my round eyes seemed to have disappeared. But the after-effects of my fall were not to do with my appearance— they were probably, as the nurse tried to explain, to do with my mind. Looking into the mirror, from the greasy mop of blonde hair to my pale hands, I realised that my state of mind was exaggerating the image. I closed blood-shot eyes and fell back onto the pillow, letting the mirror drop on the blanket.

All the hours of satiated fatigue didn't make me say to myself 'I'm wasting my time—I should be doing things out there.' The weeks before my attack I hadn't been spent making anything of my life, so I wasn't wasting any time by being in hospital. If I had been at my hotel-room instead of a safe hospital I would have, for the first time, had to face horrible home-truths. I tried to convince myself that it was my imagination, that everything was as it appeared to be, but I soon found my way to the haunting thoughts of the people I loved leaving, laughing and lying. The smiles of destroyed friendships; Kathleen had always been scheming, she had always known how to get around me. This time I could only assume that she had taken some form of natural revenge. But it wasn't just the girl who I've known for so long, it was Julie too. It was an impossible situation and gradually I knew that they could do what they liked—I had no say in any of it. I loved them both and maybe this was a fair end.

And so as the light went out I could only wonder—now that my career had fallen so badly and I was so alone—whether there really was anything that people like me had to live for.

21

They say things always feel better in the morning. In some unfathomable way they did. I looked forward to seeing Julie in all her newly acquired glamour—she looked beautiful in costumes chosen, by Kathleen, from New Bond Street. But what I most wanted was someone who was straightforward, and Julie of all the people I had ever known, was that. All the lies and suspicious glances had been draining me. However, my reward for such renewed optimism was Julie not, after all, turning up. Calling the hotel, now I was feeling fitter, I heard only a recorded message—my recorded message. I didn't leave any words after the tone. Asking for company felt ridiculous—couldn't I cope with hospital on my own? Besides there was always a nurse to talk to in between her calls. The hours seemed to have gone quickly—though I had done little in them. But I was angry and hurt about my morning's eager anticipation.

Mornings became days and submerged in a culture of soap operas and chat shows, I gave up on love and companionship, and withdrew. The TV, whether it was Teletext or Hollywood, brought me my smiles, truck-loads of smiles that lasted for seconds. Only sometimes did the lonely evenings and nights cause tears to annoyingly well up in my eyes and even more rarely did uncontrollable weeping drive me to late night radio agony-aunts. I soon began to know the presenters and learnt their foibles and odd senses of humour. In the mornings, I was the one who ordered the flowers for my room, from a little florists' shop on the street-corner. To the doctor, who called every day, and my pleasant nurse, I gave the impression of being happy and ready to approach the race of city life.

Nothing caught my attention in the newspapers—no pictures of long lost friends making it big or small on the financial pages. But I followed the leading political stories and scandals; the cabinet reshuffles and the demonstrations. Sometimes exciting stories of new natural disasters on the other side of the world or fiery riots, ten miles away, would enrapture me. It was a sorry life of bored leisure, of never admitting boredom—only trying to interest myself in subjects thought previously mundane. I had got used to this room, with its four imposing white walls. I had grown accustomed to seeing the faintly pretty nurse take my pulse, her eyelashes groomed for her evening out, and the doctor, always with airs of seriousness. The nurse looked naïve compared to a doctor who was so obviously ambitious. I felt that the doctor knew some of what I had known—even his strides to the door were expressions of his desire for power. He was studious too, anxiously learning from older medics that sometimes past through. He was a little like myself, some years earlier in the agencies. All in all, it was an ordered, even regimented, life and it was with mixed feelings that I looked forward to arranging my own life. What I most wanted was an evening out at a restaurant, to sip after-dinner coffee and watch the clientèle look wistfully at each other about the tip. I remember how in the top London restaurants, a pile of credit cards would crash onto the table, after a meal, as everyone offered to pay, each one trying to outdo the other. I remember Osman always having the newest cards and how they always seemed the loudest.

They were all pleasures that seemed commonplace to the average person out there, but for me they were unapproachable. On the last night of my stay, checking the metres of hospital-bill thermal printout and touching my hands to sense their tightness, I looked back at how well I had coped. No-one had been in to see me, the carnations that my last visitor had brought me were by now rotting in a rubbish tip. In the two and a half weeks that had felt like months, I had become thoroughly used to the smell of disinfectant. Even the enforced lack of smoking with its accompanying withdrawal symptoms was alright.

Nevertheless, I was missing my room, my views, even my neighbour, Mr. Lewin. Dressed in clothes that I had to have bought for me by the nurse, I picked up the clip-binder from the end of my bed. On it was drawn a beautiful graph showing my financial reckoning, day by day. I handed it in, paid and left. I didn't taken another glance back. I had taken a couple of very short walks during my stay but this time there was no-one to restrain me. I didn't seem to be able to walk as fast as before but, so the doctor told me, this would be temporary. The taxi I had ordered took me to the hotel. The suit I was wearing was made from measurements that I luckily remembered. I had it done in black so it looked formal and I could use it again. Stopping at a bank to retrieve some money, I was slightly shocked to see how so much had been withdrawn by the two girls.

The weather, a glorious near-autumn day of sunshine and blue skies, cheered me up. Passing through tree-lined roads, gazing at the bistros and cafés of South Kensington, I recovered my love for the city. Suited boys and designer-dressed girls on their lunch-breaks—they all looked so unaware as I watched from the taxi with such optimism. Walking into the hotel, after generously tipping the driver, I realised I was happy. The spring of the foyer carpet on my new shoes, the tame soporific air of steadiness in the eyes of the businessmen and even catching my lame but rather handsome reflection in one of the mirrors didn't stop me from feeling both satisfied and eager as I asked the concièrge for my keys.

I listened at my door to hear if anyone was in—my keys were the spare ones. The room looked like a tidied mess, the maid must have hated these girls. Otherwise it was empty. I walked straight over to the window and looked out: already clouds had begun to obscure the sun. The scene hadn't changed, all the buzzing cars, the trees, albeit with a few fewer leaves, still reached into the sky. I turned around and looked at my room, my back leaning on the window. 'Home!' I thought, not worried about my new search for security. I took my jacket off and sat down, trying to catch my breath. The way I coughed, anyone would think I was about to die. Anyway, I left the room in shirt sleeves, a tie loosened about my neck.

"Hell..." my words stopped when Mr. Lewin's door opened.

"Yes?" an imposingly attired man asked pleasantly.

"Is Mr. Lewin in?" I asked.

"No."

I realised that Mr. Lewin must have checked out. "Oh, I'm sorry, my friend must have left."

"I suppose he did," he said, now seeming annoyed. I apologised again and left for my room, ready to inspect the post. Apart from credit-card bills and a couple of pre-recession invitations from companies in America, there was nothing of interest. Just as I was relaxing, taking care not to be tempted by the glass decanter filled with cognac or the packet of twenty on the coffee table, I heard the door open. Turning around, I saw Kathleen. I didn't notice her boxes of new clothes, only her beauty. I seemed to wilt in front of her.

"Oh it's you. Sorry, I mean, how...how was," Kathleen stuttered, "when did you get back?"

"Just a couple of minutes ago," I said, "so what's the news?"

"Nothing much. Julie and I have been going to parties and...well we were just waiting for you to come back." Her lies hadn't changed. I felt close and uncomfortable, I didn't want to ask her why she had never come and visited me. I didn't reply and she went into the bathroom.

"I see we have a new neighbour," I said.

"What?" she couldn't hear through the door.

"I said I see we have a new neighbour," I said it louder, straining my voice. She opened the door wearing a half done up blouse, her skirt around her ankles.

"Yes, we have a new neighbour. Look I'm getting changed— can we talk when I've got ready?" she said, angry and sounding so reasonable.

"Where are you going?" this time I was annoyed.

"Our neighbour, as you like to call him, is having a party—okay?" she said, quickly doing up her buttons and closing the door, nearly tripping over the skirt. Any mood of cheerfulness had vanished. Now, I could only look forward to seeing Julie. Kathleen came out of the bathroom and began to search for earrings.

"Where's Julie?" I asked.

"She's meeting me at the party," she said, seeming to have calmed down. But with this sort of response, I decided to take the car-keys and drive. I'd have dinner at a restaurant that I hadn't been to for a long time. Kathleen knew the place and I told her before I left, although her only care was pinning up her hair and which mascara to use. When I saw the car, with it's new dents and scratches, I felt like throwing them both out tomorrow. Cars come before anyone else, I joked to myself, thinking about what my father would have said as I manoeuvred myself out of a terrible parking position.

22

A t last I was back in the scrum of the traffic, rather than just a naïve *voyeur*. Shouting profanities at other drivers and hurting my nerves, I swerved from lane to lane and made an illegal turn into Oxford Street. Often distracted by the thousands of shoppers, I waited at lights too long, much to the helpful disgust of taxi-drivers. I wasn't bothered about policemen today and, besides, I needed to see people, normal, everyday-people, carrying company-defaced carrier bags and broken umbrellas. I turned into Soho and began circling the roads looking for parking, at first delighted by the setting but soon tired and hungry. I got a space eventually and after fumbling with change I was soon walking about Leicester Square admiring the tramps and cinemas. Sitting at a bench made me a *voyeur* all over again and I adored it. There were no walls to break my confidence, no disinfectant to upset my sinuses. But pleasure soon merged into self-pity and my meal was turned into a lonely drinking session. How I'd like to shake it all off!

Double after double, and eyes closed, the room began to turn around and around. The white tablecloths inspired by a *nouveau* way of eating and drinking were moving erratically, and somewhere lodged between the images, when I momentarily opened my eyes, was Julie. She would be the only person to notice my elbow slipping off the table.

"What are you doing?" asked Julie, angry but worried, and the thought of someone caring sobered me up. I stood up and kissed her on the cheek.

"Just celebrating my leaving hospital," I said humbly.

"Well I've come to take you back, take you to the party.

Sometimes Kathleen's so impolite," she said employing a tasteless understatement. I mumbled something and she paid the bill, after rubbing the whisky off my chin with a lace handkerchief. I was too drunk to feel the pleasure of sitting in a cab with Julie again, I just smiled at her, and she sort of smiled back. I hadn't taken my doctor's advice, and paid for it in the embarrassing moments in which I tried to kiss her, exploding in a fit of coughs. Ever-wonderful, she asked me whether I was okay. Thank God, I wouldn't have an attack that night. Back at the hotel, after being helped all the way, I staggered into the party. "Are you sure you want to go in?" Julie asked me before knocking. I nodded, as if the occasion was meant for me to prove the state of my mind.

The faces inside seemed to differ considerably, each one looking like they should have been somewhere else. Many of them danced in the middle of the room to a hard drum-machine, their faces bathed in a sheen of sureness. But like any shined objects, at certain angles they looked flawed, insecure, maybe even dangerous. I had already picked a seat, I wasn't here to pick anyone up and if I did the person would have to get turned on by ill-looking men. Julie had gone to get me a drink, and she soon appeared with a glass of *Perrier* for me and a glass of wine for herself.

"Why didn't you visit me when I was in hospital?" Now I had the courage.

"It's complicated, well...Kathleen said it wasn't advisable for us to see each other...I mean for me to see you," she said fumbling the same way I had with the parking meter.

"So you do what she says?" I asked, my words sounding less distinct.

"You don't understand, we're friends, we respect each other's wishes—that was her wish," she said, sliding her left hand to her temples and then over her hair.

"And what if it hurts someone else in the process?" I asked impatiently.

There was no answer, just an emotionless shrug of her shoulders that made her look more like a witch than the second-most beautiful girl I had ever seen. She walked over and began talking to a suited gentlemen in the corner, back to her pleasing, vivacious self. Suits and bad dresses, how I despised them all of a sudden!

"Hello, I'm Morris," a man in a silk suit introduced himself to me and with a faint heart I shook hands. "I'm your new neighbour, we ran into each other this morning," he said, as I remembered his manly features. There seemed to be so much confidence trapped between the high cheek bones and black crew-cut hair. His eyes glinted with over-seriousness, the sort that is asking for a laugh no matter how sincere his words were.

"Oh yes, sorry about the mix-up. I've been in hospital for the last couple of weeks."

"Are you alright?" he asked, flexing his cheek-bones again and looking worried. Why he was worried for a man he had only just met I wasn't sure—I could have been a bastard or a dole-scrounger.

"Yes, just a little tired," I said, sounding ill.

"You should stay off the alcohol, it's bad for you," he said as I began to prepare myself for an onslaught of alternative medicine promotion.

"What do you do?" I asked, trying to stop the course of the conversation.

"I mean I used to drink a lot, but now I don't need a drop to feel good," he said as I noticed the double-jointed thumb of his left hand. "What do I do?" he said, "I'm in the music industry." I began to recognise his face, perhaps fooling myself, the way one does when one makes a new acquaintance.

"A pop star?" I asked.

"No, a middle man. In between the disc jockeys and the record labels," he said, "What do you do?"

"Oh, I'm retired," I said in a resigned manner, before he smiled. I suppose I hadn't aged so much after all. He could have started talking about how terrible it was to be thrown on the scrap heap after the age of sixty-five. I suddenly realised, as I looked at Morris, that I didn't want to talk to this man and, for that matter, didn't really feel like talking to anyone.

"That's what I'd love to do," he continued to speak while I wandered.

"Sorry?"

"I'd like to retire, but...well you never have enough money do you?" he asked.

"No, I suppose you don't," I replied, "look I'm sorry, but I'm quite tired, would you mind terribly if I left. I know it's impolite."

"Sure, I understand. I had forgotten you'd just come back from hospital. There's lots of drink, lots of girls , but if you're tired then I don't want to stop you. Besides, I'm sure we'll be seeing a lot of each other," he said sounding like another saintly Mr. Lewin.

I got up and asked an oblivious Kathleen, locked in an embrace with a nobody, whether she had the keys. She pointed, smiling and squinting, to her handbag before my hands stumbled through it. Finding the keys, I closed the bag and looked around me. My glances lasted only for a few seconds, long enough to see Julie dancing surrounded by applauding people. It was upsetting to find myself so cynical, so I left the superficialities and inconspicuously closed the door behind me.

Locking myself into my room, crouching with my back to the door, I looked around—I had all the keys.

23

After my head had recovered as much as it could, I eased myself up, using the door for leverage. Employing a strength that made my mind go blank, I pushed the sofa against the door. Brushing my teeth and undressing in the bathroom, I felt those long-lost joys of privacy—when there was no disturbance. After turning out the light and resting for a few moments, I got up and called the concièrge to tell them I must not be disturbed—on any account. This time, I flopped onto my bed to sleep without interruption. The sheets still retained their fragrance of perfume as I began imagining knocks on the door.

24

Kathleen

Gosh, London has something special about it! There's a boom in this city that rivals the twenties and it's poignant to dance the night away in the Savoy to a jazzy trio as the champagne is poured into crystal. Morris Castle says it's not the same, that the balls are now special occasions for charity rather than regular nights of decadence—but then what does he know?

A for *him*, he's moody and depressed as usual, eager only to stop the fun by telling us about hospital bills and the slow drop in share prices. He's loaded and he's thinking he doesn't have the cash! Still, I have a couple of things to thank him for. Julie was his girl and it *is* his money. Julie seems to the luckiest thing to happen to me, she's terribly loveable and sweet and even quaint after the sophisticated belles of Bel Air. She's my constant companion, we shop together, get dressed together. Without him, we've had a great time, romantically driving in the countryside in Michelin-starred restaurants. If only Tony Pakula knew what I was doing!

In one way I feel a little sad that me and him didn't hit it off. The first nights were really cool, talking about old times and toasting Claret. If I'd only got here earlier I would have saved him from all this trouble. He seems to have just got himself in with a bad crowd. This Osman guy, I met him and laughed in his face, he's just another of these insecure little English ex-private boarding school show-offs who don't have a clue.

I suppose it's kind of symptomatic of the boom that so many young and inexperienced adults suddenly end up driving fast German cars, never learning the style to drive them. I was used to it in LA. There were still social classes there but instead of breeding and history their inheritance relied on money. Over here, I was surprised to find aristocrats selling off paintings and stately homes to working class do-gooders.

There's a dizzy sense of history here which one can't get in LA, and with it a certain quaintness in those small streets and the Georgian mansions. They try to fake it over there, putting up mock Tudor and mock Athenian which makes it a lot more fun but also makes you realise you're not seeing the real thing. I'm surprised he didn't buy one of those cosy places in Chelsea instead of living high up in a place one can never call home. I suppose it's just one of his many eccentricities and while they might have been endearing before, they now just stink of self-pity and uncertainty.

Julie's coming to my table, now brandishing what looks like heavy volumes of fiction but which are, in fact, a selection of glossy titles from the hotel bookstore. It's fun taking part in the fashion world, buying the season's clothes and this year's darling designer as if there were no tomorrow and it's fun, too, wearing them and being watched in them. I must admit I miss work sometimes but Julie is so wonderful, so warm and easy-going that I don't feel alone anymore. I suppose leaving LA succeeded in that and, apart from a few problems, the excesses of the US Military and a certain career-doomed young man, I'm proud of my decision. Life, it seems to me, is about being in the right place at the right time and, for me, London in the late nineteen-eighties is the place to be.

It's late now and Julie has gone to find an earring that she lost. My mind is spinning to the strains of the Maria Callas being pumped through the speakers as groups of people sip at night-caps, talking about their pleasant evening and the far off destinations that the idle rich talk about. The sight of the

Grand Marnier on the silver tray almost makes me bring up my dinner. I really have had too much champagne. I'm also a little uptight because I'm out of coke and it seems much more tiresome to get it here than in LA I start to think about him as I move my fingers and tighten the muscles in my ankles. He *is* still handsome, even though he seem to disregard, purposely, his appearance. His dark suits may not be well pressed, but they're beautifully cut. The problem, I think, is that he doesn't notice me the way other men do. He's interested, in a patronising sort of way, in my career, in what I'm doing but doesn't care for a new dress or piece of jewellery I might have bought. Anyway, me and Julie are good together for everything. I'm not even looking for a lover anymore—no girl has given me climaxes like she has.

I'm not unfeeling and I recognise that a career is more important to him now, but he seems incapable of enjoying himself, the way we all do. I pity the guy, I hope he'll cope and he finds his way out because he's definitely starting to cramp our style. It's important that he stops all this rot, at least, if he wants to have half as much fun as we all our, in this glorious and enchanting boom. Oh God, bless the boom!

25

I awoke around mid-day, somewhat of an achievement for me, and stirred the sugar into my black coffee, gazing over the city and hoping that somewhere, Julie and Kathleen were suffering.

The window was blurred with water and the dark, thundery sky allowed the lights of cars to shine; to travel and to merge. There were no pedestrians to dance to the radio's unknown classical music, only hundreds upon hundreds of paired lights, turning from amber to red as they braked in unison. Already, my enforced seclusion was beginning to tax me—the long, complex symphonies of, as it turned out, Mozart only staved off the need for people for an hour. By then, the drops of rain outside were echoed by tear drops on my cheek, an unrestrained effect of my emotions that, I hoped would flush my illness away. I plugged the phone in and, to my surprise, it began to ring. The romance of weeping on silk had started to fade as sniffles travelled through the house-phone-lines.

"Hello..." I said catching my melancholic reflection in the window panes—a naked reflection that summed up my disenchantment.

"Yes, Morris Castle here," said Mr. Castle, "is Kathleen there?"

"No, no she isn't," I replied, keeping calm.

"Julie?"

"No, she's out too. I'm not sure where they are."

"Ah, you're the fellow who came to my party."

"Yes," I said, charmed that he remembered me.

"You don't sound too well, I hope you're better than you were the other night."

"Yes, thanks. It must be the pollen in the air or something," I said, speaking and glancing outside as if courting insanity.

"What are you doing today?" he asked, as if finding a new purpose for his call. I imagined him brushing back his black hair and looking at his appointments' diary. How organised and confident he seemed to be!

"Not much. How about a drink somewhere?" I asked, eager to go somewhere with a disinterested party.

"I told you about drinking," he said as I remembered his comments and then suddenly became worried about myself again. "Yes, of course, I'll meet you," he said in perfect public school-speak.

We arranged the time, about an hour from the time the receiver rested. I waited for a while, in case someone—Julie— had been worrying and phoning me, but it seemed that I was being optimistic.

As uniformed as a Mayfair businessman, I stepped out of the lift sensing a new, healthy vanity. It was with meticulous care that I buttoned down my collars and shaved each bristle on my face. Mr. Castle was already sitting on one of the chairs when I entered the lounge on the ground floor. He had outdone me in my excuse for dandyism, dressed as he was in a suit by a British designer. He seemed a nice man, even a good man, but I was probably swayed by his eyes which looked at me with a subdued respect. He seemed alone, too, and anxiously confided in me about his worries in the present financial climate.

From a classically brilliant public school background, his upbringing had always been focused on his career. It was, of course, understated, even shunned since success in any business sense was still apt to upset the Stowe establishment. His parents found subtle ways of cajoling him into business, supplying him with friends exclusively from business backgrounds and leaving fill-in tax-deduction counterfoils around the house. It all taught him *style* and he grew up a confident, double-breasted suited young man whose hand-in-pocket stance had been well learnt. After cautiously swallowing his martini and then coffee, intermittently folding his hands and letting his brown eyes follow my coffee cup, he neatly raised his button jacket as he got up. His hands were stretched deep into the pockets of his trousers; the latter, baggy and turned up enough to make a weaver cringe. He told his tale with gusto, how he had got through the Cambridge exams and grew past a brief period of adolescent wavering. He told the story chronologically, right up to his recent series of failures in the music field. He had started singing at college but his friend, a famous but talentless musician, pipped him at the post, being marginally more gifted than him. He spent a few years collecting demo-tape rejections and attending fruitless 'old-boy' meetings, eventually resigning himself to the post of music-bureaucrat. He seemed to take pleasure in his business' deviousness, not so much excited but proud about the daily underhand dealings with radio DJs and night-clubs.

"What, you're...what you *were* in is much tougher though. There's more money in advertising, private equity and investment banking, that's why. Still, I dream...dream that I'll eventually die in a big Chelsea mansion with someone I manufactured in fame accompanying the funeral cortege. Yeah, the drawing rooms will reek of expensive, hand-rolled Havanas. And I'm conscientious about it too, it broke my mum's heart when I said my name didn't sound right."

Before Morris Castle appeared (a juxtaposition of Morris, his first car, and Castle, probably from a feudal history lesson at Stowe) there was Jon Richardson.

"It may be riskier, but in the corporate marketing field you don't get to meet so many artists, real artists."

"A lot of them defect to advertising and marketing in the end Morris," I replied.

"Sure, a few of them. It's a means to an end. With these industries they can get their artistic message through to the masses, the units shifted."

Morris then began to name-drop at high speed, his conversation beginning to soak in its cynical corruption. He soon saw that his titbits on famous stars meant very little to me. My views on a particular vocalist or musician could hardly be changed when I didn't have any views on them in the first place. He even tried to make me interested by admitting that he didn't really have an interest in music now.

We were briefly interrupted as a man dressed similarly to Morris quickly said hello. Even in the few minutes he was with us, he found time to consult a small electronic device that gave him the latest details of all the world's major stock exchanges, currencies and commodities. "I have to run, Morris, ciao!" he said, leaving in a hurry.

"I've talking enough about myself, man. Tell me about your life."

Ha! My life.

26

I couldn't lay out my life for someone I didn't know—I skimmed the surface, speaking of my childhood, my near-meteoric rise and fall in a flat matter-of-fact way. He seemed to sympathise and sat motionless, looking serious and interested as a diva-like woman unpacked her cello in the far corner.

"So what will you be doing tonight?" he asked, after a pause in the conversation.

"Well, as I said, I don't really want to do anything. They say that you need two years to recuperate from bereavement and this fracas was kind of a bereavement. I don't know...I don't even want to leave this hotel," I said, finally.

"You don't want to do anything!" he said, emphasising the word "don't" in a sarcastic tone. "I think you should get out of here for a while. I have a couple of tickets for a new club that's opening up. Why don't you come along? I know when I'm depressed that a night-club is the best medicine," he said. Even though I wasn't sure about his last remark, he persuaded me easily. His endearing nature was refreshing after so many despicable people.

"Where is it?"

"The West End—where all the good one's are," he answered, "you won't regret it, there's even an Australian soap-star-turned-singer live on stage."

There was little I could reply with. I thought about it: 'A real live flesh-and-bones soap star!'

"Look, I have to go upstairs and catch up with some work,"

he stood up and shook my hands, "some of us aren't as lucky as you," he winked. "I'll knock on your door at nine, okay?"

I nodded and watched him walk to the lifts, feeling better after our conversation and eagerly anticipating the dressing-up.

After finishing my drink, I left the restaurant to the strains of the cello that played to no-one but the player. I walked out to breathe in the un-air-conditioned breeze and bought the *Standard*. A major US bank had gone into liquidation on the front page and my heart needlessly fluttered in the lifts. For a few seconds, I sat on the sofa and skimmed the pages, settled by another drop in oil-prices. It was over soon enough and after calling for some champagne I went into the bathroom to apply a variety of men's facial creams in the mirrored cabinet. Later, I put on the suit I had bought to leave hospital in. I looked forward to the evening but was apprehensive of seeing anyone I knew.

I needn't have worried, there was no-one apart from a few hundred similarly looking strangers all dancing and preening. In the cab, Morris had asked what I though about the news; was there anything he should be worrying about? I laughed and took great pleasure in calming his fears. After all, banks aren't like playing cards.

"Morris, when one bank goes down, like say Continental Illinois in 1984, everyone becomes wary. The Japs and Krauts aren't going to suicidally leave. They're cleverer than that," and that was the end of our discussion. All the same, Morris said that because of the falls on Wall Street, there would be fewer men at the club.

"Usually, there are more of them," he said looking around in the stroboscopic wilderness, "still, all the more girls for us, eh?" he shouted.

Through the drugged smoke, I watched temptresses being chatted up by more rectangular-faced boys. We only noticed them when the conversation dulled or when the hard beat of the music was turned too loud. There was little to be serious about, however, and Morris' joints and the touched-up draught from the bar intruded regularly. I smiled to myself about nothing at all when Morris disappeared for a while.

"Well, man things aren't too hot," said Morris, returning, a little glumly.

I suddenly thought of his friend and his electronic device. "What was the news?" I asked, still grinning.

"You see that girl?" he pointed to the middle-distance before he took a swig from a large *Jack Daniel's* bottle.

"No," I replied.

"Well, anyway, she turned me down. That's the fifth time in a row. I don't take that from nobody, she can just fuck off...fuck you!" he turned and raised two fingers as I had a convulsive fit of laughter.

"You know your problem, Mr. Castle?" I said jokingly.

He turned to me, his head at a strange angle, waiting for my diagnosis.

"You just take life too seriously." He patted me on the back and smiled, handing me the bottle.

"Yeah," he replied, sounding younger than he was, "Man, don't you feel sorry for what *you've* been missing? You're a great guy so why should you get stuck around two daughters of bitches?" he continued incoherently.

"I mean...this, all of this," he slurred, pointing around him, "this has been going on since the beginning of the decade, nearly. You seem to have shared only in the pain, not in the wonderful, wonderful, God-damn wonderful happiness."

I smiled back, easing him to the seat and staring out at a girl at the bar.

"Two tabs of ecstasy and seven pints—you're heading for trouble, darling," I hear her friends say, "really bad trouble."

Smiling and hoping that I'd be too drunk to know it when the club closed, I watched white uniforms pass me, happy to spend another five hours buzzing with my heart pumping to the screaming noise.

I was surprisingly quite sober when Morris and myself arrived at the hotel, sober enough to know that it was Julie's handwriting on the note that lay in the 291 box behind the concièrge-clerk. Still, I was too tired to read it and, waving goodbye to Morris, I opened my door, put the message in my pocket and undressed. I was soon asleep, dreaming about the club and its happy people.

I awoke again at midday, squinting in the bright sunlight that filled the room. Blindly fumbling about on my bedside table, I finally found a dusty pair of *Raybans* that I had bought many years ago. After my eyes had got used to the dimmed light, I picked up a newspaper and began to read alternate pages, each one of them uninteresting. It now made me drowsy to read about another American bank and I soon put the paper aside, sitting still and wondering where I would go and what I should do. Suddenly remembering Julie's note, I went to the bedroom and picked it out from my trousers' pocket. Hastily, reading it, I stared at her new phone number before walking to the phone and dialling.

"Hi, is Julie there?" I asked in a matter-of-fact way.

"Yes, hi! So you can't recognise my voice anymore?" she said jokingly.

"Well, your accent has changed a little."

"Well, anyway, why don't we get together? I mean, let's get some dinner—I mean lunch. Are you better now? You sound better."

"Oh, come on."

"Only a little."

"Anyway, why don't we get together? I mean let's do dinner, or maybe lunch. Are you better now? You sound better."

"Yes, I feel much better...have a bit of a hangover, though. Where are you staying?" I asked, trying to avoid the issue of my indirectly throwing her out.

"I'm staying with Kathleen...we're both renting a flat at the bottom of the New King's Road," she said, sounding a little ashamed of it all, "near Parsons Green. I've still got a pair of spare keys I got from downstairs. You must have wondered about how all our clothes suddenly disappeared?"

"No, not really. You mean *I'm* making all this mess," I joked, angry that they could get a pair of keys. I had been so proud of controlling my apartment again.

She laughed as she asked me whether I knew parsons Green. I said that I did, if only vaguely.

"I'm much better off now. We're both working, side by side at this estate agency in Fulham Road. I think it's better this way...not relying on you and everything. It was bloody stupid how you paid for everything. Kathleen hasn't used your cash-card once since we started work."

"Oh, I didn't mind."

"Yeah, we minded," she replied.

"You mean you minded," I said before she again began to laugh, "anyway, when are you free?"

"I've only got this evening off, can you make it?"

"Well, you know I'm pretty busy," I replied sarcastically. We arranged to meet at the Dôme, a bar where the pair of them hung out. I put the receiver down with an unintended thud and wondered why I had accepted so readily. Had I a strange thirst for sadness, a need to twist the thorn already in my side? Or was it reconciliation that I healthily looked forward to, inspired in part by the optimism of my new friend, Morris?

"Well, you enjoyed it, didn't you?" Morris said, after I let him in, "and what about the girl you danced with? Huh? Huh?"

"I can't remember that much," I replied, sheepishly watching the creases in Morris' suit travel up his leg. He looked quite unaffected by his night on the town, no sign of any hangover—instead just brighter, sparkling eyes and a just-shaved faced that smelled of blueberries.

"I thought that would be your excuse. You purposely looked drowsy so that you could say you didn't remember anything. She wasn't that bad looking!"

"No, I'm sure I didn't dance with anyone—you're the one."

He laughed, "who's talking about dancing? I like you, you're cool about everything, I don't know whether I preferred you when you were lost and depressed though," he patted me on the shoulder. "One point, though, I've still gotta teach you, and that's clothes. They're an expression of yourself, so let me show you what you should buy. Are you doing anything today?"

"What about you, what happened to work?" I replied, wondering whether to feel insulted.

"Oh, I can't be bothered with that, today. Besides, I was on overtime, last night," he laughed.

"I'm meeting someone at six."

"A girl?"

I nodded, smiling and beginning to dread tonight's meeting with Julie.

"You sure don't waste any time, do you, my man?" he paused, "come on, let's go shopping, your appearance is important," he said the word as it were 'impotent'. "And I'm going to tell you what's in and what's out. Look at that shirt."

I looked at my shirt. It had come this morning, freshly laundered in a plastic cover.

"I mean, you've earned it, so why not have the best?"

I agreed, not quite sure about what he was saying.

"Is that today's paper?" he glanced at the bold headline, "oh well, not to worry, it'll sort itself out, heh?"

We took his car and before he started the engine he turned to me and said: "If this car were a girl I'd marry it." The tone of his voice was faintly annoying, something that he could turn on and off during the course of a conversation.

"I have one too," I said, noticing the difference between the way we spoke.

"A Porsche? Which model?" he inquired.

"A red one...I think, yes, a red one."

"Ah well, that's the difference between an expert and an amateur. I know about the engine of this car, the gearbox, the tuning. I know how it *breathes*. I know when a part is being lazy or is about to break down. It's like a factory in there," he pointed to the engine, "luckily these German cars are excellent, but it doesn't stop me from knowing about them. If only the Germans owned the British car industry. There was plenty of research that went on before I went out and invested this kind of money on a lump of metal. I don't pay that sort of sum, what with the price, the petrol consumption and insurance, without being damn sure it's really good," he said in a serious, monotone voice.

"You said that the parts were lazy?"

"What?"

"I just wondered why you called them lazy."

"Well, I don't want to get philosophical-like about it all, but I see the whole system like a factory or even a good society. Here I am, controlling the thing and over there are the employees. Some are more important, of course. See this computer in the dashboard? Well, you know all the sorts of marvellous information it can give? That makes that employee extra special. It's an odd way of looking at it, isn't it, my man?" he said, not making much sense. Then, he started the car. Smoothly, his hands glided over the steering wheel and as he pulled out he began to talk ardently, but still without any change of tone, of the wheelies he'd done and how he'd overtaken police cars at high speed.

But all his stories, accompanied by a loud *Pioneer* behind him and complete with spit on the windscreen in front of him, seemed irrelevant. As he spoke, I nodded my head to give him the impression that I was acknowledging his points. Inside, I felt like a tolerant saint, or at least a saint without the courage to fight back.

27

Once again, Oxford Street lay ahead of me, its shops sparkling in sunshine, its people dulled. Morris walked slightly in front, expecting to be followed. His suit shined a little as he adopted the Alexander position, shoulders back and stomach in. He took me to one of the department stores, cordially holding the door for me.

"I think you need a good suit," he said before he began to educate me on those vague, changeable fashions. I was growing embarrassed—his voice was loud enough to attract people's attention. Fighting our way through crowds hung on plastic carrier bags, we made it to the escalators. I was to be stung by electrified static every time I leant on a coat-rail for support. Morris loved acting the father, his cheek muscles twisting as he talked to me, every so often being distracted by a girl in a designer-dress.

"Can you wait a minute," he said when he had chosen all the clothes and we were standing in a queue, my credit card in hand. I turned to see him chatting away to a pretty girl, who smiled and pouted alternately. When I had passed my card to the lady at the counter and she had driven a machine across it, I turned and saw that he had gone. It was already after five and not wanting to be late for Julie I left the shop and waited in another queue. Fumbling through the carrier-bags full of suits, filled by suits that I would never be able to wear, I found the receipt—a lot of money had left me for ever. A couple of people asked me whether they could take the next cab because they had an urgent appointment and I carelessly consented.

I was ten minutes late when I had finished watching all

the shops along the King's Road, a few emptying and closing. I had put the bags on the floor of the taxi and had stretched out, yawning and rubbing my eyes, occasionally trying to catch my reflection in the rainy glass. I paid the driver and hurriedly walked into the Dôme, bending my lapels up and brushing stray blonde hairs off my jacket. The Dôme was filled with young hopeless-looking people, smoking themselves into nervous coughs and smiling gently at each other, talking about how wonderful their social lives were in previous years. I listened and watched them, some of them watching me, while I waited. Why was Julie so wrapped up in all of this? Maybe it was the difference between Tottenham and Chelsea that interested her, but I still couldn't understand how she had changed so quickly. Many of them looked beautiful—deceptively attractive, one realised after one heard any length of their conversation, or for that matter any length of their silences. One of the girls, who was sitting with a group of fashionably dressed glancers, had a small dog that kept running around the bar, licking peoples legs and hurling itself into people's crotches. It was funny, funny enough for me to laugh but as I took another sip of the cold German beer I remembered the carrier-bags. 'The driver had been wearing an anorak,' I thought to myself, quickly realising that he would soon be wearing much more than that. But then, he would make better use of all that fine wool.

Tony, a barman from Cleveland Heights, Ohio served me, smiling for a second before sliding across to the next customer, a highly coiffured female who balanced her cigarette like it was a wand. Tony liked it here, but as he filled cups with coffee, the frown on his black, bearded face was as sad as no-one else's in the bar.

Dressed in blue jeans and a T-shirt with a smiling face on it, Julie arrived and smiled and said things like: "This is so amazing," and "I'm so glad you came," and "we have so much to talk about." I nodded and became self-conscious standing up against the wooden bar.

"What'll you have to drink?" I asked.

"I'd love a Margarita," she said smiling, warm and happy

that she was seeing me. I remained at the bar and left her to find a seat and gaze at the crowd I had just been watching. What with the filled bar-stools it was difficult to order, but somehow I managed to attract Tony again, and it was only a couple of minutes later that I had salt over my hands, slowly landing the cocktail glass on the table—in front of my wonderful Julie.

"So what *have* you been doing?" she asked, flirting with her brown eyes, as her large circular ear-rings of steel, wavered.

"You first."

"Well, I've got this job and it's very boring. You know, hours on my feet, serving clients. But it's money and it's experience— and I'm a lot better off than a couple of months ago. Kathleen is brilliant, I'm so glad we met, she has this real ambitious streak. I suppose it's rubbing off on me. You know, I want to be something. We've got this great place, too, it's not furnished yet but soon it'll look great," she said, sipping her Margarita, her secretary-red fingernails wrapped around the stem of the glass. "What have you been doing? You look much better now, you needed that rest in hospital, I think." She didn't seem to realise that I had been ill in hospital, not faking and staying away from the world.

"Yes, I feel much better. I've just come back from doing some shopping. You know Morris, the man who had that party the other day? Well, he said that I had to get some respectable suits, ones with turn-ups and Italian cuts. The thing is I left them all in the taxi, over six hundred pounds!" I said laughing to myself.

Julie twisted her mouth and said almost severely: "that's more than I earn in a month." It seems that money is a subject that one doesn't joke about. At least Julie was honest, someone else would have laughed and hidden their jealousy, "but I'll soon be getting more. You watch, I'll have a Porsche one of these days," Julie said, her lips straightening as if this was a sinister thing to say.

"I'm sure you will," I said, patronising her—well, it was better than offering her a 911 and damaging her pride. "You know, I'd love it if you came back and stayed with me again...."

She paused, "don't ask me that, please don't. I'm doing really well at the moment, now why did you have to spoil it all? If I came back to you I'd lose independence, something I need right now. Kathleen's been very good to me—as have you—but I've made commitments, now. Maybe things will change over time, but I don't think so." Her eyes dipped as her lashes shivered. "My arm got caught in the underground door this afternoon," she said raising her elbow and rubbing her arm.

The conversation was uneventful after that; she had to leave soon afterwards because she was meeting someone, and she had to be up early in the morning for work. I walked her to the bus stop and watched her wave to me as she jokingly frowned and then winked at me. It was nearly nine and the bars and pubs in this strange section of the land of money were full. One could detect the fragrance of branded nicotine from here. I walked passed the boutiques, listening to the faint melodies of coin-stacked juke-boxes. I could still smell the tequila on my fingers as I reached Sloane Square and flopped onto the taxi seats. Twilight had ended and the shop facades of Sloane Street and Knightsbridge glistened with lights and mirrors before the silent driver and my leg-crossed self speeded around the park. I asked the driver how I should claim lost-property and as I paid him I found my little packet of drugs skulking in the corner of my inside pocket. I walked back to my room and, using a kitchen knife, cut the piece in two before eating it.

28

Hallucinatory accounts will bore you and frighten me. The radio buzzed in front—I was incapable of switching it off. My limbs ached and terrorised me as I wiped the sweat of my face with the sheets. It could have been one of those sorry bed-sits, if it hadn't been for the Laura Ashley sheets and wall-paper. The news oozed out as I discovered that it was three-thirty in the afternoon. Once I had staggered out of the room, I realised that the maid must have already come and gone. The curtains were open, exposing brightness. I called room service and drank the delivered coffee with a twisted smile. I didn't want to meet anyone today, but then no-one *really* wanted to meet me. The thought of getting a job jarred in my brain. It was as if I still wanted orders, a company that would guide me like a child. I thought of embarking on a life of philanthropy but this, too, seemed dull. After a shower and spraying the obligatory cologne I went downstairs, even now wearing a suit and tie. There was at least one check on my wandering scheme-less life, an appointment with my accountant.

I sat in the foyer reading some newspapers until the designated time, bewildered by all the pages of strikes and colour photographs of night-time riots. All the same, I decided to forget them: there were only two reasons for these pages of righteous journalese, either the journalists had nothing to cover and were making it all up or this was a temporary situation that would soon be quelled. If it was a temporary situation, it gave me a chance to focus my anger on the unions and their aggressive idiocy. Still, I'd have to admit to being more than a little alarmed by the newspapers' small maps of London showing the riot zones—and how close they were to my hotel.

"Hello, how are you? I heard that you weren't too well," the accountant, Mr. Handers, said as he took his raincoat off in my room.

"Quite well, I've recovered now thank you," I replied. Mr. Handers was wearing his usual blue suit with his white, stringy, hair carefully combed back over his dirty-ivory skin. His eyes were dull and grey and he stood very upright, filling the room as he spoke. He had always taken great care that every syllable should reflect his Etonian past. He had been my accountant for years; Osman had suggested him. Alex Handers was the son of a life peer and yet his nose was aristocratic. His pompous contempt for the unlanded gentry showed in every twitch and grimace of his face.

"You...well, if you don't mind me saying so, look rather weak, tired. Are you really quite alright?" he said looking quite concerned. After all, my death wouldn't comfort his salary.

"Yes, I'm fine, it was just a late night, last night."

"Ah, I see," Handers said, "well I've come to talk about some quite serious matters, your various investments and so forth. The situation has changed quite dramatically over recent months, doubtless you've been keeping up with the events in the newspapers. I was quite surprised, in fact, not to have heard from you," he continued.

"Er, no, I haven't," there had been no Financial Times in the foyer either and I had no idea what was happening.

"Well, then, let's take it slowly. I've written a few suggestions down," he passed me a buff-coloured folder, "a few suggestions regarding moving your money about a little, spreading your risks and so forth. And I'd actually like you to look at them."

"Sure, that's wonderful. I'm sure that everything will be fine...now, would you like some coffee? I've just bought some macaroons."

"Um, really, I don't think I can, old boy. My next appointment is quite soon. It's been a busy couple of weeks. All these financial losses...everything's been a little poor, lately. And how the situation will progress, well it's somewhat unpredictable."

"Stock can go up as well as down, eh," I laughed. I tried to decode all his possible understatements, "Well, I'm sure everything's quite satisfactory, why don't you just decide on behalf of me? Where can I sign?"

He smiled, "it's not quite that simple as that, this time. These are all, of course, quite sizeable investments. Now, I don't want you to go changing accountants but in this turbulent time—so many businesses hitting the wall and all that—every decision I make isn't as solid as before. Perhaps, a professional stockbroker would be of use. You see, we really weren't ready for the October 1987 crash and most people are now altering their plans and portfolios in case there's now something else lurking around the corner. It would probably be better all round if you look after yourself for the immediate future." This was the first time that Handers had said anything like this. I still remember visiting his office, looking at one of the secretaries as I wondered how my first half-million was to be invested. Back then, Handers screamed confidence and told me that he would never let me down. Just to impress me, we sealed the deal with a bottle of Roederer Cristal champagne that he had specially wheeled in to his baronial-like office. But that was five years ago in a relatively undeveloped Mayfair.

Just then there were knocks on the door. I apologised to Handers and went to open it. It was Morris, telling me that all the power had been shut off. He was shouting, almost shrieking. I turned to Handers and he turned to me.

"I thought this might happen—it's the strike, the union must have voted the wrong way. Don't worry though," he said, smiling with an expression of utter self-satisfaction, "unlike other businesses, we don't keep our accounts on a computer. Your records are all quite safe, no techno-rubbish systems in our practice."

The thought of a power-cut, the whole city surviving on businesses with power generators, hadn't sunk in. In an ignorant daze I introduced Morris and Handers before the latter said

that he had to rush off. It was the first time I had seen Morris
without a suit on—just an open-collared blue shirt and slacks. I
invited him in, he seemed in quite a panic.

"No clubs, no computers, no concerts—and where has that
man just gone?" he asked, when I'd cooled him down with the
warmth of a glass of Scotch.

"Who, Mr. Handers?"

"Yes, Handers, whatever his name is, how is he going to get
downstairs? The lifts work on electricity you know. What, do
his offices have a gymnasium as well? He'll probably get a heart-
attack going down that many stairs."

I told him that I had forgotten and only a couple of minutes
later, Handers returned, telling us that the lifts didn't work.

"Hello, is that the concièrge? Well, when is the power
coming on?" I asked impatiently. He told me that it would be
an hour and a half before the generator could be turned on. It
seemed as if my meeting with Handers was turning into a party;
too bad that it wasn't Julie that I had met up here. Stranded on
the highest floor with no lights and with an accountant and a
music exec was not my idea of good company.

The room slowly darkened and the conversation rapidly
deteriorated with a heart-felt, but strangely comical, soliloquy
from Handers about the economic situation. I had never
thought of him as belonging to the school of economic
pessimism, forecasting crashes, bangs, wallops and whimpers.
He was more emotional tonight, as if to separate his personal
views from his professionally detached ones. He talked about
over-leveraged buy-outs, of how the October crash had given us
all a respite, of the American deficit and of a looming crisis not
merely tied to shares but rather embracing every aspect of the
world economy. More personally still, he talked self-piteously of
how he should have emigrated to Japan and earned more money
while the boom was on, his eyes, sad and mournful.

There were no candles in the room so, as Handers paused,
Morris went into his room to see if there were any there. When
he came back into my room one could only see shadows and
Handers and myself heard Morris sigh as he walked into the

sofa. I walked over to the window and looked out. The cars were still moving in lines of red and orange lights although, very soon afterwards, there would be no traffic lights to keep any order. Even then, the cars seemed to govern themselves pretty well when the traffic-light batteries ran out. The hotel towards the left already had their generator powered but apart from this beacon of light the distance was a shady, lightless swamp. Morris suggested that we try the third suite on this floor, so the three of us trooped out and along the corridor to the cheapest of the suites. The hallway was pitch-black—we couldn't even make out the features of the woman who answered the door.

"Thank God there's someone else on this floor, my husband went downstairs to get some postcards, what's happened to the power?" she said in a thick Texan drawl. I watched with amusement as my accountant and Morris fought over their leadership qualities. Mr. Handers, older and more confident, explained to her what was happening. It was obvious that she didn't have any candles, and instead we all came into her room. Strength through numbers, she called it, as she apologised for not being able to give us three gentlemen any tea. I was quite enjoying it all. The whole situation gave me an indescribable joy, watching professionals squirm—I was even thankful to those unions. Mrs. Canderson tried the concièrge and nearly fainted when she heard that they couldn't get the generator working properly and that the current power used to run the internal phones would soon fail. But like all moments that transcend the dull twangs of modern life, it was over in a couple of minutes. The concièrge must have been mistaken.

Mrs. Canderson told us that we would have to stay for tea, as her first guests. She looked in her late-forties, sophisticated in a white dress. Everything she said reminded me of visiting my grandmother. It was as if we were resigned to never really communicate, just long-skirt around a lot of flat issues. She was quite big and with an apron on looked like a symbol of the middle-American dream. As she went into the kitchen, I averted my eyes to look out of the window. The city had been submerged in a Luddite disorder for over an hour.

29

That must be my husband now," Mrs. Canderson said, getting up and spilling a cup of tea on the carpet. "Damn!"

After some hasty introductions it turned out that Mr. Canderson was in insurance, although his face conjured up images of the New York Stock Exchange. He looked younger than his wife, his blue eyes like pearls, cultured and maturely surveying us all. Handers left almost immediately, mumbling something about another client as he closed the door behind him. Morris, however, was enjoying the whole thing, now, drinking the scalding Darjeeling in loud slurps as poor Mrs. Canderson looked for a towel in the bathroom and began mopping up the tea. "Do these power failures happen quite often over here?"

"No, this is the first for a long time," I replied, turning to Mr. Canderson who was sitting on my right. I had turned to look out of the window.

"Wonderful view, ain't it?" the big American said proudly.

"I'm afraid he has the best view out of all of us," Morris said, pointing to me, "How long are you over here for?"

"Oh, just a couple of days. I sure hope they get the electricity out here sorted out, the computers must be going haywire." Mr. Canderson said before his wife suggested we put on the television in case there was any new information. It seemed, however, that they were transmitting nothing, all the channels radiating a clamorous black-and-white blur. Eventually, after some smalltalk in which Mr. Canderson seemed to be acting the part of a Texas tourist board rep. , Morris and myself left.

We parted outside my door, his saying that we must get together again and asking whether all the suits were alright. He didn't apologise for his sudden disappearance though. Back in my room, where the view was far better, I leant on the window and watched the turmoil outside. I hadn't put the light on and for the first time I could see stars, previously obscured by the lights of the city, making patterns in the sky. I went to the bathroom and washed my face before leaving the room and the hotel in search of a newspaper-stand. The last editions of the *Standard* were out and I bought a copy, seeing as the headline was: "POWER CRISIS IN THE CAPITAL" on the front page.

I stupidly walked towards one of the cafés around the corner as the newspaper began to wrap itself around me. The wind was becoming annoying, so I folded the paper up and put it under my arm. Remembering that any café in the vicinity would have no electricity, I returned back to the hotel and took the lift to the hotel-restaurant. It was full of people, all recounting tales of experiences in lifts, on escalators in big department stores and in traffic jams. Mr. and Mrs. Canderson were there, too, but they hadn't seen me. There was only one seat beside the window left and that was in front of an extraordinarily sad looking person already on his liqueur. He left only a couple of minutes after I sat down and by the time the waiter had come to ask for my order, half an hour later, I still hadn't decided. I had been looking outside like a lot of the other customers. It was so wonderfully dark.

Concentrating my mind, I managed to finish my meal quickly. I was still in a kind of daze—all those news stories had affected *me*. They were causing events in my life. But these were the passing throes of paranoia and as I sipped my coffee, while watching the ten o' clock news, I realised that the electricity-dispute would be short-lived. However, there were other industries in which disillusioned workers (or union-intimidated innocents) were ready to walk out. It seemed as if life was dancing to the mundane beats of politics. But since I had no allegiances, my shares could fluctuate in value from time to time: I would always have enough stored away. For me, the worries were about supplies of volts, of food, of water, of gas—just the essentials that allowed me to waste my time from one week to the next.

The hotel was still using a generator to power all the floors with light. For some reason the traffic lights hadn't begun operating and the streets were completely empty. I wondered how I'd sleep without the double-glazed hum of columns of cars! And raising my head I couldn't make out where the park ended, there were no lights to wall it all in—just a submerged blackness, allowing a few silhouettes with the aid of a nearly full moon. I could hear music, very faintly, and realised that it must be Morris having another party. 'There seems nothing to celebrate,' I thought to myself as I turned out the light, for a change valuing its company. I left the radio on and tried to get some sleep. Inevitably, it was only an hour or so before Morris came knocking on the door, asking whether I had any ice. It wasn't a very good excuse for waking me up and nor was the one about him thinking I was still awake because the radio was on—but then he was quite drunk, drunk enough to let his tie fly half-mast. He slurred his howling voice as he told me that the electricity had been shut off again and that his party was really livening up in the dark. I sighed as I walked into the kitchen and gave Morris the ice-tray, filled with cold water. Morris almost fell over me, it being so dark, as he then belatedly invited me to his gathering, smiling as he admitted to buying lots of candles, all the candles the hired courier company could carry. I was too worn out to accept but I walked him back to his room. As he opened the door it looked as if the room was on fire—so intense was the light.

30

I walked around the block and picked up the car, returning to the hotel to pick up the luggage. After I had reached over to the bus-boy and tipped him, he threw back the change and it all sunk beneath the leather seats. I ignored him and drove off to the roundabout, wiping the rain off my face. When I arrived at the station, Julie and a comically shy Kathleen were already there, standing with their hair wet and combed around the sides. I put the luggage in and Julie squeezed in the back.

"Well, where now?" I asked, not knowing what I was doing there, not knowing what we were going to do and not knowing what to say. I didn't want to strike up any conversation either, I had nothing to say to Kathleen and she had nothing to say to me.

"How much money have you got?" asked Julie.

"Why, how much have you got?"

"It's just we need to know what we can afford, then we can go and look for it. Have you got a pound?—we can see if there are any jobs," said Julie before I fumbled in my pockets for a coin. Kathleen opened the door and walked over to the news-stand and bought the newspaper while I asked Julie what we were looking for. She told me that we had to find somewhere to stay and, after being prompted, that they had no money. After I told her that I wasn't going to pay up and that even my finances weren't in order she frowned and told me that she would have to go back to her parents and stay with them. It was difficult for me but I just nodded my head. Once the ever-silent Kathleen had got back in the car I drove them in silence back to Julie's house. It was one of those embarrassing silences, punctuated

by semi-colons and full-stops—the conversation of weather.
The fragrance of rain and gardenia filled the air and Kathleen
silently stared at the wet windscreen, rubbing the carpet with
her heels. I did find myself asking them about their jobs and
how they enjoyed them and how they had lost them but my
surprise at monosyllabic answers gave way to carelessness. My
annoyance at Kathleen was compounded as she gave jerky sighs
when I didn't get the clutch down correctly.

They didn't say anything as they left the car and after I saw
the door shut on the suburban semi' that I remembered well,
I got lost trying to find my way around the East End. There
were no landmarks, all the rows of houses looked the same with
the exception of a few doors painted red and a few front rose-
gardens painted yellow. Finding myself on a main-road I battled
on, driving through an early darkness, arriving in the middle of a
storm of lightning and hail. But even the main-roads were empty
and the only people I saw on the pavements were vagrants as
lost as I was. I stopped at a petrol-station and asked directions,
shocked at the prices and the politeness of the attendant. Back
in the centre of London, I checked into one of the hotels lining
the streets of Holborn. The door-man had first put his arm over
my chest, blocking my way into the foyer, but once he saw that
I had just got out of a Porsche he apologised and showed me in,
much to the disconcerting delight of some laughing students
walking behind me.

The room was austere by the standards of my previous one,
but I was so glad to lie down somewhere that it didn't matter.
The only view to be had was of the car-park at the back and a
few offices. At least there was a light to stop me from feeling
depressed about the dark sky with its loud weather. I put on
the TV but flipping the channels didn't change the chat-show.
Downstairs was an over-decorated sitting-cum-dining room.
I ordered a bottle of their best wine and a light meal of fish,
cooked in that hunger-inducing nouveau style. All my payments
were by credit-card, I had run out of any cash some hours ago.
There was only one person also eating and the waiter was taking
it in turns delivering the courses. She came over and asked for

a light and not wanting to be disturbed I told her somewhat angrily that I didn't smoke. So guilty did I feel that, after a few more glasses of wine, I walked over to her table and said I was sorry.

"Oh don't apologise, everyone's a little touchy these days, it must be the weather," she said lighting her cigarette on the candles that graced each table—possibly a post-power-cut decision on the part of the manager. She was wearing a black-and-white checked suit and had a wonderfully fashionable haircut—greased back black hair at the sides and a sort of quiff at the front. Her face wasn't quite the right shape to be pretty but the way her finger-nails were manicured and the way her make-up was put on gave a distinguished look to her mannerisms. It was odd but the way her lips moved slightly as she twitched her head a little, from left to right and then back again, was charming.

"It looks as though we're the only people in the hotel," I said feeling out of control and sensing my pupils dilate. Through a drunken haze she seemed very mysterious.

"Yes, would you like to join me?" she asked confidently, raising her hand to point to the chair.

"Why don't you join me, I have a bottle of wine—it's too large for me to drink on my own." And she carried her glass of sweet liqueur to my table.

"That must have been expensive—have you seen the prices? they're all quite shocking," she said twisting her wrist and swirling the wine in the glass that the smiling waiter had brought. I told her that I never looked at the prices and she replied that I should, especially now. She was quite a tycoon with her company diversified into shipping, oil, textiles and though she said she was born in Paris her accent was undetectable. Her only speech impediment was a fine lisp which came into conversation with words such as 'really' and 'tomorrow.' After the bottle had been emptied, she said that she was rather tired and that she had to get some sleep. "Maybe we'll meet tomorrow," she said as she walked to the lifts, her heels slipping onto their sides. When I had put my last glass down, I noticed that she had left her cigarettes behind. I took one out and lit it for no particular reason and was just about to put it out when the waiter came and told me that they were closing the restaurant and that they didn't allow smoking. Apparently, they were under strict orders from the manageress. I picked up the receipt and put it in my wallet, deciding to take a little walk to aid my digestion. It had stopped raining outside and the streets had that clean feeling as they basked under a clear-night sky. I had only walked half-way around the block before I saw the students who had laughed at me, as I checked into the hotel, along with a collection of other young people all lying in sleeping bags and listening to the radio. I said nothing, scared that any of them might use the knife that lay beside one particularly large man, who was watching me as if I was an intruder. They were all sleeping, or trying to sleep, in a little outside bay that the architect must have constructed for a reason. Casually, or as casually as I could, I turned around and walked straight back to the front of the hotel, having to ring the door-bell because the porter had gone back in.

"Have to be careful, you know. Do you know how many yobbos come here and attack the likes of me?" the old night-porter said, looking very awake and alert. I told him I didn't and walked in, cold and scared. I rushed to the lifts and on getting out saw my tycoon-friend opening her door.

"Hello again, you left your cigarettes," I said feeling deep into my trousers for the box.

"It's alright you can keep them," she said smiling.

"Er, what's your name?"

It's a funny place to ask," she said giggling to herself, "I'll tell you tomorrow. We're bound to see each other, you know I don't usually stay here—it's just that business is very bad at the moment. All the girls have left because no one can afford them." She was taking off her shoes and throwing them into her room, lowering her head to her calf and looking up at their flight. Turning around she said "Good night," and blew a sarcastic, if flirtatious, kiss. I started realising what sort of place I was staying at and who exactly she was. The hotel match boxes didn't say anything so obvious as "our girls will give you a good time," but this was no church.

31

When I awoke, at about six 'o' clock in the morning, I was blue with cold. Calling the concierge, all the man would tell me was that company policy is to charge for heating only on request. Angrily I threw the telephone outside, soon landing in a cleft in the window and then a few feet outside, below the sill. It had been open all night. I carefully hauled it back in, in case the cord broke, and began dialling Handers' number. A secretary impolitely shoved me off with the words "Mr. Handers is not at the office at the moment." I told who and where I was and got dressed, telling myself that I must check-out from this go-down soon.

The manageress, or the woman who I thought was the manageress, was just leaving when I arrived in the hotel restaurant. She didn't see me and I hadn't the strength to meet her again. Soon after they had delivered a soon-to-be-cold cooked breakfast, my name was called out over the PA system. It was Handers on the phone telling me that he had moved all his affairs and had left his company. In fact his new place was the Hulton Tower—suite number 291. I said nothing and he had to prompt me with re-assuring sentences like: "The company's paying for me, I couldn't afford this—not even you could—you know that." As I stared across the floor of the hotel at the cleaner, dressed in a blue house-coat and using a broom for light-less fag ends, I wondered whether there was anyone to depend on. I laid the receiver down and thanked the girl at the concierge, my eyes aglaze with fury and panic. There was no need to talk to Handers any more, he had taken my address so that he could send my accounts. After that our business with each other was over. I took the receipt for the breakfast and walked out into the cold and misty morning, looking for somewhere permanent to stay. The faces on the street whirled past me—everyone was concerned with their affairs, everyone was concerned with just living.

I found a place to stay after a passionless conversation with an estate agent. He wasn't surprised that I needed a house now—NOW! I walked into a square, observing the lawn and entering into a discourse with a tramp whose blood-stained nose was as sharp as was the bluntness of his mind. I took a sip from his vermouth, exchanging my packet of cigarettes and not knowing what disease I was picking up. I was waiting half-an-hour until my finances could be checked by the agents. They were, thankfully, all in order and for the sum of my balance I found myself in a small room with a bathroom, almost already waiting for the thirty year lease to expire. I had long-since picked up my baggage but I phoned the hotel one last time to check for any messages. There was one, from Julie, and it broke one of my strings to hear that her phone number was the one I had had for so long. It seemed that it was now Julie and Handers who would be enjoying the views over the city. But it wasn't Julie who was staying there it was homeless Kathleen—this I understood after phoning the suite—the purpose of the call only to tell Handers to start arranging for the selling of my shares. In the meantime I would rely on borrowed money to fuel myself and my car, the car that should have solved everything, for I was promised other-worldly pleasures.

The short-lease flat was in a corner of Notting Hill Gate, where my only sight would be the daily street market and my only sound, the sound of buses taking what few workers there were to the few numbers of jobs. I wasn't interested in the verdicts deciding the fates of my former colleagues; White, along with the rest of the board sentenced to a year in one of London's surrounding jails, others from rival agencies condemned to the dignity of the dole-queues, and still others, the younger ones who made the tea, sentenced to working for the big company that at last ruled London. These street markets, too, were a symbol, just as was the huge garden that I saw from my window, they were symbols of the society I once respected.

My room was furnished in dull shades of green and brown, decorated like an institution, with the usual smells of thrown-out rotten fruit lingering from dust-bins below. It was not a shameful residence but after what I was used to I had all the reason in the world to feel abashed at the sight of my first visitor—Julie. She had been crying, Kathleen had left her and only for reasons of money. Handers had welcomed such a pretty girl and, according to Julie's murmuring and sobbing words, it was all part of their plan. And yet Julie still felt guilty. I had no pity for her, but the glints in her, now, chameleon eyes, had some attraction.

"I know there's no reason for me to come to you, I know you won't take my apologies. My parents will give me no advice, I can't tell them anything, they don't know anything. I really don't know what to do—in a way it's you're fault, you got me out of the rut I was in, and now I'm back with more problems than before—I shouldn't blame you—you hate me don't you?" she said, her last sentence rising as she seemed to realise who she was talking to.

"I don't hate you," I said before she shrugged her shoulders like a child and seemed to make for the door. "Stay."

"Why, you've made it clear..." She stopped and gazed at me, as if her whole world was being taken away from her, and left, leaving the door to knock the door-frame. There was nothing I could say to her anymore. From no amount of exchanged confidences would begin trust, our relationship had ended. There was too much of Kathleen in what she said. And, strangely, it was Kathleen who I still had affection for—not her.

After carefully navigating myself down the uncarpeted stairs I came back to the room with a bottle of scotch, bought with the loose coins, at an off-licence on Portobello Road. As I unwrapped it I could hear shouting in the hallway. I opened the door and saw that a man was lying at the bottom of the stairs, one of his hands clasped in a policeman's. Another policeman was standing next to him—he was kicking the man. Quietly walking closer to the stairs I saw the blood over his face, the bright whites of his eyes, surrounding terrified pupils. My first thoughts were to walk back into my room, as silently as I had walked out. The policeman was shouting. He was telling the man to go back to Africa. The other officer stood motionless beside, holding a truncheon in his free hand. I didn't turn back and as the shouting policeman raised his helmet, the silver reflecting on the walls in streaks of light, his eyes turning blood-shot. I pushed my hand onto the banister and reached the other to the hall-light switch.

"And who the hell are you?" the black-suit screamed, for he wasn't a man of the law any longer.

"I live here. What has this man done?" I asked, unfaltering, surely there must be a reason after all?

"Drugs, rape, we'll have him for everything, we'll pin every crime for the past year on sambo," he ranted, eyes aflame as if on a drug, before he lunged his boot once more.

"But what do you mean pin?" I said, squinting as the reflection blinded my eyes. And that was all I had to say before I was hauled into a van outside, bruised but still laughing in my knowledge that I was innocent. Both myself and the alleged rapist were guarded by two policemen. They were keeping our hands up while they searched us. Finding nothing they spat out words about strip searches. I could say nothing to my fellow companion, who I was beginning to feel empathy with. We just stared at each other and sometimes gave away a smile. It was funny, the whole event seemed funny—it was only when I saw how deep the gashes in my friend's face were that I flinched, my mouth straightening. Mr. Roeng didn't move his tired, brown eyes as he smiled—only his short eye-lashes flickered every so often. He could hardly move his thick lips, so much were they bleeding. When the van had stopped he put his hand on my arm reassuringly, as if to tell me that it would all be alright.

Dragged like prisoners of the Algerian inquisition, we were taken into a room full of men and women, all holding their pupils central, moving their heads to watch us come in. The man I was with knew a few of the prisoners and they smiled back at him. We were the first to be taken into the office of the Sergeant, a man, different and cleverer than his colleagues, whose job it was to calm us down. It turned out that my friend was a community leader, trained in law. The blood on his face had dried up, his wounds not as serious as they looked. But he sweated as he verbally attacked the officer in front, arguing calmly and logically. The Sergeant's white roman nose twitched as his deep socketed eyes stared through us, looking from my friend to me and then back again. The lawyer did the talking until the officer raised his hand and asked us to shut up. The kindness was over and the ultimatum flew over his paper-crowded desk like a small storm—he could pin any of the crimes, that week, on us, he could re-arrange evidence, he had that power and if we didn't keep silent we would find ourselves taking the rap for any number of crimes. The leader went on talking, ignoring the threats.

"Look I've warned you. Now if you don't shut up and sign the statements under your noses I'll get that nice officer who sculpted your cheek to defend himself. Simple. The charge will be resisting arrest and you'll end up with brain-damage. Now shut-up and sign. Your friend is more sensible, so why don't you, Mr. Roeng, keep those lips sealed. This is your last chance."

I told Mr. Roeng to sign for my sake and after ten minutes we were let out. Walking through the stark corridors, on the way out, I felt scared—too scared to form thoughts. I shouted for a taxi and went with him to the casualty ward of the nearest hospital. The journey was completely silent. We waited in the waiting-room for an hour, while he showed renewed signs of pain. We didn't say anything to each other, myself not wanting to sap any of the strength the police had left in him. Once he had gone, I read a few issues of Vogue lying on the table, just flicking through the pages of glossy models while my eyes slowly closed.

32

This room, too, was full of people; women and children, some crying, but most of them in control of their inhibitions. Mr. Roeng had been away an hour but I was too tired to feel worried. I sat and squeezed my temples, slowly looking around me. Flaky cyan walls surrounded the fluorescently lit waiting room. A shoe-less child was playing with a doll on the cold, black floor. In the stuffy haze, my eyes soon closed, not wanting to look any more. I was woken up by Mr. Roeng, gently tugging at my jacket-sleeve. We had been in the hospital for over two and half hours. I watched the stitches that the doctor had sewn in his face as we escorted each other out.

We had lost a night in all of this, the birds were loudly singing and the clear ultramarine sky had left frost. Mr. Roeng couldn't talk easily, it hurt too much, so I had bought a pad of paper and a ball-point pen at the hospital shop—all my money coming from overdrawn cash-tills.

"Is it normally like that?" I asked in the taxi, "I've just moved in."

He smiled and began to write: "It's been like that for the past few years, it's just that it was always the residents. I never thought they had the stupidity to get a person in authority." I nodded and told him that he had better relax. It was dark and monochrome in the back of the cab, I could only see the outline of his face and his dejected eyes, the silhouettes of the stitches making it all look like a film-*noir*. He was still strong enough to walk up the stairs to the flat, and before we parted I told him that I'd come and see him tomorrow. After a few minutes

I collapsed onto my bed and went to sleep, the noise of the markets outside, already preparing for the day's trading, ringing in my ears.

I woke up at about three o' clock, a winter's dusk just beginning. I changed my creased clothes and walked slowly to Mr. Roeng's door. The hallway was dark and smelling of a light disinfectant—and there was no reply. Leaving the flat and walking amongst the rows of litter I entered one of the small cafés that dotted the sides of the streets. A few punks were sitting at one of the tables looking sad as they fidgeted with the ash-tray, their elbows reflecting in the laminated table. I asked the waiter for a cappuccino and sat mentally trying to list my thoughts while the drone of the coffee-machine got louder and louder. I still had the bottle of scotch, securely wrapped in brown paper and tucked into my raincoat pocket. I took it out and added it to the cappuccino after the waiter left a cup with the receipt. No-one minded—I didn't look like the tramp, opposite. My seat was beside the window but my view was obscured by a tower of card-board boxes lying in front. I began to feel guilty about not knocking louder on Mr. Roeng's door, what if he was in trouble? What if he had collapsed? But I comforted myself with the certainty that he was a strong man and he was the last person to let himself just fade away. He had a *cause*.

I paid and left, my feet once again dragging through the rubbish, a lettuce leaf scuffing my right shoe. There was a note on my door when I reached my flat. Mr. Roeng had gone to work, he'd see me later in the evening. Pleased, I went into my room and called Handers, again asking whether he had got rid of all my shares. He had, and half the money had been transferred to an investment account, the other half to my current account (both at one of the two banks seemingly still in business). "But I warn you, I sold them all at bottom-value," he said. I decided to go and get some shopping done. I wouldn't be able to live my life from one restaurant to another anymore. I drove the car past the rows of 'For Sale' boards hanging beside each house. Everything from bed-sits to penthouses were being sold, everyone just wanted to get out. The falsely air-conditioned atmosphere in the car was hardly a depressant, it was rather like watching television, changing gears like switching channels as I drove over shards of glass. And the famous Knightsbridge department-store, too, had ventilation. The food selection was no different, however, to the one I had near my flat and after buying eggs, bread and cheese, I walked back to the car-park loaded with plastic bags, unemotional as I had forgotten that the last time I had bought necessities was years ago.

Feeling comfortable and secure in the squeaky leather seats I drove back, the city by now illuminated artificially. Inadvertently, I had driven to my hotel and as I made a full circle around the roundabout I couldn't help smiling as I raised my eyes to the suite at the top. They were my windows, luminously visible from Hyde Park Corner.

Back in the flat, after storing all the food in the old refrigerator and then preparing some, Mr. Roeng knocked and came in.

"I'm sorry it's all such a mess," I said, looking around at the half-closed suit-cases and my unshelled scrambled eggs.

"Don't apologise to me, I'm not your mother," he paused as I tried to stop looking at his stitches, "anyway, I just came round to say thank you. If you hadn't come out, I don't think they would have ever stopped kicking me. It took courage to do what you did—or maybe naïvety. Don't you know the police kill?" he spoke slowly and seriously. Though he could only have been in his mid-thirties he made me feel like a young boy. He had the build of a boxer and his body's agility seemed incongruous, given his measured speech.

"How are you feeling?" I asked.

"Doing alright—I'm well enough to work," he seemed to deliberate on whether to stay or not. "How come you moved in here? What happened to you during all this trouble?" he asked.

"Oh, I was laid off like the rest of them. It's just that I had a little money stored away. All this shit though," I put the frying pan down, "they'll take power, won't they? It'll be like 1984, a brave new world or something," I was getting carried away.

"Oh, I'm not sure about that, you might be pleasantly

surprised. Still, there's trouble until then, that's true," he smiled and then nodded his head gravely, "well, I've got to go to this meeting now. You look a little dispirited, huh? Well, what's new around here?" he said before making his way out, softly shutting the door.

I had never met anyone like Mr. Roeng before. He seemed almost too self-assured, as if he had been cut from the most brilliant executive material. Why was he so optimistic about the future? Catching my breath, I fell to the floor and looked around the room. With the light on, it didn't look too bad at all. It reminded me of my parents' home which was nice. Well, the bathroom of my childhood-home, anyway. I turned on my small radio and listened to the news—I still hadn't unpacked the television and hi-fi. Even though I felt that owning a hotel-room meant I was freer to move, I had still succumbed to buying spare electrical luxuries—the TV in the hotel didn't have all the added extras. At last I had a use for them all. Turning my attention to the news-reader's words I heard the reports of child-rapes, family-slaughters and Irish bombings. Mr. Roeng had said that he supported the IRA, something that shocked me. But all of it did—foreign wars, the interventions I didn't understand, or seem to understand. To listen to a Government minister speak was now to endure lies. I scratched my head and lay back on the bed, reaching to switch off the radio, but all it did was to fall onto the carpet, the volume higher, the news the same. The bed-springs creaked like only a bed in a pre-furnished room does and with a pleasant feeling in my stomach I put the brown paper-bag over my head and closed my eyes.

Like the previous night I was awoken by the sound of shouting, this time outside my window: policemen questioning people on the roads, shouting down to them. I closed the window firmly and tried to shut my eyes, the radio still buzzing with excitement. The new clamp-down was on drugs—police had been drafted in from all parts of the country to stop children from being infected by the poisons. But from the yells coming through the thin window panes, it seemed that the clamp down was on freedom not hallucinogenics.

I got up, turned out the light and lay for hours, listening to the conversations, the breaking glass, the drunken shrieks, trying to cover my ears with the pillows.

"Hey, you awake?" asked someone outside the door, fiercely turning and rattling the door-knob.

33

Yet again there were more troubles to weigh on my mind. Pathetic dreams of a family with Kathleen haunted my nights, living in a house like my parents' and even ending right: children looking over my grave. I nearly laughed in my sleep. But maybe when I was still in my hotel looking at the rings my coffee cup made on the window sill, before I raised my eyes to look over the city—just maybe I could have taken a chance at finding it all so comical. Now, it was too late. Now was when I opened the door, finding out who that voice belonged to. I could feel the tension in the door-knob, him turning it around and around, as I pushed my fingers into my eyes to pick out dirt.

The man on the other side smiled, his stitches still in place but seeming to unravel in front of my eyes as he whispered. "Sorry to wake you. It's the police again, they're coming to check everything for drugs. I'm owing you a favour: if you have drugs then get rid of them."

I told him it was alright, that I had never possessed drugs. And he replied that it was in his interest to check, he couldn't take any chances—if one of his acquaintances was on it, then he'd get the blame. I said that I understood and watched him limp up the next flight of stairs, about to knock on the next door. Shutting my door, I sat on the bed and waited for officers to pour on my room. I wondered what Handers and his friends were doing, easily persuading myself that my room must, at this moment, be filled with coloured lights, ultra-violet to red, and dancers munching crisps as they slowly fermented at another party. Rubbing the blanket with the palm of my hand, I looked out and watched the officers leave their vans.

It was not long till I was paying my second visit to the crumbling police station on De Pressland Road. This time Mr. Roeng was reassuringly sitting beside me. He whispered, in case the cops heard us, "They like drugs, they deal in them. The more people that are out of their heads, the better it is for them. I can't blame people, apart from escapism—what the hell is there to live for?" The plastic room was filled with frightened faces, staring as if to say 'this ain't my fault, it's society's.'

They had found 25 grams of D-Lysergic Acid Diethylamide in a small, transparent bag, lying in one of my drawers as if it was an old, odd sock or some exclusive talcum powder that I had spilt. As guilty as a coward, I was made to remain in the yellowish room, among the tramps and attackers. The hard plastic seats made a muffled stab at all of our backs as the room bided its time, everyone waiting for their call-up. Mr. Roeng, who waited until he had to leave because of an early-morning meeting told me that the police must have sold it by now. There was obviously some huge mistake, they never took three or four hours before questioning. "Maybe one of the officers has stolen it," Mr. Roeng said laughing, although behind that facade of coolness, I could see that he was disappointed in me. He didn't let me explain why there were twenty-five grams of illegal substance in my room, only the facts: who did I get it from? where do they live? when did this happen? are you an addict? Every question was short and simple, never allowing me to explain the events leading up to the arrest. There were only two policemen guarding the room, both of them standing by the door and looking around with disgust. When Mr. Roeng made for the door they told him to sit down and wait—it was only when he showed his identity card that one of them left to ask the Sergeant.

Once he had left it was only a couple of hours before I reached a room—the cold, grey walls the same as the day before. I was shivering as I saw my questioner's wrinkled face, highlit by an over-starched collar. Trembling as he spoke, I was worrying too much to try and actually understand what he was saying. I nodded at each convenient break in his sentences, mumbling a 'yes' or a 'no' where I thought it necessary. He told me that the situation wasn't as bad as I thought, this much I understood. They had indeed 'lost' the evidence, just what Mr. Roeng had told me might happen. Again I nodded in agreement with my questioner as if to say 'of course, it's been nearly four or five hours—that's plenty of time to lose a small piece of evidence. Besides I know how busy you officers are."

He smiled and said that he was glad that I saw things his way. "Off the record, of course, I want to tell you that it is almost definitely the case that the evidence has been mislaid. Now should it not eventually be traced, you can go about your daily business without a worry. Strictly off the record, this is a highly irregular procedure and," he cleared his throat, "the officer responsible will be seriously reprimanded. I couldn't allow your solicitor to hear all this, I'm afraid. He's bound to cause trouble, mess up our little deal, as it were. And then you would be in jail and I would be demoted."

His stained eyes looked straight at me while he said all of this, his patrician nose quivering with pleasure. He got up and opened the door, even posing to shake hands with me before I walked through the grey corridors smelling of urine and dust and finally arriving on the outside steps. Even the cold air didn't wake me up from this brushing-down and I solemnly let my thoughts leave my head as I got on the night bus that Mr. Roeng had advised. It was empty and as I sat listlessly looking at my reflection in the windows, ignoring the shops and pedestrian lovers, I began to realise what was happening.

34

L ate September and the first letter to fall through the letter-box was an invitation—of all things a house-warming party to take that mind of the previous night. There was only one person—or rather only three people—that could have thrown this joke at me and their names sat on the piece of white card like they were from a stand-up-comedian-manual. As soon as I saw them I decided not to go. But for all the meanness and deceit, the invitation had cheered me up. Yesterday I had escaped. For now, I persuaded myself that things would soon settle down again. Mr. Roeng and myself went and had a cup of coffee at the café behind card-board boxes. His dimpled cheeks raised themselves as his huge smile showed me how lucky I was.

"Well at least there's someone on your side, I suppose. They must have sold it to one of the people in the waiting room or maybe put it away in a vault to be planted on someone else. It's all terrible but at least you're safe," he said. I told him about the invitation and gave him a little of the background to my relationship with the three-some, wondering at the pettiness of the problem as I explained it to him.

"Go! It'll do you good to get out of this...all this trouble." So at last I knew that his smile was for my safety. The trouble was still out there, the trouble would be there every day until the little bubble burst and a change finally came. Some innocent would be convicted for my crime, and being just as concerned as Mr. Roeng about my safety, I didn't mind. It didn't take long to change my decision about ascending in a lift to that dark tower and seeing Julie, Handers and Kathleen sipping *Pimm's* and worrying about the price of the latest watch. I could neatly side-step the problems and, though probably not a good idea, go to the hotel and feel at home again.

The sky was a deep shade of blue, hidden by black clouds that occasionally covered a moon, high up and white. I'd been travelling by bus the previous few days, the journeys I made were few and small—just to the café, the off-license and the supermarket. But tonight, after going through a car-wash, the blue cylindrical brushes scratching at the paint-work, I left for the hotel in a Porsche. I parked the car outside, smiling at the doorman, before he put his hand on my shoulder and asked me whether I was staying there. He hadn't recognised me and probably thought I was a thief. I showed him my invitation and he pushed his cap up, off his furrowed forehead. Rubbing his flattened nose and winking he told me to go on.

Back inside, I loved the smell of the mats below me—the fragrance one finds in a carpet shop. It had been hardly any time since I had left the revolving doors spinning as I turned my lapels for the rain, looking up at harsh grey skies and listening to the thunder of the cars passing by me—yet it felt like a decade ago. The mirrors in the lift with the restaurant menus hanging beside the doors sat the same, a few inches higher than eye-level. When the metal doors opened I felt like returning to the ground again. What I was doing had no purpose—it seemed just for Kathleen.

I didn't turn back, curiosity decided my path and the music blared out, fixing my attention to the door, making me think of a nouveau riche semi' with a new record player. I didn't know the man who opened the door, he just smiled and asked me to come in. As he closed the door—my door!—he leant against it, turned around and told me I was early. He had a perfectly formed face, accompanied by the light blue eyes of an eighteen year old, both stained in blood, probably by the gin he smelled of and spat out—he was drunk.

It was Julie who first came out of the kitchen, holding a glass of white wine, not noticing me and rather looking for magazines to put away. There was no-one else in the room and already my eyes had directed themselves to the window facing the park. The view was interrupted as Julie, crouching, got up to take a sip from the glass, pausing to look at her fingernails and straightening her red dress. As she smoothed out the creases she saw me, smiled and walked towards me, walking as if she had spent the last few nights practising with a volume on top of her head. "Hello!" was the word I got and that was the word I returned. She hadn't the style or the presence of the girl in black that I occasionally saw bending down in the kitchen—now I could compare.

"You're early," she said before my first name, "Alex isn't here yet—they make him work like mad back there." As Julie spoke, Kathleen looked up from the floor of the kitchen. She smiled, got up and brought a tray holding a carafe of red wine.

"I know you like red," Kathleen said in the softest of voices, before she went to the sofas and sat cross-legged, looking towards the window.

"That's the best part of this place," I said. The waiter was in the kitchen uncorking some more bottles. Kathleen and Julie looked at me as if they didn't know what I was talking about. "The view...the view is the best part of this room."

"Well, we do get room service as well and that's hard to come by these days," said Kathleen, "and they have a hair-dresser. What do you think of my hair? I just had it done downstairs—it cost a fortune."

"I think it's great—a bit punk but we're rebels," they smiled. Julie looked at Kathleen's haircut, a wedge shaped box of dark brown hair gelled sideways and moussed to the front. I looked at it too—it made no difference, there was something intensely likeable about that hateful mind, never stirring above those sparkling pale blue eyes of hers. There was a long silence, awkward and coarse, all of us sitting around each other on the hotel-owned sofas. The music had been turned off by the tuxedoed hired help and only sometimes did he venture in to place another bottle on the white table cloth, hanging over the table like there was a corpse under it.

"Alex tells me you're based in Notting Hill Gate now—is it a big place, no I suppose not," said Kathleen after a while.

"No, not really—just a modest apartment. And you? how do you find it back at a hotel, it must have been sad leaving your new place what with all the stuff you were buying for it."

"No, it's fine thank-you," Kathleen said in a sarcastic tone before both of them began to laugh, giggling and gurgling their impoliteness in my direction.

"It's not you—it's only such a funny situation," said Julie, eventually stifling the hysterics and patting Kathleen on the shoulder to make her stop.

"Yes it is, isn't it?"

Handers—or Alex as he now seemed to be known as—interrupted my ordeal by poking his head out from under the boxes and bottles in his hands. "Hello gang—and how are all you lot?" he said awkwardly, sounding younger and flamboyant. When he had put down the packages I could see that his face looked younger too. He was no longer the strutting city gent, walking stiffly and waiting for tube trains to big-but-nowhere-suburbia. "And how are you, so glad you came," he said to me cavalierly, showing that he couldn't care one way or the other whether I had turned up or had decided to sleep in the street outside. Increasingly feeling uncomfortable I shook his hand, mine sweating at the palm. His perfunctory manner would continue to annoy me through the night but as he opened some of the boxes, each containing a dress or a piece of jewellery I wanted to leave. He looked at the two girls like he longed for them, no doubt he had them. "Where's the music gone? I told you to find some records...Johnson!" he shouted to the butler. Humbly he arrived with a gin and tonic and motioned his hand towards a pile of record bags lying beside an ancient hi-fi system. "Now look, they had better be good, we don't want anyone complaining that the records we buy are all out of date," he went on, rubbing his chin, the lines on his face deepening.

It wasn't long before middle-aged men in suits of colours ranging from shampoo-lather white to green lamé were dancing with their arms in the air, palms held horizontally. Their glasses sparkled under the hired lighting, flickering under different coloured strobe lights, their white shoes making twisted movements on the carpet. Others were groping at their call-girls or girl-friends, the latter smiling and lifting up their dresses for hands to curve around before they decided it was time to cool their partners down. All were inanely smiling like they had suppositories shoved in them. Handers had even bought dry ice to fog the air more—no doubt to prevent me from seeing where my friends were. I watched with mild amusement, hidden by the layers of funny fog, at the women's clothes cut to reveal bare thighs or cleavages as their ugly faces gorged quiche or became submerged by terrifying men's faces. Inconspicuously I sipped my scotch and soda, wondering when I should leave, when I should go and look for Kathleen, when I should call on my energies to socialise.

I felt guilty as I sat waiting to be stared back at. But my looks must have be those of a tired man, worrying about every thought that entered his mind—not those of a man hungry for sex and bent on clothes that were in fashion. It wasn't long before my attention was diverted to a corner of the kitchen. The door insulated the sound and as I pushed it open to take my glass back, someone, whispering, asked me who it was. Inside, the religious ritual of rolling the joint was in session, surrounded by open-mouthed men eager for a high and gradually grasping the unimportance of the side-affect of impotence since the single women had already been paired. Kathleen walked in and excitedly asked what type it was, before consuming most of it. I had no interest in these matters, it was of little use to me. Opening the door, Kathleen put her hand in mine and asked me why I was aimlessly walking from one room to the next.

"It's my home, I think of all these rooms as part of me, part of the results of my years of work. I used to live here, to put up with the maids and the bad cleaners, to drink out of china coffee cups and watch the view," I said, getting carried away.

Expecting her to tell me that it was her place now and that I had better accept things, I was confused and overcome as she kissed my ear, leaving a warm smear. "I know," she said holding both of my shaky hands, "I know."

35

Carrying my overcoat towards the window, sliding past couples glorying in the ecstasy of epilepsy I took out a small automatic camera and aimed it at the scenery outside. A smoke-focus of blades of light lay in strands on the film. I ignored the girl putting her arm on my neck, asking what camera it was, and untangled myself, walking through the haze of ultra-violets and phosphorescent greens.

The dancers were still shaking at midnight. Others, too tired, were sitting watching the others, drinking Bloody Marys and choking on peanuts. The part that I played was merely to watch my friends find their grooms while I swirled my overcoat around myself and left, my mouth tingling with gin and vermouth.

I wished I could have stayed—instead of walking out into a night, cold and flooded by devious dealers of sex and narcotics. I used to watch these people from my window but there weren't as many then. All my observations were now numbed by the lingering sounds in my ears and the smell of all that smoke—the stench of rich, dry ice had placed itself in my coat. Driving away I thought of the aimlessness of my situation and, for the first time, of leaving for America. Arriving at the flat, the fragrance of dry ice gave way to that of stale cigarettes. Mr. Roeng wasn't in and so I turned the television on and waited for inspiration. However, there were only a few moments until I fell asleep, this night soundly.

During the night, there had been fewer noises outside and in the morning the market was in a deep silence. Purgatory had at last arrived. Now it was only a matter of time....

It would be my last trip to the hotel. Repeating the journey of the previous day I was to collect the papers that I had left with Handers. After that, my business was over. After that I could leave this town—maybe for somewhere with more hope.

36

Kathleen

Snow had fallen early outside and the dull walls were interposed by streaks of light. Yet the room seemed tedious. Three figures were standing by the window; one of them, a man, whom I once loved. Of the remaining two, one of them was a close friend, the other was the owner of the suite. I removed the red-stained cigarette from my lips and made myself concentrate, firstly on a photograph lying on top of some hand-written papers, to my right, and then on their faces, in front. A few minutes later the silence was interrupted, just for a moment, and the panoramic view became illuminated. The broken pane of glass was glinting, reflecting light all over the room. There were now only two people, one of them in tears, leaning outside the window, gazing at the pavement as the harsh breeze blew through the room, blowing all his papers away.

Reproach

"They who have put out the people's eyes, reproach them of their blindness."
John Milton

Through the haze and it's you. But that's all it is, the rows of drinks, the blues and greens. The wet tables meaning to fall like the mats. The mirrored wall at the other end and the reflections of the orange. Those colours dominate. The tints and the shades. And you turn around but it's nothing. The floors, the wooden floors for the echoes and then the walls. But then the time arrives, the people. And the silence fades away, no longer is it the casual wipes of cloths and the filling of pumps. Empty for a long while after the time but as the hours, which you don't see, lengthen the filing and filling begin. The shades of colour on the faces, reds and violets.

The evening should be alight with fears as the blood fills. The worries over tomorrow and the worries of tonight. The haze is the smoke, lying softly over it all like blankets and covers. As it leaves the lips and the stains of red and finally reaches the other side. And then the box turns on, and the coins fall. The notes begin, mental and musical as the room fills again. And then all the breaths, the hazes and the sounds turn it from the empty silence. It escapes out from the bottles and boxes until it rolls. It's dizzy when you feel the phlegm and the noise, all the noise, lying in front of your smoke. Hands over your face, your hair at the front, soaked in the new, your forehead supporting the squints of eyes, toughened from sunlight and glasses. And over the nose, congested with the smog and into the dry bleeding lips, sore from the glasses again. This time yourself, you pour it. But a stronger label can't really help that. Another order and you're by the register and looking down at the rims with their writing and they're waiting there, wondering what the talk is and why it's him. But you pour eventually and hand it to him, touching his hands almost lightly as the metal reaches him and you lean against the back and bring the glass up to the chapped lips, and feel them burn. Burn and burn as it reaches the mouth and the lights. It's only some hours left and you can reach your room and stretch and then lean over for the machine and break a tape in. But the coins aren't enough and the eyes don't last long after the time is up. And the talking, the mouths, focus. Zoom into them, their smiles and frowns, the listlessness and the sickness.

But now the boy at the table is looking back and you have to turn away, and the gesture is sweeping until you're staring into a violet mouth, the one I said. But it's only, it can only, it is a mistake. But eyes can see you through and when you turn back to see him still watching you wonder what it is all for. Smile like the counterfeits until the lashes reach into your eyes until you're red. But the other is still watching and of course it's only last orders. Because that's what they come for. Meeting can't happen when the time is nearly up and the only want, for now, is another volume. And you ignore the corner, your eyes seeing it in there, rolling roll-up paper and it's not tobacco. But you're not the owner.

So you laugh and light as the song you want is finally chosen, and you laugh again because the numbers on that neat box are all wrong and the selector didn't mean it. But you can smile once more at the frown around it and take the drags like they were all that mattered. But he's coming to the main one now and the time is over. It's only a box of matches though, and tells me cheers.

The time is finally up and all that are left are the final wipes and lock-ups. After that these tired blocks of ice can close. Feel the door swing back as the breeze catches your shoulders and step closely as you circle past the lights of the city. Silent apart from the noise of cars and trucks speeding past. No music to accompany it all by until you reach your room, green-washed walls to the lift and the closing of doors as you get to the mirror and watch the prince of the senses, fumbling with the buttons.

Only the buttons of the lift before the smooth treads of the carpet to a white-washed room. Or greyish when you pull the shoes off and push the clothes off, until you collapse onto the springs, reaching only to press another button for the tinny sound of music through portables.

Close the ice finally and feel it all moving in your stomach. Can't sleep, just fall. And the night turns to blue. Light and bright, with a nearly straight line for a cloud.

It's time. The kettle awakes more and you pour it, looking out over a city still bounded by greens. That hazy sun the weather-men talk, it moves through trees here. And the people. The streets are filled, masterfully filled with people hurrying in usually one direction and then the opposite one come evening. And the dirty reds of the buses, brightly reflecting so it touches the insides of your eye. But the flints are gone and you reach for the matches and strike them. The small window stares at you too long and when you've tired, though you never will, you look into the small reflection, upright on the table and apply the strokes to your face. Occasionally you glimpse out again, maybe to vainly push the window one more fret and then you again. The liner runs until you squint and reach for tissues before you dress and give up. The water has cooled and as you look into the cup and feel the wetness of your cheeks you decide to leave, to leave that loose hair and leave the room. No hellos except one in the small lift, the stench remaining from last night.

You are so conscious now of the stickiness of your face as you squint again because the 99p blades are lost. You look at the legs for a while until you reach the store set amongst the shoppers for buying the aspirins. The assistant doesn't stare too long and her impoliteness is her excuse. You ignore the news-stands as you swish past it all and ignore every stare that comes your way. You don't even bow your head to make sure the wind runs up the right way. And you are moving with a soundtrack spinning through that mind until you reach a bus-stop. Get on knowing where it's going, you know. And it's jump up the stairs as it speeds along because it was only a traffic light that stopped it. Ignore. Press onto a seat, but it isn't the back. Move your hands to the back of your head as you realise the blades or shades are in the lining. Push them over the ice and gaze into the faces of hundreds. But the time runs like the wind that so many speak about, and you know it's only a couple of hours until you return to the work, hoping you'll meet someone who knows about the futility. There's been hot weather that suddenly reached out over the week into your bus and you watch those beautiful expressions change when the driver hits the unexpected curb.

Rise and walk down, pausing as the bus begins to halt until you get there. Walk in and have a drink that isn't allowed. Starve yourself and sit looking at the headlines that you bought without thinking, ignoring the old face of the seller on the way.

Suddenly, because it is, the rumours begin to fill the already smoky atmosphere as twilight returns. The ties in evidence as the rumours are the bomb. And as night falls, this is no ordinary night at the bar. The doors have been locked as the scare begins. The police in evidence outside as the room hushes with murmurs. The defusing of the bomb is the order and we are the victims. So the doors have been locked and the screeches of a stray car are like bullets hitting your spine. How long are we in here?

2

A romantic image. Trapped and this time the eyes are looking different. It's the knowing. She looks with worry. He looks with hesitation. Conversations easier to strike up now. Easier because of not knowing what the next minutes will tell. She asks for a light and it begins, classic you suppose. No one can see you clinging to your counter and watching the uneasiness shift, from bombs to moves. Worn-out chess analogies and the quiet skies, completely still. What's underneath? A complete and conscious concentration as they move like symmetry tasting the tops of the glasses and gently tipping it like threading a needle. Different? You can't hear but the eyes are different and maybe this is the only circumstance that can give conversation its extra airs. Fear that should be there all the time, that is there all the time, now slowly uncovered as the room recovers slightly from the initial cries of the owner: "We have to lock up, there's been a bomb and the services are trying their best to defuse it."

That's all that's needed, for the couples to silently scream at each other. The real romance is suppressed but it has been just a few minutes from the message. One girl is crying and her friend is smiling with embarrassment as she puts her arm around hers. You give it a couple of minutes and look down at the newspaper, past its rapes and murders and to the wider world. It is only that that affects. The two people's blasting. It has only been a couple of minutes and you, the satellite, watch the arms go around with caution. But the symmetry is consistent. And this time the lights go out as ten lighters knock their flints and you help take the candles out. But for a while it's a misty darkened twilight with the yellows of the lampposts poking through and the flicker of a drag from a cigarette, with the sad accompaniment of tears. As you light the first, the shadows begin to waver, orange light through the glass of a half-full bottle. The arms are still there as you take another candle and deliver it to a boy, alone and expressionless. And then a pair of girls, sensitivity hidden and more silent than usual. The fear's rising as the shadows sparkle and waver for a cracked second as a breeze blows from the window. The candles are out now and back at the bar it's only the expressionless boy who asks for a drink because the flicks tell him to. Detections of slight sycophancy as you sit down with a cold glass of clear water. It's dark now and the only light is from the re-lit candles. The mirrors at the back give the room lights of curaçeo and menthe, scotch and vodka, an alcoholic séance almost. And the girl's talking more confidence finally. And they're reading each other's palms now.

You walk beside the tables until you reach the window on the street and see spotlights, lighting the quite alone man fixing one of the bags, there are more than one. You'll know the face now if that's the last job he ever does. And you can hear a police radio, confidential remarks that there are probably more bombs spread in the shops, and then you hear the reply: to defuse one at a time. But some coins have dropped and the sick chart splutters into the ear-drums. Turned down, it's true. And the owner beckons to you as you are asked for a light. A policeman is at the back, wanting a drink. And you carelessly pour it without a question. And meanwhile the owner turns the box off and turns on a portable radio, that in between reports of no consequence explains by implying. No-one's prepared for it as you walk back to the girl who wanted a light and see she has one. "What's going to happen?" sounds a silly question but you answer slowly, faltering a few times because you hear a sound— just another car. Girls in leather jackets, you turn around to see that she isn't the only one. Fashion again. You turn back and she smiles. So all the confidence is shattered by the thought of death because it isn't accepted, because freedom isn't recognised.

But you draw a chair up beside her and say that you're sure

it'll be alright, just the way anybody would have said. (I admit to you that I don't know that it will be alright.) She says it's just like a book she read in which the optimistic times meant that no-one worried. And the end? They all died, but you're quite sure that we won't. This decade has enough of the people in this room to last forever. "Who wrote it?" you ask but she can't remember. You only asked to put the ball in her court, you turn around and see the others talking more. Only a few are left sitting, looking into their glasses for consolation. Training hasn't been given to us for this inevitable situation. We should have seen it coming. And we hear an explosion and crying in here. The owner closes all the shutters under orders from the men in blue, and you help. You watch for a few seconds before the shutters close and see the ambulance taking away. "There's another one," the owner whispers to you as he tells us all that we'll be let out soon.

You're glad, glad that some of these are here, you sweep the air with my hands. You close them and forget the candles that have flickered too soon to remember a hot summer's evening in a litter-strewn central high street with its ices and coffees. You remember the way the cafés stared at yourself. But you open the eyes and see the girl not seeming to miss you, maybe it's worry. All that experience, they must think deep down, all the people they've met, every gulp of air taken as you talk, what was it all for? Was it just meant to die in a freak bombing in the centre of London? It probably was, the fatalism continues. Possibly rash, you walk back to the table, as she smiles. Then you sit and her girl-friend appears from somewhere and they talk. There are a few at the windows trying to peer out and see what's going on, but the owner or king soon tells everyone to sit and calm down. The nearest to the window dies first, I suppose he says, until you realise that it might help his profits. Who are you? You work here and mumbled dangerous conversation continues until you see someone in the hazy distance who you think you've known before. Ear-rings I think. You smile at the confusion, what do you do then? That's what you ask, returning like you're normal. Secretaries, should have seen by the bright fingernails. Where?

A company. It would sound interesting to others. Looking and leaning over towards you, the one you'd seen before and again you get that annoyance from your two clicks. You stare for a while until it seems almost stupid and a smile turns away.

Do you find it fun? No it's terribly boring, but who's asking who? Well, guess then. The radio drones on and comes alive when we hear about riots further down, officers hurt. I smile again and again, it seems because I don't give a damn. Tell me it was inevitable. But that sounds like I'm tightening the leash. Well so what? You don't expect you'll have much longer. They all think they're so right, so pathetically right, reading and working like bastards raised on the newspapers. You start tearing it and decide you're going to look down, right down at it, but you see the person again. How long before you meet, you wonder? The awareness hurts, really stabs when the being goes to the bar in a long black clothes and asks the owner for a drink when of course he calls you to serve. "What do you think's going to happen?" the being says. You can't think that you've heard it before really because the inflection is different.

"I'm not sure. But I suppose we'll soon know," you say, not meaning to sound half-empty.

"That's a bit pessimistic," being says smiling again. A smile beating you to pieces so you can't tell if being's posing for a shot of a camera or a gun.

"Well I'm not sure," you repeat myself," are you afraid?" you ask.

"Yes," as the smile stops.

"What's your name?" you ask and hear it, and then you swap. "Well, why are you afraid?"

"Don't say it like an analyst," being smiles to prove joking and you forget the features of being's face, noticing the hair toss, "I don't know, but if something goes wrong we're going to die," she said, seeming to believe it. "There's nothing we can do. We are all totally powerless."

I'm surprised that people can tell when they're powerless and when they're not. Only a few fear planes. "Yes, but surely there's something we can do."

"What?" being says before a pause," is there a back entrance?"

"We were told not to use it." You think the person was scared, of you maybe. But then it occurred to you that if the thought of a backdoor was hurtling around the being, could it be in the minds of the others, would there be a stampede to the door? But of course not, like the horoscopes, it's all destined, so if there's a backdoor exit to freedom, read as stability, someone will stand up, swirling a lager maybe and shout: "Backdoor."

"Well can I have a drink then?" person said as you noticed the fingers close up and delicately binding a five-pound note.

"No charge," you said, turning your head around while the measure was delivered, just before you took some money out of your jacket pocket and slotted the fare into the register. Probably saw it.

"Won't you have to pay?" being asked.

"It doesn't matter," you said as being took the glass and drank most of it.

"Well you're already buying me drinks. Maybe..." and the sentence tailed off until something flew through one of the windows on the other side, a rock or a bottle. A sudden collection of screams as the seated customers ran back from the windows. Someone's jacket had orange juice on but that was all. Being panicked and leant forward putting arms around you over the table asking you what had happened. When the screams had stopped and the murmuring had subsided being took arms away, smelling of an ordinary perfume, and blushed. You opened the bar-hinge and let being through and you both stood behind. Almost as on a tube, the insiders stood shaking, some of them with there face in their hands, others looking like they've locked themselves out. And in front there were empty tables, neatly aligned with just a few chairs upset, and a few drinks over the floor, broken glass lying close by. You couldn't see the friendly projectile, probably just a pebble and yet it caused so much emotion. A few must have thought it the end. And you wonder whether I'm cold not to react in their way. What happened to your emotions? They're ruling me, the right ones, the deep-downers. Drink and look tough or they'll scream. Maybe it's past that now, maybe they're starting to come to terms with the real emotion, especially when you see a boy cry, leaning against a radiator, not bothering about a cigarette, just standing with his hands in his eyes, not caring anymore how other people judge his actions. Arms around, you must look like a statue, you can bear all of the stones that come your way. The bobbies are putting up some sort of flimsy wire netting to protect the precious windows on the world.

Remember, the candles, no wonder it was darker. So it wasn't the stray pebble that led the eyes to feel the darkness enlarge. The owner, desperately worried, by now, goes and re-lights them, and the room brightens a little until the others smile at you, with your arms locked and your eyes locked on the candles. The radio stopped some time ago, and you expect they've got the radio-station. Oh how I remember the piteous Oxford Street rushes on a Saturday. Fooled and fools. Seven across again, Forward—Reg's pros! An anagram that's probably far too obvious and one that you'd have replaced. "I have to phone my partner," was a funny remark from your companion. You could smell the scent and feel the smoothness of being's hands, and your white-shirt was like a lip. The phone wouldn't work, of course. You wondered whether this was all in the historical scheme of things, it seemed that way, if you squinted some more through the smoky haze, lit by a dozen candles and looked further through the windows, listening to the noise of the police. You thought being was lying. But you say it'll be alright and the arm returns, and the lips move as if being knows that both of you won't ever see the Seine by moonlight or feel the velour of a cinema seat or watch the ripples in St. James' Park. In fact the decision is all about her, these are your last hours, and you almost wish and know they are.

3

Of course it isn't. This isn't the melodrama that you or I have read. We won't see blood, the lyrical blood that we watch on television. Surely we all know this. But the boy who still cries, jeans and a designed pull-over on a white shirt. Looking a mess, the way all those wear it on the shopping streets. Well, now there's a kind of silence, nothing but distressed looks and you feel as if you're being strangled. Maybe they're studying the tables that you have over so many weeks. They can see the chips and splinters, but for most the shoes are more important. Finally we've reached the underground stage. Like in a train, you have silenced, a few read a free magazine to calm them but the writers are rubbish in a gutter. The smoke now turns to mist, and the windows, firmly closed, blur as the rain falls. A hard noise, the sort you can't hear on a Saturday night because of the noise of conversation. Relaxation after work, but they don't realise that *this* is the work, not the sentences that they serve at the electric typewriters.

"Can you draw?" you feel like asking, because the scene is full of that tension. You look to the left and see dimly lit candles reflected in the glass light-shades. Above them some pictures, art thrown to the ground by the clutter and the frames. New York galleries, probably. And then turn towards the right, over the dark tables and single candles in the middles. Look up and see the flickering shutters and the gaps netted with wire. It's all empty here but a bigger turn leads to the people about thirty or so—I can't count them- all standing in strange ways, huddled together in front of more pictures. And then the black ledge where your hand rests, wet with beer. Some empty glasses on the sides and then you look at her face, quite listless. You look further and see that in one of the corners, one I had not seen, is the pure and delicate silhouette of your manager sitting nearly straight, his hands over each other, lying on the table, his face looking as if he knows what's going to happen. It's all those small stories on the second page, they've all built up this mess. Because when you're young, your pure responses are not like the love of stability. Now, those men and women on the sides, they *love* the permanence. More afraid of that small occurrence, like a broken paving stone pushing you off balance.

Wisps of string-like smoke leave a candle that's just gone out. The owner rises and tells you all that he's got some packs of playing cards, asking if anyone wants to play. Tension-relieving, I suppose. You laugh a little, an hour, you have sat waiting and now the cards are coming out. He goes behind the bar table and gets some boxes. Meanwhile a policeman comes from nowhere and tells you all to remain quiet. The room which had that slight murmur after the idea of a jack and an ace falls silent. Slowly, like a lying patient to a relative the man tells you to remain calm and that you might have to stay here for some time yet. Some serious groans interrupt him. "If any of you are tired, you might as well try and get some sleep," he says, "it'll be alright", he tells the boy who's by now using a handkerchief that a girl has just given him. He must be about eighteen. The bobby leaves and moves his eyes when he sees the owner pass him. The policeman leave through the backdoor.

The king hands the boxes out to some of the others. I can't understand how he chooses which ones to hand it to. When he comes back to the bar he hands you one of the packs. And you give it to being, in a ridiculous way. It almost reaches up the sleeve. Being opens the pack and puts the packet on the table and then shuffles the cards. You're too interested in watching the others, seeing them open the little boxes and look and smile at each other like a group of children at a nursery. It's too late to tell them that the rainbow does have an end, they won't understand me. I wonder who will end up with who. One girl at the end has sat on the floor leaning on the wall behind her, trying to close her eyes and trying to ignore the others, by now exchanging cards. You decide that you don't like it at all. You like being, the one who's still shuffling. You walk over to the fridge and go on the other side of the door that lies behind the bar to open it. You are noticed as you conspicuously come from the door with a bottle of champagne. The owner smiles, he doesn't run towards you, strangling me or punching you. You untangle the wire frame over the cork and the cork flies through the air and hits the window on the other side, making a light clicking noise. Some laugh, some who hadn't noticed the bottle look up, startled. The glasses are ready and you pour six or seven. Blank expression, you have one. Being takes the other and a few of the bravest take the rest. Clink.

You drink it quickly and lay it down on the table. Haven't tasted this for years. You yawn and close your eyes, you think some of them are looking your way. Authority, and the owner bowing his head. You open them for an instant to see which boy and which girl, then glance at the orange sky coming through the shutters. The noise of cars and lorries and men, the noise of breaking glass. You close them again, opening them with a start when you hear a vacuum cleaner turn on, the owner sadly pushing it up and down, the noise is horrible. An engine or a giant insect, or a giant blowing along a straw. Close the eyes finally and think of *De Chirico*, open to see it just like Melancholy. You wonder, should you help him?" You've got to go to work tomorrow," being says.

"I suppose they all do." You look towards a boy reading a newspaper in the corner. Being's still sipping the champagne. The boy has stopped crying. Bang! As the glass shatters and the tiny blocks look like stars on the dark floor, flickering as the candles do. You can see the pictures better now. You ignore your companion like being does you and walk swiftly to one of the tables. Some bottles, messages soaked in gasoline fall through the open windows and broken shutters. The wind keeps blowing and one of the candles nearly falls into the arms of a fire. You save her and put it out. Bringing it back, you light it, a hard strike and the gentle stroke on the wick. It lies next to the other one. The network of boy, boy, girl, boy, girl, girl, girl, boy, until the end of the wall stare, now at the wall they are facing. The owner still sits, like nothing has happened. You say something to your companion, but being's left for the cigarette machine.

The vermilion turns to a deep gold as the flames begin outside. Now, the scents of carbon, wax, scotch, smoke and cloth, sometimes perfume. The wind still harder now, blowing you like in a fast car. Small blocks of glass scatter across the dark wooden floor....They soon flicker like galaxies of stars as the candles light, then dim. The pictures are brighter, you almost pick out a few faces along the wall when they turn around. The taste of wine in your mouth lingers. The noise of trucks and a hundred people, pushing and colliding with each other outside. An officer, red stains, walks and stumbles to a seat, there is no front door. He is followed by ambulance-men helping him. The candles seem so far above the bright stars on the floor, the perspectives are lost. "The situation is under control," he says to us and you feel that you should laugh. The radio, before fading away, far behind the trucks and sounds of bottles hitting roads is louder now. Liverpool, Birmingham, Glasgow, the other networks have realised. This while the blank faces of the spiny people on the wall crouch. Water appears, but the tears have ran it all out. The flames are brighter and then dimmer. The faces, white like sheets, expressionless with their short hair and bodies in black with maybe silver buttons. They look like nothing, nothing human. No one sees the boy who walks behind me in the dimness. The sound of a siren, without use. You don't hear the gentle bell of the register in the corner as he takes pathetic notes and leaves, you hear the steps, out of the back door.

Many hours separate you from the warm views of the city and the bed-springs. Eyes, almost crusted in the smoke feel like crying. That bang, the one that breaks the shutters until they filter the wind, scared you. But it's not only you, and the fear stays for but a second. More faces lit by a golden light, the pictures are clearer now. "Have you cotton wool?" an officer, who has just come to you, asks. I feel like telling you about pharmaceutical companies. You say nothing. It's all falling apart, more medics rush in as the smell of kerosene comes in. The sound of the hundreds outside seems louder now, and the uniforms that fall into the arms of the chairs, tripping over the abandoned vacuum cleaner, are glazed with blood. The flames are gone again and the room falls into darkness like the one that gave the boy his escape. There wasn't much in the register though. The playing cards have all fallen to the ground, Kings and Queens in front of stars below high candles like crude surreal art. So again it is only the candles and the reflections from the floor, tiny pieces of bright glass.

In front of this scene that develops from silence, to radio, to wind, from darkness to orange to yellow, from wax to spirit are the two candles. You blow at one. It wavers and glows until it's out.

4

It reminds me of a man I used to see walking along Cheyne Walk every Friday. It was always the same night, every time and he always held a white candle in his left hand, unlit. Rainy winter evenings, not too cold, beside the river, very much alone. More concentration needed to cross the roads entering the bridges. Battersea and Albert. The usual reflections, shiny streets and the yellow merges of the car lights. Sometimes a moon easing the lamp-posts, cold lanterns, old and black again. The candle and the one that's lit on the counter. Steps on and on walking nowhere, passing no-one and pausing only to look at a driver or passenger winking through the misty windows. The wrong reflection usually—all of them seem to look at him. Trying to get it out of his head, but a view over the grey walls and into the black water leave it strong. The idea, that's it. But candles are so much of it. Holding the umbrella, he can't move his hands to his face, stroking the stubble. A cigarette limply clinging to the lips, dry and then wet. A fog, a fifties style. Until I couldn't see anything. Thin outlines of trees and the benches like dark temples, risen on blocks of cold concrete. He walks to the walls and looks down. I see it from my window, high above. Binoculars help. The umbrella tips to the side and I can see him, leaning on the wall, a hat rim deep in water. Gazing into the river, the lights of the offices in the corners of his eyes, ignored. He folds the umbrella, zoom in to his wet hands, rubbing his black coat. He leans the umbrella against the wall, still holding the candle, and falls.

I did nothing, like I do now. The room is the same, the haze, the soft fragrances. You dream for a moment, like so many, that you could lead the lonely entrepreneurial existence of a ladder ascender, but too soon—reality. They tell you that this is love and you say it is, then they tell you this is success and you believe it, never questioning. The noise of the sirens that you had forgotten, that you don't need to take notice of, begin again. You don't mind if this really is the end. You were tired of the headlines, the smoke. And suddenly all the senses don't matter. Calm silence. "What's going to happen to us?" being's confidence falls through before saying it to you, hand in your hand. No one says become, like in books.

No wonder death never mattered, it is all dying for the last time. But not in physical ways and desires. Aware minds will always be unhappy until they realise. You don't, or you haven't, like the nights spent in bars where you don't work. With friends that you had, sometimes. Talking, thinking you're taking them into your confidence. "It'll be alright...", how many times must you lie, and why? Worry sweeps the room but no outpourings of doubt and the experiences and accomplishments still to be made give way. It's still not too late you say to myself. You'll say if I say first. "You work here, has anything like this happened before, ever?" and you think and finally find something new, it has been happening ever since you were born. Crumbling like cake that you can't pick up. It finally meant something, all those fragments like the ice-like glass that can't be picked up. They just lie there, untouched and crying out to be. Until, in a still society they can cry no more. "Where were you born?" you ask.

"West of here. I grew up there," being says, the realism again. Being doesn't ask why you ask. You have seen it, you tell her, the greens and greys of the West, and the dark greys of the skies that always sit waiting. Still too early to confide, you think.

"I was born in the village hospital. We lived on a farm, it was all very normal and I left when I was nineteen. London always attracted me. Everything happens here..."

But everything happens everywhere, you glory at the generalisation, meriting a distinction. The sound of a missile, the ones that hurtle over you towards far off continents, that you, too, have visited. They're only planes, though. There's no moonlight anymore, not the sort your speechless friend walked in. But the whirring of the engines, for the sound isn't quite that, continues, seems to, for ever. With this, this riot in front of you, a bar-counter separating you from it, it seems like a missile. You're not tired anymore, the calm calamities are just that, they don't touch you inside. Nothing can, it's like finding an empty field after so much rush. It's almost like our images of death, images like a child's queries on sex, or a fatalist with dice. The sirens fade away like your ears from being's conversation, now listened to by serious eyes that stand next to you. You never were silent, like the officers told you to be, is this why we were punished, or is it a God?" I remember when I first saw the lights, I was taking a taxi from the station—I didn't know what the underground was," and nor did a Russian. Because all these submerged facts come to the surface, onto the hands that you can't feel, sitting neatly on your life-lines. Fatalism never leaves us, that's why this was inevitable. The hope that should have been despair. Tell me about this Love. And they tell you it is. Mouths open, interrupting being's statement, pleasure, you suppose, but it isn't like they told you. The attractions of a stolen desert-city where the films come from, where the word reaches its lows. The couple and its demise. The tongues no longer at the roof of your mouth. Where it should be, you know, especially when your eyes are only looking forward.

You don't like the barrier, with its transformed sand and its blackness. It stifles. It comforts when we lean, close together, scents strengthening, almost overpowering but soon you know that you're escaping, a too easy escape. Like the ones that they give you, you now invent your own tailored pleats for your situation, one that lands in your life as so many you hear, this summer. Flames again, and here you see and look closely at something that means more. Wavering body forms, painted tips, transparent still, but it burns, blowing your flesh away, worthless like it is. Hot sensations, cold at first, until your mind finds out, the eyes squint, cheekbones advancing up screaming towards your foreheads. Arms around a back, soft material and zips. Unlock and check.

A queue's building like blocks. Gin? Lager? So the drink is what they're after eventually. Like an illegal jazz club, that serves drink when there's no license. Money from sweat-spread fingers, greasy coins for the cool and sometimes violent shades that make the glowing of the spectrum behind you. The measures delivered, the drinks starting to lower and again it is all back to normal. They're even edging nearer and around the glass on the floor, sitting on glass-strewn chairs. Talk and a kind of social. And again, the qualms of touch. Toneless. Jack is his name, the one that begins to talk, greying hair, quite old, fifties again or sixties. Too old, it seems. Talking to you, away from the crowd, leaning on the bar (being has left for the crowd, now playing cards!). He isn't afraid of death, not at his age, he tells you. You suppose it's obvious though some would say that after so many years one begins to value life. But after so many years, experiencing so much, you realise it isn't worth anything. You don't agree. You still want 'to change the world' for yourself. Although that's only at the back of your mind as you spend nights pouring drinks. You're putting it off for a while, maybe next year when you have enough money, you think. How would it be to make *the descent of the spirit to the heart of the senses* from a clean white sheet and a burnt match or a pen? You can't tell, it only happens to a few, you know. Oh to collocate all these minds! To shake them out of their torpor. But it's only as you raise your glass to them that you become a fit of frustration and anger. It's all underneath.

You must have felt it too, like radioactive snow falling behind your back, but don't believe it. He's a writer, he tells you, and you have no reason to disbelieve it. He writes plays, but the last was thirty years ago. "How does it feel?"

"It feels like nothing else. "You knew it. To express the thoughts of a scene so well and well, you digress. He's asking about you and you reply that you were born in London, an orphan, but aren't we all? Laughs. You remember hot summers and the smell of trees blowing the sunshine away. And the waterfalls start again as a hail of bottles rise into the night sky, lighting like planets this time. And you can't see the frightened faces of the boys who throw them, out of the pent-up frustration that many speak of and few reply to. Is it the homes we have given them, is it their dying parents without doctors? Or is it that they have no place in this walking famine, just like us all if you dared to admit. "National conscription..." You hear some of the words that are all too common, regiment them so they can have their own silver buttons and unite their problems with a lover who doesn't understand you. The relationship, and how it cries to be forgotten. It won't and will never work but they won't understand, they can't even see the power of the frustration in the eyes, that must be sparkling behind the broken shutter still blowing forward and backward, glimpses of light but not the whites of their eyes. And the irises that reflect distortions, because it is the relationships on the other side that are the distortions. The shutter has caught alight, like the spark of love when they tell you that that is what it is all about: the responsibility. You laugh as a man throws his lager over the shutter, it drips until you turn to look at the fight, the man used another man's drink. Suddenly there are fast movements as punches are thrown, a regular brawl that breaks none of the ground, the tables or chairs. Noses bleed, as their relationships save them. But they don't, not really.

Everyone watches in silence, as the drama continues, it all looks like a wreck, the haze and the four seducing silhouettes, shouting at each other and calming each other down. They come to you for refills expecting your nice face to give in and give it for free. The cards have stopped too.

5

Oh come on, just a couple of drinks," he says, thinking you have a say in any of this. The boys wink at you to prove their points. Well, you won't and they take their wallets out soon. Fast-earned cash and fast-spent too. The girls smile back and then they walk away. It all ended sweet and asleep. Your friend comes back after a while and asks you whether you've heard anything. You haven't. Right now, you feel that your place is not a bus-ride away. It doesn't need you feeling a cold metal bar or shuffling in your pockets for change. You live upstairs, now, not even the owner knows. Laugh, because it's almost funny. This isn't an occupation 'for-the-moment', you want to live it through, right to the end. All these walking monotypes, they are friends, friends that you love and hate. It doesn't matter if you live up or not, because it might as well be further away. Trivia, the trivialities that make people think they're having fun and times still go on. Now, the trivialities are taking place at an even more unique time. As they are spoken they seem more wasteful. Being holds your hand across the table and you take it back, making sure you can see your reflection in the mirrors behind you as your turn your neck, smooth and gliding.

"You're scared now," being smiles, white teeth, eyelids lowering.

"Why? Is everything alright now?"

"Yes," being's drinking. Your eyes are stinging, you don't have the time for a five-minute-infatuation as you pull out a handkerchief from your bag. You're noticing it more and more now, noticing lovers and loners, always glancing at you for a change but not making any moves towards you. You've pulled the particle out of your head, and it rests, neat and folded, on your handkerchief, while you smile a constant smile but a smile that can't work like the one being gave you. "Where do you live?" velvet-toned inflections again, more like sleeping with velvet death! Quite nearby? That's the answer, a lie, of sorts. "There's no point in me going home when this is all finished..." Not an unfinished sentence, not the awful ones that you can't answer now because you're worrying more than anyone about the stray stones and fires and water jets and explosions. You're worrying and the rest are thinking of tomorrow and the problems of transport. You thoughts too, sort of. You're not going to answer, squeezing your hand being leaves for some other cathedral of gullibility, seeing through the pretty lashes etcetera.

They don't work, how many times can you lie to yourself? Some more police rush in, almost storm in like pathetic precipitates, you don't remember what they said. It's too obvious and you won't analyse their stupidity, not even when they confuse you all with rioters and one of the boys gets hit in the confusion. Rushed off, you know, straight there. Probably for a TV first. "Look at what these extremists have done!" will be the cries of the impartial. And it was just one short-sighted policeman, just out of training. You said you weren't going to analyse, not them anyway. You branch with those bodies in sweat, a bottle in a left hand, erased of any milk and kindness and in the right hand nothing. Just a hand with cropped fingers like *Liechtenstein*, ready to give the other force. The stance, legs slightly apart, a white or grey shirt. It flies and hits a uniform pocket and the flesh smells as it shakes until it bleeds and the frame of the man in uniform falters, stumbles, falls. And then he is carried away.

That is all outside, fields of close bodies in the imagination, never wavering and never hurting. They've done that all along. But motives are not clear, because motives born out of frustration are always never clean and sure. It isn't straight, they aren't, and they aren't flat. Structure after structure and then maybe someone can understand all these bodies fighting bodies in a year far beyond the wars or the battles or the escapes or the trials. The trials are going on now, and just as they fared outside, in normal life, they fare as badly now. Not like humans again, not like them at all. "I can't find anywhere to stay, can you help, please?" being asks as if you will leave this bar turned hell.

"But how do you know you need a place?" you ask.

"Of course, of course we will," you hand the handkerchief, but tears should never dry. "Please?"

"Yes, you can."

"Thanks. I'm not with anyone, you see my friend, my girlfriend went to meet someone. She was going to come back, but, but then all this happened."

"It's alright."

"You know, I was still acting cool, you know what I mean, but it all didn't end as soon as I thought. I'm not usually like..."

"It's alright," you persist until being doesn't need words, the fear is in being's arms and hands.

"We're going to start evacuating groups of five," a policeman shouts at you all as he enters. He chooses two girls sitting nearby and begins to look in the still dim room for the other three. Being, with the beacon of solitude, looking for a place, rushes to the tables, bumping into them. They all lie about ten feet away. Being crashes into a few, but by the time the officer has chosen, it is too late for being's cries. It's so melodramatic. You feel normal, quite normal. It's stuffy, no more than in a small club, and aspects such as smoke, haze, dim light and a very faint smell of blood create no more than the hint of danger. Some help being up, the officer won't change his mind and he takes the lucky five out of the backdoor. The five, foolish as they had been when they entered, oblivious and lovers of trivia, obvious and divorcees with love, the real one that time, they leave smiling at every boy that their eyes reach, sometimes checking makeup until, at last, they leave you. You're not sure for what, of course. As for being, well you expected it. Being's talking to someone else now. I lie to the reader less than they, the big they, lies to you.

There are such fine lines to cross. The tossing of her hair, or the tossing of his last week, the lips and the hands, they are small steps into the lies. You shuddered under them, just a few moments ago, and now it is only a neatly trapped piece of dirt under the fingernail that is required to relieve diseases of the mind. A cigarette is now trapped between your lips. You're staring at someone, not able to take your eyes away. It's a trap, and a trap that some just don't grow out of. It is not the most serious of the traps though, that would give to much importance to it.

A lot of them are drunk now, drunk and you served them, drunk like the services you suppose. They rush off to toilets sometimes—just to throw up, and you come back stained. You almost wish that the last unshattered shutter is destroyed, the air, you need the air, but nothing out there is going to help you now. The officer never returned for the next five, you wonder what happened to those charming debasers?

Don't shed the tears.

6

So it goes on and on, this interminable ending. An ending, passionless and smelling of corpses slid amongst one another. It's reminiscent of a chivalric knight fighting for his country. Human relations that don't exist, showed up, minute by minute, showed up for what they are. The talking is truly as oblivious as it was, the faces as they were. They're not even the bodies, just an id, or two. There's a knife, clean and deep, lying on the counter. You use it to cut up lemons for your friends' gin and tonics, or even white wine if they want. It's a clean blade, you didn't use it last night, and you take it with you, for your journey to the backdoor. As if journeys can be so important!

Sweeping feet over a floor, thinking that you'll either use this sharp tool against a customer or use it against yourself. It doesn't matter, not really, they're indifferent to you and so you might as well be to them. And then across the room someone is calling out, screaming out words, that you can't hear. No notice. Another scream and still everyone carries on sitting on the ground, sitting on the chairs, smoking their cigarettes, drinking their glasses dry. He won't be heard and nor will you and you soon sit down behind the counter never seeing the backdoor. The slow decay of conversations, stale and burnt. The misuse of qualities like imagination, for they have none. Sometimes how easy they are to fight and meet. You weren't very violently suave with being. No, you seemed too interested, making remarks to feel important. You're a conformist. You walk over to being and ask whether all's alright. Being says: "Yes."

"Come on sit down," being says, a regular flirt of blusher on your cheek, "I'm sorry I ran away like that."

"You don't have to apologise to me, we've only just met," you laugh, probably staring right under her eyes at the flickering tears. Half-lit are your faces, the eyes vibrating.

"No, I was, well I was talking and it must have seemed like...oh never mind," being says, stuttering and pausing because being doesn't know how to behave and there's none of the exits that being must be so good at using, just when being leads them on. Two boys come and sit at the table. It's wooden and it is quite dark. "Hello," being says with a smile as big as the one I got.

"Hello, what's your name?" one of them, the more revolting one, asks. They swap, just like everyone does with their intelligences when they go to school. And they start talking and you sulk, like a spoilt child, hurt by a corner of a banister or grazed on a stair. They're soldiers, and meanwhile at the other table, two yards away, you can hear money changing hands and cards being shuffled until they spill. Cries of joy when one wins, just like your two little soldiers, the sort that think they're very right. But you're too tired for all this now, you cover your face in your hands and catch words or phrases from the conversation, sometimes sensing a sigh from your right, and sometimes a smile from your left. They don't carry swords, they never do these days. Out of uniform means they go into another. They have blood stained brains like the rest of you, they're fools debasing every potential, corrupters. And they smile as if they are like all of you. They smile because they are, because you are all death camp orderlies with sick veneers of love and humour. How do I convince? So this beautifully concocted situation, this wonderful orchestration of a dramatist's talents—it hasn't brought a different, more noble angle, to all of the girls on the walls, or the boys in chairs. Nothing has happened. A few tears, a few base emotions that even your teachers couldn't touch but now the bar returns to the scene that graced it hours before. Yes, there's flirting and there's forgetting, there's blood and there's sex but after that you might as well be unconscious co-operators.

This time someone is hurt—this time it's visible evidence, clear and real. A girl who you had noticed earlier, quite pretty with dark brown hair and a small upturned nose. Well this time it's the blood of the physical that dyes as with silk. She lies motionless at first. At first, because you haven't paid enough attention, at first, because you're still shocked that they've penetrated here. Shocked because the sound, the sound of a bullet? I don't know. Just a sound that has silenced the room, finally some sort of gut-feeling. It demands some unique response. She's moving, but no-one else does. They're just watching. Just watching her lie on the table that she must have been blown onto. Her feet limp at one end, in the air, a heel apparent. And who tells me that thousands are for charity, you knew it was for tax or something other than care. And they finally come

"Bastards they stopped us police we have to get her out of here
hope the police don't stab don't hit don't charge they can't."

And the wrong ones, again and again, the military wings of a government walking their lies and flying their scandals until they blind you, blind burns of the eyes. Melting as you see her call, a sweet beautiful cry as the two men in the white carry her passed you all. You stare, they stare. Passing the tables, passing the counter and out by the backdoor into a cold night, that is turning redder. Redder because their is no violet. And the tears are rolling down your cheeks for her. For you all, because they have no reaction, they can't understand. And still the constant sound of objects landing on live bodies until hearts seem to shrivel—you must have blanked it out from your mind. And the swords, cowards with shit in their mouths, carry on talking. Even being frowned at their senses. Bad shapes, the senses. You, even the skeletons of the soldiers, rattle towards the back, leaning, all of you, on the bar counter, close and touched. Seduced with the action, the killers laugh and put their thick arms around her. Cliché, I believe, because a life which is no life tends to be.

But when the tears are stinging your face and you have no time for the detachment of a professional victim, then you feel ill and down. You think of friends that you used to know. Occasionally one that was close for a month and who died in one of the battles that we don't hear about in the decade of the media, occasionally he comes to mind. But as one of the boys creeps up to the box to drop some of his coins, music appears. Depressingly reminding, sadly nostalgic and all the time eating away, just like it does to any of the thirty or so present. Still present in a room. They're talking again, exploiting the closeness to violate spatial abilities until they are of no use. Nothing happens for a while. You're thinking, sure, you're thinking all the time while the scene to your left and right doesn't change, thinking but *rahmenerzahlung* isn't necessary. So you look at the clock, strain your eyes until they hurt like they're falling out, hanging on a vein, strain until you can see a thin second hand. A hand lying at two or three. A hand without progress, a hand without a movement.

7

And still the colours. The colours of the clothes you ignored. Greens and Greys, colours of no description soaked in the fire of circumstance. Anoraks, matching jeans' uniforms all helping in their little ways to kill any uniqueness. But it's the light blue that is worst. Colours scarred with metal as they lift glasses and seem so innocent. As if it has nothing to do with them. Reminding me this time, of the sense of touch—when you kiss the lips of a photograph or see the fingers clasping a trumpet. Trumpet because someone did drop a coin in the machine of emotion, trumpet because the records are all mixed up on the juke box. But then the sorry individual in a blue suit, with a moustache too normal, well he didn't know he was selecting the castanets and jazz of *Miles Davis*. He shouldn't have got up, he feels now. These vibrations in the air lead to minds feeling more pessimism, not less. And he smiles as he walks back to his friend in a buff-coloured jumper, watched by everyone else. Watched because the others are rightly scared of their stupidity and coping equipment. They sit close to the shutters, far from the rest—non-conformist stupidity—not insolence.

And now the cigarette-machines empty, piles of nervous boxes lying on tables without width, maybe slightly resonating with the sadness, the purest kind, sonic sadness. The long track ceases after six minutes leaving the room, at last, affected by something 'with feeling'. You didn't cry this time, though, not even when the false laughter of fear died in the last breath of the instrument. Maybe the trumpet, with its falsely bohemian curves, wasn't there at all. The man never existed, your mind wandered and wondered until you wanted to know what its effect on the crowd was. Even if it was just your mind—the blue-suited man with a cloned companion for company—the effects can be seen now.

"What did you say?" you ask when being mumbles something, away from her patronising patriots, after walking through the maze of thirty. Annoyed, it sounds. Annoyed because it's frustration at seeing it over and over again. "What did you say?"

"I've run out of matches—so have my friends. Got a light?" being says embarrassed. You say nothing and light a match to being's head.

Didn't you say that relationships, where the art of imagination must be at the extreme, can't be mastered? Even when you're in the top-deck of a bus watching a sleepy couple kiss by the railings on the side of the road. Even when they smile as a green jersey knocks into them or an exhaust pipe stains them. They won't know, they won't be able to imagine. Just when you think you can, it falls apart.

You ignored it before, like you do so often, when you concentrate on particular nuances and their implications, but some suits are still discussing business, exploiting a situation with a powerful lady or a rich man. Even now, after all your senses having been filled with the bizarre, even now, they're acting to exploit—while the talked-to show their discomfort inside by peculiar smiles—not giving much away but enough for me, your picaresque friend without home or background. It's like you landed two days ago, maybe replaced someone's body, you don't like this one. Too muscular and fit, it makes you ignore things. Catastrophically bad judgements will always lead to disaster. Your confidence from another planet is beginning to be regarded as self-love. So quick to come to extremes of black and white about character and so slow about society, the people around you are changing face. The liberals for life are kneeling to green bottles like they're gods. A television is on now.

No-one's eaten for hours. You're alright, though. For them, the shuffling of feet illustrate cravings for sandwiches. Animal instincts at last! Now it's only sex, sleep and death left. Human nature to the fore and how much fun it is to watch, when you prove to yourself that you're not like them. But how much sadness is it to see that you are so powerless to help them? Straws in some of the drinks are wavering until they reach open lips. People are thinking that this will end in calmness. But serenity is nowhere. Noise is hiding.

Hidden until you concentrate harder. You need an ultraviolet awareness like the one I referred to before, as ultraviolet as the blackcurrant on the bar. Or, rather, as invisible portions of the bottles behind you. They all lie in line, untouched, not even the screeches or the sirens have broken them.

You seem to have forgotten about the matches that light up every four minutes, but there's plenty of time. You almost wish, like them, that we were all released. But, no, they don't like the final release, this event has been like shooting up into your arm. And so you actually wish you could stay. Maybe you once wished this would happen, but the crowd who were trapped would have been different. Different as hell. Not even the girl in lightly-washed hair with the striped-trousers would you have kept. Not the boy in tight black jeans. You wouldn't have wished for clasped hands. You didn't want blouses slightly undone.

At least there's a lot of coffee, you'd have kept that, even if there's so much that it makes you drowsy. It's the owner, trying to act nicely, for a change, giving customers lots and lots of what they don't really want.

Slowly the line, leaning on the bar, sit down, still sloping. There's so much talk now, so much ruffling that it's a blur—just like when this whole mess started. "It's probably," that was as much as you could hear. Probably what? A publicity stunt? No, that would be clinging onto the refuge and refuse of this two decade period existence, the sort you see on the sides of double-decker buses or in tubes or from your office on the fourth floor or on the television or on lights. When the menu-cards lying on the bar begin to be read as they get up and down, that's the time to worry about them. It's not only food, it's boredom. Boredom only strikes the least aware, rising like broken glass, formed from an empty mind, unable to analyse. Characters, you can't fill them out anymore. They're all too similar will be the excuse. You feel bad about saying 'stereotype' or 'covered people.' So many different backgrounds all leading the well-trodden path to normative, lazy back-of-the-mind ambition.

The pink make-up which you touched on is illuminated for barely a second when the strike is up. The cloning of fashion is not shallow analysis or thought, because they are extensions of character and demonstrations of lack of self-confidence. Especially when they smile in groups and frown when alone. You're sitting on a chair, hoping that they don't see you staring at noses and cheek-bones. But they can feel it burning them until they get the wrong impression of your motives. Well, you've missed the lovers hovering in some of the corners. You can't see them because they're crouching. You can only see the broken shutters, straight ahead, blowing in and out—never stopping because the beat or breath will feign life until the last minute.

The denim, pearl-earring-ed one puts her hand to her cheek like some mad pop-star with a crush. She says nothing to her companion, lying with his beautiful haircut and the white shirt with the red stripes. The coffee's making you drowsy, even if medicine bottles say no. This time your eyes feel as if they're cloning for the last time. How the body hides suffering! No-one knows the suffering whether it's khaki rain-coats or white handbags, whether it's the brushed hair of the town-crier or the business-talk. Something interrupts your wandering, the barman with the other shift walks in from the backdoor and asks me what's happening. I tell him and he says that it's terrible. Exact words. Terrible. Well, he says that at least he won't have so much work and I ask him about the backdoor and he says that if old silver-buttons tell him not to use it, he shan't. Surprise? No, you're not surprised, even the audience, who stand as he enters rushing questions about doors aren't really surprised. Traps always have escapes—it just depends on the courage to use them.

"In search of America's greatest dream," says a matchbox.

You think the childhood of this body, spent rolling over New England fields, where the light is a strange yellow ochre and it seems so safe. So safe, because the mat that you lie on is like your mother's arm. But that was in the last months of the sixties. Now the solitude that you, or this body, feel is not wanted. Not usually, but when you're trapped with caricatures who tire of being interesting, then you want loneliness. Probably in front of the mirrors of the bathroom when your zip's stuck or your heel has fallen off. Like breaking manicured nails, the floor is crushed by the sighing of stilettos and the used-up ash. Very neat, the foreground anyway. Only the distance can remind you of a painter. Perforated windows exist to laugh at you. They're objects with more emotion than your friends. America's dream search? It was a newspaper cutting stuck on the wall, sometimes illuminated. Probably the owner's nostalgia. But now it's like a jungle. Densely covered by leaves, the constant bolts of mosquitoes on your body stinging until you're like them. Tiny flies as you try and lie down on the dry-mud ground, smelling of arid decay—just like the legends of saints. Taking a water-bottle, made of rock, to your mouth, you wake up because it's only vermouth. The television was never on because your industrial love for electricity had died premature. It almost looks like the room's empty when everyone's under me, leaning on the metal bar on the bottom of the counter. Empty, you feel as if you're the only one here. Alone in a room where fighting outside rings true, rings too real. Every sense you thought of is now not shared by anyone else. The smells, the lights and the sounds, they all belong to you and it's only you that's in such danger. In a creased white shirt and dark jacket that you feel close to you, you are rigid, staring straight ahead.

But the clock didn't work, you said that the hand didn't move, so time might as well be out of the room too. You're watching silhouettes outside in stances of solid anger, frozen like the branches of those Capability Brown trees you see in Hyde Park or the leaves in different positions lying on a Japanese garden, only there to be looked at. No more. You can see a tuft of sparkling hair and again the sounds penetrate once more. Dressed in monochrome, like you, the hair covers the eyes as being looks at you, rigid as ever, to see or confirm your insanity. A white pen-like cylinder pressed against a forehead, not worried when you stare back. The whites of the eyes are like fear, the fear you saw before, the one you thought had turned into one of the stubs. Mouthing 'Hello', time comes back into the room. Communicative, half-open lips show you that you are no longer alone.

Why do you say it again and again? Why do you say that you might as well be alone for all the company you get here. It could be an empty ballroom, empty apart from yourself and being, dancing the hours under imaginary ceilings reaching into the sky, ceilings painted gold. There are some in London, near Piccadilly, where the ambience is imaginatively bad. Black taxis ringing the cloakroom, it feels like, until you suddenly you realise it's another siren or another burglar alarm under stress. I wonder about the slow creeping dawn. Collages lie at the end of this room, pieces of glass, tinted in black and orange, brown and green. How reflective, at least.

Jackets with baseball names soon ground you, you miss seeing the room fill, from empty to full, the smell of the floor being cleaned or the lights being switched on or off. That is what's missing here: the light. Again powerless. The candles have been out for a long time, the occasional gust of the smoky night breeze is just enough to extinguish the flames. You watch the candle for some minutes after you light it, watch the flame until it wavers like the shutters before it dies. And it all seems so civilised, like watching haircuts down an expensive London Street or wondering whether people will eat at the glass furniture in the boutique windows. So obvious that the American colony serves coffee, not tea. How it all looks so empty, only the girl standing and visible. Continuous present without a madam to introduce you. Intellectual unit, you can't talk to anyone because you've seen it all before in books. This time you strike your fist at the bar-counter in frustration, frustration with the hand of circumstance, timeless and as beautiful or ugly as someone with scarce looks. But what about the straight ahead?"

Hello," mmmm, such soft inflections of the voice, and art you've mastered.

"It's been hours, do you know what's happening" being asks. Bits of conversation, unanswerable until you die. Sweeping the hand again, repeat after repeat. Bothered by claustrophobia? you will be when you realise that those are just mirrors, but then today a reflection of affection can be picked up in a second.

8

O nce upon a time. No, that isn't the way to start it, it isn't your doodling that'll turn doodles into art. You wonder where the pencil came from, anyway. The graphite, worn down, the paper dead in black. Annoyed, because you can't see the sketches properly and you talk as if it isn't really you. Well it's not, especially when you're getting to know this boy, asking for the last option available. Available from you, that is. If only they'd see their grand-scale folly, you think.

One long scale and the twang of the bow, flying through your fields. The recessions have now continued for so long that you've become blind, another handling of the wet eyes with a television screen. And the news-types, the interviews of the youth of classes beyond. An accent that you're used to, the American accents in your body, the one that says 'Noo Joisey', it too finds its niche in the beauty of a Hampstead road or a Harvard lawn. You only remember all of this, because this Yorkshire accent of the boy brings it to the mind. Bitter isn't it? Smelling of the artificial now, probably the news-type that poisons you all. Sporting muscular bodies, where sport is an only past-time, in the North, of course. Where the ghosts of brass bands blow across the industry of different fields. Slowly they all group like the finale, the last bar of the finale. It makes you think it is, the third movement in the event. The two girls and this boy, the two national-lovers eager to dispute their facts, and the sad owner with a classic black, drooping moustache.

Families to convince, that there are. Sisters to tell. You have none of that, and it is for you, instead, to convince them all. Alone for twenty minutes, not exact, and then you adapt.

Adapt until you find that your body feels like there's a weight clinging to your lobes, and the veins in your hands have stopped pumping. Isn't this the time to start worrying?

And then, just when you think it can't happen to you, the sadness of seeing someone you love die, it happens. It will strike at all times, when you know that it is you who's responsible for your actions. Is it being who's gone up in flames over a trivial accident? Well, it was surely, truly, beyond your attitude and your controls, well then you just imagine how you'll forget it when you're an old man leaning on an arm-chair and thinking of the betrayed. Betrayal is all around, this time it's them, tomorrow it'll be you to yourself. The soul is theirs, not religious, but modern and individual, some kind of lonely subject. Say, years of growing, when the memory doesn't fade and you, one day, in a big castle of strength, relive it all, moment by moment, like the dreams you should have every night, replaying just a day. And you forget the little accidents, somewhere in the sixty years, the small infatuation that you have left behind, maybe at a party at which you acted so suddenly. Or maybe an insignificant place like the one you now watch over. Watching and hoping it'll all end now, because all those that one love, well it can go up in flames like the fate of this being with the oblivious stuck to her temples. Think of a far away countryside where you grew up, lying on rocks by streams and brooks with nothing but the noise of the natural for company, far away from the offices and shops and progress. The London that you loved all that time ago, now in the sepia of the movies, rocking you till you expire. You realise that you were, that you are, not alone. There may be no-one who can explain like you do, all those events, because only a minute of your times, your happiness, your agonies can be told by those that were involved. In the depths of freedom, you've been lying abandoned and desolate like each blade of grass that wavers. Doleful, bleeding hearts endure. Try and remember the notes of song, or the taste of an air or the ultimate: a use of your prince of senses, to imagine those days well before.

For the people that have lived in a single street all their lives, theirs can only be less of the bleak reflecting on events when you were younger. For them the scenery didn't change. While for the lights-hunters that leave with ambition and excitement for the cities, for them, they can see so much. Books teach the single-streeters too, and whatever and however they cut the sentimental, this majority cannot cover the sorrow of endurance from themselves. At last you close your eyes to dream.

A countryside that has been written about too often. The brooks and the smell of mud and flowers. Meeting no-one but your future. How innocent, really, you were then. When you had no ideas about the wretchedness and the glory of freedom. Lying on this rock, now, you are so glad that you had the courage to fight them all off, to use that freedom and to turn it all upside down. It wasn't at thirteen that you realised your teachers and masters were wrong. It was at three or four. And now, walking up a hillside path, still quite alone, looking over at the view of the closed down North, empty factory buildings made of wood, rooves black set against a sun-set, you gloomily nod about your correctness. Being died you know. You had known being before, playing when you were children, beside disused barns. And then it all goes black. There really can be caricatures of the good and the bad. No, not of the good, but there are so many that are bad out of their own choice. Being's dead, as being's carried off. Still, you suppose, to have walked with being's friends is to watch from outside. Being's last glimpse was of a world finally and hearteningly destroyed. City-men, joining hands in expensive cars, falsely secure and you have forgotten your romantic despair, of the sort when St Julian kills his parents or seeing your life in a grand finale of the last cry as one based on hatred and fear. Lie to yourself, and lie with yourself, is this really what you are all to live for? Couldn't dead mothers have written it down for you before they died. Is being's last breath in an empty room?

9

When the boy who stole walked through the backdoor
that no-one uses, your mind entered that cold grey
register on the table at the back. Those notes that
you spend hours earning, thinking sometimes about how it
would be if the cash-till around the corner began to spew out
thousands of pounds because of errors. The drugs of security,
and how secure will that boy who ran through the back be?
It's not security, wondering who your friends are and why they
like going out with you. Green notes now that people spend
time over, spending maybe two years in a foreign job. Builders,
perhaps. Earning respect that shouldn't be paid, earning
experience that isn't really there. Unless safety problems and
the lack of trade unions force the earning of death. It seems
so far away from the dream of the country, but only until you
pass the last rock and you reach the summit of some small hill,
overlooking a giant valley of green grass, and there that giant
white carcass of a stately home. There is the money that you
seek.

And when you hear about the rich becoming poor and the
poor becoming rich, why should you feel your face flush? Girls
look at their fellow's gold rings and the boys wonder whether
diamonds are big enough. Emeralds that don't glow, and
sapphires that can never match the colour of their eyes. Yes,
the richness of art, when the value has been stamped over the
signature, how do you spell without a £ mark? The coins that
you threw at a busker playing a taut violin, money for emotion.
And then you have to go back to the fields, rather better should
they be Elysian, the fields of New England, and a short walk

to the beloved screens of Americana. Watching long-told-of consumerism flash and reflect in the pupils of such grace. Well, you never sought such prizes.

Do you charge her for the match you lit? Of course not, but you are not the one who wants the millions. To think, that the executive lounging in the corner like he does, haunting a glass of gin, to think that he is not worthless even here. The situation, with its bombs and bottles foretelling your destruction, it has not levelled you all like in Revelations. The guy's still quite respected. And surely the testament to this truth is his friends eyeing, still staring, at worthless gold, strangling the finger that has typed out...what's this? A resignation? A bit of melodrama.

The sign of the strong currency is as serious as the cross-bow or the sign of peace. Here, and slowly you realise it, are the roots of the problems so apparent today. Crazy, these noises, that ring while you try to sleep amongst the broken glass on the floor. Mad, and you don't accept it, you aren't somehow responsible. How could your wallets be a cause of such misery? All the forms of art, the sound of the saxophone that lingers somehow, with its curves permanently in gold light, the paintings that hang framed in silver, and the books that are lined with gold leaf— they are all in this circle, buzzing to the radio waves and signals of pagers and devices transmitting options and derivatives.

And the human nature, the existence of which you no longer believe in or that you have learned to despise over the past few hours (you realise it can be the false argument in a line), some of it is there. And the parts that make it up, food, sleep, health even. They all require the beloved state of the wild businessmen, shrouded behind their deathly facades of compassion and care. I don't care about the businessmen, says a song you've heard. And now, look about you, out into the street with their cars, up into the sky with their jets and into the buildings around, all infested by the investment, and torn by capital. You're so slashed that your wounds ache. You can smell the carpet, the arid affluence of men who fly their lives on arsenals of telephones and computers. You wear no rings of wealth and no gold-buttons on your jacket to glint in mates' eyes. But the conditioning around cannot even allow you to be noble.

Well, even if you do try to be, isn't it just the way the bell rings on the register? All these successes which lead to insults and cries of the kind which use French. But all one needs is a single chandelier, it'll remind you of why you were told not to be like it all. Why was it so important, all the parables of rich men and needles? The oppressed were oppressed, no more melodrama being says, still wondering about her fiery death. And once more, how many times must you say it?, You look out over the crew as if they were an expensive cruiser floating against a wind. You never conveyed that sense of pride behind a bar, did you? The pride going on nerves because you imagine it being like *Casablanca* or some romantic ideal. The piano, improvising jazz and then passages out of beat poetry doggerel. You had to have some Scotch eventually. That evaporating taste and sensation feeling that it will calm the nerves like the promises in films, the films you mentioned. You swear, you know, you promise you can hear it, a piano. There it goes, repeating scales over and over, sometimes a chord that isn't in the books. But what about the printed shirts, that's what reminded you of it. This time engraved and painted like the coins you should have shuffled in the register for your Scotch. That's one ethic abandoned, theft, and now it must be their turn.

It's more vulgar than you thought. You can hear the crowds of people.

Fuzzy cheekbones and quiffs and you realise what was imagined. Briefly you wondered whether she—you can't remember who, exactly—would suddenly arrive at your station and say things like "He's asked me to marry him—what should I do?" and you could have answered "How do I know, I've only just met you." But that's like the stuff you read in novels. Someone's just come over to you, though.

"I'm getting bored, when are we going to get out of here?" drunk you believe, caricatures they all are—but this one you like. And 'like' is the strong and sincere in a world of bad meanings.

"You don't really like those people do you?" you ask.

"No, but you seemed as if you didn't want to talk."

"Well, I don't normally have situations like this on my hands."

"What's it like—working here?"

"Interesting, I suppose. I don't really ask for more," you say with a hint of sarcasm.

"Really?"

"No, but people don't ask for much these days."

"Pessimistic again! I'm happy but secretly I want to be rich and famous, and so does everyone here."

"Maybe. But only in the back of the minds, they should have it up front."

"(sexual gesture) But you just said you didn't ask for more!"

"Yes, but I know and that's enough."

"I can see why I didn't carry on talking to you." There's a bit of flimsy hand-touching going on now.

"No, not pessimistic. I'm not." you say. You are, and the futility with which you describe and continue to describe is proof.

"Do you want to dance?"

"No music, but thanks, so you are different!"

The piano, that rings in your mind, saxophones left-behind, is still there but no-one else can hear it.

"Of course. Once I get the money I'll go to America and learn it properly, well I'm not sure that I want to. I just want the delights, not the work for it."

"So don't you want to marry someone rich?" You smile because sex-conditioning will always remain. Everything always remains someone once said.

"Not really rich. Just enough, you know?"

A nd the piano vanishes, with all its trimmings of Jelly Roll. And only because of the generous eyes of the uniformed 'good-guys' who so befriended the one in front of you. It ties in with the money too until you suddenly stop to think about that life where awareness was stifled, encouraged and again stifled. Childhood, adolescence and maturity. You have an emotion that is hard to describe because it makes you as speechless. Clouds grey over the sky. Lightning strikes later when your chance for response is long over. And in the same way you remember and eloquently tell yourself what you should have said, like adolescents with platonic friends. It takes you only a few months to erase it. The jazz from the piano has turned jealousy into pain.

"Come on cheer up, you still look sad. People used to tell me that, until I told them that I can only look sad. Some eyes are just sad, don't you think?"

You nod. "You the barman?" the painless torture administered with just three words from our friend the Corporal. You nod again.

"Any chance of any drinks. What's happening here? I have to get up in the morning," he says, like it's your fault. It is.

"It's not his fault, silly," says your friend, smiling.

"What do you want?" You ask, no longer attending to customers the way you are supposed to. You don't give a fuck what he does.

"Pints of bitter. And you can't charge us, we never knew what we were letting ourselves in for when we came in here, eh Twiggy?" he says, the same one. Then he looks over to his smiling wretch of a friend. And you thought the small branches of a tree were girl's names.

"Come on," he says impatiently because you haven't moved.

"Get out of here. You scared of it out there, that why you want a drink?" you say, in front of that noisy back-drop of sirens and breaking glass. You say, knowing they could kill you with a fist. And they smile in a so funny way at your friend who smiles back, too stupid to know anything and you're so stupid to care.

"You don't pour us something and I'll give you one of these," and you move your eyeball, insolently, looking at his hand that must have hurt so many kids in the playground, that must have sent him time after time to the headmaster's room crying.

"Never mind, come on we don't want to start a fight. He's just tired," the other says apologetically, still with a bit of hatred.

"Yes, we don't. Jack and Twiggy," she introduces you to them as if you care for experience or relation any more. Just let me out! you think.

"They're in the army. They fought a couple of years ago in the war," she says proudly as if you can remember it.

"Unlike you civilians, we've seen blood and we've seen death. Deaths of friends even," Jack says, you knew that was hate. Hate and cowardice mixed like the cocktails they want. She becomes serious now. You've seen death, not the romantic type on a green battle field with blood coming out of all the parts, but in the mind. That friend you talked about before, he died in one of these jaundiced wars that aren't even given a second look by editors. You knew him, you understood him. He had no choice, and these bouncy fakes say they've seen death. They don't know that friends are the people you can meet without having to do anything

"Was it terrible?" she says acting her part.

"Well it was good experience. Now we've fought we know what it's really like. We're ready for the Reds now," and I'm sure you misheard. You're not interested in this anymore, you don't want them. Why, when these people tell themselves that sorrow is irrational in the world of a living standard? You're now old enough to be bored with the beauty they used to tell you about, old enough to be uninterested in the flirtatious flings, old enough to know that this room is full of the last people you shall ever see, even.

"But don't you miss women when you're so far away?" she says, succeeding in calming the Western savage.

"Oh yes, god we miss them," he smiles to his partner. That's Jack glancing at Twiggy, like he would when he saw Twiggy's corpse on that green battle-field, thrust amongst grey rocks and grey seas. Like he would when he realised he was without food and that Twiggy was dead. "So, you got a boy-friend?" he asks.

"No, why?" she says. You're surprised at the steel of her gaze and the concentration of her eyes and the twists of her body.

"Oh, just wondered," he says before you have to laugh at how she defeated him.

"Don't go away," she says, before you can leave for the shutters to check on what's going on. She says that and you stay to hear the rest of the military strike only to be ignored by her, because the sophistication and innocence of her eyes and the contours of her eye-lashes are looking him up from knees upwards.

You walk around them, Jack makes a gesture like 'get out of here we're busy', and you walk in front of the others to the shutters. You walk alone and get to the end, crushing glass under your shoes. The scene hasn't changed. The continuous present will never die, not when everything's so stagnant and immovable. Still, the black silhouettes of policemen and ambulance-men and still the dark figures of the stances of discus throwers ready to launch their well-aimed missiles on us. Storming the gates and if only you could get out to enjoy the aftermath of chaos. The window-ledge too, covered in broken glass and you see your finger bleed as you foolishly wipe the glass off onto the floor. Not a deep wound, just a cut, just enough to stain the ledge and glowing glass and see the red light flicker like a red pen-light torch on decayed batteries. You can't feel the pain anymore, not when you know you're dying, the last leagues of <u>Verne</u>, sinking fast without even the knowledge to re-live. Re-live dreams of boys and girls who you should have known better, foolish once again. You never learn, and you turn to see couples in classic embrace. No, bitterness it isn't. You're seeing the vulgar shades better than Technicolor. Foul tastes in your mouth are symptoms of one emotion. When the lashes quiver, and the oblivious decide, that is jealousy.

II

If you say they aren't conscious of what's going on around them, you mean the friends in the room, you're wrong. They're conscious of everything, even the soldiers and her with their spontaneous laughter. The handshakes that you failed to mention, maybe that was the reason for your asking to bleed. And when someone shakes your hand in that hard macho way, don't you wonder: what are they so afraid of?

And when is the moment to realise that your mind is held together by splinters of selfish greed? Only the sexual impulse and so to the ultimate failure of Love, personal love. When you look back at some of the eyes, with the famous tricks of lingering after introductions taught years ago, you desire. But is that really the wooden greed you talked about before? You have no greed because you understand that it fails, you understand that the impulse which you mention is only a way of reaching the ideals of existential subject-subject. Is that the greed? You stop thinking of these conclusions, learnt through all your mediums, stop because the lines advance, nearer and nearer. You retreat back to the bar and the scandals being discussed. How your life seems so dull now! The stories of relationships with friendly eccentricities and the surprise. And sure, that brief interest is false, choosing to lie. If only greed was as simple as wanting more scotch when you've had enough. Had enough because your walk back from the window was a journey of stumbles and falls. No wonder they're laughing, they wouldn't dare risk the sneers for a breath of the fresh air. The fresh air of a street filled with smoke, fire, petrol and the smell of burning metal. It's better than in this hole. It is no longer a bar, the stools lie broken. You wish they could be fixed. The drinks and cigarettes are long finished. How you wish for them. The haze is not the light sort of one you stroll into, it is a funny, dense fog of dirt. How you wish it were clear. And yet you're quite alright, the physical in control, the mind in control. You're prepared for the future now, even if it is only like a soldier coming out of a trench to advance into gunfire.

You've spilt the drink now, the blood filling till your brain seems to burst with that awareness without bounds. It doesn't help you think more clearly, but it doesn't make you think less clearly either. The physical lets you down by using fatigue. You can still see the two figures, masked by uniform, chatting away as if they have all the time in the world. Again your mind leaves for the image of the Cheyne Walk man. Your rooms, until the rates became too high, still rising out of the pavement with its views of murky Thames-sides, you loved it there. And like the object it was, you received other objects: friends and lovers. 'And how many complicated problems lay in wait?' you thought each morning. There was no sense in it, even then, you lived for the next day and believed that when you came across a sudden change in life-style, just for a day, it was a blessing. A feeling that you believed was inexplicable, just something deep inside seeking something that you didn't know. But the talk that you spent your time in was of no consequence, talk of subjects, with only one asset: strict banality, just as those idiots who believe discussion is not amusing. The girls and boys in this room, roped together in some hope that the thrown-away potentials can be put to some use, are useless, now. All those smiles don't even touch you anymore. All that stupid flirting, when all they're offering is a death of emotion, death of self and the massacre of the mind. Smiling lips and lingering eyes, the sort that used to fall into your greed, are worth nothing. They are all now as free as marionettes.

You ignore the others now, and take a rest from such lust. The music of the bobby floods in, while the violence plays like a never-ending symphony of strength. Doctors, lawyers, accountants and the unemployed: they're all here. Almost a

Noah's Ark, but there'll be no dove to tell you when you're safe.
"Isn't this terrible," the doctor asks you.

"Yes."

"It doesn't look too good out there. I checked outside and
it looks like we might never get out of here. All I saw was fire,
just a continuous blaze of yellow fire as far as the eye can see," he
said, with that worried expression. Professional worries which
don't amount to much.

"Well, you got any confessions?" you laugh as you say it.

"Yes, I do. Funny how situations like these bring people
together."

"I hadn't noticed," you interrupt.

"No, but, well anyway I was going to say that it's such a
cliché to tell everything to a bartender...look I didn't save
someone out there."

"It doesn't make any difference, we'll all be dead soon. You
said so," you say because when you speak that horrible arrogance
now sidles in. I told you I was right.

"I said that, sure," now you can hear his American accent,
"oh you're no good. My name's James," and you introduce
yourselves like this was all very formal. "Good to meet you."

"Yes."

"Why were you looking so sad, even before I told you about
what's happening out there?"

"Oh something..." you say and he smiles.

"I only came here last week. Holiday. I live in New York,"
he says.

"I was born over in America. I never saw New York, not
properly," you say.

"Well, looks like you're not going to," he says with the
famous professional detachment as a flame falls into the room.
"Gosh, that was close!" he says as if he's seen three strikes on
the diamond.

"Are you a private doctor?" you ask.

"Yes. I'm an expert on..." he mentions some word with
twenty letters, "it's a mouthful, but I've always been interested
in it. I've contributed papers. You just a bar-tender?" he asks.

Just a bar-tender? How the insults seem so kind when you've just met.

The real talk of great decisions and thousands of pounds is being decided by four tied men crouching some miles away. They're in a stance that still allows the disengaging of business cards. It looks like a match made in hell. Surely someone could have the dignity to stop shouting advertisements amongst the injured? But if your life is for notes, it is acceptable that they take advantage of every situation. The roles of others who act differently to exploit their situation from the angle of their project: Gigolo, artist, writer, businessmen, thieves. Only the postman or physicist is unable to take their advantages. The rest are thieves, scrounging what they can from a doomed building. And then the doom is not because of a San Andreas Fault. It is the doom caused by your faults. Faults, prejudice all for the technocratic master emotion. I want it, I want it now. Give it to me. Give it to me even if I have one already.

Please: leave me <u>my</u> avarice.

12

And now you come back from your three sins. Three futile sins that matched the mood of this almost speechless, touchless love affair while a war of sorts rages outside. The sun is rising and yet it must be the imagination. An imagination in the mood of one going without sleep for five days. An imagination like the one you believe in when no water passes your lips for a week. These aren't moments of charming melodrama that you describe in a phase of depression. The romance that lies here isn't the situation, which—as I have tried to prove—is of our making. Surely, when you annoy the patriot with your remarks of self-confidence and existential arrogance and when he strikes you on your arm—this is not romance. Not even your eyes, that linger on only one now, are the eyes that glint of romance. You try to put a price on this inner world that you let yourself into and realise that there is no price for the luxuries of wooden seats, drinks and friends without words.

Your eyes feel like crying now, watching the face ignore you. The haze still stands, of course, but when the physical rebels you have no choice. The object that throbs behind your forehead as you continue to pump yourself with alcohol it doesn't want. You're waiting for an event beyond your control. The other barman with transcendental suave has begun talking some who are crouching below the bar top. Oh how that image of the backdoor swings into your mind like the fairground rides that you do pay for. Almost adventure-like. Thoughts of belonging when you look into the faces and soon realise that we belong to no-one. They're tired now, tired enough to believe it and know it. Tired enough, for vanity, when they rush into the toilets and come back with slight differences. The film-stars never seemed to have to care about vanity, and that terrible look in the morning, that's what they say. You can see it all much better now because the room's brighter. The time really has passed. And all this time, you have heard sirens, breaking glass, screams and shouts, then silence. Screams, then silence. Screams, then silence. On and on until you realise that the silences hurt most. Your heart almost jumps to the offer of such salutary silences. Many are asleep, a light sleep, but eyes can't be closed when vocal chords seem to be crushed outside. Outside, they are using police batons.

The avarice, all the sins, they don't matter, they don't enter your mind. You've forgotten already and you don't believe that fickle love is worthless. You try and remember the times when you feel freer in space, moving from place to place for no reason but your loves. Sultry brown eyes and drooping mouths trying to act like they are the victims. Next time, if there is a next time, you shall act differently. No more shall you act the clown and fool, no more because of them, the talkers who can charm demons. This normal hate that descends after the high of an infatuation. Crouching, trying to hide behind crowds, scared after you know them that well. Eyes that never seem to linger that way anymore. So fair, so nice they all seem. Can't I see it, as I rub the collars of my shirt? Hiding and not realising it can't be a game. And now the sparkle of the diamonds on the floor dulls so they look like black stones. Black stones, like the ones you step over to cross that brook. Jet-black like his hair. Black like now never to be dug up coal. But now, it has taken a time, they don't matter. They don't matter because you've seen inside them all, inside their facades and surfaces to the robot-core, lying beating in flesh. "They say we'll soon be free," says being.

"I don't care," you say when you realise that it's all ending. Ending and crumbling like a day's weather moving from sun to dark, dark clouds. Overcast days in this great city, overcast like the players in this room. All those memories of the simple days of childhood, when even your freedom was not known. As the last shutters fall apart and the last bricks are exposed, you can feel something new. Something glorious as you feel the foundations fall, feel the ceilings fall, feel the sirens take over your heart. Overflowing senses, the smells of damp gutted wood. The sounds of sirens and silence. The taste of dust. The touch doesn't exist. And the last, the sight of such a chance going to waste.

A Taste of Money

"In all these movements they bring to the front, as the leading question in each, the property question, no matter what its degree of development at the time."
Karl Marx and Friedrich Engels, 1888.

Leymann sat at a corner seat, waiting for his friend and waiting for the cocktail hour to begin. It was late afternoon and from the window he could see half-past five commuters walking to their stations in the cool air. He was comfortable, unusually so. The seat had a plush, springiness that made him feel safe and faintly aristocratic and American. He wondered whether it was the novel he was reading—the torn cover of a 1920's novel dangled on one side of the marble table. His eyes were watering slightly but he was used to that. He believed it something to do with the industrial cleaners that were dabbed on the acrylic carpets once a month. He had been feeling miserable, the past week, looking out from his office towards the Telecom Tower in the distance, wondering where there was any reasonable height from where London—minus tower—could be seen. He presumed not.

His meeting, this evening, concerned his job, the one that made his life feel stale and musty. Each morning, when he visited new houses that had to be torn down, he looked around, feeling that the damp on the walls, the sagging ceilings and the broken, decaying floorboards all resembled the state of his mind and heart. He had grown tired of it. His divorce, only pending at the moment, made it possible for him to drop responsibility from his CONS list as he made his decisions. It was a lucrative post. Most of London's housing was being pulled down. Not since the sixties and the public housing boom had so many buildings been brushed away. Motorways, too, were flourishing, circling the cities with snails' pace commuters. The only headache was pushing unnameable squatters and the like from properties. This was where Leymann came in even though he no longer liked doing it. He was bored and tired of it and his choices seemed limited. There was nothing he felt specifically wrong about his job, neither the equity nor the demolition. It was just that this job, along with all its so-called 'perks', was like a slow injection, of the flu-jab genre. He worried that if he didn't get out now, he'd live to be a regretful, old man.

Jocelyn nudged the wheel of her BMW before the car turned into a shabby street, South of the river. She had had an energetic day. There wasn't a minute in which her mind hadn't been ticking over some new problem or dilemma. Her work, though she was at the top of her particular ladder, was similar to Leymann's. It had the same number of rungs and seemed to shake on its pivot when things were going badly. However, she displayed or felt none of his dispiritedness. There wasn't time to think, there wasn't the time for any nervous deliberations. Decisions were made at a quick pace. They were calculated and once they were made that was it. Now, there was not a moment in which she could change her mind about 'everything'. She was tapping on her steering wheel, while dictating to her machine. It was a letter, quite a long one, and as she oscillated on her brake pedal, she slowly moved her lips staring at the road, waiting for an accident.

She had decided that Leymann was to go. That was the only reason she had accepted his invitation, she assured herself. Finding a parking space—she was lucky in parking—she took out a lipstick and began pouting in the car mirror. There was a spot on her left cheek, too red to disguise. She rubbed it a few times and listened to the telephone ring. It was her solicitor. Yet more legal enigmas presented themselves to her. Her divorce was taking years. She threw the phone down disdainfully, having to reposition it soon afterwards. The rare moments when Jocelyn felt out of her depth usually concerned her divorce. Occasionally, a phone-call from a lawyer would throw her completely out of synch. Sighing, she dialled her mother's number. "What the hell am I doing all this for?" she said commandingly to the dashboard.

Mr. Roeng stood outside his shack and watched schoolchildren gather around a bench before moving to the bus-stop. Most of them were boys, the youngest only five. He rubbed his hands together to warm them up and watched the group of grey blazers enlarge and grow louder. The younger children, while not overjoyed, seemed more enthusiastic than those of ten or fifteen, he thought.

Leymann was still waiting. He had been there nearly an hour and in front of him stood a sheet of tissue paper upon which sat a sickly Bloody Mary in a twenties' style glass. As he took the tissue paper away, his hold on the glass lapsed and the drink then lay in a pool on the table. He winced and dabbed the corner of the tissue in his eye as a waiter descended. He looked away from the waiter, out of the window and wondered whether Jocelyn had had trouble parking her car. He'd been musing once more on his decision—after all it was a revolution in his life. He liked Jocelyn, she had always been courteous and friendly towards him. While he sat at the office, which wasn't very often as most of his time was spent at properties, she would stream past his desks in one of her flower-print dresses, smelling of chewing gum and expensive French fragrance. She wasn't pretty, her features were too rounded and the way her hair was done it sometimes made her look like a Christmas pudding with a ribbon around it.

"Your book, sir," the waiter said to Leymann as he held out the volume, now blood red in colour.

"Oh, er...thank you." He placed it on the table next to him noticing that the waiter had crumpled up the torn cover and was using it to wipe down the table.

"Mum, how are you? I'm in a terrible state. Work had been so busy, have you heard from John? He hasn't called me in weeks. I haven't even seen the girls properly for months," Jocelyn said. "I mean, what's the point of all of this? I sit and work all day so John can while away his hours. The only time I see the kids is when I've come from work. And then all I do is tell them off. God! And when they go to their father's, he takes them to the cinema and the fair. They worship the bastard while he sits and does nothing, nothing at all.

"Yes, I know he's a nice man. We've already gone though all of that. Look, I'd better go—I'll call you tonight. Okay? Bye," and Jocelyn had finished her outburst, letting her mother get away with only a few syllables. Then she got out of the car and went into the newsagents to buy some gum.

They began to play music in the bar and the customer-audience went from one to fifty.

"Hello, would you like another drink?" the waiter asked.

"Yes, thank you. Half pint of lager?" Leymann said, his words rising in pitch. The waiter promptly left his table.

There were now three others seated around Leymann's table, each with an exotic cocktail in front of them. He stared at the lemon, lying in a syrupy brown liquid in front of him. It reminded him of a house he had visited yesterday. Everything was brown or yellow, the wallpaper, the curtains, the carpets — where there were any. There had been a tramp living in one of the upper rooms. He remembered the blankets he was using and how they were stained with blood. He was quite an expert at getting people out of houses without having to resort to the courts. It wasn't that difficult, of course: most of them were breakable human beings. Others were already broken: alcoholics and mad people that had been thrown out of wherever they had been before. Leymann remembered a documentary he had seen. "Care is expensive," a woman had said. Jocelyn had always told him to wait, to wait until the decorators were in. "Then you at least have others on your side for backup. If that doesn't work, let the courts do it all," she would say. She was right, too. The job was usually quicker with builders and decorators on one's side. But it was easy for Jocelyn to give advice. She only saw properties after they'd been done up, when there was no more weeping, when the desolate homes were made beautiful. "Each floor now has a video-entry phone and a microwave cooker and if you don't think they're beautiful look at the way the light glides into the room, the way the shutters seem to lift the sunshine so it glints in all the right places. It's like a film, like a Hollywood film," Jocelyn had once said.

There was no doubt about that. But it wasn't Leymann's job to market, to swan through homes when they were glossy and neat. It wasn't really his job to hang around the finished home at all. He was allowed to come to the press launch, if he didn't get in the way. But once the press had arrived—the big teethed men and women from magazines—he had to go. He remembered taking an elegant cocktail glass, only meant to look nice and not to be used, and filling it with water and how Jocelyn had told him off.

The houses would smell of flowers, huge bouquets from alluring florists in Knightsbridge garlanded every room. As he sipped his water, he'd wrinkle his toes, savouring the carpet through his soles and then press the video-entry phone button. A sharpish image would appear, the size of a paperback and he would watch the cars meander about and the trees sway a little. An hour later, the journalists would rush in, saying that video entry-phones were more fun than TV. Leymann believed they were right, he felt that watching the curious fixed camera image, silent and matte, was like eavesdropping.

Spotting a copy of The Tatler, she grabbed it from the shelf and began anxiously flicking through it.

"Gotta pay for what you look at, madam," the tough looking man said.

Jocelyn looked at him for a moment, eyeing the areas on his face that were shadowed by his flat blue hat and put the magazine down. She had bought the gum already and walked out, listening to the man shout at her. "Fuck!" she said, walking towards the car, "cat food!"

It was much darker now, car lights were on and the streets were less crowded. Leymann remembered his brother, the one working for a security agency. He would be starting work now, carrying out real eavesdropping. He rarely spoke to him, these days. Perhaps, he shouldn't really have told Leymann what little he had. Even a brotherly disagreement seemed now to turn into something about national security. Leymann recalled how his brother had come to mention his occupation.

Jocelyn was fond of Leymann. From the day she started work she had always seen Leymann as a man with potential. There was more to it, she liked the curve of his face, the way his brown eyes were inset at an unusual angle. But there was something stopping them from being together. Their lives weren't timed in the same way. Jocelyn worked the lunch-breaks and Leymann was, anyway, out most of the time. During the past few weeks, everyone in the office had seen Leymann change. He was becoming less confident, less tough. Jocelyn felt a little guilty. She wondered whether she should help him in some way, offer him more backup. Now, however, it was already too late and he had to go. The cashier read the price out again, holding out the cat food receipt. Jocelyn apologised, noticing the cashier's crocodile brooch and taking a mental note.

Leymann had been early, he had known it when he arrived. However, his message to Jocelyn was slightly ambiguous, as if relating to a previous time when they had found themselves alone with each other. The implication was the that the meeting was to take place a little earlier than specified, Leymann thought. It was only a half-hope, though. Had he even really expected her to remember?

"No," murmured Leymann to himself, "no, no, noooo."

Those at neighbouring tables stopped talking, looking straight at Leymann for at least a few seconds. Then they resumed their conversations.

It was about a fifteen minute car journey to Leymann's bar. The short cut was through some small roads by the river, past big, deserted warehouses, lit only by a few street lamps. Many lamps had been smashed by the gangs, the groups so beloved by local paper feature writers. Jocelyn remembered the broken glass on the roads and regretted using this route. It had been some three years since her daughter, Evangeline, had disappeared and broken glass always reminded her of those ensuing weeks of hope, expectation and final despondency. "It was a learning experience," she coaxed herself into believing, pushing on the accelerator.

Leymann was laughing to himself, laughing uncontrollably. Usually, he would have sacrificed his life for composure in a public place. His brother had said that once. Etiquette, or some sort of personal etiquette, was an essential cogwheel in what made Leymann tick. He had inherited it from his father and it was part of a persistent agony.

He was laughing for a reason, though. He was thinking about his prospects if he left his job. If there was ever a good time to be unemployed, it wasn't now. Despite the reported highest economic growth of all time, Britain seemed in a kind of interminable decline. It would be a year before he would even be eligible for dole. Legislation prevented all but the richest from leaving a miserably employed life.

So now he laughed because it seemed funny, mad even, as mad as the people from the closed down asylums. He had made some provisions, even saving a little money, but it was only enough to allow him to eat and pay bills. Still, his decision still stood: why do something that made one indifferent to all the beauties of life?

Jocelyn pulled over at the side of the road, recollecting the scents of medical halls. The sedatives had had a sweet smell and they must have soon calmed her down. Her daughter had had a round face, too, one with innocent eyes and tiny lips. And while she relived flashes of pain, with only the small light in the car switched on, groups of children, only a few years older than her daughter, gathered around her car.

"Can't you understand anything? You can't live on nothing. It's bad enough the way your flat looks at the moment. What do you expect from life, anyway? I honestly don't know. That damp on the ceiling of the sitting room—don't you have any pride?" Leymann was remembering a conversation he had had with his brother.

It had been a lengthy one. He recalled the sound of morning birds calling as his brother left the house. Leymann's throat had been sore on that day and his brother had been talking about his work. It was reasonably fascinating—Leymann conceded that—but bugging people's telephones was hardly a nice way of making a living. His brother would tell him of blackmail plots and assassination attempts on union leaders, all in the enthusiastic tones of a thriller fanatic. It didn't bother Leymann much, even when his brother suggested Leymann himself might be under surveillance. His phone was, anyway, erratic, only working on certain days and at certain hours. This unreliability was not due to neglected final notices but rather some local inefficiency. He faintly recalled an article he had read about how the new cable company was having problems.

Jocelyn started her car with a lurch, swiftly changing gears and staring straight out in front of her. The boys scattered quickly and only one was grazed by a fender.

Leymann often thought of travelling abroad, though the brochures thrown through his letterbox seemed more like elaborate jokes than the beginning of concrete plans. He liked to look at the pictures of sandy beaches and coral blue seas. They sparkled especially on television advertisements, where character seemed to have a very easy time of it all. Things seemed easier on television. They only ever had a few things at once on their minds. Leymann's mind, however, was always on many things and devoted to each was only a shallow sprinkling of emotion. There was no one thing that wholly absorbed his mind. The closest it came was Jocelyn who, as Leymann paid for yet another drink, kept summoning his thoughts. "It would be fun to lie on a beach with her," he thought, even then ending his idea with an "I suppose". It was a catchphrase for him. Leymann closed his eyes and rested for a few minutes.

Drops of rain began to splatter Jocelyn's windscreen. She concentrated on the road as thoughts of her daughter faded away. Casually, she switched on the radio and listened to the evening news bellow from the speakers at the back of the car. The news was serious but not unusual and Jocelyn paid little attention to it. Only financial indices and property price fluctuations had any bearing on her life.

Leymann looked at his watch. It had been given to him by his long deceased grandmother. He started to think about his family, the members whose screams lay at the back of his mind like smouldering cigarettes. Nearly all of them talked as if they had just digested the text of a book of symptoms. It was as if every minute was spent outdoing each other in their prescriptions for Leymann. They had so much advice but none of them had amounted to much, Leymann thought. One couple was different: a mad aunt and her husband, an uncle whom he had never seen and was rumoured not to exist. The aunt suffered from schizophrenia and she would refer to her non-existent husband with great tenderness. Many years ago, during a family argument, the aunt produced her husband's National Insurance number as proof of his existence. The family still didn't believe her. Perhaps he did exist, but only as a garbled computer error in the bowels of a mainframe. Whether he did or not, the couple were Leymann's favourite relations.

Leymann watched the rain outside and the belisha beacons turn on and off. Passive smoke was beginning to make his eyes water and he wondered whether living like his uncle wasn't a better way of coping with the world.

"Damn!" shouted Jocelyn, not only because a driver had cut her up at the traffic lights but because there was a fire at 63a Keir Hardie Avenue. Property Developments PLC owned number 65 and Jocelyn, head of the company, didn't want the fire to spread. It wouldn't do to delay the survey so Jocelyn felt obliged to visit the scene. After all, what was the point of a mobile phone other than to shoulder responsibility? Within a couple of minutes, Jocelyn was there. Like an ambitious reporter, she lurched out of the car and ran towards the fire crew.

"How did it start?" Jocelyn shouted, blinded by the spray of the hoses.

"Don't know," said a fireman, peering above his yellow helmet.

The rain was getting heavier and the smell of burning intermingled with the scent of wet tarmac rose around her. Number 65 looked fine—until she entered the premises, a huge key-chain dangling from her handbag. The hallway, no longer musty, resonated in a damp mist. It was as if someone had tried to kick-start the house into freshness by spraying the house with water in the hope that it might come to life. But, like a dead plant, the house's response was cold and silent. Jocelyn ran out towards the fireman.

"What's happened to number 65?"

"Oh...we aimed a hose at the wrong position. Must have gone into the wrong house. Shouldn't have left the windows open, though," said the fireman before returning his eyes to number 63a.

Jocelyn remembered opening the windows herself. "Why do things always have to be a mess?" she asked herself. No matter how organised she thought she was, something always turned up. Just like on a partying Saturday night, she reflected, no matter how dressed up and confident she was, all it took was a squeaky irregularly shaped toy on the stairs to shatter her resolve. She didn't want to be here. It was dark, wet and cold. Running to the steps of 65, she eased the key in and locked the door behind her, holding her breath and looking away. She put her head in one hand when she got into to the car. Her hair was soaking wet, a thin stream of London rainwater edging down her neck and onto her back. She moved her shoulders up and down in a massaging action and stared at the mirror. There were thick, dark lines under her eyes and her nose was shiny. Her makeup had run but her watery eyes sparkled.

One of Leymann's small numbers of friends—he didn't make friends easily—had once suggested that it was his parent's divorce that had unsettled him as a child, may have been responsible for his nervous temperament. Leymann rejected this but wondered about it for days after the conversation. There was definitely a fortnightly clash that had frightened him as a child. His mummy and daddy would be in the same room, trying their best to look away. She would scream and his father would try to ignore it, maybe fingering his glasses before turning to Leymann. In turn, Leymann would stare up at his father and begin to sob. Looking around him, Leymann wondered about the parentages of those around him.

His hands were clammy and his head began to twitch, a nervous affliction he had gained from his brother who had later discarded the habit. As he floundered, his polyester shirt rubbed on his neck like a damp cloth wiping off spilt milk. He had never felt comfortable with his clothes, either.

Jocelyn had got into the practice of talking to herself. The bouts were at first a little inarticulate but after some weeks she found a fluency with herself. The car quite stationary, she would listen to what she considered a finely tuned Home Counties' accent for fifteen minutes at time. Her voice had been trained. "A fine voice," her mother had said, "needs well roasted potatoes and good Sunday sprouts." Her mother had tried to train Evangeline, Jocelyn's ill-fated daughter. It seemed such a waste of time, now—aspirations as much as the expense of small school blazers and private nurseries. The smell of rain and wool in the car reminded her of dark winter afternoons, outside Evangeline's school and inevitably of the particular afternoon when she failed to appear.

"Mr. Leymann?" said a crisp voice in the bar. Leymann looked up, his eyes distinctly vexed like those of an animated dog negotiating an unconcerned master.

"Yes?" he answered.

"There's a message from Jocelyn..." the well-dressed member of the bar-staff began to talk. It was a short speech but enough to make Leymann reach for his book and plastic briefcase, ready to depart. He was unhappy about his failed meeting. It was not only that he had wanted to tell her of his resignation, he had wanted to see her. What with their different lifestyles, he hardly ever saw her and, today, he missed her. Her hazel-brown hair was tied in with his fate. She was confident. She seemed to offer a life of little trouble, even though Leymann believed he would be prepared to suffer for her.

He twitched once more, anxiously wiping moist Bloody Mary from his book onto the table. The threesome in front of him looked at Leymann in turn, waiting for a fourth companion to join them. He had been waiting for Leymann to vacate his seat, eager to get into the conversation and show what he knew about the topics under discussion. Leymann apologised to him and went to the till to pay.

"Can you pay the table please, sir?" a woman in black and white queried. Leymann nodded and came back to the table, searching for the plate his waiter had deposited for him. The four suited men looked at Leymann as if there had been a mistake. The fourth man, the most uncomfortable of the group—he may have assumed that Leymann was coming to claim back his chair—looked with wide open eyes at him. Leymann didn't feel like talking. He had had a wasteful hour or so and was not in the mood for offering explanations. Luckily, he had the right change. He took one last glance. Two of them had moustaches, modern-looking moustaches, and had been chatting about one of the women behind the bar: "You know, Jack? That guy, he was so pissed...he wanted to fuck and just..." Leymann stopped listening and frowned, not knowing why. They smiled a lot, Leymann thought.

As Leymann walked out of glass doors, he yearned for Jocelyn.

Each turn of the 291 bus seemed to mean more than before. The bare trees reach out towards him like clawing, outstretched hands. Afforded a birds' eye view, he watched the black, wintry expanses of parkland and the people outside blowing illuminated mist from their mouths. The bus shook vigorously as the street lights flickered, some filaments cracking to the roar of a thousand motor engines. Inside the bus, meaningless graffiti covered the seats like reflecting pools of disturbed water under the advertisements.

Leymann breathed out uneasily and got up, steadying himself on the cold steel handrails. As he slowly pushed the button to let the driver know he wanted to get off, he could see his drawn curtains and, lower down, the gun shop and the florist's. They lay side by side, each occupying half the space of the other shops on the road. The air in his flat was a pleasant mixture of rare flower scent and unused gunpowder, all rising like steam through the floorboards. Leymann's main grief was the noise. Double glazing was an unaffordable luxury. He wanted to forget the world in this castle of his, not listen to its un-oiled wheels grinding through the nights.

Jocelyn regretted cancelling. She hated the idea that she cared about what she looked like in front of Leymann. They were there to talk professionally, not to stare into each other's eyes and flirt. She liked Leymann, she realised again. Her two other daughters were with her father tonight and should Leymann have pleased her sufficiently, she could have invited him back to her place. As she pressed the automatic garage door button, she smiled.

Leymann put his case on a chair and began to make some dinner. For most of the week, he relied wholly upon frozen food for his dietary needs. It was a well-rehearsed ceremony: the stinging fingers as he pulled a carton from the freezer, the lighting of the oven with a long match, the depressing wait. Leymann knew he wouldn't like the result—he never did—and yet, at the supermarket, the images of colourful, beautiful, gourmet food on the boxes seemed to beckon him. He meditated on the well-cleaned aisles and the rows of enticing food, the Warholian soup cans and Henry Moore butchered meat.

His cookery books had never been opened. He had been frightened off by over-protective relatives, afraid that he would hurt himself. All he seemed to have inherited, regarding food, was an unselective addiction to additives. He was now emptying half a plastic container into the waste disposal unit, listening to the whirring machine munch away and spit out a bad piece of beef. He had lost his appetite, now engrossed in a TV chat show. Leymann used to dream of being on a TV chat show, especially the one hosted by John Barleycorn. He felt sorry for himself. He was observing the springiness of the chair that the bottom of Barleycorn's guest had just met. She had a vulgar, disjointed face, powdered and yet greasy. She was talking about intuition and telepathy, about how women were more telepathic. "It's just that we're more daring," she continued.

"And what of the after-life?" asked Barleycorn, anxious not to sound too serious.

"I firmly believe in it. Last winter I was driving through the Lake District at night. It was freezing and ice covered the steep hill that I was driving down. As I came towards my house, I saw my mother at the door. 'Silly thing, fancy worrying about me and coming out into the cold!' I said to myself. Then I remembered: my mother had died two years previously."

The chat show host was now listening to a detailed account

of how his guest's mother had given her a racing tip and how the guest had become very wealthy. Leymann bit his nails as pictures of her mansion appeared on the screen. He looked around him. It wasn't a bad flat. It was just that he had such little time to care for it.

Two twenty year old boys were eating at an expensive restaurant in the West End of London. Both wore black suits and brightly coloured ties and both of them were talking about aspirations and handicaps. Sebastian, taller of the two, didn't care much for Frezzle, partly because he seemed to remind Sebastian that he, himself, was a misfit. They had met at school. Frezzle and just yesterday decided to abandon his university course in favour of taking banking examinations.

There was silence as another bottle of white wine arrived at the table. Sebastian had been vaguely worried about his looming examination failure but the smile of the pretty waitress made him forget. Frezzle, meanwhile, was uninterested in the shortness of her skirt and was instead regretting that he was missing John Barleycorn.

Jocelyn had a big, four-bedroom house. As she entered, she picked up the morning's mail from a gingham-clothed side-table. Jocelyn cursed the privatised mail system and ripped open a letter addressed to her neighbour, sighing as she took out a glossy photograph of a cat. She turned it around and read the pencilled handwriting, 'Hello Dolly!' and placed it back in its envelope. Jocelyn put her arms around her waist, unzipping her skirt a little, happy that No one was around the house. She was a little hungry but her weight was more important than that so she ran upstairs and changed instead.

Jocelyn was proud of her clothes. Even for her, they seemed an expensive item on her household budget. As she unbuttoned her blouse, she sat on the edge of the bed. Her skirt was at her ankles as she looked in the mirror, wondering why her underwear was so dear and then taking pride in it. Gently, she unclipped her bra-strap and let her breasts fall a little. She stared at the mirror, her hands on her skirt, feeling the quality of the wool.

"I'm really tired," Leymann said to the telephone.

"Aw, c'mon, just down the pub," said Tony, a friend he had known since the age of six. It was a fight but Leymann got the better of it. He dreaded their evening meetings. They were entangled, tortuous journeys, usually with seven or eight others, none of who seemed to speak or understand Leymann's tongue. Since Leymann had landed his job with Property Developments PLC, two years ago, Leymann's language and aspirations became incompatible with those of Tony.

Tony was a clerk at the local postal company. He hated his work and cared more about what he called, 'the finer things'. His taste in clothes, music and partners was acquired from his younger brother, a slight, uncoordinated man who parted his hair at both sides and had left the area to work in the City. Tony used to talk about him for hours, about how he was helping him to monitor his share portfolio wisely. Leymann would sit in silence, nodding and thinking about whether to book an appointment at the job centre. Tony's brother drove a fast German car and made lots of money, so Leymann was told. However, Leymann had never ever seen him. He had a vague memory of a four year old boy running around the neighbourhood, smashing dolls on the tarmac outside Tony's parents' house. Other than that, he didn't seem to exist. Tony, himself, admitted to not having seen him for over five years. He said that his brother often flew away to magical sounding places like Hong Kong and Singapore.

Leymann paced the short distance between one wall and the other, remembering the way he did it in vacant properties. He'd stand, all 5'2" of him, and point out sections of the floor, counting in his head with his lips quivering to a tape recorder. The lengths and widths of these rooms, even when approximate, were of some use to the battalion of architects and planners back at Property Developments PLC. The most alarming thing, as he would stand atop a carpet of beer cans and cigarette stubs, was the glassy stares of itinerant groups of squatting young boys and girls. As their eyes focused on him, he would sense danger, though these gentle, almost broken down, youngsters hadn't even the energy to take a rubbish-bag out. He remembered the sound of sniffling and coughing and young dogs barking. After noting down the figures, he'd march out, avoiding eye-contact, and speculate uncertainly on where these people would go.

Loddington is a Northern town. The closure of the bus and railway stations left the town unconnected, her residents wholly reliant on private transport. In a telephone box with its customary smells of urine and sugary soft-drinks, Jonathan, a twenty-five year old man with weary, grey eyes was waiting for the phone to ring. It was cold. His fingers protruded from some cut-off acrylic gloves that smelled of old vegetables and fruit. He worked at the market on Sundays, casual labour that propped his dole cheque up, five pounds for six hours.

Jocelyn hadn't bothered to wrap herself in her silk dressing gown. Instead, she walked around the dark room in her panties, tidying up and looking for a telephone number. She went to the dressing table and, finding the yellow square, read it. As she memorised the twelve figures, she sprayed some French perfume onto her armpits. Stomping towards the phone, she looked out of the window. Her chintzy room, looked out onto a large garden. She could see two people in the window of the nearest house. Jocelyn was curious. There had been loud noises coming from that house all evening. She carefully angled the pane and peered out, catching the reflection of her own body. She had been comfortable without clothes on, freer and now she felt embarrassed. As she reached for her gown, loud screams radiated from the window. It was a man slapping a small girl.

Jonathan was becoming impatient. His friends were at the pub and all of them thought that the Employment Seekers Scheme, a new government programme, was futile. Jonathan's counsellor had told him to wait at the booth at the appointed time. There was a company in London that was prepared to offer him some work.

Leymann sat down again, flicking through a property magazine. He spent many nights laughing at the prices of houses in central London. He couldn't understand how so many people could afford to buy bedsits, with 15 year leases, for nearly a million pounds. As he sipped a cup of tea he watched a game show.

"Okay, boys and girls...heh...a cryptic clue for a clever crew: where in Paris can you not see the Eiffel Tower on the horizon?" asked an over made-up man with brutally white teeth. There was a pause and then a buzz. "No one?" his face fell, "on the Eiffel Tower, of course!"

Jocelyn closed the window and drew the curtains before dialling the number.

"Hello? Jonathan Mans...ill?" Jocelyn stuttered, listening to the peculiar tones indicative of payphones.

"There's no Jonathan here. Look, I'm half-way through my dinner, so if you're selling water filters or mobile phones, I'll ask to you to hang up now, thank you. Just because its a payphone, doesn't mean it isn't a private number, you know," a woman in Loddington said.

Jocelyn replaced the receiver and dialled again, thinking about the thousands of pounds of tax incentives offered to those hiring unskilled labour. There was no reply, this time.

Jonathan had left. He had been tired lately and wondered if he was getting some sort of ulcer, given his stomach ache. For a twenty-five year old he had the air of someone who had seen everything. He had experienced terrific falls in spirit, this year. His girlfriend of ten years had left on a battered bicycle for the South. Jonathan hadn't heard from her since and he had only really lived for her.

Leymann wished he had Jocelyn's number. If he had the number he could have begun to explain his feelings for her. He had realised that he would have to go to work the next day—just one day more. The thought irked him. He remembered waking up that morning, feeling happy and free.

But he had to turn up. His curriculum vitae would be damaged if he didn't and he didn't want to burn all his boats and bridges. 'There are radical steps and then there are radical steps,' he murmured to himself before turning off the television.

Jocelyn couldn't remember how many times she had been profane this week. She just had to contact this man from Loddington. Too much was at stake and as her stepfather had once said, 'some say that the Inland Revenue is real charity, giving from the rich to the poor, but I say screw them for everything.'

Gently, she eased the dressing gown off and got into bed. The sounds of shouts or screams (she couldn't tell) rose again and she remembered the open window. After closing it, she lay down and looked at the red marks where her underwear had been and at her legs—her best feature, she thought—before opening a best-seller. Seeing the name of a cologne, she said to herself: "I must buy some of *that*."

Leymann was frightened about going to work. He had to go to a council estate and bargain with an unemployed father of three. He wondered whether his decision to resign was because he didn't want this case. His assignments had all been getting grimmer. Just thinking about the facts of this one made him feel ill. Why had the man decided to buy the council flat in the first place? Didn't he know that the British motor industry was in decline? Didn't he read the papers? And what about his family? It's winter and the gas, water and electric had already been cut so how were the family functioning? Leymann asked himself some more questions, sighing as he had done so many times during the course of the day. He set his alarm clock, believing he wouldn't wake up.

> *Young boy in knife-shock horror...pensioner raped...£5000 of goods stolen from...schoolboy beaten for 12p.*

Leymann read from the local paper in bed.

"She moved sexily with thoughts of romance. In her short jacket, he could see her bosom, ripe and fulsome like..." Jocelyn was enraptured. She knew the novel was unbelievable, silly even, but she kept on reading, twisting from one side of the bed to the other and repositioning the book in her hands.

Jonathan was brimming with hope despite the absence of a call. He longed to move to London and his stomach turned in expectation.

He was quiet in the pub as his friends laughed and joked about it, his best friends with remarkable passion. He knew it was their way of expressing sorrow rather than ridicule. Surely he knew it wouldn't work out the way he had wanted it to, things never did work out anymore, they seemed to say. Through the smoky, bittered air of the bar, he looked past the jukebox and to the comedian.

As he walked back across a field, it began to rain. The grass began to turn into mud and instead of running, Jonathan slowed down, the water trickling into his eyes. He was taking deep breaths, smelling the damp grass and cold, fresh air. His face grew red as he looked across at the black ground. He felt water rising in his eyes. He considered what his parents would think. It had been one month since his girlfriend had left and since that day he couldn't afford a place of his own. Moving back with the family was a strain. His mother would understand: before going to the payphone she had told him not to hope to much. His father had been silent. All his large, black eyes ever seemed to look at were newspapers, these days. He scanned them as if they were maps, guiding him carefully on some night-time journey to Utopia. As Jonathan looked up, tracing the pole star from the plough, he knew his father didn't know North from South and that a map would never be of use to him.

Towards one o'clock in the morning, Jocelyn and Jonathan were still awake. Jocelyn was still reading, skipping the occasional page to get to the end of the book. She had forgotten to switch the burglar alarm on, had remembered at page 250, but had been to tired to get up. Jonathan was lying awake, looking out of his window, suffering from a combination of insomnia and excitement over whether there was still a chance of getting the job. He would stare outside until the warehouses on the hills in front of the house became visible, silhouettes against the morning sky.

By twelve-thirty, Leymann was asleep.

Next door, Mr. Atkinson pressed his spectacles to his eye sockets and peered at the sports' pages. It had been a quiet day and there was no cash in the box he kept by the kitchen sink. Shaking his head at the coverage of a football match, he turned to an advertisement for a satellite television dish.

The radio began to buzz at seven. Leymann jumped out of the bed and turned it off just before the final news headline about an indefinite, nation-wide social security strike. Leymann began to wonder why he had got out of bed so exuberantly. It was going to be a horrible day. But at least he had the courage to fight it.

Jocelyn lazed about in bed. She didn't need an alarm, progress in her career had allowed her lie-ins. She remembered how at boarding school her greatest treat came on a Sunday, when she was able to stay in bed till seven. By her late teens, she had loved to get up early, there had been so much to get up for. Boys, tennis lessons, accountancy courses, all these things and so many more, made for a regular daily stride to the left of the mattress. And now she had the time to sleep late, she couldn't enjoy sleep properly. Every night was restless. She could never remember her dreams.

Jonathan was back at the payphone waiting for the call. The counsellor had said it would be either yesterday or today. The sun had only risen half an hour ago and he shivered in the booth as he ate half a chocolate bar. Path after path had closed, gates had been shut, every step seemed accompanied by an aggressive murmur. He felt that if there was no phonecall now, he would kill himself but he knew he never could.

"Hello, is that Jonathan?" Jocelyn said, still lying in bed, now with a stick of chewing-gum enveloping her tongue.

"Yes...yes...that's me."

"Well? Are you the seeker?" asked Jocelyn impatiently, catching sight of a magazine about food on her side-table.

"Yes."

"You don't say very much, I hope you're better than you sound," Jocelyn spoke louder and more sternly as she heard an aborted interruption, "be at the office by five, this afternoon. That give you enough time? Not sure where you are exactly, but that's when you've got be down here, okay?"

Jonathan found some words: "The address is on the card, right?" But Jocelyn had already hung up. Jonathan was shaking. A light fall of sleet blew from the West as he raised his knuckles to his nose. He had been conscious of his accent on the phone. The woman who rang sounded like a television announcer raising her vowels out of proportion to her consonants. Green turned to white as Jonathan gazed over fields, hills and junk yards, wondering how he'd afford the trip to London. Dick Whittington seemed the only lasting legend from his childhood, not counting Disney films. It was the greatest of dreamy stories, coming from nowhere and making it big in the City.

It's only a short walk from Highgate Hill, where Whittington turned away and back, to Archway Bridge, suicide bridge. In a few hours, Jonathan, curious and shaven, would weigh up his chances. He'd never see the Bridge, only the seductive view. He knew then that the towers of steel and glass would never let him down.

The first hour of Jonathan's first visit to London would be spent in a cell. He reflected on his travels, that hour, the walking leg of the trip, the coach leg of the trip, the train leg of the trip. He remembered his mother's eyes, tearful, angry and as desolate as everything she had ever known in Loddington. He hadn't wanted to ask his parents for train money. He thought he's be lucky. He thought his life was now part of a lottery accumulator. After all, he never bought lottery tickets because everyone in Loddington knew the lottery was scammed the poor. Couldn't this be a way of winning without a ticket?

Leymann ate a piece of burnt toast, covered in a thick layer of gelatinous strawberry jam. The gun shop, downstairs, was always the first shop to open on the street. Innocent-looking men in their twenties, dressed in battle-fatigues vied for first-entry and supremacy. Whose Nazi badge was biggest? Whose boots were comfiest? Leymann looked at his brother's guitar-case on the dining-table as he flicked through his record collection. "Keep Music Alive" it said in a yellow circle.

"Keep Ammunition Live. The spray-can is mightier than the sword but not mightier than the handgun." Jonathan read the graffiti on the smoky windows of a train-carriage.

Jocelyn was laughing, a shrill emanation that beat like a toy tambourine. She was watching breakfast television and was laughing at what she thought must be the jokes, as cottage cheese and toast crumbs dropped from her mouth. She wiped it on her dressing gown sleeve and meandered up the stairs to get dressed. Within an hour she was at her office, co-ordinating, organising, bulging with confidence. At the back of her mind sat a niggling worry, the trouble over Leymann. She would have to see him today—she wanted to—and tell him about his redundancy. Until then, Leymann could be measuring up the flats. The company had bought part of a council estate and after a lot of trouble vacating most of it there was now just one flat to discharge. The whole estate was now inoperable what with its severed utility supply and dangerous structural flaws. "Well, Leymann might learn at least something from this business before he leaves," Jocelyn thought, "we offered everyone a fair price."

As she looked into the dressing-table mirror and down at a framed photograph of Laura, her eldest daughter, she thought about how similar Leymann was to a little child.

Just a month ago, Property Developments PLC had run smoothly and profitably. Jocelyn would find a property, using her contacts at London's many estate agencies and council housing departments. Her lawyers, burly, young law graduates with low fees, would take care of the contracts and then it was up to Leymann to handle the tenants and squatters. Leymann accomplished the task with great confidence. He had never been privately educated but had somehow picked up the tough, brash skills required to show who was boss. Leymann had bloomed in the face of inconvenient tenant-trouble. Even in co-ordinating architects, builders and plumbers he was quick-witted and composed.

The other fifteen or so staff had all looked up to him. He seemed to know more than anyone about it all. It was all the more surprising, then, that he of all people should be undergoing a mental crisis. He was the dependable anchorman, not a junior employee to be distressed about. But because Jocelyn cared, more than she admitted to herself, she felt a twinge of guilt about sending him on tough assignments.

Leymann put a record by Mahler on the turntable, wondering whether the Sex Pistols wasn't really what he wanted to hear. Within ten minutes he was out of the door and back on the trundling bus, watching the same branches, now no longer stretched out but curled into fists. The graffiti, too, had changed, now no longer indecipherable. Leymann felt stronger, as if this day could be beaten into shape, like a slab of red hot iron.

Jonathan had been sitting idly looking at the other passengers, mostly influenza-ridden commuters sniffling their way to London. Jonathan thought about his mother as he looked at the woman in front of him, offering the teat of a milk bottle to a baby in her arms. But within a few minutes of jumping on board an inspector caught him. As a hand had touched his right shoulder, he thought of his friends in Loddington. One in particular shoplifted for a different reason to the others or appeared to. He seemed to actually have a love-hate relationship to the hand of conviction. A grabbing palm on a shoulder could send the same kind of spine-tingling fear as plunging on a roller-coaster.

It had been pointless arguing and Jonathan had resigned himself to an uneasy pilgrimage to North Holloway, from where he was taken to Highgate police station.

He was eventually let out with a warning. The constable wasn't as terrible as he feared. 'Let's give it another try,' Jonathan said to himself as he went down the stone stairs of the police station, shielding his eyes in the harsh North London sunlight.

Jocelyn wasn't at the office when Leymann arrived. As he brushed past the glass entry door, he said hello to Jenny, the receptionist. Before today's visit, he had to deal with a host of development contracts and reports. It would take him about seven hours, with only a short break for coffee.

☙

Jonathan resumed his journey, cursing himself for not spending twenty pence on a paper. When the train finally stopped, he had counted hundreds of pylons.

Jocelyn sweated. Nervous about meeting Leymann, she now felt guilty. She wanted to see his face and yet she had interrupted her journey to work, parking her car outside a run-down office block. She procrastinated over a light blue attaché case, using her mobile phone. It was about four in the afternoon that she broke for a round of smoked salmon sandwiches. Phonecalls from her ex had compounded her problems over Leymann. Every time she heard from him, she felt an uncomfortable ache in her stomach.

It wasn't long before Leymann's cool imitation of nonchalance faded away. As he looked through the papers, spotting a piece about a family without a gas supply, he felt desperate. The message from Jocelyn had been like a sentence. One more day in hell. She wouldn't see him till six, this evening. He was expected to finish off today's work by then. As he passed a young man studying his underground ticket beside the reception desk, Leymann's pack of paper handkerchiefs fell from his pocket.

"Your handkerchief, sir," said Jonathan, raising his eyes like those of a pre-Raphaelite angel.

"Thank you, thank you very much," Leymann answered, surprised by the courtesy. Leymann had a patronising affection for Northern accents. His ex-wife was from Yorkshire and though saddened by thoughts of her, he loved it when he recognised the pronunciation.

The glass front door and the wall-to-wall carpeting of the reception area impressed Jonathan. As he stepped forward he knew that fawning was mandatory, that it didn't matter who it was, even the subordinate-looking man who dropped his pack of handkerchiefs, they were all target-voter. If he was to get on in the company, he knew he had to unlearn the difference between the genuine and the dishonest, whether while offering sentiment or receiving it.

Inside, an anger at the clerks around him smouldered. The diamanté on a woman's dress or a man's gold tie-pin was all it took to catch. But Jonathan was as quick to extinguish any flames.

When Jocelyn had wrapped up the leftover crumbs of bread and salmon in polythene, she remembered Jonathan. The Seeker Scheme involved the possibility of government inspectors' visits so Jonathan would have to be employed, or look as if he was, if the company was to enjoy the tax advantages. With no vacancy to fill, or job for him to do, Jocelyn would have to figure something out. She put the cling-film parcel into the glove compartment and realised she had long decided she was too tired to go to work today. Her eyes felt sticky, last night's unwashed mascara clung to her eyelashes like monkeys on branches.

Reports and contracts completed, Leymann cleared out of the office. He escaped the confines of an ozone-filled underground train, warm air permeating his brown suit, and climbed to street-level. His heart pounded dangerously hard as he stood to catch his breath. The stairs had shaken him up enough to worry him. Looking around the effervescent thoroughfare, he breathed in heavily.

"Jonathan?" asked the frail-looking receptionist. She was only about twenty-six, but lines underscored her eyes and her wispy blonde hair made her face look thin and square. She looked at Jonathan sympathetically. He was wearing a light blue suit of his brother's that had been bought from a discount-store in Loddington. When matched with a thin, short white shirt and over-slim red tie Jonathan looked like someone poor, dressed for a magistrates' dock. The tie was crooked and the shirt looked grey. The suit hung badly with its bulging pockets. This was what Jenny noticed about Jonathan.

As an incoming cloud obscured the midday sun, Jocelyn entered a pub. "Whiskey and soda," she said at the bar, wondering about the effects of sun-up alcohol on her diet. The landlady, a strong-looking woman with long black hair, listlessly reached up and pressed the glass to the tip. It was only a minute later that Jocelyn returned for a refill.

Leymann knocked, his knuckles in a state of cold shock as they hammered the wooden boards. After a few minutes, he heard the sound of someone descending stairs. He could only just hear it what with the noise of hurtling traffic saturating the air. The footsteps were slow, like a bag of potatoes balancing and then plunging down a staircase. A man of about seventy moved the door a little and peered out at him. He was wearing a rare pair of government spectacles, one lens cracked as if drawn on by a cartoonist.

"Yes? If you're from the developers, the answer is no! We're sitting here until they demolish it. It's our home — two hundred and fifty of us — and we'd rather be eaten alive than by two dozen bulldozers than yield to you." He said it slowly, giving Leymann time to looking him up and down. Leymann's face fell as two elderly women also arrived to join him by the door.

"But this isn't your property, you're stealing," said Leymann, at first shouting and then becoming more calm. He was surprised at the figure of 250. Other developers must be vying for space here, he thought. He also couldn't tell how his words were being taken. He fell silent

"Not our property? Nonsense, I'm British and this is Britain. This is my country," he paused, "you know you can't go buying and selling land just so rich foreigners can buy luxury apartments." Leymann didn't expect the man to have enough energy to say a word, let alone a sentence. This outburst, along with the two nodding ladies was disconcerting. Leymann felt the thud of his heart again.

"Gerrof! Young upstart", said one of the women. That was all it took for Leymann to retreat and retrace his footsteps, glancing at the pieces of timber strewn around the gardens. Once he might have persevered. Beside a slat-less fence a brightly coloured estate agents' board proclaimed 'SOLD.'

"It's a very friendly office. And if you don't cross anyone they'll be more than generous to help you out," said the receptionist, stuttering a little.

"Does that mean I've got the job?" asked Jonathan timidly.

"I presume so. Miss Hanwick called in this morning, but she's always very busy," Jenny looked at a note distractedly, "here it is. Yes, you start today." Jonathan began to think about where he would stay tonight.

Jocelyn Hanwick was on her sixth drink and was tipsy. She had never done this before. As she sipped and gurgled, her mind turned to Malcolm Benson, private investigator, a man in his early thirties with ubiquitous tanned, rippling muscles. He had stormed through the pages of last night's 400 page book. Jocelyn's posture had sagged. There was No one in the pub apart from the landlady and Jocelyn watched her in case she was looking at her as she wiped down the bar. The landlady wasn't looking. She sat down, cigarette in one hand, magazine in the other. Jocelyn thought of Leymann and the way his trousers hung. She brimmed with confidence now. She felt she was in a position to tell him that she wanted to love him, to spend time with him. Rubbing the pockmarked wooden table with her red-tipped fingers, she straightened her collar-less blouse over her shoulders and raised her hair a little with a right palm. Jocelyn's unbalanced walk presaged a stumble into her car.

Leymann began to think about brandy. Once again, he was looking at graffiti, this time on the lower deck of a bus. He wondered about whether the bus driver's presence made graffiti-artists scared, resulting in strange lines and shapes instead of readable epithets. Upper decks used always to have something readable, even if it was only "John 4 Jane" when he was at school.

He walked from the bus-stop to the pub in a kind of daze, opening the door with an uneven twist of the wrist. He was nervous and cold. The listless bartender with the long, black hair was never very pleased when a customer arrived. The agony pages of a cheap women's magazine held her interest much more than the people who walked around the surrounding streets or even those who caught her gaze.

It wasn't long before Jonathan, jacket-less and sleeves rolled up, was engaged in his first pursuit for the company. The subtleties involved in fashioning ready-to-drink coffee seemed tedious. Jenny, the receptionist, who had seemed somewhat cold, was now quite emotional when she spoke about teaspoon numbers and water volumes. She reeled off the figures solemnly like a scientist announcing exponents. Jonathan listened like a new boy in a new class, feeling gradually more indifferent...

As he crossed the artificial corridors, by-products of open-plan partitions, No one looked at him. He felt wounded as he laid the polystyrene cups on their crowded desks. He found it more tiresome than challenging to remember whether cups were to be black, white, sugared or unsweetened.

Leymann gulped down the brandy and looked at his watch, delaying his trip to the family with no gas. He glanced at the Constable on the pub wall and then at the window where, though a black micro-blind, a stream of white light shone, like in a refrigerator. The walls were covered with paintings by nineteenth century artists, careless photographic reproductions scarred by layers of nicotine and tar. There were no other customers here.

Jensen leant back on his leather chair. The weather on Wilshire Boulevard was, as it had been all week and all year, sunny and bright. From his office he could see the traffic. He sucked at a generic-brand cigarette and glanced out again. Police officers had stopped a black man in a car. Hearing an exhaust backfire and interpreting it as a gunshot, Jensen flinched, then relaxed sufficiently to say to himself: "Ah! This could only be America!"

His office was always cool and clean. Its pink walls offered a perpetually rosy outlook on life, as long as he was at work. This morning, he had been downtown. The area always made him feel uneasy. From the milling office workers of Pershing Square, it was only a wrong turn before the unleaded motorcar vapour became thicker and blacks and Latinos seemed to be on every avenue. At first sight, they looked relaxed and worn out, their bums leaning on car bonnets or flaking walls, their limbs like unused machinery. But these men had tinted diamonds for eyes and they shone at passing motorists like warning signs. For all their easy-going deportment, a television news education made them look dangerous and strong.

Jocelyn was about to buy Jensen's company. Property Redevelopment Inc. was an international concern and Jocelyn always wondered why expensive homes were confined to Beverly Hills, Bel Air, Pacific Palisades and Malibu. She didn't know very much about Los Angeles, but did believe Jensen's company had the potential to expand Eastwards.

As she sifted through the contracts and deeds, she remembered her honeymoon, her first taste of the easygoing West Coast. Although her schooling had been expensive, her parents had never been able to afford the far flung summer destinations of her peers. Her honeymoon memories were marred by the presence of her husband. His ever-flowing words, packed with patronising nuances, had hurt her every kilometre of the freeways. But it had been her first time in the state of love and California. Jocelyn grimaced and looked out of her windscreen, wondering why she did all her work in the car. Was she really scared of her affections for Leymann?

A meeting, presided over by a deputy, was in progress in the bowels of Property Developments PLC. Jonathan sat still, looking at the plastic buttons of a beige phone. He wanted to call his mother. Her worried face had terrified him before he left. She always had a sad, damp look about her but, this morning, she looked as if she was on the edge. Jonathan was very close to her and, though there was no particular tragedy to set her apart from most mothers in Loddington, she seemed to have been consigned a melancholy hand. He pitied her.

Leymann decided he was ready. He got up with the same exuberance he had that morning, striding out of the pub with brandy-induced confidence. "One of the greatest acts of this party is to have given the chance to millions of people to buy their own council homes," he remembered Jocelyn's words. He wondered about Jocelyn's thoughts now. Leymann, who felt weary of missing her, thought up a response: "It's better than that, one day soon we'll own them."

"You bastards! We can't even warm our baby's milk bottle. Sell off *your* fucking property, it's our fucking gas. What the fuck do you think you've been doing?" These were the friendly words that greeted Leymann. Bargaining would be difficult, he surmised.

"Er, I'm not from the gas company. I'm actually from Property Developments PLC. I'm afraid that we actually own your house, not you," Leymann said softly before an eight-year-old boy came out and kicked him in the shins and then punched him a few times, hard and sharp. A few seconds passed. The boy, screaming and waving a Stanley knife madly in the air, was taken back in by his father. The door slammed shut, leaving Leymann stabbed in a heap outside, pools of dark blood gathering on the concrete slab that made up the pavement. In previous years, it was always Leymann, the most fearless in the office that could handle these situations. "Get a strongman?"

"No, that's okay, I'll handle it," Leymann would reply saving the company money and often, time. Leymann sometimes decided to deal with even the more dangerous cases. But, now, something had made his weak and easy to defeat.

Jonathan's eyes converged on the phone. He was fidgety about using it: he remembered the receptionist's monologue, "if you don't cross anyone."

Jensen's office was in a nice part of town. The air was fresher, cleaned by the rolling Pacific nearby. But there was always a perceived threat of violence. He didn't even feel safe on the freeway he used to get to work. But the Los Angeles Jensen lived in was actually safer than he knew. Freeways bypassed areas that were less safe, gated communities disqualified the insolvent. He chuckled as he recalled a humorous bumper-sticker: "Don't shoot, I'm reloading."

"Mum," said Jonathan.

"Jonathan, where are you? Did everything go well?" asked his mother.

"Yeah, they gave me the job."

"That's fantastic."

"Yes, but the police," Jonathan was interrupted by a tallish man of about the same age. His moustache was straight and his grey eyes glared. As he jammed the receiver back into its cradle with a light pressure on thumb and finger, he tipped a cup of sweet, black coffee onto Jonathan's suit. It had been a mistake. The man's stringency dissipated as he looked at Jonathan as if to say sorry. In silence, he went back to his meeting, papers in hand.

"Jensen, how are you?" Jocelyn asked.

"I'm fine, baby, how are tricks with you?" Jensen's Midwest rising timbre was hard to lose.

"Not too bad. I called to ask about the account number."

"Okay, darling, hang on," Jensen rustled some paper and tapped at his keyboard casting his digits. "So, when you coming around? LA misses you, Josie."

Jocelyn had always hated diminutives. Jensen was one of the few friends of her husband's that she talked to and he was thoroughly dislikeable.

"Come on, Josie, I miss you. You're still not attached, are you?" Jensen asked.

"Actually, there is someone. It looks as if I finally am. A guy called Leymann..." Jocelyn realised that she mentioned his name not only to shake off Jensen but also with a degree of wishful thinking.

"Yes, Leymann," she repeated.

Leymann crawled along the pavement, his arms clutching his stomach bruises. Exerting slow pressure on his right foot, he made his way to a payphone. Using all his energy, he raised himself and pulled the heavy door open. As he lent across a horizontal shelf of black painted metal, he looked at the digital display, his nostrils flaring in the stench of urine and stale cigarette-smoke. When he bent his arm sufficiently to pick up the receiver, he glanced at his reflection: a blood-stained, grey face with black marks for eyes returned his gaze.

Jonathan wiped his suit off with a piece of tissue and began to worry. He wasn't so agitated about the stains on his brother's suit. What troubled him was the effect on his mother of a truncated telephone call. Jonathan was so astonished when his mother's voice faded away that he couldn't remember whether he had mentioned his fracas with the police. He didn't want to remember that he had. Why had he to confide in someone about his journey, let alone his mother? The one piece of advice she had drilled into him from an early age was never to get involved with the police. Even when he once left his wallet in a corner of Loddington, she had reprimanded him for thinking of going to the station. Jonathan thought her actions odd—an unfailing trust and respect for the boys in black was not untypical in Loddington.

Jocelyn mused upon her conversation with Jensen. She realised that now was the time to see Leymann.

Jensen looked out of the window again. Dreamily, he got up and left his office, locking his office door.

"I've got to get my car fixed," he said to the smiling, blonde receptionist who jumpily put her nail-file away in a drawer of her desk. Her plastic jaws expanded a little as her neck contracted with a nod.

Jensen was soon in his Japanese car, depressing the electric window button. On the passenger seat was a pension folder detailing all the payments he'd made over the years. At forty, Jensen would be part of a new breed of retired men and women. He'd be able to spend his hours lolling about at the inherited home in Connecticut or settle down somewhere safer like San Francisco or Santa Barbara. The lump sum ratified a third option which often played on his mind. He harboured dreams of going to Mexico for life of easy money and easy sex, where his money would go further than in America. He might not have seen anything of Mexico except Acapulco but emigration appealed to him.

Both the ear-piece and mouthpiece had been removed from the telephone. Leymann let out a low-volume grunt and fell onto the concrete floor, pushing the door ajar.

Jocelyn's reactions had been dull and numb ever since leaving the pub and it wasn't surprising when she hit her car into a passing lamppost. She wasn't hurt but a compact disc ejected from her dashboard like a Frisbee and her phone jumped from her handbag to lie in a contorted heap in the well of the passenger seat. A police-car happened to be nearby, the constable inside burning his tongue on a cup of tea. He started up and sidled beside Jocelyn's car, opening her door and opening his eyes wider as he saw Jocelyn's thighs and uncovered suspenders. Jocelyn's heart was beating fast. She eased her way out of the seat and put her arms around the policeman, eyes closed and moist. The russet-haired constable smiled and strategically placed his hands before turning an angry and repressed red colour.

The police-vans that ran up the surrounding roads didn't seem there to help anyone. Thick iron gratings covered their windscreens and inside, police sat dressed for riots clutching tightly to Perspex shields. By chance, such a van passed Leymann's telephone box. The men in the van had been grumbling at the junction, debating whether to start the siren and jump the light. One proposer caught sight of Leymann.

"Fucking tramp!" he shouted as he hit the accelerator pedal and unilaterally reached over to switch on the siren.

It took an old man with a white beard to help Leymann. Though his eyes seemed dull and tired and though his curly hair was well groomed, the shabby jeans and fraying nylon sports jacket gave away his credit position.

He was black and Leymann made a half-hearted attempt to back into the booth on his bottom when he saw him. The man didn't say anything as he picked Leymann off the ground and eased him towards his house on a nearby estate. Leymann, vaguely conscious, realised his injuries were hardly serious. He felt slightly ridiculous, supported by the stranger's shoulders as his calf muscles propelled him forwards. The steps were painful though, and Mr. Roeng's strength was surprisingly comforting. He breathed in, gaining the smell of Mr. Roeng's aftershave. Leymann ceased to feel cold.

Jonathan, after a few failed attempts, sat on a strangely shaped black office chair. He had begun to relax in the strange posture the chair dictated, his knees resting on a kind of plinth. He nevertheless feared the moment when the staff meeting ended.

The largest man in the office, his tie inclined thirty degrees from his neck, had earlier advised him not to make personal calls, not even to touch the phone. He had given his order harshly: Jonathan was not to used the device under any circumstances. The receptionist dealt with telecommunications.

Jonathan, however, forgot his orders again and picked up the phone on its fourth trill. He was late enough to hear the triggered office answering machine. Accompanied by the outgoing recorded message, he heard Jocelyn screaming. "Hello? Who's that? Who the hell is that?"

"It's Jonathan," said Jonathan, trying to be heard above the answering machine recording, now reciting the company's fax number.

"And leave your name and number..." continued the machine.

"Hello?" said Jocelyn. "Damn!"

Jocelyn hung up the phone before dialling again. This time, Jonathan obeyed the fat man's orders.

Leymann settled into an ancient, fabric-covered armchair, the only chair in Mr. Roeng's room. In between despairing gasps, Leymann observed the ceiling, wet and pockmarked with umber puddles. A warm, dilute solution of chicken soup was proffered to Leymann's lips as Mr. Roeng began to speak.

"You're hurt pretty bad. I haven't got any cloth to bandage you up but there's a skip outside that might have something," Mr. Roeng smiled, scratching his head.

Leymann nodded, not understanding the relevance of the skip and worrying about the state of his carer's mind. "Can I use your phone?" Leymann managed to ask.

"There ain't no phone here," Mr. Roeng laughed, in sawtooth waves. "You know how much those things cost to install, these days?"

Leymann nodded again and gulped down the soup. He soon burnt his tongue; the soup was still boiling at the bottom. "I think I should just wait by the roadside. There'll be a taxi soon." said Leymann, wanting to leave the stifling congestion of the room.

Mr. Roeng smiled again. He thought to himself: "this guy can't walk, he'll probably soon run a fever. But he's going to try anyway, so why not let him."

Leymann was soon back at the junction, hugging his wounds and looking sick, hungry and dishevelled.

Jocelyn smashed the phone down, chipping the receiver. 'At least all the phones work, these days,' she thought. Over recent months, all the payphones had miraculously begun to function in the areas Jocelyn lived in and around.

Though she wasn't hurt, Jocelyn though it best to visit her private clinic for a check-up, just in case. The kind policeman was willing to drive her there in his squad-car. Siren-on, his eyes glancing at Jocelyn's lap-seated hands, he ignored the scent of whisky that circulated in the car. Jocelyn should have been glad that he hadn't breathalysed her but she was fuming. The constable hadn't allowed her the use of his car-phone.

Jensen flipped the sun-blind on his windscreen, whistling to the sound of the radio. In the traffic jams, he looked through a crisp copy of the LA Times, reading a story about the Queen of England and her dogs. Jensen saved all the stories he read about on England in a scrapbook.

He headed for somewhere associated with safety, a pink cathedral-like shopping mall guarded by armed security guards. Speeding through the underground car-park tunnel, he was thrilled by the foot per foot descent under the desert floor. Finding a space, he clicked off the radio, now buzzing more fiercely from the earthquake-proofed concrete around him.

Though Leymann stared intently at the cars passing by him, his mind had wandered from his task. As vans and estate-cars zoomed towards a roundabout to his left the light drizzle spattered his trousers. The sky had darkened. His heart ceased to beat so hard and he wondered why not.

When the fifteen frowning members of staff had finally regrouped in the office, Jonathan was exiled back to the reception area where he had begun, along with the prematurely old receptionist. He looked at her black business suit, at the curves of her breast. The jacket looked expensive and of a type he had never seen, fitted and yet not fitting. Under the desk, she fidgeted with her feet, her heels lifting from her stilettos, exposing a heel-ladder. She ignored him as he sat motionless, worrying about accommodation.

As Jocelyn lay on the bed, the policeman was curtly told:

"That will be all." Jocelyn looked up to the white-coated doctor, his gold cufflinks glinting faintly in the fluorescent light. He reminded her of Malcolm Benson. "How I wished I had that novel here," she thought as he asked her to unbutton her blouse. As the doctor, a mess of black hair and light, almost colourless, grey eyes, lowered his stethoscope, Jocelyn held the two sides of her blouse to her shoulders, proudly gazing at her underwear. As the doctor carried out the examination, Jocelyn began to think about Leymann. In front of her was a large colour television, with stand and video recorder. A huge bouquet lay on a table and some cordless telephones beside her pillow lent an air of luxury to the room. Outside she could watch a quartet playing beside a wreathed waterfall. Further on, she could see swans gliding on an artificial lake.

As the doctor shoved a lolly-stick into Jocelyn's mouth, his long fingers almost leaning onto her chest, Jocelyn wondered how Leymann had fared with his assignments.

Jensen stood quietly in the lift. There was something wrong with the air-conditioning in the mall complex: it was set too high and the air, just meant to circulate, was rushing quickly through the building. It unnerved Jensen. He worried over whether the perfumed mall breeze presaged tremors in the earth. He walked quicker than usual on marble floors glittering from spotlights. He usually felt safe here. Even the LA uprising couldn't suppress the melodies of in-store credit computers.

He purchased four halogen light bulbs and a couple of three inch screws from an electrical department and went to the all-nation food fair area to drink espresso with some Korean food.

A burnt out *Fiat* slowed down and came to a halt beside Leymann. The car was stained a blend of brown rust and military green. The man inside, in his late fifties with fine lines engraved all over his face, tipped his trilby. Leymann had one eye open and watched the man lean over, his brown coat distending, towards the passenger door. As it opened, the door fell, slanted towards the surface of the road. Only Leymann's hand seemed to separate the car door and the tarmac. The ferrous oxide dust stung Leymann as he lifted himself up, raising his hand along the side of the door.

"Hurt?" asked the man with a throaty East London accent. Leymann nodded and climbed in, surprised as the seat sank to the floor. "She's not much, but at least it's a car. Can't do without them these days."

Leymann motioned to him as if to say 'I didn't mean to complain'. At five miles an hour, it was like going a hundred.

"Have you anywhere to live?" asked the receptionist suddenly. Jonathan had been staring at the carpet for nearly an hour, seeing little Rorschach men with big bellies in the patterns. After his trance had been interrupted, he answered with a pathetic shake of his head. "Have you any money?" she asked in a kinder, tuneful way. Jenny had been watching Jonathan while he stared downwards. Jonathan had a toughness about him that she found attractive. He seemed very different to the other men at the office. She was tired of their moaning about their lives and though Jonathan was a subordinate, he was interesting. She wiped a blonde wisp of hair from her forehead, exposing brown roots, and said "You can stay with me until your first cheque comes." Jenny surprised herself as much as Jonathan.

"Thanks," he said, slightly embarrassed.

"Just until it comes," she reiterated, remembering the dangers of allowing a stranger into her flat.

"That'll be all, Miss Hanwick, you're ship-shape." The doctors always talked in clichés here but Jocelyn fretted a little over whether the idiom was a reference to her figure. "You've got a couple of minutes till the hour is up. The cashier's desk is just outside," he said, handing her the bill.

Jocelyn grasped it between thumb and forefinger, watching him leave. 'It was nice of him to keep time,' she thought, placing the bill onto a silver plate beside her and buttoning up her blouse. To tuck it in, she got up and unzipped her skirt a little. As she straightened her skirt, the russet-haired policeman walked into the room.

"Where're you going?" asked the old man.

"Hospital...home?" Leymann replied softly.

"Where's that you say?"

"Hospital!" Leymann found the strength to shout.

"Alright by me. I wasn't going anywhere really anyway. The one round here's closed but there's another one not too far away," he said, moving his frail, blubbery hands around the steering wheel. "I guess it's all on my way."

The hospital, a gigantic prison-like structure made of grey rock and punctures for windows was noticeable because of its swirling queue, wrapping itself around lampposts and vandalised phone-booths. As hail spewed from the sky a hundred or so lit cigarettes gave the line of people the form of a many-eyed snake.

"I'll pay you when I get home—please? Kids from the estate...they stole my wallet..." mumbled Leymann, wiping a stripe of blood from his cheek. As the car drew nearer, Leymann saw what looked like dying men and women. He would never get in there. The best he could do was go home.

"Ten pounds," said the man, rubbing his frayed Tweed trousers, "twenty, actually."

Leymann nodded and looked out at a navy blue Rolls-Royce in front of them. A pale-skinned man in a dark green suit was driving, a hand hanging out of the window clutching a cigar like a baton. Leymann turned to his driver who had begun to talk.

"God, am I in a state, too. You know, I was in Ireland a few months ago, my mum was pretty ill sitting there in her house. She had saved up for my trip home. Anyway, I visited a dentist there, you know just to check up on the molars and gums. Anyway, everything was fine, I brush my teeth three times daily, you see, always looked after them," he sloped towards Leymann and showed him his teeth. "Well, last week, I went for a check-up around here. They're going to charge from next month so I thought I'd better get myself done before I can't afford it anymore. I'm entitled to it, you know? Well, guess what he gave me. Nineteen fillings is what he gave me—nineteen! It took me till today to return to the place, that's where I just came from. The fillings had been falling out, every day since the check up. All his drilling had been for nothing. Well, it turned out that he gets paid per filling. He must have made a pretty penny out of the social on my mouth. I goes to see him today and he calls the police, saying I'm harassing him. I scarpered. But what hurt most, what's most painful...oh, the drilling."

Leymann fell into a light sleep, sore in the gums.

Jensen drove to a supermarket. He grabbed some polythene bags from a dispenser and began to fill them with fruit. "You know where that fruit comes from? That's smuggled fruit, out from under a shower of bullets and bombs," screamed a man who had sidled beside him. Jensen ignored him, dropping the bags and turning away towards the dairy refrigerators. Security guards rushed up towards the man and bundled him away, out of the store.

Jensen smiled nervously and returned to his bags, weighing them on a machine.

"Just hang on there for a few minutes," said the receptionist, lifting her skinny frame off the chair and walking into the main office area. Jonathan felt empty. The day's traumas had got to him despite Jenny's generosity. When she returned, they walked in silence towards the lift. "It's not very big, but I expect you know how expensive it is to live down here," she said.

"No, I don't, really. I mean I don't, not at all," Jonathan replied. "I haven't the slightest idea," he tried to upgrade his accent. The receptionist laughed.

"And what are you doing in here?" Jocelyn asked, smiling at the policeman. He didn't answer. He put his helmet on the bed and sat down beside it, putting his arms around Jocelyn and forcing her towards him. "Hey, what's that for?" she asked, flustered and abraded.

At last, Leymann had arrived home. His driver shook him a little before he awoke.

"Ten, I mean twenty pounds!" he said.

"Yes, I'll go in and get it. Just wait," Leymann got out of the car and went as quickly as he could to the flat, too tired to glance at the gun shop.

"There, sir, notice how the Effoleber has its weight distributed evenly? Notice the smooth contours of the handle?

In America, they call this one the Sunday Night Special," said Mr. Atkinson, owner of the Torpedo Gun Shop. The potential customer held the Effoleber and stared through the fine wired sight. He swung the gun around, watching the objects in the shop blur into elongated shapes. "Er, that's enough of that, sir. Never point it at a person," Mr. Atkinson said to the barrel, "they must have taught you that at the gun club."

"Gun club?" asked the man in the green anorak.

"Yes, you've been a member of a gun club?"

"Yes, of course, here's my license."

Mr. Atkinson nervously brushed his fingertips on his tweed lapel and examined the card. He was nervous. For the first time in years he had handed a loaded gun to a customer.

Leymann tumbled about the room, limping across his floorboards in one direction and then another. "Where had he left that twenty?" he thought.

"Where are you from then?" asked the receptionist.

"A town called Loddington."

Jenny nodded blankly, "Jonathan?" she said.

"Yes?"

"Do strange girls help you out in Loddington, then? I just ask, because your mind seems a long way away. Not many people in London would have taken you in, you know. You're pretty lucky."

"I'm sorry, I don't even know your name. Thank you. Thank you very much for what you're doing," Jonathan said, watching her move towards his corner of the lift.

"I'm Jenny," Jenny said, smiling sweetly. She left the lift first and Jonathan followed her out of the air-conditioned office block.

Only that morning, Jonathan had been terrified of this building. Its stone front had inspired panic and horror. Through a hundred or so windows, Jonathan had seen shadows, crouching, standing and sitting. The shutters on some windows swung about in the wind. The message 'CHRIST' was emblazoned upon one set of panes, the letters all different colours. Though it would be obvious to the average pedestrian that the letters were a remnant of last year's Christmas decorations, Jonathan had been alarmed by the sign.

"I think that's in order," said Mr. Atkinson, pushing his forefinger into the centre of his glasses' frames. He had had twenty-twenty vision for nearly all his life but a short spell fighting Argentina had left him with problems. The disability was negligible thanks to his glasses but it was still permanent. He would have had to leave the army soon anyway, his father had just died and he was to take over the family business. He still spent long enough in the services to get a medal and Mr. Atkinson's love of weapons and his knowledge of them made it easy to make the change from using guns to trading them.

Business had taken off when he took over the firm. Mr. Atkinson settled down well and nursed the idea that he would one day marry Mrs. Blueheart's daughter, Caroline. He and his brother had played with her as children. While Caroline's mother tended her florist's shop, they would run through the park and play games. When they were younger, Caroline had always been closer to Mr. Atkinson's brother, Arthur, a strong-minded peacenik rebel who was said to have sped on his father's death by his loud and impracticable proclamations on pacifism.

However, Mr. Atkinson still had problems. One of them was his flourishing inability to decipher the fonts on some gun-certificates. This predicament was less serious that one might think, at least Mr. Atkinson said so when caught out at gun dealer conferences. Since his father had set up shop in the early twentieth century, only twelve recorded deaths had ever been traced to the shop. "Twelve accidents in nearly a hundred years!" Mr. Atkinson muttered to himself, sometimes. "I wonder how many cancerous deaths are traceable to that tobacconist's over the road," he would wonder.

"Now, are you taking this one?" asked Mr. Atkinson, watching the man aim the gun at his shop window as a rusty *Fiat* hooted outside.

The policeman threw Jocelyn onto the bed and tore Jocelyn's skirt, peeling it off as his other arm pulled roughly on her blouse. His hand then pushed onto her mouth. Suddenly, he got up and walked to the door and locked it. As rain began to pour on the pavements outside, turning grey stone to black, Jocelyn reached for the phones. Outside the door, a nurse was counting notes in surgical gloves before depositing them into a safe. Along the corridor, a chef was hardly cooking mange tout. And on the first floor, three old men and a woman sat in a waiting room that looked like an *ancien regime* drawing room.

Jonathan's cheap, unframed rucksack had been looked down upon in the office. Men were supposed to carry attaché cases and not look like inter-railing tourists. He put the rucksack down on the pine floor and looked about the small flat. He began to feel sorry for Jenny. The room was sparse, oddly shaped Le Corbusier objects that seemed like broken chairs were the set-pieces. The walls were white and all the fittings were black.

"Decorate it yourself?" Jonathan asked.

"No, I didn't actually. One of my friends from school became an interior designer."

"Oh, is she going to do it all up?"

Jenny didn't feel like discussing design. 'If Jonathan couldn't tell it was a beautiful apartment, why explain?' she thought.

"It comes with a string of bullets, special offer this week," said Mr. Atkinson.

Leymann stumbled about the room, as if dancing to the Mahler record that had been repeating softly since the morning. Leymann often kept a record going to scare off potential burglars.

"Shall I pack it?"

Leymann found the envelope.

"Sir?"

Leymann heard a shot.

Jensen waited in the line of cars to pick up his shopping. The mall had induced a headache and though he was all for returning to his Santa Monica townhouse, he found himself passing the cross-street. The final act of the Jensen-managed property company concerned a new construction in Malibu. Driving back down Wilshire and onto a stretch of Ocean

Avenue, he saw the sun high up over the pier. 'Bag-people', those who had unadvisedly left neighbouring states in search of fame, fortune and bread, scrambled alongside palm-trees as the Pacific mirrored the richly coloured sky. A large boat, possibly a warship, sat still in the distance as the sounds of a fair penetrated the air. As Jensen drove down the steep carriageway to Sunset Boulevard, he pushed a CD into his dashboard.

There were none of the usual smells of disinfectant in the hospital—only a thin veil of expensive perfume. As the policeman stood, half-naked and trousers dangling, Jocelyn reached for a button on the telephone. The receiver had been knocked off while her underwear had been wrenched down. She wanted to scream. Jocelyn's skin felt cold and taut, dark bruises building up over her skin. As someone tried the door, a drop of blood from Jocelyn's nose fell onto the starched cotton sheet.

Mr. Atkinson walked towards the broken front window and looked out at the *Fiat*. The car was sloped towards the ground. The bullet had ruptured one of the front tyres and the driver's head had dipped towards the steering wheel. The customer had run out, holding the gun, seemingly worried about what he had done. After a few seconds in which he leant into the car, seeing the driver nod happily, he ran off, finding a dazzling black taxi.

Leymann tried to rush downstairs. Instead, his leg refused to move and it steadfastly clamped itself to the floor, leaving Leymann to lean on a table and view the offence from a window above.

Mr. Atkinson rubbed his hands through his greased hair before taking off his perched spectacles. He looked tired and, despite all the time he took over his appearance, weary. Slowly, he paced towards the phone, an original Second World War military telephone used by the Royal Air Force. The police would be on the scene with the usual promptness, some forty-five minutes later.

Jocelyn's finger had been on the buzzer for a few seconds, her arms held by the muscles of the policeman. He hadn't noticed the commotion. He concentrated on his actions, stiffly punching Jocelyn in the eyes and nose, while kicking her in the

crotch with a well-built boot. Around her legs, scratches filled
with blood. As the smell of sweat rose, Jocelyn's tears and blood
mixed up and ran in lines towards her mouth, now covered and
biting the hand. The taste was bitter and execrable.

Jenny lay on the long sofa, her hands on her face as she
yawned loudly, kicking off her shoes. Jonathan watched the
balls of her feet move from side to side. He was exhausted and
he had just about enough energy to look down. His trousers
were scuffed by mud and stained in coffee. He slumped into an
armchair.

"Well, what would you like for dinner?" asked Jenny.

"Oh, anything. I don't feel that hungry, really," said a
starving Jonathan. He hadn't enough money to buy lunch and
had sipped at a vomit-smelling powdered soup he found in the
office instead.

The rescue was well underway until the policeman pulled
out a knife. As Jocelyn sobbed and yanked the sheets to cover
herself, she watched the staff back away from the policeman in
the invoice-hall.

Jensen's car had sat in a traffic jam for nearly half an hour.
He was glad when he finally got a chance to speed through a
stretch of Sunset. To his left was white sand, above him mountain
rock and across the intersection a few jacarandas. The music
riddled the air with electric guitars. The windows were wound
fully down and as he watched the assorted restaurants, singles'
bars, fast-food places and the crests of Pacific waves, he realised
he would miss this place, if he ever left. A sandy track, leading
off the road, took him towards the beach and what he liked to
think was a small and exclusive hotel cum dating agency. The
boys and girls were, from the fancier end of Venice to Malibu,
perfect specimens. Tanned, muscular surfers strutted about on
the sand, their damp blonde hair dripping into ice blue eyes.
They were *beauty* as propagated by innumerable magazines
and commercials but Jensen's proximity tended to conjure up
loneliness. He hadn't found any friends since he came out here
ten years ago. Sometimes, he thought the salary more than
made up for it, other times, he shook his head. Los Angeles was

a city of promises, each one like a gift from Pandora. It was only after the uprising that he mulled over escape.

As a yellow moon ascended the ecliptic, the *Fiat* stayed still. Leymann applied disinfectant to his wounds and watched out for any sign of the driver. He had relaxed a little, beginning to feel a little more comfortable. He thought about the driver and how odd it was that he had come to his aid. Leymann would never have picked up a hitchhiker. His expectations about Jocelyn receded as he sat down, his feet resting in a plastic tub of water. The protruding hairs on his ankles began to float as he fell asleep.

Rose poured out a glass of rum. Outside the bar, greenheart and wallaba trees provided shade for a dozen workers, Indians and African Americans. The morning's rain had subsided and all through Georgetown the fresh fragrance of wet vegetation filled the air. She was a little tired but was vaguely excited about tonight's date. As she watched more workers from the sugar plantations and coffee mills arrive she thought about the morning's profits. If it hadn't been for her inheritance she would never have been able to afford this slow and easy existence.

Jonathan and Jenny sat in front of the television, eating a peculiar goulash from a tin. As their spoons jingled, Jonathan thought about his mother's cooking and how Jenny's seasoning was so strong. John Barleycorn was at his best as he tapped a pair of drumsticks onto a scale of milk-bottles. Jonathan turned to Jenny.

"Do you like this programme?" he asked, glad he'd broken the hour's silence.

"Yes, he's gorgeous," Jenny replied, dripping a little sauce onto her jacket.

"No-one watches him in Loddington. He's such a drunk."

"That's the fun of the thing. Drunk chat-show hosts. What a brilliant idea. It has the highest ratings, too, you know. Listen to all the laughs. His producer knows Sharon from the office. He's won a British Academy Award."

"My mum knew Omar Sharif," said Jonathan before the TV

competition got into full swing. After a few minutes, both of them became briefly restless before sinking back into silence.

John Barleycorn, the grey-haired drunk who made the housewives smile, was glaring into the camera.

"I'm afraid that cue doesn't project the right discourse," Barleycorn whispered to the floor-manager in a thorny Etonian accent.

"Cut...choo!" someone shouted with a cold as a stripe of blusher was applied to the host's nose.

"And end of the break, go!" said the floor-manager.

"Weel, I mean! Who's today's guest there, huh? Who do you think? Ha ha hee hee. Hic, hic," Barleycorn said to the camera. Beneath twenty bright lights, the smell of industrial cleaner rose from the floor and an audience of one activated the canned laughter. The director stifled another sneeze.

A policeman on a bicycle finally appeared beside the *Fiat*. Mr. Atkinson had been waiting, totting up the day's accounts. For the next hour, the policeman sat with Mr. Atkinson, waiting for an ambulance. The old man who had driven Leymann had suffered a heart attack. As the policeman had pulled the door of the car opened, the balding man fell out onto the road, his useless skull fracturing.

Under light sedatives, Jocelyn relaxed. She felt happier, less in a rush. A very light hangover floated in her head but to the doctor she was either a woman of strong character or someone who was refusing to face up to her violent attack. Her physical injuries were surprisingly not severe: minor but very apparent facial bruising and abrasions on her thighs. Despite the strength of the policeman, he had inflicted less damage than Jocelyn had feared. Her sexual organs burned a little but her main wounds were in the psyche.

After the doctor had administered dressings, bandages and painkillers, Jocelyn called her ex-husband and asked to speak to her children.

"Hello, mummy."

"Hello, darling, how was school?"

"Alright."

"What did you have for lunch?"

"Peas, er, roast lamb. Mum, are you okay?"

"Just a little tired. Put your elder sister on."

Laura Hanwick was thirteen, last month. She had grown up with a confident, if spoiled, command of her surroundings. Her blonde hair was long—her father never took her to the hairdressers', but her face was as round as her mother's. She had been having difficulty with her French lessons and Jocelyn had been paying large sums of money for extra tuition.

"*Bonjour, ma petite fils,*" said Jocelyn, coolly remembering the French classes of years ago.

"Mum?"

The hotel cum dating agency, or Malibu Love as it was actually called, had been constructed by Jensen's company. It had been his final project and he had shares in it. It wasn't big but rather, intimate. For the past month, large businessmen of all ages danced the evenings and dollars away while the handsomely paid girls from all over metropolitan LA yawned.

Jensen left the car and shoved the door into place. His jacket rippled in the air as his English shoes crumpled the sand.

Rose was closing up and just before she left, her handbag poised on her shoulder, the phone rang.

"Dammit, Rose, I haven't talked to you for ages. I haven't talked to you for a long time," drawled Jensen, who was sitting in a comfortable, light blue chair and smiling at a tall brunette who was filing her nails behind a counter.

"Jensen!" Rose screamed, then calming herself down, said "this is a surprise. I thought you'd never ever call again."

"Come on sis', we're the only family we have," Jensen replied, unpacking a box of light cigarettes. Jensen hadn't talked to his sister for nearly three years, ever since she had dropped out of a New York university. Though South America interested Jensen, he had always felt it no place for her sister to be making a life. She was too young and hadn't even completed her education.

Rose smiled. Every day seemed to be lazily happy but

this phonecall, coupled with tonight's date made today extra special.

Mr. Atkinson didn't speak. All the previous shootings that traced back to his shop had been far away: Northern Ireland, Europe, the Americas. The policeman mumbled "terrible thing," as he held a small square mirror in his right hand. It had been used to check the driver's vital signs.

Before the ambulance reached them, Caroline, from the florist's, came into the shop, wearing faded jeans, tennis shoes and a T-shirt with the words "Summer of Love," emblazoned across her chest. A small gold crucifix hung below her neck. At her arrival, Mr. Atkinson smiled, eager to forget the day's misadventures.

"Leymann?" This is Jocelyn."

Leymann had awakened on the twelfth ring, surprised to find his phone miraculously working after so much inaction.

"Hello, Jocelyn, how are you? I'm afraid today didn't go very well, at all." Leymann coughed and splashed in the water beneath him.

"Leymann, listen. It doesn't matter."

"It doesn't?" Leymann replied, puzzled.

"No."

"I'd like to see you."

"Well, come on over," Jocelyn said. Her voice was sweet and deep. She wanted to see Leymann as soon as possible.

"I'd love to, Jocelyn. But I can hardly move. One of the tenants gave me quite a hard time. I suppose I'd better get some rest. You could come over, to mine," Leymann had never asked her home before and was surprised as he suggested it. His face flushed.

"Oh, Leymann," Jocelyn said reflectively, "we are in a mess, aren't we? I can't move either."

"What happened to you? Gym accident?"

"I don't think I'm strong enough to talk about it. I shouldn't talk about it," she said, pausing, "rape."

"Rape? What do you mean?" Leymann replied, amazed at what she was saying.

"I had to confide in someone, just say the word, you see. But I don't want to talk about it. You understand."

"Where are you?" asked Leymann.

"The Purple-Cross."

"Oh."

"We've always been close, haven't we?"

"Well..."

"We have, Leymann. I want you to understand that. I haven't been as close to a man since my husband."

"But we never see each other," said Leymann, intrigued.

"Yes, but more of a psychological attachment...telepathic, you know?"

"Er...yes," said Leymann, shaking his head.

"Do you like it at Property Developments?" Jocelyn asked, tightening her grip on the receiver.

"I did."

"What do you mean 'did'?"

"Just that. I loved it in the beginning. It satisfied my hunger, my ambition...I could even use my leadership qualities. Now, after seeing everything. I don't know."

"Well, I suppose you've seen your share of everything," Jocelyn whispered.

"I suppose," said Leymann, weakly. He had always been weak with Jocelyn.

"Leymann, I've worked hard on this company. I've worked damn hard. Daddy gave me a start but if I hadn't had him, I could have got a loan on the house. I've had a few, I've had few advantages," she paused, "I had contacts through school but that doesn't diminish anything I've achieved. Those tenants, the ones you saw today, their thinking is screwed. I don't want to seem harsh but..." There was a pause. "I'm not so special, you know. And I know that there are some genuine cases out there, the company even does a yearly charity day. But, basically, Leymann, anyone can do a decent day's work."

"I know," said Leymann, puzzled.

"And I know you know," smiled Jocelyn, "that's why we're

so close." There was a pause as Jocelyn recalled the events of the day.

"But there is something difficult...oh, it's so difficult to explain. It's like being imprisoned by my own words. Leymann, you've been becoming a little disillusioned, I've noticed that. It's as if you've maybe seen brighter things, other than work, I mean," Jocelyn drawled.

"I haven't."

"well, anyway, I'm not as strong as I seem. I'm tired, too, Leymann. I've everything I need. I could close down the whole thing tomorrow. I could sack the lot of them. I'd still have enough to live on. I'm safe, my daughters are safe."

"But, what's wrong then? Apart from..."

"It's difficult, I told you."

"Try," said Leymann softly. He wondered whether he loved Jocelyn more, the less she spoke.

"It's like...insecurity. I'm in property, the mainstay of security. If you don't have a house you've got nothing: nothing, at all. And yet, for me property just makes me feel insecure. Then there's Evangeline, there's...oh, there's just so much. I don't think I'm going to stay sane much longer."

"And your divorce, how's that going?" said Leymann, not quite following Jocelyn.

"Don't Leymann, just don't?" He felt a chill down his spine, as if he was being told off..."At least, we talked. When we get better, we'll meet," Jocelyn changed the subject, suddenly becoming colder.

"Yes, I'd like that a lot. I could take you for dinner somewhere, perhaps?"

Jocelyn laughed. "Can you afford it?"

"Of course, I can," Leymann replied, thinking about his pending resignation from the firm. He couldn't tell her now.

"Anyway, I might be going away, so you might have time to save up."

"Away?" Leymann said, ignoring his own annoyance at Jocelyn treating him like a child.

"Yes."

"But we're only just beginning our friendship."

"So we are," said Jocelyn, growing tired, her eyes blinking quickly. "Goodbye Leymann, bye."

As she replaced the receiver, Leymann sat in his room, dreaming and in darkness, wondering whether to go down and see what happened to the *Fiat* and its driver. Soon afterwards, Jocelyn fell into a depression.

She had liked talking to him. She felt she was better than him and it always pleased her to talk to people that she saw as weaker. That's why she must like him, she thought. She usually felt better after chatting with him. But now the phone was down, there was nothing to save her from her imagination. Why did she have to suffer? And why did she have to hurt. Her mind wavered, images of the rape flitting in and out of her head.

It seemed as if Jocelyn's strength had finally cracked and its shiny pieces reflected nothing but self-disgust. She reached over to the bedside drawer and pulled out a sheet of letter-headed notepaper, scattering a few others on the carpeted floor. The pen, as the notepaper, was engraved with the name 'Purple Cross'.

Dear Leymann,

It seems so silly to write to you but I felt, the way things are going, time will pass too quickly.

I have always admired your courage in dealing with people, the people we have to deal with, the angry, horrible people. You could empty a block quicker than anyone. You always had a strength about you. I hope you learned things from me, too. But now, I'm in trouble. Don't you get that feeling? When everything seems to be at a loss? All this seems so sentimental, adolescent even, but that's just the way I feel, right now. Remember when we used to go to that bar? It was just the two of us and we — I — always had a wonderful time.

I don't have any old friends now and I have always felt you understood things. Please understand me now. We will meet up but for now, I have to tell you: both of us are being hunted down. The dogs know our scent and for me, I fear it's too late. For you, it's different. Don't you know it's true when I say that we're two of a kind?

Your friend, Jocelyn.

The writing was careless, indecipherable at times. Jocelyn put the page into an envelope before she fell asleep, drained from writing something so different to a building firm memo. To her it didn't seem meaningless or hackneyed, to her it seemed as deep as the literature she read. It was a declaration charged by emotion and sensitivity.

Jonathan had noticed that Jenny had fallen asleep. Her empty, white bowl lay on the floor, half under a black table strewn with magazines and newspapers.

A sitcom was warbling on and Jonathan switched to the news.

Four more factories closed in the Northwest, today. A spokesman for one of the companies involved blamed poor profits and high labour costs.
Pause.
Tens of thousands of people were affected in London today by a strike at social security offices. Management claimed that seven out of ten worked, despite the union's claim of a 90% walkout. Most affected were the sick and elderly. An opposition spokesman said that strikes in the social services were a regrettable action...and on a happier note, a talking dog shouted its head off in Newcastle's...

"Oh, shut it off!" cried Jenny, waking suddenly.
"It's the news."
"The Feast Lenders is on the other side!"
Jonathan turned the channel and sat in silence during the show, watching Jenny rise a little as she gawked at the set.

Jonathan wanted to go to sleep now but felt too shy to ask where his bed was.

"How've you been, Caroline?" asked Mr. Atkinson cautiously. The ambulance had left in a storm of sirens and the policeman had trundled away and back to the station.

"Alright. I only came for some sugar."

"How's the florist's?"

"Fine, we're doing a lot of wreaths. Funny that," Caroline said, making a puzzled face, "Mr. Farmer's is raking it in." Mr. Farmer ran the funeral directors nearby.

"Oh."

"How's Arthur? Heard from him?"

Mr. Atkinson flinched when he heard his brother's name.

"Haven't heard from him in quite a while."

"Too bad. You know, I've said this before, I'd love to have had a brother like Arthur. It was nice when he was next door."

"So what have you been up to in your spare time, then?" asked Mr. Atkinson, changing the subject. Anxious not to sound like a father he asked Caroline whether she had been to any rock concerts.

"Not really. There's one coming up, actually, but it's at Wembley Stadium and you know how much they cost. I'm just living, I guess," she said, putting her hands in her tight jeans and lifting her T-shirt a little. "It's terrible what happened to that man, though," she looked out of the window, "not the kind of excitement we really want, is it? I suppose that's what's bound to happen when you run a gun shop, though."

"Well," Mr. Atkinson smiled, "this sort of thing doesn't happen very often, you know. That customer was just a bad sort. He stole my gun and all. That'll put a hole in this week's takings."

"See you, anyway," Caroline said, turning to the door with the bowl of sugar in her hand. Mr. Atkinson tried to think of something to say, something that would make her stay. He couldn't and Caroline left the shop and receded from view.

As Rose walked back from the minister's house, a white, temple-like colonial home, Jensen was sitting beside the beach.

He had found a black rock to perch on and he was watching the waves darken and reflect reds, purples and yellows. The skies here were at their most brilliant at sunset, the LA smog fuelling a violently-hued canopy of colour. If the young and fashionable youths of Melrose Avenue or Santa Monica became tired of vegetarian restaurants and the neon, all they had to do was look upwards.

The air was clean and the fragrance was not so much salty as flowery. Jensen was missing his sister, wondering whether he had failed her a little. He remembered seeing her weeping after their father's funeral, amongst the massive limousines. Now, the Pacific foam began to splash too close and Jensen got up, turning his head...Malibu Love was yielding other people's credit.

In the dim light of the table lamp, Mr. Roeng sat in his armchair, biting his lip. He was reading the work of an American professor. Increasingly, he would turn to American academic work for salvation, looking at sociology in particular. For a while, he had been delving into Eastern mysticism, buying strange pseudo-philosophical deliberations published by strange sounding firms. He had tired of them and felt that going back to more materialistic inquiry would now offer him more.

Rain-clouds spattered water on the corrugated iron roof. Mr Roeng became distracted. He kept losing his place in the book, his mind forgetting beginnings of sentences on reaching their ends. He thought about his younger son, Carl. Mr. Roeng hadn't seen him for a couple of days and was determined to wait until he came in. Each strange sound was carefully thought about before its reverberations ceased. They weren't the sounds of Carl's sports' shoes.

Since Carl's mother had died, after a spectacular misdiagnosis and misapplication of anaesthesia, Mr. Roeng hadn't been able to cope properly. He spent some of each day devising new ways of budgeting.

Mr. Roeng's limbs had been attacked by arthritis a few years ago. Before that, he had been quite an influential community leader in West London. Now, he was condemned to sit around the house and, above all, not spend too much money.

"I'm really tired, Jenny, the day started at five-thirty for me, you see," Jonathan said in a fit of courage.

"Of course, Jonathan. You don't mind sleeping on the couch, do you?"

"No...it's warm here."

"Okay, as soon as this is over, I'll get some sheets and blankets."

Jonathan nodded politely and continued to read an article about the nation's sexual habits in a women's magazine. His eyes drooped as the blood in his eyelids turned the sparsely decorated room into a reddish blur. He rubbed his fingers. They were grimy, the skin rubbing away with the dirt.

He began to fantasise, remembering how easily his skin had rubbed away when playing his friend's guitar. It was the strap that did it, grating away at the shoulder-blades as the guitar was strummed. He imagined himself playing in front of his secondary school, bare-chested with a *Fender* slung around him like a machine-gun. The music was harmonious, moving even and his peers cheered loudly for him—the greatest accolade Jonathan had ever sought. He smiled, looking around the hall and at the faces, thinking about how simple and wonderful school was, where happiness was brushing past the girl he had fallen for. Suddenly the strap began rubbing like a razor across his spine. His peers watched on, dancing and singing as the spotlights became brighter and brighter.

Carl couldn't have phoned his father. Even if Mr. Roeng had a phone, the chances of finding a working call box were slim.

Kitted out in his red baseball jacket, a pair of 501 jeans and a pair of expensive trainers, he was loitering with his friends. Together, they made up a frightening bunch of crew-cut youths. Their clothes were expensive. Ranging from eleven to twenty-one years of age, they had all become disillusioned by crushed fathers and mothers or unsuccessful bigger brothers and sisters. They believed themselves to be tough and some of them bore battle-scars. There didn't seem anything constructive to do, night-clubs and bars were all too expensive. The local youth-club had long been closed down after the council needed space to house twenty pensioners. However, Carl and his friends still pursued a variety of hobbies.

That night, the youngest of the group had crouched between the rails of underground trains, spraying their trademarks on advertisements. It wasn't so dangerous — trains were infrequent. It was a pastime that had eventually become tedious. Often, they would open their shoplifted spray-cans in readiness and then just gaze at the porcelain hoops that lay beneath the live rails.

But, by now, Carl, six feet tall with shaved eyebrows, was gulping down hot chips, the salt and vinegar stinging his palette.

The night air was cold and foggy, the lights of cheap takeaways and bars glowing. "Not much action tonight," he said glumly to his friends.

"No," replied Robert, stealing a chip.

In murky light, Jensen sipped at a Margarita and watched his Malibu Love clients. The room was saturated with perfume and sequins and as he looked through *LA Weekly* he listened to the girls talk. Though they were supposed to be giggly and flirtatious, their talk was very serious.

"How are you Jensen?" asked one of the tall women. She had a sharp, angular profile, a black bob that could have been a wig and green contact lenses.

"Okay." Jensen didn't like talking to anyone here. The talking was left to a fifty-year old Californian woman named Labilia whose walking was aided by a multicoloured stick. Her hair was badly dyed brown and her face had undergone two face lifts, presents given by clients from years ago. She was an ideal employee. She lectured the girls on appearance, etiquette and sexual safety. A workaholic, she would be there by one thirty in the afternoon, parking her faded grey Chevy in the car-park.

"You're not here often, are you? Not these days, anyway."

"No," Jensen replied, returning to the properties for sale column.

The conversation stopped there. Labilia caught the green

eyes and wafted her own hand towards a seventy year old looking man who had presented his wallet at the cash desk. A Los Angeles Club membership card fell onto the thick reception area carpet.

The girl with green eyes moved swiftly towards the scene, bending down and looking up at the man from the floor. The black dress she wore ended only a few inches below her waist and the man surveyed her sheer-covered knees and thighs. She grinned and motioned to the wallet.

Leymann had woken up uneasily. His head was aching and he had waited for around three hours before deciding to get up and look for medicine.

While he tipped a bottle of analgesics towards his left palm, he looked out onto the road. The *Fiat* was still there, the light of a pink streetlight clinging to the bonnet. The sound of an engine broke the morning silence. It was Caroline, still in her T-shirt and jeans, emerging for an old 1970s-styled car. Caroline looked up and smiled, her head swaying from side to side. As Leymann secured the cord of his dressing gown, he saw a bottle of some kind of spirits in her right hand. The car sped off and Caroline rushed towards Leymann's front door, downstairs and out of Leymann's field of view.

Leymann had presumed she he had gone home, to the florist's. It was with some dissatisfaction that Leymann got out of bed again, this time to answer the door.

"Leymann!" she shouted as she climbed the narrow stairs, "you up there? Of course, you're up there!" she laughed.

"No, I'm actually in hell," Leymann whispered to himself,.

Caroline giggled, jumping up the stairs, two at a time. When she arrived in front of Leymann his face shiny with sweat and sprinkled by stubble, she quietened down. They stared at each other for a couple of minutes, her mouth straightening a little.

"Just thought we might have a quiet drink," she said, the timbre of her voice rising until her request turned into another fit of giggles.

"It's a bit late, Caroline, or a bit early, I mean." She frowned.

"But, we might as well, there's no way I'm going to work," Leymann said softly, his voice deepened by sleep. His headache had already begun to evaporate.

Once Caroline had sat down beside the dining table, she reached for a packet of cigarettes from the coat she had tossed to the floor. Leymann switched on the lights and looked on disapprovingly.

They began to talk about Caroline's mother whose impending trip to India had been a rumour that had spread along the whole street.

"Terrible what happened today," Caroline pressed a hand to side of her lip and looked at it to ascertain the circumstances of her lipstick, "that car and the shooting, did you see the funny man's face?" Then, she began to laugh again.

"What did happen?" asked Leymann, concerned but distracted by Caroline smoothing her T-shirt over her breasts.

"I think the driver was shot, he was so bald!" She watched Leymann's face fall a little and then shook her head into a state of composure. Leymann slowly approached the table and sat down, cupping his face in his hands.

"Oh, come on, it might not be serious at all. What do I know, anyway? I just saw the people milling around the car. Did you know that guy or something?" Caroline sipped from her bottle, watching with alarm as Leymann's frown turn to tears.

"I owed him a tenner," Leymann mumbled.

Carl walked with three others. Even the late night shops were closed by now and the streets were empty. They had mastered a special walk: each step of the way, their bodies would jiggle upwards and downwards. It was as much to do the with the feel of their loose-fitting clothes as their soft shoes. Carl didn't care to return to his father's place. Apart from it being so cramped, it looked like it was going to rain and rain never let him sleep except when the corrugated rattle beat in time to the counting of sheep or fast cars.

They were on their way to the squat. Carl had slept there most of the week. He liked it there. It was a large four bedroom house on three floors. Electric heaters and hot rings on a fire hazard stove kept the air unhealthily warms and dry. The electricity company had forgotten this house and appliances were on day and night. The floorboards were all either bare or black wood speckled by lines and dots of lighter shades of paint.

Though there was a busy road nearby and the floorboards were fragile and splintery, the house seemed luxurious. Carl and his friends were astonished about living in such large rooms. The largest rooms they had known till then were assembly halls and gymnasiums. It was the other three who had found the place and bought and fitted the many-levered lock. In the front room on the first floor, a ghetto blaster sprayed bass through the house. As Carl rolled a joint, one of his friends made some tea.

"Jonathan!" Jenny said walking into the room in her slip.

Jonathan awoke drowsily. He had been dreaming about Loddington. "Yes!" he said with a start.

"You were sound asleep. I've brought you some blankets," she said, laying them down.

Jonathan attempted not to look at her body. It was slim and well-kept. Though her face looked old to him, Jonathan was attracted to her and wondered what his friends in Loddington would have made of the situation. Jenny smiled and waved goodnight before walking into her bedroom.

Sitting in a chair beside the dressing table, Jenny looked into the mirror. She applied a little night cream around her eyes and thought about her house-guest. She wanted him to like her and decided that she might have been too cold and brash during the day. He certainly seemed safe and she had no regrets about inviting him home.

Jonathan unwrapped a couple of blankets on the sofa and was soon asleep, his shoes dangling from his feet and his suit indelibly creased.

Carl and his friends sat in a circle. Their pupils were glassy, the whites of their eyes rheumy and bloodshot. They would remain in their positions even after the cassette had stopped. As Carl stubbed another roach into one of the holes in the floorboards. Everyone else stared out through the window. It would be dawn soon.

Jensen drove on. The streets were brightly spot-lit, as if they were successive stages for the homeless. Every decametre, there were new actors. Jensen hadn't turned on the music, choosing to think instead. He hadn't worked hard enough today and he would have to make up for it tomorrow.

Caroline slept on the sofa. She had fallen asleep in mid-conversation. Leymann decided not to wake her and crept painfully out of the door at eight-thirty in the morning. It had been while chatting to Caroline that he realised he would have to go to work today. He had reports to file and what with Jocelyn in hospital for an ambiguous ailment, he would have to fill in. If he didn't think about the pain, he could now walk quite easily. However, some signs from yesterday were there. He felt almost feverish and he had no desire to eat.

A relentless stomach rumbling escorted him on his bus journey. The park looked pretty, all pale yellow and dark green grass shining with dew and sunlight. It was all just as if he had never really made the decision to leave the company, as if his life was more entrenched than ever in Property Developments PLC. Nearing the office, he felt a little stronger, as if prior events had reinvigorated him. Perhaps even his old stamina was returning to him.

Jenny played 'hard-to-get'. She woke up at the normal time, spent an hour on grooming, ate a piece of toast, drunk a cup of coffee and left the flat. Jonathan was left dozing without an alarm clock. However, thanks to the morning traffic jam, the sound of hooting had disturbed him. The stainless steel watch his mother had given him when he was thirteen was always reliable and he was soon up. Quickly, he folded the blanket and washed up. He carefully propped his rucksack against the sofa, looked about the flat as if having lost something, and went out.

Sleep still clung to his eyes and there was dirt under his fingernails and on his teeth. In the dark of the stairwell, he recoiled at the smell. The disinfectant made it seem as if, at any moment, a patient might be wheeled through the building.

Sunlight streamed through black shutters and still Jocelyn didn't move. Outside, the busy traffic, all one person cars and lorries and machines, moved slowly in lines.

"Miss Hanwick?" asked the nurse. Jocelyn raised an eyelid and gazed at the pretty, private nurse. Jocelyn did not answer, merely opening and shutting an eye.

Jensen slept well to the purring all-night music-channel from next door. Just outside, a tramp unzipped his trousers and emptied his bladder on the roots of the palm trees. Further East, the flaming lights of warehouses glimmered and some tens of thousands of men in their thirties slept quite soundly in tents. Nearby, a new night-club attracted a fee-paying couple of thousand to its stroboscopic wilderness.

Leymann sat at the word processor, generating his report. Yesterday's visits may have been unsuccessful but they all had to be set down and filed. Today, he'd call for police backup and see how those unwilling to move would respond.

Jonathan had always had a good memory. His uncle had taught him systems for learning, when to employ mnemonics and the best times of the day for remembering. He looked out of his correctly selected bus in earnest and clutched firmly to his ticket and the change that was all the money he had in the world.

The sides of the streets were filled with brown water. A sewage pipe had burst early in the morning. Jonathan looked at the schoolchildren walking on the pavement. They were being showered in sewage as juggernauts caught the gutters. Species of fruit he had never seen shone from fruit-seller's stands and on one street-corner stood an old man surrounded by people. He was wearing a khaki, forties-style raincoat and a pair of black framed stone-glass spectacles, grey locks of hair intermittently covering either lens. One cigarette hung from his mouth, then two, then three, then four, all at the same time. To applause, he then swallowed and seemed to regurgitate them, whilst they were lit. A couple of coins bounced into an empty hamburger box beside him.

Further on, a small boy in a navy blazer was being hit about the face by two others while a boy in jeans and a white jacket emptied the small boy's pockets. A man, eccentrically dressed in a blue suit and long red neckerchief was walking while he talked into a portable phone. All the time, Jonathan vibrated with the bus. He was excited about his vantage point. Loddington had too few buses to make them worthwhile carriers.

Smoking, despite the signs, seemed permitted. The top deck was lit up by a sun strewn dusty light. Jonathan, an occasional smoker, asked another passenger for a cigarette and a kind looking old woman with silver flyaway hair picked one out of her pocket and lifted it up in a shaking hand.

"Give us the cash for it, then," she said before Jonathan handed her his coins.

He lit the end with a book of police station matches that he had picked up the previous day. It was curiously light and he felt as if he was inhaling icy air. None of the enthusiasm he had expected from the nicotine came to him. As the bus stopped at a traffic light, the muddy gutter water was a patchwork of red and brown. Lowering his eyes, he saw a wrinkle-scarred man sitting on a short brick wall beside a pool of blood. His right arm was poised on a large handkerchief that covered the top of his head and flapped over one eye. The other squinted, only opening wider to gaze down at the scarlet mottled grey slabs. On his other side a frowning skinhead sat looking at his watch, perhaps waiting for an ambulance. Jonathan looked towards their feet and saw crooked paving stones.

"Hello, Jonathan," said Jenny, exposing a few teeth as she smiled.

"Why didn't you wake me?" Jonathan asked, half angrily.

Jenny put her finger to her lips as she saw Leymann abruptly limping through the door. When he was further into the office heartland and behind a partition, Jenny spoke. "I don't want to give the impression I'm seeing someone from the office, do I? It's a violation of rule 72."

Jonathan's mouth formed a circle as he sat down.

Carl, Errol, Johnstone and Robert had slept quite soundly on their mattresses. A small black-and-white television set, its back nearly torn off, played a Dvorak symphony.

"Errol, you awake?" asked Carl, standing on his mattress in a pair of red-heart-on-white-background boxer shorts.

"Now I am," he replied, peeping his head over a cold and damp flower-print duvet.

"There's that march today, council cuts. Council cuts, council cuts," Carl repeated.

"Will you shut up? It'll just be some boring long walk. I'm not going."

"This one looks serious," Carl said, interrupting his chant, "loads of people from the estates. Everyone'll be going. Come on, I'll buy you a pint if you go. Fair?"

"I'll think about it," said Errol before submerging himself in the duvet and returning to a dream of Selznick proportions, set on a desert island. Errol sat on a rock, looking out into a turquoise ocean as naked island girls massaged his back. The only thing that troubled him about it was the nagging feeling that he had picked up the cinematography from a current television advertisement.

"Come on," Carl said, "let's join my brother inside. And Johnstone's. Let's show them he's not the only person to refuse to wear a tag. Errol, it'll be a riot." Carl spoke more plaintively. "There'll be girls."

Carl stared at the test-card as his body tightened. The other two boys left for the next door room, where it was warmer.

Caroline made some instant coffee in a plastic party cup she had found. Leymann had bought the cups when he began renting the flat. He had the vague idea that one day he would have a housewarming. Caroline's T-shirt was stained with grey patches, the cotton smeared like a chromatogram. The coffee was hot and she held the cup from its topmost sides before leaving it half full to go to the bathroom.

The bath and basin were all off-white. The carpet was a black particle-flecked grey. A tube of toothpaste and a few disposable razors sat on the basin dimples below a shelf carrying a cheap aftershave.

The denim had a good feel to it, Caroline thought, as she pulled her stomach in and tugged her jeans to her waist. Her thin hair had set wrongly during her sleep and squatted in clumps at the back of her head. Looking into the mirror, she lifted her shirt to see how the alcohol had affected her skin. Her small breasts sat still, aiming forwards as she tried to rub some sticky patches off her stomach. Then she left the flat with the cup in her hand.

"Caroline?" shouted Mr. Atkinson who was outside his shop, putting out a new sign: "SPECIAL OFFER: STUNGUNS HALF PRICE."

"Hi," she said daintily, walking past him and into the florist's.

Mr. Atkinson had liked Leymann when he first moved in to the block. He seemed to have a military man's quickness of mind. When problems like burst mains and gas-pipe explosions had broken the calm, at least on weekends, Leymann had taken charge and acquitted himself valiantly. But the recent Leymann, aimless, lethargic and discontented made Mr. Atkinson think of a shirker on AWOL. Now, he was watching Caroline, Mr. Atkinson's childhood sweetheart, climbing down Leymann's stairs, looking dishevelled and perhaps abused. Mr. Atkinson was enraged. He decided to have a word with Leymann when he returned.

Laura Hanwick was sitting in a fast-food restaurant, a milkshake the size of her head on the table. Laura hated her father. He had been sinking into an ever deeper depression ever since his belle, a twenty-three year old art student, had left him to do a business course in America. Laura looked at the dentist's endorsements on the milkshake container and thought for a moment what it would be like to live in America.

Laura's hatred for her teachers had swelled. She didn't like the way they all smelled and sniffled in tattered tweed skirts and jackets. She felt that her school marks all tended to be inversely related to the effort she put in. Even the school buildings seemed decrepit and gloomy, all barely vertical red brick walls masking rows of wooden desks that looked as if they had suffered mortar-fire. Her father made things even more difficult by constantly reminding her of the cost of the school fees and then sending her out of the house, saying he wanted to be alone. Thus, Laura's truancy had snowballed. She was, these days, forever running through hedges on the Eastern borders of school grounds and out into the cafés of the local village.

She was sitting with her friend, a particularly ugly child with greasy black hair and a puffed up face. Her parents worked overseas, in Southeast Asia, for the government, and she hardly saw them. She was busily scoffing her second cheeseburger and reading the paper. Laura stared vacantly out, as a line of chocolate milkshake lengthened under her nose. She took another puff from her cigarette.

"See the grand prix last night?" asked one of Leymann's colleagues.

"No," Leymann replied, turning to the tall young man whose moustache was drooping today.

"Very good. Heard you had a hard time, yesterday?" he asked, puffing on a slim cigar and eyeing a bruise on Leymann's face.

"Well, sort of," Leymann said, "not really, though. You know how it is sometimes."

"Unlike you to have a tough day, isn't it?"

Leymann considered whether his younger colleague was trying to rile him or just engage a senior in conversation He had been taking a break, closely reading the local tabloid paper. The front page showed a line of women queuing up at an emergency social security office, their children in their arms. The headline, "UNIONS DON'T CARE", sat above it. He shuffled for the weather pages.

Jensen sat on his rowing machine, busily swinging his arms on the oars. In the background, a disk provided music as 'Good Morning, America' flickered in luminous wide-screen colour. After a glass of orange juice he ran out to the car, holding his mail.

At the petrol station he read a letter from England, the pages tinted red from his sunglasses.

"Got some money to help the needy?" said a small Latino boy, who had run onto the forecourt.

"Oh, fuck off back to Tijuana where you came from," an annoyed Jensen replied.

The letter was from Property Developments PLC, telling him that Jocelyn would be unavailable and that a man was taking charge of the transatlantic deal. The company was still prepared to meet the present terms and arrangements and hoped that all contracts would be honoured. A new contact at the office in London had been arranged should he have any outstanding queries.

Jensen drove off, thinking about his conversation with Jocelyn. He wondered if he had been too forward. 'Was Josie snubbing him?' he thought.

At the office, too, Jensen was uneasy. There was No one at Jocelyn's house when he rang and what with the workload being slim, Jensen was left to ponder and let his mind wander. He wanted to try Jocelyn's ex-husband's number but he had fallen out with him many years ago. Jensen had always believed that she had been treated badly by him. The ex-husband, it seemed to Jensen, was more interested in sleeping with as many women he could than anything else. Jensen believed that adultery was a sin.

Carl and his friends stood together, buffeted by the crowd. Thousand upon thousand had come to the march, which had now been halted. A line of riot police stood in front, shields and visors gleaming. In the crowd people were continually moving as organisers handed out legal advice leaflets and paramedics administered first aid for bruising, fainting and dizziness. The demonstration had been scheduled to end hours ago.

The black, white and brown heads seemed to engage in a sinister dance, all pushes, pulls and mysterious contortions. The crowd seemed to have the leisure time to spend the night there.

Carl stared out provocatively, looking directly into a

policeman's eyes. To Carl and his friends, these men and women who stood before them — their faces uniformly white — were not merely agents of repression, they were to blame for everything that was wrong in their lives, past and present.

A few sound-systems on the pavements played out drumming and bass-lines that matched participants' heartbeats. The smell of leather, dirt and even hot dogs rose from the road as three boys in their twenties shattered signs that had been held up high during the march. They then somehow piled them in front of a local bank branch. As women shouted, fists aloft, a first projectile scored a direct hit.

It was a slow day for Mr. Atkinson. It was made worse by the defective central heating. He had been sweating all day. The stun guns, rejects that he had got at half wholesale price, all sat grimly in their boxes, stunning No one. All the while, he was tempted to go next door and pay a social call to Mrs. Blueheart and, of course, Caroline. As he plucked petals off a daisy that had fallen from a delivery van outside, he wondered about Caroline and the passions in her life.

After typing a couple of letters, some long housing inspection reports and reading a copy of Property Digest, Leymann was left staring out of the window. He could see building workers catcalling, cement-mixers churning and the sky begin to dim. Leymann felt well, as if his lost confidence had regenerated itself. Even writing some of the reports had been fun.

Jonathan had been busy with the coffee, taking a new pride in delivering the correct mixtures to the right desks. By immersing himself in his work he quickly forgot Loddington, his parents, his friends, even Jenny who would, now and again, coquettishly smile at him. Even the man with the moustache seemed more agreeable.

"Ah, so how are you finding the work?" asked Leymann, as his fifth cup was laid in his hands.

"Not so bad, sir. I didn't know I'd be doing coffee but..."

"Work like this and I'm sure you'll have the best of

promotion chances," Leymann said, grimacing a little at the state of Jonathan's attire.

Jonathan looked sleepy. The same lines he had noticed on Jenny had appeared as faint scars under his eyes. Jonathan liked Leymann, he was the only one who seemed to talk with him. He had a slightly annoying paternal air about him but he seemed warmer than the others.

"I always like to get the newspaper," said Laura's friend.

Laura looked at her for a moment. She knew that her friend only bought it to look grown up.

"Subversive is what my dad says about these people, look at them," she said, rustling the pages. She tossed the newspaper at Laura who had begun to study a boy at another seat. She looked down at the late edition of the local tabloid. A large colour photo of a black man with his mouth open covered the first page. Inside another picture from the same riot showed five soldiers with raised batons over a group of four boys handcuffed on the ground.

"Come on, let's get out of here," said Laura after failing to attract the attention of the boy in the adjoining seat. They left the paper behind and a young man in a striped uniform scrunched it into a ball. He played catch between his hands for a few seconds and popped it into the dustbin, filled with hamburgers and long plastic straws.

Carl had finally arrived at the hospital emergency centre.

Jensen opened the diary on his desk. The failed actress brought in a cup of steaming coffee and Jensen smiled. Tonight was his singles' night, a dinner in a night-club organised for professional single men and women. His secretary returned to her mahogany-finish desk and opened her daily chlorofluorocarbon package, swallowing the processed scrambled egg at breakneck speed. Outside, palm leaves swayed in a brisk wind and a Buddhist canvassed for support. The leather squeaked under Jensen.

"Fucking hell," said Robert in the wide open space of the

hospital waiting room. His sharp manner contrasted with the laid back insouciance of the others. He was larger than the others and his friends found his emotions easier to tug upon. They steered their heads to the ground, watching insect journeys on the floor. The fluorescent lights glinted disquietingly from the magazines on a badly built table beside them. Behind a sheet of bullet-proof glass, a receptionist filed her nails to keep awake.

"You boys with Carl Roeng?" There was a pause as a white coated man waited for a response. "Do any of you know whether he has health insurance?" The boys slowly raised their heads.

"No, I suppose he doesn't," said Errol after blocking an attempted punch from Robert. Errol had become the group's spokesman. "Why, should he?"

"No, I just wondered. You see, we have a very good emergency centre here. He won't have to wait for more than an hour and he won't be in pain. He's already on anaesthetics now. Anyway, it's just that we might have to keep him under observation and, well, there's no ward space for him."

A pair of policemen came through the doors as Robert faintly remembered a story about Carl and his mother, something to do with putting people out, perhaps something about gas or a chemical.

Out of gas and water rose these flowers. The deep, rainforest scent flooded the room. Wilting tulips sat evilly smelling alongside sweet pink roses; flower-less green plants shaded exotic cacti and tubs of plant food; a large grey cash-register shielded a girl of uneven pallor from any customers that might venture in. Behind her, a curtain of sansevierias hid the white wall.

Caroline often picked off the chocolates, what her mother called the European chocolates, from the display counter. She had tired of every centre except the brandy liqueur which continued to spring a surprise. Her mother, Mrs. Blueheart, was having her late-afternoon nap, the hours of which lengthened day by day.

When a benefactor—Mrs. Blueheart never called them customers—who wanted to buy some flowers entered the shop,

Caroline would wistfully watch as if observing a fly. Then, she would light a cigarette to kill the scent that had attracted the shopper in the first place.

"Do you know which hospital Jocelyn's at?" asked Leymann.

"Er, I've forgotten the name. It's on the tip of my tongue. Let's see..." The moustached man continued to think. He was frowning and looking at small scraps of yellow paper on his desk. He couldn't remember. Leymann would have to wait until tomorrow.

Jonathan had been doing an errand and had found a packet of cigarettes in the lift. There were four left and so far he had restrained himself from lighting one. The only box of matches was on Jenny's desk. He was hungry and each sandwich his co-workers unwrapped was like a stab in the navel.

"Not having lunch?" asked Jenny at the time when families around the country were putting their youngest children to bed. Busily eating a thin slice of crisp bread and some yoghurt, she didn't wait for an answer.

Jonathan watched her eat her high fibre, low fat meal, with abhorrence. He had been on his feet all day and only now had been able to sit down at a seat. It was meant to be for waiting clients but he had made it is own. His suit, creased and stained enough to attract passing glances, had carved itself into the fabric of the chair. Without a shower, he felt groggy and unkempt. His hair floated greasily above him as he stroked his rapidly developing beard. His tie was scored by creases and falling apart. His eyes had darkened and Jenny showed a hint of fear when, after a few seconds, he answered, "No."

Mr. Roeng sat breathlessly in an armchair. Putting his hand to his mouth to cough, he let the white, plastic bags fall to the floor. Inside them were assorted packets of powdered soup, cans of beans and a carton of milk. Hoping that Carl would return soon, he had spent a few pounds on a two-pack of strong lager. If buying beer would endear him to his son then he would, even if it prevented him from buying a second-hand paperback he had had his eyes on for a couple of weeks.

Listening to a large radio, he mulled over the news.

The last item considered the riots and it got Mr. Roeng thinking about what he wanted for his son. He thought about how quickly Carl had become apathetic and indifferent. When Carl was younger, his teachers said that he used to mediate in his peers' arguments and that he was bright for his age. But as his teens approached, Carl changed. Mr. Roeng suspected it might be his own imagination but he thought that Carl's maturing inertia could even be seen on his face. Carl's eyes lost their sparkle when he had been out playing with his friends. In due course, he dropped out of subjects that his father had seen his son fascinated by only a few years previous. "Heroes," said Mr. Roeng as he heard the numbers of injured and the single fatality.

Leymann replaced the receiver. It was without precedent: the police couldn't come to help him vacate the property till next week. He picked up his briefcase and carried it out towards the lifts, smiling at Jenny and Jonathan on his way.

"We've come to arrest Carl Roeng," the officer said to the receptionist. Robert and Johnstone had left for Mr. Roeng's place while Errol had sat patiently on an orange plastic seat.

Leymann's ears tickled. The bus worsened the problem, vigorously vibrating as he clung to a pole. From his pocket, he took out a much-bruised apple and looked at it before rubbing it on one ear. Leaving the bus, he saw the silhouette of Mr. Atkinson taking in strings of bullets from a cardboard box outside the shop. Nearby, queues of schoolchildren issued from chip shops and confectionery shops.

Mr. Atkinson watched Leymann jump off the bus and trip slightly on a leaf of lettuce that had been meandering across the pavement from a vegetable-seller. Moving his hands to his spectacles, Mr. Atkinson stared at Leymann's worsted trousers, then at his hands and the shoddy looking case he was carrying. It was these spiny legs and clammy hands that must have wrapped themselves around Caroline's naked body, he thought.

Robert watched a woman on the bus. She was about forty but looked older and was half reclining on the neighbouring two-seater chair. Her brown hair was messed up and her black top had slipped off from her shoulder, exposing a red rash. Lower down, fishnet stockings adhered to her legs. So short was her skirt that it looked like she had nothing to cover her crotch. She smiled at Robert, following his eyes down to her underwear. Then, she straightened up, crossing her legs, moving her hands to her lap. Her face was brimming with powder-less makeup. Robert imagined making love to her as her thickly painted lips twitched to the flicker of the passing streetlights. She looked down and unzipped her purse, a much weakened plastic case with a broken steel fastener. Robert saw condom packets and green social security literature peep out amongst the brown change. She was looking for something and had taken out a loose photograph of a man holding a baby.

Robert returned to thoughts about Carl and his father. As he looked out of the window, over Johnstone's shoulder, he saw the woman, now outside, talking by the bus stop to a tall man with a small head. She was laughing and smiling.

Johnstone was silent. He presumed that Robert, too, would be thinking about Carl. As they passed Keir Hardie Avenue, Johnstone peered at the sign and then at number 61, the squat. Its lights burned in the darkness.

"Evangeline?" said Jocelyn, almost sprightly in tone.

"Mum? It's Laura."

Jocelyn lay corpse-like, her silk dressing gown, caught on the cotton sheets as if by static. Dark curves had settled below her eyes and they reminded Laura of a Spirograph set she had been given when younger. All the foundation colour had gone from her mother's face. Her colour matched the writing paper on the table beside her.

Laura was wearing her green school uniform, her hair tied back under a jade coloured boater. She had changed in the toilet of the restaurant and had taken a taxi, dropping her friend off on the way. Unaccompanied children were technically not allowed into the wards but for a small surcharge, the hospital tolerated bending the rules. The receptionist had pointed to a charge card and smiled nervously as she was paid.

"Evangeline," repeated Jocelyn, as she watched Malcolm Benson enter the room.

Carl lay across three plastic chairs, mumbling about his favourite football club. His bloodshot eyes were trained on the ceiling, a yellowy mass of dark patches, cracks and smears. Beside him, a grey-haired man, bathed in pullovers, spluttered phlegm into a polystyrene cup of green tinged soup. A tired nurse stood in the corner of the room telling off a queue of patients. "Behave, otherwise it'll take longer," she was saying with a sore voice.

"Hello, Mr. Atkinson," said Leymann when he had crossed the road. A heavily laden lorry caused him to wheeze a little as he asked, "see the paper? Looks like we're in for a recovery." Leymann referred to piece in the finance pages of the evening paper.

Mr. Atkinson winced. The faulty street-lighting wavered and, in the darkness, Leymann's face became grotesque. A scent of garlic wafted through the smog and around them. Leymann remembered once having had one of Caroline's garlic mushrooms at a friendly dinner with Mrs. Blueheart. Perhaps, Caroline was trying out her favourite recipe again.

"I saw Caroline coming out from your place, this morning."

"Yeah, she was really drunk, last night. We had quite a good time. I was pretty tired, though...seemed like I went up and down all night," Leymann replied, remembering last night's painful climbing of the stairs.

Mr. Atkinson stared angrily at Leymann for a couple of seconds before entering his gun shop in silence.

Leymann went to his flat and found that he had recovered his nervous twitch. For a while, he breathed in the smell of cheap spirits rising from his sofa. Then, just as he decided to cook up another frozen meal for his waste disposal unit, the phone rang.

"Leymann? Tony here," said his friend who worked at the post office company.

"Oh, hello."

"Haven't seen you for ages, what do you say we go to the pub?"

This time Leymann relented.

Jonathan surveyed the office. Jenny had told him to wait for her since she had some things to type out. Jonathan was uneasy and tired of the cycle of apprehension. The office was like a battleground and he was like a lone, infantryman amongst enemy cavalry and heavy artillery fire. The day had ended badly, after all. Jonathan had been given a chit in a brown envelope, notifying him of his monthly salary, pay that would be meagre enough back in Loddington. Jenny's keyboard-tapping gave way to silence. She eased herself out of her chair, yawned and left for the ladies' toilets on the floor below. Jonathan stared at the unfinished typescript and then at her patent leather handbag. He had planned this venture well, grabbing the bag and opening it to insert a card that he had written on and removing her house-keys and a twenty-pound note. All the time, his eyes were on the lift doors, a pair of shiny grey walls about to be sprayed on by ageing cleaning women.

Jenny zipped her skirt back up and looked into the mirror as she washed her hands. Through the haze of airfreshener, she decided that she would be extra nice to Jonathan tonight. He was a tough boy but also terribly innocent and it was up to her to make the first move. She was sure he liked her—she knew that he sometimes stared at her—but she realised that he would never try anything.

Jenny wished she had taken her handbag with her. Her powder and lipstick were in it and her lips had lightened since her lunchtime snacks. In the lifts, her thoughts returned to the subject of home furnishings and carpet colours.

Mr. Roeng was reliving a death-in-custody court-case he had won. His client had been a mother of three. It had been soon after Mr. Roeng's wife had died and he had been intensifying his legal work. Looking back, it had been paradise to live where he had. Everyone knew each other. Pleasant glances were exchanged instead of the neighbourly grunts he got around here.

In the middle of the housing complex, a man from one of

the large houses across the road had left a burning rubbish pile. Slabs of foam, tube-less television sets, broken microwaves and slices of wood lay banked up, charring or flaming. Around the knoll, Mr. Roeng's neighbours greedily gathered things that tumbled off the heap. One short but muscular man in a denim suit, his face scarred with age, sat on a tree stump and nursed a burnt hand. His eyes, lit up by the flames, were filled with melancholy as he saw others seize what he desired. Robert and Johnstone, not the youngest in the crowd, jostled with the takers. Robert was laughing as he held a table up in the fiery air. The table-legs scratched at his jeans as two residents looked on, hoping they might benefit from his heroics.

"Come on, Rob," said Johnstone, who had become a little sentimental. Johnstone had grown up in this area. His mother still lived in one of the nearby shacks. The flames were all that lit the scene and the thick black smoke billowed up into the sky.

From his window, the man who had started the fire watched on. He had decided to throw away the useless junk that he had collected over the years. To exact the highest price from the property developers, he wanted his house to look sparse and so bigger than ever. He would buy new microwaves, televisions, videos and home computers for the next house. A home was not a home without them, especially when one had children.

He watched an old man smile as he held a broken radio, grasping it using his shirt cuffs in case he got burnt. He watched others, mostly silhouettes, as his wife called him for dinner. The sight of his rubbish being reached for and desired made him feel comfortable.

Mr. Roeng, too, had begun to watch the bonfire of technological vanities. He had woken up to the smell of burning plastic. Quickly filling a basin with an intermittent stream of water, he had cautiously looked around his room for signs of fire. It hadn't been long before he was on the doorstep, watching the flames. He gripped the heavy, oval water container and sighed.

Leymann was listless. He regretted his decision. "Er, two

lagers, please," he said to the barmaid after puncturing a wall of suited men.

Tony sat with two post office colleagues. They were chatting about government surveillance cases that had gone wrong, the conversation beginning with a general grumble over the extra work that the government was giving them. The subject didn't interest Leymann. As he guiltily laid the beers down on the table—he hadn't the money to buy a full round—he thought about his brother. A flickering TV set sat on a hanging plinth, displaying images of the American McCarthy era with dubbed music of the time. The secret services certainly seemed more lucrative now, he thought.

Mr. Roeng stumbled back in surprise. He seldom had visitors and all words seemed foreign with an unused vocal cord.

"Mr. Roeng?" said Johnstone, whose father had once known Mr. Roeng quite well.

"Hello, son, what's happened?"

The world had become dark but for a shard of feint stroboscopic light. Mr. Roeng looked at the boys' faces. Johnstone saw it in Mr. Roeng's eyes. He knew.

Jensen ate a pastrami sandwich while flicking through a magazine that the receptionist had left on his table by mistake. As he looked at the stylised advertising-framed pictures, he felt as if his clothes no longer fit. Each interview, each feature seemed to paint the world in happy colours. Families were always strong and supportive, millionaires either seemed to have made it easily or have coolly inherited it from loving parents. Either way, despite all the money, they seemed unaffected by it. They were simultaneously down to earth and shining in the sky.

"It must be because I'm doing nothing, Jensen thought to himself. Apart from the contract with Property Developments PLC, there was nothing much for him to do. He grimaced every half hour as he remembered there was no urgent need for him to be searching out for new development opportunities. For years, he had gone seamlessly from one high-rise project to another. There was a time lag to recouping the profits so there was no rest if he was to keep the earnings' juggernaut rolling. Money from his last three or four projects wouldn't reach him before he got to Mexico, if that's where he was going.

Jonathan stopped for breath under the canopy of a glass tower. His mouth watered as he saw the windows of the restaurant on the ground floor. Heads bobbed up and down over shallow, long-player sized plates. Heaped cutlery magically greeted their mouths, one utensil after another. He wouldn't eat here. One of the moustaches blurred by cream belonged to a Property Developments man. Jonathan had noticed him before, how he worked late into the evening. Now in shirtsleeves and eating alone, he looked vulnerable and unparalleled.

Sebastian, dressed more casually than Frezzle, had just learned that he had failed some of his most crucial university exams. Frezzle wondered whether this was connected with the seemingly sudden lengthening in Sebastian's brown hair as he explained what news he had about his life. Mainly, this concerned Frezzle's father who had said to his son he didn't care anymore about whether he was gay. As long as his son passed his banking exams, just as he had done decades before, Frezzle would be given a house. "If I pass them, that's it! No more threats. I'll have my own place, no mortgage and no ties. I'll be free," he said, slamming his beer bottle down onto the wooden table.

Listening to all of this was Sebastian's escort. Lena, an ambitious girl from Loddington, often cried. Wearing a white blouse and short black skirt, she rested her high heels. She remembered reading in one of her mother's magazines, many years ago, that height was status. That's why she bought the high shoes, the first thing she bought upon arriving in London. She was a bit disappointed by the lack of difference between London merchandise and that nearer home. There was little between the shopping experience on the streets of London and in the shiny thousands of square feet shopping malls of the North. Shopping in London was done outdoors and there was no moat of car parks, that was all.

After shoes, she went for a haircut. A beautiful, but

expensive, black bob hung around her head. Men she met in London told her she was beautiful. They would remark on the combination of black hair and hazel eyes, or her long lashes and faultless lips. They told her she could be a model. Lena put it all down to her height.

Leymann took the occasional glance at Lena when Tony's conversation became unbearable. He tried and failed to catch her attention.

Sebastian, the failing undergraduate, had a large face and had taken to wearing sunglasses indoors. His loud and haughty laugh echoed around the pub. His father ran a prominent chain of fruit-sellers and every time his name was in the financial pages, his fellow students would taunt him. In the past year, he had become a loner and in the past month or so he had begun to regularly hire escorts when in public. He believed there was a philosophical justification that underpinned his actions. He was convinced that a crucial change in the relationships between men and women had occurred roundabout the time he was going through adolescence. Women now frightened and intimidated him and this he blamed on the nineteen-sixties.

Lena had seen the advert in one of the evening tabloids. It was just when life had taken a sharp swerve for the worse. Most of the people on her estate were older than her and had paid a subsidised price to own their own flats. By the time developers had come to offer them money to move, the mostly retired residents wanted to move to the country. Losing in the ballot, she left for a bed and breakfast while the council tried to find somewhere to re-house her. In the waiting time, she fell into debt, just the escort agencies began to boom.

Choices were always easily made by a confident girl of thirteen. Where so many people around her displayed their stress symptoms by being unable to make decisions, Laura just strolled through them. She decided that her mother didn't want to talk. To each word Laura uttered, Jocelyn could make no response. Gently, Laura unhooked her hand from her mother's and left the room to descend in the lift. It was getting late.

Jenny sat and stared at the piece of card: 'Sorry Jenny, I am broke. I have taken the house-keys so that I can pick up my rucksack later. I'll return the twenty pounds when I get some money. The keys will be under the doormat. No money in this — Jonathan.'

Her first reaction was to believe Jonathan was a coward, just like all the men in her life. Then she began to wonder whether she had been too harsh on him. After all, he was new to London. Maybe she shouldn't have treated him so strangely. Finally, she thought about tonight's dinner—that was her last twenty pounds and she couldn't seem to find her bank card.

"There was a cheque for thirty grand and my colleague— you met Mike, right?—well, he jacked the whole thing in and just nicked it!" Tony laughed, as falling from his cigarette. He noticed that Leymann was hardly listening. "Come on, Leymann. Cheer up. Anything wrong? How have you been?"

"Alright. It's been a tiring few days," Leymann had been thinking about Jocelyn as he drank more, "the other day I got into quite a mess." Tony rearranged his cigarette pack and plastic lighter on the table. Leymann could see Tony wasn't interested. A little later, Caroline and Mr. Atkinson came into the pub. Caroline looked bored and detached as Mr. Atkinson sat beside her at the bar. He was grinning and soon pushing a huge, red cocktail towards her. Mr. Atkinson looked different, he was wearing a baggy leather jacket and loose fitting jeans. Caroline wore what she had the previous day.

"So, Frezzel, there's some philosopher that I'm sharing my rooms with. He's a real drongo. He doesn't go out much and doesn't seem to do anything except read and write." Frezzel laughed.

High up in a gothic, fortress-like building, Jules Handers sat writing. On his desk lay a hundred paper booklets, some typed, others scrawled on in black ink. A glass of vintage Bordeaux perched on a side table as the man read a newspaper, being careful to look through the lower portion of his bifocals. Outside, by the courtyard, the fragrance of Cuban cigar smoke wafted along a hallway as drunken screams and laughter rose from the boats on the nearby river. On his shelves lay books on philosophy, on literature. They were new books. A well thumbed copy of his favourite poetry book lay beside a back issue of a men's magazine and further away a copy a journal entitled 'Culture'. A Bob Dylan record lay flat on the turntable. The man's hair was prematurely balding, his eyes a faint blue and his nose a flattened pug shape.

He looked at the Rothko poster on the wall and then out of the window before settling his eyes back on the desk. An internal memo reminded him about tonight's meeting. A group of the college's leading lights was to discuss the state of language. The meeting was to be in his rooms and apart from buying the wine he hadn't prepared for it. He was to give a talk and he wondered if the pages on the desk could be used for it. They were outlines that he used to remind him of recent developments in the new relativist philosophy and cultural theory. His mind wandered, now focusing on the state of his carpet before he mused on the use of a single tea-bag to make six cups of tea. "Blessed are the pure in heart: for they shall see God," he said to himself, recalling St. Matthew. "Or shall they see financial rewards?" he added, deliberating upon his purity and its unjust recompense. There was something troubling him about a sponsorship deal he was negotiating with a large South Korean corporation. There was to be no large sign but there was still to be an office in the courtyard. In the free market world, at the end of history, he speculated, property was the one lucrative thing his college owned. Looking over at a picture of his relative, Alex Handers, he mumbled to himself: "The more intelligent a man, the more capable he is of suffering."

Jenny walked past some restaurants, thinking about Jonathan. Occasionally, as she pushed her hair back because of the wind, she caught the eyes of large businessmen leaving cafés, all looking harsh and unsatisfied. On one street corner, a tall black man in cycling gear was giving tickets out. A pop group was filming a video in a nearby night-club and needed extras. Jenny didn't feel like going but, as she passed him, she took a ticket anyway. Neon lights and tourist bureau de change signs blurred around her as she looked at it, wondering to go.

Mr. Roeng hadn't been outside the area for months. The only times he left his room were to walk in the housing complex's grounds or to shop at the supermarket. Robert told him that they'd have to skip the fares on bus and Mr. Roeng suddenly felt regret at buying the beer for his son. As they passed the bonfire, small children poured water from used paint cans to quash the blaze. On the bus, Johnstone removed the petals from a daisy he had picked from the fire illuminated grass.

It was late when Laura arrived home. Her father wasn't in and an impoverished baby-sitter was seated on the sofa, watching TV while Laura's younger sister slept soundly in her bedroom. Laura put her key on the mantelpiece and rushed upstairs. She was too hungry to eat. After undressing and brushing her teeth with an ineffective electric toothbrush, she lay in bed, twiddling the knobs on her Walkman before going to sleep to the sounds of an emotional psychologist giving tips to transvestites.

Jonathan's eyes clouded over as the bus journeyed to Jenny's flat. He was lucky that it had arrived as he reached the stop. Fiddling with the keys, he pushed and pulled at Jenny's door, entering uneasily. Quickly and quietly, he gathered his things and put his rucksack on his shoulders. The room was scented with an expensive perfume, from a bottle given by Jocelyn to Jenny at an office Christmas party. Jocelyn had tired of the smell.

Jonathan went into the bathroom and twisted the taps before cupping his hands. The water refreshed his face but he wanted to use the shower. With an air of curiosity, Jonathan entered Jenny's bedroom and sprayed a little perfume on his neck. The smell was feminine, though the label said it was unisex. Jonathan hoped it wouldn't linger.

Looking around at the messy bedroom, he reflected on how luxurious it was. He thought about his parents' bedroom in Loddington, where everything was old but not old enough, frayed but not frayed right. He felt uncomfortable now and went to write the word 'thanks' on a notepad. He placed the keys under the inside-doormat and left.

Lena tried to drink as many non-alcoholic cocktails as she

could and kept asking Sebastian for money to buy crisps and peanuts. Usually, her clients took her out for dinner, she had never expected to be wined at a pub, especially somewhere so far from the West End of London. She yawned and kicked her heels, looking around the pub at faces she didn't know: Caroline, Mr. Atkinson, Leymann and others. She couldn't wait to be home in bed.

"Aye...bastard," said a boy in a jacket priced at one tenth of the average annual wage. He was in a group of about twelve similarly dressed young people. Conspicuous in his stained suit, Jonathan looked up from where he had been sitting for hours, wondering where to stay. "Good threads, funny...heh!" one said to him. Another, with a plague of acne along one side of his face, began to shift his foot around, kicking Jonathan in the groin, his arms and stomach. Jonathan sighed and watched blood roll from his nose as a fifth visit hit his face. Squatting on the ground, a faraway look in his eyes, he saw a woman in a fake fur coat in the distance. A little boy stood shouting on a corner.

The streets near this fight were brightly lit. The area had once been a centre for sex shops and shows but had changed over the years. Recently, it had come to be a locale dependent on the advertising industry, its restaurants and bars, its video processing studios and photographic suites all living off the art of selling. Down Jonathan's street, a police van fortunately braked. A constable rolled down his window and shouted at the group of boys: "Come on, fun's over, let's get out of here, nice and quickly." The group left.

Lena dropped her glass. Sebastian had been spiking her drinks all evening. Caroline had left the pub by now and Mr. Atkinson sat reading a gun magazine that he had brought with him. He didn't acknowledge Leymann's presence.

"Well, I think I'll be going now," said Leymann to his friend. Now, Mr. Atkinson, sipping from his three-quarters' full pint of bitter, cautiously looked towards him. He suspected that Caroline had left to meet Leymann, secretly behind his back.

It was chilly and Leymann unfolded the collar of his overcoat as he walked down the street. Beside him, for twenty seconds or so, were rolling hills, a trace of the original green belt land he lived on. At night, on this pool of pre-development earth, there was a surf of dark silence. Only the noise of a duck or a park-keeper's car could sometimes be heard. As he jangled his keys, listening to his footsteps, he wondered whether he would ever see Jocelyn again. He wouldn't go to work tomorrow.

By the time Robert, Johnstone and Mr. Roeng had arrived at the hospital, it was closed to relatives and all new cases. Vandals had attacked the main operating theatre some months ago. They destroyed thousands of pounds of equipment and because of this the ruling body had decided to prohibit visits after a certain hour, even for relatives of the seriously ill. They couldn't afford to risk the new equipment. As drops of rain began to fall, the three of them sat at a bus-stop, praying.

They eventually escorted Mr. Roeng back home. Outside the shack, Robert and Johnstone stood nervously looking at the remains of the bonfire.

"Let's go to that guy, what's his name?" Johnstone said, breaking the late night hush.

"No, I don't feel like it much. You can go, I don't care."

"Oh, it'll be fun. Come on."

"No," Robert looked to his shoes, "I think I'm going to visit my mum. You go, though."

"You think Roeng's going to be okay?"

"Which one?"

Jensen ordered three different dishes of Thai food at a restaurant by the ocean. The choice of food in LA was an unchanging wonderment for him that served to kill his depression. Even so, he mused, the ethnic cuisine was a poor sop for all the crime and poverty caused by immigration. After pouring out some sake from an American-style pitcher he looked at the palm trees and ice-cream parlours outside. He thought about Jocelyn and four or five other professional women with whom he was infatuated.

"Jensen?" said a man in an Iranian accent. Jensen flinched and then relaxed. He had built a house for the man in an expensive suburb of the city.

He was looking older, his face overweight and haggard in different places, perhaps the result of two many saunas and Jacuzzis. The man spoke to him for a little while about how he was worried about his wife and children who were back in Tehran. It seemed he wasn't able to return to collect them, thanks to missiles coming from Iraq. The conflict would last longer than both world wars.

"How's the house?" he asked unsurely as he was trying to remember the man's name.

"Oh, the house! No insurance. They said it was an earthquake zone."

"Everything's in a fucking earthquake zone here," Jensen smiled.

"Anyway, I sold it. I'm staying at the Beverly Hills. The insurance companies don't like Iranians, you know."

Jensen reflected on the man's nationality and decided that as long as a foreign national had enough money it didn't matter in the least where he came from. "Join me?" he asked. The man was meeting someone tonight.

"Leymann? Don't you ever get tired of life. Don't you?"

"Well, sometimes."

"I mean, I just wonder about you nine-to-five people. I run the shop for my mum sometimes, but I couldn't imagine selling flowers every day for the rest of my life."

"So you take off the state?"

"I suppose I do. But the state doesn't offer me a way of life I want. The least it can do is keep me alive."

"I don't know," Leymann said shaking his head, "all you do is go out and get drunk every night."

"Not every night, Leymann. You sound like my mum."

Pause.

"I just wondered, because you seem so assured and confident about things. They don't seem, things don't seem to trouble you much."

"What sorts of things?"

"Just generally...just general things. I mean, I see you in the supermarkets sometimes. You're very organised, aren't you? You carry around a list. You don't drink much, do you?"

"You've been watching me. That's interesting. Well, yes I enjoy a drink, if everyone in the room is drinking."

"You have that twitch, though."

"What twitch?"

"That funny thing you do with your neck and shoulders. You kind of lift them up and twist. That shows a kind of inner tension, I suppose."

Leymann pondered his twitch. He didn't think anyone had noticed it. He worried over what his work colleagues must have thought.

Caroline took a cigarette box and some cigarette papers from her jeans' pocket. "Want some blow?"

"Er...no, thanks. I don't think that's very good for you."

"Got asthma? Any relatives that have?"

Leymann nodded.

"Well, this cures it. Either that or it saves it from coming on. Honest." She licked the paper with her tongue.

Leymann thought about this for a little while. His first reaction was to take a paternal air and tell her to get out. But he was tired and after his decision to quit work, marijuana seemed of little consequence. A few years ago, he would have snatched the stuff from her and given it to the waste disposal unit. But he was slightly drunk. He had had to be to not turn Caroline away from his door.

Caroline burnt the black and began sprinkling it onto the cigarette paper, along with some tobacco from a stripped cigarette. It was the early hours of the morning.

Leymann edged closer to her, looking at her brown pony-tailed hair, her thin T-shirt covered frame and her slim waist. Confidently, he put his arm on the back of the sofa and around her. Caroline looked up from her rolling and smiled at Leymann. Only a private home and property allowed one to do this, Leymann thought.

After spooning out the leftover peanut flavoured sauce from a small steel bowl, Jensen attracted the waitress' attention.

The scent of spices and the sake-heat in his stomach was intoxicating. Paying the bill with a grey credit card, he got up and walked to the car.

"The weather in downtown LA is dry and clear. Tomorrow, there'll be hazy sunshine and a maximum temperature of eighty degrees Fahrenheit. Air quality will be average in the coastal areas and poor in the valleys. Next on KBW291, the latest track from..." Jensen switched to his CD.

Jonathan got up, wiping his nose on his suit. He had read about a hostel in the area and decided to try his luck.

Leymann and Caroline laughed together.

Jensen drank a few beers in a bar in Hollywood. A football game purred loudly and the chatter of unshaven men with big bellies filtered around the room. The secretary from his office had suggested he go here. He wondered whether he's taken the addressed down correctly. Jensen made a half-hearted stab at searching for the address in his pockets. Bars for professional people were nearly always side by side with bars for the poorer classes. He resigned himself to breathing in the smoke and listening to police sirens playing outside.

The gates to the hostel were steel and shut. On them was a battered sign, drawn on using an unsound stencil. Jonathan could see was a dark alleyway, lit up by a single yellow workman's spirit lamp. A few riot barriers lay scattered about like obsolete machinery on a factory floor. The blood was still dripping from his nose and he felt dizzy. He stumbled in surprise when he caught sight of a group of boys, about his age. He hadn't noticed them. They had left the cover of deep, black shadows.

"You'll have to wait till seven, tomorrow," said a tall boy with sunglasses perched at the end of his nose.

"Only five more hours," said another, his arm in a loose sling that also carried a batch of untidy newspapers.

Mr. Atkinson sadly stirred a mug of cocoa. His flat was gloriously rococo in some parts. There were velveteen covered walls. There were modern prints of young girls with flowers by artists he couldn't remember. The there was a plastic kitchen floor with holes in it. Hygiene, where it mattered, was not one of Mr. Atkinson's strong points. Once-white cupboards were layered in dirt, grease and vegetable oil. The squatting plastic bin-liner contained nothing but tin takeaway cartons. Two black crossbreed dogs, stinking of faeces and urine, fought over a fallen rib. The soft scent of paraffin, used by Mr. Atkinson to clean his guns, also perfumed the air.

Sebastian drove his convertible sports' car at high speed. The leather seats squeaked as Lena and Frezzel were pulled around. They chatted to each other distractedly as Sebastian, his sharp blue eyes staring ahead, thought about how little time he had left in London. Just another day and he'd be back in his rooms, chatting with his tutor and queuing up at the canteen.

With the breeze blasting her hair into her eyes, Lena took gulps of air. By the time they got to Sebastian's she'd be sober again. Frezzel seemed interesting. She recognised his insecurity and ambition.

Jenny had been listening to the band with some satisfaction. A slim, young boy with short brown hair and thin lips had bought her five drinks. As they danced, she stared at the shiny mohair of his pressed suit.

"I find these places really superficial and shallow," the boy said when they had sat on chairs overlooking the dancefloor.

"Me too. I don't know why I came in here, really," she replied

"Me too."

"Well..." Jenny smoothed the hair on the side of her head with her fingertips, waiting for him to say something interesting.

"What do you do?" the boy asked, not letting himself be distracted by the music or the dry ice percolating in the club.

"I'm a property advice consultant," Jenny replied, her mouth straight and her eyes sparkling for a few seconds under the light of a stroboscope.

"Yeah? You're going to have to give me some tips. I'm

thinking of moving." He seemed impressed. He tried to subtly look Jenny up and down.

"What do you do?" Jenny asked, taking apart a cocktail umbrella.

"Arbitrage. I work at Piggobank...yes, I know what it sounds like."

"What? That banking sounds boring? Some might say the same about property development." Jenny strained to hear him more clearly. The music was getting louder.

"No...er...I didn't mean that. I just meant that most people laugh at the name, Piggobank. It started off as a bank especially for children. That's why it's stuck with the name."

"Oh."

"Want another drink?" he said, pushing a silver can to his lips. "No problem," he mouthed, wondering whether he was making any headway. He was slightly anxious about what time he had to be in at the bank in the morning as well as worrying about whether his girlfriend would be at the club.

"No thanks, that's okay," said Jenny, before looking towards the stage and seeing the band step off and move towards where they were sitting. "Well, alright then."

The boy smiled and walked away to one of the bars, trying to hide his face with his hand as he pushed his way through the crowd.

Two heavy bouncers stood at the doors of the club. Beads of sweat roped themselves down their necks and past their spiny bow-ties. Jensen showed both of them his membership card and ID and they granted 'good evening.'

His blood raced as he pushed the lime into his beer bottle. There were fifty or so suited men and women chatting at small circular tables. At the bar, where the glow of music was brighter sat two women, sandwiching a man in a sailor outfit.

Leymann had flinched when, earlier on, Caroline had kissed him on the cheek. Now, he lay asleep, not used to the excesses of dope. Caroline lay beside him, gazing at an all night comedy programme on the television she'd moved in from the hall. She had had a vague notion of seducing Leymann. For her, marijuana had the effect of a strong aphrodisiac. However, she was now wondering whether she should leave. The T-shirt she had so exuberantly taken off was under Leymann's hind regions though and she didn't feel like disturbing him. Occasionally, his dry, relaxed fingers would twitch, exciting Caroline's breasts, where his hand lay. As long as the movement wasn't too extreme and the programme was of slight interest, Caroline felt a few pleasant sensations.

Laura dreamt of birthdays. She thought about the moment when the lights were turned off, curtains drawn and she was required to exhale. This ceremony warranted her staying up late, she thought.

As the pair departed, leaving for the swimming pool at the back, Jensen approached the lone sailor.

"Buy you a drink?" he asked, noticing the Mondrian-grouped medals on the front of his tunic. The sailor nodded, swivelling his stool towards the bar.

His face was oval and clean-shaven. Hair that had once been Brylcreamed back was now white and thin. On of his eyes was paralysed, a motionless brown iris set shallow in its socket. The other eye was a sharp green. They gave him a knowing, arrogant look. His suit was clean, a navy linen accented by gold buttons and borders. His lips had geometric curves and his hands were smooth but for a scar separating a thumb and a forefinger.

Ordering only a glass of tap water—rare in a part of town that was used to sucking from the mountain springs of France and Switzerland—he began talking.

"Leave lasts only a few days," he said in deep South Carolina intonation.

"I see," said Jensen enthusiastically, "I don't know much about the services."

"You ought to make it your business to, if you want to fight for God's own country and get those reds," he paused, "it's mostly boys from our states that understand, you see...not you sophisticated Southern Californians. Jobs are pretty scarce down there, you know? You been East and South of here?"

Kane held a reasonable navy rank considering his age and family. Jensen failed to hear it.

His job, aboard a nuclear-powered submarine, was a crucial one. After years of code-courses, he now constructed the daily series of characters required to launch an assortment of devices from an on-board atomic arsenal.

It disturbed Jensen a little to know that someone with such apocalyptic power frequented the same slightly pathetic places Jensen did. But as a tune he recognised mixed in, he relaxed again.

Jenny had hardly looked at the band. Behind the battalion of cameras, the rigging crew and the extras had been a foursome distinguishable only by their lack of charisma. They were there to mime. The managers had advised them that it would be better that way. Otherwise their audience might detect differences between their recorded presence and their actual live performance.

They'd had a string of hits, parading themselves up the charts with a certain regularity, at least for six months. Bones, the lead singer, had changed his name from the one given him by his mother. He had told the press that he didn't want to be thought of as quarter-Scandinavian and that Eric rang too much of Eric the Red.

But Bones was an apt *nom de guerre*. They jutted out from him. His face, in shadowy light, looked like a miniature photograph of a contorted gymnast, his rear sculpted like the seed of an avocado.

"Jenny's a nice name," his voice was young, almost falsetto.

"Thanks," Jenny replied, anxious not to seem awed by the fact that she was talking to a famous pop idol and that he was agreeable at that. She wasn't awed, in any case. She was quite conversant in the transient nature of fame, impure with marketing men. It was money, not notoriety or publicity that Jenny sought.

Bones had been talking: "...you know, my father runs a sportswear shop in Canada. The first records were all made thanks to him. He gave me forty thousand dollars—peanuts.

But, then, he didn't want to spoil me. Don't you hate that, when spoiled kids...I don't know." His Canadian accent slowly emerged.

Jenny listened, searching for a mirror and happening on her misplaced bank card, in one of the recesses of her bag. The young banker supposed to be getting her a drink had disappeared.

The passing trains, rather than the stench of antiseptic, disturbed Carl's sleep. Dimly lit up by the streetlights outside, the ward had a late summer feel to it. In the middle of it was a desk at which a solitary nurse was straining her eyes. Carl heard music in the distance. A page of squared paper floated to the floor.

Mr. Atkinson found that he couldn't sleep. At an antique wooden table, he sat reading a gun catalogue, sometimes noting down a metric calibre down in pencil or looking out of the window.

Caroline softly tiptoed out of the room, holding her T-shirt. Leymann was sound asleep.

Pausing only to lift her arms and thread them into the shirt, she left the flat and came out into the cold air. Tonight would be her mother's last night before her trip. From tomorrow, she would have the place to herself.

Mr. Atkinson watched Caroline leave Leymann's door. She seemed to look satisfied, almost sated. He winced, got up, drew the curtains and went to bed.

Jonathan slept soundly on a piece of discarded foam. A couple of boys around him lay down, dissecting his rucksack, looking for change and finding a loose apple. The boys sniffled a little and got up, stretching and squinting in the morning light.

Errol slept alone in the squat. The casualty nurse had ordered everyone out after the waiting room had had to be converted into emergency bed space. Errol didn't bother to scream or shout, like some of the others. He just shrugged his shoulders and left.

Jenny bought a drink for Bones and sleepily listened to him.

"What did you think of the video...well, it's difficult to tell what it'll be like. I mean, once the company edits and rearranges it, it'll look completely different, certainly not just a few guys miming on the stage of a night-club. Those special effects were used in a Coca Cola advert...you're quite tired, aren't you? Why don't...look, why don't you come back to my place for a cup of coffee. Everyone thinks that stars always have someone around them but, hey, we're a lonesome breed."

Jenny grimaced.

Kane walked out by the pool-side. Shaped like a giant heart, it had large red dollar signs painted on the bottom and they curved and swayed as the breeze shook the water. Nearly everyone was back indoors. Los Angeles grew cold at night, this time of year.

He peered into the pool, standing on the side and leaning against the trunk of a coconut-less palm. The bark felt dry and irregular to the touch. Kane stared out and watched the occasional insect, lit up by the moon, drop from a leaf and into the pool.

Sebastian and Lena said goodbye to Frezzel at his door and left. They were headed for Sebastian's father's place and when they'd got to the flat, Lena said that she should probably be going home now.

"Nonsense, it's by the hour, isn't it?"

"Well, yes."

"And I can pay, so don't worry."

Lena settled down in an armchair and breathed in the bouquet of antique books. Sebastian's father was touring India and since his departure the drawing room had taken on some of the paraphernalia found in Sebastian's Cambridge rooms. Upon the large Iranian carpet lay empty cans of beer.

"What beautiful books!" cried Lena.

"Yes, I told the old man to get them. He was doing a deal, some large fruit company. One of the directors gave these books to him as a present. They belonged to someone in the Caribbean.

Not that my father's particularly interested. He's more interested in the spiritual, Eastern things, you know. They help me though, what with my studies." Sebastian then threw a guava at Lena who had been glancing at her watch. Her daily wear contact lenses couldn't track it and she failed the catch. The fruit landed on a large volume of company reports.

"So what makes a girl like you become an escort? I mean... why not just stay where you were, where your parents were... Wood...Loddington—isn't it?"

Lena smiled briefly. "Life's different up there. I like London," she said, regretting her responsiveness.

"I like London, too," Sebastian replied, sitting on the arms of Lena's chair, alert and awake at the sight of her garter belt, "it's just that...well, you're not exactly from a rich family. Why would you want to go lower, as it were?"

Sebastian smiled, swing his legs and lifting a china coffee cup to her lips. He looked at her thin blouse and the lace beneath it.

"Look, I didn't want or mean to hurt your feelings or anything. I am really most terribly sorry," Sebastian paused, "yes it's seventy-five pounds, here's eighty...look, please stay." Lena brushed him away and stood up, straightening her skirt.

The door slammed shut. The cup had dropped.

Sebastian sunk to the rug and picked up some of the broken pieces. "Such a stupid, common little girl," he said, rubbing blood and porcelain chips on his jeans.

Lena was out on the street. The morning light gave Mayfair's buildings a dreamlike quality. Picking a taxi from a line, she got in and looked out at the passing shops and offices. The streets were empty and the ride back to Hackney would take a matter of minutes.

Jensen was troubled. All his daytime hopes of losing his loneliness had evaporated like the spirits that his body had broken down. Slowly, he walked across the small dance floor and out into the garden. Kane was sitting on a sun-bed, smoking a joint and staring up at the sky.

"You don't see many stars in LA. It's the smog," Jensen said. But Kane wasn't looking for stars.

Jocelyn sweated into her sheets. She was feverish. During the night, a left or right eye would flicker. Outside, the branches of one of the manicured trees would brush up against the window pane.

"Name?"

"Jonathan."

"Date of birth?"

"Twenty-six, zero-seven, sixty-"

"That's the twenty-sixth of July..."

"No...I mean..."

"N.I. number?"

"N.I.?"

"National Insurance?"

"Here."

"Do you have any other form of identification?"

"I have a birth certificate."

"Not acceptable. Too many forgeries. Passport?"

"No, I haven't ever been out of the country."

"I'm afraid we can't let you in."

At the entrance to the hostel sat a scowling volunteer member of staff. She wore clear grey spectacles and although only about twenty-eight, had the airs of someone older. For the past week or so, she had been breaking the social security strike. She believed it was unfair to take it out on the customers. Picketing prevented her from going to her own office. It wasn't so much physical prevention as emotional. She hated being glowered at and told that charity destroyed all that it sought to help. So she travelled to charity-funded hostels, lodging herself in doorways and alleyways, keen to manage the running of these private refuges.

At this hostel, other volunteers would repeatedly tell her that her presence wasn't wanted. But, as if fighting a lone cause, she would appear at the gates at the same time every day and seek to vet prospective clients.

The hostel staff were, overall, a kindly bunch. Most of them were unpaid volunteers whose job it was to give the homeless a cup of tea and a roll and place to stay for one night before sending them on their way. Sometimes, the pressure of work made them irritable but the sight of anyone being turned away made most of them feel uncomfortable. One woman volunteer, who was just back from a holiday in Latin America, had tried calling the police when the blackleg turned away a disabled boy.

Robert had felt embarrassed when he arrived at his mother's house. She, however, was wholly indifferent to her son's sudden appearance. She opened the door with a flash of recognition across her face before silently turning around and walking back inside. Robert gazed at the old, broken tricycle in the hallway. The red paint had chipped off since he had rode it as a child. It was still in action, though. Robert's toddler cousin now used it.

Jenny sat in a thirties' style armchair whilst Bones made two cups of coffee and poured some champagne into a couple of glass beakers.

"This is my old flat. Before I made it, I used to live here and I sometimes come back when I want to do some thinking. I used to write a lot of my songs in here, Jenny."

"Really?" Jenny had never heard any of his songs properly, let alone his lyrics. "Nice guitar," she said, pointing at a guitar balanced on a stand.

"It's not the best of my guitars, but it's the one I know best. Give you a song, then?"

Jenny turned to look around. The carpet was a made of a thick tapestry-like fabric, as if a white floor had been covered by decades of crushed vegetables and tomato ketchup. There was only one window and over it lay a stained fly-net. The bulb was low power and yellow. The fridge, filled with twenty bottles of cheap champagne, emitted more light when the door opened.

Boom! Boom! Boom!
Let me get you into my room!
We can do it all night!
You know, it'll make you feel alright!

Jenny laughed a little, staring at the hole in the guitar. Then, she suddenly began to wonder whether Jonathan had locked up her flat properly when he had left. Almost simultaneously, she thought of a black man who lived on a lower floor. He had always been courteous to her on the occasions they'd passed each other on the landing but, somehow, she was worried he might have ransacked the place.

Leymann beamed. He thought about the joy of waking up at an early hour and not having to suffer as the alarm clock rang. The joy was unparalleled in modern life, he speculated. After dozing for a while, he jumped out of bed and pulled morning material from his letterbox. It had been a long time since he had had the time to properly read a paper. He had been piling them up in a cupboard for a long time, as if he was establishing a research library or a birthday newspaper company, like the ones advertised in the classifieds.

Leymann leafed through to the back pages, passing the for sale 1930s' radio cabinets and worn out lawnmowers. He took a quick glance at the daily quotation, today's was from Somerset Maugham. "How the gods must have chuckled when they added Hope to the evils with which they filled Pandora's box, for they knew very well that this was the cruellest evil of them all, since it is Hope that lures mankind to endure its misery to the end." Leymann wondered whether the quote of the day was a crack by the editorial staff or the work of a daily, lone classified space buyer. He turned to the national paper.

A last minute hitch in the peace deal being negotiated in Moscow appears to have scuppered an arms' limitation treaty concerning WRS bombers. The strike continues and a woman jumps off a tower in North London, leaving two children orphaned. An increase in social security spending was ruled out yesterday by Whitehall officials. A new report by the Looms Foundation says that breathing in too deeply could cause a strain of the rare Bloomer's Disease found in one in ten thousand in the UK. American-backed Contra rebels have mounted another offensive, burning three villages to the ground in Central America. A policeman has

been gaoled for life after abducting and murdering four child
prostitutes. The Queen visited Australia, yesterday, where a
small aborigine girl...
House prices leap again.

Leymann remembered how, when unemployed, he would read the papers cover to cover.

Errol woke up with a pain at the bottom of his back. He had slipped off his mattress in the night and onto mark-inducing floorboards. His hunger was exacerbated by the knowledge that nearby shops were always vigilant. He had already discounted queuing up at one of the designated church halls for a food parcel. Instead, his strategy came to him from the openness of the windows. He could make out the sparkle of silver from across the road and had heard the sound of two cars leaving earlier in the morning.

The glints were only imitation silver. Polished chrome taps were good impersonators. Errol manoeuvred himself through the frame and discovered that the tension in his back had gone. He tramped about the kitchen, looking at the jars of tea, coffee, sugar and salt. He sleepily glanced at the busy interior decoration. This house and his squat were identical in shape. Perhaps, the garden was a little bigger.

Errol eyed human-like sculptures through the double glazed patio doors, each one copied from the same female body. Turning back he saw a message on the refrigerator, on the back of a brown bill-envelope. "Darling, your lunch money. Mummy made some French toast which is in the fridge. Use the microwave!"

"Anyone there?" someone asked from the hallway.

Leymann realised why he felt happy. The smell of Caroline's hairspray triggered off an image of her. Leaving his place in the paragraph about Lebanon, he looked up and thought about his situation. He thought about what happened with Caroline the previous night, registering that Caroline was now gone, Mr. Atkinson owned a gun shop and Mr. Atkinson was in love with Caroline. Leymann frowned.

"Bye, mum," Caroline said.

"Goodbye, sweetheart," said Mrs. Blueheart with watery eyes, "I'll write. Please be good, don't go too mad while I'm away."

Mrs. Blueheart stroked Caroline's gold crucifix before giving her daughter a giant hug.

"Time to wake, patients! Time to wake!" said a rotund nurse, blue blanket wrapped around her uniform.

Carl looked at her before lowering his head and gazing at the patient next to him. He wore square-shaped lenses, framed in clear grey plastic and was wearily reading a local newspaper. Carl smiled on seeing a poorly reproduced photo taken at yesterday's march.

From the windowsill, one could see a small private bus. Parents ushered in their children, armed with pack lunches. The trees that stood above them were bare and spiny. Boys played conkers once the bus was moving, a few in the back lighting up their first cigarettes of the day. They were all too young to miss their parents or even to be nervous, so it looked. Boys bathed themselves in the company of other boys. The only moments they spoke to girls were due to shortages of 'tabs'. Girls always seemed to have more of them.

Sebastian woke up slowly. He was a little excited and a little apprehensive about going back up. A year at college hadn't left him comfortable with boys and girls and this was now compounded by his own academic failure. He was used to treating people as he wished.

As he packed a large, patterned overnight bag with bottles of cologne and unread textbooks, he thought about how his friends seemed to have limitless adaptability. He was tense from the strain of being pulled by school, family, his peers and his class.

"Won't be a minute!" he said, breaking into a false grin for the taxi driver.

Errol looked at the young girl who was staring back at him.

"N-N-Nigger!" Louise snarled, through fear and revulsion.

Errol didn't flinch, startled by the look of innocence on the child's face. He extended a faltering smile, trying to put her at as much ease as a robber could. He felt the muscles on his lower leg tense.

"Get out n-n-nigger," she said, her consonants sharper, this time. Stopping herself from crying, she blurted out "my daddy says you don't belong here."

"I'm sure he would," Errol said, looking around at the room. She would have it lucky all her life, Errol thought to himself. "It's no wonder all this crap continues," Errol muttered to himself. Errol put the envelope with the girl's lunch money into his pocket and watched Louise break into sobs. Running out of the front door, after a twitch of the catch, a page of newspaper dropped and fluttered down from the hallway table.

Louise walked up to the page and made out the headline: 'Immigration: Rivers of blood run high.'

"You know, Jenny, you're a really nice girl," said Bones. "Some boys think that sex is all that matters, like the other guys in the band, you know? But I don't think so. All I want is a girl for sharing, you know, for sharing stuff. I like to tell her my problems, you know, my feelings. Sure, the songs have a lot of sex in them, but that's the way they like it, people like it, you know? Me, I'm a really feeling type of guy."

Jenny listened. She was a little scared to leave now, what with Bones' monologue. She had decided to exit at the first strum of his guitar but somehow she had let things linger too long. She resigned herself to staying and watching him move closer to her. The only affection Jenny felt for him was by way of his room. Working in the property business made her acutely conscious of it. She kept thinking to herself about how mad Bones was to keep a hotel room on instead of using his money to buy a second property. She thought through the tax disadvantages and calculated that Bones would still be better off, allowing some leeway for income estimates. She wondered what it was like to be someone so reckless with money. She thought about the attractions of living in a hotel-room, or on a short lease. Her eyes caught those of an actress on a poster on the wall.

"Boom! Boom! Boom!" Bones was singing again.

"Dad?" said Carl, barely standing up as the sound of sirens blew over the estate.

"Carl! How come...your friends said you were hurt pretty bad." Mr. Roeng gasped. "Thanks," he said, turning to the paramedics who had delivered his son to his doorstep. Carl limped to the sofa.

Carl had apparently benefited from the faster throughput at the hospital. He tightened his grip around the conveyor belt analogy as he wearily heard a paramedic explaining something to his father. Mr. Roeng nodded as he heard the recommendation that at least a week of rest in bed was needed for a full recovery. He listened with sleepy eyes, his lip drooping. Outside, other patients in the van were awaiting door-to-door delivery.

Laura decided that her mother was more important than school. She made the decision easily. Double French lessons held no sway with her. She took a bus, knowing that taxi-drivers were often too inquisitive when taking young people in their cabs. She stepped off on a street lined by clothing-shops. The French names on the labels here were full of grammars and codes, all more complex than anything to be found in her classrooms. She believed she had a good command of them and that this comprehension required a much steeper learning curve than any subjunctive.

She had long concluded that a capability for truancy was intimately related to money. With it, she could camouflage age with subtle lipsticks and eyeshadows. Her eyes would sparkle when she boarded the bus and the driver asked her whether she was young enough to use a child ticket.

Jonathan was told he could have a place at the hostel that night, as long as a more urgent case didn't surface. This meant him waiting out the whole day in the cold. He became numb with the chill as it gnawed away at his cheeks and legs. None of the other boys outside the hostel spoke much. A couple of them would sometimes point out a passing sports-car model and argue about engine sizes before sinking back into silence. Jonathan spent most of the hours with his eyelids sealed down, only elevating them when he heard a siren or the sound of a passing laugh. The clatter of building materials all around him sounded like a humming chuckle that provided a good base for the sound levels.

Any remaining fairy-tale dreams of meeting Lena had been bleached away. He knew he had been naïve regarding all of that. He could hardly remember her face in his mind, any more.

Lena sat in the escort agency offices, biting her nails as the other girls were told of their assignments. She was feeling quite pleased with herself, what with yesterday's earnings.

Usually, a this time of day, the girls would look at each other's assignments and say things like "Aren't you lucky?" or "Gosh, I'd love to go there." This was especially the case when the assignment involved foreign travel. Otherwise, these interchanges were more fake and really just ways of summoning up enthusiasm. There were quite a few students working now and some of them swapped knowledge about tests and essays. Others talked about how boring their unemployed boyfriends had become. Those from other countries who hadn't work permits remained quiet. Lena listened to a couple of girls in one corner of the room chatting about whether it would be better to go it alone and work on the 'phone-card' business. This involved paying a small commission to someone to place cards advertising services on telephone booths. Once a girl had a regular income, this kind of move was perceived as being more risky. Unless one had a nice home to live in and do business, any career reconfiguration was forbidding. But around the office there were always rumours of six or so friends taking in thousands of pounds, enough to pay the rent at an expensive central London apartment and a host of card-boys to promote the services.

Lena got her card and was relatively happy to get a job involving the escort of a television executive to an awards' dinner. That guaranteed meeting a few interesting people, she thought.

Caroline was happy to see her mother go. When she was on one of her excursions. She was able to enjoy some semblance of independence. Though her mother rarely knew of her escapades, Caroline felt as naughty and secretive as she was taciturn in her farewells. Mrs. Blueheart said this would be one of her last trips abroad. She said she was getting old and tired and that life would be downhill when she got back. Caroline suddenly felt a little sad about this confession and offered a "nonsense, mum!" She realised she actually felt quite proud. Her mother had always been more adventurous than other mothers she knew. They would go to Spain or France whilst Caroline's mother would save for longer to explore remoter regions of the planet.

When her mum left, Caroline sat in the bath, drinking sweet sherry from a bottle and dripping it over a magazine devoted to pop music and fashion. She looked at a jeans advert and the curves of a boy's bottom. Her eyebrows rose and her mouth twisted when she saw anything faintly sexual. At other times, she would compare her body, lowering the magazine, to those of the airbrushed.

"Hello? Leymann?"

"Yes?"

"This is your aunt...Leymann...remember me?"

"Yes, of course, I do. How've you been?"

"Never mind how I've been, pet. How's about coming for some tea this afternoon? Your uncle would like a word and, anyway, it would be so wonderful to see our successful nephew again. You've been keeping well, I trust, my dear?"

"Yes...quite."

"Never mind, pet," interrupted Leymann's aunt. "I'll expect you around four, alright. It's just that I...well, it'll be alright, what with work, four o'clock?"

"Yes, that's fine."

Leymann was happy to accept the invitation. Apart from the video he wanted to rent and see, there was little that he had planned for today.

Jenny walked to work. Battered flyposters emblazoned with Bones' name and photograph lined her way sometimes, and, at one junction, an ambulance sat waiting for an accident victim to be hauled in. Beside it lay a car with smashed front end.

She had touched up her makeup in Bones' room, feeling tired as mascara flaked into her eyes. Now, she was one of millions, trundling in one direction or another, occasionally checking analogue watches. The pavements were darkened by rows of FOR SALE, FREEHOLD and TO LET boards. From above, they seemed to fan commuters to their air-conditioned destinations. Some faces were taut, hungering for cigarettes or coffee. Others were flabbier, thinking about their families. Then, there were those thinking of nothing, blank from morning reams of newspapers and carton orange juice. When many had begun their journeys, the now cloud-blocked sun had been locked off, hidden by horizons of semi's and car-parks.

Troubles hung in many minds, a child failing at school, perhaps, or an obsolescent mother causing rifts. 'Why else was No one smiling?' Jenny asked herself before moving her cheeks upwards to create an artificial grin. As a hooting car stopped in front of her, a fist spurted from an open window and her cheekbones fell again.

Jensen drove away, moving down the Drive and looking over at the boutique windows. The pleasant dusty evening twilight, with its neon sky and reflecting, orange sunlight, had given way to harsh blackness. Unless one was in a house or at a party, LA became like a promotional film for a detective series. Cold, empty and frightening, the monotony of a thousand red and yellow bulbs fed Jensen's loneliness.

Laura walked into the department store with a confidence that could be traced back to her private school. It was at school that she had learned to walk. The shop, empty apart from a few residents from the surrounding streets, seemed to contain only wives and daughters. Beautiful fabrics sat taut around them. The rails and fittings, all shiny, looked as if they were alive and energetically vying for floor-space. Clothes were folded up so that by the time one had looked at them one felt embarrassed tucking the sleeves back and deciding not to buy. Laura cautiously lifted a jacket from a coat-rail and discovered that it was chained to it by chrome links. She let the strain subside and touched and savoured the wool.

Lena had tried working as a seamstress once, but the conditions had been too harsh for her. She always felt lucky not to have been able to sew too well. The factories off Brick Lane where she had gone to try and get a job looked like lost remnants of Victoriana, except that all the faces there were brown. The rooms, about twenty by ten, had around fifteen overlocks. These machines were antique, constructed when 'built-in obsolescence' hadn't been coined. Threads of different colours weaved in and out of the points of oscillating needles. Bangladeshi women operated the machines, supplementing the income of their husbands and families. In an adjoining room, more women cut cloth. The patterns would arrive at the back door, almost as soon as metropolitan designers had shown them off at glossy shows.

The odour of rolled and cut fabric made the air stuffy. Microscopic threads bred in the white walled workshop. At its edges were pinned patterns, old sewing machine advertisements and faded fashion stills. Everlasting light-bulbs, hooded with dust, had lost their luminescence and the workers squinted through their thirteen hour shifts. All around, the noise of the machines blasted out like angry modern classical music.

For hours, Jules idly watched the boats. The previous night's meeting had gone well. "History has ended," was the battle cry and over the sherry afterwards, all gathered had agreed.

"Hello, Jules," said Sebastian, opening the door and settling his bag on the ground. Jules nodded seriously, swiftly opening a textbook to show that he had been deep in thought and not just staring out of the window. "Had a good few days on your own, then?"

"Actually, I and a few colleagues have been engaging in a little study group. Quite a lively debate, as it happens."

"What? Sherry and cheap wine?" Sebastian replied, flicking through his mail and throwing away a letter from the Dean. "I mean, that's what you do, isn't it?"

Jules didn't feel up to any argument and decided to ignore

Sebastian's teasing. "Oh, here are the books you ordered. I looked through a few. Rather good. Everything fucked up and so on."

"Have them. They're all duplicates. I only ordered the stuff because my father told me to. Have them as a present. And thanks."

Jonathan had at last asked whether someone in the queue could keep his place. Not eating had given him an intense, chafing headache. The constant muttering of car-engines exacerbated the problem. The hours had been like those of an insomniac's in bed. Jonathan felt as if he was falling further and further away from reality. Waiting in the queue had even made him temporarily forget Jenny's twenty-pound note. He hadn't had the confidence to ask anyone to keep his place to go and get some food. But, as he was trying to summon up the courage, he fell to the pavement and was helped up by those on either side of him. He finally sprayed out his question. "Will you keep my place? I just got to go to the toilet."

"Most people do it right here in queue, or at least I have seen some. Sure, we'll keep your place."

No matter how many times the staff shined the surfaces, they never seemed to gleam. Behind the counter, star-clad men and women, one star for each merit, served the lines of people. From school children to unemployed families on a day-out to the owners of large companies to the homeless with a sudden pound, they all left the tills holding hamburgers high. Jonathan had found himself actually smiling when he saw the logo of the place outside the door to the restaurant. He ordered more than most after momentary speechlessness at the head of the queue.

"Don't let me see you slacken!" said an assistant manager. The Ph.D. student slunk back to her post and spat into a hamburger before wrapping it, bumping into the space-conscious fittings as she slid it into the purveyor-unit. For Jonathan's carefully examined tender he received above-average food.

Rapid Eye Movement had ceased. Jocelyn could see no moving images when she slept, only two motionless pictures of two ten pound notes, one for each eye. She studied the Queen's face. She looked surprised, her eyebrows hoisted peculiarly too high as her hair curled ever-upwards, almost launching her crown. The Queen's robes gave her a resemblance to Superman, though a tired and worn one. Past the anti-counterfeit, psychedelic patterns surrounding an ornate thistle, she focused on the little Britannia in the lower left corner. The cross on her shield looked askew.

Leymann felt pleased with himself as he looked out at people that seemed dour and melancholy. He felt free and subject only to his own whims. Instead of a barrage of bureaucratic orders he could only hear effervescent silence. He was no longer worried. He was no longer haunted by visions of homeless youths and shoeless toddlers on desolate looking fields. Money that he had saved would be more than enough to see him through to his first dole cheque, if, indeed, he needed to claim the dole at all. He had always been good at inadvertently preparing for hibernation. Injuries from the other day looked, by now, slight.

Jenny missed Jonathan as she bought a cup of coffee from the machine. Jonathan had tended to the duties well. He had perhaps even become indispensable. Others in the office missed him too and the coin-counting queue to the self-service cup dealer was a unison of frowns.

"Where the hell is Leymann?" said the moustached man, striding about the office and looking at his watch. Most of the others shook their heads before returning to their telephones and typewriters. "Jenny? You seen Leymann?"

Jenny flinched as she heard her name being called. This man, now assuming control of Property Developments PLC was disliked by everyone. Jocelyn had been tough but fair, Jenny thought. The fat man was tough for no reason at all. "No, I haven't. He hasn't called or anything."

"Well, can't you get in touch with him, then?"

"He doesn't have one, sir. At least, it doesn't generally work very well."

The man left, strutting elliptically and sniffing.

Errol looked out of the window and at the other house as

he unwrapped a slice of processed cheese. He had seen the little girl opposite leaving for school, clinging to a leather satchel and some paper money. She had never realised that Errol lived opposite her. The robbery's impact on her life had been trivial, Errol thought to himself. Then, he began to worry about Carl.

They had known each other since they were seven. The large school still appeared in their dreams. Sporting heroes and blackcurrant lollipops were common symbols for them and even when they had been apart when Mr. Roeng had worked in West London, their reunion had been smooth. The same intriguing girls had enchanted them, the same TV programmes had excited them and the same economics had exhausted them. Errol had been the first to visit when Carl's mother died.

It was around that time that his circle of friends felt crushed. They all held that there was nothing they could do, that all their childish enthusiasm for the world had only been just that. Around the time of Mrs. Roeng's death, itself emblematic of their sorrows, other events added to the grief. There was a sudden fracture. It issued a shared suspicion that the whole community was being hunted down. Fear was at the core of this and when all the hopes and aspirations, even for those who had gone onto further education, came to nought, people began to live only for the next day and sometimes only the next hour. Breaking and smashing things, even telephone booths, would become the most exciting hobby practicable.

Leymann thought about what to bring his aunt. There was an old packet of Rich Tea biscuits at the back of his cupboard and Leymann brought it out, observing the sell-by date before he pushed it to the rear again. Wearing a pair of jeans and an open-necked shirt, he counted out some money and transferred it to his pocket. A letter from the phone company squatted on his doormat. It was a large twelve inch package with the word "URGENT" upon it. He slashed it open and read out what was due. "Two pence," he said to himself, glancing at the eighteen pence stamp on the envelope.

The florist was closed so Leymann walked around the back,

ringing the Blueheart's bell as he looked over at the clothes' lines and shabby backyards.

Mr. Atkinson was reading a military equipment catalogue at his desk. The day had already been a busy one and he had had a hard time catching up with the morning's post.

Mr. Atkinson, who usually refrained from selling anything to customers who looked young, had sold two handguns, that morning. The clients had looked under thirty but their certificates and identification all seemed in order. "We want to join the SAS. Both of our fathers were in it," the energetic one in the army jacket had said, "there's no point in us wasting valuable training time."

This brought a smile to Mr. Atkinson's face. He had wanted to join the SAS as a teenager. "The finest fighting force in the world," he had spiritedly told them.

Turning away from his catalogue, which didn't seem to cure his general unhappiness, he stared at a brown, unopened parcel.

Caroline was wrapped in a towel. She had dropped off after eating a large salad.

"Caroline! Hi," Leymann said, surprising himself about how young he sounded.

Caroline gave Leymann a hug, saying hello and keeping the towel above her breasts.

"Er, I came to see if I could buy some flowers or a box of chocolates." Caroline sleepily kept her arms around him.

Jensen stopped at a little, out of the way, all night restaurant. The prices were cheaper but the fittings were the same fifties' shapes and colours he was used to in Hollywood. Tail-lights glittered through the windows and across the torn upholstery. He felt hungry and he knew that apart from breakfast cereal and a few jars of pickles there was nothing at home. He didn't want to go to one of the chain hamburger restaurants but now, as he saw old men sitting alone with their mugs of coffee, he felt regret. Two boys who had driven in from a night-club sat eating French fries, wiping their makeup off onto a napkin. They were giggling and puffing as they passed Thunderbird under the table.

At the booth, an ordering platform of speakeasy proportions, a Chinese American unrolled a steel blind.

"Yes, sir?"

"Quarterpounder and French fries. Well done. Black coffee." All the time, Jensen was wondering why he was doing this. It was quite a ride to Malibu Love but at least he would have been around people he could talk to or at.

"Thanks," the man said, before he roughly let the blind fall. He heard some disconcerting laughter from behind him as his change fell and descended a small slide into his hand.

"Now Carl, I'm going to make you feel at home. You haven't been spending a lot of time here lately but well, you know, I am your father. All I want is for you to be happy. I bought you some beer."

Carl smiled, in repose and queasy with Valium.

"...of course what with the Valium I don't suppose you'll be needing any," Mr. Roeng laughed, "I'll turn the radio on, shall I?"

Carl wanted to shake his head but he was too tired. By the time the switch had turned, he was asleep.

...Israeli troops opened fire on UN peacekeeping forces in Southern Lebanon, riddling an armoured vehicle with artillery and small arms' fire, the UN said today...maybe you'd like to talk about that or maybe a new survey out this morning claiming that nine out of ten of those between sixteen and twenty have never joined a trade union...Phone 291 2910...most washing powders are taking advantage of the new chemical technologies that give us whiter sheets. However, Antenna washing powder contains WRK, the solvent especially formulated in our labs, Antenna, you know it's right, you know it'll be white...right, first caller, Leelan, hello, I'm calling about your test match coverage.

Jonathan slumped back into his position in the queue.

Feeling sick as his stomach expanded, he thought of Jenny. He decided that, after tonight, he would have to find a way of returning to his parents' home. It was impossible to live in London. Property Developments had been a joke and even those nice to him seemed odd. Everyone he had met seemed to be wearing poorly constructed masks.

Leymann's aunt lived in a medium-sized detached property. Before she retired, she worked in a restaurant in Camden Town and Leymann, ever conscious about property prices, had long puzzled over how she could have afforded such a home. As if sensing his bafflement, she would always say, unprompted, that her husband had received a large tax rebate and that he had been paying life insurance premiums since he was eighteen. His aunt said that Leymann's uncle had always been scared of death, even as a child, and discovering that there was an insurance industry had been a revelation.

"Auntie?"

"Yes, dear?"

"How is it that you don't have any pictures of my uncle?" asked Leymann, wondering why he had never asked this question before.

"Ask your Uncle, Leymann, don't be rude, now."

Leymann looked around the room, at the tables and chairs.

"Darling, what is it? Are you alright? Don't be shy with you aunt, what's wrong?" As she spoke, she patted the armrest of her chair. Leymann stared at an alabaster egg.

Mr. Atkinson suddenly felt dizzy. His head moved in a circular motion as he lifted himself into the air, blindly stumbling and crashing into the door. The Falklands' syndrome attacks came after longer and longer intervals. As his face lay pressed against the pane of the door, he saw blurred cars and lorries, a small child playing with a football and a Union Jack flutter above a spire. A letter, typed and with two creases, was in his hand.

Jules had come back from the Arts' Cinema where he had seen the latest blockbuster from Hollywood. He sat down in silence for a few minutes, structuring his thoughts for the onset of essay writing. After a few sips of cold coffee, he left the room again, walking down the stone stairs into the courtyard.

"Hello Laura," said a nurse, counting credit card receipts at the till, "how've you been? I love your jacket."

"Fine thanks," Laura replied, stiffening her back at the attention. She was sure that the jacket was too big for her.

"Your mum's doing wonderfully. She can leave today, if she likes. I dare say, though, that if I had the chance of a little holiday, I'd stay a few days longer here. She looks much more relaxed than when she came in. Have you noticed?"

Laura listened to what the nurse said and hauled her satchel over her back before walking into her mother's room.

"Laura! You came to see me...shouldn't you be at school?"

"Oh, mummy, are you alright?"

"Of course I'm alright! I've just been sorting things out in my head. I feel quite refreshed again. How's your sister, is she enjoying herself? Has your father been looking after you? Poor man, he must be rushed off his feet."

"Daddy..."

"I've been a bit hard on him, you know. I've been thinking, I've been very, very hard on him. Anyway, it's all behind me now. I'm leaving for a little holiday and if you want to come."

"Where are you going?" Laura asked.

"The States."

"I don't want to go."

"Well, never mind. You can come during your holidays, if you want. I'll be staying with Uncle Jensen. You'll have a great time, this summer."

Laura frowned.

"Oh don't worry, darling," Jocelyn said before hugging her.

Jensen had been a little irritated by Jocelyn's call. He was glad she was coming but the call had awoken him after just a few minutes of sleep and felt like a stab in the shoulder. Jocelyn sounded different, too. She sounded even a little nonsensical.

Mr. Atkinson held a gun in his right hand and the letter in his left as he sat on the floor of the shop. He had pulled down the blinds and the room was very dim. He considered various options in his head. Mr. Atkinson was having a crisis. It wasn't only Caroline, though she was always going to be entwined with any crisis in his life. More generally, his life seemed to be heading nowhere. The silver and gold coloured glints from the triggers and gun barrels sparkled like candles as they caught shafts of sunlight. He looked up to them and realised that even his interest in guns had waned. His hatred began to focus on Leymann. To Mr. Atkinson, Leymann had something of the traitor in him. He had seen this type before, a Philby of a man. He had liked him, had had a great deal of respect for him and now he had defected.

He thought about his brother, Arthur and his innocent dislike of guns, his loathing of the gun shop. "Property is theft," Arthur had said to him once. Images of flat green land and Antarctic ice flows perforated his mind. He thought of the Falklands' War.

He looked around the room, at its shelves and neat rows. Increased violence on the streets hadn't helped the sales as much as he liked to think. Hunting wasn't as popular as before and Mr. Atkinson, while trying not to think about it, also knew that in this area, kids still used knives and bottles and crow bars. His father might have been proud of him for continuing the trade as long as he had but Mr. Atkinson knew that he'd never realise the turn of the century dreams of a weaponry department store.

The crisis was all in his hands. The Torpedo Gun shop was to be repossessed. It was everything to him. He had lived above it all his life. He had been born down the road. He had known the area when it was all just green fields.

"Land," Mr. Atkinson said simply and softly before a bullet passed cleanly through his brain.

...Welsh Guardsmen who had found worn tufts of hair on their hats have requested for new bristles. Apparently, the hair comes from the underbelly of the yak, found in China. Urgent pleas were made to embassies after stocks of hair in England were found to have been depleted...

"Carl? I've brought you a glass of milk," said Mr. Roeng.

Carl silently sipped from the glass and his eyes closed. In his daze, he wondered about Errol and why he hadn't come and visited him. He began to worry for his father. He looked pathetic and forlorn, a hopping figure anxious about helping his son. Even while Mr. Roeng read, he looked fitfully at his son to see if he was comfortable. But what Carl cared for—somewhere to live—was beyond Mr. Roeng.

Jenny read from a property magazine, drinking cold tea and looking for flats. The one great loss in her life was that she couldn't afford a mortgage. Her place was like an immovable taxi with a deafening meter. She could smell money being burnt when she slept. Each morning, she thought it was the day that she'd find somewhere more long term. Slow transportation from the outer suburbs crushed her. She was slowly realising that her only option would be to move away completely, leaving Property Developments and the sophistication of the city altogether. But she couldn't leave.

She remembered the sunny days when she used to walk more slowly to work, when she had time to glance at late commuters rushing coffee or couples savouring it. Often enough, those couples would walk into Property Developments, their visit the outcome of long deliberations. They would enter, one partner less sure than the other, and leave, as a rule, both bewildered. Only those with a rich relative to put up a deposit for them were really serious about signing anything

Jenny didn't get on with any relatives, rich, dead or otherwise. A pride prevented her from seeking help from any of them. It never harmed her to look, though.

Caroline had been looking at the pile of chocolate boxes in the shop. The shop was doing a promotion and she wondered whether it was the low prices that had attracted Leymann to the shop. Like the striped multicoloured ribbons tied around the boxes, her emotions were mixed. She wondered whether she'd been used. She wondered whether she wanted him only if he didn't want her. She knew that her real affections lay elsewhere in any case, with Mr. Atkinson's brother, Arthur.

At first, Caroline thought there had been a car crash or that someone had dropped a heavy box. However, the sound was stranger than that and then the years of watching television detective episodes helped to enlighten her. Quickly, she walked up the stairs to her room. They were uncarpeted and littered by stems and leaves and, occasionally, the petals of cut flowers. In her hand she held a Belgian chocolate. As she put it into her small mouth she thought about the sound. Its flash had faded enough to create doubts that it had ever happened. Standing on the landing, towel about her, she licked melted cocoa from her finger.

In her room, she dressed to an instalment of a practical joke programme with hidden television cameras. A secretary was using defective office equipment and the camera was filming her responses. It reminded her of Leymann's mumbled speech during his sleep. He had talked about his brother and surveillance and cameras. As the secretary began to punch a broken franking machine, her discomfort was transmitted to Caroline. She switched off the set.

In a red turtleneck sweater and jeans, she walked out of the back door. Here, in a backyard that had been unused since her childhood, the odours of rubbish and dust grew in the wind. She remembered boys playing with bows and arrows and toy guns and how the arrows landed in a yard that seemed so much larger. Time had made even the washing line seem shorter. She remembered the picnics organised by both families, the Bluehearts and the Atkinsons, in fields further on and the many dreamy summer afternoons of innocence. That was before the two families fell out. Caroline's mother had always blamed it on the proximity of the two. "It's all the fault of our housing," she would say.

Caroline thought it was more to do with Mr. Atkinson's mother. She became an overprotective woman after her husband's death and seemed almost jealous about how Mrs. Blueheart had coped with her divorce and subsequent loss of husband. While Caroline's mother had taken evening classes and learnt about art and crafts, Mrs. Atkinson had chosen the television as her therapy. Mrs. Atkinson would ridicule her neighbour's attempts at education, saying that there must be something wrong with a woman who couldn't keep her husband. Caroline now knew the irony of such accusations. Arthur had confided in Caroline that his father was always having affairs when Caroline was too young to know what affairs were. She now appreciated Arthur's alienation. She was unsettled by her knowledge of what had gone on behind the Atkinson's blue-curtained facade.

Around the corner, a fish and chip vendor was scooping thick chips into handmade paper cones as schoolchildren offered pocket money and relished the heavy pouring from salt-sellers. From exotic flora to rubbish and now ascetic acid, the wind blew scents all around.

Through the gaps in the shutters that she would shortly be pulling up, Caroline saw him on the floor. The beam of light focused on his eyes, blazing like fires as smoke settled around him.

Leymann looked at the many photographs, framed in silver and scattered over the antique chests and tables. Lavender potpourri, like confetti, lay in small baskets and the aroma entwined with the smell of Madeira cake on his coffee plate. A wedding photo he hadn't seen for years recalled his wife. She was pretty in the picture, wearing the dress that her best friend had worn a few months before. Next to her, Leymann, fresh-faced and aglow, smiled absurdly as if his seat was on fire. One had to look hard to perceive any lines on his face, all a long way from the present scarring crevasses and grey pallor. Leymann cursed, blamed and hated himself for not posing correctly for the elusive instamatic that had preyed on him that day.

"More cake, dear?" asked his aunt after a lengthy silence.

Jensen's annoyance had retreated overnight. At the top of his condominium, dressed in a stripy dressing gown, he looked at the bright sapphire sky and felt the warmth. On a white, plastic table lay a carafe of orange juice, squeezed by his daily. He sat down and looked upwards, smiling with satisfaction. The Pacific twinkled in the corner of his eye.

The previous evening's receipts from Malibu Love and

the thought of being reunited with Jocelyn had reinvigorated him. He shot a glance over the stone parapet and down at a sunbathing blonde and turned up the volume of his radio, madly waving his tumbler.

"Okay, get out of here, you fucking nigger. If you think we're paying a penny to get you out of here, you've got another thing coming," said the fat man. He had been watching the house for a couple of hours, checking on the need for reinforcements. He realised that one youth would be no match for him and a scythe.

The fat man had been glad to find Leymann absent at the office. He had never liked him. Now, he had the chance to prove that Leymann was superfluous at Property Developments. He relished what he saw as a virility test. He had stopped off at his flat and the first weapon he found was a sickle. His flat was full of interesting Russian souvenirs thanks to his grandmother who had left after the revolution. Only when he put it on the back seat did he wonder how he would explain it to any vigilant policeman.

Errol, who had been watching television, thought that the shouting was another of Johnstone's stunts. Errol never found them very funny and this time he was angry. A favourite cartoon was climaxing with a mouse-detective nearing victory. What with Carl's accident and everything else, Errol tried to excuse his actions a few hundredths of a second after they were committed. There were surely mitigating circumstances for throwing the set, already only loosely attached, at the person prying open the door.

"Oh God! I'm sorry...you alright? I'm sorry...nice sickle." Errol could just see a glinting curve from a gap in the squatter-boards. He was frightened. He couldn't think of why Johnstone hadn't remembered his key. They had spent a long time fitting the lock to the house and it seemed inexplicable that he'd smash up the door to get in.

Silently, pink faced youths marched in, too numb to feel the temperature gradient. Inside, they lined up once more, waiting for a self-satisfied looking woman to dole out cups of tea and biscuits. As the first few boys sat down, they began to talk, the first time they had exchanged words all day. They spoke in rushed sentences of towns and cities, villages that sounded like brand names. They spoke of broken marriages and beatings. They spoke of fights and ghostly night-time encounters, of living without shelter. But more of them still were happier to settle down in front of a resounding television set, careful to cling onto their polystyrene cups. They thawed as if the images were flames.

Jonathan was one of the quieter ones. More than anything, he was startled by the numbers of those like him. The past day he had felt self-piteous, always on the verge of tears and now he surveyed the commonness of his condition. With some spite he saw others summoning up smiles and laughter. He didn't eat his soft to the touch biscuit, preferring to watch the screen. He didn't take any of it in but he felt in some ways happier. Soon, he would surely be back in Loddington, drinking on the tops of hills with friends, viewing the desolate countryside with a grin. He began to think about his days in London as nothing but a small unsuccessful adventure. Jenny was a distant memory, she almost felt like something conjured up by his imagination. As for the capital, there was no love lost between them.

"You know, your uncle is very proud of you—we all are. None of this family have amounted to very much," she smiled at the empty armchair, "the property business does seem an exciting way to earn one's living. It's always on the news these days. There was a programme on it just the other day. There was a bedsit somewhere, about the size of our loo and do you know how much they were selling it for? Eight feet square or something, really?"

"Where was it?" Leymann asked, watching his aunt's wrinkles join and unjoin like waves as she looked a little irritated by his answering questions with questions.

"Central London somewhere, in the borough where they were moving all the poorer families out. You know how much?"

"Tell me."

"Well, I will," she said, "and it's already been sold as well, in case you were thinking of buying the place," she laughed, "I mean there wasn't even a kitchen. The man on the television said that any bachelor with that kind of money would be able to eat out. It's actually a bit sad really. I mean, that means that people on the bottom of the property ladder, I mean people like ourselves, I mean you for instance, well...actually, who would want to live up town. There's all the smog."

Jules walked along the perimeter of the lawn, wondering why he felt broken-hearted. Floodlights shone up the spires of the chapel to the lightning conductors as the sound of a choir bled through the stone.

Sebastian showered, inhaling the bar of soap he had bought from London. It conjured up reflections for him, of his childhood in one of the British African colonies. The pink oval induced super-eight in the mind. There were ochre plains where black migrant workers picked crops, large white houses and fanned colonial artefacts, a grandmother who mumbled. Sebastian always felt that scents had a greater effect on him. In a new packet of white bread he could smell the whole of America.

He thought of Frezzle and about how he was being bought a house and then about his own extensive choice of places to live in. He wouldn't miss his cramped university rooms, he thought. "I'll be alright," he said to himself.

"Bones!" exclaimed Jenny, astonished to see him in her reception area.

Bones had spent the day writing a new song. He had found the tune for the chorus quite easy but, so far, he had only written two lines of lyrics. After Jenny left, he returned to his luxury hotel to write. A burly woman from room-service had delivered food and drinks every few hours and by the end of the day the beer cans resonated to his singing. It was over joints and club sandwiches that he had begun to lose confidence in his work. He started to wonder whether he could recapture his talent. 'Boom! Boom! Boom!' had been punchy. It hinted at a latent eroticism, as one music journalist had put it.

Jocelyn still felt unbalanced. She had tipped the taxi-driver three hundred percent, had irregularly checked in and was now seated in first class behind a row of empty glasses. She hadn't even gone home to see her younger daughter or check on how her maid was coping. She hadn't even checked on the bills. Even when Laura had hugged her outside the hospital, Jocelyn had just smiled inanely.

An older woman at an adjoining seat, her spectacles at an exciting incline, tried to make conversation. She was the wife of an American farmer and was returning from a wedding in Paris.

"She's been a friend since I was...oh, years. And then I thought, why not go and see London? It's so close, these days and, you know, I'd never been before. Anyway, I was only there for a couple of hours. You live there?" she asked, excitedly sipping soda water.

Jocelyn nodded, unable to keep a vodka and orange steady in her hand.

"I thought of having some champagne. It's all free, after all, but thought better of it," said the older woman, "after all I couldn't very well afford much in London. It's so expensive there, so terribly expensive. Even champagne is cheaper in LA. It's all triple the price."

Jocelyn nodded again before leaning away to look out of the window, at the Atlantic.

"I'm not from LA but my daughter lives there," the older woman said, producing a small photo-wallet from a snakeskin handbag. As she flipped the plastic sheets, she pushed her glasses up her nose and noticed how thin Jocelyn was. "You sure do have a beautiful figure. Did you have a good dietician?"

"I better be going now," said Leymann, looking at his watch. He reflected on why she was his favourite aunt and was now worried over what his other relatives must be like.

"You won't stay for dinner? I've made some shepherd's pie."

Leymann declined, feeling that the visit had already delivered the requisite catharsis. He had quite forgotten the traumas of leaving his job and, as he walked out into the cold evening, he felt unfettered and almost autonomous.

"Your uncle will be sorry," his aunt said on the doorstep before she turned back towards the house. "You will be won't you? You would have liked to talk to your nephew wouldn't you?" she said fantastically to an empty chair. "Before you end up in a home," she added cryptically.

Sebastian's father, Alec, had entered the plane at Dubai, a city with no skyline but a Hilton hotel that resembled a lone vertical sock. He always took economy class. He credited his success to thrift. For over an hour, he had been chatting to Mrs. Blueheart, having shortened her name to 'Blue'.

"So you've never been to India before, Blue?" asked Alec.

"No, but I've been doing a lot of research. I have this folder," she replied, taking out a file of magazine cuttings and photocopies made in her local library.

"Don't worry about back home, Blue. I'm sure your daughter will look after things properly—at least if she has anything of your intelligence," Alex said reassuringly.

Mrs. Blueheart giggled nervously, feeling awkward in a seat that afforded such paltry space.

Caroline didn't accompany Mr. Atkinson to the hospital. There didn't seem any point. Her first reaction had been to think of Arthur. The death of Mr. Atkinson would surely bring his brother back to her. And then, as the ambulance drove away, she wept. She cried for hours, drying her face on her sweater, again and again. The policeman had left her alone, remembering what he had learned on one of his courses: it's always best for grief to express itself at the earliest opportunity.

Jonathan slowly fell asleep, not hearing anymore.

Johnstone had never seen anything like it before. He was used to surveying this patch, looking for even the most dubious signs of vacancy. The block that had astonished him was a fifties' model he had seen many times before. Today, it had transformed from concrete to some other kind of stone. It was of the same proportions and yet it was nothing like what had stood there before. Instead of square shapes for its stairs and windows, there were curves, instead of greys and mottled charcoal colours there were whites, pinks, oranges and reds and seemingly everywhere, glass. Below a Romanesque arch fluttered a fabric sign offering the building for let. Surveillance cameras roosted in the windows nearest the pennant.

Diners' babble thundered about the restaurant as Lena pulled another superfluous cigarette from the packet on the bar. She hadn't ordered a drink as there was no guarantee it would be paid for. She just watched the waiters arrive and collect their orders, sporadically smoothing out the creases in her borrowed black dress.

"Lena," said a large, smiling man in his fifties. He had adopted a possessive tone of recognition, as if after some unclear loss. He was balding with an extraordinarily small nose. His slightly bulbous eyes remained dull and swampy as the shallow laughter lines crinkled his face.

"How did you know what I looked like?"

"I could tell. You must be Lena. My name's Mr. August. We've been matched by fate."

Lena sighed as he took her hand and grandiosely kissed it. 'We're not matched by Fate,' she said to herself, 'that's another escort agency."

"Johnstone! I'm glad to see you," Errol said, looking up from one of the books he had found lying around. He had been reading for over an hour. "I think that this is the guy from the property company."

"Yeah?" Johnstone replied, until now feeling pleased with himself because his mother had given him some money and the consequences were on his feet.

"Nice trainers," said Errol, changing the subject.

"So, what...he's been lying here for an hour?"

Errol nodded.

"You sure he isn't dead?"

Errol shrugged his shoulders. "All I know is that he was going to attack me with that sickle."

"Pretty blunt instrument, heh?"

They devised a plan. Johnstone told Errol about his

discovery, a refurbished and transfigured block of empty flats, and then they set about getting their things. Now that the television was broken, there were just some mattresses and mugs, some cutlery and a few heaters to move. They climbed the stairs to see if there was anything they could use to burn the place down.

Laura sat with her friend, fiddling with a beer mat and feeling dejected. The barman stoked the pub fire and the flames lit up her eyes. Her friend, the diplomat's daughter who never had the chance to even miss her parents, was uneasy. Usually, they went to the pub later in the day, when it was more crowded and they were less conspicuous. At the moment, a barmaid was staring directly at them, trying to discern any signs of youth. The barmaid eventually outstared Laura's friend. She, too, had once passed herself off as older at a pub, chain-smoking and pulling hems to lengthen her skirt.

"So what do you actually do?" asked Lena, suspiciously.

"Well," Mr. August paused to intensify his smile, "I make decisions. I'm in television." He dropped some ice into his brandy with a pair of tongs. "Do you like the club? I didn't want us to meet at too public a place."

Lena twisted to peep through the stuffy cigar smoke. The room was lined in wood, a succession of Victorian cartoons flowing across the walls. As elderly members spluttered Lena noticed that all the waiters and bar-staff seemed to know her client. It was unusual for a customer to take her to such a traditional style club.

"It's nice," she said.

"Actually, it's only since last week that women members have been allowed in."

"I see."

"So, have you ever thought of going into television?"

"Well," Lena grimaced, "perhaps." Her frown had been a reflex. Now, she composed her perma-smile again.

"Well," Mr. August said, embarrassed by his opening gambit, "if you ever want to, you can always give me a call at the office." He took out his card and gave it to Lena. She put it in her small handbag. "There, business over," he smiled again.

"Mr. August?" a young man with short tufty blonde hair interrupted.

"Peter, how are you? Lena, this is my accountant's son," Mr. August said as Peter mentally undressed her.

"Hello," said Lena politely, turning quickly back to Mr. August.

The air-hostess had disappeared, relaxing in a special aisle and talking to her colleagues about which drunken businessman had been the most annoying. One of the hostesses remembered a cushion-request and got up to deliver one.

Jocelyn hadn't needed any. The first class cabin was quite comfortable. She was still bruised but the large doses she swallowed induced sleep and unconsciousness for the most part. A pair of plastic headphones clung around her ears, buzzing with a comedy radio programme. All the time, her American neighbour was chatting to her.

Jenny was always being asked where people were. Just as she had decided to do something, whether it was reading a magazine or stepping out with a nice musician, she was expected to locate the whereabouts of every employee. This time, the missing person was the fat, moustached man. He was supposed to be acting manager in Jocelyn's absence so his non-appearance was something of a calamity. It was probably costing the company a lot of money.

"Shit! I need these authorised, why did he have to go and do a job that he wasn't even meant to be doing?" said a smartly dressed boy.

Jenny knew why he had gone to make an eviction round. The fat man had always struck Jenny as being insecure. "How much is all of it worth, then?" she asked.

"It's a fucking auction. He knew it was today. It's over four million pounds, six houses in the West End," the boy paused for breath. He was almost screaming, "the money's due tonight. Can't anyone else authorise...oh fuck it. It was just that it was such a prime site. Have you got a contact number for Jocelyn?"

Jenny shrugged her shoulders, looking over at Bones who returned a mystified gaze. He had never understood office life. There were only two offices he ever visited. One belonged to his record company and the other his manager's. But these offices, once one was past the busy secretaries and assistants, were just like friends' houses: lots of music, beer and recreational drugs.

Carl felt desperate. He wanted to die and he knew he wasn't seriously injured enough for the task. The hours had made him reflective. He would have liked to see some of his friends. Hanging over his father's bed was a red and white baseball jacket, the word 'RAIDERS' and the number eleven still discernible through the ripped fabric. He had been wearing his best outfit the day of the attack. He remembered the day he got it. Johnstone's girlfriend had bought it for him with a stolen credit card.

The place had got cold and Mr. Roeng, who was more used to it, took off his pullovers and covered his son. The acrylic fabrics, stitched with shiny thread, attracted the dust. Carl breathed it in from the jumper under his chin as he tried to ignore the radio. It was a charity broadcast that was running on all channels, money was to be raised for a variety of causes. Mr. Roeng forestalled complaining to his son about the uselessness of charity.

"Wake up, Jocelyn," slurred the American lady, "more complimentary champagne's here, finally." Despite her nudging, Jocelyn was unavailable for comment.

"The dirty old man in 7c pinched my bottom," said a hostess as she poured out some sparkling white wine.

A tall black building, imposing and shadowy amongst a sprawling city of white bungalows. Little people walking to and fro, many of them holding hamburgers. Jonathan was one of them, though he was not moving, merely looking upwards. In his dream, he spent hours trying to look up and through the building, though the panes across it were black. Only one of them was transparent and Lena was clearly

visible, laughing with some of his Loddington friends and
drinking ale as clouds passed under her chin.
"Mum!" Jonathan shouted at one of the passers-by.

Leymann had walked past the bus-stop after briefly
peering at the small figures that made up the timetable. It was
cold. Waiting beside a metal post in an open-neck shirt for a
subsequent bus that was, anyway, unlikely to arrive could mean
a visit to the doctor. Usually, the situation made him miserable.
There was nothing to do but wait. The uncertainty was worse at
night, outside the office. There was not only the niggling doubt
about whether the bus would ever come but also the increased
volume of sounds around him to think about. Was someone
watching him? Was he about to be mugged? Should he save
the trouble and spend next week's fares on an immediate taxi.
These uncertainties at the bus-stop used to be symptomatic of
Leymann's indecisiveness. Today, he just walked past and the
act made him feel conscientious. In addition, it meant that he
knew he was no longer subject to the whims of an under-staffed
bus-station. He took a taxi.

Errol had sat in the basement of the house for hours. With
each strike he had time to think. The matches would flash
across the damp, wooden room, illuminating a row of electrical
meters. Below them sat empty beer-cans and cigarette packets,
bygone litter stained with age. He sometimes heard noises
from upstairs, perhaps the groans of the man whom he hadn't
properly seen and whom he was now trying to burn.

Johnstone was standing outside, leaning on mattresses and
watching for even portents of movement. Looking up at the
houses opposite him, he watched warm, soft light glow about
candelabras and walnut dining tables. In one house, a dinner
party was in progress. He could see the glints of silver as he
wrapped his neck in a scarf grabbed from his sports' bag.

"But Charles, there is no empire!" laughed Esther, before
leaving the table to check on the dessert. She looked back at
the faces of her friends, scarlet with alcohol. It was peculiar to
be giving dinner-parties, she thought. It was only a few years

ago that she had been going to dinner parties with her parents. Now, at the age of twenty-eight, stretching a black dress that had been fine just last year, she felt as if she'd gone from child to aged hostess. She opened the pre-packaged puddings into bowls and popped her head around the door to observe the state of her guests' plates.

Back in the kitchen, as she put a slice of kiwi fruit into her mouth, she spied a group of some forty or so people though the window. She vaguely remembered something the baby-sitter had said about Louise seeing a black man in the house and how he had taken her lunch money. Esther was used to her daughter's ploys. Usually, Louise was given what she wanted, extra money that she could spend on her doll house or record collection. The mother didn't have much time to spend with Louise, although she always gave her what she wanted. Career progression kept her perpetually busy and tired. It had been easier when she had just started at the company, or at least she thought so, with hindsight. Now, there was always new blood in the firm, working at top speed and making more money than she found herself making for the company. Since there was no security of any kind, she could be sacked for falling below a quartile. Last week, her friend was escorted out the building. The stress was starting to tell. On seeing the gang outside, some of them holding sticks and flaming bottles, she dropped a china plate, filled with ready-sliced strawberries.

Johnstone had chuckled when he saw his friends and the friends of his friends arrive. They had been due to come over anyway but once they heard of the situation they left and returned well equipped. He surfaced from the basement and accepted a can of beer. The crowd made him think of the past when he seemed to have many more friends, when even the parents of his friends knew each other.

Lena smiled at the paparazzi and security cameras as she entered the hotel. She recognised many minor celebrities milling about in the foyer. Women's faces were shiny from makeup, lit up by sequins and satin. All hair was still. Mr. August lit up a large cigar and Lena's eyes began to water a little.

*John Barleycorn here...how are you all. Well...I'm your host
for the evening and this is the ballroom of the Hulton Hotel
in London, where, in a few minutes, the first of twenty
awards will be presented to media luminaries. See you after
the break...fuck, what's wrong with the autocue, Bill? You're
making me look like an idiot.*

Bill struck an electric box at his side.

"Hey, come on what do you say you young beauties come
back to our place. We're having a party, we only came to the pub
to get some more booze."

Laura looked at her friend. The man speaking was one
of three handsome teenagers who had come to their table.
Each was wearing smart, newly pressed clothes. Laura's friend
was pleased: the barmaid had stopped surveying them. Laura
thought a little before gulping down a glass of icy, sweet alcohol.
She looked around the pub. Fast music was vibrating around
them but the room was filled with large middle-aged men
sullenly drinking from pints. "Come on let's go," she said to
her friend, who always found her decisions plausible. When
Laura made a decision, she was transformed by her confidence
and determination. Her friend took her chewing gum out and
scrunched it into an ashtray before gulping down her mineral
water and following Laura outside.

Kane drew the curtains and lay on his bunk bed. Once, the
submarine had made him feel claustrophobic. Now, its strange
light and unbalanced movement made him feel at home. He
was used to the lack of privacy, the disjointed shifts, the harsh
workouts and, eventually, it was the land mass of North America
that seemed alien, not the submarine.

"Leymann!" shouted Caroline, who had been waiting for
him. Leymann smiled at her, jiggling his neck, and then paid the
driver. Caroline began to holler.

*It's one-thirty in the afternoon, Pacific Standard Time. I hope
you enjoyed your flight and the crew and I would like to wish
you an enjoyable stay in Los Angeles or a smooth connection*

should you be travelling elsewhere. The temperature at LAX
airport is approximately eighty degrees Fahrenheit with
bright sunshine. Thank you again for choosing to fly..."

Jocelyn stumbled down the aisle with an orange vanity case
and a stewardess on each arm. Images of the rusty red rocks of
Nevada and Arizona flared in her mind. It wasn't until the first
set of stairs that she woke up, the Stanislavsky-technique smile
of the President beaming from a framed portrait. "Welcome to
America," it proclaimed.

The hushed silence of the immigration hall jarred with
the ringing aeroplane noise in Jocelyn's ears. Draped flags
stained with red, blue and white hung from the ceiling as
armed officers questioned nervous visitors. Beyond the desks
lay speedy conveyor belts and Jocelyn pushed her hand in her
pocket to retrieve non-existent quarters. "BE WISE, RENT
A TROLLEY!" it said beside a row of them. Jocelyn had no
currency.

"Bloody ridiculous, isn't it?" said a woman with a North
London accent to Jocelyn.

Leymann sat on the seat usually reserved for Mrs. Blueheart.
All week, Jocelyn had been on his mind, her disappearance and
her phonecall. Even now, after this explosion of violence, just
next door, he was thinking of her.

Caroline sat on the floor, again crying. Leymann remained
calm about Mr. Atkinson's death. It was the letter from
the developers that threw him. All the learning at Property
Developments PLC hadn't taught him to be concerned about
his own precarious housing situation. He had overlooked
the personal implications of a small revolution. Over a short
space of time, council houses had been sold off, new mortgage
instruments and enterprise zones had been created and homes
had become gambling assets. During this time, compulsory
purchase orders had flourished, interest rates had shifted,
entrepreneurial housing co-operatives had been born and local
government had become a handmaiden to a philosophy.

"Two days, Caroline, what are we going to do? Can we contact your mother?"

Caroline shook her head, poking a finger in her eye to save the mascara from stinging.

They looked around the room, at the potted plants, the cellophane-wrapped bouquets, the chocolates. Leymann thought about his options whilst inwardly cursing Mr. Atkinson about the fate of the little half gun, half florist property. He concluded that he must have known about what was going on far in advance of this letter. Mr. Atkinson must have hidden the order, he thought.

He speculated on whether he could stay in one of the many empty Property Developments' properties. Or maybe his brother would know of somewhere. Or maybe his aunt would die. He reproached himself for giving up his job.

Lena and Mr. August had settled down at one of the large circular tables scattered over the marble floor of the hotel's ballroom. Big spotlights shone onto the stage and sometimes swivelled towards the audience. One of them caught Lena in its glare just as Mr. August was offering her some whisky. "I call it Jonathan rather than Johnnie's," he said, "I just do. It sounds more comfortable than a glass of Walker, doesn't it?" Mr. August gently pushed away Lena's hand to get to the bottle. Others at the table proffered tense smiles.

"Jonathan? Yes, that's a nice name," she said, too softly to be heard under the drum roll. He'd live and die in Loddington, she thought to herself. He was provincial. She let her mind wander and speculate on what Jonathan was doing now. She wasn't sure whether it was the poor, drawling, Billie Holliday cover or the whisky, but she felt, for the first time, she was as naïve as her parents had accused her of being. For all the laughs, there had been no point in leaving for the instability of the city.

As John Barleycorn announced an award for new talent, Lena felt sorry that she had never learned how to play an instrument or sing. She looked at Mr. August, clapping loudly and noticeably, as if the award winner was a protégé. He'd be of no use to Lena, whether it was because she hadn't sufficiently impressed him or not. A veil of fear coated her face. The confidence that had flowed, on entering the hall, had evaporated. What was she doing here? She had nothing in common with her dinner-partners. Even her place mat, a steel, engraved pyramid, had no letters on it.

Jensen sat in the airport lounge, looking at the bar and the customers buying beers. He was tired and the proximity of alcohol made him feel a little sick. The airport, with its black plastic seating and abundance of Mexican looking men and women made Jensen feel he wasn't in one of the whiter areas of Los Angeles. It feels like a different country, he thought to himself, looking around at the crisis-ridden faces. He wondered why so many of them looked worried and decided it must be because many of them were waiting for illegal immigrants or drug suppliers. Jensen didn't like the airport, at least not the arrivals' lounge.

Some fifty feet above him, well dressed international travellers were preparing for departure, shopping at boutiques and choosing presents. Jensen frowned and snarled as he denied money to a beggar before a security guard escorted the man out.

Laura didn't reply to the boy's questions. As the old car slid along a suburban road, the diplomat's daughter wished she hadn't come. She tried to attract Laura's attention as one of the boys slid his hand onto her knee. But Laura was staring straight out of the windscreen.

"Cigarette?" asked one of the boys.

"Thanks," replied Laura, turning to smile at her friend and sensing none of the danger.

To her friend, Laura had a blank, faraway look, as if she was thinking about nothing at all. But she was thinking. As she dipped her head for a light, her friend alert to the scar on his hand, she thought about her mother and her father. It seemed that her parents had never been further away from her than now and that they had never had less in common with her. The world must have changed so much since their childhood, she concluded. They would never be able to understand what she felt or thought. She sucked hard and knew that she loved them both, especially Jocelyn. But whatever her affections, Jocelyn, she decided, would never have any relevance to her life. As she felt the heat in her lungs, the car trundled over rough ground. As she realised how alone she was, the car stopped in a deserted field.

Leymann had made a decision. It seemed a long time since he had so firmly dug a position but he was completely convinced that he was right. His aunt wasn't going to die. She would live for another twenty years, believing that her imaginary husband would soon receive his massive insurance payout.

His brother, like the brother of his friend, Tony, didn't care what happened to him. Whether bugging phones or moving large sums of money about the earth, they were too busy to distress themselves. One didn't interrupt a bricklayer at work and his brother, like Tony's, was laying bricks all over the world. Leymann smiled, remembering a shoddy architect.

If Leymann was to find a way out of the mess, he thought, he would have to go and seek out Jocelyn. He put Caroline to a fitful sleep, laying her on a mattress to dream of Arthur, and left the shop.

"Jocelyn," said Jensen, softly, hugging her and expecting to breathe in expensive European perfume. Taking charge of her bags, the hospital disinfectant inflamed his nostrils.

"How are you, Jensen?" Jocelyn asked, sheepishly.

"Yup, great. You're not too well, though, huh?" Jocelyn smiled. "Still, if you're not too tired, I'd like to take you to see one of my developments. Actually, it's my last development. It's my dream-place."

Jocelyn was too exhausted to shake her head. She shuffled alongside him in the car-park. Jensen had got older, she thought, less moveable and even fragile. His hair was still smooth but there was a scar of hair-dye above his right ear. In turn, Jensen, was dismayed to see Jocelyn. She looked pale and uncoordinated. She walked with a limp. Her eyes had lost the sparkle he remembered and were now ringed by blue-green semicircles. Her lips seemed almost burnt. Jensen tried to put it down to the poor weather in England.

Carl wished to be with his friends instead of ailing at his father's home. When Carl thought about it, he realised that his father had annoyed him ever since his mother died. Carl's hopes and dreams had seemed completely different to those of his father. But now, a couple of hours of silence had begun to breach the fissures between them. Carl suddenly saw that any hopes he might have were unrealistic. He resolved to fight less, if at all.

Mr. Roeng mouthed the words he was reading, sometimes whispering a phrase. He thought about how wonderful it would be to have a bath. "Clean, clean, clean," he began to recite as both of them listened to the screams and shouts from the nearby shacks. Mr. Roeng smiled and watched Carl drift away.

Errol wanted Carl to be there. The excitement of a hundred flaming torches, the clean scent of white spirit and the tearing of fabric all made it seem as if this was a battle not a skirmish. More and more people were joining in and, despite the drunkenness, the rows of people from surrounding estates and squats looked like a fairly well drilled infantry battalion. There was a moment when it looked like the football supporters who had emptied from the pubs were about to start picking fights but even they joined in. A few councillors arrived with some television cameras. The councillors used megaphones to cry out for what they called 'useful action' rather than murder and arson. Some groups of people who had brought banners with slogans about property rights chanted against them. At first the councillors were pelted with rubbish and sticks, just as the police had been.

Errol looked up and watched, gasping at the number of people that he could see. Some of them held torches that shone across the lines, others catapulted things at the riot shields. Opposite him, the windows of expensive houses had filled with people.

And quite far off, on the horizon and on the top of a hill, sat a wall of uniformed men and women, holding shields and guns.

The crowd attempted to propel Errol away but he was rooted to the ground, staring at the sharp line of silver. He could make out no faces, just the onset of a volcanic-like flow.

Johnstone dipped a rag into a bottle and lit it, passing it to Errol who felt the powerful heat. Looking up, again, he saw the wall charge.

"It seems like ages ago. It was ages. It was ages since I was here," said Jocelyn, staring out onto Lincoln Boulevard and the flat regions beyond it. "How do you think I look, Jensen, honestly?"

"Beautiful, beautiful, especially so when considering you've been on a long haul flight," Jensen said, his eyebrows at acute angles from the top of his nose. "Why? Is that Leymann fellow at the office tiring you out?" He laughed and then laughed again when he saw the bumper sticker in front of him: "THE MAN WHO DIES WITH THE MOST TOYS WINS."

"No...Leymann's not tiring me out...Jensen, could you turn the air conditioning on. I'm a little hot."

❧

Jonathan woke up suddenly, not because of an unusual sound but because of the sudden minute's quiet. Cars and lorries carrying fruit had whizzed past the hostel as he had slept. Newspaper vans distributing their computer typeset pages and the isolated screams of late nightclubbers would continue through the night.

But, in that moment of silence, he raised his head and squinted in the apparent darkness. He saw two boys moving together in a single bed and one boy stalking the dormitory like it was a bank. He strained to lift himself and shift his legs, wondering whether he was watching tricks of the light.

Waiters moved Lena's empty wine bottles to the centre of the table rather than taking them away, as if to complain about her voracious drinking. Minutes earlier, she had felt a pleasant spinning sensation in her head. Now, she was shivering a little, her mouth drooping and her eyes filling with rivers of vessels. She tightened her fingers around the stem of her glass as a TV camera swept beside her, chasing a winner to the podium. She tried to get up, lifting herself halfway.

"Get down, Lena!" said Mr. August sternly before smiling at the others at the table.

Lena only vaguely heard him and didn't care to watch his abrasive gesturing. Unbalanced and like an eccentric old lady with a pocket-sized umbrella, she walked blindly past the tables. Guests' eyes were by now turned to the stage rather than her.

Leymann, now with a steely concentration, tried to remember anything that might tell him where Jocelyn might be.

Leymann:-Bloody hell! Last night was a bit tough. Three black men threatened me. It took a fuck load of persuasion to get those out of there. They didn't want to leave. It was only when I offered cash inducements that they said alright. They gave in.
Jocelyn:-Things have become a bit tougher, haven't they, Leymann? I'm sure you'll be able to cope, though. You've never had that many problems over the years, have you?
Leymann: -Not as such, I suppose.
Jocelyn:-I don't know...things seem to be easier in America. When I got married...that was one disaster...I went to LA... a friend of my husband's was there. He was a nice fellow, charming. Anyway, he had just bought this plot of land by the beach. No hassle, nothing, just a straight deal. There's so much space out there, you know. There's so much building and there's still so much space. Everything's just so crammed in here. It's a better lifestyle, it's just easier to make the money.

Leymann recalled the conversation loosely, like remembering seeing a playing card somewhere where it shouldn't be. He leafed through the previous day's tabloid, looking for cheap flights to America. 'America would solve all of my problems,' he thought, 'and all the airfares seem ridiculously cheap.' He shut the paper and slept to the sound of a western.

He slept soundly, better than for a long time. He dreamt of

his ex-wife and then Jocelyn. They were all at a roulette table, the smell of sweet perfume, green baize and stale bourbon abnormally distinct and overpowering. In the course of a few hours, Leymann, his arms around Jocelyn, had been winning more and more of his ex-wife's chips. His ex-wife sat motionless and for some reason she wore a croupier's cap. Her eyes were covered by shade that the chandelier couldn't assail. Then, she began tossing chips into the centre of the green mat's squares, each arc perfectly timed.

The submarine was surfacing for emergency repairs, a common inconvenience. The more expensive the parts, the more defective they became. Kane slept through the elevation thanks to a bottle of vodka living under his pillow.

Usually, the beaming sunlight and the sight of the sparkling Pacific of the San Diego shoreline came as a shock. The first time Kane had resurfaced after a long underwater sojourn, he felt as if he had been dead and he had been raised into life. Colours seemed sharper, faces more complicated and women more beautiful. Today, Kane just scrunched up his eyes and shuffled across the quay, jumping onto his bunk when he got to his quarters.

"Hey, Kane! Want some snow?" asked one of the group of sailors who had been playing cards near him.

Kane looked at the stacked dollar-bills and nodded before some stubby fingers showed him a playing card to grab. It was an unused joker with a white line.

Jensen didn't take the freeway, preferring to take the long and snaky Sunset Boulevard up to Malibu. Jocelyn had been silent for most of the journey, lazily closing her eyes and occasionally being startled by the glare of the sun. As they reached the ocean, the hot glitter made Jocelyn thirsty. She conquered her craving, beginning to think of Leymann, his stamina and his subtlety, and how he had her love. Leymann unlike Jensen didn't seem like just a man.

Jensen beamed as they drove into the forecourt of Malibu Love. To him, it looked like a project realised but to any passing tourist it looked more like a partially completed building.

Jocelyn saw it as such, only briefly glancing at the wooden props, and moulded steel surfaces. It seemed undressed.

"Well, Jocelyn, this the dream. This is the dream...realised." Jensen began the sentence with confidence, even with a little of the passion that he used to be able to create and summon up as if by sleight of hand. The sentence ended, however, with a croak.

Jocelyn grinned, pushing one of Jensen's spare pairs of sunglasses onto her nose.

"You see the way the surf flicks like that? That's unique... unique to this village, as you English would call it."

Jocelyn didn't identify any curious wave motion. Nothing seemed unique here, no oscillation or surface tension. It seemed just as any brochure-ocean should. With a dumb expression she stared at the rocks that littered the sand, turning to hear a story about Jensen and his father.

Jonathan crept out of the hostel after a quick wash at a limescaled basin. The streets were empty, waiting for the tramp of office-workers. He crossed over to Chinatown, startled by the drizzle.

The hot coffee burnt Lena's throat. She hurried the fried egg on toast to the cadences of other escort girls. It was an all night place they often finished up at and though she seldom enjoyed the others' company, she sometimes went, starved after a night of stealthy avoidance, carefulness and alcohol. Sometimes, on the early mornings that she felt depressed and disgusted, she would go anyway and sit apart from the others, perched on one of the window seats. From it, she could see Chinese unpacking vegetables and standing around smoking.

The previous night had been a bit of a disaster. There was a fifty-fifty chance of Mr. August complaining and not paying his dues. She sat there, worriedly watching a boy of about her age gazing at outdoor menu signs. He put his rucksack on the tarmac, wiping drizzle from his hair and counting change from his pocket. He looked like a tramp to Lena except that when she peered at him more closely, he was wearing a suit. Putting his rucksack back on, he asked directions from a postman who looked him up and down a few times before pointing a gloved hand to the tube station.

Jonathan had begun his return to Loddington.

BOOM! BOOM! MAN SOLICITS PROSTITUTE
DRUGGED POP STAR IN SEX SCANDAL
US DEFICIT REACHES NEW HIGH
JOHN BARLEYCORN ILL IN HOSPITAL—AIDS?
MASS LONDON RIOTS — SIX SHOT DEAD
DRUNK POP STAR IN SEX SCANDAL
AMERICANS HONOURED AT AWARDS
TRAGEDY OF TWO GIRLS, BLONDE AND
BRUNETTE, MURDERED IN FIELD
SOUTH AFRICAN TOWNSHIP VIOLENCE
FLARES UP AGAIN
THE COMET REPORT:
Bones, famous young singer in the band Tearful Blue Icicles, solicited a young woman, Jenny, last night outside his luxury suite at a West End hotel. An undercover journalist from The Comet secretly posed as a butler, bringing pint after pint of lethally strong beer to Bones' lavish pad. At one point, when your fearless Comet reporter interrupted the lovers, Bones was brandishing a sharp kitchen cleaver, pretending to cut an orange. At another point, Bones asked our reporter for 'coke' (a slang term used by pop stars for the opiate cocaine). When your reporter told him it was too late and he didn't know where to 'score' it, Bones gave him the address of a seedy, all night restaurant in squalid Soho.

All the while, busty blonde, Jenny, from North London, smiled and giggled as she unbuttoned herself. Smiling and giggling are recognised symptoms of long term drug abuse. See page 17 for what Doctor Doolie says about the evil of drugs.

WIN! WIN! WIN! YOUR CHANCE TO SPEND A WEEKEND AT THE PLUSH LUXURY HOTEL WHERE BONES SPENT HIS RAUNCHY NIGHT OF PASSION. SIMPLY FILL OUT YOUR FREE

GAME CARD IN TOMORROW'S BRILLIANT COMET.

Jensen lay on his bed looking at the ceiling after showing Jocelyn to her room. The driving had drained him and he presumed her silence meant she was fatigued too. He had only ever slept at Malibu Love once before, when construction had only just begun. Back then, he had been able to feel the sand beneath his toes.

Jocelyn couldn't get to sleep. She took some pills but they just made her toss and turn more violently. She took her key from the side table and left, walking down the stairs after seeing the 'Elevator still in construction' sign. There were other women bustling down the stairway, all in either short skirts or tight shorts and they looked at Jocelyn with skepticism.

"Can I help you, miss?" asked Labilia, multicoloured stick in hand. "Oh, it's you, Jensen's friend. Darling, couldn't you sleep?"

Jocelyn nodded.

"I can't blame you. The noise is so intense, isn't it?" she laughed, "sometimes I hear those bedsprings bounce so much, I can feel my own heart try to keep in time, you know, darling?"

In her long white nightie and stiletto shoes, she looked like an ageing starlet, now spotlit by the few lights from the car park. She wandered towards the water, expertly lifting off her shoes, and looked to her left at the giant cove. She chuckled as she remembered reading something her daughter had left for her. "Nowhere is the pursuit of happiness more unabashedly materialistic, and perhaps no city in modern times has been so universally envied, ridiculed and, because of what it might portend, feared."

Leymann packed a hold-all with a few essential items before sitting down in his armchair. He sipped from a mug of tea and looked around the room, dark from the overcast afternoon. As the rain pitter-pattered on his window, he looked at his small book collection, most of its constituents from his brother. Before Tony had moved out and into the West End, he used to be a librarian, stealing titles for him. It was because of this that Leymann had a randomness to his reading.

Above the bookshelf was a photograph of the Property Developments building, its staff forging smiles in front of it as Jocelyn accepted an award for business from the Prime Minister. She smiled similarly beside her bodyguard.

"Bye..." Leymann said uneasily to his room as he locked the door and ran down to the telephone box.

"Jenny?"

"No, Jenny's not here today. Leymann is that you?" Leymann cupped the telephone in both hands. "Haven't you read the papers? It's all over...The Comet," she rustled some paper.

"No, I haven't. Look I'm phoning from a box, so I have to be quick. I wondered...could you check on the addresses of the building developments in America...it's the big one in Los Angeles I'm thinking of, and some of the smaller ones. Jocelyn was dealing with them."

"Okay, I'll try to be as quick as I can," she tapped at a keyboard, "there's one here, shall I read it out? Well, there's a notice here about the purchase of a small company in California. Jensen...is that it? Well, there are some sizeable housing complexes in West Hollywood, Culver City, Watts, Venice and then there's some commercial property in downtown districts. There's one development in Malibu. I'm not sure this is a complete listing. Leymann?"

Leymann inserted a coin and the telephone replied with a flat minor tone. Looking over his shoulder to a long, wet queue, he decided not to call back.

Protecting himself from the rain, he perched his bag on his head as he ran to the bus stop. Amongst a crowd of school children boarding private school vans, he looked over to the Torpedo Gun Shop and the shuttered down florists. From the ground to the top, there were no lights to brighten the building up.

He sat at the back of the upper deck and looked at the back of passengers' heads before turning to the windows. He examined the misshapen trees, their branches like torn tendrils.

Below them a drenched man had set his chainsaw going and behind him a line of discarded limb-like structures shone with rain.

Where had his hardy, rugged self withdrawn, he wondered. Was there a slow disintegration or was there a blunt discontinuity? He tried to use his knowledge of mortgage payment plans, front and back loaded, to analyse himself. The only answer could be that he had been blind for a long time. And yet, now that his eyes were open, there was nothing to see, no glaring truth or answer. Instead, it was as if he had drifted away from a secure path and was now enjoying getting lost. He had put his trust in love before and yet again he chanced his happiness on it.

"Can I help you?" asked a frail newsagent.

Leymann looked around at the magazines and tobacco. "Yes, I saw your advertisement in the paper. I want a one way ticket to Los Angeles."

∾

"Well, how about we go and visit my sister in Guyana...you deserve a rest, even though I don't really know why. You're not going to tell me, are you?" asked Jensen, sitting with Jocelyn at an outdoor breakfast table.

"No, Jensen. I just had a few problems...England isn't as nice as before. Well," Jocelyn laughed, "if it was ever nice before."

"Right, and if you're going to have to stick out some violence, better here than there. Here's where the big bucks are, Josie," Jensen replied, rubbing his right thumb and forefinger together, "more mango?"

"Thanks...I must be feeling better. I've recovered my appetite already."

"You're still a little bit sad, though, Josie?"

"That's my expression. I always look sad."

"You didn't say that when you and John came out here... long time ago, huh?"

"That bastard," Jocelyn said angrily, "he gave me...he did nothing for me. He thought I'd be dependent on him and all the time, these days, it's him who's dependent on me."

"How is he?"

"I don't see him much. Sometimes, very rarely, he looks after Laura and her sister."

"I saw pictures. She's a beautiful little girl, Josie."

"She's going through a bit of a stage, lately -you know, the way teenagers do."

"Yeah."

A couple of tall, blonde boys, carrying glistening surf boards, marched out from their neighbouring beach house. Jocelyn watched them wade into the water and drift into the distance, floating and then rising. It seemed such a natural action as the ocean spray, foam and spindrift blew around them.

"They can surf better than they can walk," Jocelyn said.

"But then, that's all they can do."

Kane's family, a long-forgotten wife and two small toddlers, were coming to visit him. He had learnt to despise them. Whenever they visited the base, they interrupted his frivolous play with money and other women. Like Kane, his wife came from a hot, poor Southern state and although he had once loved her, the Pacific depths had let them drift apart. The navy, with its advantageous pension and mortgage schemes and family protection structures was supposed to have saved his family. In the end, it had helped to kill it for him. He had seen too much incompetence and too many scandals to believe in the flag at reveille. The other submariners clung to flag and faith and left him nothing to clutch. Today, on another monotonously sunny Friday, he had sufficiently advanced his plans for self-destruction.

He met them sulkily, hardly listening to his wife's remarks or noticing the cake that she had baked him. Very briefly he complimented her on her clothing. She was in a starched green dress that looked cheap compared to those of the women with whom he had last fornicated. He lifted up his youngest and told him that he was in for a treat. He had hired a lightweight plane. The children were still too young to get very excited. They were fitted inside the small cockpit, crying and shaking.

As Kane pulled back the throttle, his wife screamed with

delight, putting her arm around him. She was used to being alone, her emotions blocked. Now, with her husband, they overflowed. Long ago, Kane would have told her to straighten up, explaining that navy wives were supposed to act with more decorum. Today, he just looked straight ahead.

The children were silent on their mother's lap, examining the naval base in bewilderment: the huge buildings, the control tower, the giant oil drums and missile silos. Jensen turned to his wife and smiled at the children before accelerating the plane. In a couple of seconds it had hit an alloy cylinder, containing thousands of gallons of oil. All over the base, sailors rushed from their posts to try and prevent the fire from spreading to one of the largest collections of nuclear devices in the world. The base seemed to drown under the weight of Pacific spray.

Leymann arrived at Malibu Love in his hired car and counted his few remaining dollars. Unfastening the seat-belt, he saw Jocelyn sitting on a boulder-like rock, secured to the sand. Jensen had gone to get some more wine and was stuck in traffic.

Leymann thought about his bus-stops, the grey overcast days when he boarded buses with school children. As he walked off the tarmac and onto the sand, he peered at the woman in a billowing white dress. He didn't know how she would react but the ride from the airport had introduced him to so many sights and so much space that there seemed little cause for pessimism.

Stepping lightly across the sand, images of his waiting for her came to mind. That was all over and Leymann had no doubts. Already he could imagine bigger and taller buildings by the ocean. It wouldn't be like England where to earn one had to go through a living death. Here was where he and Jocelyn would hope and, one day surely, taste money.

GOOD MORNING, BRITAIN

Censorship is never over for those who have experienced it. It is a brand on the imagination that affects the individual who has suffered it, forever.

Noam Chomsky

There was a garden at TV Centre. He remembered a children's television programme that nurtured the garden from seedlings to bushes and trees. The aim was to teach children about botany. Each week, soil was painstakingly levelled and branches were pruned. Flowers were fingered as young viewers learnt about nature. One week, the entire garden was vandalised and destroyed. He laughed when he remembered this.

Jonathan had been a lucky man. He still had dreams of falling now and then, a hangover of some harder time. But by chance, he had got himself a life in the capital.

Apart from the day of his interview, Jonathan had never been to Television Centre. He knew that the world's first television service was launched there and he had seen the building on thousands of programmes as a child. Twentieth century British history had often been made there. But he had never seen how much the building looked like a ship, one that might wearily tell tales of iceberg collisions and lightning. When Jonathan arrived at the interview, he was too nervous to search around too much. His recollections of the place, as he returned on the tube, were only as if he had been in a series of exceptionally open-plan offices. TV Centre had been like a hollow shell.

Interviews at the Corporation were called <u>boards</u>. It was a measure of how far Jonathan had come that he knew this. Jonathan's <u>board</u> was in a shabby office. Next door to it, a man toyed with a video-recorder. He was surveying the latest footage from the world's war-zones to censor actions too unpalatable for the country's breakfast tables.

There were about seven people arranged in a semicircle in and as he entered, the irises of his eyes must have looked like skidding pebbles as they cast about the room. His glance was quite involuntary as he was quite expecting there to be a number of people. He had seen a few <u>boards</u> before and had heard about how they went at the bars where he had met journalists over the years. He had even experienced one, at a different office, in a different time. That attempt had not been successful. During conversations with the <u>board</u> members he realised that his knowledge of world news, current affairs and history had little bearing on the invitations to the <u>board</u>. He hadn't had any idea about for what programme he was being interviewed. That <u>board</u> came about because Jonathan had had the good luck to work as a silver service waiter at a party to launch a new charity and there he had met a famous television personality. The man's fame stretched as far as the county lines, but in a county where the capital is the capital of the country, his fame was sufficient to secure a <u>board</u>.

That time, the <u>board</u> of seven or eight shuffled their papers enough to cause a breeze as he had entered the room. The other candidates for the job had filled out proper application forms, detailing qualifications, hobbies and referees. What reached the top of the interviewers' papers when Jonathan had entered the room was a single sheet of paper, hand-written and outlining to the presenter that he had met him at a party, that the famous man had got rather drunk but that there were no hard feelings. Eyebrows had searched the ceiling when the breeze subsided.

This time, Jonathan had done more work than before. He had researched a plan. He had a dim memory of a long ago office he had known which had neglected their forward planning. Jonathan believed it to be the reason for their failure. His plan was to impress upon each of the <u>board</u> members that he was not human, not such a hard task given his character. He was sharp and self-conscious and sometimes it felt like most of his brain was concerned with how to get ahead. Jonathan's interview method would involve showing a complete disregard for correctness. There would be no pleasantries. He would try to appear as if, for him, other humans might as well be stone, albeit stone from which blood could be obtained.

Jonathan surmised that any imitation stone required high pressure, in this case the pressure of "truth", the stuff that television believed it knew most about. Jonathan would have to seem weighed down with it and he believed that if one used a barometer calibrated by time, he was surely, by now, made of stone.

For the <u>board</u>, the truth was also like a pearl. They wanted someone who could dive deep enough to net the oyster, sharp enough to then cut it open and devil-may-care enough to chuck the oyster away once the pearl was out. Living things were as nothing compared to semiprecious truths. This was how Jonathan explained news coverage he had seen

Jonathan, himself, was not sure what truth was.

When it came for him to sit down in the chair he looked around, realising that shaking hands would exhaust the time permitted for the <u>board</u>. He folded one smart, dark suited leg over the other, adjusting his tie as he did so.

"Hello, we've all got copies of your CV in front of us. Perhaps, you could tell us your experience in television," said a woman who would later turn out to be from the human resources' department. He glared at her.

"Please?" a man said, thinking that Jonathan was merely nervous as opposed to acting tough.

Apart from the human resources manager, the others were all men. They dressed differently, with concessions to the twentieth century's sixties, seventies and eighties. Their faces were taut, ready to bounce back any raindrops or flippant remarks.

"If I've come here to be asked about my experience," Jonathan turned to the woman from human resources, "I shall leave now, if you all don't mind," he replied.

There was a slight pause as one of the number looked upwards and smiled, as if with recognition. "I'm terribly sorry. Why don't we start with a hypothetical story?" He was taller than the others, leaner and yet puffier in the face, with red eyes and yellowing teeth.

"Very well," Jonathan said, allowing his tone to soften.

"The national currency has devalued, how do you treat the story?"

He looked up, then across the pairs of eyes awaiting him.

Stifling the urge to say he couldn't give a toss about the national currency, Jonathan told them what a serious matter such a crisis was, whom one would call for comment, whom one would call for facts. In this way, he alerted them to his understanding that fact and comment were different.

"I see. And how would you try to balance your report?" said a man, wearing a thick woollen poncho.

"I would ask spokespersons from the other political parties how differently they would have handled the events leading to the crisis."

"A million people die in Africa," another man said, this one with blue eyes that sparkled in a fat thick set face. "A million men, women and children die in Africa, and a train crash in London kills ten people and—it is a good news sort of day—seventeen people die up north. What's your lead story?"

"Ten in London, followed by the story in Africa."

"Good. And your reasons?"

He waited, perhaps for Jonathan to say that Africa was where black people lived and people north of London were not immediate concern. There was an answer on those lines that Jonathan had formulated but he could already tell that some of the men were concerned that he was reckless. They seemed confused that he was offering them the right answers but along with them, strange distortions of his face. "The local-ness of news is more important than just cold figures of casualties."

"Er, deaths."

"That's right, deaths. There's no point in ordering stories just on the number of deaths. A million is important, of course. But our viewers want to know about British people, English people, London people."

"Of course, if the seventeen up north had died in a particularly gruesome way, perhaps a serial killer, it might be different?" the lean man said, moving his head as if confiding something in Jonathan.

"That's right," Jonathan said, stony faced, knowing that these policy decisions were matters of pragmatism in a busy newsroom more than anything else.

After two more questions, Jonathan looked at his watch and said he had another appointment. Human resources looked troubled, having stared at him ever since Jonathan had spat out the word 'deaths'.

He left the interview room and noticed that the staff working in the newsroom shared an important news gathering feature, the ability to focus along with the ability to ignore.

Jonathan wouldn't remember what he did after the interview: a kind of electronic hibernation was how he lived. He did some freelance crime reporting and newspaper sub-editing to earn his living expenses. He was lucky to know a few friendly commissioning editors and because of a unique housing arrangement, he had no rent to pay.

He tried to monitor every news programme. He would concentrate on word-choice and running order, emphasis and picture selection. As the days went by, he became more unsure, gauging that the chances of his getting the job were slim. But he was lucky. A month or so after the interview, he received a letter and a plastic folder. The letter said he had been appointed as a producer, the folder said they could terminate his contract when they wanted to.

Jonathan celebrated by having dinner at a local Indian restaurant, shifting the pages of the Radio Times magazine. He had hardly any friends so he asked one of the waiters to sit with him and have a beer to toast his success.

On his first day, he wore his interview clothes, not realising the complex dress code that sets producers apart from reporters and reporters apart from production assistants and porters. On the tube to an area of the capital known as White City, he felt himself involuntarily nodding to passengers he thought were heading to Television Centre, rather than to the sweep of government housing adjoining it.

He had a purposefulness about himself when he marched into the air-conditioned room that sat beside the main gates to Television Centre.

"It's my first day, I don't have a pass," Jonathan smiled at the fortyish woman behind the counter, then glanced at some people sitting on the couch. While the receptionist turned away to select a file from the cabinet behind her, he looked at those waiting, at their cheap clothing and their unhappy faces. Presumably they were cleaners or porters on short term contracts, waiting to clock in at the appointed time. Jonathan remembered when he had jobs like that.

"Do you know which department?" she said, bring the lenses of her large clear plastic glasses closer to her eyes, magnifying them some four times.

"Yes, Good Morning, Britain," he said.

"Do you have a phone number? Well, I'll look it up...here it is. Hello? I've got a person here who says he starts today. Right. Okay." She laughed a little as Jonathan signed the list and was pointed towards a black machine constructed of steel.

In a few seconds he was walking through the security scanner. It was the kind they have at airports, except that there were no signs calming those with pacemakers. He didn't know it then, but it was the only such security feature at Television Centre—anyone in a taxi could get through the main gate without a pass.

That day there was a problem with the main front doors. Wooden blocks had been placed crossways against them to warn anyone who might think of pushing their way in. Others wishing to enter, including a news-reader, a comedian and an actor in costume, as if from a Victorian literary adaptation for the screen, walked through a side door and he followed. After a circuitous ten minute stroll through some corridors he found himself by the front doors again. Looking up, he noticed what looked like asbestos caving in from the ceiling. Since everyone around him was by now wearing masks, he hurried away.

In the corridor, Jonathan passed a newsagent, a dry-cleaners, a barbers' shop, a travel agent, a photocopiers' and a wooden case filled with awards. Then he met the group of four lifts on the ground floor. It was crowded here and illuminating. The settings for lifts in news organisations can say a lot about the efficiency and prioritising of newsgathering, he thought. He had read that the management consultancy firm used by the

Corporation was working on lift-settings. Jonathan was already very much looking forward to their research.

Unlike at some other offices, seven minutes' wait didn't cause anyone to take the stairs. They waited patiently, watching the spin of the three digital numbers adorning the tops of the lifts. Jonathan thought they looked like graphic devices for teaching children about memory.

Inside, the crowded lift, a male computerised voice announced that they were on the ground floor and then read out the date, the time of day and the outside temperature in case a passenger hadn't seen the ominous electronic displays by the doors. These acted as state-of-the-art reminders that the architects of Television Centre had foreseen the birth of a new window tax some time in the late twentieth century.

After a twenty minute walk, he found the right room. The door to it was emblazoned with a big "no smoking" sign and what looked like an old promotional sticker that had been designed to advertise the programme when it was launched a decade or so before. Behind the door was a room the size of a middling church hall, brightly lit by mercury lights and furnished by paper-strewn desks that had been jammed together. There was a computer terminal beside each chair and a couple of video editing machines stuck in *en suite* cubicles.

"Hello, I'm joining the team," Jonathan said politely to a man dressed like a secondary school mathematics' teacher. He was flicking through the last of what looked like his holiday snapshots. His bushy eyebrows turned up as if to escape the static electricity issuing from his double-breasted blue suit.

"You're the first to arrive, why don't you sit down and log in to the computer, so that you can find your way around?" he said, turning to look at his exposures again.

Jonathan sat beside what was the main table in the office and looked down at the grimy keyboard. He smiled as the computer recognised his name and password, his eyes resting on the top right of the green screen monitor. It was here that flashing capital letters announced new tragedies from around the world.

Nuclear—France-Test-Urgent
Sport—Glance
bc-fin-money-newyork
XMS DAVIES ARGENTINA
NUCLEAR-FRANCE-TEST-URGENT
BC-USA-MURDOCH
+ROVER CAR PACK
Yugo-Bosnia scheduled
C* 2300 BOSNIA ATTACK
EU HUNGARY COA
bc-oilprice 9-5 0489
Corporation C MOROCCO-FLOODS 2=
BC-USA-MURDOCH

These were "wires", news-stories penned by correspondents and news agencies from around the world and of all the wires being sent into the Corporation's computer system, these wires were deemed "flash" or "priority", which meant they were the most newsworthy items currently available.

He selected a different "queue" on the system, one relating to the morning breakfast programme. Under the military-style heading "Debriefs", was a list of dates. He accessed the most recent:

"Another good programme.
Oh, there's a leaving party at one o'clock for Sam Jones, who's leaving to take up his new PR post at Arbiter.
First off, Ireland. Not a good news day, so I suppose it's passable. Bad cut to David though. Is Camera Two all right?
Alfred's piece was good but why no real people. This isn't a text book, it's television.
ALFRED writes: fuck you, I'm leaving
EDITOR writes: Yup, either that or you're fired.
Newspaper reviewer guest was crap, banned from now on. Too many puffs for his own paper.
And can they please use the Tokyo feed time. We've only got

it for a few more weeks, why can't they get some pieces about funny Japanese or something?"

As he read through it, some of the other newcomers arrived. They looked sheepish and rich except one of them who turned out to be a trainee who wasn't being paid.

"Right, we're doing a course this week. We didn't have one last year and we think a lot of people didn't know what to do for the first couple of months which was a shame. Hopefully, this time they can start out a bit better," the teacher-like man, Peter, said. "If someone can give me a hand with some of these boxes, we can go down to the room we've hired.

The corridors of Television Centre were a maze but no one admonished Peter for moving too fast. Instead, the group of new boys and girls tried to stick together as best they could as they followed him down into the basement, some seven floors below the main office.

❧

"Right, we've still got some people to come, but we had better get a start on," Peter said. It was then that Jonathan realised how stern the man was, how he could ask whether you wanted a cup of coffee and make it sound like he was threatening your mother. During the course, Jonathan realised how strange it was that he should have this effect, he seemed to have so little cause to be angry.

"Now, I remember when I first came to the Corporation. I had just left Bolt Today, a trade paper. Anyone read it here?" Everyone in the room shook their heads. "Well, it's a pretty good paper, deals with construction projects, usually in the Gulf, Arab countries that kind of thing. It was a good grounding in journalism for me because it gave me a firm grounding in the need to be accurate. Accuracy, that's important at the Corporation."

Jonathan took out a pencil from his inside pocket, noticing he was the only person in the room without a clean pad in front of him. Accuracy, he told himself, was important.

"Now, let's start by going around the room and announcing names and new jobs and where you've come from."

"I'm Elizabeth and I worked on the Children's Cartoon Network. I'm going to be news producing here", said a petite blonde woman who looked like she had scrubbed her facial features away that morning.

"I'm Nigel and I've just graduated. I'm going to be producing, as a trainee though." Nigel looked downwards. He was wearing a thick jumper and his stomach and eyes seemed to be separate only by twelve centimetres.

"I'm Sally Colon, I worked as a production secretary in repro on the fourth floor and I'll be researching here."

"I worked at the Management Consultants firm, MacKnife and Faytel"

"I've just graduated from Durham in history"

So it went on, each description eliciting a kind of surprised sigh in the room. A couple of new recruits had copies of the Daily Mail newspaper in their bags and three of the group had rolled up copies of Hello! Magazine in knapsacks. They all seemed like reasonable people, Jonathan thought. He liked them already.

The men seemed deliberately to dress down as if to demonstrate that hardworking journalism was their game, not the vanities of television presentation. And yet, their dressing down was too calculated, almost as if they had been dressed up as a new fashion trend, one that encompassed a new mood of awkwardness, disorder and colour-blindness. The women all dressed up, their ambitions not so well concealed. Their jackets and tops were too new, the cases they had brought in too shiny. One thing the men and women shared was a decisive rejection of spectacles. Uncomfortable eyelash fluttering would benumb the week-long course. Participants, it seemed, already knew where to pigeon hole themselves. There were naive men, boffin men and men with authority. For women, there were pretty women, glamorous housewife types and older "sensible" women. In this class, the women tried to be pretty types whereas amongst the men, there were twenty year olds trying to look like seasoned ex-Vietnam reporters and forty year olds trying to look like bouncy travel reporters.

"I'm going to start by showing you a video that they shot in the office that should explain the sort of days or nights you are going to have here." Peter said, bending down and checking the connections between the video recorder, the television monitor and the wall socket. After a little head-scratching he was on the phone calling an engineer. After silent anticipation had reigned for half an hour, he called another. The first had got lost in the TV Centre labyrinth. After a while, there was a knock at the door and a man in blue overalls carrying parcels and letters came in looking alarmed.

"Hello," he said looking around the room, "this is the first time I've seen anyone in this room and I've been delivering mail here for twenty years." He went to the back of the room and the class followed his slight frame as it crouched. Then, they all noticed the six foot pile of buff coloured envelopes and tan coloured bubble packs. He laid some of the letters down beside the dusty pile and then walked back to the door. "Bye, then." He said.

After half an hour, a fuzzy video image came onto the TV monitor and Peter told the class that this was the best he could do for the time being. And so the film began. To the tune of some xylophone music, a man read a newspaper. Then there was a green screen like the one Jonathan had been using earlier and then the man was leaving the office and getting into an estate car that shot off out of view. Back in the office, Peter, himself, could be seen co-ordinating, pointing at things, looking glum, looking pleased. A researcher frowned with a reporter. A journalist carried a tray of steaming polystyrene cups. Eventually, a new team arrived, followed by presenters. Presenters liaised with editors. Suddenly the theme song to Good Morning, Britain segued from the xylophone music and the two presenters "wished a warm welcome" to viewers. Then Peter switched the television monitor off and smiled.

"Quite good, wasn't it?" he said. The xylophones still resonated in his pupils' ears.

"Now, I'd like to introduce Dave who's a cameraman...he should be here in a few minutes." After a silent couple of minutes during which faces nervously turned, Dave walked into the room, carrying a tripod, a video-camera and a lightweight waterproof bag. "Dave, always on time, huh?" said Peter, his words hanging in the air for a few seconds. "Well let's start with what annoys you most about television producers when they're with you on a shoot?"

Dave, his check shirt collars peeping from under a grey pull-over, did not look happy. There were umber marks on the knees of his jeans that matched the shade of the few hairs on his head that were not grey. His eyes looked tired and weary. His face looked as if it had been thumped into shape by a Playdoh machine.

"Hello." The sound of his voice was as if he were in a far off lavatory-cubicle. "I'm Dave, I've been here thirty years and I'm going to show you what cameramen, camera people, do when they go out with you on shoots." He began to set up the tripod and camera. "The first thing to remember is that our equipment is very expensive, so though you must help us carry it, you had better carry it safely. Look at this."

We all inclined forwards to see what he was doing.

"This is a fluid head. It costs a lot of money. So don't put it in the way of other people. I remember one producer taking it out of the car boot and placing it in the road. The whole thing was ripped off. RIPPED OFF!" he said, his voice emerging from the cubicle and into the wash-basin area, just for an instant.

"Now, there are 'x' basic shots. Head and shoulders, interviewee; head, interviewee; reverse two-shot; and that's about it, or at least that's all that you have to worry about. I don't want to see any budding Spielbergs with me like last year. Then there are noddy's, when you speak to your interviewee and I shoot him, saying nothing and vice versa. Also, remember that because it's not film that we're using," he looked down for an instant, tears glistening on his eyelids., "we can hardly ever shoot an interviewee in front of a light source, such as a window. Also, if there are going to be computer screens in the shot tell your cameraman to bring a 'shutter', that stops the screens from flickering.

"Now, sound." Dave had recovered his composure. "We've got radio mikes, lapel mikes and boom mikes. Usually, the mike on the camera can record atmos."

As he spoke, his gaze wandered to Peter whose furrowed brow and deep-set eyes were levelled sternly at Dave.

Meanwhile, the others in the room, except for the seasoned-looking twenty year old, whom Jonathan noticed had a packet of Woodbines cigarettes in his padded waistcoat, were frantically writing Dave's words down.

"The most important thing to know is don't tell them what to do, tell them the effect you want. There's nothing worse than a young producer ordering around an experienced cameraman," said Peter, "any questions?"

"Hi, I'm John. How often has your camera gone down in the past thirty years, then?" asked the man with the woodbines, smirking and then turning his head from left to right as if seeking approval from the rest of the class.

Dave turned sadly to Peter, his moist eyelids stretching as far as they could go. There was silence.

"That'll be all then," Peter said and Dave quickly began to pack away his things before sloping off.

"Right, now onto the next video," Peter said, pointedly ignoring John who was whispering to Elizabeth and crossing out some of the notes on her pad with a smile.

"Hazards. You will encounter many hazards and there are a number of courses such as Bullet Penetration 0200 and Swampland 530 and Air attack 50. But, I've always thought that it isn't the war-zones that are the most dangerous. Everyday scenes can be the worst. Take a look at this."

The class peered at Peter's rolled up sleeve and then they peered a little closer in confusion.

"I got that graze, on a splintery door post in Guilford, shooting a piece about the rate of inflation." Peter said. With his left elbow pointing to the class he used his free arm to reach over to press the play button on the video recorder. By the time he had lost balance and fallen to the floor, the film had started.

It was in better focus than the previous one and began with a series of bright explosions before the title "Hazards" scuttled up the left hand side of the screen. A Six O' Clock News presenter began narrating.

"Hazards and hazard control are part of your job. There are no honours for getting killed on an assignment. Take a look at this." There followed two minutes of men and women getting their limbs blown off or cut apart. Gun shots, mines, building demolition, detonated bridges, helicopter crashes were all shown. Perhaps the most interesting segment involved three journalists standing two yards apart from each other on a field.

"Okay, keep calm," said the first.

"Just don't move, you keep saying. Well what should we do then?"

"Look, Harry just walked onto that pebble and he was fine. Just follow him onto the pebble. The white one over there."

"What pebble?"

"Look, just follow him."

Each of them walked one step forward: they were all immediately killed.

"Now that's not the way to do it," Peter said later, before emitting a loud chuckle.

In another segment, a multi-storeyed building was on fire, the sky seemingly illuminated by fireworks. The film cut to a correspondent Jonathan had seen on television for years. He rapped his knuckles on a hotel room door. He was shouting an Arab name, imploring him to come out and go filming with him. "We've got to, they have to, come on!" he shouted.

When the man came out with his gear they went and found another Arab man in the canteen, a sound-man by the looks of his equipment. He immediately got up and joined them, walking through a hotel lobby.

"I remember telling them, go closer, go closer," the reporter said beside a destroyed wall, obviously in daylight and filmed much later. "I stayed back and then," the reporter looked down and paused before returning his eyes to the camera, "there was a bright flash and both of them were killed. It was terrible."

Only John was smiling when the video ended. Peter then handed out some laminated cards, covered in yellow and orange symbols. "This will be useful. Keep it on you and you can tell what kinds of hazards are around you. It describes what the markings on missiles, planes, mines and shells actually mean so that you're not caught out."

Jonathan shivered slightly as he imagined himself digging in a minefield to look at what stickers were on the mines beneath him.

"Now, they obviously give you a kit when you go into a dangerous area and this is it," Peter said, proudly lifting up a small cloth bag. Inside it is all you need to protect you against the hazards that may await you. There's a pair of eye-protecting goggles," he took out a pair of cheap looking imitation Ray-Ban sunglasses.

"There's a life jacket." A dusty orange bib failed to inflate as he yanked a cord that had sprung from the bag. Peter then began to blow on what looked like a kazoo.

"There's a bar of chocolate," a fragment of Cadbury's Dairy Milk chocolate, the size of a small finger nail was unwrapped and consumed.

"There's a sun hat with protective covering," he brought out a floppy white sun hat, the top of which was made of yellow acetate, the kind one finds in file-dividers.

"A box of matches with which to light fires." A small hotel matchbook was produced.

"Some plasters." A single waterproof Elastoplast in a small cellophane packet came out of the bag, "very useful that's been," Peter added.

"Various screws and bolts, a bottle of ink, another whistle, some aspirins, a packet of playing cards, a roll of film, a cotton-reel, three pairs of handkerchiefs and a woollen mitten."

So strange was the recitation that Jonathan, too, was now writing the contents of the "hazard" bag down on a bus ticket he had found in his inside pocket.

"Obviously, a proper half-day hazard course will be paid for by us so that you will have more training in this field."

"So, what happens if someone gets hurt while we're shooting? I'm on a short contract, so I wondered what sort of insurance we get," John asked. He was for the first time looking perturbed by the show.

"Oh, you're fully insured. However, you'll find out more on your course. But the camera, the rest of the equipment, that's definitely all insured. So don't worry about having to stump up the cash to pay for a forty thousand pound camera when you get blown up," Peter smiled.

"What about previous accidents?" asked John, refusing to let go, "what happened to them?"

"Well," Peter smiled, "I know of one story where a producer was out filming on a public street and he left a tripod in a dangerous position. An old lady tripped over it and sprained her leg and then sued."

"Sued the producer or sued the Corporation?"

"Sued the producer in the end," Peter mumbled before saying sternly, "The Corporation isn't there to protect you."

Jonathan looked troubled.

❧

There is no map of Television Centre.

Jonathan asked receptionists, personnel departments, secretaries, production assistants and they all said that, unfortunately, there was none and, in addition, there were no plans for ever producing one. Another producer who had been getting lost a lot joked to his editor that if, somehow, everyone at the Corporation died, they would have to send explorers into the building to map the place out, in the manner of Vasco da Gamma or Columbus. The editor stared at him for an instant and then left the newsroom. Jonathan didn't laugh either.

The office, though, was mapped out. On one set of twelve desks, pushed together, World Service Television News people sat at all times. On a set of four desks, sat the Good Morning,

Britain people and on a set of eight sat production staff from an odd lunchtime programme that no-one knew anything about.

He was assigned the Good Morning, Britain desk and sat at the computer, still baffled by the news-wires flashing on the screen. A bit of exploration of the computer system offered stranger things still. There were diaries, one for foreign news that usually concerned America, Japan, France, Germany and Italy. Another was for home news, and each day's entry began with a list of royal engagements throughout the UK. There was also an Economics diary, perhaps the best kept of all and one that was certainly more international. And then there was a special asterisked queue devoted to detailed information about the rapes and murders of a particularly grim serial killer who had been convicted some years ago.

Another queue was reserved for staff comments, a place where mutinous employees deployed stinging invective against their bosses. Jonathan laughed out loud on reading one comment about an editor.

His amusement was interrupted by the arrival of a researcher and day editor. They were each carrying copies of the far right Daily Mail, the newspaper of choice amongst many staff. Mondays, Jonathan would learn, were different. The first weekday was reserved for earnest reading of The Guardian newspaper, which published its television jobs' section on that day. Also in the hands of today's shift were hot-off-the-press copies of Ariel, the Corporation staff paper.

"Well, read the papers then," said the day editor who later introduced himself as Julian. "We're story hunting and if you don't find anything by eleven o'clock I'll send you out to do the new chocolate bar that's being launched by Clover's. Apparently, it's soft on the outside and hard on the inside."

"That sounds great," said Anne, the researcher, "have you had one? Will we get any to taste?"

"They sent me a whole box. I brought some in last week… it must have all gone." said Julian, peering over a loose gossip column page from his paper. Now, come on, settle down and get some stories. I'm going to have my hair cut and if you haven't got a story by the time I get back, it's chocolates."

"How about this?" Jonathan asked, "this bank that's gone under. There's a final judgement that comes tomorrow?" Jonathan was interested in banks. Over the years, he had accumulated a few thousand pounds in savings through thrift and solitude.

Julian put down the paper, his hazel eyes looking like they were deep in concentration. The researcher looked up from the newspaper she was reading. In the silence, Julian began to peer upwards, as if searching for dirt on the ceiling.

"I'll tell you when I get back, but try phoning for some comment." Then he got up and left.

Jonathan looked around the office. All the important stories were continuing ones: wars, budget crises, cease-fires and so forth. During the day, they would have to take "feeds", three minute video-packages that had already been completed overseas. They also had to call up and reconfirm guests that had been booked the previous week to appear on tomorrow morning's programme. The package they had to come up with was an "extra", a piece to fill up the air time or, if luck would have it, an unprepared-for news story that looked like it was going to break in the night.

"This is GNS!" Pause. "Reports are coming in of new shelling in Sarajevo. Casualties unknown at the moment." The announcement came over the Tannoy speakers that sat like gun-turrets on the newsroom wall. For an instant every person in the room halted in hope. The interregnum that lay between the activating of the announcer's microphone and the movement of his lips to speak was a long one. Suddenly, in that pause, everyone became part of a huge lottery syndicate, the balls in a Brownian spin. Would he be announcing imminent nuclear Armageddon or the arrest of a soap star?

But, today, the balls landed like clay for the kiln. What the announcer offered was merely news that had already been served on the wires. Over time, Jonathan would realise that this made a mockery of the Tannoy-man's urgent tone. Though he could say the words 'We are getting reports of...' like Orson Welles, he could never match sombre mood for information. Perhaps his worst performances were when he had to announce the "To be or not to be" of public address announcers. No week passed without the urgent recitation: "This is a test! This is a test!"

The bank story Jonathan had picked up on was not new either. It had broken years before as the worst bank collapse in history. What was new was that there was going to be a court ruling that might compensate savers at the bank. This was his story, or at least the story the newspapers were pursuing. He selected a name from the list of action groups on the computer and dialled.

"Hi, I'm calling from the Corporation. We're looking to do a story on the court ruling tomorrow. I just wondered about your thoughts, which way it's going to go and so on. And whether there was anything new that's come to your notice?"

"Oh, hello. Yes, yes. Shut up, Harry, it's the Corporation, hang on." There was a pause, a dog barking, the sound of a police siren. "There's quite a bit. You see we've got papers showing the Bank of England was completely negligent, that they withheld information, that the whole regulatory regime there is useless."

"Well, obviously, that would be very interesting," Jonathan replied.

"You people usually want a saver, I can help out there. There's a good woman who's been quite active. I'll call her and tell her to call you back. In the meantime, perhaps I can fax this stuff over to you?"

"That would be great," Jonathan replied, already looking forward to Julian's return. He smiled at the researcher, who looked up from the paper and bit into a crisp.

Julian returned with a fiercely short haircut, making him look like Peter, who had been quiet all day, just mechanically tapping numbers into a nearby computer. Julian agreed to go ahead with the story and told Jonathan to get moving. Jonathan arranged two interviews, one with an investor who had lost everything and another with a banking analyst at one of the City's merchant banks. "Always get an analyst," said Julian.

"And take Jane, she's the assigned reporter, you'll find her in the Economics Unit on the other side of the corridor. And call John, who's our camera-person," said Julian, as Jonathan declined a cup of coffee from a researcher on another desk. The offering of coffee was an intermittent comma that punctuated life in a newsroom without a coffee machine. Not an hour went past without someone asking a select number of people whether they wanted a cup of coffee. Even to Jonathan, who had started life in London making coffee, he would come to see that the offering of coffee was a momentous ritual.

Right across from newsroom was the Economics Unit, a place that inspired fear in producers because of its power and the strength of its views. Those who were employed there were known to have close links to the Corporation hierarchy and they were also known to have a single view about how the economies of the world should be run. Their office was much neater, a sign in itself of the power of the department. In it, reporters sat waiting to be collected by producers, *en route* to the car park downstairs. Jane was fortyish, toothy and with mousy, flyaway hair.

"Hello, I've just been told you're one of the Breakfast reporters, we're doing a piece about the court decision over the collapse of..."

"Yes, I know. Julian told me. Right, let's go. Have you got some cuttings?" She stared at him suspiciously.

Jonathan handed over a copy of today's newspaper and as she glanced at it, he could tell she regarded him as so much grime.

"It's quite interesting because the real story is to do with the Bank of England which let the bank continue for longer than it should have," Jonathan said, excitedly.

"Hmm..." she said dubiously.

"Well, I told John, who's our camera-person, we'd be down in five minutes."

"Well, we'd better get going then. I know John, I haven't

seen him for a while." She smiled a toothy grin, as if her whole set was about to leap out and fall on to the keyboard of her computer terminal. Jonathan walked towards the door, noticing the other reporters, each sporting either sceptical or smiling mouths. Some of them were reading tabloid papers, others chatted loudly on the phone in confident but at the same time, unintelligible, voices.

"Are you coming with us?" Jane asked to Jonathan's surprise. She was pulling herself into her long black coat.

"I thought I would," Jonathan replied said rather unsurely.

She moved her head as if taken aback and then slowly nodded with a frown. She was a quick walker and was out of the office and at the lifts a minute before Jonathan, even though they left the Economics Unit at the same time.

"There's really no need for you to come along you know," Jane said to him as they waited, side by side.

"But I know the people we're going to talk to."

She said nothing more and they entered the lift listening to two presenters analyse the merits of two makeup artists.

"Did he say we'd meet him at the car park?" Jane asked.

Jonathan nodded.

"That's in the basement. Look, I've just got to talk to the travel agents. I'll meet you down there in a second. Alright?" Her smile, because of her teeth, made her look like a frightening walrus.

Suddenly she'd vanished from the lift at ground level. Jonathan, alone, had arrived at what looked like a forbidding cellar on a lower ground floor. It was lit by bare light bulbs that trailed cables along the adjoining corridors. Balls of fluff, knee-high, blew about like tumbleweed and the scent of rotting wood infused the air. He ran down the corridor, thinking he saw exits further down only to find they were tricks of the lights. Where the walls were shinier, they looked like gaps. Eventually, he found a Sellotaped hatch and broke through it. He travelled through another corridor, passing the now usual hanging-from-the-ceiling asbestos-like foam. Further on, he passed noisy rooms where the walls were flaking. They housed deafening generators and shrieking air conditioning motors. Just near there, he discovered a door that led into what looked like a dimly lit garage. It was the car park. In one of the four or five spaces, Jane was already seated in an estate car, looking at her watch whilst she talked to John the cameraman. She scowled at Jonathan when he came to the window and waved a free hand at the pair of them.

"Hi!" he said, "Hi, John."

"Hello, you can probably squeeze in the back there, but be careful not to bash the tripod," he said, turning to Jane and letting his eyes rise to the roof of the car.

Jonathan scrambled into the back seat of the estate car, putting his mobile phone, some clippings and his notebook on the passenger seat.

"Right, where are we going?" Jane asked.

Jonathan gave John the address. The cameramen responded by drawing his pullover sleeves back from his wrists and starting the car. Jane leaned over and pressed a button on the dashboard which caused bright light to pour in from the where a large steel door was opening. They had left the building.

"It's a little like Batman," John said to Jonathan, "working up on the seventh floor and than taking a lift into the basement to drive out of the centre." John laughed, quietly at first and then progressively louder. With each new volume increase came more spittle on the windscreen. Then, quite suddenly, the whooping subsided into silence and John began to wiped his face clean with a handkerchief.

Jane raised the subject of her children and John responded by talking about his. They ran through what types of clothes their children liked, what toys, what foods.

Carefully choosing his moment, Jonathan spoke up. "So, er, the story for today," he interjected.

There were a few moments of silence.

"So, John, had any luck finding private schools in your area?" Jane asked

"Not really thought about it," John replied.

"I haven't actually. Although, one has to get them in early if one wants a place, that's what my friends say."

"Sorry," Jonathan interrupted, "the bank story will need some..."

"Was Harry okay about you going away to do that series? I remember you were having some trouble," John said to Jane.

"Oh yes, it was fine."

"It's actually quite complicated, the..." Jonathan tried to interrupt again.

"That's good, it is quite tough on family and friends, isn't it?"

"You see, the bank..."

"I suppose it is. Oh, look at that driver over there."

"The questions should..."

"Nice weather today, better than yesterday."

"Jane, I..."

"Do you remember when we were out shooting in, where was it?"

In the cramped space allowed him by the tripod and assorted video equipment, Jonathan, so rebuffed, began to doze off. He wasn't used to getting up so early in the morning and this first day had already made him drowsy. He only awoke when his car-door suddenly opened.

"Asleep? We're not going to get any filming done that way, are we?" Jane said, holding a menacing video light attachment in her right hand as if about to smash it over Jonathan's head.

He clambered out, looking up and down the suburban street. Straight ahead of him, he watched Jane forcefully rap the knocker of a dilapidated-looking door. Repeatedly, she pounded it like a winning prize-fighter.

"Hello, Mrs. Clam, we're from the Corporation. Excuse me." Jane had barged past the frail woman, pushing her out onto her doorstep to pick up the broken knocker from the patio.

"Shall I make some tea?" Mrs. Clam asked, looking up at John, who was carrying the video camera high on his shoulder.

"Tea, that would be lovely," he replied, marching in.

Mrs. Clam sadly fingered the gold coloured knocker for

a few seconds and followed the camera-person inside, gently closing the door.

Jonathan walked out onto the pavement and balanced the tripod in his fingers, his other hand trying to grasp his notes and a mobile phone. It took a few attempts but he eventually managed to get to the house and gently tap the leg of the tripod on Mrs. Clam's door.

"Hello, Mrs. Clam," he said when she had answered, "we spoke on the phone." Jonathan looked down at the trail of muddy footprints now decorating Mrs. Clam's fraying living room carpet.

"Yes, come in. Your people have just gone in," she said politely. Mrs. Clam was short woman with straight grey hair on the sides of her small head and a clump of dyed brown hair on the top. She had a smooth face, small eyes and a button nose and made Jonathan feel as if though it wasn't her fault, she thought he was somehow extraneous to the filming.

Inside, there was a desk, a white sofa and some plastic chairs. On the mantelpiece of the thin, hallway-like room, were photographs of children and an empty bottle of brandy. The bottle was green and smart looking as if its presence were to lend the room some charm. Opposite the mantelpiece was the sofa. It sat, fluffed up, under a framed A4 size magazine page depicting Van Gogh's Sunflowers. Jane jumped onto the sofa and lay down, her walking boots hanging off an arm rest where they scuffed some yellow sheeting that covered a side table.

"I'll have some Earl Grey, please," Jane said, letting her head fall on the other arm rest. She picked her hairclip from her head and began to examine it, accidentally pulling a tablecloth off another side-table with her elbow.

"Oh, don't bother about that," Mrs. Clam said, collecting the broken crockery that had crashed down to the floor. She held up a detached and somewhat ornate teapot spout and looked at it for a moment.

As Mrs. Clam's fragile body disappeared into the kitchen, John began shifting objects about in the room, occasionally looking down at his feet to the mud that he was dragging across the carpet. "Whoops-a-daisy," he said.

When the cups of tea emerged, Jane and Mrs. Clam sat down and were "miked up".

"Sorry, there was no Earl Grey, I could have gone out and got some from the shop only I have to pick up my son from school at four." Mrs. Clam frowned a little.

Jane looked unconvinced and lowered her head to her clipboard. "I'm recording this on my tape recorder for my own use so don't worry," she said cryptically before placing a small Dictaphone at her feet.

Jonathan stood in a corner, watching the interview.

"So how has the bank collapse affected you?" she asked to Jonathan's satisfaction. This was the opening question he had wanted to advise her to ask in the car.

"Well, it's been a bit hard..." Mrs. Clam's head was inclined towards Jane's feet.

"It's pretty hard for everybody, you know." Jane interrupted sternly.

"Yes...yes, of course. Well, as I was saying it's been a bit hard but it's hard for most people. We're losing the flat, you see." She looked up.

"Why's that?" Jane asked angrily.

"Well, my husband, Johnny, he borrowed some money for his business and he used..."

"What?" Jane asked, wrinkling her nose and looking as if she couldn't believe what she was hearing. "He borrowed money on the house?" She tittered a little before looking stern again. "Didn't the man realise that that would be risky? Putting you all, your family at risk?" Jane asked, more incredulously.

"Well, it was a good business. We had lots of customers and the rate offered by this bank was good, so yes...it's all a risk and in the end I guess, well, we were just unlucky." Mrs. Clam's eyes were slightly watery and had begun to sparkle under John's lights. She looked younger.

"That's right," Jane said in a coaxing, comforting way.

"Although, it was terrible when the bank went under.

Johnny was convinced the Bank of England had been negligent, they hadn't bothered to supervise this bank properly. He had papers showing they knew it was going under but the Bank of England refused to do anything about it, until people working there got the money out of the bank. The thing is Johnny was trying to campaign and then he had this tragic accident and..."

"We can pause there if you want," said Jane, even more comfortingly. There had been a loud click as Jane switched off her Dictaphone midway through Mrs. Clam's speech.

"Well," Mrs. Clam, said, large tears in her eyes, "the papers were gone. It's all so terrible."

"Here," Jane said, offering Mrs. Clam an arm rest cover she had untangled from her boots. "Wipe your nose on that. You'll feel a lot better. Anyway, so to recap, both you and your husband realised that this whole thing was an almighty risk. What happened, this whole saga...well, basically you've been unlucky. If you'd been lucky, we wouldn't have heard anything about you."

"Unlucky. Yes...we have been terribly unlucky. Some people are lucky and others are just unlucky I suppose. We took a risk and we lost. It's like the races, really," Mrs, Clam looked almost cheery. "Although, I don't know why it was us that had to lose our savings. I suppose it could have been anyone losing their savings...it's just been God's will really," Mrs. Clam forced a smile.

"John, you got that?" Jane said, smiling and looking satisfied, her front tooth sticking over her lower lip.

"Let me just check," John said before playing the footage back through his headphones. As he did so, Jonathan glanced into the distance and suddenly noticed that behind Mrs. Clam there was a glinting gold-coloured candelabra and that the camera shot must have included it. Jonathan would think nothing of this, nor the small enamel brooch on Mrs. Clam's collar until he got back to TV Centre.

"Right that's fine," John said.

"Why don't we take a set-up shot, say in the kitchen," Jonathan asked Jane, "perhaps pouring water into the kettle."

He had noticed that the kitchen fittings looked old and that if Mrs. Clam was the "saver" in their piece, it was right that she looked in some way affected by the collapse of the bank and the loss of her savings. The kitchen looked old and worn, the fittings either chipped or faded with age.

"No, I think we've got what they, I mean we, want." She turned to Mrs. Clam. "Thanks," she said tersely.

"Er, what time will this be on television?" she asked, her eyes still wet and now looking down at the full china teacups in her hands. She didn't seem to have the confidence to look at who she was speaking to in the eyes.

"Trowbridge between six and nine in the morning." Jonathan said, trying to appear cheerful by smiling.

"Oh good, Johnny and I do love breakfast television. It really wakes us up."

There was a loud crash as John casually put his foot into a toy boat, made of plywood, that had been sitting on the carpet. The boat splintered in his large hands as he picked it up. The sails ripped as he inadvertently pulled them the wrong way. Bits of wood spun onto the floor which John then crushed with his boot as he tried to stop them from moving. Mrs. Clam urged him not to worry. "It was only a bit of rubbish my husband made for my little boy, I was wondering what to do with it anyway," she said, taking what was left of it from John and putting the pieces down very carefully on one of the plastic chairs.

Jane put her coat on and swung her sleeve into the full teacups which scattered across the carpet like shrapnel.

"What an awful house," Jane said to John when they were all back in the car, "so cluttered. No taste."

It took about three quarters of an hour to reach the City of London and in that time, Jane had softly played back her Dictaphone and noted words and phrases down on a sheet of paper. Jonathan tried to look over her shoulder but it was in shorthand that he couldn't decipher. He tried to tell her about the Bank of England angle to the story a few times but there was no reply to anything he tried saying.

A light drizzle began to fall to the ground. Besuited men

and women with worried faces stood beside pelican crossings as the floodlit bank buildings behind them glowed. Umbrellas collided and briefcases jostled as the melee navigated orange traffic cones, building materials and giant cable reels. Above these city workers there was a collage of intricate scaffolding rising to the sky, the result of a huge bomb, a year ago.

"So where's the best place to park?" Jane, asked, turning to Jonathan. "That's the fucking producer's job, you know."

"Er...well, I suppose a National Car Park, or a parking meter if we're lucky," he said rather unsurely. He felt as if he had let the whole crew down by not thinking of where they would be able to park.

"It's okay, I can drop the stuff off at the office and find a place further away if necessary," said John, calming Jonathan's nerves.

Like so many in the City, the office block had been built to have the gravitas of a cathedral. The concièrge desk was made of steel, the lifts were Perspex, in the centre of the building were waterfalls and high above was a sheet of diamond-like glass.

The three of them got their name tags in exchange for their signatures. Jonathan put his on his coat, Jane put hers' in her handbag. Then, a security guard took them up in the lift to an ante-room filled with antique French furniture. Jane sat in one of the chairs with a blank expression, gently painting her mouth black with a ball-point-pen she was chewing. Jonathan looked at one of the paintings, saying the name "Jason" to himself, so that he would remember it when he came through the pine doors.

"Hello, Jason, I'm the producer, this is..." he said, as a double-breasted figure came in.

"Hi, Jason, how are you? Did Jenny and Tim like the dinner party?" Jane moved in front of Jonathan, pushing him away with some force and interrupted Jonathan's introduction. She winked and wiped a little of the ink from her face as she sought to remove a stray wisp of hair.

"Yes. It was wonderful. How are Len and the kids? Little Timmy must be quite grown up," Jason replied, looking up and kissing Jane on both cheeks.

Jonathan took a seat and watched them talk, listening to the sound of car horns from outside and the sound of the vacuum cleaner that had been brought in. He looked out of the window to his left and saw the five o'clock change of the City. The faces of those walking the streets turned from white to black as battalions of cleaners arrived for work.

Jane and Jason were on the subject of the news piece they were doing. "...Just the usual stuff, a look-ahead to the court decision. Anything you're unsure of, we'll stop the camera and do it again, all right Jason?"

"Anything you say, honey," he replied, brushing dandruff from his lapel.

John had set up the tripod and camera, had taken a white-balance to set the exposure settings in the camera and had switched on a light with a diffuser. Wires trailed across the furniture, matte landscape paintings on the walls turned shiny.

Jason's secretary, a short brunette with stress lines on her face, came and asked Jonathan how long they'd be. "Not long," he told her wearily. He felt tired, the feeling of being nonessential thwarting any excitement about the story he was producing. He watched Jane take out a powder compact and her hands begin to twitch about her face like a car-manufacturing robot.

"Want any, Jason? No, you look naturally beautiful," Jane said, using her forefinger to tuck her tooth in.

Laughter lines crunched on Jason's face before he looked down to a piece of paper in his lap, occasionally fingering the microphone cord that hung from the middle button of his shirt.

"Right...don't you think that tomorrow's court case will put an end to all the speculation about conspiracy theories and the like over the collapse of the bank."

"Er...yes." He suddenly looked a little nervous. "Hang on," he said, raising his shoulders and straightening up on the chair. "Okay...I think that the decision reflects the city's propriety and sense of justice. Sorry. I think that TOMORROW'S decision WILL reflect the city's sense of justice in these matters, it will reflect the fact that the city wants to get its house in order, that if there's a problem, the city can sort it out." Jason sucked his cheeks in and looked more serious. "After all, the City is a wealth-creator that's for the benefit of us all. Any type of bank collapse is hard, but these things do happen. Not very often, obviously. But that makes it all the more important that matters are cleared up quickly and efficiently. There are those who blame the auditors, the accountants, the lawyers, the government, big business...even the Bank of England itself. But I think that when the papers on this affair are opened up in fifty years' time, we'll all find out that nothing strange happened. This was just a case of betting gone wrong."

"That's great," said Jane.

"And let me tell you this," Jason said, his brown eyes sparkling below his floppy brown hair, "it's the savers I feel sorry for. But feeling sorry for them doesn't absolve them of some blame. After all, they thought that the overdraft rates at this bank were good, they decided to save or borrow there. In a sense it is their," he emphasised the word, "fault for not looking into their own financial affairs more carefully. If they had, the auditors, the lawyers, the accountants wouldn't have had to be called in to clear the mess up...and clear it all up they did...most efficiently, I believe."

"Thanks."

They were back in the car.

"Jane, why didn't you ask him about the Bank of England? Why didn't you ask about the leaked documents he showed you? What's wrong with you?" Jonathan felt exasperated. Somehow, they had seemed to lose the main thread of the story.

"Look, I've been in television for fourteen years, do you think I should listen to how you want this story done, or you should listen to me? I'm the seasoned reporter."

John chuckled as he turned the steering wheel.

Back in TV Centre, Jonathan was on the fourth floor, the place from where programmes were beamed across the globe and the place where programmes were stitched together. Jane had recorded her "track", her voice-over, onto a tape reel and had left him with a script and suggested pictures. Most news packages contain what is called library footage, the pre-recorded stuff with which producers can illustrate scripts.

"Not more library footage," said the videotape editor, a rough looking large man who was reading a book that was as unfamiliar to Jonathan as the thousands of pounds of equipment in front of him. "You know, less and less stuff is being filmed. Eventually, we'll be using pictures of 1970s' high streets for a piece about inflation figures in the twenty-first century."

"Too right," Jonathan replied, not quite understanding what he was talking about.

"Hello, library? I'd like some pictures of high street banks as well as the bank branches of the collapsed...oh, you knew? Great. Oh, also, pictures of the Bank of England and the Serious Fraud Office."

"These the rushes?" asked the picture editor.

Jonathan nodded, looking down at the two encased tapes on the desk.

"Right, let's get the package started. Is this tail-out?" he said holding the foot-wide tape reel.

"I'm not sure," Jonathan answered, images of animal tails in his mind. The glow of the electronics was unsettling him.

The picture editor "laid down the track", copying the voice of Jane from audio-tape to videotape, before looking for the "synch", segments from the rushes that showed the interviewees.

Mrs. Clam looked bright and cheerful in the nice lighting that John had shone across her living room. In close up, the scene reminded Jonathan of a baroque period drama.

"Doesn't look too hard up," said the picture editor to himself as he spooled through the tape.

The cameo brooch she'd been wearing had transformed into what looked like an antique diamond. It glittered as Mrs. Clam breathed. Behind her, a gold candelabra sparkled like a fitting from the Orient Express. Even the natural light looked as if it was a scintillation from the equator.

"We'll just alter the sound levels a little," the picture editor said, "there's some rustling. These cameramen are deaf, I reckon sometimes."

As he slid levers and pushed buttons, Mrs. Clam all of a sudden began to sound less cheerful and more resigned. But there was another effect. The vowels of Mrs. Clam's actual words began to linger longer, just a little. Her working class accent began to change, fading in and out. There was more twiddling and then, as if by magic, Mrs. Clam began to pronounce her words in a more Corporation-English accent. She sounded curiously calm.

"You can go if you want," said the picture editor. He spun the controller on his video editing machine like someone forcing a drawing pin to rotate on its tip.

"I'll check the computer," Jonathan replied, logging in and watching the news flash on the screen. In one of the queues was what was known as a "handover", a list that the day editor, Julian, had left on the system so that the night-editor knew what had been done during the day.

After some paragraphs detailing satellite "feeds" from Sarajevo, Washington and Tokyo and some live links to the studios in Westminster and one in York, where a body had been found, there were details about his piece: "should be a good one, Jane's on the case and it should have been cut by eleven tonight."

Jonathan asked the picture editor whether he wanted anything from the canteen but he said he'd be on his break in a little while and told him not to bother.

Jonathan left the cold of the editing suit and took another tour of the Television Centre. He felt a pang of guilt about leaving the news area. He worried that anything could be happening in the world while he walked and that he wouldn't know about it. It was partly the guilt that caused him to nearly choke on the food in the canteen, when he eventually found the place. By the time Jonathan had returned to the edit suite, the editor had left, having finished the piece and left the times at which titles ought to be placed on the screen to identify speakers. Jonathan carried the tape upstairs and left it with Harrison, the night-editor, who told Jonathan to go and get some sleep. He had been working for sixteen hours.

"Good morning, Britain. It's January the…"
Jonathan listened to the morning broadcast as he shaved.

"Today's news headlines: It's day 30 of the serial killer trial. Witnesses are expected to be called in at nine o'clock. More fighting in the former Yugoslavia, peace envoys say the stalemate will soon be broken. And the biggest banking disaster in British history, what lessons can they learn? Stay with us for all the news, weather and sport."

Jonathan tried to time his morning routine so that the only package he saw in full was the one he had produced the previous day. He bit his nails a little as the announcer read out the cue he had written. What followed was a devastating news package about the vindication of city analysts and regulators. Mrs. Clam exploded onto the screen as a minor aristocrat who was a bit of a moaner. Jason, the banking analyst, had been transformed, vaulting into view as a hero of the age. Here was a thrusting city man, as knowledgeable about finance as he was young and as his suit was well pressed.

Jonathan scratched his head a little and went over to a framed picture of his mother and kissed it.

"Oi! Jonathan!"
Jonathan flinched.

"Food. Food, man! Food, know anything about it?" asked Julian the next morning, eating a soggy bacon sandwich.

Jonathan looked up at him from one of the morning papers and nodded.

"Good. I think we should do something on the food scare

stories, call some people up, find some facts. Facts, facts, facts, get a move on!"

"Would you like some coffee?" asked Anne, the researcher. Until then, she had been busy filling in the bingo cards that had come with one of the newspapers.

"I'll get some today," Jonathan said, reaching into his jacket pocket to see how much change he had, "what would you like?" He knew what it was like to always have to be the one to get coffee.

The coffee bar was located directly below the newsroom. It was a bustling place where there were seats only for the cashiers. Old and grey-haired, they would sit together by one of the two tills counting out change as if they were blasé hospice dwellers counting the days they had to live. A pair of coffee machines had been fitted at the back behind a tray rail. They were impressive to look at, fresh beans in clear plastic funnels on top and spouts underneath labelled "cappuccino", "espresso" and "white" and "black". Underneath them were polystyrene cup dispensers. The machines only delivered one cup of coffee at a time so long queues, sometimes involving fifty or sixty people emanated from them. On getting to the front they would smile a little as they pressed the required buttons only to frown as they topped their cups with a plastic cover. The fresh looking beans on top were, it turned out, nothing to do with the process of making the coffee. They remained motionless the whole time. The watery coffee being dispensed, meanwhile, was always soupy and scented of essence.

Alongside the till, staff stared at the array of odd biscuits and crumbly cakes that seemed as if from another age. From the sleepy eyes of those juggling their polystyrene cups, Jonathan recognised the use of coffee as a drug. Most of them were technicians although producers and presenters came to the coffee bar too. The system was remarkably democratic: presenters who had to be on-air in a few minutes were not permitted to jump the queue. They didn't seem to mind much. Even those who were trailing microphone cable around with them were calm as they looked for their change.

The top presenters were even more sedate, seeming to prefer chatting to the cashiers than the nation. Jonathan wondered whether the cashiers were the only constants in the presenters' news-riddled life.

Senior producers did, however, sigh and pull faces when they were at the back of the queue. Peter was one of them, gripping just a Kendal Mint Cake and staring angrily at the rounds of sandwiches before him. Only those on the business and marketing side of the Corporation were spared the community feeling of queuing together and so there was a subtle hint of solidarity about the "buying of coffee". Jonathan heard the presenter at the head of the queue telling one of the cashiers he had seen state-of-the-art coffee machines being wheeled into the corporate suites on the top floor.

"The message is simple. Beef is off. The terrifying thing is that Creutzfeldt-Jakob disease takes a minimum of 10 years to incubate, and the BSE scare only began in 1986. Over the next few years, tens of thousands of people could start to display symptoms," declared a professor. Jonathan had phoned up one of the leading microbiologists in the field. The professor had told him that whereas Britain suffered this problem, European countries reared beef with high levels of a banned growth hormone, clenbuterol. American beef, meanwhile, has been routinely treated with five different growth hormones including "the controversial bovine somatotrophon." As for pork, he said that Britain still uses the recently banned antibiotic, avoparcin. As for poultry, about a third of all supermarket chickens contained high levels of salmonella, compared with less than one percent of Swedish and Norwegian chickens, he helpfully added.

"What about vegetables?" Jonathan asked, gazing down at his cold beef and salad sandwich.

"Well, according to the Ministry of Agriculture, carrots have unacceptable concentrations of pesticides. As for potatoes, half of all potatoes recently sampled by a working party on pesticide residues were found to contain residues of Aldicarb, a highly toxic insecticide which is suspected of being able to mutate genes."

"Mutate genes?" he asked.

"Call for you, Jonathan," said Anne, interrupting and pointing at her telephone receiver.

"Look, can I get back to you. I've got all your details, perhaps you'd be available for interview tomorrow morning?"

"Hello, this is the Meat Consultancy," he had picked up the other line. "I hear that you're doing something on the food industry. Well, I can put up our chief executive. I can get him for you. So you're one lucky producer. He's a Mr. Bark..." as he spoke, Jonathan could see Julian waving his arms about in broad circles and mouthing the words "get him, get him."

"Great," Jonathan said, seeing Julian fall out of his seat in the corner of his eye. "It would be good if he could come on the programme."

"Julian," Jonathan said, when he'd put the phone down, "there's a microbiologist who's keen to come on the programme tomorrow, only he's not in London. Do you think they could get a feed for a live interview for tomorrow?"

"Where is he?" Julian replied, getting back onto his chair.

"Leeds."

"No can do Jonathan. I've done the quota of feeds for tomorrow. Tell him we're doing some other late breaking story but leave his details in the contacts queue in the computer for future use," Julian said, furiously typing in handover notes, filling out expenses' forms and accounts and preparing to disappear to interview staff under the Corporation's staff assessment strategy. "Got a farmer yet? Well, find one and go and ask him how it's affecting his farm. Get one who's nearby, too. Pronto!"

Jonathan looked under the "Farmers" entry in the computer:

Farmers
1.   *Horace Cliff   High Farm, Essex—Good on food issues*

2. *Johnston Duff   Drainage   Lane   Farm—Not   very articulate*

3. *Spencer Johns   Clamfort Farm, Yorkshire—Stutters*

4. *Dora and Ely Staines Shepherd's Bush Market Farm— V.Good, near Television Centre.*

"Hello, is that Ely Staines?" Jonathan asked, "I'm calling from the Corporation."

"Oh, hello. Yes, this is Ely, would you like to do some filming today?"

"Well, yes," Jonathan said, surprised, "we're doing a piece on how safe Britain's food is and I wondered whether we might be able to arrange an interview about what the main issues facing farmers are?"

"That would be fine, what sort of time would you like? Any's good with us."

"Well, we're just exploring the idea at the moment. What do you think are the issues?"

"Well, you tell me."

"Sorry?"

"You tell me. I mean I only see what I read in the papers. Why don't you bring around some of the latest information and I can have a look at it. I mean," Ely laughed, "basically, I know what's going on. There's been a big scare and now it's affecting farmers."

"That's right."

"Well, we're not exactly in dairy farming down here, more flowers. But we're farmers alright."

"Sorry, Ely, I seem to have another call. Look I'll get back to you in a few minutes."

"Fine."

"Hello, this is the Meat Consultancy. I'm sorry to disappoint you but Mr. Bark won't be able to be interviewed after all but I can put you through to him if you want some background information. I'm very sorry about this. I really thought you'd have him for your report. It's most annoying, actually."

"Mr. Bark here," said another voice on the line.

"Oh, there he is. You've got him, after all."

"Hello," said Jonathan, somewhat confused about who he was talking to. "I was wondering really about some facts about BSE, when it began, the possible causes and so on."

"Yes, well, it's a pretty difficult problem, BSE. No doubt about it. The problem is, of course, that no-one knows much about it. I mean, I think it's quite frightening, well, it seems that it might be frightening, as it were. I mean, we've been doing some research of our own and, well, it doesn't look good at all, I mean, it looks, well, quite frightening. Of course, our research...well, obviously, we couldn't appear on television doing interviews saying anything about all this stuff. Maybe, we'll be looking to do some TV when our report is finished. Sorry, I can't help you."

"So you're quite worried?"

"I wouldn't say worried, concerned would be more the right word, off the record obviously."

"Is there any information you could perhaps fax to us on the research you've done?"

"Well, that would be doing your job for you. No, we can't fax anything to you. You know how it is. Now, I've got to attend to some other things so as I said, we'll no doubt be in touch when we release our report."

> Yr Mn Date Day...................   When   last
> modified and by whom
> 95 09 25 Mon.................. Fri   Sep   22   16:11   1995
> pleeburn
> 95 09 26 Tue UNITED NATIONS!!   Fri Sep 22
> 12:52 1995 nutman
> 95 09 27 Wed JENNIFER'S BABY DUE   Fri Sep 22
> 01:00 1995 nutman
> 95 09 28 Thu.................. Fri   Sep   22   13:07   1995
> nutman
> 95 09 29 Fri MONETARY MEETING   Fri Sep 22
> 04:49 1995 nutman

95 10 02 Mon................. Thu   Sep   21   12:32   1995
nutman

95 10 03 Tue MURDER TRIAL VERDICT   Fri
Sep 22 12:12 1995 nutman

95 10 04 Wed................. Thu   Sep   21   12:08   1995
nutman

95 10 05 Thu Harry's DRIVING TEST   Thu Sep 21
12:33 1995 nutman

95 10 06 Fri CEASEFIRE ANNIVERSARY Fri Sep
22 09:53 1995 nutman

95 10 07 Sat IMF ANNUAL MEETING Mon Sep 4
11:15 1995 nutman

95 10 09 Mon................. Wed   Sep   20   11:28   1995
nutman

95 10 10 Tue NUTMAN'S BIRTHDAY   Thu Sep 21
12:36 1995 nutman

Jonathan entered the details of when the Meat Consultancy
report would be out into the Corporation diary queue of the
computer. The diary was the starting point for day editors and
planning editors. They had to make sure that on every day of the
year there was something that the news could cover should no
story break. The list was odd in that personal annotations had
become mixed up with international affairs. Thus journalists'
dentist appointments and driving tests had become mixed up
with the anniversaries of cease-fires and the summings-up of
judges at the High Court. As he flicked the down-cursor button
on his keyboard, the Tannoy announced the discovery of more
mass graves in another part of the world. Jonathan noticed that
Julian could see he was looking somewhat distracted.

"Look laterally, Jonathan. Laterally, that's the way to do a
story if you're having difficulties," said Julian. "Look, why not
just get a vegetarian, someone who has an axe to grind about
meat."

A few hours later, after another long car journey through
the streets of North London with another reporter and another
camera-person, Jonathan was back in an editing suite on the

fourth floor. The reporter had left after the interviews because
he had an early start the next day, going to Bosnia. The camera-
person had been a gentle, quiet man, in his forties, wearing a
weary expression that communicated his lapsed ambition to
be a film director. He had talked on the way back to Television
Centre about the Corporation, how it had changed. "It's still the
best, you know. That's the problem. It's the best of the worst."

Jonathan nodded seriously as the camera-person swung his
steering wheel. "I don't suppose I can use your phone, can I?"
he asked.

"Who do you want to call?" he replied, "you know it's my
phone. They took away the Corporation one. If it's a personal
call, of course you can borrow it."

"Well, it's just that I thought I should phone in to the
newsroom, in case there's an urgent story. You know...and we
happen to be in an area where they need a camera"

The camera-person laughed, fumbling for cigarette. "You
remind me of how it used to be," he said, "no-one does that
nowadays. We don't have the same pride in the profession, you
see. No, best to knock off at the earliest opportunity, I'd say.
Get the mediocre job done and get home to the wife. I've just
done an eighteen hour day, you know.

"I remember when we'd race to get a story," he took a drag
and turned to Jonathan at the traffic lights, "when we'd park
on a double-yellow line if the story needed it. Now, I wouldn't
do anything more than I'm told to do. One of the resources'
cameramen parked on a double yellow line a while back. It was
big civil disturbance or something. What did he get out of his
heroism? He had to pay for his tickets out of his own money.
Another was a few miles an hour over the speed limit. He was
rushing to get to the scene and he got the story, pictures of a
shooting in the West End or something. What did he get out
of it? Points on his license, that's what he got. The Corporation
never helped him out, not like they used to when we were all
staff cameramen. For him, that was it: his last story and the end
of his livelihood. He couldn't drive around anymore.

"I thought you producers would hear about all this sort of

stuff. You heard about the New York shoot you people just did? That was a classic story.

"Some of your management consultant people, some of the big cheeses had the bright idea to re-use videotape. Hilarious one, that. Your boys went to New York. Huge story about the President, massive budget. Hotels, Plane tickets, car-hire, you even had to pay a sum to get with the President's entourage. What happens?"

Jonathan shook his head.

"Nothing. Absolutely sod-all. They were re-using a videotape. What a cost-cutting manoeuvre!" He chuckled. "To save twenty pounds for a new videotape, they had lost a hundred thousand on the whole shebang. Plane tickets, accommodation, salaries—all for nothing."

When Jonathan said that he had heard the Corporation wasted its resources in the "good old days", the cameraman smiled a weak smile, as if Jonathan was an enemy who would never understand.

After the customary quarter of an hour wait at the lifts he "booked in" the tapes of the interviews. A bearded man with large droopy eyes angrily got up from his computer where he had been playing a fast shoot 'em up arcade game. Then, he stumbled about the small office, taking out red, blue, green and yellow stickers, pens and pieces of card from various shelves. These he used to classify the two tapes Jonathan had brought in by laboriously noting down reference numbers, gluing cards and sticking stars and squares onto the video cassettes and their boxes. Then he copied the numbers down onto a clipboard. "Quite a system you got there," Jonathan said, watching the man settle back down to his computer game.

Since the reporter had gone to prepare for Bosnia, Jonathan was to "voice" the package. He was shown into a place called "SRU" by the picture editor, standing for Sound Recording Unit. It was here that newsreaders, top correspondents and sometimes celebrities urgently came to get their voices onto magnetic tape. Jonathan's first "take" was not good enough. At first he put it down to the restrictive nature of his jacket and his excited saliva glands. He felt slightly embarrassed and began to psyche himself up for the job.

"No, it's not you that's the problem," the picture editor said, opening the door of the small room. "It's this," he said pointing to the microphone. "You have to push a little, just a touch, on the Sellotape, otherwise I can hear a crackle. "Oh and you have to jiggle the sign a little if you want the 'IN USE' sign to light up outside the door. After banging some buttons on the console in front of Jonathan with his fists, he went back to the editing suite to record the voice.

When Jonathan knew his picture editor was recording, he began to read the script that had been written for him. He had been on a course on voice-overs and he read the way he had been trained, speaking the words as if not understanding them, emphasising syllables counter to the meaning of the sentences they were a part of. It was the weak phrases that needed to be pronounced as if they were most important, he remembered.

After a quick and glutinous meal in the canteen where he watched sad newsreaders sip at goulash, the picture editor played back the finished tape in the suite.

"Yes, sorry about this. It's just that the library shots were terrible. I'm afraid we had to get hippies from the sixties for the vegetarian shots. They just didn't have any of the New Age Travellers...they're all out for a documentary someone's doing in the other building," said the picture editor, his 747-like editing console hidden by piles of old-looking videotapes. Jonathan noticed that the shots of the hippies looked like older video footage. The colours looked strange and artificial. Viewing the tape for the first time, he remembered to listen and watch only for what his trainers had called 'televisual style' and not for 'content'. He knew it was important to concentrate on the look of the piece in isolation from what it was saying.

He soon realised that in this removed context, the package looked extraordinary. The whole thing ended with a disturbing white line moving down from the top of the screen, revealing the Royal Wedding of Prince Charles and Lady Diana Spencer.

Jonathan looked troubled on seeing that the tape had been used before.

"I was wondering about that, where do you think it came from," the picture editor asked him as he haphazardly peeled back one of the many overlaid stickers from the box where the tape had come from. Jonathan peered at the box. The label that drew his attention was one written in bold red capitals: "DO NOT ERASE. ROYAL WEDDING RUSHES MASTER. KEEP FOR LIBRARY."

Good Morning, Britain. A very warm welcome to the programme.

Jonathan wiped the sleep from his eyes and finding himself drained, went to the kitchen to make some coffee. Timing the running of his stained bathtub and the boiling of his steel kettle, he settled down on his bed in time for the TV-piece billed as "the food scare and what to do". His name was announced inaccurately—something like Cow instead of Jonathan—to over a million people, a few seconds later.

Here's Simon, one of the millions of militant vegetarians in Britain.

"*Well, I started being a vegetarian when I was at University. Now I eat onions and potatoes, no meat at all. That's because it's poisonous.*"

The camera tracked through the kitchen, lingering on potato and onion skins in the rubbish bin to the strum of a sitar. There was then a cut to a group of long-haired young men and women chanting around a fire.

"*No meat. No meat. No meat. Aaaargh. No meat.*"

Spirits run high here about the meat scare although most people look upon this band of young rebels as a curiosity.

"*Well, we think they're quite funny. I suppose they'll grow out of it all when they've left college,*" *said a woman in a green hat, interviewed in front of a chemists' shop.*

But what does the local butcher think? Will the new anti-meat-eating tendencies in Britain catch on or is it a fad?

"*No bother at all. Mostly they're out stopping fox-hunts. It doesn't stop the customers coming in. There's been a slight decrease in sales this week, but any case that the media trumpets does that. My message is to the TV people like you, stop destroying us, we all know it's safe."*

The butcher was carving up a joint of beef. Then he was unloading carcasses from a lorry. Then an animated graphic came onto the screen.

"There is no proof that there is any truth in the current scares about meat" That's what the Ministry of Agriculture said to Good Morning, Britain.

But as long as there are people that are against eating meat, protests and misinformation will probably continue.

The final voice-over accompanied pictures from the sixties endeavouring to be pictures from the nineties of more long-haired men and women dancing to psychedelic music in flares and short dresses.

"No meat. No meat. No meat."

A piece of jargon that Jonathan had heard, perhaps than any other in the canteens and tea-bars of the Corporation was "co-siting". He knew what it meant, loosely translating it into English as "moving", specifically moving the Corporation out of central London and over to Shepherd's Bush. People in the canteens would complain about it, not only because it was harder to get to the new site but also because of the how much the move would cost. Salaries would have to be kept low because the new site would mean the Corporation spending more on taxis and coaches for interviews and audiences, ferrying them from central London and out to the suburbs. Jonathan read in Ariel that the management consultants, who themselves were moving to central London, said that co-siting would indeed be cheaper. Jonathan understood the argument to be that though the news might not be as speedy as before—news was usually made in the centre of the capital—the management consultants themselves, who needed instant access to the restaurants of the West End would be able to work much more efficiently.

One early symptom of the co-siting to come was the use of taxis at TV Centre. Since the hours for producers were so long, their transport had to be paid for by the Corporation. A memo in Jonathan's pigeonhole the previous day told him that staff should take unlicensed minicabs where possible and that freelance staff were not permitted any late night transport. Jonathan believed that this memo had influenced his editor's decision to lead the next day's programme with the state of public transport in Britain. It was either that or the announcement of the latest crime figures for the Shepherd's Bush area.

"Planes, Trains and Automobiles," Sara, today's day-editor, announced, "seen the film?"

Whilst Sara chatted to the day-researcher about the film's merits, Jonathan began dialling the number for News Information, the Corporation's own press cuttings' department.

"Er, can you give me some of the more recent feature articles on transport and transport policy…er…my authorisation number…yes." Jonathan looked to a large poster on the wall, below the faulty clocks that were supposed to tell the time in different parts of the world.

The poster was a legacy of the internal market and consisted of a forty figure alphanumeric code. Each department was allocated a unique series which to quote. It was meant to stop employees feeling they were part of one entity and instead make them believe they were competing for resources, against each other. Competition, it was hoped, would result in "efficiency-gains" as those departments which ordered the fewest cuttings, used the least research and Corporation resources would triumph. Jonathan knew very well the significance of a news-producer ordering cuttings to research a story. Some departments had cut 'deals' with News Information whereby the department paid less because they required so much research. Good Morning, Britain did not have any deal, partly because departments with deals usually suffered worse research. If News Information wasn't getting paid as much, they weren't so keen to use the more expensive tools such as computers for searching for keywords.

Jonathan remembered all this as he recited the forty figure authorisation code. Then, he waited. He waited some one and a half hours before he was rung up and told to go and collect his cuttings. This week, the News Information department was located about half a mile in a northerly direction. Consultants were still deciding one where to position the Corporation's research departments. Jonathan knocked on the door and waited for a few minutes.

"Hello?" said a man dressed in leather motorcycle gear. He was the only person manning the whole department. Sitting amongst the resounding telephones and coffee-splashed keyboards, he enlightened Jonathan about how the redundancy programme was progressing without any prompting

"Sorry about that. I have to keep this motorcycle courier job, otherwise I'd have nothing if they phoned me and said they didn't want me to come in. I was just out on a really quick job. You know how it is. Look, here are the cuttings, what I could get, you know," he said, offering Jonathan two A3 size sheets of paper, "sorry there aren't more, it's just...well..." he pointed to the flashing lights on his telephone before putting his hands to his ears and then answering a call. "You want what?" he said, "some cuttings on Yugoslavia?"

AEROPLANE SAFETY FEARS—CRAMMING THE SEATS IN
BRITAIN'S PRIVATISED AIRLINE HEEDLESS OF SAFETY CONCERNS
PRIVATISED AIRLINE IN DIRTY TRICKS CAMPAIGN
RESIDENTS VOW TO FIGHT NEW AIRPORT TERMINAL
UNDERCARRIAGE DROPPED FROM THE SKY
BRITAIN'S RAIL NETWORK SOLD FOR A PITTANCE
EFFICIENCY = DEATH : SIGNAL FAILURES ON BRITAIN'S RAILWAY
BUY A TUBE STATION—AND NAME IT AFTER YOUR COMPANY
THE END OF RAIL INFORMATION
RESIDENTS FIGHT OFF STATION CLOSURES

*THIRD LONDON UNDERGROUND STATION
CLOSES
"KEEP THE PRICES HIGH TO DETER
PASSENGERS" SAYS SPOKESMAN
RAIL CHAOS BLAMED ON TEETHING
PROBLEMS
THE LESSONS OF CLAPHAM AND KINGS CROSS
: PRIVATISE
RAIL CARNAGE MASSACRE: HUNDREDS DIE
RAIL BLOODBATH
THE GREAT TRAIN BUTCHERY
AIR POLLUTION IS KILLING OUR CHILDREN
GOVERNMENT SAYS DON'T LEAVE YOUR
HOME
WORLD HEALTH ORGANISATION SLAMS UK
AIR STANDARDS
OUTSTANDING NATURAL BEAUTY TURNS TO
ASPHALT
MORE ROADS MEAN MORE CARS MEANS
MORE ROADS
PROTESTERS STOP NEW ROAD BUILDING
RISING ASTHMA CASES BLAMED ON AIR
QUALITY
PRIVATISED BUSES ENDANGER PASSENGERS
AIR KILLS*

Jonathan looked at the press cuttings while his assigned reporter entered the newsroom and chatted to Sara, exchanging photographs of children. Jonathan set himself the task of coming up with one interview by the time they finished.

Francis, a man from a transport think-tank, answered the phone on the first ring and said an interview "down-the-line" was all right. Jonathan thought he spoke well about the need for an integrated transport strategy across Britain. However, the man was more cagey about privatisation, not seeming to want to come down on a side.

"Well, it's not proved. Privatisation of the buses has

increased the number of buses. Fares in some areas have fallen. It's true that our survey results show that passengers are waiting for buses for longer and longer times and that bus accidents have risen sharply, but that doesn't mean much on its own," Francis said.

"According to cuttings I have, congestion has got much worse in towns with privatised buses. And in some areas, competition has led to the monopoly of one privatised bus company in the town, one that charges more and offers less," Jonathan said, looking down at his desk, feeling quite good about how eloquent he sounded.

"Yes, that is true but it's too early to say. What I can say is that the government puts too much into roads and too little into public transport infrastructure." Francis batted the subject to and fro for a while, on his own. For a moment, Jonathan idly wondered where the money came from to support the think-tank....As Francis spoke, Jonathan looked it up in a reference book he had found propping up one side of his desk.

"Hello, I'm Hugo, your reporter, I'll be in the Economics Unit," a large man creating a shadow said.

The trick of producing television programmes, Jonathan decided, was to speak to the reporter before he or she walked off to the Economics Unit. If he was lucky enough to meet an assigned reporter in the newsroom, he knew to try and keep them there. The Unit buoyed up the confidence of reporters, Jonathan thought. They needed the camaraderie that cackling to themselves about incompetent production staff gave them. They liked producers having to come in and haul them from their barracks. They liked the cowboy-in-a-saloon silence when producers walked in, the comradely laughter as they walked out. But Jonathan wasn't quick enough. Hugo had vanished.

"Er...Hugo," he was half-way in through the door of the Economics Unit and Hugo was chatting with Jane, who was apparently being complimented on her reporting of the Bank collapse story earlier in the week.

The room became silent as Hugo, about six feet tall, got up from his chair to receive Jonathan. "Yes?" he said, before looking at his fellow reporters on either side, "what are we doing today, then?" He flashed an angled smile as if from a horror film. Jane giggled a little.

"We're doing a transport film," Jonathan said as various reporters raised their eyebrows, "about transport in Britain."

'Not another one,' seemed to be the silent response of the reporters. They began to form a circle around him.

"Look, Hugo, let's go into the newsroom, where I've got the cuttings," Jonathan said quietly.

Hugo looked quizzically at the colleagues surrounding Jonathan before slowly beginning to pile his papers into a file. "I'll be there in a few minutes," he said, waving his hand at Jonathan, who had broken the circle and was running towards the door.

"As soon as possible," Jonathan shrieked, catching the door in his face and the glance of Jane who was staring at him as if he were something disappointing in the canteen.

Jonathan waited nervously in the newsroom, smiling as Hugo entered, half an hour later.

"Sorry about that, then. Right then, what's the story then?" Hugo asked, when he had sat down at a nearby desk. "I mean what angle are we going to look at, then?"

Jonathan looked puzzled at his reporter's use of language. "Well, it's the whole thing. The editor brightly came up with the title 'Planes, Trains and Automobiles'," Jonathan whispered.

"God, what an old story, then," Hugo wrote something on his pad.

"Well, it did seem a low news-day," Jonathan replied, not quite sure of what he himself meant. Wire stories marked urgent were flashing up on his screen every sixth of a second.

"So far, I've got someone from The Transport Initiative, a think-tank. We can interview him down-the-line and what they really need is you to go and..."

"Oh, he spoke to Sara," Hugo said, "she told him they didn't need this for tomorrow because of the extra story on Jimmy."

"Jimmy?" Jonathan asked.

"The boy that's gone missing. Anyway, they still need the

story, then. It's just not for tomorrow morning. It'll be for the following day. We've still got to turn it around quickly, then."

Jonathan looked towards Sara who had been listening to them between bites of her salad. "I'm not on shift tomorrow," she said.

"Well, it would be better if there was some continuity," Hugo said, "would you want to produce this tomorrow? I'm on for it."

"Oh, I didn't mean it like that, I'd be happy to be on the story for tomorrow, it looks like being a good story," Jonathan said, trying to gauge where the conversation was going and what they were talking about.

Sara laughed, "all right then, go to it."

Jonathan was beginning to feel insecure

Hugo and Jonathan began talking about the project and they both decided they needed, in addition to the transport think-tank man, someone from the privatised buses, someone from the privatised railways, a resident who was against a new Air Terminal, some "vox pops" (impromptu interviews with passengers) and someone from a rail-user's organisation.

"how about someone from the rail unions. There's a strike looming..."

"No, no, no, no, no," Sara interrupted, "they make boring television, you must know that. We don't want any weird regional accents either," she said.

"I agree, then," Hugo chipped in.

"Alright then," said Jonathan.

Over the next couple of hours, Jonathan and Hugo "phone-banged", making many calls. Jonathan realised that if there was to be no union man, the only way he was going to get the main points in the story across was by interviewing someone from the main opposition party. After a while, Jonathan scratched his head, unable to reason why groups fought shy of saying they were against privatisation. "That's party-political. Let's stick to pollution or asthma," one environmental group spokesman said to him.

"We're not interviewing any politicians. They're boring

and we've got more than enough on our screens," Sara laughed to applause from the researcher. "Real people, that's what we want, real people and their experiences, That's what we want, not more politics."

Hugo almost ran out of the door to get to the town of Concernt. Jonathan had discovered that a new privatised bus company had just taken over there the previous week. Jonathan decided to interview a junior transport minister "down-the-line", against his editor's previous wishes. When she heard, she consented. "You're probably right to do so. Don't let anyone know I said it. You're probably going to be critical of the government so it's best we get their side of the story. Good work. It's all in Producers' Guidelines. Keep it all nice and impartial."

Jonathan looked uncertain for a second and then returned to his desk. He would go and interview the minister via a link on the fourth floor and then go and join Hugo in Concernt before travelling by train to interview Francis, the man from The Transport Initiative consultancy.

Jonathan made his way down, on his way holding doors open for nervous producers on daytime news programmes. They stumbled about the building, balancing piles of tapes between their knees and their chins. Jonathan helped a few of them pick fallen tapes from the floor.

The editing suite itself was having problems. The picture editor mumbled technical terms to himself as he went from one corner to another, checking connections and applying gaffer tape to loose-looking connections. A fuzzy and then slowly clearer image of a government Minister began to emerge on the screen as the clumps of sticky tape grew bigger on the leads. Jonathan held a microphone between his fingers and watched makeup being administered to the Minister. The suite was quite dark, illuminated only by a colour and a black and white image of the minister and some jade green graphical waves on monitors.

"Hello, Minister, can you hear me?" Jonathan asked, bending forward.

"Yes, I...er..." the Minister fell from his chair and then tried to retrieve his ear-piece.

"Hello...this is the recording engineer, we're getting a bit of hum can you check the mikes?" said the picture editor, snatching the microphone from Jonathan's hand to speak.

"Hello, this is scar," came another voice, "this studio has that problem, I'm afraid. The Sellotape does that, do you wish to continue?" It was a voice from a control room that was co-ordinating the feeds to Television Centre.

Jonathan nodded authoritatively to the picture editor.

"Right then, Minister, can you hear me?"

"Yes, I can hear you," the Minister said, his small eyes gleaming at the lens. Under a greasy grey curl his face came over as bright pink, something that the picture editor tried to amend with complex-looking electronic image manipulation equipment at his side.

"I can go and get the colour adjuster," said the picture editor, turning to Jonathan who was now squinting at the monitor, "but we might lose the feed."

"I don't think that'll be necessary. This is fine," Jonathan replied, putting his hand over the microphone.

"That's a lip-mike, by the way. Your upper lip is supposed to touch the panel, there," the picture editor said to Jonathan. Jonathan looked over and thanked him for the advice.

"Now, Minister, I'm going to ask about various aspects of transport policy. Anything you want to go over or that you're not happy with, we can just...er...redo, alright?."

The Minister nodded with a broad smile over his face.

"Right, firstly, what do you say to critics of the privatisation programme, those that complain of new monopolies being created?"

"Well, you know, we've put a tough regulatory regime in place that's working and more importantly must look to the public like it's er...let's go over that one."

"Right, what about those who say you're just creating private monopolies?"

"Well, we've introduced a tough regulatory regime including local people, local users and they have powers, tough powers."

Jonathan watched the Minister blink. There was a pause. "But critics say that apart from the monopolies that are being created, private companies are cutting corners on safety procedures as well as closing down track and stations because of what they see as inefficient lines." Jonathan was looking at an article he had found and tried to read it in the dim light as he spoke.

"Look, they all know what British Rail and the Underground system and the Bus services were like before, they were inefficient. What they now have is a modern, efficient system, new trains, new signs. Those that are complaining, I think you'll find, are the unions who are angry that their power has gone."

"But what about the number of accidents," Jonathan read from a list, "at Clapham, Purley, Glasgow, St. Helen's, Forest Gate, Salford, Wembley, Falkirk, Morpeth?"

"Accidents and losses of life are always regrettable, but you're not telling me that there weren't accidents before privatisation. I mean there were far more accidents before the privatisation programme, they funded privatisation, they help the public take charge." The Minister seemed to have lost his way during this answer.

"What about general transport policy across the UK, are you not building ever wider roads and designing your transport policy around roads?"

"You can't un-invent the motorcar. Everyone likes cars, they're fast, convenient and with catalytic converters and so on, they're relatively good for the environment. Don't you know, we've planted more trees, the roads department, than any other department, lining the roads with them, that's what roads do. Roads are the lifeblood of a modern society."

"But what about the recent research showing that air quality is damaging the nation's children?"

"The air was a lot more polluted when there were factories, that's what we say to the people who say that cars are damaging children's health," the Minister laughed, beads of sweat beginning to glow under the lights of the studio, "you're probably too young to remember the days when one couldn't see in winter because of the pollution. Those days are over thanks to us. We are the green...the party of the environment. Private cars produce much less pollution than buses. Ask the public what they want and they will always say cars."

"What about the Sites of Special Interest, the Areas of Outstanding Natural Beauty that are being destroyed because of a road building programme that will have to be continuous if it is to keep up with demand?"

"You've put your finger on it."

"Sorry, Minister, could you possibly start your answer with the topic in question. My questions aren't going to be on the finished piece so they need sort of, self-contained answers."

"Sorry, OK, ask me again," the Minister said, taking a handkerchief from his pocket, blowing his nose and putting the handkerchief away again.

"What about the Areas of Outstanding Beauty?"

"The thing about our roads' policy is that it is trying to satisfy demand. People want roads, that's why we're building them. As for where they are building the roads, well, that's not the point. If people want roads, they build them. And don't forget that it's thanks to roads that we've got more trees."

The interview went on in this vein, ending finally on the topic of airports.

"Airports, we can fly, so we fly. Aeroplanes are marvellous things and if we are to retain our position in the world we need planes. Privatisation has led to our airline, the British airline being the envy of the world. The accident record, the prices of goods in airports, the age of the fleets, it's all nonsense. It's safer to fly than cross the road."

Jonathan nodded, thanking the Minister and waiting for the tape to be logged and smothered in coloured stickers. "Thanks," he said to the picture editor but he was already busy dubbing war footage.

"How was our slippery customer?" asked Sara when Jonathan returned to the newsroom.

"Slippery, I suppose," he replied, not feeling he had got what he wanted from the minister.

"Hugo called to say where he'd be," Sara threw him a piece of paper, "good luck!"

She was now handing over the day's news to the night-editor who had been called to come in a little early because of a corruption scandal involving the Department of Trade and Industry. The night-editor was soon sitting where Sara had been, leaning on the desk and mopping up the detritus from sandwiches and salads eaten during the day. He wore a blue suit and thin red tie, proudly, it seemed as he was careful to follow the crease of his jacket as he hung it up on the coat rack by its loop. It was from his skin that Jonathan could tell he had spent most of his life awake when the sun had set. Years without sunlight, strange brews of Corporation coffee and odd nutritionally null snacks had taken their toll, not to mention the stressful live programme editing. He barely noticed Jonathan putting his things away. The night-editor knew that Jonathan's piece played no part in the next morning's game and therefore ignored him. The night-editor again began to wipe his desk, this time with even more force, as if from this direct pressure the desk would yield a quiet, comfortable night of editing, inserting graphics and on-time guest-arrivals.

After the customary wait at the lifts, Jonathan sneaked out and left TV Centre, pausing only to peer at the politicians waiting in the reception area on the ground floor.

He had timed his departure well, and the one-train-an-hour had just parked in the station when he arrived. The train was crowded, though, teeming with late night office workers on their long journeys across London. A few of them stared at the mobile telephone he was clutching. It turned out that he needn't have worried about it ringing.

Like animals in a snowy part of the world, the crowd headed for the mainline British Rail station. An announcer called trains and made muffled announcements. Children wailed as the queues wound their way from outside onto the main concourse, around metal bollards and strips of fabric littering the concourse.

The video monitors, sprinkled about, let viewers know that a hitch had disabled the information system. Jonathan's portable telephone didn't work, so he began to hunt for a call-box, one that took change instead of a card.

"Hello, Hugo?" he said, when he had got through to him at his hotel.

"Yes, hi, Jonathan, how's it going, how was the Minister?"

"The Minister was fine, he circled around the topics, never really answering anything. The longer the interview went on, the more nonsense he was talking," Jonathan felt freer to talk about his feelings, out of the office.

Hugo laughed.

"Look, I think I'm going to have to take a taxi. There's no service to Concernt."

"All right, well, I'll see you at breakfast then. I'm going to get an early night so I'll be good and fresh for tomorrow's interviews," the sound of a cocktail lounge piano tinkled in the background as well as laughter and the crash of glassware.

"Excuse me," someone said, opening the door to the telephone booth, "it's an emergency, can you hurry up," the woman pointed to what seemed to be her child, lying down on a blood-stained floor.

"Yes, sorry," Jonathan juggled his folder and his phone, "my mobile doesn't work, otherwise you could use this. The call-box says no 999 calls." The woman looked at Jonathan angrily and then was distracted by a tired-looking member of the public who had rushed forward. He was, Jonathan assumed, a doctor as he was soon treating the child. "Why don't they bloody clean this polish up?" said the man, as he bandaged the child's head.

"It's not my fault," a cleaner said, joining the small crowd, "I'm the only cleaner on shift."

Jonathan walked away, wondering whether the cleaner might be a good interviewee before quickly realising that his piece would lose 'focus' if he was to interview everyone connected with the railways on the programme. He had read about the importance of 'focus' in a book about television production that he had read. In a passage he could still recall, the author had advised that the professional producer always cuts out anything that might be too much for the viewer to handle. Four minute packages should be equivalent to the amount of information one could get from about twenty words of newsprint, he remembered.

Jonathan began to feel cold and he tried to revolve the toes in his shoes to aid circulation. The air was frosty, despite the thronging crowds. On the way to the taxi rank he had noticed two camera crews interviewing five half-dressed teenage boys. He looked back and caught sight of two blonde women interviewers smiling alternately. Jonathan presumed they were sharing the "feed" back to a cable news station. A crowd had gathered around them all, push-chairs acting like barriers and behind them perplexed-looking men with attaché cases watching the proceedings as if they were part of a horse-race they had betted on.

One of the women interviewers shrieked, causing even the station-announcer to pause for thought when he mumbled about more cancellations. The interviewer then ran her hands through her wavy blonde hair before pumping a fine spray onto the sides of her head.

The wait for the taxi was complicated as Jonathan had to select one that took credit cards. He had no cash of his own, only a Corporation credit card, as he hadn't been paid. There were at least a hundred or so men, women and children waiting outside now, all of them pressing against the steel railing that bordered the curb. Eventually, he found one and heatedly negotiated with the driver to force down the price of the journey. Jonathan was relieved to hear that the cost was only ten percent higher than if he had bought a single rail ticket. He had been fearing the wrath of the stern production manager whom he would have to discuss his expenses with when he returned to London.

Unfortunately, the traffic, even at nine in the evening meant the two hour trip would grow to more than five hours. Jonathan slept through most of the journey, despite the chill, the horns and the sound of the taxi's radio.

"Can you turn it up a little?" he sleepily asked the driver

as the muffled sounds of a World Service Radio presenter announced the time.

> *This is the World Service from London. The headlines at zero-one-hundred GMT.*
> *An earthquake in China may have killed as many as one hundred thousand people.*
> *There are rumours that as many as one million people may have been massacred in Africa.*
> *The German and French Governments have announced that they are encouraged by the Berlin Summit, despite doubts about the timetable for monetary union.*
> *The US Central Intelligence Agency admits that with the Israeli Government, the United States may have intervened in the affairs of Guatemala during the 1980s.*

Jonathan felt warmer and smiled, all of a sudden feeling good about working in news.

"You know, we should get some shots of the interior of the hotel. I was doing the Magna take-over bid, the other day and library had very few shots," Hugo addressed Jonathan across a breakfast table. He seemed distracted, as if he was keeping something from Jonathan. No longer looking tall, he was chain-smoking, not bothering to stop the smoke from entering his bloodshot eyes. Jonathan, too, was distracted, watching the cars on the motorway from the restaurant windows. It had been a long time since he had spent a night in a hotel and he was still uneasy from not waking up in his own bed.

"So how did it go with the bus company, yesterday?" he asked when he had snapped out of watching the tailback.

"Well, they're running quite a successful operation up there. There are two main companies competing for customers and prices have come down and the roads seem full of buses. Most of the people I interviewed said that it was all quite a success. I think we could go down the 'people said it wouldn't work, but now people are complaining that there are too many buses instead of so few' angle. There were loads in the high street."

"Yes, but Francis at the Transport Initiative said that this always happens at the beginning. Once the battle between the bus companies is over, then one company emerges as a monopoly."

"Well, that's the future. I think that's a bit complicated, you know," Hugo, bit into a piece of toast, "I mean, well I just wondered whether you're more used to documentaries. It's just a little piece, you know."

"No, not really," Jonathan replied.

"It's just too much to get into, that some time in the future there will be monopolies," Hugo said with a pained expression on his face, as if he had got to his car in the morning and discovered that his car keys were back at home. "Look, anyway, the Transport Initiative man will say a lot of that. We might still get the point in."

They regained their awkward silence. Jonathan wondered whether Hugo's bumbling use of language would affect his piece to camera. Hugo wondered whether he'd get back to London early enough to go out to dinner with his wife. He stubbed another cigarette out into the overflowing ash tray and looked over at the menu on the table, searching for the price of a Bloody Mary.

"Waitress! What is this? I asked for toast, T-O-A-S-T!" Hugo broke the silence as the waitress collected their plates. She stared back meekly, then turned her head as if looking for support from other staff.

"Oh, it doesn't matter, just clear it away. You won't get a tip, though."

Hugo smiled and nervously sipped his coffee, a dribble coursing its way down his chin as he shivered. "Fucking morons," he said to Jonathan.

"Look, I was wondering, Jonathan, when do you think we'll get back to London? I don't normally do this, but...well...it's just that it's my wife's birthday and we're supposed to be going somewhere nice."

Just then, Jim, the camera-man appeared, with all his bulky equipment. At the same time, a woman of about forty with brown hair tapped Hugo on the shoulder. "Going today?" she frowned, "I thought you might be here another night. Well, here's my card," she looked nervously at Jonathan and then back to Hugo, "see ya," and walked away, out of the restaurant.

"There you are," the cameraman said who had been watching the exchange. "I had breakfast in the room." He looked as if he didn't want to be there with Hugo and Jonathan. "Humph," he said, sitting down. He wouldn't say much more for the rest of the day.

"Er...Jonathan, about when we would be in London?"

Jonathan ignored Hugo's question, thinking that he would be in a better position to respond when they had done a bit of shooting. He got up and the rest followed. Then, there was a big bang. Hugo had tipped a table over, crockery and all.

৵

"Son, I think, it's the license people," said a feeble voice behind the front door of an above average sized semidetached house, "Just coming."

Jim assembled his camera gear on the pavement outside. Hugo looked into the sky, not realising his feet were gently crushing early crocuses in the garden of the Claymores.

"Hello, Mrs. Claymore," Jonathan said, when the door opened, "we're here to interview Francis." Mrs. Claymore was an extremely frail woman, perhaps in her late nineties and was wearing a faded pink twin-set. Her eyes hadn't lost any sparkle through age, Jonathan thought to himself.

"Would you gents like a cup of tea, I'll go and make some. Francis is upstairs." She left the door open and arduously made her way down the hallway with a Zimmer frame, down to the kitchen at the back of the house.

"That would be lovely," shouted Hugo down the hall, "bloody deaf codger," he said to Jonathan.

They walked up an old, chipped stairway, Jim, scarring the fraying carpet and pockmarked walls inky black with his tripod.

Francis was much older than Jonathan had expected. His

beard and small eyes made him look weasel-like, as if he was perhaps a magician from a children's book. He looked as if he had had a hard life, as if he was not that much younger than his mother even if his voice as sprightly as a man in his twenties. Jonathan looked up, above the leather armchair in which he was sitting, at a banner made of green-and-white computer listing paper. "Transport Initiative—The Consultancy For YOU!" he read.

"Hello, mother's probably making the tea. I hope she is anyway, she's getting a little absent-minded. Ho, ho, ho, ho," he laughed like an actor doing breathing exercises, "do come and sit down—a bit closer if you don't mind, my hearing's not what it used to be."

Jonathan nodded and tried to get eye-contact with the man. Just as he was about to speak, Hugo said, "so how've you been, Johnny?"

Francis smiled, "fine, how's Shirley?"

"Oh, fine. So, anyway, this'll be very short. Just a quickie about roads and transport generally. I went up to Concernt to look at how things were going there, with the buses." Hugo had barged past Jonathan to sit on a seat close to the interviewee.

"Yes?" Francis looked interested, "it feels like ages since I've been out of here." Jonathan's mood had changed from one of surprise to resignation and he slumped into one of the other armchairs and listened.

"It's great, I mean, there are a few problems, but nothing really pressing."

"I see," Francis said, smiling then looking up as his mother entered the room with a tray of china. She seemed to be juggling with her frame and the tray and soon plunged to the floor.

"Oh, damn!" she said.

Jim made a kind of grunt as he saw the cup of steaming tea roll towards him. "I think there's still some in it!" he said, before leaning against a fragile bookcase and taking a hearty sip. Mrs. Claymore gradually raised herself with the aid of the frame, propelling Jonathan away. "I'm quite alright, young man," she said, angrily.

"Oh, right," he replied, picking up the cups and saucers.

Mrs. Claymore stood, leaning on her frame.

"What about the rate of accidents for buses?" Jonathan found himself asking before biting his lip. He felt self-conscious, as if he always sounded negative and uptight about things.

Even Mrs. Claymore looked at him in alarm. Then there was silence before Hugo and Francis began chatting. Mrs. Claymore, looking satisfied that she had helped out, eased herself up a little and migrated sluggishly out of the room.

"Right, are we rolling?" asked Hugo. Jim, looked up from a thin book he had been reading.

"How do you see transport policy in Britain?" said Hugo, calmly.

Jonathan noticed then that Francis was sporting a red polka dot tie. Francis had been slouching before and his V-neck pullover had obscured it as it twisted around the knot.

"Well, it's complicated, the government has been good at some things, bad in others. I mean, privatisation isn't something that's essentially wrong. But there have been problems, even they concede that. If I take them one by one. Firstly, roads. We have spent far too much pleasing the roads' lobby, trains are important after all and it will take time for the railways to get to grips with privatisation, the accident that killed a hundred people the other day is proof of that. But roads are good too. Yes, roads are useful. Basically, we need a good transport system so that business can work, not a bad one so it can't. So there are many sides to the debate."

"That was great, um...competition is good for transport isn't it? I mean, different operators competing. It all brings the prices down?"

"Yes, I think so. I mean, not if they cut corners. But then these new privatised companies do think about more than just money, don't they? I mean there might be some operators who feel that to compete, they need to reduce signalling staff or guards in trains and so forth. That wouldn't be a good thing. But then there are other private operators who offer more services than before. Swings and roundabouts, you see, that's how it's working today."

"Right, well, that's great..." Hugo looked back to Jonathan, "anything else, in particular?" he seemed to be asking for reassurance.

"Well..." Jonathan hesitated, "what about those that say any privatisation means that companies are no longer part of the community and that private companies are basically about making money, that that's their first and most important goal. Isn't it wrong in principle?"

Hugo gave Jonathan a tired look, turning to Francis and raising his eyes to the ceiling.

"Well, er...do you want me to answer that, Hugo?" asked Francis.

"Only if you think it's important. I think we've already covered that point," Hugo said, turning to Jonathan.

"Well, there is a case for that. I mean, privatisation does lead to companies thinking only about profit and around the world, it has meant the destruction of communities etcetera. But with the proper regulation...I mean, that is the way the world is, in a sense. That's what people want so, I mean I wouldn't say that in principle it's wrong. I wouldn't go that far...it's not helpful to just be negative about it," he looked over at Jonathan, "that's all I can really say about that. You see, in a modern, functioning economy, money is what it's about. And good transport."

"Okay, let's stop there," said Hugo.

∽❧∾

They were double-parked outside another semidetached house, this time in a *cul de sac* in West London. At the end of the street was a pair of cast iron doors. Overhead came the roar of jet engines, every thirty seconds. The mobile phone of the cameraman had rung on their way to a railway station and the day producer on duty had informed Jonathan that the whole project had to be reconsidered.

"But we've already done some filming," Jonathan said.

"Yes, I know. Look, so soon after a train accident, we don't want to be doing anything on trains. Why not concentrate on planes and cars, instead. Planes always look good and there hasn't been a crash lately, has there?"

Hugo was mostly silent when he heard the news, only pausing to say he knew that a story on trains would be out of the question. "The story you wanted to tell will now have to wait until after the inquiry. Perhaps, we should just call the whole thing off," he said firmly before retreating into his shell.

At Jonathan's insistence, they had gone to film a Mr. Dawnes in a small back garden. Jonathan gazed at the wild weeds and grasses and the solitary apple tree, watching everything shudder every thirty seconds. He had to brush the hair from his face because of the wind that rose up as the planes screeched by overhead.

"Sound's fine now. Rolling." Jim said.

Suddenly all was quiet.

Jonathan had advised Jim to position the camera to get as much sky as possible in the shot. But, now the tape was rolling, no planes came, so they waited and waited. After a while, Hugo began the interview. Not one aeroplane flew overhead as they spoke.

"It's not that noisy really is it?" Hugo asked for openers. Mr. Dawnes scratched his head and looked up at the sky like a farmer in a drought.

"Well, it's terrible. I'd like to see some of those airport executives living here," he paused, as if expecting the rush of engines. Nothing happened. Hugo asked a few more questions.

"Jonathan?" Hugo said, when he'd finished his interrogation.

"That's fine, I suppose," he replied, having counted on the noise.

When Jim had stopped the tape, his headphones still on his ears, a jet duly stormed across the sky. He fell onto his back amongst the weeds, his headphones pulling both camera and tripod on top of him. "I'm alright. I'm alright," he said, brushing the mud and blood from his face. "I was in Vietnam," he said, laughing a little.

Jonathan smiled, thinking that now they had some sound,

they could always mix it into the interview. In the back of his mind, he had been worrying about the ethics of mixing in the sound of planes from library footage.

Hugo had been facing the other way during Jim's somersault. "Noise wasn't as bad as we thought, Jim. Managed to get that in one take," he said, pulling the apple tree down to the ground as he picked a fruit.

"I'm afraid I think a new Terminal at Heathrow would be an excellent idea," Hugo said to the Mr. Dawnes who was looking unhappy.

"Well, the noise is usually," Mr. Dawnes voice sounded weak against the sound of Jim's tripod decapitating a garden gnome. Just then, another jet thundered across the sky.

"It's too late to go and do the interview all over again, just to get plane noises," Hugo said, looking up at the glint in the sky. "I'm not sure it would be proper in any case. Also, I'm having dinner with my wife..." Hugo put his pen away and began to pick at his teeth with his fingernails.

Jim cleaned himself up in the bathroom while the others waited in the hallway, listening to him cry out as if being stung by a bee. Mr. Dawnes spoke up. "Hugo?" he said, reaching into his inside pocket, "I wonder, whether I could give you my card. You see, I'm trying to run a consultancy service, just starting it off. I thought...well," he continued nervously, "you, what with your job and everything. You might be able to give me a bit of help. Clients...you know? Could you?"

Jonathan, slightly surprised, looked at Hugo who was smirking contemptuously. "I'll take the card," he reached out his hand, "but I'm not promising anything!" Hugo moved closer and whispered "and my services aren't cheap either."

"Thank you, thank you so much," Mr. Dawnes said. Jonathan scratched his head, feeling he had lost control of the production.

A sound like that of detonation howled from above as they drove away from Mr. Dawnes house. Jonathan looked up and out from the rear window and towards the airliners.

❦

Planes, Trains and Automobiles, Hugo Boyen-Bassett reports on Britain's transport. That's after the news in your area.

Jonathan had slept only for a couple of hours even though the night producers had taken the piece over from him to cut when he had got back to TV Centre. But Jonathan wanted to watch the piece as it went out and he forced himself awake for it, before then resuming his sleep. The graphics looked superb, he thought to himself, watching a plane whizzing across the screen, then a train, then a car.

...Those are all the underground lines facing delays this morning. Meanwhile, there's no service on the following Sensation-Rail in association with Gleeb's Pharmaceuticals' routes...

Jonathan dragged himself from his bed and bunched up the curtains in his bedroom to eclipse the shard of sunlight cutting through the room.

...And problems at Heathrow, the Uncle M hamburger airport, as...

Jonathan looked at the ceiling as the scream of horns outside his window became constant.

...And the usual story in London. All the main arterial routes are jammed. Very slow progress on the...

Jonathan turned the volume on the television up.

I'm standing in Concernt's main bus station and it's a busy place, I can assure you.

Hugo grinned to the camera.

There were those that said it wouldn't work but here at Concernt, no fewer than seven bus companies ply their trade, competing with each other and forcing down the fares.

Hector Bayside, Chief Executive, Loader Bus Services

Well, it's been a success. I mean when they started there was just one bus service, now there are seven and we are rapidly becoming the leader here. Some routes we're lowering the fares to almost nothing. From Gant High Street to Bleedstone it used to cost one pound sixty, now we're charging just five pence.

Back to Hugo, walking down the high street.

But it's not only the fares that are going down.

To the musical accompaniment of a song 'Let's get down

on it," buses flashed across the screen, shoppers entered and exited through glass doors, the sun glinted on colourful chassis. Then, it was time for vox pops, interviews with random people on the street.

Well, it's great, innit? Loads of them.

I never really take buses, but it looks like there's more of them.

Excellent, that's what I have to say, absolutely excellent.

Then the piece cut to a large airliner flying through blue skies. Then it cut to the interior of the plane. Jonathan thought the shots were strange. The camera seemed to negotiate with the plane, hovering, in sharp focus, around the logos on seats, on the logos on the food trays and on the logo on the fin.

This brand new X400 plane is the pride of its airline company. It took more than ten million man-hours to research and make, with safety and comfort the paramount concerns. That's meant jobs for thousands of people. But what about the people whose houses it flies over. Not a problem, you might think, especially given that so much of the research and development of the plane was geared to minimising noise and pollution. But, surprisingly, there are those who still complain, just as in the nineteenth century there were those who said that man should not travel above forty miles an hour.

Title: Mr. Dawnes, houseowner.

Well, it's...er...not been very good.

The interview was intercut with Hugo's grave noddy's. This had allowed the night producers to use Mr. Dawnes' answers like a palette from which to paint any picture they chose, stopping Mr. Dawnes lines of argument short with a quick cut to Hugo. Their composition was of a sad young man who disliked progress.

Later, Francis, looking like a short wax model, eyes made of glass, was soon staring out of the television. After his equivocation, the anchorman in the studio interviewed a live guest from a United Nations organisation who told the interviewer that the Government had deliberately routed motorways through areas of Outstanding Beauty and Sites of Special Scientific Interest because it was "cheaper" to do so. He claimed that the countryside as well as the British people were being poisoned.

> *Interviewer: Surely, you don't mean that? Aren't you just acting irresponsibly, scaremongering?*
> *Guest: I don't believe so, no.*
> *Interviewer: But we do need roads, don't we? I mean, I dare say you travelled to our studios by road.*
> *Guest: Yes, I did.*
> *Interviewer: Well, there you are then. How can you tell people in the countryside, let alone those in Britain's cities, that they don't need roads?*
> *Guest: I was merely saying that in the long run these schemes will prove far more expensive, in terms of health problems and so on, let alone the devastating environmental impact...*
> *Interviewer: Well, I'm afraid we'll have to leave it there. These are interesting times. Thank you.*

Jonathan soon realised over the weeks that conversations in the newsroom, like in any other workplace, were more often to do with day-to-day home-concerns. He, like the other producers lived by a strange timetable: intensive days and nights followed by days and nights that were entirely free. Whereas Jonathan, like most office workers, had once pined for his twice-a-year weekend breaks, Jonathan now found he not only had time but also the money to go away every alternate week of the year. The *quid pro quo* involved a complete commitment whilst on duty.

Jonathan had been fortunate in learning how to be organised over the years. For those who weren't, especially those who were juggling a family at home, a four day shift could be highly disrupting. Night shifts, for instance, meant that shopping and household chores might have to be done in the early hours of the morning.

From what he heard in the newsroom, he found that when on a four day shift, most of the other producers didn't bother to clean up their flats and houses. They preferred to sculpt crazy paving across their carpets with the aid of pizza cartons, silver foil containers and other take-away detritus. Others managed in other ways, those with children paying for the aid of full-time nannies. What these schemes all required was life not throwing up any surprises. A rocky marriage, plumbing and electricity problems, a burglary or fire—these could destroy any routine. Jonathan now had such a problem, thanks to his landlord. Now, after a series of unfortunate events, he found himself lying in a sleeping bag in Peckham.

He told the day editor that he wouldn't be able to come in due to his housing problems. His words were treated like moral frailties. The editor was disgusted that others, with family commitments, with a whole range of commitments, could get in to work on time and he could not. His disgust was not only due to the short-manning levels in the newsroom but also to the fact that Jonathan was destroying a complex rota pattern that had been carefully devised with the aid of the most powerful microcomputer in the office. As the editor told Jonathan of war reporters who had left for conflicts without knowing where they would be living when they got back to Britain, Jonathan remained silent, trying to calculate his incompetence.

The effect of his interference with the newsroom rota was his transfer to the world of the night shift. Night shifts were where news packages were really constructed, where scripts were used like pallets from which to paint pictures of the planet. This was where graphics were hitched together to focus on a key point. This was when the scripts that would end up on the presenter's autocue were honed and finalised.

As he walked through Peckham he looked up at the sky, lit up by burning cars below. The trill of distress-signals— rape alarms, burglar alarms, car alarms—rang through the air. Shattered glass lay strewn across the broken pavements where the homeless lay in boxes and nylon. The smell of burning and fast food intermingled. Illuminated advertising hoardings towered over the streets of bankrupt shops. As the sirens wailed, he took out his company credit card and bought a ticket for the last night train to White City.

TV Centre was a shimmering hive of activity when Jonathan

arrived. Cars painted ministerial black were creating traffic jams and producers for the late night flagship news programme, 'Newsnight' waited anxiously by reception doors. Politicians and pundits rushed to and fro, mobile phones sang out loud and taxi drivers stood by their cars trying to spot celebrities. It was the end of another news day, with the issues first raised at breakfast were lain to temporary rest. Within a few hours all would be silent and motionless save the quiet newsroom computer beeps of stories from faraway time zones. During the next artificially lit ten hours, Jonathan's would see green characters and numbers whenever he blinked.

THE HANDOVER—page one
Not much around I'm afraid.
<u>Inflation/Bleeney</u>
Chris Bleeney saves the day and dives in to rescue us from a sick (and absent) Frederick. This piece will also run on the One. Looks ahead to tomorrow's RPI—
the last ones before the Budget. Chris will link it directly to interest rate cuts and what it means for the Chancellor's budget options. Interviews with
various shop people. Thought they could trail—Sophie producing and in control.
<u>Updates:</u>
Daniel Seweel has done an interview for World with the Belgian Prime Minister, which may be worth a clip if he has said anything lucid about EMU. Editor has bet him a fiver this doesn't make it on!...There's a challenge for you.
<u>Sushi/Darts</u>
This is due to come over on the regular Tokyo feed...but suggest someone gives the Tokyo office a call fairly early on to establish how it's coming and check that everything is in place. They may be feeding it to Tokyo from Osaka and then feeding it on—or hopping it via Tokyo directly...if that makes sense.
<u>Education live</u>
Schools closing down. We've got the head of the school in

question on the programme. Plus a minister. Brief piece looking also at options for parents, whether they should save up for private schools or whether a new scheme from the government offers the best way forward. Headmaster is driving himself in. Mobile number and other details in special handover. Possible lead.

Jobs/Shisthe

Nice piece from Harrison pegged to Prince Charles and Board of Trade President's visit to Germany to try to drum up investment into the UK. Full of outraged German's furious that their jobs and money should be lost to Britain.

Rapist/McLaughlan

Piece on the hunt for escaped rapist. He's been down to Surrey where he's interviewed the police and local residents. Full of residents saying they're afraid he's out.

Music/Jones

Good piece about screaming girl fans of new pop groups. Interviews with psychologists about why they scream.

Mollusc phono

The consortium, Nigeria PPP (of which Mollusc is part) may announce whether they are going to go ahead with their plans to obliterate Ogoni land or not. They had a meeting today and they are watching the wires avidly—nothing as yet.

Meanwhile MEPs started meetings today (Wed) with various MPs with both left and right wing leanings lobbying for sanctions against Nigeria. There will be a debate tonight and a vote tomorrow morning. From the UK, the two MEPs from the UK out there are Jon Gleethmore-Jones, Con who will do us a phono in the morning from Strasbourg and someone else who might not be available (CHECK!). Tel numbers in handover. Said they would phone him at 10.30 (11.30 his time) so call him tonight if you change your mind. NB for gfx: no still of him in the building, so have booked a line from MMA (graphics' studio in Millbank where they have one) to graphics here at 10pm–10.15pm.

Contact at Millbank is Delia on 3222. Glenys Cynon is also out there and she may call in as they hadn't got hold of her before. Also the perpetual bid in for someone from Mollusc. Have asked for a track from Brussels—Celia has great hopes for results from the producer out there, Donald Adriasson—whose father works for Mollusc—who is doing his best. Pics have been fed from Strasbourg, which has been used in Jane Amelian's six o'clock piece.

Papers

Jonathan Bluestock—all booked.

Sports

Check with Steven—the tapes were late yesterday!

The night team comprised a night-editor, a director and two producers. Jonathan had never met any of them before. The night-editor, Theo, was a sheepish, tense looking man with chestnut hair. As he perused the handover on the computer he nervously wiped his desk clean in quick light strokes, mumbling the words "What a mess. What a mess," to himself. The director was a small woman with brown hair named Ivy, who smiled and tapped vigorously into her computer before the night-meeting. The other producer, Trowbridge, looked gregarious, chatting away on the telephone in a loud haughty voice.

For half an hour, the night team sat watching the monitors placed at opposite walls of the newsroom, their headphones rattling in their ears. The night-editor mumbled to himself occasionally remarking "good story" or "bad story" during the 9 o'clock News. Other members of the team simply stared, their expressions blank.

Afterwards, they adjourned to a small box-like office at the end of the room that doubled as the chief editor's office. Empty wine and beer bottles lay around the desk which was scattered with faxes and ring-bound files. Theo turned down the television in the room, so that the music video was inaudible, and sat in the chief editor's chair.

"All had a good sleep?" he asked, when the team had settled on the grey settee that lined the tiny room.

Trowbridge answered first : "No, I couldn't sleep at all. The road was being dug up and then my girlfriend called because she'd forgotten her car keys. It was terrible. The noise of the road, chug, chug, chug. Then the phone, ring, ring, ring. And then there's the hole in my curtains and every time the wind blows a bit the aerial on top of the flat keeps squeaking. And my alarm clock went off in the middle of the day. My answering machine doesn't work. Someone's doing some work next door. The gas-man came to read the meter..." It was a rambling response and was only stopped by Theo lowering an outstretched palm to silence him. Ivy then spoke up and said she hadn't slept much either.

"Right, pretty quiet night tonight, or should be. Chris has done us a boring inflation piece, Ivy you can handle that. It looks all cut to me. But it needs graphics...where is the graphics person?" Theo asked, raising his voice a little.

Just then a woman with red hair, dressed in a clinging black suit came through the door, made up as if she was going out to a party.

"Hi," she said, smiling, "sorry I'm late."

Theo looked down at his notes. "We were just talking about you. We've got quite a bit of graphics. There's an inflation graphic to start with."

Jonathan looked down at his printout, his mind wandering a little as Trowbridge had turned the volume of the television up to keep track of the plot of a popular soap opera that was now on air.

During Theo's résumé of the night's tasks, he apportioned different stories to each of the team. Jonathan was to look after Education, Sushi and the Papers. Trowbridge was to look after something called "SPIXING", a role that involved close liaison with the night picture editors on the fourth floor to make sure that all the stories were in a fit state to be broadcast at the correct time. Other producers would be arriving at various times during the night to take on other stories, with one reporter on standby should any news need covering in London overnight.

Jonathan sat at a desk and looked at his notes, listening to Ivy talk to Theo about problems in the Studio.

"Yesterday, there were lighting problems. But the worst moment came when a camera began rolling across the studio floor. Something to do with the wheels, apparently. Julie was having a cup of tea at the other side of the studio and you know, suddenly we had a tracking shot of her eating a biscuit instead of the latest world news round-up."

"Stop!...Stop!...Stop!" shouted Theo, who had been typing on his terminal during Ivy's summary, "did anything go right?" Theo looked worried and already drained.

"Well, as I was saying, after that the keyed-in images," 'keyed-in' images, Jonathan knew, were pictures and graphics that sat above the shoulders of presenters when they were on-screen, "ended up being mixed up with Julie drinking her tea."

Trowbridge, meanwhile, had been typing out his SPIX list, a rundown of every videotape needed for the morning's transmission, along with its length and who was in charge of it.

Jonathan walked over to the fax machine in the centre of the room and examined the piles of paper it had churned out. Most of the faxes were from public relations companies. These were mainly attempts at engaging producers' and editors' interest to get commercial products endorsed on television. There was even one from Mollusc the company who wouldn't put up an interviewee for the piece on Nigeria. It was a six page fax asking Good Morning, Britain to take note of "a new Mollusc green environmental award scheme for British businesses that showed awareness of the planet's problems." But there was no further information about Mollusc's operations in Nigeria.

Perhaps, the most interesting fax was entitled "Corporation DUTY LOG", which was an exhaustive list of all phone calls received during the previous 24 hours from members of the public.

Corporation DUTY LOG — Page One
CONFIDENTIAL — NOT TO BE SEEN BY ANYONE OTHER THAN STAFF

Good Morning Britain

"Informative" said a caller from Gwent who wouldn't give his name.

Christmas with Pigsy

<none>

Elevenses with Sue and Lloyd

AG said she enjoyed the item on toe-nail painting very much, could there be a repeat showing so that more people could see it? BF said why is so much sugar always used in the recipes featured in the programme? LJ wondered what was wrong with Lloyd's hair, is he all right?

Regional News

HJ commented : What an excellent programme, well researched and well written. Keep it up!

One O'clock News

FD disliked the term "animals" used to describe spiders in the package about unusual pets.

SE said why is it that Conservative politicians are always questioned more aggressively than Labour politicians. She also added that more good news would cheer everyone up, particularly as the weather is so gloomy.

WR said that the piece on Sudan was biased. "It was biased because..."<unintelligible> he said.

TS commented that the presenter looked "particularly beautiful" today and that she should be given more work on other programmes as she "adds sparkle." "I like her a lot, couldn't we see her bottom half? Just the top makes me want to..." <unintelligible>

HD asked why there were no royal stories today, especially as the Queen was visiting an important garden centre.

WR said that the term "decimate" had been used incorrectly as its meaning was "to cut by 10%."

The Dollops

Billy R from Buxton complained that this week's

episode was quite unsuitable for children. He said that
the antics of Dollop bunny were "pure titillation."

Drugwatch

RW asked why so many programmes were about drugs
these days. He said that drug education programmes
were actually just promoting the use of drugs and that
they should all be stopped immediately and that their
producers should be "locked up."

Killer Motorcrash

SW said he greatly appreciated the programme but
asked why there weren't more close-ups.

Vets

TQ commended the programme for showing the
profession in a good light.

Lottery

IO asked why he hadn't won when he had some of the
numbers that were announced on the programme.

Sex Fantasy II

HD complained that there was too much sex on the
television and that, in any case, this sequel programme
was not as informative as the first.

"You know our editor calls in every day just so there's one
positive response to the programme in the log," said Ivy, over
Jonathan's shoulder. "I'm Ivy, by the way. You probably know
that from the handover, though. Would you like some coffee?"

"No, it's okay. Actually, I was just about to go down to cut
the Education piece."

"The red tea-bar's closed tonight," she said, still standing.
"It's such a pain, we'll have to troop off to the white one every
time we want a cuppa," looking up from one of the Log pages
she had lifted from Jonathan's desk. "Oh, hello Felicity," she
said, turning to greet one of a group of other night producers
who had arrived and had begun rifling through the pigeonholes
by the door. They were all pale women with sleepy eyes and were
dressed in black trousers and V-neck pullovers. As they shuffled
around the room, finding their places, Jonathan was startled to

see the same kind of crushed ambition he had once known. It was all around him. The only moments when they all smiled would be now, as they excitedly opened envelopes containing either their payslips or notifications about jobs to which they had wished to transfer.

Jonathan got up and went to stand behind, the night editor, Theo and waited for him to stop looking at his monitor. "I'm just going down to cut this short education piece," Jonathan said, realising that Theo wasn't going to ask why he was standing up beside him.

"Right," Theo replied, eyes still trained on his screen." Bernie and Harry are down there in two and seven...seven, right Ivy, sorry Trowbridge?"

"That's right," Trowbridge said, cupping his hand over the telephone receiver into which he had been chatting.

"The sushi piece is coming over on the five-four-five bird, but you can find some footage to fill in the blanks before then. We'll talk to Tokyo a little later. Try and make that one look good, Jimmy loved the idea for the piece."

Carrying nine Betacam SP tapes, each the size of a large hardback biography, a twelve inch reel of audio tape and thirty or so loose pages of paper, Jonathan walked precariously to the door and out towards the lifts. According to the computerised voice, the temperature outside had dropped to minus two degrees. Jonathan dropped the tapes a few times as he navigated the fourth floor and when he finally got to his editing suite, there was crash as everything in his hands landed on the rough carpet.

"Hi!" Jonathan said, looking up from the spinning reel of audio tape into the dark cockpit-at-night like light.

"Hello," said Harry, about forty years old and with short grey hair. Harry had his long face aimed at the commercial satellite channel on one of the tiny monitoring screens in front of him. "Is it going to be a busy night?" he asked, switching off the satellite channel and putting a blank tape into one of the video recorders at his side.

"Doesn't look especially so," Jonathan replied, shivering in the brisk air-conditioning, "apart from the five-forty-five feed from Tokyo."

Harry laughed, "Oh that's fine, but we're not presenting the show from New York or anything are we?"

"No," Jonathan said, arranging his tapes to the side of Harry's video editing console. The desk was already quite full of tapes, each one shining in the green oscilloscope light. "This piece is about the closing down of some schools." Jonathan stared at the controls. Like other producers, his knowledge of these suites was virtually nil. He depended on the night picture editor like he did the ground not to cave in.

"Is there a script?" Harry said, casually.

Suddenly, a black man in his twenties, wearing overalls and pushing a vacuum cleaner opened the door and began moving around the room. Jonathan peered out of the suite door-window and saw that other cleaners were gliding around the fourth floor, all of them black. The storey looked like a scene from South African apartheid.

"The script, yes," Jonathan said when the man had left, "the day reporter and producer left this track and this script."

"Well, just sit down and watch me go," Harry said, imitating a drawling American accent as Jonathan sat at the computer terminal on a small desk at the back of the room.

He looked at the wires flashing like fast Morse code on the computer, noting that it was around half past midnight. The news on the screen was a world away, Jonathan thought. Things didn't seem in any rush. He looked at Harry, entwining the audio tape around the heads of the horizontal reel-to-reel machine, the strange light fittings above him sending thin shards of illumination down on to the editing wheel which Harry would soon be spinning.

The voice of the reporter started up: "Some say that Britain's education system is facing collapse. A new report out today says that lack of government funding is leading to the closure of schools. That means overcrowding for pupils such as Callan. Synch. Then second paragraph."

As Harry stopped the reel from spinning, Jonathan said to

him "Harry, how about you take out the first three words, so that it begins with 'Britain's education system.' I think it's just a bit punchier, that's all."

"Fine by me, you're the producer," said Harry, rewinding the reel, "so you don't want the 'some say that...'"

Jonathan's terminal beeped, the top line of the screen announcing that an internal computer message had been received. He pressed the 'message' key:

johnson	*Trowbridge here, how's it going down there? we want to do some editing.*

Jonathan replied that things were going fine.

johnson	*Theo's a bit off tonight, don't you think? What have we*
johnson	*all done wrong?*

He said that he didn't know.

ollson	*Ivy, here, Jonathan. Did Theo show you how to put VT details in?*

To Ivy, he replied that he did not even know what she meant. She said she would come down in a few minutes. Jonathan had learnt that this messaging facility formed the spine of the Corporation. Every minute of the day, beeping electronic signals commented, notified and revealed. Everyone seemed to believe the system was confidential. Jonathan was surprised by this as his first taste of information technology had been at the social security office. He knew how deadly the tools of information were.

Nevertheless, extra-marital affairs, chat-up lines, salary negotiations and sackings were all part of the traffic on the little first line at the top of the monitors. Even Corporation management used the system and Jonathan suspected that this was an explanation for the corporation's computer department escaping expenditure cuts. With wires, the computer department held the reins of power in the Corporation.

"Hey, we're missing some library here, we need some more primary school pictures, you have any?" Harry asked, again very casually, in a voice that seemed designed not to perturb.

"No, I'll call library. Which reminds me, I'd better see

graphics about the insert in the package." Jonathan swung out of his chair and left the room to walk over to Graphics, a section of the fourth floor.

It was also a dark place. However, it was decorated in polished black sheeting. Jonathan gazed up and saw skulls and bones stuck on the ceilings. Below him, netting sprawled on the floor. A fluorescent eyeball glinted in his peripheral vision. In front of a long desk of computers sat a couple of men and four women all dressed in black, their hair set so it emerged vertically from their scalps. Their faces were smeared in blue and green makeup, picked out by flashing blue and green lights placed strategically around the room. Eerie music played out from a ghetto-blaster as more bones were scattered around the floor. The monitors in front of these people showed pictures of mutilations in Bosnia, photographs of political leaders from around the world, multicoloured computer-generated graphs of unemployment figures and prison statistics.

"Hi," said the graphics woman who had come up earlier to the meeting of the night team. "What do you think? Tonight's horror night," she said standing and smiling, fangs instead of incisors curling from her top row of teeth.

"Yes...er...I just though I'd better give you these figures about school closures," he held up a photocopied table of figures. "I need a graph for an insert in my package."

"That's fine," she said chirpily, looking down at Jonathan's groin area. "Give me an hour." She sat down on a swivel chair and laughed as she began to type onto a keyboard.

"How's it going, Harry?" he asked when he had rushed back into his editing suite. Jonathan had been excited by the graphics department, the staff there seemed to show an imagination that was lacking elsewhere in the building.

"It's fine except for the school footage, wanna see it?" he asked.

"Sure."

Britain's education system is facing collapse. A new report out today says that lack of government funding is leading to the closure of schools. That means overcrowding for pupils such as Callan.

"There's too many people. Sometimes the teacher can hardly hear us and some of us have to sit on the floor instead of on a chair."

But ministers challenge this, saying that more money is being spent on education than ever before.

"This report is a nonsense. We reject its conclusions entirely. As far as I am concerned, this think-tank is a no-think tank."

Opposition leaders, meanwhile, call for an independent inquiry into education standards.

"Harry, can you just rewind it so I can take the Astons?"

"Oh, the Rileys, sure."

'Astons', Jonathan knew, were the titles that came up on the screen, to identify speakers and interviewees for the audience. He had read that they were called Astons because the computer used to create titles was once made by a company called Aston. Before 1980, the titles used to be called 'Rileys', after the previous company that supplied the machines. The book Jonathan had read on television production had noted that producers seeking to impress their colleagues by their long-service should refer to them as Rileys, whereupon they could say "oh, that's what they used to be called before you were even in television."

The timings of Astons were crucial. One second out and they might the wrong people. Wars, Jonathan was assured, had broken out because of a misfired Aston.

Ivy arrived in the suite and asked Jonathan to adjourn to another room.

"I didn't want your picture editor to think you didn't know anything," she said sweetly.

"Thanks," Jonathan replied.

"Well, look, here is an example of VT details. If this is inaccurate," Ivy looked worried, her small face scrunching up, "we and me in particular are all screwed."

"You've got the right times for your Astons, yes?" she said.

"Yes, I was quite careful over that," Jonathan replied, somewhere in the back of his mind beginning to panic.

"Right, so you've got the spellings and timings. Now what you need is the first and last three words of each package as well as the total duration. That way, I can be alerted as to whether the wrong tape is in the machine in the first few seconds of the piece. That's supposed to stop any joker from broadcasting a pornographic tape," Ivy laughed. Ivy went onto explain that each news piece had a "page" in the computer that popped up on the director's console when the programme was being broadcast. "Those last three words are important, too. They tell me that the nation will be watching either a black screen or a frozen last frame if I keep playing the tape.

By the time Jonathan was back at the suite, a row of tapes was growing on a shelf, each one a package to be broadcast on Good Morning, Britain. At the top of the programme, were the 'heads and teases'. These comprised six tapes, three of which contained enough video footage to illustrate the morning's headlines and another three to "tease" stories in the programme that were not as well "pegged" to the day's news. "Don't go telling me the headline pictures when we're just about to go to air, okay? I know that some producers like to show how professional they are by waiting till the last minute to cut the headline, just to show they're aware that the headlines could change at any minute."

On his computer screen, Jonathan scrolled through the running order of the programme. In the corner, flashed news wires from parts of the world that were awake, the larger land masses of the earth. But the Asia and even Australasia would feature little in the morning's running order, even less so the stories coming from Africa. Non-coastal China was merely a blank space, it could have been just an area of ocean bordered by Russian and Australian landmasses.

"You wanted some tapes?" said an earnest man who had just swung the door open to the edit suite, "we didn't have much of primary schools, I'm afraid. We've got some public schools, I mean private schools and there was a documentary about some inner city schools which Newsnight were using. Maybe that'll be of some help. Otherwise, I'll have to go to Brentwood."

Brentwood was another key term on the night-shift that Jonathan had been warned about. It was the video librarian's flare. It signalled that there was no possibility of getting hold of the footage. Theoretically, it meant that the librarian would have to take a taxi to the nearby suburb of Brentwood to get the tapes. But that would leave one less librarian at Television Centre for up to three hours which was unfeasible. In an emergency, the death of a celebrity for instance, the competition would beat the Corporation to broadcasting a video-obituary. A librarian mentioning Brentwood was a decisive full stop to making an interesting looking video package.

"Fuck, it's U-Matic," said Harry as he put the large videotape into the machine.

"Sorry?" asked Jonathan.

"God, you know, U-Matic," Harry said. "It's an older video format. See this? And this?" he held up a Betacam and a Hi-8 tape, "well, this is better than this which is better than this," he said, dramatically tossing the tapes, one by one, into the bin at his side.

After retrieving the U-Matic tape and pushing it into the machine, they sat watching a crowd of young children gather and sit down on the wet tarmac of a car park. When Harry turned up the volume levels, they heard a head teacher saying something to them through a megaphone. As Harry altered the bass, they heard him informing the children that the school was to be closed down. "It's good," Jonathan said.

"Yes, but look at all this." Harry pointed to the flicker and the lines and the visual noise of the picture. "It's a cut story, so it would be impossible to edit anyway. Look at the quick cuts. That's what they leave us these days, cut stories instead of the original rushes. With rushes we use to be able to get something at least." The reporter's voice then came on explaining that this unfortunate school had to be closed down because of local health inspectors.

Harry changed the tape.

I want to be a captain of industry.

The stark words came from a nine-year old boy in an Eton-collar. "What do you think of this? It doesn't illustrate the collapse of the education system very well, but at least it's on Betacam," Harry said, spinning through the tape. "You know, I can't understand why the Corporation can't just film the local comprehensive for a few hours. It's only down the road from here." Harry spun on, trying to look for shots that might be passable. Jonathan watched the screen intently, too.

"Perhaps, we should use the prep school shots, the ones of the playground, they don't seem to be in uniform there," Jonathan said, "that is if there really is nothing in the library from a government school."

"It's ridiculous, I was cutting a piece only last week about comprehensives. I can't believe they just trashed the tapes." Harry had swivelled around, stirring tea in a polystyrene cup.

"Hey, guys, sorry, to disturb you. Man, can I just check something with you?" It was Trowbridge, holding a tape, "sorry to interrupt, Jonathan, it's just that it's some feed stuff from Bosnia that just came in on the bird. I just want to check it's not too hairy, you know?" Trowbridge laughed.

"Sure, go ahead, we're still not sure what we're doing in here," said Harry, looking back at Jonathan.

The room darkened to black, before being lit by a sequence of images of gaunt civilians being shot at by snipers. A bus garage was blown up, some children were having their heads hit by the butts of machine guns.

"Better turn the colour down a bit, for a start," Trowbridge said as the two-tone pictures filled with the first of video's three primary colours, "wonder who's fighting who," he added.

Even Harry was being less sardonic as he sipped his tea. "I don't think they can use the close ups of the body parts," he said, as the camera lingered over shattered arms and legs lying on a road.

When the image of a soldier firing a machine gun between the legs of a small girl came on to the screen, Trowbridge swore. "It's good shit. Can you make me a copy for me Harry? The sound's not too good, though." They watched more explosions. The sound had cut out now. "But I don't think we'll be using it for tomorrow. Have you got the sound effects tape? I think we'll just run the shooting noises over the piece to camera as wild track. That way we get the extra tension." Harry gave Trowbridge the tape, saying that such pieces were a bit hackneyed now.

"Trowbridge, it's a bit corny now, isn't it? To have a reporter standing up in a street with gunshot sounds in the background?"

"Just do it, okay?" said Trowbridge, slamming the door.

"My mother always says to me when she sees shots like these, what on earth is the reporter telling us all this in the middle of a street during a gun battle," Harry mumbled, inserting the sound track.

"There, that's that done. Now back to education," Harry played the piece. It focused on new saving's schemes for parents who wanted to send their children to private schools. "You know what gets me..." Harry said when he'd finished editing in some images from Eton. Then he stopped.

"Go on," said Jonathan, looking up.

"Well, the private schools are registered charities anyway. It's the poorest that are subsidising your Eton's and your Harrows, you know."

"Yes, I've got the cuttings on that," said Jonathan.

"Hiya Jonathan," said Ivy, "How's it going?"

"Oh fine," he said, a little glumly.

"Now, don't forget that if it's a tight 'in' or 'out', put it down on the page so that I know if we have to be alert or not in the gallery. And if the graphic is liable to be covered by the little clock that tells our viewers not to be late for work, give the times when we should switch off the clock and when we should put it back up again."

Jonathan remembered the little clock that sat in the left hand corner of the screen during transmission of Good Morning, Britain and was amused at how it was affecting his life.

Ivy settled down where he had been sitting as Jonathan sped off to the graphics department. He was pleased by the graphic. They had done a good job, the statistics of school closures written in script-style on a graphic of an exercise book with a spring-type spine. He confirmed that each point was revealed in time with the script and then began to rub his head. He had bruised it. Some of the decorations had collided with him as he had entered the door to the department. When the graphic designer stopped the tape, Jonathan turned around suddenly, feeling the heat of someone behind him. There, in front of him was a man dressed as a vampire hammering an ice-pick hard into a fish head. Noting Jonathan's alarm, the designer mumbled something about the Common Fisheries' Policy. "It looks very good," Jonathan said.

"That's Dudley, he's intern-ing with us from an art school... and pretty smart he is too," said the redheaded graphics woman, swivelling around and patting him on the bottom.

Jonathan made his way up the stairs, past the bustle of presenters and producers running down to put programmes out on World Service Television, and looked at his watch. It was one-thirty in the morning. Jumping out onto the balcony where Corporation staff chose to smoke, all was quiet. From where he stood he could see all the way to the Canary Wharf tower, a light on its pinnacle flashing like a heartbeat. Before it was the West End, Centre Point signalling the all-night bars and clubs of Soho that were just opening for business. To his left and right were the suburbs of north and south London perched in orange-mercury light, intermittently speckled by the indigo of sirens.

"Newspapers are here," said Theo, hoping that with that the office would seem more busy. A burly black security guard had banged a huge pile of second editions on one of the newsroom desks, "let's try and get that part of your job done early, all right?" Theo turned to Jonathan, looking angry and nervous. "Is it your first time on nights?"

"Yes," he said, "but I've looked at some of the computer help files."

"That's good."

The 'papers' job entailed choosing five headline pages, writing a short script for the presenter to précis the themes and then giving clean copies of the newspapers to the Graphics Department so that they could go up on the screen. According to the handover, the initial papers' segment on Good Morning, Britain usually contained three broadsheet newspapers and two tabloids. Certain papers were banned, unless there was a very good reason for featuring them. The left-wing Morning Star was prohibited. The pornographic Daily Sport was also forbidden, though the Sport was still bought for the newsroom, just in case. The other proviso to "doing the papers" was that it was a flexible. One of the computer help files had advised that "stories of note" could be featured instead of a newsy headline page if they merited attention.

Jonathan began to type up his script. As he reached the end of his first ten word paragraph, the two presenters, Catherine and Peter, entered the newsroom. Suddenly, a kind of enforced studiousness struck the staff, as if no-one wanted to acknowledge their arrival.

"Hello," Jonathan said as they both sat down, opposite each other and next to him.

"Hello," they said, pleasantly, before setting down pieces of fruit on their desks.

"Sleep well?" Theo asked, frowning at Jonathan for trying to make verbal contact with the on-screen talent.

"Yes, thank you," they both replied in unison. Then they turned to each other and began chatting.

"I had drinks with Sir Colbert, yesterday evening," Peter said to Catherine.

"Oh, was that nice?"

"Yes, he told me a funny story about how he and Harold were so drunk a few years ago that they couldn't find their way home properly."

Catherine laughed.

Both presenters wore no makeup. Peter, tall and with chiselled features, sported an unshaven face, looking confidently relaxed. He rubbed his chin as he flipped casually through his copies of the tabloids. He had been a war reporter in the nineteen-sixties and had been in television journalism for over four decades. Catherine, petite with short brown hair, had only started at the Corporation a few years earlier but seemed already charmingly cynical about the industry. She studied the broadsheets and looked as if she was reading with much greater concentration than Peter, as if she knew she had to keep up with him. "Is it my turn to get the doughnuts?" she asked him.

Theo talked to Trowbridge about a wire that had flashed on the screen regarding a massacre in Peru. "Do you think it's important? I mean you went there on your holidays."

"Life's pretty cheap down there," said Trowbridge, "don't mention it unless nothing at all else comes up."

"Sorry," said Theo, "I don't know what I was thinking, between that and the national strike in Burma I haven't the faintest idea about foreign stuff."

"We've already got Nigeria, besides. Heavy shit, you know."

Peter looked up and grimaced.

"Have you seen this memo, though?" said Theo. "It says," he began reading aloud, "'Corporation producers are advised to exercise considerable scepticism of any information provided to the corporation by Greeno, the environmental organisation. After the oil platform disposal incident, and subsequent apology by Greeno, we can no longer consider that co-operating with this organisation is in keeping with our charter, i.e. maintaining our impartiality."

There was silence, interrupted only when Peter asked Catherine what colour jacket she was wearing for this morning's programme.

Jonathan having chosen his five stories, had tried to précis the most salient points.

"No, no, no, no, no," said Theo, holding the printout Jonathan had made of the script at arm's length, "for starters, include a couple of tabloids, I mean the story about the pop star and the school girl is a good one. And, why all the foreign stories, who gives a shit? And so what if one paper has done an in-depth investigation into education, we've done our own separate one on today's programme. And the first line of each script-let should repeat the headline so that viewers can match up what comes on the screen with what they hear Peter and Catherine saying. Remember it's television, it's only up there for a few seconds and everyone who's watching has only just got up."

"That's if anyone is up to watch the programme," said Catherine, smiling at Jonathan.

"I'll knock it about a bit," said Theo, ignoring her, "And you can forget the homeless piece, too, that's not a headline, that's just a stale old story."

"Hello, London, this is Tokyo, we'll be ready in three minutes," said a NASA-like voice coming from the speakers in the editing suite. On the monitor was the logo of a Japanese television company.

"Okay, we have bars," said Harry, referring to the row of coloured vertical stripes on the monitors.

Jonathan looked down at a fax that had been sent from the Tokyo correspondent, a Mr. Charles Darts. Stories from Tokyo, Jonathan had surmised, especially those during the recession, always centred around strange customs and odd goings-on. He looked at Darts' cue on the fax:

> *Japan is hosting a 'Sushi-a-thon', to see how big a piece of sushi can get. You certainly won't see pieces as big as this at your local. The seven-day event will see the Japanese coming in droves to witness the measuring and weighing of thousands of types of fish. As Charles Darts reports from Osaka, oceans of Soya sauce and mountains of rice will be consumed this weekend.*

"You ever eaten sushi?" asked Harry.

"No, you?" Jonathan asked.

"Yeah, but I don't like it much. Raw fish is an acquired taste," Harry twirled the knob on the editing machine. "You know, I remember when Charles was a trainee, all those years ago," he added, wistfully. He was on the fast track here. Are you on the fast track?"

Jonathan looked down at the fax again and scribbled the words "In" and "Out" on it, ready to write down the first and last words of the piece.

"Hello, Tokyo here. We'll begin soon, are you rolling?"

Harry pushed a switch, "We're rolling, ready when you are."

Jonathan looked at a clock on the wall and stared at its hands. It was five-forty five in the morning. When the Darts' piece was in and he had entered the details for the package into the computer, Jonathan went back to graphics to check that the newspaper pages were all correct.

"Hello," he said, brushing what appeared to be flour from his shoulder.

Some of the graphics' people laughed. He looked up to see a tin of powder placed strategically above the swing doors. At first he thought it might be asbestos but he soon knew it was merely part of the Graphics' Department's nocturnal prank schedule. He went over to one of the monitors and looked at a newspaper front page. "Fine?" said the graphics' woman, sipping whisky from a plastic cup. Jonathan checked through his script.

"I think there's a problem over the one in the Mail," Jonathan said, "the script's about Princess Diana's new hair style, but you seem to have put up an article about the Chechnya death-toll."

"Oh, sorry, I wasn't concentrating. Which page of the paper is the Diana story?"

"One," said a vampire, pointing to the front page of the newspaper he had picked up from Jonathan's pile.

"So are you going to dress up for our next one? We're doing heavy metal tomorrow night," the woman said, putting the front page face down onto a pane of glass and focusing the video camera that sat above it.

"I'm not sure, er, it's just that we have to meet the guests," Jonathan replied, looking at the ghoulish crowd turned towards him.

The woman laughed. "I suppose it might put the frighteners on them, eh?"

"Hi Trowbridge," Jonathan said as Trowbridge came through the other pair of swing doors that opened out into the graphics department. "Had a good night, so far?" he asked.

"It's been okay. Kathleen? Have you done the rape stuff? I just want to check the figures."

"Alex is doing that," the graphics' redhead replied, flipping through the newspaper images one last time.

Just then, Theo bolted through the doors Jonathan had entered through, covering himself with the rest of the white powder. "Hey," he said to him, "get upstairs to the gallery, I've got to sort out a Mollusc phono, they want to come on. You," he put his hand on Kathleen's shoulder, "get a logo together."

Jonathan ran out and abruptly halted, just near "TX", the room from where tapes were broadcast around the world. He could hear Ivy's voice being relayed from the gallery, the place where the director and producers manage the output of the programme while it's on air. "And forty seconds before titles," she said. Around him, people were running, charging between editing suites. One woman was on a settee, crying, a videotape with its tape hanging forlornly over her lap. For himself and the host of other night producers coming on shift through the night, this was the time of reckoning.

"Where's the sports? Where's the fucking sports?" someone screamed.

The shouting grew louder, one man hollering to another who had just slipped as he raced from an edit-suite with pictures of a just-launched Space Shuttle. Video editors, who had been so calm through the night, were shouting abuse at their machines as they spun their little editing wheels like truants at a video arcade. Only in TX, where the tape operators responsible for putting in the right tapes at the right time for transmission, were relaxed. A couple of them opened cans of beer. Another showed anxiety only because of a problem with his Walkman. "Bloody batteries," he cursed.

On Jonathan's right was "RCR", a kind of management

room for all the resources on the fourth floor. Overnight, their chief responsibility was producing what were called "clocks", the little leader segments on each videotape that were the first indication to a director that a tape in a particular video player in TX was the correct one. Usually, it was too late to "put the clocks on", leaving the director no option but to watch a black screen or the first frame of a package in the gallery and hope that it would play out fine. RCR, around six in the morning, was a place where people shook their heads. At this time, young men and women assistant producers would implore RCR staff to find them an editing machine that worked, a monitor that was functional, a place to take in a feed from some distant place. RCR, the name and the room itself was interchangeable, would in turn, laugh the words, "you should have come in earlier," or "why doesn't your editor hire more suites?" or "it's your own fault, why are you working for such a run down organisation?"

Only in moments of crisis was RCR famed for its ability to make something from nothing. Jonathan had heard that most RCR people had worked at the Corporation for more than twenty years. They were notoriously cynical, believing that financial cuts had destroyed the Corporation. In their opinion, they were now working for a sort of hospital television station that would be hard pressed to report on a fire in the casualty ward, let alone an international catastrophe. They also blamed young producers for what they thought had happened. "Why are you working here? Don't you realise that you're being paid peanuts, that there aren't nearly enough of you to put out a professional looking programme? Don't you realise that the Corporation can do what the hell it likes because people like you want to work at the Corporation regardless?" This was their line of questioning tonight to a young man who was pressing the point of a pencil into his left thumb. But, and this was what counted, Jonathan had been told, RCR always rose to the challenge in the face of a major story. Last time, it had been the Brighton bomb that hit the hotel where leading Conservatives were staying during their party conference. A "links" vehicle, a mobile unit from which one can feed stories direct to TV Centre, had got itself lost around Brighton and it was only the fact that RCR was quickly able to reallocate other resources and work for a steady 36 hours that the Corporation was able to get any news at all. As someone at RCR was to tell him, the Corporation relied on members of staff to sacrifice their health, taking drugs if necessary, to rise to the level needed to cover a big story.

The screaming was now growing louder. Producers, now cloaked in white powder and fake blood, scattered themselves along the corridors of the fourth floor. As the howling grew louder, Ivy's voice, fed through from the gallery and into TX said "and cue titles." The music for Good Morning, Britain began to grow louder and then, very faintly, Jonathan could hear Peter, the presenter, saying "Good Morning" to the nation.

"Excuse me," he interrupted the argument between the RCR man and yet another assistant producer, this time one whose fist had been bloodied by his repeated banging on a tape-strewn counter, "can you tell me where the gallery is?"

As Jonathan ran up the stairs, he could feel his shirt sticking to his body. To reach the gallery, he charged past doors that warned about authorisation, the rules of trespass and high voltages.

"Where the hell's Theo?" yelled Ivy, turning around for an instant from her console, "are we doing the Mollusc phono?"

The gallery was directly adjacent to the studio, with a glass pane to separate them. So as not to put the presenters off, posters and bits of paper had been tacked onto the pane. But this wasn't what Jonathan noticed first. It was rather the cinema-like darkness he had been transported to.

He was standing at the back, a production secretary to his right. In front of him was a long table that looked out onto a bank of sixty or so television monitors. At the table, in the centre, were Ivy and four other people. A further dark pane of glass on Jonathan's right separated the gallery from the sound engineers.

On the production secretary's desk were a couple of computer terminals and a few ringer-less telephones with orange lights attached to them. They reminded Jonathan of cold war hotline phones. They were directly connected to the studio and to the presenters. If Peter wanted to speak urgently to someone, he could push a button under his desk and talk to a producer.

But he wasn't paying much attention to the phones, he was looking forward, upward and to his right. It was there that one could see what the country could see. One monitor showed what they were broadcasting, another what the Corporation's rival was showing. It was the rival monitor which attracted most staring in the gallery.

"Use the European MPs first, then we'll use Mollusc," Jonathan said to Ivy before turning to the production secretary and asking her for reassurance, "that alright?" Jonathan began to sweat.

On one of the many small monitors was a group of MPs, on another a graphic image of the logo of the Mollusc Oil Company. The production secretary who Jonathan had just spoken to, on the right of Ivy, held up a stopwatch and counted out the last seconds of the inflation package. As the interviewee, Lawrence Chancellor said "and that's no mean achievement on the part of the Government. Their record on inflation is second to none", the secretary counted down from seven. "Out words, second to none," she said.

Directly in front of her was the autocue screen, a monitor showing a scrolling series of words that could also be seen by the presenters in the studio. This, Jonathan had been told, offered suffered glitches and had to be manually twiddled when it began to scroll the words too quickly. Sometimes, it had to be reversed when a presenter coughed or swallowed some words.

Now we go over to Brussels where, as you heard before, a campaign against the activities of the Mollusc Oil Company as well as the Nigerian Government is gathering strength.

The first MEP began to speak about the cases of five Nigerians who had fled to Britain for safety, but who were today to be deported from Britain. A red light lit up on the desk behind him. The production secretary motioned for him to answer it as Jonathan offered her a puzzled expression.

"Hello, N1", he was referring to the Corporation gallery number thanks to a fading sticker on the receiver.

"this is Donald Adriasson, what's going on, why aren't you using Mollusc? I spent hours getting my father to get someone from Mollusc, what's happening? Where's Theo?"

"Yes. We've got them, they're just waiting now. Mollusc's on the phone line," he signalled through the darkened windows of the sound booth as if to say "have we got them on the line?"

"Look, Mollusc said they'd only come on if they went first. They're launching a new green scheme at the petrol stations, today and they wanted to be the first to be interviewed. They have to be first."

The sound man tapped on the glass screen between them, signalling that the line had been lost. Just then Theo rushed into the gallery, waving his arms about and icing a line of script pages across the floor. "Argh," he shouted, causing a momentary stop to all activity in the gallery, "What the hell happened? What happened to Mollusc?" Theo snatched the phone from Jonathan.

Then another phone went off, this one buzzing. "Hello, this is the Home Office, we've just issued a press release on the wires. I thought I'd better tell you that it's for release as of now." Jonathan quickly realised that the not letting Mollusc on first had perhaps influenced the Home Office's decision.

Theo was now talking quickly to himself, tapping wildly on a keyboard, flicking down the "queues" of stories that were coming up. Donald's voice, rising in volume, could be heard coming from the receiver held between Theo's elbow and stomach.

"Right, we're going to Sushi, hear that TX? There's no phono," said Ivy into her microphone.

Jonathan had moved to the desk behind Theo and was trying to locate the Home Office wires' queue. "Theo," he said, "Theo!...That was the Home Office, they've just postponed the deportation of five Nigerian refugees."

Theo was nervously looking at the red digital clock below the two broadcast monitors. As if hearing him by accident, he told Jonathan to write a short script. "Charlene," he said to a production secretary, "create another page between 202 and 207."

He quickly typed in the script beginning with the words, "We've just heard from the Home Office that…"

"Sophie?" Theo shouted at a producer who had just entered the gallery, "Get graphics to do us a Home Office comp, for a statement." Then he told Jonathan to hurry up and run down to graphics with a printout of the statement.

When Jonathan had returned from the depths of the Gothic graphics department, he could see Theo, on the phone to Trowbridge in one of the editing suites. "Get some pictures from Sophie's piece and find anything on some Nigerians who were due for deportation. Anything, do you here, this is urgent."

Since Theo wasn't telling him to do anything, Jonathan watched the programme. A harsh police identikit picture of a rapist perched itself on the screen. On their rival, a frothy, blonde woman danced around a multicoloured studio lit by vivid spotlights.

The rapist has terrorised this small village with this five-year old girl saying she's frightened to go out of doors after dark. Police are warning women to stay indoors at all times, if possible.

Over his shoulder, he could see that whilst Theo tried to keep track of the timings of pieces and interviews, the right hand corner of his screen flashed the word "messages" as fast as he could answer them. Jonathan couldn't see all the messages clearly but he got the impression that Theo was being messaged by programme editors, managing editors, directorate managers and other senior staff. They were all in constant communication with each other as the programme was broadcast. The higher the level of the person he was emailing, the less profane were Theo's messages.

Prog editor :what the fuck's going on in the rape piece, where was the second Aston?

Theo : Screw you, there are more important things. Did you hear about the Home Office?

Man Editor :Good work on the rape, nice human interest angle. Good work

Theo :Thanks, trying my best!

Prog editor :And what's this fluffy sushi piece doing?

Theo: I dunno, that was arranged by the day team and we lost Mollusc so we had to quickly put Sushi in.

Prog editor: So all you do now is copy the day team's work, huh?

Theo: No.

Prog editor :Perhaps, we should talk after this programme has gone out.

Theo: Fuck you!!

Prog editor :You're fired.

Dir Manager :Excellent sushi piece. Congratulations!...My wife liked it very much, too. She's just got a machine!

Theo :What do you mean fired?

Prog editor :just joking!...Theo, aren't you being a bit defensive? Still, see me afterwards

Just then Ivy swivelled her chair around, "How much longer with the headmaster?"

"How long have we got?" Theo asked one of the production secretaries, sweat dripping from his ears.

"You've a minute in hand."

"Give him thirty," said Theo before turning to Jonathan to ask what he thought of the interview and then turning back to reply to some more messages. Theo's eyes were blood-red.

So how do you characterise seventeen years of Education policy?

Well, er...

Well, sorry, we'll have to leave it there. I'm sure that one thing everyone will agree on is that this debate will go on and on. Catherine?

Thanks, Peter. Screaming girl fans are back again. The new groups...

The package began with some black and white footage of

The Beatles, singing "She Loves You", whereupon the Directorate Manager emailed Theo to give him more congratulations.

Dir Manager: Excellent, I thought.

Theo: Thank you very much. We put a lot of work into it.

It was ten o'clock in the morning and they had been on shift for twelve hours. The programme had ended. Tiredness had turned into a general confusion, as producers slipped on staircases, tipped cups of coffee over on dog-eared scripts or talked like rapid machine-gun fire. Some read newspapers, although there was nothing Jonathan hadn't read in the morning's batch. Others tapped on their keyboards like dripping faucets. There were two things that everyone, even the presenters, Catherine and Peter, were now waiting for: the debrief and an invitation to sit with the editor of the department, perhaps sharing a morning glass of wine or beer with him.

The keyboard-tappers were using two keys on their keyboard, one a "cursor-right" and the other a "cursor-left". They were checking whether the computer queue called 'Debriefs' had been updated by the editor. At around ten past ten, a new queue appeared, with today's date as its title. Trying to "go into" the queue was impossible, however, as the editor had locked it. Usually, Jonathan was told, this meant he had either forgotten to unlock it or that he was checking with a more senior management official about his comments.

"You know, Jonathan, not everyone cares about the debrief. Those with staff jobs couldn't give a toss. Mind you, have you heard about the Newsnight ones?" Jonathan said that he hadn't. "They're terrible. After each programme, the entire team assemble in a semicircle. It's a bit like a board except it's the other way around. One editor is interviewing all the staff. Anyway, every night someone ends up crying because of what the editor says. And the weird thing is that whilst you're being slammed, no-one else can help you."

The queue had been unlocked.

Debrief—first producer set
Not bad for a quiet day.

Peter and Catherine looking relaxed, but why strange camera angle first thing?

Led on Education, not great but at least we showed the country what some private schools look like. School headmaster was boring though, don't let him on again. That's despite Catherine's ever wonderful questioning.

Then straight into hard economic story from Chris, perhaps a little complicated for the morning. Should have emphasised the interest rate cut more, that affects our viewers more, makes 'em happy that they're paying less for their mortgages. Then, a wonderful piece about the sushi record breakers in Osaka. Fascinating.

Harrison Shisthe, barely in Frankfurt for two hours goes to work on the Krauts. Excellent piece, full of angry Germans, both from the banks and in vox pops.

Peter handles the link to Rape expertly. Again, good real people interviews, showing how frightened they are. All in all left a nasty taste in the mouth. Good work.

Then Screaming girls story, perhaps a tad dull? Haven't we seen this before? Nice use of The Beatles at the beginning but that seemed to be about all. Although, the phone rang in the middle of it so perhaps I should take a second look.

Then: disaster. We piss off Mollusc after all the work that Donald Adriasson did to get them on <u>board</u>. What happened? Full investigation will follow. Instead of Mollusc we go to enraged Euro MPs, who say sanctions are the answer. Or at least, they're supposed to say this but hey, what's this? We talk about five Nigerians about to be deported from Britain. Good story, all of a sudden, and we're making news. At last, a real Britain angle. Excellent quick work from Theo on getting the Nigerian library footage onto the screen. Still thought we could have had Mollusc on, though.

Papers—Bluestock gives us the usual, what good value.

And Sports late again—if it happens again we'll chop it completely!

And we're gone...

So went Jonathan's section of the long and rambling debrief. Through his tired eyes, he felt strangely happy about the comments of his editor. Other producers sat back in their chairs, exhausted and either looking deeply worried or satisfied. Jonathan knew that every debrief was the beginning of an open access forum. Anyone could complain about what the editor had said—but there were penalties for this. Because everyone would be able to see the comments, everyone would know the relationship between complainant and editor. Debriefs, as Jonathan saw when he looked at the previous day's examples, took the temperature of staff disagreements. He didn't want to risk any ire from the editor. He wasn't feeling brave and he had no desire to alert the editor as to the ins and outs of the Mollusc story. Jonathan suspected that, in some harsh sections of the debrief, the editor seemed as if he was actively encouraging complaints, perhaps from protégé agent provocateurs.

From coffee bar gossip, Jonathan knew that some of the most angry complaints against the editor, now popping up in the debrief, were from those with jobs to go to, outside the Corporation. They didn't care about criticising the boss. He looked over and saw one exhausted producer frantically tapping on her keyboard. He knew that she had no other job to go to and was puzzled at her angry denunciations of her editor, now popping up on the system for everyone to see. As he saw tears in her eyes, he realised that because of her fatigue she must have suffered a temporary loss of judgement. He wouldn't see her again.

Ivy had been the first to complain, though because it wasn't about the journalism of the show, her debrief comments didn't destroy any of her career prospects. She protested that the "funny camera angle" was not her fault. It was the funny angle or no angle at all, she wrote.

Jonathan's extreme exhaustion was now waking him up. He was fidgety, his eyes were blinking faster, his heart had sped up. He began to feel proud about what had happened to the deportees. The Tannoy had announced the Home Office's decision to postpone the deportation and he knew he had had a rôle in it all. Not choosing mollusc may have even saved some lives.

While he was considering this, Catherine and Peter came into the room, flushed and refreshed by their performance. They had the airs of survivors. Fears that they might dry up on camera, that their voice might not sound when they tried to speak, that a long seen-off twitch might have returned, that they might collapse in a fit of sneezing—they had all been unfounded. Interviewees had all been relatively sane, with none of them fancying monosyllabic affirmative and negatives to complete sentences. The autocue had run relatively smoothly, the tapes had been the right ones, the lighting hadn't failed and they had told the right time to their audience.

Catherine put her hand on Jonathan's shoulder and spoke to the team, "let's go into the boss' office, then," she said, her other hand fumbling for a packet of cigarettes.

Quietly, they all trooped into the corner office, where the editor of the programme was talking heatedly on the phone. Theo, the night-editor, looking drunk from the exhaustion reminded Jonathan of the escaped convict featured on the local news bulletin in the middle of the show, except that he was muttering to himself. The crowd of producers rubbed their eyes.

Peter lit a big cigar and pressed buttons on a remote control unit. "Damn, how does this thing work?" he said, trying to retrieve a recording of the programme.

Catherine smoked a cigarette and chatted to Ivy about how if her husband ever discovered that she was still a smoker, her marriage would be over. Trowbridge watched the boss who had put down the phone and was now typing into his computer.

"Good show, I thought," he said, when he'd finished. The editor looked at the team suspiciously, like a headmaster who was trying to seem relaxed. "Open some wine," he said, looking around until he motioned for Jonathan to look in the fridge beside his desk, "there should be some beer or some white in there."

Peter successfully rewound the tape and now played it

at low volume, fast forwarding it through every bit of the programme that did not involve him.

"Good interview," the boss said as Peter's interview with a rape victim played out.

"She was good," he retorted.

It's terrible, an experience that no one can imagine except...

"By the way, I had drinks with Sir Colbert, yesterday evening."

"Still with the same wife, is he?" the boss asked.

"I think so. He asked after you, wondered whether you were free for dinner in a couple of weeks time," said Peter, tapping his ash into a beer-bottle that Trowbridge had just emptied.

"Not sure. The wife's being a bit strange at the moment. I think I'm sort of gated," the boss looked up at Catherine.

"Well, perhaps when the time comes."

"Sure," said the boss, a frown becoming a smile towards Catherine, "stop it there, will you?" he said to Peter. Catherine was interviewing the MEPs on the tape. She watched, impassive except for the biting of her lower lip. "Actually, I had dinner, yesterday, with Cleo Warner," the boss said when Catherine stopped being on the screen.

At the mention of this name, both Peter and Catherine looked up. In his tiredness, Jonathan ventured an interruption. "Cleo Warner?" he asked.

"Managing Head at Director Level of News and Current Affairs Daily Programmes Factual Directorate Stories Plurality Section with extra responsibility for news action prospects," the boss, said smiling at him as Jonathan carefully lifted the cork out of a bottle of white wine, flinching at the bouquet.

"He said he wants to come and look at the operation here, see what's happening, how we keep our costs down so well."

"I could tell him that in a minute," Catherine said, trying to pat down a few strands of hair above her ear. She had had blonde hair when she came into the office at three. Now, it was a kind of golden colour, what with it's centimetre-layer of hair-spray.

"We still going out tonight?" asked the boss, winking at Catherine. Peter puffed harder at his cigar as producers nervously sipped at their alcoholic drinks. Behind them the morning's news was already being shouted across the room, news that was little different in tone to the previous night. A new shift had just sat down at their desks, preparing for their morning meeting. It would take place amongst the empty bottles that Jonathan and others would leave behind.

Catherine smiled back at the boss.

As the minutes ticked by, producers slowly trickled away, fighting either the tears of tiredness or the urge to butter up the editor, for fear of accidentally insulting him. As he left TV Centre, the daylight made Jonathan feel like a shattering pane of sugar-glass.

"Goodnight," he whispered to the security man who was checking the passes of those entering on foot at the entrance. He gave Jonathan a faint acknowledgement before looking bothered by the interruption.

The journey back was uncomfortable. Though rush hour crowds had subsided, there were still troubled faces on the underground. They belonged to the late, the unwell or the jobless. Jonathan eased a smile at the newspapers they were carrying. All covered yesterday's news. Tomorrow they would be covering what he would tonight. For the rest of his journey, Jonathan's eyes remained shut, his fingers rubbing against each other.

Jonathan bent down to retrieve the key for his temporary accommodation from beneath a plant pot, the litter of the street still scuffing his shoes. Once inside, he had no difficulty falling asleep in the zipped-up bag, despite outside shouts and pneumatic drills. Unlike normal night shift periods, Jonathan could enjoy more than five hours sleep. His slumber lasted twenty hours with a short break for a sandwich at midnight.

Jonathan was assigned a day shift, not because he had performed badly on nights, but as a way of "breaking his resistance" to working at night. Jonathan knew that the job wasn't just about working after dusk, it was about being able to work 9am to 1am one day and 9pm to 11am the next. His boss sometimes worked shifts of more than twenty-four hours.

"I'm too tired," grumbled a producer in the newsroom.

"I have friends who are junior doctors and they have more free time than me," the editor snapped.

Jonathan laughed as others worked in silence. Shift work had many effects on news coverage. One, in particular, was its impact on coverage of those working in the National Health Service. There was a view in the newsroom that newspaper stories about nurses' long hours were pretty feeble. "How could anyone be working harder than us?" was the consensus.

But, on this day shift, it was a "quiet" news day and the day editor, Durward, had lost an aunt the previous evening. He was wearing baggy, multicoloured, woollen clothing and it was rough as if he this wearing it was a ritual. "Awful, awful, awful. They took hours to come," he said, for a moment pained, "and the emergency department. It was horrible." He paused to compose himself and took a sip of coffee. "Get on the case, man," Durward continued, pointing to a new survey he held in his hands. It was embargoed till the next morning.

Cordelia, the researcher, looked at Jonathan from across the desk and smiled, before dialling a number. As Durward flicked through the Daily Mail, he stroked his blonde beard with great seriousness. His yellow eyes had lowered, scanning the brightly laid-out horoscope page with concern.

"Who's the reporter, today?" Jonathan asked, softly.

"Marsh. He's next door in the reporter's room," Durward replied, turning to the racing pages.

"Marsh's a real sweetie," said Cordelia. "By the way, Durward?" she said, trying to catch his attention. "Durward?"

"Yes?" Durward looked up from the paper, annoyed.

"Did you see the piece about blacks and the police?" Everything stopped for a second as a cleaner who had been vacuuming in an editing suite looked up. "The piece says that," Cordelia continued, "one in every hundred and fifty whites in Britain is stopped by police compared with one in twenty blacks."

"Oh, give over. Everyone knows that blacks are stopped more often. That's old news," Durward smiled at the cleaner who returned a puzzled expression. "Now, Cordelia, get on with what I told you to do. You obviously have a longer way to go than I thought before you become a producer."

Cordelia muttered something about how she had been encouraged to come up with ideas and that there didn't seem much point if she was going to be shouted down whenever she spoke up. Jonathan watched her smooth her brown hair over the back of her head and tap her pen on her pad a few times. "I was only..." she began saying.

"Shut it!" said Durward, banging his hand on the table, before returning to his paper.

Jonathan began to make a few phone calls. He soon discovered how difficult it was to get statistics about the National Health Service that agreed with each other. After a while, Durward suggested that he take a camera crew to a casualty ward that evening and gauge "first-hand" the pressures facing an accident and emergency department. "That'll be the way to do it. If we could get what I saw last night on..."

"That's not too good an idea, Durward," Edwin, the planning editor interrupted. He was sitting at a nearby desk, devising schedules and rota patterns. He looked annoyed, his eyebrows arched about his eyes. "There's no way we can give you a crew tonight, it's just not a possibility. Why all the fuss about the NHS all of a sudden anyway?" he asked.

"I'm hear to day-edit, alright?" said Durward, straightening his tabloid with a flick of his wrists and ending the matter.

Jonathan phoned the reporters' room. "Hi, Marsh? I'm on the day-desk today, just across the corridor. It looks like we're doing a piece, a sort of general piece pegged to a survey, about the health service. So, if you want to..." Jonathan paused.

"Oh, yes, sure. That's wonderful, I'm sure I can find a lot of information. I know quite a few people. I'll call you in about half an hour, is that all right?" Marsh said, his words hurried, but confident.

"Yes, that's fine," Jonathan replied. While he was on the

line, Durward began motioning to Jonathan with his right hand. At first, he couldn't understand what Durward meant to communicate with his curved fingers and the lateral movement of his palm. His mouth had formed an 'O' shape through which he was whispering a kind of grunt. Jonathan smiled back at him, understanding Durward's alarm at having so little prepared for tomorrow's programme. It was eleven o'clock in the morning and Jonathan imagined tonight's meeting between day and night-editors, the excuses day would say to night if day bequeathed nothing but a blank sheet of paper.

After Jonathan had been to the stationery cupboard, in a room where a producer was irritably fast-forwarding a tape of some more war footage from the former Yugoslavia, he sat back at his desk and began to dial. He had consulted the computer database and after an hour or so of calls had some possible interviewees and a pile of faxes.

"Marsh?" he asked, holding the last corner of a tuna sandwich that Cordelia had got for him.

"Hello, any luck?" Marsh replied. "By the way, why don't you just come over across the corridor instead of phoning. I don't mean to sound..."

Jonathan recalled the reporters' room, 'just over the corridor', as Marsh said. He knew that he was going to have to get used to entering that room, with all its reporters gossiping and plotting. Trying to buoy up his confidence, he reflected on the ridiculousness of being frightened of them. He lifted himself off the chair, squared his shoulders and marched out the door.

Again, the effect was that of a cowboy entering a saloon in which he was not known. The hubbub died down the instant his fingers left the door handle of the room.

"Marsh?" he asked as a group of ten reporters stared back, as if waiting for Jonathan to break into a jig.

"Hi, I'm Marsh," a neatly attired man of around twenty-six replied, "why don't we go over there." Jonathan flinched at his politeness.

Marsh escorted him to a small cuboid office hidden at the back of the reporters' room. When they'd sat down, Marsh smiled at Jonathan in a half plaintive, half patronising way and began to speak of his morning's work. He had a striped blue collegiate tie on and would, from time to time, flick its tail. As he did so, he would then look down and then look back at Jonathan with confused grey eyes, his sharp, angular nose making a shiny arc.

"Well, I haven't found much at all, alas. The Department of Health gave the usual figures which show that the Service is performing better than ever. More patients, more beds, more doctors and nurses than when the Conservative Party took office—all that sort of stuff."

"I see," Jonathan replied with a sense of anxiety, his calf muscle suddenly in a nervous spasm.

"But of course, they always say that, so I don't see why that should be a problem, we still have a kind of story. The only problem is finding people who use the system, if you know what I mean. If we can find something out, we're home and dry." Just then, Jonathan recognised what he had been trying to for some minutes. Marsh didn't seem to be like the other reporters. He had the demeanour of someone who had been picked up from somewhere else and planted down in the reporters' room. Despite his confidence, he looked surprised and a little bewildered. He looked as if he was in a constant process of trying to come to terms with an astonishing adjustment of circumstances.

"Well," Jonathan said, looking down at the scrawls across a double page of his large new red notebook. He paused for breath as Marsh flicked his tie again.

"I've got some statistics about beds: Since the present Prime Minister came into office, London has lost one in five or fourteen thousand beds. If one takes it from 1986, forty thousand beds have gone. And if you take it from 1979, when the Conservatives came to office, two out of five beds across the country have been cut. Since 1990, that comes to a cut of one in six acute beds across the National Health Service."

There was also some material he had got about teaching hospitals and Jonathan quickly reeled it off. "Saint Bartholomew's and the Middlesex are to be shut down. Guy's and Saint Thomas' are to merge. The Royal Brompton heart and lungs centre and the Royal Marsden cancer centre are to be shut. And the Royal National Ear, Nose and Throat Hospital is to be merged with the Hospital for Tropical Diseases."

Jonathan continued to tell Marsh about what he had found out. He explained the tax advantages that had been introduced for employees wishing to opt-out of the NHS and into private medical insurance policies. Marsh's head had been steadily dropping but, on hearing this, he spoke up and flicked his tie. "That's terrible," he repeated quietly.

"Between 1984 and 1994, the NHS has each day recruited 10 senior managers and lost 30 nurses. Since 1990 there are eighteen thousand three-hundred and forty more managers in the NHS versus fifty thousand fewer front-line staff in hospital wards and nineteen thousand and twenty fewer nurses in training. But the best statistic of all, if we can get a crew, is that around sixty hospitals are now turning patients away." Marsh remained silent, so Jonathan continued to speak. "I thought we could go to one of the hospitals that are turning people away."

"That's a really great idea," Marsh declared, "perhaps makeup downstairs could do something and I could go in as an emergency patient, to see how long it takes for me to be seen or something."

"Well, I'm not sure that would be quite ethical," Jonathan frowned, "but, yes, something like that. I'll have to check Producers' Guidelines."

"Oh, another reporter from one of the daytime shows did it a while ago. I think it was...maybe it was on ITV. Anyway," he paused, finding something of interest on one of the eyes of his brogues. "Actually, this might not be too easy a story to do. I remember, a while back, that it's very hard to get permission to film in hospitals." His face creased up in thought, bulges of skin collecting under his eyes. Then, he untied one of his laces and tied it back up in a double knot. Jonathan looked at the felt pinboard behind him and scanned the images of various reporters. They were glossy photographs cut from a fashion magazine.

Under each were the reporter's name and the shop from where the clothes they were wearing could be bought.

"I do have a friend at the Clarence Trust in Chelsea, perhaps I'll call him," Marsh said, suddenly so excited that his face was feeling wet, even from a yard away.

Jonathan returned to the newsroom, which was now nearly empty. "Where's everyone gone?" he asked.

"Oh, it's Darren's birthday, he's having a knees-up at Joe's Wine Bar in Shepherd's Bush," replied a weary-looking presenter from the world news television desk, "if it wasn't for the stupid time differences, I'd be there now. Still they left me this lager. Want some?" she asked before smearing the can with her lipstick.

After a few more calls, Jonathan managed to get interviews arranged with a professor of hospital management science, a government spokesman and an opposition one. He was encouraged by Marsh's attitude. Unlike other reporters, he seemed interested and engaged in the story, even genuinely moved by the statistics he had gathered about hospital staffing and the bed shortage. Jonathan knew that Jane and Hugo would have laughed at his recitation of the figures. They would have complained that his statistics were open to abuse by political parties and that it was best if the piece ignored them completely. Statistics, Jonathan had learnt, were liked more in the graphics department than in the newsroom.

Cordelia had been shouted down recently for suggesting a story about the methods for calculating unemployment figures. She had claimed that the system had changed thirty-two times over the past seventeen years. "Your job is to get the latest data and the reporter's there to present it," a producer had told her. "Simple as that. Leave ideas about figure-fiddling to more in-depth programmes. That story comes around every couple of years anyway, and only when it's a particularly bad news day."

"But how will people know whether the figures are correct?" she had asked.

"Look, we don't want to have to give everyone a lesson in

mathematics every month so that we can teach the public how to interpret the unemployment figures, alright?"

Jonathan had felt bad for her during this exchange, believing that the programme's audience were fascinated by data analysis, if only because they thought it could make the difference between jackpots and torn-up lottery slips. Marsh didn't look like a betting man, Jonathan thought. He seemed genuinely interested in the National Health Service and that, Jonathan anticipated, would make for a good report, his best yet.

After quick interviews with government and opposition spokesmen, both of who opposed the other just the way Jonathan had expected, they went to the hospital.

To get to it, they walked a brightly polished marble path to the main building. Rich foliage brushed at their shoulders as they advanced, the sweet fragrance of tropical flowers filling their lungs. An artificial lake gleamed beside them and on it, two swans glided past a luxuriant willow. Further, at the other bank were flamingos casually walking on turf fit for a cricket square. The sheen of the chrome on the front door temporarily blinded them and they turned back to witness the flight of a bird beside a floodlit waterfall. Jonathan, Marsh and Arnold, the cameraman, listened for a minute to a string quartet gently bowing under a white canopy of flowers. Their black bow ties fluttered in the breeze and Jonathan sensed that something was not right.

"Er, Marsh, this is a private hospital," Jonathan said, watching the palms above him sway about a radiant sign announcing the Clarence Trust.

"Sorry?" said Marsh, looking perturbed.

"Private. It's not a National Health Service hospital."

Arnold turned his head towards Jonathan and said he'd park the car and have a look anyway as they might be able to get some shots.

"No," Jonathan said firmly, "this isn't the same thing at all."

"Well, how was I supposed to know that?" replied Marsh,

adopting a very different tone to the one Jonathan had become got used to. "Look," he whispered loudly, "my friend Alex very kindly gave us permission to film here. I think it would be a great shame if, after all the trouble he must have had to go to, we just decided to pass up the opportunity. He even said we could film some of the new electronic scanning machines, the magnetic resonance thing. Put it this way, I don't think Edwin will be very happy if we've got Arnold to come out and film and you decided not to use him at all."

"I think that settles it," Arnold said, as he looked down at his shoes and rubbed his face with his hands.

The reception area was huge, lit from the sky via a transparent ceiling. Nurses and doctors smiled at the three of them as they sashayed across the marble floor, dressed not in uniforms but smart city suits. The only tell-tale sign that it was hospital apart from the sign above the reception desk was the cornucopia of stickers advertising different types of credit cards and the costs of some common operations beside the cash-till.

"Look, I know it's not quite right, but we can get some shots here and then go and see an NHS place afterwards to fill in if you want to," Marsh said. Jonathan was searching the atrium with his eyes.

"Welcome to Clarence," said a tanned, fit looking man with an American accent. "I am Baden and this," he held out his palm, "is where ill people become well again, where lives are saved and where some people, after a hard week's work in the office, come to recharge their batteries. This way."

After they had followed Baden through some empty and clean corridors, they arrived at the scanning room. As Arnold lit the room and tested his camera, Baden's face slowly lost its smile.

"Well, just a short interview would have been nice, you know, I mean for the Clarence. We are laying it on for you, you know." He pointed to a cloth covered tea-trolley overflowing with cakes and sandwiches. "But, if the Corporation doesn't think we're good enough, then so be it. Alex," he turned to Marsh, "thinks very highly of you and he'll be mightily disappointed that you didn't want to interview any of the doctors or nurses."

Marsh glared at Jonathan and turned to Baden, "I'm very sorry, Baden. You're right, we wouldn't be getting the feel of it. Perhaps, I'll do a quick piece to camera." Marsh looked at Jonathan and came over and whispered that it was just in case they couldn't get a good piece to camera in an NHS hospital. Jonathan sat down in a leather Chesterfield and consented. Marsh walked over to a Victorian desk and angled a gold fitting to illuminate a blotter. Then, he began to write his piece.

A tall, blonde, clear-skinned woman wearing glossy red lipstick and what looked like nothing but a lilac, knee-length silk bathrobe had entered the room. Jonathan smiled at her nervously as Baden talked to Arnold about how the scanning shot could be set up so to look as interesting for the viewer as possible.

"I'm sorry, Baden or whatever your name is, but no-one is going to tell me how to light a shot. I've been in this business for quite a long time, you know...I know what looks good and I certainly wouldn't tell you how to do your public relations job, now would I?" said Arnold angrily.

"No, no, of course," Baden replied in a calm monotone voice. "What I was giving you were merely suggestions. Lana, here, would make any shot beautiful, in any case," he smiled. He turned to Jonathan who was shaking his head. "Well, if you don't want her, you don't have to have her. We just thought the shot would look nice with her, that's all."

Lana smiled and fluttered her eyelashes, not saying a word. Jonathan found himself looking at her three inch high heels.

"Sorry, Baden, I understand what you mean. It's just that it's my decision. Ultimately, it's up to us, not you." Arnold turned towards Jonathan, "that's me and ultimately my producer, no-one else. That doesn't mean that if you come up with a good idea, we won't use it, it just means that the final decision is ours, right?"

Jonathan nodded in agreement before picking up a glossy woman's magazine from a gold table at his side. Remembering that he should be finding a hospital to do some more shooting in, he flipped open a Corporation mobile phone and began dialling some numbers.

After twenty minutes, during which Arnold took footage of the model being conveyed through the scanner and the resulting scans on various computer screens, Marsh stood up in front of an operating table. With the bright halogen lights shining above him like an alien spacecraft, he began to speak.

"The crisis in Britain's hospitals is something we all take for granted now. But some hospitals are managing their finances so as to minimise wastage and maximise the healthcare of their patients. This state-of-the-art hospital is only one of thousands springing up to fill a need. Harnessing the latest technology, the facilities at the Clarence enable doctors and nurses to diagnose and treat patients efficiently with less waiting time. Gone are the lacklustre wards famous for their fading paintwork and faulty fittings. Instead, interior designers and architects have created an environment dedicated to the well-being of patients. And customers come first."

Marsh delivered his script to the camera in one take and Arnold congratulated him on it before they packed the equipment back into the cases.

"Thanks," Arnold said to Lana, as he gave her his card.

Back inside the estate car, Arnold and Marsh were chatting about the shoot.

"Brilliant, wasn't it? I think the piece to camera should look really good, if you got it right, that is," Marsh joked.

"I got it right, don't you worry. It'll look good, what with the girl in the background going through the machine as you while you were speaking."

"It's good to have movement in a shot," Marsh said, turning to Jonathan. "But, as I said," he looked more serious, "if we find that it doesn't work, our first priority is to use one from a nationalised hospital."

Jonathan felt betrayed and ignored him. Instead of replying he told Arnold how to get to the Panford Trust, a hospital that had opted out of council control to receive funds directly from central government. Jonathan knew it wasn't perfect for the report, but it was the only place he had been able to get permission for filming. Jonathan had wanted to film a hospital that hadn't opted out, one that might have been more representative but time was against him.

"Any idea where we can park?" Arnold said, peering down a side street of double-parked cars and construction vehicles.

"Not sure, I'm afraid," Jonathan replied, cursing himself.

"Never mind, we can park down that street over there, by the boarded-up shop. They say in constant use, but it looks pretty deserted to me."

"OK, but if we're towed away, you're paying," Marsh joked, dryly.

Soon, they were all speechless. Hauling the equipment up towards the hospital, they slowly began to see the crowd of a hundred or so people queuing. The line ended at what looked like a pre-fabricated concrete outhouse. Ambulances, their sirens switched off but their blue lights violently flashing were parked in a row around them. Stretchers, half revealed, looked like hot dogs falling from buns.

As they came closer the dripping red lines on people's faces became clearer in the dark grey light.

"Excuse me, we're from the corporation," said Marsh, trying to make a way through the meleé for Arnold and Jonathan.

Weary looking eyes curved upwards and injured limbs shifted to make way for them. Soon, they were beside a dirty reception-desk, vivid stickers advertising the brand names of different medicines adding the only colour to the bullet-proof glass. A one bar fluorescent bulb, itself advertising the popular drug, Prozac, lit the impatient face of a nurse whose throat was too dry to be audible.

She motioned for them to wait and Marsh and Arnold moved away to the nearby collection of sponge-sprouting vinyl seats. On two of them lay a muddy sleeping bag, a bearded man's face peeping out from one end. On another chair sat a woman in a shawl, checking the pulse of a baby in her arms and next to her was a worried man in a black suit, biting his nails as the veins in his eyes darkened. The stench of illness and soup pervaded the air. Jonathan tried to adjust the rate of his breathing.

"We can't really film any of this," Arnold said to him, his voice dry at first, "it's a Producers' Guidelines thing, you know."

Jonathan nodded, remembering a personal rule he had made, not to intrude into personal grief. Suddenly, there was a flurry of people around them, jostling for space, pushing and shoving. Then, they all froze. A smart man of about thirty, in a gold tie and double-breasted suit had arrived. He had heavily gelled shiny short black hair and as he greeted Marsh, Jonathan couldn't help feeling that it was as if he had sprung from the ground. Even those limping with the aid of others had stopped their journeys when he appeared.

"Good evening, so good that you could all come. Sorry about the directions, you were supposed to come through the Darlington Road entrance, it would have been easier for you to park there," the man said, "as you can see we're very busy indeed. Perhaps our busiest for some time. I do hope this won't take too long."

The man had a square jaw and an aquiline nose. Though his light fabric suit and fresh face gave an impression of relaxed corporate style, beads of sweat had gathered above his upper lip. They were now so large that they were dripping into his mouth.

He escorted the crew into a rectangular, off-white room with a big table occupying most of its space. At the far end was an armchair, covered by a dusty sheet imprinted with the name of the hospital.

"If you'll wait here, the Trust Chief Executive will be with you in a few minutes."

The three of them stood for a few moments in silence, trying to compose themselves after the carnage they had just witnessed. Arnold was the first to move, setting up his lights and having to check for potential difference with each socket. "I'll have to turn this off," he said looking at the bare bulb in the centre of the ceiling that was giving out the colour of old lemon squash. "The wiring is screwed up in here," he said.

Marsh looked up and then back to his clipboard, mouthing words to himself, going through the questions he would ask the executive.

"I think the first thing he should answer is the criticism that these hospitals were bribed by the government to opt out and that after opting out the funding just hasn't been there. Not as promised..." Jonathan said, watching Marsh write in his notepad, "also we should ask why waiting times have gone up and why the opted-out hospitals need so much more management staff and so many fewer doctors and nurses."

"Absolutely," Marsh said sternly, "those are the key questions. It's hell out there, isn't it?"

Once Arnold had placed a few diffusing pieces of plastic over his lights, he sat down in a rickety school-chair and asked Jonathan whether this would be the last assignment as he wanted to get home early tonight. "I've got to be up early tomorrow... holiday, you see. And not a moment too soon."

"Oh, you're going away. Where?" Marsh asked, interrupting his silent lip movements.

"Indonesia, Bali. It should be nice, ever been there?"

"No, I know a friend who was there trying to cover a war story down there. East Timor? Anyway, he was a bit of a nutty guy, actually."

"What? Is there a war down there? It's very beautiful, isn't it?" Arnold asked, as if for reassurance.

"Yes, yes. Quentin came back with loads of pictures. Actually, he ended up holidaying there himself after his assignment was done. Plenty of girls there, not that he was much interested. He came back a bit of Buddhist," Marsh said, flicking his tie. "I couldn't work that out myself. It's a Muslim country, isn't it?"

"Muslim?" asked Arnold, sounding worried.

The man with shiny black hair now returned and made an announcement like the compère of a Weimar cabaret show. "And now, the Chief Executive of the Panford Trust." Jonathan looked over to Marsh. The doorknob turned a few times. After some pushing sounds, it opened.

The Chief Executive was a short, grey-haired man with a ruddy, fatty face. He shook hands with everyone while two white-coated men with stethoscopes brought in a plastic chair. Then he sat down and they shuffled out of the room backwards, the ghostly summonses of their bleepers echoing around them.

"Sorry, I'll have to re-light this, if you're there. You couldn't sit on this chair instead?" asked Arnold wistfully.

The Chief Executive looked towards his assistant for approval.

"That should be fine, I think. Fine, fine, fine," said the assistant.

Once he settled down, Marsh began to fire his questions. The Chief Executive answered in measured and eloquent sentences, pausing for thought before delivering each Ciceronean clause.

"Why the opt out?"

"I don't think that opting out is necessarily the issue here, if issue there is and, after all, that in itself is an issue. Interest groups, those that want to lobby for this and want to lobby for that, those that like to complain, although there are some that approve of things we are doing, well, those interest groups, those ones that I referred to before, they would like everyone to focus on, rather as a decoy for whatever ideology they wish to press onto the public imagination, the things that are negative. What surely, really counts here—and I don't think one will find many who disagree with this or at least one would be hard pressed to do so—is good and efficient healthcare."

"What about the charge that you have recruited management personnel at the expense of front-line ward staff?"

"Again, this is a charge that certain groups wish to use as a means of ideologically dominating the field of debate. They want us to live in a strange, mythical past where the old values that failed made up what now seem, to some, like a golden age. What counts now, and I really do mean now, is healthcare.

What if, and I just want to pose the question, here, what if better healthcare can be administered by fewer doctors and nurses? If that was proved, if that was found to be the case, if we all discovered that this was so, would any of you prevent that better healthcare? Would you punish those patients, such as the ones you saw waiting outside, would you make them suffer because you thought that more doctors would benefit them? I think that would obviously be a very irrational way of going about building a modern, efficient health system, don't you? Look, we are nearing the end of the century and many old ideas that we have used like security blankets, for too long—yes, for all too long—they have been discredited. We shouldn't be fearful of this, we shouldn't fret that things we have long clung to have now just blown away in the light of new circumstances, new dimensions, new paradigms. For so long now, this country has poured billions of pounds into a system that has been failing the population at large. What hospitals such as ourselves are doing is delivering first rate healthcare to customers, regardless of offending certain interest groups and politicians. We've had to take tough decisions but as I'm sure you saw as you came in today, customers are still coming to us for our expertise—they are not deserting us for, say, the hospital in the next borough. I might add that that hospital hasn't opted out. We, by contrast, are an efficient machine that's competing within a modern healthcare dynamic which forces managers and chief executives to take harsh and complex decisions that form the structural, body and mind foundation upon which our society functions."

"That alright?" asked Marsh, scratching his head and turning to Jonathan.

"Well, how about why the queues and waiting times are longer?" he suggested.

The Chief Executive smiled peculiarly as he looked over towards Jonathan. "Look, we can't help what we've inherited. What we were given was a shabby, clapped out old system which we are making anew. Our targets cannot be achieved overnight, these things take time. Rome, you will remember, if they still teach classics at school, was not built in a day and certainly would have taken longer to build if money had been as tight as it is today. Wait and see is how I respond to that, wait and see. Remember, the old system was a ruinous one with bad management and old practices, now disposed of forever by the winds of time."

At this moment, Jonathan suddenly wondered whether the man in front of them had been in charge of the hospital before it had opted out. "Were you not in charge of the hospital before the government changes to the NHS?" he asked.

Again, the man smiled, faltering annoyance in his eyes, "I wasn't in charge. I wasn't in charge and I can say that categorically. I was not in charge—definitely not in the way I am in charge now. There were tiers of local government, regional health authorities, the so-called mechanisms of government that were accountable to the local area but were instead just swathes of politically correct dogmatism. Besides, in the system that was here before there was a certain structural problem whereby every member of staff was dis-empowered. Today, everyone who works at the Panford knows that they own a part of the place. They feel it. Just look at the fast food canteen, to take an example. There's a pride in the beef burgers they provide. Look how different that is to the old cafeteria, where the food was shoddy. I admit that now."

Jonathan looked down at his notes. 'Ask about five fold increase in salary,' it said. It would sound impertinent, he thought. This was the only hospital that had agreed to an interview. What if he was risking the Corporation's future ability to interview Panford staff? Would the Chief Executive call his editors and complain about him?

"What about your salary?" Jonathan mumbled, "what about the huge increase in your salary?" As he said it, his heart beat faster and Marsh flinched, putting his clipboard down.

"I see," the Chief Executive replied, his voice much louder than before, "I see." Arnold slowly moved a dial on his camera. "This is the gutter level the Corporation is descending to these days. It wasn't like this, you know," he paused and composed himself, wiping his lips with the side of a forefinger, "what they are doing is paying me the market rate. If you have a problem with that then you obviously want a hospital run by substandard staff. Managing a hospital takes leadership, and leadership costs money." He began to free himself from his lapel microphone, "I dare say you weren't around back then, in 1945, when the health service was beginning," he began to tangle the wire about his tie. "No-one's saying this is all perfect you know, but my God…is it a crime to want to help people?" At that, he glared at Jonathan to the sound of a siren and stormed out leaving his assistant to blush and stand up.

"Get that?" Jonathan asked Arnold.

"Yup, but you won't be using it. Producers' Guidelines," Arnold said sternly, "if you want bad sound quality actualité, you should be on World in Action," Arnold smiled.

Marsh looked at Jonathan nervously as the Chief Executive's assistant began helping Arnold to pack some of the equipment away, "I think it would be best if you got off this property as soon as possible, we have patients to treat. I don't think we'll be well disposed to do anything of this kind in the future."

Some weeks later, Jonathan was in the newsroom one late afternoon, typing in a cue to a piece about global warming. The day-team had received satellite photos of the "hole in the ozone layer" above the earth and the editor said they would make a good end to the next day's programme.

Jonathan sipped at his cup of coffee and noticed a piece of paper peeping from a pile of faxed duty logs and press releases. It was a memo, posing a question about the safety of the Corporation's polystyrene coffee-cups. Someone had noticed that the inner coating of the cups bubbled up after coffee had been poured into them. Jonathan peered down into his cup and then listened to the fizzing polystyrene.

"Hello boys and girls," shouted out a reporter and producer as they came in through the door. They were carrying videotapes. "We're just back from the Toxall car factory."

"Oh, yes. How did it go?" Jonathan asked, his tongue checking his palette for any remains of the coffee.

"Really well," replied the reporter with gusto. He was a tall, earnest-looking man of about thirty and had bent down to pick up a fallen cassette.

"I see," said Jonathan.

"They gave us some promotional video material of the research and development for their new car. The whole thing is pegged for the launch tomorrow. It should look great." The producer looked like the reporter's twin, about the same height and age.

Julia, the researcher opposite Jonathan who had been busily scanning the media jobs sections of the newspapers looked up at him. She was smarter-looking than most of the staff in the newsroom. Her shiny blonde hair, pale lipstick and dark trouser-suits were, Jonathan assumed, precursors to her obtaining a reporter and eventually anchor position on one of the news programmes. However, she seemed a little shorter than the required height and also a good deal younger. Her face, though, was perfect for the presenter's job, no feature was out of proportion. Instead a flat, mannequin-like blankness seemed to emanate from her bones..."Your cuttings are here," she said tersely, holding a sheaf of photocopied pages, precariously held together by a paperclip.

The Toxall producer and reporter peered over Jonathan's shoulder, snatching a glance of the pages. Jonathan thought he detected a hint of unease as they scanned the top page. The 72-point tabloid headline announced a strike ballot at the Toxall factory. "Ah, the nineteen-seventies, eh?" said the reporter, "doesn't News Information have anything more recent than this?"

The producer said nothing as both he and Jonathan looked further up the page to the date of the cutting.

"I think you'll all find that that's yesterday's paper," Julia replied, stroking a strand of hair from her face. "Get much on the ballot in your story? The strike?" she asked, "get anything on that?"

The producer and reporter looked at each other for a moment, as if they almost didn't understand the question.

"Well, isn't this your responsibility?" the reporter recovered, scowling at Julia.

"Look, I'm nothing to do with your story. I'm here to get other parts of the programme together. You were down at the factory for Chrissakes, didn't you interview any workers, even about the new car?"

The reporter made a sipping sound with his mouth and turned to the producer.

"It doesn't matter. Don't worry about it. We weren't there to cover the strike. We were there to do the new car," the producer said calmly and at that turned around with his tapes. The reporter followed him quickly to the door.

"Bloody researchers, they never do anything," the producer whispered to the reporter as the left.

Jonathan sighed as the door shut. "This is terrible, Julia, it's going to be one long advert for a car."

"Glad you can see that, most producers can't see anything except their pay-cheques," she replied, smiling and, he thought, a little flattered that he had spoken about a story with her. Jonathan knew the relationship between producers and researchers was meant to be like that of confused teachers to bright pupils. No matter how ingenious the pupil, even a dim-witted teacher should never give way.

Using the find command on the computer system, Jonathan searched down the list of wires for any references to the Toxall factory. Sure enough, yesterday's wires were full of news about an impending strike ballot, some even on the lines that the ballot would mar the launch of the new Kepler car. Jonathan was moved by the mistake and angered.

"It's as if someone's paid us to do their PR," Jonathan said, loudly. It was the first time he had raised his voice in the newsroom. A few producers on other desks turned around and then got back to their work. A presenter for the World Television News service replied sarcastically that he thought all home news was just PR.

"You see those tapes behind you, over there?" Julia said to
Jonathan, casting the jobs' pages of her newspaper to the floor.
Jonathan looked over to the window sill full of videotapes.
Each one was marked "AWN" and, as Julia explained, was from
a firm called "Authentic World News." "AWN supplies us with
a regular ration of PR. They're all beautiful. There's wonderful
footage of cars, supermarkets, factories and chemicals. You've
probably been using it as wallpaper," Julia continued, referring
to images that could loosely illustrate parts of the narrative in
a script.

"Ever notice what we use to illustrate pieces about
inflation? Well, they do. Use one of their shots and you'll get
pristine pictures, almost film-quality, of cash registers at the
supermarket—perfect for a script that talks about inflation
going up or down. Only there's a catch. Why do you think
AWN send us all this free stuff? I'll tell you. They do it because
the cost's hidden in the pictures. Supermarkets have paid them
to make this stuff. That's the reason the footage is covered
in logos, plastic bags, signs—all advertising the company....
They're getting ads onto the Corporation.

"Sure," Julia continued, lowering her voice a little, "your
editors may say that you can't use any of that AWN stuff, but
why is it there, then? Why don't we just throw it all away or re-
record over it. That's because with all the cuts we don't have all
the footage we need. As a producer, which are you going to use?
A badly framed shot, taken decades ago or an endorsement-
laden shot that looks like it could win an award?" She put her
finger to her lips, "your editor knows all about the use of these
pictures but it's all hush-hush. There's an unspoken agreement.
I mean, obviously, you'll get reprimanded if you just cobble
together a load of big budget adverts together and call it an
impartial news story. A while back someone made something
about the launch of a new soft drink which virtually told our
audience to go out and buy it or they'd die. Obviously, you can't
do that. But, something nice and subtle, something that makes
the piece a little glamorous-looking. You're in." Julia laughed.
"But don't tell anyone I said so and always protest the use of it

at an editorial meeting. You'll get points for that. They'll think you're innocent and editors love that." Jonathan imagined his editor shopping for jelly.

Just then, Harriet, an anchor on the World Service Television News desk came out of the boss' office. She looked over to Jonathan and beckoned seductively beside the door. The seductiveness came from the way she was dressed—like many female presenters, she looked like a sophisticated cocktail waitress. Only close up could one see the layers of TV makeup. Presenters always looked incongruous, Jonathan thought to himself. Unlike producers who wore peculiarly poor-looking clothing, perhaps to impress the boss about salary considerations, presenters, at least from a distance of seven yards, looked like posh male and female prostitutes plying looking for business.

"Hang on a second," Jonathan said, inappropriately fingering for change in his trouser pockets before putting the finishing touches to a script. When he looked back up again he saw Julia coming out of the boss' room. He hadn't noticed that she had left her researcher seat.

"Boss wants to see you," Julia said with fake discretion.

Jonathan's pulse began to race. His palms began to sweat. He put the cap on the pen he was holding. "Right," he said uncertainly, pushing a just-arrived cup of scalding coffee off his desk with his elbow, "that's fine."

"GNS, testing, testing," said the Tannoy, forcing his heart to skip a beat.

Jonathan walked up the newsroom and threw open the door, looking around the small rectangular space. He hadn't seen it since the morning's debrief session after his night-shift. On a desk strewn with empty wine and beer bottles, the boss' head was just visible, emerging with a phone on his ear. While he spoke, his stubby pink fingers thumped on a computer keyboard, itself tainted by months of coffee-spillage. When he saw Jonathan, he abruptly ended his phone conversation, slamming the receiver down hard before reclining in his chair and placing his hands behind his head.

"Aha!" the boss said, giving Jonathan a jolt that the boss

must have noticed, because he reduced the volume of his next remarks. "Sit down, relax," he said, casually. Then he rummaged about in the jacket hanging on the back of his seat until he found a cellophane-wrapped cigar.

Jonathan sat down on one of the five cushions that made up the corner-sofa.

"Hello, how are you?" Jonathan asked.

"Never mind that," he replied, blinking bloodshot blue eyes under short eyelashes. Lighting his cigar a few times, he put his hands on his bulging stomach and groaned, his face becoming reddish and puffy.

Jonathan tried not to look straight at him. Instead, his gaze faltered around some piles of official internal memos, clustering about the empty bottles.

"Looking at the latest crap I'm getting from the sixth floor? Well, it's crap, everyday there's more of it. Have some if you want, maybe you can use it for memo paper." He held out fifty leaves of A4 and harshly stapled it with a gun.

Jonathan raised his eyebrows and took the pages, the thought floating in his mind that all the boss had called him in for was to offer him free paper supplies.

"Julia told me you spotted the strike at Toxall, that you were even quite annoyed."

"Well, not annoyed," Jonathan replied trying to downplay what could have sounded like an insult against his colleagues.

"No? Well, you should be damn fucking annoyed. We don't send people out of here so they can miss important stories like that. It's hard enough getting the budget for a crew to go and cover a fucking story let alone paying for one to go out and hash up the whole fucking thing. You know, I don't think we've really spoken, but your prospects are good here. There's a lot of stuff around and you know, well what with all of this fucking crap... well, I haven't had the chance to tell you that there's soon going to be a vacancy in New York and, well, you could be out there." He winked. "Yes, you could be out there."

Jonathan smiled, not wanting to seem overkeen....He knew his boss was dangling the most prized offer a producer could get in front of him, but had a vague suspicion he did this to every producer that came through his door.

"Anyway, why I called you in. Firstly, I hated one of the pieces you did on something. I can't remember now, but it was just fucking awful, just not television, I mean you wouldn't get an intern producing work of that quality. It was horse-shit."

"Um, do you know which story?" Jonathan said, his palms beginning to sweat.

"I don't know. You should know. Why should I know? Who fucking knows?" He looked out of a false window for a second. "I've got all this to do, so how should I know about some fucking story we showed weeks ago? Huh? Well, how should I know?" he held out a large organisational chart.

"Er, yes?" said Jonathan, uncertainly.

"Basically it was the graphics, I think it was the graphics," the boss softened again. "Far too much information for a viewer to take in. It would have helped if the script matched the graphic a little better, too. But that's all before, you know, we don't just fire people here for a couple of mistakes, it's water under the bridge. You hear?" his voice rose. In this way, Jonathan felt as if he had embarked on an ocean-journey in a boat needing of repair. The phrase 'couple of mistakes' flashed through Jonathan's head.

"So what I've called you in here for, apart from to slam you for the bad, fucking work you've been doing, God, it was awful. Well, what it's all about, what I'm trying to tell you is that I wondered if you want to act up. That means we don't pay you the full whack for the job, but you get experience that'll stand you in good stead. I want you to be assistant editor, or at least shift as an assistant editor. And the first fucking thing that entails is that you're going to cover the end of the cease-fire in Northern Ireland. I..."

"I don't think I've done the Northern Ireland hazard course..." Jonathan interrupted, encouraged by his boss' news.

"What does that matter?" the boss grimaced, "I ain't never done no fucking course, and I've been there loads of times. Don't listen to many people, okay? You're a nice boy but you just listen to too many people, that's the fucking impression I get. Anyway, I'm telling you, I'm fucking ordering you. You're going. That course you're thinking about costs too much for this department. It would fucking bankrupt us. Anyway, so basically, you're rota-ed in next week for Northern Ireland. So go home today, and get a few nights' rest. Come back on Sunday and try and hitch together something so that we've got something for Tuesday's programme, something human interest-y. Alright?"

Jonathan nodded, waiting to hear him say something else.

"Well, that's all then," he said, beginning to dial a number on his phone.

Jonathan sat on the plane, excited about his first trip on an aircraft. It didn't take him long to get used to it and he was soon thinking about how different everyone had been treating him in the newsroom, since his promotion. Producers were now careful to greet him when they entered the newsroom, offering him coffee at more frequent intervals. Some wanted to chat with him about their lives outside the office, even inviting him for a drink with them when he got back from Belfast. The greatest change was in the reporters' room. Whilst they weren't all friendly towards him, quite a few of the younger reporters were now keen to smile and ask him how his work was going. As for the presenters, he couldn't tell whether they thought he had been promoted prematurely or they had expected from the outset he was in the fast lane. Only Julia was the same towards him, as cynical and as seemingly bored of what he said as before.

As he signed oaths about the Prevention of Terrorism Act, Jonathan thought about how working with Paul would be. He was one of the regular anchors for Good Morning, Britain in London and the star of the show. He was one of the oldest people in the office and was personable and casual, with the airs of someone above petty office politics.

It was only when he got into his hotel room and phoned London that he found out that Paul was ill and that, instead, a reporter would be flown over the next day. To find this out he had to wake up the deputy editor, late on Sunday night, something that wasn't appreciated. Jonathan's blossoming panic was hardly diminished by the news that the reporter would have to be briefed about the story on the day of shooting.

"Can't I just get the main Northern Ireland Correspondent?" he had asked before being turned down

"Correspondents are for Newsgathering, not Good Morning, Britain," said the deputy editor, surprised by Jonathan's naïveté about Corporation organisational matters. It was Newsgathering that hired reporters within the internal competitive market recently set up at the Corporation. Correspondents were directly accountable to Newsgathering.

"Just because there's a correspondent somewhere doesn't mean any old producer can use him, you know. Correspondents will only do the bigger stories, unless they're seconded to Newsnight. Didn't anyone tell you that?" the deputy shouted on the phone. Jonathan said goodbye and flipped the channels on the cable television in his room, lying on the bed and wondering how the story would proceed. Though one side of his curtains was lying in a heap on the carpet, the room was clean and well kept. By his bedside was a channel guide, including a large list of prices for pay-per-view adult entertainment. Switching the set off, he took a bottle of mineral water from the mini bar and turned on his laptop computer. He was cheered up by the fizz of the water, the noise of the auto-dial modem and the field notes for Northern Ireland he retrieved from the main Corporation computer.

INFORMATION FOR BELFAST
First, don't be scared by Belfast. Don't bring with you all the emotional baggage about violence and war. It's a safer city than London and you're more likely to be shot in London than Belfast. Having said that, here are a few things to bear in mind while you're out here.
Northern Ireland is a part of the United Kingdom. It was partitioned in 1921 after Eire got separated. Though none of

the main UK parties field candidates in the province, MPs are elected at UK general elections and then represent their constituents in parliament. The main groups are:

Democratic Unionist Party. Led by Ian Paisley.

Ulster Unionist Party. Led by David Trimble since 8 September 1995. The former party of government in the old Stormont.

The Alliance Party of Northern Ireland. Led by John Alderdice.

Social Democratic and Labour Party. Led by John Hume. The main Irish Nationalist party.

Sinn Féin. Led by Gerry Adams.

There are a number of other groups, though these have little support in the province and can thus be discounted. Note that Sinn Féin MPs refuse to represent their electors in parliament. The main grievances of the parties are as follows:

Sinn Féin and the SDLP want a united Ireland, that is Northern Ireland to unite with the south. Whilst the SDLP adopts a more moderate tone, Sinn Féin represents the political wing of the provisional Irish Republican Army (IRA).

The Ulster Unionists, Democratic Unionists and Progressive Unionists all want to preserve the union with mainland Britain.

The following guidelines should also be of use. They were to me and by following them, I made my stay here a pleasurable and enjoyable one. Ulster people are friendly and generous and I had a wonderful time talking with them in pubs and clubs, I hope you do too.

1. Don't go into a café or bar in a Catholic area and ask how you can meet people from the IRA. That's how they do it in the films. In real life, you're liable to get told to fuck off or worse.

2. Better still, stay out of areas controlled by the Provos. It's dangerous. This is especially true at night.

3. Unionist areas are much safer

4. Always first get permission for filming from the Ulster Constabulary. They are nearly always helpful and will point out any dangers that you may not have foreseen. They've been around for a while and know all the pitfalls for journalists intent on covering the province as if it was a war zone.

5. If you make contact with someone on the Republican/ Terrorist side, never accompany them on an outing away from the main city centre area. Not only is it foolish for safety reasons, your work will not be broadcastable anyway, so why take the risk?

6. Re-Read Producers' Guidelines—if you've forgotten your copy in London, get one sent out, your editor will appreciate your request.

7. Always co-operate with the armed forces stationed in your area. If you don't, no-one is going to help you. Don't believe American journalists stationed here that by disobeying them you'll be a hero, more likely you'll be escorted back to Britain and your assignment won't be completed.

There followed a list of good locations from which to shoot views of the city as well as the names of journalists and experts with their phone numbers. Jonathan's boss had wanted a 'human interest' angle on The Troubles, so Jonathan thought a good start was to do a piece about a project that some big multinational companies had set up to try and rejuvenate Belfast's commercial life. The companies had begun planning about four months into the unilateral cease-fire that had been declared by the IRA. This investment, aided by the British Government's encouraging tax regime for businesses in Northern Ireland, as well as the influx of American money was expected to boost the province's chances of avoiding an economic slump.

Jonathan had rung quite a few of the companies behind the consortium and was to interview one of the chief executives who happened to be on a visit. After keeping up with the news in Bosnia, via the CNN station on the hotel television, he drifted asleep to the jingle of the World Service.

He met the reporter, Hirst, in the breakfast room of

the hotel. As if still following a night shift pattern, Hirst was alternately drinking whisky from a silver flask and sipping hot coffee.

"I'm glad it's the Europa. This your first time?" he said, his eyes rising just a little above their so far floor-trained gaze. Jonathan nodded, picking up his glass of orange juice.

"I was here, I mean, I've been here," he said, swaying his shoulders and brushing the hair on the side of his head. "Yeah, it's a terrible place. Terrorist isn't the right term for them, thugs more like. The Europa hotel," he motioned with his hand, "this is the world's most bombed hotel, it gives me a kick just to have a drink in here."

"The most bombed? It can't be. Surely, Beirut…"

"Nope, it's the Europa alright. More than Sarajevo's Holiday Inn, more than the Commodore in Beirut, more than the Hilton in San Salvador. My brother covered Beirut at the Commodore, I know," he said, tapping his nose with his forefinger.

Jonathan listened to Hirst's stories about Belfast, thinking about a friend from his hometown who had once come there as a private. He felt it was odd that apart from the armed soldiers at the airport, the green country port of Belfast didn't seem to connect with Hirst's hellish descriptions. In fact, the more Hirst spoke, the more certain Jonathan was that Hirst hadn't read the notes for Belfast on the Corporation computer system.

"It doesn't look that bad, I mean considering what I thought it was going to be like."

Hirst laughed, "that's because you haven't been anywhere. I'll show you around. I'll show you what makes this awful place tick." Hirst took another swig from his flask.

"By the way," Jonathan hesitated before changing the subject, "I'm not sure how to put this but are you going to shave, before we're on?" Jonathan had just seen a shard of sunlight illuminate his reporter.

"You think so? I mean, you are the producer but I think it gives the whole thing an edge, you know, gives the viewers back home an idea of the fear that pervades, yes pervades, the place."

"No, I really think it wouldn't be appropriate, not for the subject we're doing," he replied, nodding to the waitress who took his plates. Then Jonathan explained the story.

"Sounds like a good one, about regeneration, good. That's good. But I still think we should go and check out the thugs in the Fall's Road, just check on them, you know, go and have a look at the gambling and prostitution rackets."

"Sure, I don't see why not, as we're here and all that," Jonathan replied.

"I also want to check out the bars," Hirst laughed.

"Oh yes," Jonathan said, "I was reading about the National Trust bar." It was a long time since Jonathan had looked forward to going to a bar. Drinking had once been an obsession and, now, he now just didn't have the taste for it.

"The Crown? No, I was thinking more about some of the more seedy places."

Jonathan smiled, his face tinted by dread.

"Oi!...I want to go through the back streets, okay?" shouted Hirst, looking annoyed and disappointed.

Through the windows of the taxi, they passed groups of young people kicking footballs, sitting on walls and queuing. Protestant graffiti glowered at women with shopping bags. Back on the main road, a Job Centre just ahead of the mall was like a whale's mouth, pouring people out. "Most subsidised place in Britain, you know," said Hirst, pointing to the line of short-haired boys and young women with prams, "look at them. More regeneration than in Brixton, but you still get the timewasters."

Jonathan nodded back at him and looked down at his statistics showing inward investment by the UK Treasury.

They got to the top floor of a shopping mall, in an office next to the Customer Services desk of a clothing store. Hirst began talking to a retired officer, now Chief Executive of the Cents and Sensibility Store on Royal Avenue. He told Hirst that things were going very well. "Even if the cease-fire suddenly comes to an end, we'll be fine," he said.

The cameraman, Don, was local and quiet. Moving about

across the floor in hushpuppies, his check-shirt hanging over a pair of brushed cotton slacks, Don taped gels to his lights.

"But, surely we've got to do something. I mean couldn't all of you business-people get together and fund, I dunno, your own militia or something, something that would have real force to get these people out, to get rid of them once and for all. People are still getting knee-capped," Hirst spat his words out.

"The Northern Ireland situation is a very complicated one. There are no quick fixes here, even the SDLP leader said that."

"Him? What's he got to do with anything, the..." Hirst stopped himself.

"Look, what's needed now is peace."

"I know that, I know all that." Hirst snapped.

"Look, I'm not sure this is..." Jonathan ventured before the Chief Executive cut him off.

"Look, don't get me wrong. I do understand what you're saying," he said, looking at Hirst, "I know what it's like when businesses can't function because of them, I know what it's been like. But I'm just saying that if we're going to get to where we want, where there are consumers turning over a vibrant economy that makes profits for us, and which then trickles down to those in need, well, there's only one way to get there."

"By this kind of initiative?" he asked, though the Chief Executive seemed not to be listening.

"No, of course not. This initiative helps to publicise who cares about the situation, large businesses like ourselves. It's to show that we have an interest in the community here. We have a commitment to this community."

Hirst nodded, "well at least we're agreed on that. It's just..." Hirst gave a forced expression on his face as if he was an Elizabethan plantation-owner arguing with his son. "It's just that they're so horrible, so despicable."

In the next taxi they caught, Hirst began to berate the films and newspaper articles he thought benefited the terrorists. Don remained silent.

"The guy that did that fiction about the Guilford Four, he

deserves the wrath of all those mothers whose children have died at the hands of the IRA."

"My best friend did some work on that film," Don said suddenly, spitting on one of the sound meters on his camera and wiping it off with his sleeve.

Hirst laughed. "I don't want to argue with anyone but I thought that was an awful film. These guys weren't innocent. Maybe to liberals they're innocent. How many of them know what it's like to see a car jumping a check point? You wouldn't fire a few rounds? It's them or you in that situation, make no mistake about it."

Don mumbled that the soldiers fired more than a few rounds.

"Look, have you been in that situation? You ever gone on patrol?" asked Hirst.

"Look, I'm nothing to do with any of this," the cameraman interrupted, "all I think is that it's bloody unfair. The soldiers pinned a fucking picture of the child they killed on their barracks wall and scrawled 'one down, a-million to go', for Chrissakes."

"Well, you obviously don't understand what it's like to be shot at, that's for sure," Hirst said, smiling before taking a swig from his flask.

The next shooting call was at a youth-centre set up by various companies. It was easily visible thanks to the twenty-foot logos of oil companies and fast food restaurants that rose from the roof of the prefabricated block.

"I'm just going over the road to fill her up," said Hirst, pointing to his upturned flask.

He was left alone with Don, whose demeanour had changed since his conversation with Hirst. "So what do you think about what's happening here?" Jonathan asked him.

"Look, it's not for me to say, I mean I just live here and shoot for you," he replied suspiciously.

"But you must have a view about it all?"

"Well, see, my personal views don't matter. They don't affect my work, if that's what you're asking. Look, this is my first thing for the Corporation and I don't want to blow it. I'm a good cameraman, that's all. Alright?"

"Sure, I was just wondering..." Jonathan tried to sound conciliatory.

"Is this an interview?" Don squinted and then laughed. "Well, I suppose if you really want my view then I just think the same way Hirst does. They're scum, aren't they, the fucking IRA."

Some of the children, milling about outside the centre turned towards them, their blank expressions hiding any response to what they may have heard.

"Language," said a priest who appeared beside the children. He was being sarcastic. He giggled along with the children.

"You here to do some filming? I'm Father Michael," he said before they shook hands. "Going well? Doing another hate piece against the poor again?" he chuckled.

"Er, no. Actually, we're trying to look at something positive that's going on here," Jonathan replied, looking down at his clipboard.

"Positive? You won't find that here. Maybe now there's a cease-fire on but even then some people are angry about it. Can you believe it? I have people asking me why the Provos have let them down, sixteen year olds asking me whether they should start their own movements, their own terrorist movements. Can you believe that? There are people around here who think the IRA has sold them down the river, that without the IRA they're powerless. 'Who'll stand up for us?' some of them asked me. Don't suppose you'd be showing that on the Corporation, will you? Probably best you didn't, actually, probably best you didn't show the attacks either. No-one wants to stir up any trouble."

Don stayed quiet. "But surely you do agree with the regeneration initiative?" asked Jonathan.

"Money, extra money is always good. But what's it for? Just so big businesses can exploit us, just so they can do us in. Can you see that?" he pointed to something they hadn't seen, a row of cameras angled towards them from an adjoining building.

"When's that going to stop? They're still scaring us, even if they don't shoot, maim or torture us as much."

"What do you mean 'us'?" asked Don, "you're a priest."

"Yeah, I sometimes wonder about that. I wonder whether I can actually do anything here, in this fucking colonial state," he turned to the children who were laughing. "The IRA isn't even pro-Catholic. It opposes religion," he paused, "but then, who votes for them anyway?"

"Quite," said Don.

"You know," Father Michael said, turning to Don who was checking the white balance on his television camera, "it's you that I don't like, the people that help people like him to distort what's happening here. Unemployment, do you know the rate, here?"

Jonathan recited the statistic on his clipboard. "Isn't that why this regeneration project is so good?"

"Look, I don't know who you are or what you know about Ireland," he said to him, "but the wages these companies are paying are less than they pay in their factories in Korea. Everyone thinks this is some kind of slave market. You know, just yesterday the police told everyone on this boy's street to get out of their houses for a strip search. That's at one in the morning. Everyone on the street!...When you were a child did anyone in camouflage knock on your Daddy and Mummy's house and point a machine gun in their face and tell them to stand on the curb in their night-clothes?"

"I think we had better go in," said Don, seeing Hirst on the other side of the street, waiting for the traffic to subside.

"Yes, let's go in. Nice to meet you Father Michael. I don't think we all quite agree, but nice to meet you nevertheless." Jonathan offered his hand, but Father Michael didn't take it.

"Good luck," the priest said, holding the back of his hand up towards them.

"Fascists!" cried the six or seven boys sitting around him on road cones.

"Whoa!...what's all this?" said Hirst who had just raced

across the road with a brown paper bag in his hand, "you and Don trying to start a riot?"

A mysterious sight greeted them when they entered the youth-centre. A well-dressed man, in a corporate blue double breasted suit was pushing some rough looking teenagers out through the back door of the room. One of the boys, tattooed and looking particularly nasty with his skinhead haircut held a cue in his hand. Beside him, an unresolved pool game sat idle.

"Sorry, are you from the Corporation?" said Alex, the suited man of about thirty-five.

"That's right," said Don for Jonathan.

"Well, we're just getting some things ready in here, do you want to wait outside just for a few minutes," Alex said, evidently ruffled, his hair mussed up and a bruise reddening the side of his face.

"We're a bit busy in here," said the boy with the cue.

Don turned and winked at Jonathan to signal that this was interesting footage, that they may have caught something here that they weren't meant to see.

"I think we'd rather stay in here. You carry on and I can begin to light," said Don, brushing off chalk from his trousers.

Jonathan walked over to Don and whispered for him not to film. "There's no point, we can't broadcast it anyway."

"It could come in useful as library material should there be a riot though," Don smirked.

Hirst had sat down on one of the plastic stackable chairs that lay along the sides of the room. He was looking studious, recording things down in a notebook between scratches of his head. Jonathan walked over to him with the aim of going through the interview questions.

"Yeah, I know what to do," he said, quickly flipping over a page of his pad and trying to cover up writing on the front page. He looked up and smiled, "just a CV. Did you see the sports-reporter vacancy in the staff magazine? You know, I haven't got a proper contract, they say that this is the way in for a staff job."

Jonathan could barely hear Hirst say this. There was a

commotion at the end of the room and loud profanities were blanketing all other sound in the echo-laden centre. After the snap of a pool cue and the slam of a rear-door, a ruffled Alex turned around, towards them. "Now, where do you want me?" he smiled.

༈

Don had labelled the video-cassettes and had said goodbye, shuffling off to his parking space. "Sure you don't want to eat anything?" Jonathan had asked after him, but the rush of traffic hid his voice.

"Well, what do we fancy tonight, then?" Hirst said at the pub.

"I was wondering whether we should meet up with some of the Corporation people up on the Ormeau Road. There's a night-club around there," Jonathan said unsurely holding his mineral water.

"The Limelight? That's student-rubbish," Hirst replied, holding an equally unsteady pint of Guinness. "I was thinking somewhere downbeat, where the action is you know?"

Jonathan finished his water and said they'd better hurry over to the editing suites and finish the package if they were going to do anything later, at all.

"Sure, sure," said Hirst, "I'll go do it, you can relax."

"But."

"No buts, I'll handle it, or," Hirst brought his face closer to Jonathan's, "or I'll tell the boys back in London you've been a pain to work with, alright?" At that, Hirst left his half-finished pint and departed.

Jonathan decided to take in some of the sights. He walked over to the Prince Albert Memorial Clock Tower and observed the stillness of the Harland and Wolff shipyard. He looked at the scaffolding on Customs House and at the door of a neo-Romanesque cathedral. Getting on to the 'Golden Mile', Jonathan wondered how Hirst was getting on, simultaneously wishing that he had had time to look into the history of the town. He paused at Great Victoria Street, wondering whether to see the famous Protestant mural on Sandy Row, then deciding against it.

In the evening, after the piece had been fed to London, Jonathan and Hirst had a drink in the hotel bar. American businessmen loudly regaled each other with stories from back home. One of them, on his fourth martini, turned to Jonathan with his wallet and began showing him pictures of his wife and children. Jonathan nodded politely. An hour or so later, the man said that he was off to find a girl at 'Paradise Lost', the club just next door to the Europa. "Want to come along?" he slurred.

"He's not going down there," Hirst interrupted, proprietarily. In his silence, Hirst had been watching Jonathan. "We're going to see the real Belfast."

After a short cab ride, Hirst and Jonathan arrived at a bar. "This is the heart of Belfast, watch your step," he said. Hirst was soon gulping down more Guinness. "Good protest singing, shame about all the crap, all the anti-British propaganda. Jonathan scratched his head. Hirst was drunk and seemed to be imagining things.

"What do you mean?" Jonathan asked, his eyes weary from the smoke and dry ice of the dance floor, "You alright?" Instead of Hirst's imagined protest singer, the Manhattan was reverberating to top 40 chart music. Most of the young people were drinking cocktails and European lager.

Coughing from a roll-up, Hirst shouted cryptically above the din: "It's better we came here, I don't think you could have done with the Ballymurphy area around Springfield Road." Hirst moved his mouth to within an inch of Jonathan's ear. "There's no poverty here, there's just corporate regeneration."

Hirst went to get another drink and Jonathan took out some papers he had picked up from the Youth Centre and began to read them in the flashing light.

Another child is dead, another child's death goes unreported.
And yet they want us to lay down our arms

Jonathan looked at his watch, wondering when Hirst would appear.

The British Government, thanks to subsidy, gives away electric shock-batons, landmines, torture equipment, missiles, helicopters and tanks to countries like Algeria, Argentina, Chile, China, El Salvador, Ethiopia, Indonesia, Iran, Iraq, Israel, Kenya, Mexico, Nigeria, Pakistan, Rwanda, Saudi Arabia, Syria and Turkey. All sales to these countries were made when they were condemned by human rights groups for torturing and murdering sections of their own population. A UK family of four's average spending per week on armaments (through taxation) is £40, just a little under the £50.43 they spend on food. No wonder that British law contravenes the European Convention on Human Rights over the use of 'lethal force.' The UK Government refuses to accept recommendations of the United Nations Committee Against Torture because they want to keep on torturing, kidnapping and killing members of our community.

"What you reading, then?" Hirst asked, gently, "you know you're a good producer, you're really professional."

"Oh, nothing." There was something nicer about Hirst's demeanour, Jonathan thought, "just propaganda, I suppose."

"So what's your next project then? I'm just asking, you know, because we've worked pretty well together, any plans?" Hirst inquired, nodding to the music.

Jonathan hesitated, all of a sudden realising that Hirst was trying to request work from him. "I'm not really sure, right now. But if anything comes up, of course you'll be on the list of possible reporters." Jonathan tried to conceal his pleasure at having a reporter, who so obviously didn't like him, begging for a job. Jonathan even got the feeling that Hirst was regretting something. He began to worry about the report Hirst had filed for the morning's programme.

"Thanks," he said, "thanks for thinking of future projects for me. You see," Hirst said, warming to a topic, "I believe that it's our job to report the truth, to get out there and show the truth, and I think you share that outlook on things, too," he paused, noticing that Jonathan looked tense and was staring away from him. Hirst turned to look towards where his eyes were pointed but Jonathan's eyes weren't aimed at anything in particular, just the bar area.

"Which truth?" he asked when he'd stopped looking at the rows of drinks, "you know, I know some truths that will never get on television."

"Sorry?" Hirst's face had crumpled up. "I do too, I know about truth. We know about truth. Look, I had to go through all that with the VT editor at the Corporation, just now. He was a freelance. I had to teach him the ropes while we were cutting the story. I had to teach him about impartiality." Hirst was slurring more, now. "I know what you mean when you ask which truth, don't take me for an idiot. I'd dearly like to say to camera that the IRA should be blown apart, that the Falls Road should be blown apart. But the truth has..." Hirst didn't finish his sentence.

"So what is truth then, just your truth?" Jonathan replied, enjoying his assistant editor status and sipping more strongly from his non-alcoholic lager.

"Just that. Truth is what happens. It's what happens."

"But, surely an event that just happens," Jonathan put his glass down, "well, that event could distort your truth. What if, for instance, someone is jailed wrongly for blowing up a pub. Reporting that will hamper legitimate terrorist searches, perhaps. Does that mean you don't report the appeal?"

A couple had sat next to them, the man looking at Jonathan with what he thought was a frown.

"No, of course not. It's a big story, a big story. Of course, I'd want to cover it if it's a big, big story like that. But, you know, we'd cover it in a particular way, in a way that would..." Hirst's words petered out as a waitress came round and asked if they wanted drinks. "Just got some, thanks," he replied.

Hirst made as if to get up and dance and then sat down again. "I think I'm going to look for another bar," he whispered in Jonathan's ear, "you don't have to come if you don't want to. It's not really related to the story we're doing. I'll probably use it for an article or something." Jonathan nodded, draining his glass, as Hirst put his fur-lined brown leather jacket on. They left together and took separate cabs.

The next morning, over breakfast, Jonathan relayed the ideas of his editor about possible other stories to cover in Belfast. It was six-thirty and Hirst was unshaven and, for the first time, not intermittently sipping from his flask. "Black coffee is bad for hangovers, I wouldn't advise it," Jonathan said, trying to break the silence with a helpful hint.

"Yeah, but I still want it," he replied, his voice down a few semitones, "how would you know anyway? You don't drink."

"I used to, Hirst. Did you have a good evening?" Jonathan was half-looking at the morning papers on the side of the table.

"Look, I don't think I'm going to be able to go on today. Honestly, I've never done this before, it's just that I don't feel very well, at all." Hirst was as pale as the sky.

Jonathan grinned back with incredulity, wondering what the editor in London would make of his producing skills. Jonathan imagined the boss shouting: "What's wrong with you? You made two reporters ill? It's not as if you're stuff is cutting edge." Just as he was mulling over his career prospects, a girl of about sixteen came over to their table, dragging a chair with her.

"Hi, Hirst, you said you'd wait for me," she said, looking over at him with a makeup-less face. Hirst shuffled on his seat, avoiding Jonathan's glance and trying to reach into his pocket.

At seven, they walked over to a communal television in the foyer of the hotel to watch the story go out. Jonathan plugged his portable computer into the wall and almost the instant the story began being broadcast, a wire flashed on his screen announcing the news that a Catholic youth had been shot on the Ormeau Road.

It's not all doom and gloom in Northern Ireland, as this

shopping centre demonstrates. Sparkling new shops in this mall are attracting the punters in an area that was once better known for its gangland violence.

Regeneration is the task. And that task is in full swing. A consortium of companies, local companies that also have an international presence are working together to rejuvenate the place. As well as the shopping centre, there are large-scale charity projects aimed at re-skilling those who have long forgotten that honest work is an option.

At The Consortium Youth Centre in West Belfast, youths are learning fast.

The signs of the various companies hovered above the prefab. They glinted in what must have been the only rushes-shot with some rosy light.

The people that come here have no hope. That was ripped out from them by the IRA. But today, they're beginning to be retrained, retrained, as one youth here said, in hope. For so many young people, all it takes is some sort of wage.

Hirst didn't say a word as he watched; like many reporters he had picked up the habit of remaining silent as his voice sounded on the TV. Yet, his mouth seemed to move as his words rang out. Only when it was over did he let the words "good piece" issue through his lips. "Good piece," he repeated to himself.

He switched off the television when the story was over, just as Peter was segue-ing into the weather.

"It wasn't the truth though, was it?" Jonathan said.

Producing had been like listening to a pianist play too delicately. Jonathan had produced four stories in all from Belfast, none of which made him feel comfortable. The reporters that came and went after Hirst all seemed to barely touch the truth as he saw it. He had been more undermined than ever over the past few days and he couldn't tell whether the boss understood how he felt about it all.

Julia showed him into the boss' office in a business-like manner. Jonathan waited patiently as the boss spoke angrily into the telephone, at the same time beating the keyboard of his computer with the base of an empty bottle of beer.

"We can't afford to lose that money, we just can't," he was saying. "I know what they can and cannot cut, and that's something they can't cut."

When he had pushed the receiver into its cradle, he told Jonathan that he had been discussing the graphics' budget. Apparently, the department had gone over budget and one of the management consultants had suggested using one less graphic designer per show.

"Graphics are what holds the whole fucking operation together. We reuse the tapes so much now that the cut stories are chocker with drop out. The bleeding lighting of the interviewees is so harsh that no one would have thought it acceptable a few years ago. The only thing we bloody have are smart graphics to liven up a fucked up piece and now they want to cut that too. What the fuck are we going to do? Anyway, how was Ireland?"

"It was interesting," he replied, "I had some trouble over reporters but."

"A good producer knows how to handle a reporter. It was your fault," he said, frowning. "I have to say I wasn't too happy with the stuff you were sending back. But, it was your first time abroad, I guess," the boss began to unravel the cellophane on a meat pie from the canteen. "Look, it's no demotion, but I want you to do a UK story. One on the utility privatisations. We've been thinking about doing it for a long time."

"Right, it's a good story," Jonathan said, not knowing much about the subject but remembering the shock of his first water, gas and electricity bills.

"I want one on water, one on gas, one on electricity and one on telecoms," he stared straight into Jonathan's eyes. Then he began pushing buttons on his telephone, "go on then, get on with it!" he said to Jonathan.

When he walked back into the newsroom there was a hush. From the faces of his colleagues, he could tell that they thought he had been given a brushing down.

"Fine?" said Julia, when he had sat down at a desk next to her.

"Yes, fine. I'm doing another series," he replied.

"He likes you then, you seem to get all the series," said the day-editor opposite him who was obviously weary of his on-the-day story making. "All I seem to get are reactive pieces." 'Reactive' was a great pejorative in the language of news-making.

Julia handed him four thick heaps of cuttings from News Information, each one annotated with either "Water", "Gas," "Electric" or "Telecoms."

Surprised, Jonathan thanked her and asked how she had known.

"You might be an assistant editor," she said, smiling, "but I reckon that I still know more than you about what goes on in this building."

"I'm sure you do," he replied, recovering from his surprise and now conscious of her flirtatious glance.

"What are you doing for lunch?" she asked, "I thought we might go to the club."

"Lunch?" he replied with a strained voice. I don't think I've had ever had a lunch break on shift. I'm not actually a member of the club."

"That's okay, I can take a guest."

"Well, then. I'll just make a few calls and we can go down together."

Julia smiled and went off to the boss' room with a pad in hand as Jonathan tried to get through to a few analysts who might be able to tell him about the water that Britain drank. After half an hour of getting nowhere, Julia and he headed down the corridor, towards the third floor Corporation Club. The name of the place was a gentle stab at sarcasm, for the Club was a shabby place. No-one from Corporation management came here to entertain or to relax. Their clubs were in the affluent neighbourhoods of central London, with drawing rooms some twenty times taller than that of the Corporation Club. This didn't make for any lack of security at the door to the club, however. The main entrance to Television Centre may have been like an open invitation for terrorists to knock out the country's main media source but the Club was like Fort Knox. Without a credit-card style membership-card or a member who had one, there was no admittance. Even famous presenters needed one to pass the guards.

The bar area reminded Jonathan of a clean hostel, except alcohol was served. He felt slightly uncomfortable before he realised that no-one around him looked at ease. They queued up at the self-service food area and Jonathan couldn't decide what to take from the little plastic flaps.

"We can sit outside, if you like," Julia said, selecting quiche.

"Yes," he replied, uneasily eyeing the clock on the wall and wondering how journalists in the newsroom would contact him should an important story be announced. There was no Tannoy system plugged in here.

"So how are you finding the Corporation?" she asked when they'd found a couple of rickety wooden chairs.

"It's very interesting," he replied, "it's certainly different to the kind of broadcasting I'm used to."

"Yes, you worked at...what was it?"

"Well, various places, just various independent firms really."

"It's certainly very different here. I've only been here a year but my other friends who work for other places say that whenever they deal with the Corporation, they're shocked."

"Why shocked?"

"Well, they say it's slow, bureaucratic, that kind of thing," Julia smiled as she bit into her tuna sandwich, crumbs finding their way down to her black skirt.

Jonathan drank some water and asked her how she had known of his assignment before he had.

He waited for her to finish her gulp and begin talking.

"You know, I think you're different to most of the people in the office. I've noticed you," she said, batting her eyes, "and let's say that I told my godfather. You see, I'm related to him. How else do you think I got the job, the competition is so stiff, you must know that."

"I guess I must have just slipped through the net, then."

"No, I think you're pretty good, Jonathan. Having said that, I don't know what 'pretty good' means, really. I mean there are some producers in the office that one always thinks of as being good, Johnny and Byder for instance. That's because they always have lots of graphics in their packages and they always try to get some humour in. But apart from them, well, to tell you the truth, I hardly ever watch the thing. No one does. I can't believe that on some mornings, people bother to talk about the trouble they're having with the timers on their video recorders. It's all such a pretence. Once one's out of the building, one doesn't want to be reminded about the bloody office."

"I suppose so. Although I always watch my pieces."

"Oh sure, people always watch their pieces," she said giggling, "but only the boss watches all the pieces, that is unless he's delegated it to someone else. You'll be doing that soon, writing the debriefs, coming in at six in the morning and working twenty-four hours."

"It must be quite difficult to do, I mean quite a political act."

"Political?" she said, puzzled.

"Well, internal politics, one doesn't want to step on people's toes. If I don't like a piece, I don't want to damn the producer and reporter to hell."

"Not if the reporter is highly respected, for instance you couldn't criticise a reporter who was already picked for bigger things, it would just backfire on you. You couldn't slag off Johnny or Byder. I've been in the office and seen an acting assistant editor like yourself shooting his mouth off about a reporter who the boss already thinks is wonderful. That was the end of him."

"I see," Jonathan looked at some Corporation staff sitting around them, "do you know who are the chosen ones, then?"

"Well, you could be one of them. You haven't done badly, have you?" she smiled.

"No, I suppose not. Of course, I'm not sure why I have done better than some of the other new people. I can't really work it out. In news, most packages are much of a muchness at first sight."

"And second sight," she replied, "after all, it's only in a war-zone or in the face of a great big, huge human tragedy that producers, cameramen and reporters really shine."

"Although, I think I try and cover things fairly, more fairly," he hazarded.

"How do you mean? I thought you people just went out and grabbed as much stuff as you could and just fit it into a report. There's not much you can do with a Sushi-a-thon!"

"Yes, but I think I'm beginning to understand which questions to ask."

"They taught me that at journalism school: how, what, where, which and why."

"Yes, and I think that it's the 'why?' that's usually the main thing," Jonathan felt more comfortable as he said this.

"Not in a three minute news piece it isn't."

Suddenly, he realised that the conversation was annoying Julia a little. She seemed as if she didn't want to be talking about work but he persisted.

"Well, for instance, that Toxall piece. I would have known to ask the people who were actually making the car, whereas..."

"What, so you're a champion of the worker?" she asked, laughing, "Come on!"

Jonathan took a few sips of his drink before Julia said that they'd better be getting back to the office.

"How would you like to see a film sometime?" she said, just before they entered the newsroom.

"I'd love to," Jonathan replied, reflecting on how the savings in his bank account had been mounting up what with the high pay and the little time in which to spend it.

When he sat down at his desk, the first thing he did was to pay some old bills. He had never got out of the habit of paying them at the last minute, when the demands went red. These envelopes he was licking were to various utility companies. Price increases since the privatisation of Britain's water, electricity, gas and telephone systems weren't something that affected Jonathan's daily life anymore, nor that of his colleagues. Occasionally, someone in the newsroom might curse a company because of an erroneous direct debit, always in the company's favour, but no-one doubted that the revolution in services was here to stay.

"You must do something about water metering, I know they did a few months ago but it would be interesting to take a look, I think. I mean, if you want to," said Jon, a day producer whose manner had completely changed since Jonathan's trip to Ireland. Jonathan could see Jon was jealous. Not a day went by without news of some corporate merger in the water and electricity industries. The papers were full of stories about bad service, increased charges, mass disconnections and board director pay-rises. Jonathan offered some thanks and phoned the video library for some material on water-metering.

"When did you say the piece was transmitted?" the librarian asked.

"I'm not sure, a few months ago."

"That as accurate as you can get? You know, you should have the TX date."

"Look, it was on water metering and it was a couple of months ago."

"OK, look, give us a few hours, maybe it's in Brentwood."

Turning to look at his clippings he caught Julia's smile. Momentarily, it made the paper below Jonathan's eyes seem boring.

Water: Manna from heaven for directors
Water disconnections.
Internet Revolution leaves the disconnected behind.
Water purity standards: The worst in Europe.
Telephone competitor goes bankrupt.
Gas prices up fourth month in a row.

Rain but no water: Privatisation and Drought.
Business calls cheaper.
Water metering—a Green revolution.
Water profits up 400%, Prices up too.
Gas prices reach new peak.
Long distance calls drop in price.
EU slams UK water Standards

"Well, I guess I'll be seeing you next week," Jonathan said, burying his face in the articles.

"Let's go and see a film, when you get back," Julia replied.

Over the next week, Jonathan travelled across the land, interviewing experts in the fields of energy, water and telecommunications. On the surface, investment in new water-quality schemes had rocketed since privatisation. Telephones, too, had become more efficient in that there were many new styles to choose from and there were new services available. Phone-users could find out who was calling them before they picked up the receiver and press a button to repeatedly call an engaged line. Only in the gas industry did privatisation seem to have been a total failure.

For his reporter, Simone, the whole series was prosaic. She had just been recruited from working in the fashion advertising industry and walking along sewage pipes was, she told him, considerably beneath her. That morning, they had been taken for a ride to the coast by some consultants from a local water company. They were plied with sandwiches and coffee from a thermos and sat around a wood-stained boardroom table in a cabin amid gigantic drilling machines and piping equipment.

"There won't be any waste on the beaches here this summer," Freddie Moroni said, leaning over to take one of the triangular-cut sandwiches. "See that?" he said, pointing out of the long double-glazed window that gave the prefab hut they were sitting in a view over the North Sea.

Simone and Jonathan peered out into the blue-black middle distance.

"That's going to be the cleanest water in the world," he said, biting into the sandwich, "except that the green environmental people will no doubt lead the public down the garden path about it." Sounds of sandwich-munching ensued. "After we've finished this, let's go and get into some suits and go down," he said, rubbing tired grey eyes.

Wearing hard-hats and white overalls over their clothes, Simone and Jonathan were lifted down into a shaft, some one hundred feet below the ground, through a hole. Both of them were alarmed as the box was lowered, swinging from side to side like a slow beating metronome. Down in the hole, they found themselves in a storm drain pipe, about twenty feet in diameter. Along the pipe, little red lights twinkled, signs to the construction workers that the pipe was not smooth enough on the inside. The red flickerings were from a laser beam directed along the pipe. A man who looked about seventy was using a plane to smooth down the surface of the pipe. Wherever the laser beam was interrupted by a bump, it lit up.

The camera-person was a heavy, thickset man who paused every time he rolled the camera, having to untangle his beard from the handles jutting from the head of his tripod. He was quiet even by cameraman standards, so silent that he didn't even seem too sure of his name and wasn't too keen on offering it to anyone. As the laser glittered, so did the nameless cameraman wander along the pipe, disappearing down a curve where water was high enough to scuff his ankles.

"What do you think?" Simone said to him, "PTC, piece to camera down here?"

"I'm not sure."

"I think it looks pretty good. Quite hi-tech, if you know what I mean," said Freddie Moroni before he looked up and saw the worker with the plane approach us.

"Hello," he said in a thick Newcastle accent, "you've come out filming then. Am I going to be on TV?" the old man wiped dirt from his chin and then began to laugh.

"What do you think?" asked Freddie Moroni, unsurely.

"Bill's my name," the worker offered a filthy hand to Simone who smiled nervously and then asked how many hours a day he worked underground.

"Ooh, I dunno, miss, usually it's a fourteen hour day. Isn't that right, boss?" he said, smiling.

"Er, no, that isn't right."

"Just joking, miss, about ten is the normal."

"Less than him, then," Simone replied, looking Freddie Moroni.

After a taut journey up to ground level, the cameraman made a grunting sort of noise to indicate that one possibility for the piece to camera was having Simone talking into a radio-mike, as she was lifted from the hole in the ground. By now, Jonathan was concentrating on the state of his shoes. The holes in soles were easy entry for what he presumed was probably excrement-overflow from the council estate closest to the shore. The piece to camera went ahead, Simone looking upwards, her radio-mike picking up her references to the massive investment-programme initiated by the newly privatised water-company.

Freddie Moroni pushed Bill, the foreman, out of the way when they got back into the room with the inappropriate-looking boardroom table. Bill had followed them up, helping to steady the tripod for the cameraman and enjoying his moments of fame as he used a trowel to spread cement over a part of the pipe floor. After his polite questions addressed to "Sir", Jonathan, and "Miss", Simone, Freddie Moroni began to bark at him.

"Look, you can see we're busy. Why don't you just get down there and get back to work. Just get out!...Now, come on, we have some pretty tight deadlines and I don't think the Corporation are all that interested in what you have to say, now, are they?"

"Well," said Bill, sheepishly but with a glint in his eye, "do you think the situation will be OK tomorrow? I mean, I know that there'll be a lot more queuing at seven tomorrow because it's the first day since the tooling company on Cross Street's shut down. Any chance you can guarantee my place on tomorrow's team, rather than being casual and stuff? Come on, I just helped you on your publicity and everything."

"I'll see you tomorrow," Freddie Moroni said firmly before physically pushing Bill out of the door and into the grey-haired tea lady whose trolley then slammed into an architectural model of the completed waste complex.

After the door was shut, the cameraman lit the subject and Simone did the interview, the sounds of earnest gossip penetrating the plastic door.

After they left the complex, they found they had some time between interviews and Jonathan suggested they go and have a cup of coffee. The cameraman said he'd wait in the car so Simone and Jonathan went on alone to find a café with swift service, overlooking a street football game.

Simone was about thirty-five and five-nine. Jonathan wondered whether to advise her against very red lipstick and then stopped himself. He rather liked the contrast between her pink suit and the grey surroundings they found themselves in. "I suppose it's been quite tough first assignment, Simone," he said.

"Not really," she paused, took out a compact and began to powder her face. "You know, I'm not sure about this. It's not that it's tough, it's just that it's all a bit serious, the stories we've been doing," she elongated the vowels of the word 'serious', 'but it's jolly good experience. The man that got me the job said it would be different, that I could really have a career at the Corporation. Anyway, it's all for the best. I can always move on to one of the independent networks, now. You see, what I'm interested in is more the celebrity-orientated stuff. It's not much fun tramping about a place like this, is it? I like drama, you see."

"Well," Jonathan said, looking out onto the shopping street, at the empty windows and squatter boards, the fluttering litter and cast iron clouds above them. "This is certainly where the news is."

A football bounced off the window and some contrite children appeared between parked cars to retrieve it.

"I suppose so," Simone replied, giving way and not wanting to alienate an assistant editor. "You're not much interested in the celebrity interviewing, then? That's where the money is, you know."

"I suppose I am," Jonathan replied, "it would be fun for a while. You get to travel a lot more, I suppose."

"I know," Simone said, excitedly, "why don't we go to one of the brand new shopping centres here, perhaps we could do a piece to camera or something about the rejuvenation of the city. You know, to cheer up the country's television-viewers. I think everyone's a bit tired of all this wintry, depressing stuff. Everyone's waiting for summer to arrive."

"They do use water, gas, electricity and telephones," Jonathan replied, gingerly.

"Well, shall we?"

"No, I don't think so. Look, why don't you go, if you want to. I've got to make a few calls, that is if the battery on this mobile will let me."

"OK, I'll meet you back here in an hour," she said to Jonathan's surprise.

When she had left, a man came towards Jonathan and tried to sell him a copy of Socialist Worker, a newspaper producers weren't allowed to cover in the Corporation's paper-roundup. As the heading was about water, Jonathan decided to buy it.

He found the style of writing curious but was interested by its assessment that there was a crisis. He found himself thinking about how his Corporation newspaper-allowance wouldn't cover the expense for the receipt-less newspaper as there was no receipt

Folding the paper up, he made some phone-calls to the Labour Party, hoping they might put someone up who could criticise privatisation. Jonathan had got Simone's bug for drama and he wanted some for the water programme.

"We don't really comment on the purity standards angle. It's the huge wage increases of the chief executives that we're campaigning against. I think that once you go into the actual business of the thing, the public tend not to be able to follow you. You know what I mean?" said the Labour Party press officer.

"Does that go for the other utilities?"

"Yes, I mean we certainly don't comment on the privatisation of the telecommunications' industry."

"I see. So I wouldn't be able to get anyone to talk about the increase in disconnections?"

"It's not something we have a release on. Sorry. I can send you our release on the Internet, that's to do with connections. I'll pop that in with the salaries' stuff. It's quite a detailed piece of work done by our research department."

"Thank you very much indeed." Jonathan replied.

Perhaps it was the coffee, or perhaps it was just that he had wanted an antagonist for the series, but Jonathan suddenly felt angry. There was certainly, as far as he could tell, no one whom he could get on camera to talk about the grave problems he had read about in the paper. He knew that interviewing a journalist from one of the more anti-government broadsheet newspapers was out as the boss didn't like pundits in series. It was only in very special circumstances that a producer could use a newspaper journalist. Hacks were regarded as competitors by the News and Current Affairs department: if a print journalist was used in a TV piece, it implied that viewers were better off reading the news than watching it.

After his fourth espresso coffee, Jonathan decided that as an assistant editor, he should be able to do things that everyday producers couldn't do. Knowing that Simone wasn't too up on things at the Corporation, that she had probably little knowledge of the Producers' Guidelines book, he decided to make a few calls and arrange for interviews with anyone who could at least voice some of the statistics that served the anti-privatisation case.

When Simone returned, carrying some shiny string-handle shopping bags, he told her that there was a change of plan, that the series lacked a focus and he knew how they could get one.

"Sure, you're the boss," she said, her face flushed from her hour spent in the biggest shopping centre in the continent.

AFSHIN RATTANSI

Back in London, Jonathan worked hard at arranging interviews with those whom he knew were considered conspiracy-theorists. Jonathan had heard these names being mocked in the office when an urgent live guest was needed. Often, the names would be pronounced in funny voices before an editor finally quietened down the sniggering by saying that these names were on a blacklist. Corporation journalists had adopted the American vernacular for guests deemed discomforting. There was no official chart for guest selection but Jonathan knew what it would look like if there had been:

APPELLATION/IMPLICATION/ GENERALLY ADMISSABLE/ FREQUENCY AS GUEST

fascist/Right wing Conservative supporting "family values"/ Yes/Regular

sensible/Supporter of the Labour leadership or Supporter of free market economic principles./Yes/Regular

commie/Left wing Labour or certain journalists presumed to support the command economy and decrease national defence expenditure. /No/Very Rarely

Nazi/British National Party, skinheads, those openly opposed to immigrant groups/No/Never

liberal/Most people/Yes/Often

Liberal/Naïve person/Sometimes/Compulsory during Local and General Elections

Spare Rib/Those seeking male-female equality/Yes/Rarely

Third Worlder/Those obsessed with anti-colonialism and racism/Yes/Very Rarely

To maximise the dramatic impact of his piece, Jonathan had selected "sensible" people, some "Nazi's and some "Commies". Even Julia raised an eyebrow when, from the other side of the newsroom, a producer shouted the names of people returning his calls. The boss was on his vacation, so Jonathan was in complete control of his series. The only thing slowing him down was what was now called "The Beef Crisis" — transmission of his series was to be postponed by a day.

With all episodes of the series edited, Jonathan sat in the office, checking last-minute facts and looking for "newsy pegs", items of news that were less than a day old which he could tack onto the cues for each piece. The best ones could make an audience believe that a series was reacting to daily events rather than the outcome of a week-old discussion with the boss.

"The boss arranged for you to see this guy," Julia said, from across the table, before she passed a business card to him, "he advised having him live, off one of your pieces."

Jonathan read the card slowly: "Dr. Charles Culloden-Pryce, Utility Consultant".

"Seven-thirty at his club, he said," Julia told him, a black canvas bag slung over the shoulder of her tight black dress.

"Is the boss coming?"

"He wanted to, he likes the man. But he's tied up at a management meeting."

"I see. Would you like to come with me?" he asked.

"Well, I was going to do something tonight," Julia smiled, 'hang on, I'll just make a phone-call."

The Babylon Club had seen better days. The allied bombing and destruction of Babylon during the Gulf War had taken a toll on membership and the place had never fully recovered from a divisive poll amongst members over whether to change the Iraqi name to something more modern and sophisticated. Still, after sewage pipes and electricity substations, prison-like editing rooms and the shoulder-ache of holding phones, the dark wooden panelling and subdued lighting was congenial. Simone, who seemed to have lost all interest in the series after she had laid down her voice on a tape, didn't mind in the least that Jonathan had taken Julia to meet Charles. She was pleased to have a free evening before she started on a new fashion series that began filming in the next couple of days.

"You'll have to go into the mixed section of the club," said the man in the morning-suit at the front desk.

"That's fine," he said, watching Julia grimace.

The mixed section was empty, the sound of chatter coming from the main men-only bar reverberating from below. After introductions, Charles opened a gold-trimmed leather business card holder and gave Jonathan a card.

"Glad you could make it. Your employer and me go back a long way. I used to do a bit of journalism for the college newspaper, you see. What would you like to drink, I think a bottle of champagne would be nice, what do you say?" Charles smiled at Jonathan's unsure glance at Julia. Charles was much younger than he had expected, perhaps in his thirties. His black hair was gelled back over his head and he smiled often, exposing shiny white teeth. He wore a dark double breasted pinstripe suit and the large lapels seemed to accentuate his ruddy ears.

"Don't worry, I know the Corporation budget doesn't stretch quite as far as Veuve Cliquot. Actually, I probably know more about the Corporation's budget than you do. I do some consulting for the Corporation in my spare time, you know."

"I suppose we are a utility," Jonathan replied, tightening a presenter's spare tie he had borrowed from the boss' office.

"Yes, but I only do it for prestige value. It dazzles quite a few clients, you know. But the serious money is all in the privatised utilities. Who would have known it? A couple of days a week advising and I can sit here and buy you champagne. Trickle down or what?" he chuckled.

"What do you advise on?" Jonathan asked, staring into Charles yellow pupils.

Julia gulped some champagne down and crossed her

legs. She seemed almost humble outside the bedlam of the newsroom, Jonathan thought.

"Well, basically various companies send me piles of papers every week and I check through them. I'm a sort of trouble-shooter. Usually, they're fine. In fact, between you and me, if I'm pretty stretched I just sign the bottoms of the pages without reading them," Charles laughed loudly. "Off the record, of course. I mean, in any case, no-one could read all of what I'm supposed to study every week," Charles selected a cigar from the waiter's wooden box.

"So what's your impression of the privatisation programme?" Jonathan asked.

"Lucrative. Obviously, I wouldn't say that on camera, but I think lucrative is the word that comes to mind. Look, let me tell you that if you've ever had enough of the hack work, these companies are always looking for experienced people to do a bit of PR work for them. Public relations, you know, is a good business and they already have lots of good ex-Corporation producers working for them. I let your boss know of the offer and even he said that he was interested. I'm not saying the job is easy. There have been some problems but, really, these pale into insignificance against the gains. Most of the problems are more to do with the presentation part of the business, anyway. I mean, look, water is cheaper, we'll soon have a choice what gas company and what electricity company people want to use. The phones seem to work much better. Basically, the whole operation has been an amazing success. It's hard to remember, now, the time when the unions were controlling everything and one's only choice of phone was red, green or grey."

"I remember that," said Julia, pouring herself from a condensation-covered champagne bottle. "I remember when every payphone seemed to be out of order."

"And as for the cellular market, well," Charles looked up at the glass chandelier, some twenty feet above them, "they may be frowned on in here, but out there everyone's using a mobile phone. In fact, if you want a good deal, I can let you have one for free. You too, Julia," Charles pushed his hand into his inside pocket and took out a black box the size of a credit card, "a bit better than your Corporation standard issue, Ill bet."

"Great, I'd love one."

"Keep you safe when you're waiting for the bus on a dark night," Charles said, puffing smoke and laughing and then coughing.

After a pause when some more drinks were arriving on a silver tray, Charles became more serious. "So, how's the series progressing then?"

"Quite well. We've got everything done, well, we've got a lot in, anyway," Jonathan replied, sipping the flute glass with curiosity.

"That's good," he said, tapping his cigar and lifting an eyebrow, "were you critical, quite critical of the programme?"

"The privatisation programme?" Jonathan asked, "yes, we were. We got Alfred Classer and Liz Borrow."

"Oh no, not the left-wing loony brigade," he said, looking over to Julia for support, "they're completely mad. What about Sir Archibald Snee? Doesn't he head a think-tank somewhere in Whitehall that would be good? Or even the Utility Network Foundation, they have some top brass analysts. I mean, my God, one of the regulators even. I think you might have made a mistake there, Jonathan. You've let in the loonies and you must know that they still think we live in the bloody nineteenth century."

"I thought I'd go about it all slightly differently, try and look at it from a different angle. It's good to be a bit original sometimes, I think," Jonathan said, feeling buoyed up by his first taste of champagne. "The package will work well, what with your live after the pieces."

"Yes, I suppose you're right. At least there'll be some conflict for your programme. But, of course, there are matters of contention that are interesting, without having to go down the path of the loony-left. I mean, there's the issue of consultants working both for suppliers and buyers in the gas industry and in electricity. There's the whole story of how the telecommunications industry is lobbying pretty hard against there being any competitors, things like that."

"Well, the main thrust of the arguments in these pieces is that, well in the case of water..."

"Water?" Charles seemed quite rattled, "well, even I wasn't all the way for water. I do very little work for them." Charles became still and a tube of ash fell to his lap.

"Well, what I was really saying was that in the case of water the problems are standards and price rises. In gas, the huge inefficiency of the new regime, in electricity generation and supply, the formation of huge cartels and in telecommunications, the huge rate of disconnections. We didn't look at airlines but of course that's a more long term story. I mean, some people say that the privatised airlines are already compromising on safety."

"I see. And this is what you find in your daily life, is it?" Charles asked, his tone harder. Another tube of ash fell. "You find, on the doorstep, people saying that everything in the utilities has changed completely since privatisation, that everything has gone to the dogs? Well, I dare say your attractive colleague doesn't and nor do I."

Julia seemed to wake up when she was mentioned, putting her champagne glass down on the table with a start. "I don't quite see what you're getting at," she said, turning to Jonathan in a doubtful way, "I mean, my water's much the same."

"But, they're going to have standpipes in the streets in the North of England because most of the water leaks away into..." Jonathan interrupted.

"I don't think it could ever get to that stage," Julia said in a low tone. "The telephones are much better. Come on, Jonathan, they are. Coin-boxes seem to work, there's the Internet. As for gas and electricity, the prices have gone up, but not horrendously. They were always pretty high, I thought, at least with the electricity."

"There, I think that's the normal view," said Charles, brushing the ash in grey streaks down a pair of pinstripes.

"Well then, haven't I made a series with an abnormal view then, a different view?"

"It's not really fair on your viewers though, is it? I mean, it's not the truth," said Charles. Jonathan waited for some words of defence from Julia.

"That's covered in Producers' Guidelines: impartiality across a channel, not in one single programme. Jonathan's right. One programme doesn't have to show impartiality: the channel as a whole has to. Mind you, that's normally documentaries, not news," Julia declared, looking towards Jonathan as she awkwardly poured some more champagne.

"Well," Jonathan replied, annoyed and reckless from the drink, "the series is signed and sealed and all ready to go. It doesn't make any difference what you think about my work, I think any producer would have done the same. It'll be up to you to rebut the arguments you see tomorrow."

"That's right, that's what all the best producers say. But all the best producers also make their programmes impartial," said Julia, smiling at Charles and pouring him a drink. "Look, I've got an editing suite in my flat and I'm a dab hand at editing. If you really want to change anything I'm sure we could. You don't want to let down your boss."

Jonathan glared at Julia, wondering what his next move should be. He wasn't looking forward to the prospect of his being accused for bias by two people who hadn't even seen his series. Right now, among the heady atmosphere of wood, champagne and cigars, he thought Julia's once silk-like hair resembled the spines of a frightening fish. He offered them hurried excuses about tiredness and left the tall-ceilinged room for the summery night outside. He even suggested to Charles that if he was to get time to hone his arguments against the points made in the series, he should go have a good night's sleep. He slept on the top deck of the first bus and thought about the broadcast on the second, connecting one.

The number of people using mobile phones on the bus had Jonathan wondering whether he was right about the angle he had taken. The bus passed a misty park. Jonathan mulled over whether the news was a place to really get to grips with complex issues. The series would shock its morning audience, Jonathan thought.

Later in his journey, with the street lights flashing beside him, he speculated on whether his series would just make others in the office jealous of him. Envy, he had detected, could deliver mortal blows in the office.

꙳

The series was a success. As Jonathan raised the volume on his television, he realised that he had had a hand in shaking up, if not the privatised industries themselves, then the media's impression of them. When the second three-minute "episode" was screened, the newspapers were headlining the first. The Six and The Nine, as the two evening news programmes were known, both repeated the pieces. He didn't need to read the boss' comments on the series in the debrief, he knew it had all been a triumph. On the afternoon of the electricity episode, the boss called him at home.

"How's my assistant editor, then? Very clever, very clever stuff. Simone's going to do a few presenting spots, I want her to go high profile, big interviews. Wasn't she good? And, as for you, you've snuck a few things through that maybe you shouldn't have. But you pulled it through. Charles was alright, he gave a good stab at it, he probably wasn't tough enough. That was the only problem, let's call it a flaw. It seemed like your personal view was coming across a little too strongly. Did you recognise that?"

"Well, not so much my views, sort of some views that aren't normally given an airing," Jonathan replied.

"Well, maybe. But remember that what we do is news not views," the boss paused, the sound of a beer bottle being opened in the background, "look, don't give me any bullshit. I know exactly what you were doing when you asked Classer and Borrow on the show. I'm not fucking stupid, you know. The management dickheads haven't completely neutralised my brain. I did start in journalism before I became a Corporation management pen-pusher, you know. Frankly, your interviewees aren't exactly Middle England's favourite cup of tea, are they?" he waited for a response. "Look, it was good work, but be careful, very, very careful. Use those people very sparingly."

"Thanks," Jonathan replied.

"Well, off-the-wall producers get off-the-wall assignments. Have I got a surprise for you. Because of your great success I'm sending you where everyone wants to be. You're going to be with Martin Mass. Hello? Did you hear that?"

Jonathan felt dread in his stomach. He didn't have a clue who Martin Mass was. "Yes, thank you," he replied.

"You've done a hazard course, right?"

"Yes."

"Well, some of us argued against it, I know you're not as experienced as some of the blokes in the department, but I'm giving you the chance to go to Bosnia, if you want it, that is." The boss gurgled on his beer.

"Well," Jonathan said, uncertainly.

Jonathan had never been to another country before. He had collected and dropped off people destined for overseas from airports, coach and rail stations but had never found the time or money to go away.

He was keen to research the history of Yugoslavia but soon realised from the thickness of recent histories that he would have no time. Most of his preparation concerned how to get there. The easiest way, so his computer said, was to get a flight with the United Nations High Commission for Refugees which had a base in Ancona, on the Adriatic coast of Italy. The RAF, German and Belgian air forces were based there, in an operation run by the British. As he sat with the printout, he sometimes looked at the pile of video rushes that he was to log and code as a squeamishness test. The rushes had just been fed in on the "bird", or satellite, and he had to check which images were suitable for Britain's evening meal viewing.

The notes on Yugoslavia would at first be over-simple and

then impossible. To Jonathan, the sentence "UNPROFOR cards are essential as usual but CANNOT be issued in Ancona, only in Zagreb or Belgrade" meant as little as the reasons for the war itself. Quickly, he scanned which Alitalia flights flew from Rome and Milan to Ancona. Then he looked at the possibility of travelling from Split on Mondays, Thursdays and Saturdays. The Split-Rome flight could then take him to Ancona via Rome but he was told he must bear in mind that because of NATO "air movements" the advertised flight duration of one hour was now double that.

Any time Jonathan wanted to devote to understanding the actual conflict was now wholly shelved in favour of travel arrangements. Another way to Sarajevo, he discovered, was to go to the UNHCR office located in a cargo-warehouse next door to Ancona's customs office. Because the sentry on the gate was likely to be a British soldier, Corporation staff would be well directed, so his printout said.

There was also a direct way to Sarajevo via the town of Split with the RAF or the Royal Navy. According to one Corporation journalist, it was thanks to Navy Sea King helicopters based at the military heliport near Trogir that a spare part for a satellite dish was urgently flown to a crew in Sarajevo, so in theory one could go via Trogir too. It was also possible to fly with the Red Cross on their "soup kitchen" flight from Zagreb. There was another way that would have made arrangements much easier but the US Air Force jets that regularly flew between Frankfurt and Sarajevo were not permitting journalists to hop along on sorties.

In the back of Jonathan's mind, whilst Jonathan organised his journey, was that, so far, a quarter of a million people had died in the fighting in Yugoslavia. The UN had issued customs warnings to all travellers:

"To all passengers on UNHCR Humanitarian airlift to Sarajevo. As weight of baggage recently has been excessive and due to incidents according to the content, the rules given by UNHCR AIR OPERATIONS GENEVA as

of 19 January 1993 and due to mutual agreement between UNHCR Split and CIVPOL of 2 August 1993 are stated below in extract as follows:
Revision 1
a. For reasons of safety and security, the following control will be strictly enforced for all passengers. Passengers and baggage will be subject to search for the purpose of determining whether the passenger is in possession of, or his baggage contains any, items which are likely to endanger the aircraft, items prohibited under applicable laws, regulations or orders, explosives, firearms, ammunition or any type of military or paramilitary material or components thereof. Such searches will be conducted at the airport of departure by UN authorities and/or by the aircraft operators/crew. If a passenger is unwilling to comply with such a search, the carrier may refuse to accept the passenger or baggage.

This part was little different from advice to passengers on civilian airliners.

b. If firearms or associated ammunition are being carried, these must be declared and surrendered to the aircraft commander for safe custody during the flight. There can be no exception to this rule. Aircraft commanders may refuse to take on board such articles.

Jonathan envisaged arms dealers smiling as they offered their guns to the flight crew so that they were in safe custody.

c. Passengers will be permitted to carry personal baggage only. Baggage is limited to two suitcases and one piece of hand luggage and should be properly marked with the owner's name. The total baggage should NOT EXCEED 20kgs.
d. Aircraft schedules will not be delayed or amended to satisfy passenger travel requirements. ALL PASSENGERS TO SARAJEVO MUST HAVE HELMETS AND FLAKJACKETS. Passengers are not allowed to bring more than: 5 cartons of cigarettes 5 bottles of alcohol 5 bags of coffee

(250g each) 6 private letters. The letters must be presented to CIVPOL monitors when check takes place. Passengers are fully responsible for the content of the letters.

A BBC journalist added:

It is still possible to fly from Split but the French armed forces who run air movements are very bureaucratic, none too helpful to journalists, and inclined to tell you after you've arrived in Split that there's a ten-day waiting list for flights.

Jonathan now tried to remember his hazard course, uneasy that a day's training, months ago, would be sufficient for his producing from Sarajevo. He shuffled his papers to look at what he should bring with him.

1. *Previous attempts by the media to accompany army convoys with 2-wheel drive vehicles have ended in tears, in one case with the vehicle having to be abandoned. You are strongly advised to acquire a 4-wheel drive vehicle if you are intending to operate over these routes.*
2. *Acquire the following and carry with your vehicle on every trip.*
   a. *6 x Crepe bandages 1 x Airway 2 x Morphine syrettes (if possible) The Army cannot supply any of the above to civilian personnel.*
   b. *Vehicle jack Wheel brace Tow rope Full jerrycan of fuel Hammer and crowbar Clear plastic sheeting and adhesive tape (temporary repair for smashed windscreens) Anti-freeze and oil Spare bulbs;*
   c. *(High sugar content) 5 litres of water fuel stove and messtin sleeping bags per person torch and spare batteries Clasp knife Map and Compass*

Body armour and Helmet Corkscrew and bottle-opener;

d.   Finally, know and mark your blood group clearly on your body armour.

3.   Military operations are designed to achieve a specific aim with the minimum of delay and disruption, and to be capable of also dealing with unexpected contingencies. If you treat your operation in a similar vein you should be able to achieve your aim, keep up with the military operation (without becoming a burden or being left behind) and to cope with both the hostile environment and hostile natives. Below is a checklist you are advised to run before starting:

a.   Attend P Info brief on operation, noting route, objective, danger areas and any specific problems advised.

b.   Ensure your vehicle and jerrycans are full.

c.   Check Oil level Washer level Fanbelt Tyre pressure and grip (snowchains may be required) Coolant and windscreen wash levels

d.   Clean Lights Windows Press markings

e.   Check your medical, vehicle and personal kits are complete.

f.   Book out with someone, leave details of who is in the vehicle, your intended route and destination and when you are due back.

g.   Finally, put your body armour on, you may not get a chance later.

4.   Give any armoured vehicles you encounter considerable room to manoeuvre. The effects of "Panzer Rash" have already been tragically and dramatically demonstrated. Armour bites!!!... Warrior and CVR(T) are both capable of sustaining high speeds on road and cross-country, up to 70+ mph. They are both capable of stopping from speed within their own length, considerably faster than your vehicle. When they stop their rear rises up on its suspension. Should you be travelling behind one when

it slams on the brakes you will impact with the belly of the vehicle. The vehicle will then sit back on your bonnet, if you're lucky!...Warrior weighs up to 30 tons, CVR(T) over 8 tons and FV432 over 15 tons.

5.   *a. Many of the tracks in use are very narrow and make bypassing a major problem. Keep at least 50 metres apart at all times. This also makes sound military sense.*

    b.   Please don't overtake without talking to the P Info staff or convoy commander.

6.   *High Risk Areas If you are told that you are entering a high risk area the following additional precautions should be taken.*

    a.   Open side windows and turn off stereos. This will enable you to hear incoming fire and possibly the firing of mortars nearby.

    b.   Remove seat-belts to be able to de-bus swiftly or facilitate casualty evacuation. c. All passengers should look outward covering a 360 degree arc around the vehicle.

7.   *For vehicles in the convoy, the following actions should be taken to ensure everyone the best chance of survival.*

    a.   direct fire or artillery fire it is important that the following vehicles do not cross the killing area unnecessarily. If you hear firing ahead but are out of sight of the contact you should immediately pull off to the side of the road, using the terrain to shield you from the firing. (There is a good possibility that the vehicles ahead will come rushing back. If it's armour you certainly don't want to be in its way.) Any accompanying P Info personnel will direct you in extracting yourself from the vicinity. In the meantime you should take cover away from the vehicle (large fuel tanks especially!) leaving your engine running. Unlike the movies cars don't

> stop bullets. Under no circumstances should you go
> forward unless cleared by P Info.
>
> b.   should make all speed to exit the killing area.
> Trying to second-guess the man with his finger on
> the trigger only wastes time. Most of the tracks
> are not suitable for zigzagging and you'll only be
> overtaken by the rest or, worse, slow everybody
> else behind you. Once you are clear you should
> go past the P Info escort and stop the car in the
> nearest cover, giving consideration for the number
> of vehicles behind you who will want to do the
> same. fire. This is the signal to increase speed.
> 4-way flashers should not be used in the danger
> areas for any other purpose

In the aeroplane, Jonathan continued to read and for the
most part he was undisturbed. The other passengers were
from the UN and were keen to read their own operations'
manuals. And so, after less than twenty-four hours he arrived at
Sarajevo airport, complete with boxes of food and emergency
equipment. He was due to be picked up by a producer who
was leaving Bosnia, as was the form when new journalists
arrived. Harry Colson, a twenty-nine year old producer had
been there for a month and was expected to tell him about all
current news events that might have taken place whilst he was
in transit. Colson was about two hours late, held up on Airport
Lane, a slip road that had earned the epithet "Murder Mile".
While Jonathan waited for him, a UNHCR truck-driver asked
whether he wanted a lift, but Jonathan preferred to wait, not
keen on leaving the terminal, what with the sounds of sniper
fire echoing around the corrugated iron walls. Jonathan had
never been so scared since his first days in London.

"Colson's mine, what's yours?" he said, touching Jonathan
on the shoulder, "name, man...what's your name?"

"Jonathan..."

"I'm afraid it looks like it's getting pretty rough for you,
down here. My job was tough and yours is going to be even

tougher. Anyway, at least you'll have a full tank of petrol," he held up a rusted vacuum flask, "and, of course, Zolin." He pointed to a short smiling man with a knapsack on his back who was chatting with a soldier by the terminal entrance. "He should help you out. He's better than some of the others, at least."

"Well, how have you found it then?" Jonathan asked, intrigued by such little Corporation solidarity. He thought Colson would have been pleased to see him.

"Scared?" Colson motioned him to one of the airport chairs dotted around the floor.

"All the information on the computer didn't really give me much confidence about the place and nor did the footage," Jonathan confided.

"It's not so bad. The Holiday Inn even has laundry today," Colson took out a cigarette and lit it with a shaking hand. He looked older than twenty-nine, perhaps because of his large size. Jonathan followed Colson's eyes downwards and looked at the tins of pasta beside his own feet and wondered if he had really needed to bring so much stuff all this way. "Let's see, what should I tell you? We've got electricity, thanks to the hotel genny. And, there's a sniper who's still doing target practice at the back of the hotel. There's three meals a day. Oh, and check out the Queen of the Danube restaurant, which is still running. There's no beer though and nothing in the markets. Though you shouldn't really be going to the markets anyway," he was speaking energetically, obviously excited about the city of Sarajevo.

"Well, if I can't leave the hotel, how can I get any filming done?" Jonathan inquired.

"Best thing is to wait for the UN convoys. Move around with them. No points for dying, you know." Colson looked up at what turned out to be a stopped clock on the wall and then at his watch. "Don't drink the water. Allan, our cameraman is pretty ill at the hotel because of that."

"Is he alright?"

"He's much better now. Basically, use the sterilisation tablets. What else? The only place to get petrol is at Kiseljak in Croatia, some people from the pool have gone to get some more. Also, do you smoke?"

"No, is that compulsory?" Jonathan joked.

"Did you bring any Marlboro?" Colson was very serious.

"Yes, I read about that."

"Well, keep a lighter on you and a torch. You don't want to be caught out when the electricity fails. Oh and don't drive like the blazes when you speed off from the hotel, just because of the snipers. If you crash the car, you'll be stuck outside the hotel like a sitting duck. Just use your head. And, if you have to come to the airport for some reason only use the UNPROFOR armoured vehicles. They're always going back and forth."

"I should probably have gone with them today, then, someone offered me a lift," Jonathan said, as a deathly firing intensified.

"Armoured cars can't stop rockets," Colson said, shaking his head, "so it's not much safer with them."

"How's the hotel doing then, otherwise?" Jonathan asked, thinking quickly of questions he should ask and looking up again at the stopped clock.

"Ten storeys high," Colson gesticulated with his hands, "except that the top five are kind of open plan," he laughed, "then there's the south side of the hotel, that's uninhabitable, the whole thing. The other three sides are open for business. Don't listen to the hotel staff though. They say that there are safe sides to the hotel. They'll tell you that rooms on the west and north sides are fine. The UN gave us an unofficial briefing about that. Apparently there's people firing at all sides of the hotel, and the Holiday Inn, well," Colson stroked his chin and smiled a stubbly grin, "the Holiday Inn has taken more direct hits than any other building in Sarajevo except the Presidency. Take room 216 on the North side, get your key in the lock, open the door and with one step, you're off of the building. That was hit with a 105mm tank shell. A 155mm Howitzer shell destroyed the entire eighth floor." Colson smiled again, while his gaze wandered to a group of head-scarved women, eyes to the floor, who had just entered the terminal building, carrying boxes.

Jonathan looked in his box for a Coke and opened it as quietly as he could before offering it to Colson.

"Don't necessarily sleep in your room, either," Colson said between sips, "there's a discotheque in the basement."

"Discotheque?" he asked, watching a young boy on crutches approach from one of the corners of the room.

"That's one of the best places to sleep. I've been staying there. There are mattresses on the floor and it's one place where you can't hear so much of the gunfire. As for the food," Colson brushed some Coke from above his top lip, "there are three meals a day, but no choice and the washing is a nightmare. There is water, brought in by the UN, but it's cold showers only, I'm afraid. But there are some good things. You're too late for the Sarajevo Sniper, if you're into that sort of thing. It's a jolly good cocktail they make at the bar. It's made of basically anything they have around. If you're a drinking man, it's mainly gin and tonics. Zolin knows where all the other places of interest are. AP are staying at a brothel called the Belvedere, at least it was a brothel." AP stood for Associated Press, one of the wire services.

"I read something about the Hotel Bosna. Does AP still have an office there still?"

"It's still there, just. It was mortared pretty heavily...needs a bit of redecorating. Oh, by the way, all phone calls in Sarajevo are still free. But that's only within Sarajevo. It's on the 071 exchange so you can't call Croatia or Serbia, though. Apparently, the lines are all routed through Belgrade and the Croats won't let Sarajevo use their microwave link to Zagreb."

Jonathan looked confused, his eyelids drooping slowly as he tried to assimilate all the information.

"Let me explain," Colson said, looking up at a mark on the ceiling for an instant, "Kiseljak is Croat and Pale and Ilidza are Serb. Right? Anyhow, you'll pick it up. Were you ever in the TA?"

"TA? Er, no."

"Territorials? No TA-experience? Oh dear. What school did you go to, then?" Colson laughed before they both heard a large bang outside. There was a pause during which Colson's short hair began to twitch and his nose wince. "Damn, no camera. I could have done with a last report. How's my stuff looking on the news anyway?"

"Good, good coverage, I suppose." Jonathan remembered thinking about how he had learnt nothing from Colson's dispatches from Yugoslavia, other than there was a lot of fighting. "Oh, there was a bit of murmuring in the office about why you were standing up in a street doing a piece to camera whilst there was firing all around."

"Oh that, that was just dubbing in the editing studio. We just dubbed the sound over. I did try to do a PTC whilst there was firing, but I didn't get it right, so we just moved on. There's plenty of good locations for that sort of stuff."

Jonathan nodded as Colson drained his can, vertically.

"I've tried to save my room for you so you should be able to take it. The windows are all smashed in, but the phone works. Anyway, if you want to phone outside Sarajevo, best to use a Satphone. Zolin's looking after it. But, don't forget, if you get separated, you won't be able to call him because calling a Satphone is technically an international call." Colson got up and hoisted a big bag over his right shoulder. "Oh, and don't turn the lights on in the room, you'll get shot."

The ochre-facaded Holiday Inn was built for the 1992 Sarajevo Olympics, not that Jonathan got much of a chance to view its exterior. He was shaken by what he had seen on the journey to the hotel and was recovering from the trauma in a gloomy corner of the ground floor of the hotel.

Only after half an hour could even look around to scrutinise what was around him. He looked up and saw Mark, an experienced Corporation producer, some twenty-six years old smiling down at him. Mark had begun to give an impromptu briefing, mostly about how experienced he was. What disturbed and impressed Jonathan was Mark's sense of excitement rather than fear. He was wearing a flak jacket that he said had belonged to one of his cameramen, now dead. "Look at the holes in the back, here and here," he said, heaving the jacket up like a matador. Whilst two others, writers for European magazines, negotiated the selling of a carton of cigarettes, Jonathan asked Mark about how long he'd been in Sarajevo.

"A couple of months," he sniffed, "I'm here for the long term, producing for the big one," his brown eyes looked upwards to the dark ceiling above in an attempt to communicate who exactly he was producing for. His lofty expression could only mean that he was producing the main evening news reports for the Corporation, with the Corporation's principal reporter. "It's good work. Once I'm back in London, she says I'll go straight to the top of the queue at the Foreign Desk, Newsnight, you name it."

Just as Mark was about to continue his talk about Bosnia, he suddenly seemed agitated. He had seen an older journalist colleague, a black Frenchman with a long face, named Patrice. Patrice came over to the two of them and looking inquisitively at Jonathan. He was taller and looked tougher than Mark. For a few moments, he spoke in French to someone who was trying to get a ride to the airport.

"Well, that's my work done, or not done," he said turning to Mark, "I'm going to Angola or maybe Rwanda. I'm sick of all this shit, of all your shit. The entire media operation in Sarajevo is a sham. We don't understand it so I don't know how our folks at home are going to. The editors I'm writing for said I was doing great work which can only mean that while I've been here, being fired at, France has gone completely mad.

"Anyway, at least my stuff hasn't been as bad as your Corporation crap. You've been doing the worst coverage of all apart from the German stations." He turned to look at Jonathan, like a pro to an amateur, "this war is about money, like all fucking wars. But I don't suppose Mark here is going to go for that angle for his blessed Corporation.... The West has wanted to destroy Yugoslavia for half a century. And now they have a maniac in power they've poured in British and German made arms. The arms your country have built and exported around the world kill more people in an hour than die here in a month." He was only just warming to his topic, taunting Mark with unconcealed disgust. "Your country is the absolute worst, your government is fucking giving away weapons away to maim and murder, it's as if they think arms are bloody medical supplies."

"It may be millions that are dying in Rwanda, Patrice," Mark interrupted, "but this is Europe and I'm sorry but Europe counts. That's where everything starts. I'm afraid that 250,000 Bosnians are worth more than a couple of million blacks," Mark continued, sadly. "You know," he said more angrily, "I think I know this place a little better than you, thank-you very much. And I certainly know a bit more than you about Great Britain and its arms' trade. Look, I was here in Yugoslavia before you'd heard of the place, I took my holidays here while you were wasting your time in Central America, like some macho..."

Jonathan detected that this was more the banter of two friends than a spiteful feud. There was mutual pleasure below these harsh words. As if confirming Jonathan's deduction, Patrice sympathetically advised Mark that he had heard that Zaire would be the next big story. At that, Patrice beckoned a thin, dusty-faced porter carrying a couple of suitcases and walked towards the crowd at the door, waiting for the next lull in the fighting outside.

"Sorry about that guys," Mark said, slapping his right cheek with an open palm and getting the attention of the two European journalists. Oh, Hi Tim!...Hi Fiona!" He looked up at a couple of British newspaper writers who had joined the group. "I was just about to explain to the new people all about Bosnia."

"Oh, we missed your lecture last time, can we listen?" said Fiona, a brown-haired, short woman with large cheeks.

"Right, then," Mark said, conspiratorially. He teased opened a box of matches. "These matches are going to represent the various factions. First there's these people, the Bosnian Government army or Arm-ee-ya Republike Bosn-eyee Hertz-o-govina or Arm-ee-ya for short," Mark's face contorted as he pronounced the foreign words, his mouth enlarging into a letter-box like opening.

"Ar-mee-ya are called OS BiH in Sarajevo. It's a potent force and is organised regionally," Mark began to place pairs of matchsticks on the table, "there's the First Corps in Sarajevo, the Third in Zenica, the Sixth in Kon-yic. Notice that it's wrong to refer to them as the Muslim Army or the Bosnian Muslim Army as there are some Croats and even Serbs in the Ar-mee-ya. Right, now, over here," he opened another box of matches, these ones with red tips instead of blue, "these are the ARS or Ar-mee-ya Republike Srpsk-a or BSA to us. The Bosnian Serb Army is all-Serb and is heavily armed. There are not so many of them though and they're not so mobile. And now onto the Croats. I haven't got any other matches, so."

"Here," said Michael. A tall blonde-haired German journalist from Frankfurter Allemagne handed over some yellow headed matches.

"Thanks. These are the Bosnian Croats which are a little more complicated. UNPROFOR are using local names for them. The main initial is HVO, the Hrr-vat-sko Vee-yecce Ob-rahn, which translates as the Croatian Defence Council. There are loads of factions splitting off from this and some of them are against each other. The HVO in Tomislavgrad, Prozor and Vitez are fighting the Muslims," he placed a yellow-headed match on the table, perpendicular to a group of blue matches, "the HVO in Tusla are fighting with the Muslims, against the Serbs. The HVO in Mostar, meanwhile are fighting everyone as well as trying to recreate Herzegovina-Bosnia, which no-one else really cares for. Then there's the HVO in Vares which turned against the Muslims and subsequently lost. Now, the HVO has officially patched things up with the Muslims, so there's a shaky federation of both of them in Central Bosnia."

"But that's breaking down," said Danny, a red-headed American who had sat down and was intently staring at the collection of matches on the table.

"Some say that, yes," Mark replied, with slight irritation.

"And the Croats," Danny drawled, "are the ones doing in Sarajevo, right now."

"Only with artillery, though. Now, they also have some

renegade Muslims under the command of Fikret Abdic who has split with the Bosnian government and commands a private army in the Bihac pocket in Western Bosnia. Right, now, if you got that straight I can start on what's happening outside Bosnia."

The group smiled nervously at each other, some tipping their glasses for the dregs of gin and tonics. Mark eased the piles of matches to one side, giving him more room on the table before beginning again.

"We have Serbs and Croats. Firstly the Ar-mee-ya Republike Srp-ska Kra-yeen-a. These fellows are all Serbs, but are under separate command. You shouldn't call them the Croatian Serb Army as Croat Serbs are not the same thing as Kra-yeen-a Serbs. Better to call it the Kra-yeen-a Serb Army or the ARSK, which is what they are to the UN. As to the Croat Army, they're huge. Well-equipped and reorganised, they've beaten the ARSK forces in Western Slavonia and are down in Knin in Southern Kra-yeen-a. Added to this is the OS, a Croat paramilitary faction that sometimes gets involved. They're the non-Bosnian remains of the JNA, the Yugoslav National Army." Mark paused for breath. "Now, for my next trick." Then he paused again and turned to Jonathan, "you see, you always get into much more detail in a war situation. It's not like the reactive home-stories you're probably used to." Smiling, he then took out a more expensive-looking black and gold match. Igniting it, he proceeded to set fire to all the piles of matches he had been setting up on the table. As they burned, the group applauded.

On Jonathan's first night, Martin Mass recounted his experiences in the Gulf War, to the eerie peal of outside shelling. Jonathan thought that he recognised Mass, after all. He had seen him on television since he was a young boy. He was a senior reporter of around fifty and had the requisite layered grey hair, shiny eyes and smooth skin. Mass looked strained tonight, though. His talk was being hampered by a young American journalism graduate, Clark Berry, who had arrived the previous day. Jonathan had spoken to him earlier and liked him. Clark had confided to him that he had no accreditation and that he had only been able to come to Sarajevo because a rich aunt had recently died. He had wanted to see a European war and the inheritance had allowed him to live his dream. To Jonathan, Clark seemed altogether more human that his Corporation colleagues. Now, there in the gloomy darkness, he was arguing with Mass about how journalism had had its worst days during the Gulf War. He was reciting statistics about real kill rates and the accuracy of Patriots.

"You know, Jonathan, this war is different. I've been covering wars for fourteen years and usually, in conventional wars, two armies face each other along a front line. What I do is basically visit the front line and then return to the hotel or TV station and feed the story," said Mass, turning to Jonathan with a smile. "Now..."

"What crap, you never went near a front line during the Gulf, you were stuck in Amman, doing nothing but transcribing the reports the US Government gave you," Clark interrupted, his stick-out ears receding more from the side of his head. "You covered the allied bombing of orphanages by telling your audience that an arms' dump had been blown up and that the Iraqis were trying to milk sympathy from the world by killing their young and parading them for the international cameras. Now it turns out they were right and you were wrong, you idiot," he continued, hazel eyes flashing with anger. Jonathan was impressed by his confidence and wished he had had time to mug up on Mass' reporting career.

"Don't blame the messenger," Martin, said chuckling before his face regained its seriousness. "What I don't understand is that even if what you said was right...well, what does that make me? What do you think I think about it, if what you say is true. I'm not evil, you know. I'm not some Satanic cheerleader, urging the bombing of orphanages. What I do is just try and do the job as best I can. You really seem to think I'm some sort of agent for the Pentagon. I've never even been to the Pentagon. Anyway, if you want to learn something then you'd better listen."

Clark looked momentarily unsettled and fiddled with the bristles of brown hair on his chin.

"Sarajevo is a big place," Mass announced, "about the size of Bristol. That's Bristol, England in case Clark wants to butt in about Bristol, Virginia or something.

"It's very spread out. What you have, basically, is a big rectangle, east-west along the valley of the river, with hills and mountains surrounding the city. There are Serb, Muslim and Croatian gun positions in the hills but down in the city, right here, all is chaos. The city-centre and the old town are divided by the river. On the north bank, there are Muslims, on the south side, Serbs."

"Yeah, and the Serbs have always been there. They haven't just arrived," said a voice from the murkiness.

"Right. Anyway, they shoot at each other the whole time. Now, we...we're on the Muslim side, a few hundred yards in from the river. That's why we're always in the middle of the cross-fire. That's what our editors don't realise when they say, stay in the hotel to avoid the battles. We are the fucking battle. And all around the city there are groups of Muslims and Croats fighting the Serbs, then Croats and Serbs fighting Muslims. If you go to Stup, near where the UN is, there's a three-way split. As for the old town, in the centre of Sarajevo you can hear machine guns and small arms' fire continuously, on and on, hour after hour. That's the sound of the Muslim gangsters. The Muslim mafias are fighting for control of the parts of the city they want to have control of when the war is over. What I'm trying to say is that I might hate the Serbs for starting it all but the whole thing now has a kind of momentum of its own." Jonathan listened to the silence, followed by the exchange of "Good night's." Outside the gunfire seemed like it was only just beginning.

The next morning, wearing their flak jackets and carrying first aid bags and food kits, Mass and Jonathan ascended the stairs from the basement. Jonathan felt tired and dirty, remembering about how he used to live in London, all the time. In the reception area, they met their guide, Zolin, a Muslim man of about thirty-five with a broken nose and a red scratch on his left upper cheek.

"We'll get a UN convoy?" Mass sternly asked Zolin.

"Yes, I've checked it all out," he replied.

Jonathan nodded and was thinking about how differently their guide was dressed. He was wearing remarkably well pressed jeans and a spotless pink sports' shirt. As he wondered how Zolin had pressed his clothes, Zolin tried to make conversation.

"You know there's a new office-block in the five mile Muslim zone? It spans the whole distance between here and where the UN are. And guess what flag it's flying? The Croat flag"

"I thought the Croats were fighting the Muslims?" Jonathan asked.

"Yes, but here the Croats are our friends. I mean the Muslims' friends."

They clambered onto the UN Convoy vehicle with some difficulty. Mass needed the assistance of two UN soldiers.

"What are the range of all these weapons?" Jonathan asked Zolin, turning to Mass to momentarily joke that he had forgotten his Corporation guide to hazards in London. Mass didn't laugh, instead rubbing his neck as if in pain.

"Well, what they do, I mean the Muslims, is fire mortars from the streets, behind blocks of flats or in abandoned factories. We, they, use the same weapons as the Serbs, all stuff from the old Yugoslav army. Mortars have a range of about seven miles, some of the bigger guns maybe fifteen miles. They can get the Serb positions from down here, you see," Zolin replied cheerfully.

Jonathan looked up at the lush green countryside that passed them, holding his right hand with his left and rubbing it to get rid of the pain. He had grazed it on the side of the truck.

Zolin made a whistling sound. "That's the sort of warning you don't get with firing," he rubbed his beard and let his eyelashes flutter in the dusty breeze. "No warning at all. It just happens. And everyone's targeting civilians so be aware that this is all happening around you." Zolin made another sound, like an eerie wind rushing through a stone corridor, "that's the sound of a shell. When you hear that you go to the floor. You've only got a fraction of a second, but at least there's some warning. And don't go looking to see where they're coming from, you can't tell because of the range of these bombs." Zolin fastidiously wiped some dirt from his left shoulder.

"You'll learn," said Mass to Jonathan in a deadpan voice, blinking a little because his contact lenses were giving him some trouble, "it's very confusing, though. It really is, even for me. You just can't tell how close they're landing and you can never tell what the intended target is. The only thing you know is that if you hear one shell or mortar, expect more in the same area. Sometimes it lasts for minutes, sometimes for hours and hours."

Suddenly the collection of UN soldiers, followed by Zolin, Mass and Jonathan ducked to the floor of the truck as it screeched to a halt. "Snipers," Zolin said helpfully, "snipers usually fire from about 800 or a thousand yards," Zolin crept upwards, his eyes peeping out from the side of the truck. "You can never see them, they hide well in buildings or bushes. Sarajevo is good for snipers. Look," Zolin eased a petrified Jonathan up by his shoulders, very slowly, "nothing, absolutely nothing to be seen. The sniper's hiding because he thinks we might shoot back. Only we're not going to," Zolin lifted the Betacam camera from another journalist's back and carefully pointed it outwards and set it recording. Without its on-board microphone to capture the sound, the footage would look like a tourist video, Jonathan thought to himself, full of quiet countryside. As the truck got moving again, Zolin put the camera down. "You know, these snipers have pretty sophisticated weapons. A lot of them have laser-sights. They can be accurate up to a range of around two miles."

The driver somehow managed a three-point turn and began

moving back into the shelled out city. "See these streets, they are like New York, all grids," Zolin said, "that means a sniper can position himself at the top end of a street and see down, along and up, right across Sarajevo. That's what a sniper alley is.

"Just like the one in the airport, you remember? The dual carriageway there is the original Sniper Alley. But some of the others are so well known, that you'll see boards or pieces of plastic with paint on warning you that you're crossing one. Don't forget, though, that most are unmarked." Zolin smiled as Jonathan shivered in the heat of his flak jacket.

After a terrifying dash into the hotel, the three of them slumped on the floor, the sound of firing ringing in their ears like booming popcorn.

There was an impressive, improvised editing suite in the hotel and thanks to the UN camera, they had some rushes. Jonathan half-listened to a journalist who was talking loudly to his editor in London on a Satphone as Mass spun through them.

"I can't get out of here. There're 350,000 people who'd like to get out of here, none of them can get out of here," he said more softly.

Eating some cold beans from a tin, Jonathan watched Martin scribble in his pad. He was writing the script he would voice over some of the pictures Zolin had got. Zolin had meanwhile arranged for Jonathan to meet a Muslim contact who was going to give them permission to travel to another part of Sarajevo and then perhaps to Bihac. The situation wasn't looking good, though. For the present time, No one, journalists or UN personnel could get in or out of Sarajevo.

"So how's it going?" asked Sam, a producer on the night shift in London whom he had never met. She was talking to him during the fifteen minutes booked on the satellite feed. Whilst Zolin tweaked the controls on the edit deck, he had two minutes to relay to London how they were.

"I mean, is it pretty hairy down there?" she asked.

"I suppose it is," Jonathan replied, knowing that if he said it was bad, he'd be recalled to London in favour of a more experienced producer or worse still, Mass and he would be recalled and the Corporation would stop covering Bosnia altogether.

"So it's another four minutes we need from your end tomorrow, along with a Martin insert, you know, thirty seconds of Martin saying that later in the programme he'll be talking to x, y and z. We might not use it though so don't get too uptight if we don't. It's just we might be using Harry in Geneva or Don at the UN in New York to talk about the current fighting, alright? And if things continue to be quiet there, you might have to go down to Bihac, okay?"

"Quiet? Down here?" Jonathan had flicked the talkback switch. Communication down the satellite feed line was only one way at a time.

"Well, not quiet, you know. Not quiet," she repeated, "but if it continues to be the case that you can't get any good pictures..."

"Sure. Okay, I'm passing it to Zolin, now," Jonathan replied

"I'm passing it to John," Sam replied

And then the images, looking something like a home video of someone's expedition to East Anglia's fen country began, along with the occasional shots of black screen where London was supposed to insert better pictures from battles that had taken place over the past couple of weeks. Jonathan frowned, looking at his reflection in the black screen.

"Don't worry, too much," said Martin, later. He was sipping gin from a small tumbler as Jonathan read through the Martin's script. "The viewers back home will get a taste of the chaos, that's all we're supposed to give them. Not answers, not history, not chat, just nibbles."

The journey to Bihac began with a misunderstanding. Plans

to advance there were spurred on by information from the UN that Bihac was not so far under attack. Everything was quiet there, they said.

But in London, commentators disputed this. In Sarajevo, people whom Jonathan talked to said the town was under heavy attack. Jonathan and Martin didn't understand this mismatch until a young Belgrade physicist, who was at the hotel to write a book about the war, explained the discrepancy. "You have heard of the famous two-slit experiment—in quantum physics? Yes? Well, Bihac is in two places at the same time, like the photons."

"Bihac," Zolin said as they sat aboard a truck on a perilous road out of Sarajevo, "is the town where Yugoslavia's Second World War resistance movement was born. We're going north-west. In 1942, General Tito began to amass his antifascist force." Zolin continued to talk as they travelled on.

Across the beautiful, dangerous landscape, they made it to the town and Jonathan saw how useful it had been to hear Zolin's history lesson. All the unity he had spoken about bore no resemblance to the town before them. Martin's cynicism had begun to rub off on Jonathan, the hatred of the United Nations, the hatred of the Serbs, the love of the small market traders in the central squares of towns they journeyed through. Martin had described them as little bright stars of enterprise sparkling amongst the deathly black of war, before writing this down in a notebook.

The razed Bihac was a UN-designated "safe area". Jonathan remembered the difference between a UN "safe area" and a UN "safe haven". There was only one of the latter, over in war-torn, Kurdish, Northern Iraq. He recalled the Corporation note to journalists:

I won't bore you with the differences between a safe area and a safe haven—though there is one—as the greater interest is in their similarity—they're not safe.

Martin pulled out a Royal Air Force map of Yugoslavia on his lap and smoothed it out. He delicately rubbed his famous grey flecked moustache. In a series of clear-consonantal phrases he ended a profane description of what he saw out of the windscreen with the words, "fucking assholes."

They were approaching the Bihac pocket, a place 25 miles across at its widest point, a little corner of Bosnia that wasn't part of the Bosnian Serb Republic. The western line of the pocket marked the international frontier between Bosnia and Croatia, though this part of Croatia was under the control of Krajina Serbs. The eastern line was less clear. All they knew about that border was that there was almost continuous fighting there.

"You know what a pocket is?" said Martin, adopting an annoyingly avuncular tone, "well, I do. I have a holiday home in a pocket." Jonathan looked up, rubbing sleep from his eyes. "Pockets aren't enclaves, mind you. You know the difference?"

Jonathan tried to remember whether he had read about the difference in any of the printouts he had mugged up. He looked over towards Zolin for help as firing intensified ahead of them.

"I'm parking the truck over there, we'd better wait for a couple of hours," said Zolin, smiling at Martin.

"An enclave can sit in the middle of a country for centuries, a pocket sits surrounded by the territory of another country during a war."

Jonathan looked out of the truck, at a long line of disheartening women distended from a water stand pipe.

"If you don't understand this, you might as well get back to London, you hear?" said Martin, angrily shouting above the roar of the truck's engine-noise.

"Yes" Jonathan replied, watching the blood-blemished bandages in the queue.

"Have you ever been to Italy? For a holiday or something, when you were little, or a little littler than you are now?"

Jonathan bit his tongue. "No, I haven't been to Italy."

"Well, too bad. If you had you might have had the chance to visit Campione d'Italia, an Italian enclave, a little piece of Italy that's actually in Switzerland. It's an excellent place: gambling, women. Oh, I had the best of times in Lugano. For me, that's what an enclave is all about. Not that Bihac is an enclave, mind, and I don't want you sending cues back to London saying anything like Martin Mass reports from the enclave of Bihac or any such rubbish."

"You know," Zolin interrupted, "this is where modern Yugoslavia began."

"Oh, boo-hoo, spare us the histrionics, Zolin, just keep the gun aimed straight, all right? We'll do the history. Listen," Martin turned to Jonathan, "people will want you to think that the Bihac Pocket and the UN Safe Area is one and the same, so don't confuse them. The Safe Area is a place for refugees to gather, and that's it. The UN has no commitment to Bihac as a whole. You'll hear Bosnians talking about something called the Bihac Safe Area. They quite deliberately want journos to confuse them so that NATO and the UN come out fighting for something that they shouldn't be involved in at all."

"But if the pocket is destroyed, what then?" asked Zolin, his attempts to brush grime from his sports' shirt more fervent and unavailing. "The Safe Area will just fill up with refugees and then the UN will just have an impossible time protecting them all."

"Conceivably, yes. But that's not anyone's concern."

"Except the refugees," Zolin checked, before sinking into silence.

In Bihac, they found they didn't have any way to send pictures back to London. The power out, the population wandering like sleep-walkers, they wandered about trying to get the best shots they could as battery-levels flashed in the viewfinder. All three of them remained quiet much of the time, except to warn each other about a piece of rock that they might be treading on or a white balance procedure they had forgotten. Zolin occasionally went over and chatted to people that were queuing for food or water whilst Martin sometimes swore.

When they realised that they couldn't get any further, Martin said that they had better return to Sarajevo and move towards the South West. For two days they waited for petrol, Martin's eyes red with the pain of unwashed contact lenses.

Jonathan and Zolin slept soundly enough, though. With the sun rising over verdant meadows, they set off, again.

"The BAFTA's ain't up there. They're East not West. Gorazde, Srebrenica. We had a hell of a time," said a reporter from one of the TV wire services. He had just been to Pale, just 20 kilometres south-east of Sarajevo.

"The Serbs are getting impossible. Down in Han Pijesak, there's what they call an "International Press Centre" consisting mainly of Karadzic's daughter, Sonja, stopping anyone from filming anything at all. What's more, she's continually fighting with her father's political adviser which means that she doesn't let him be interviewed by the press. The power's off more or less the whole time and there are no phones, no gin, no anything at the Olympik Hotel. Have you been to Pale, yet?"

"Er, yes, just for a short while, at the beginning," Martin said, lying to the wire service man.

"Oh, then you'll know all about the bloody Zvornik Bridge."

"Yes, it's pretty terrible there."

"I couldn't get any of my provisions in at all."

"So what's the latest from there?" he asked.

"It's all rather funny, really. Karadzic lies in till around one o'clock so the press conferences are never on time."

"I see."

"Well, I've got to see whether I can get a call through to London. Martin? I'll see you down here in about half an hour? Alright?" Jonathan asked, feeling woozy and wanting to go down to the discotheque and sleep.

Martin didn't answer preferring to stare vacantly at a bottle of whisky that a newly arrived journalist had unpacked.

Jonathan walked along the corridor, the sound of his shoes banging across the floor like in a hospital. The Satellite Phone had been recharged on electricity that the hotel had had for the morning, so he didn't need to swap batteries and tinker with screwdrivers, which is what happened the last time he had to use it.

"Hello?"

"Sarajevo? Mass, Martin Mass?"

"I'm producing down here. It's me, Jonathan."

"How's it going? We've heard the peace negotiations are going quite well."

"You mean in Geneva?"

"Yeah, I suppose so. Anyway, the boss isn't in. But he was muttering something about getting another producer down there to take over from you. Are you not getting on with Mass too well?"

"He's alright, I mean it's okay. Everything's okay. It's fine, really fine."

"Well, that's not the impression back here. Apparently, he's been complaining that the boss has dispatched a real greenie."

"I see," Jonathan, replied, a volley of sniper fire sounding outside.

"You not too keen on guns?" the producer at the other end joked. Jonathan speculated on how far his star had fallen in the office. The voice on the other end of the telephone didn't seem to reflect his position as Temporary Assistant Editor.

"Well, look I'll tell the boss you rang."

It was the first phone-conversation with London he had had in which he hadn't cut them off first. Slowly returning to the bar area, he saw Martin chatting with what looked like another reporter.

Jonathan approached them and realised that Martin wasn't going to introduce him. "Hi," he said, trying to be friendly. "Look, Martin, it seems the boss wasn't around."

"Yeah, I know that. That's because you're going home. Meet Peter, your replacement."

Peter, his seriousness flashing in guile-less eyes, spoke up. "Hello, I'm a trainee. The boss told me to tell you that you've been doing sterling work down here. Now, it's time to give some others a chance. I've just graduated, you see, and, well, this looks like the best kind of experience there is, what with working for Marty and everything."

"I see," Jonathan rolled his eyes leftwards. "Well, it'll probably be a few days before I can actually get out, what with the flights and everything. How did you get in?"

"No, that's all sorted out. Don't worry, we've arranged a UN car and everything," Peter said with his constant look of concern.

"You're in luck," said Martin.

"I see."

At that, Martin and Peter turned to face each other and began chatting about guns and artillery. "That one's bloody good, isn't it?" and "the RK 20 or RK 26 is the one. Blam! Blam! You know? I tested a real sucker out. But you've got to admire the Kalashnikov, I mean, these things are like fucking Leicas, built to last." As they spoke, the sound of shelling got sluggishly louder.

There was a chill in the office when Jonathan returned. He could feel it in the sweat on his shirt. For the first hour, he tapped randomly at his keyboard, his mind blank. He was surprised to be pleased about wearing properly cleaned clothes. The previous evening, he had felt satisfied and happy at the comforting accompaniment of police sirens. Echoes of past shelling made everything feel nice and safe.

Jonathan had been in a place that he hadn't understood before and knew even less about on his return. He now thought not about any specific Yugoslav faction nor about Martin Mass. Instead, he thought more about the emphasis and judgement instilled in Corporation journalists. He recalled Patrice, the reporter now in Rwanda. He remembered Clark arguing with Mass about the genocide there that had killed ten times as many people in the past six months as in the entire Yugoslav war. He pondered on whether he would have come back from Africa with the same ignorance as he did on his return from Sarajevo.

A face he didn't recognise winked at him. He was in the

middle of a long conversation with Marsh, the duty planning editor, trying to persuade him about something. "Do you want any coffee?" he asked Jonathan, presumably unaware of the battle he was in for at the coffee bar downstairs.

"I'll come down with you," Jonathan replied, noticing that Julia and the boss were still in conference.

"Hi," said Marsh, "great work, great work over there. Well done."

Jonathan smiled back and followed the newcomer out of the newsroom.

"He's awful, that guy, Marsh," the new face said.

"Take care. I could be on his side. Duty planning editors are important people, you know," Jonathan advised.

"Yes, of course. You're the Assistant Editor, after all."

"When did you join the team?" Jonathan asked, opening a pair of swing doors.

"Last week. I'm just a trainee. But, Christ, they haven't told me much. They just sent me to Thorp nuclear power station and told me to get on with it."

Jonathan nodded. They were now in the queue and the newcomer had lowered his volume.

"You know, the kind of stuff I dug up was unbelievable. I mean there's more radioactivity that comes from Sellafield then anywhere else on Earth. The Irish Sea is bloody well the most radioactive sea in the world. It's worse than Chernobyl."

"Well, looks like you got a good story then."

"No, Marsh says it's all old stuff. I mean it is all old stuff. It's all been known for ages. He says it isn't news. He wants me to do a piece about, something to do with different privatisation strategies."

"I'll have a word with him," Jonathan said, as they carried out steaming polystyrene cups up the stairs.

Sellafield is the largest source of radioactive discharge in the world and as a result the Irish Sea is the most radioactive sea in the world.

There is no commercial demand for Thorp's products Uranium and Plutonium. THORP can produce up to 5.5 tonnes of plutonium a year. A nuclear weapon can be made using less than 10kg.

Sellafield was the site of the western world's worst radioactive leak in 1957, when it was known as Windscale.

Childhood leukaemia is 14 times the national average; Skin cancer is rising 50% faster than in the rest of Britain. Multiple myeloma, a bone cancer linked with Plutonium exposure, is increasing at the same rate as it did in Hiroshima and Nagasaki. Cumbria has the highest rate of acute lymphoblastic leukaemia in England and Wales. The overall cancer rate for retired Sellafield workers is 30% more than the national average.

Jonathan read the sheet he had given him and took it in to the boss' office, where Julia was sitting, writing in a notebook.

"Hi, Julia, how are you," he said, noticing that Julia had swapped her all black dress-code with a fuschia livery.

"Fine, things alright?" she said, slanting her head and wrinkling her mouth.

"Yeah, fine."

"They say it takes a few months before you're back to normal," the boss said to Jonathan from behind his desk. "Well," he turned to Julia, "get the calls done then, come on, toute de suite, Julia."

"Now, where were we?" the boss looked up to Jonathan.

Julia shut the door and smiled at him through the window to the office.

"Yes, I just wanted to say that the coverage from Bosnia was wonderful. You and Martin really did some great things, in the circumstances. I hope you didn't think we were dumping you when you got your orders to come home. I mean, you understand that we were trying to give some others a chance, you know," the boss was talking to Jonathan while tapping quickly at his keyboard. "Damn! Damn computer. Hang on a second, have a beer, there are some in the fridge, if you want."

"No that's fine. A bit early for that," he laughed, nervously.

"So, any ideas for a piece? I mean, you could take some time off if you really wanted. But, it's just we're pretty short of staff, at the moment."

"Well, there were a couple of things. Firstly, I noticed you're doing some stuff on Thorp."

"Oh yes, the new guy, what's his name? What about it?"

"Well, I hear Marsh isn't giving him much leeway."

"Oh, Marsh. Yes, he's a bloody ass, sometimes. I'll tell him. Yeah, the new guy seems quite bright," the boss, unscrewed a miniature whisky bottle and began swigging it down, "don't worry I'll tell Marsh what to do. I guess he wants to take the new guy through it slowly."

Pleased at what the boss had said, Jonathan asked him what he had in mind for him.

"Well, I heard from Martin you were interested in Africa."

"Well, not interested, particularly. I mean, I'm not sure I want to go there so soon. All I was saying to Martin was that a lot of the foreign journalists seem on the way there." He began to wonder about how Martin had such good communication with London, all the way down in the hell of Sarajevo's shadowy Holiday Inn.

"Look, I'll be straight with you," the boss, rubbed his temples, blinked his left eye forty times or so and began typing again.

During the interlude, Jonathan looked at the new additions to the boss's noticeboard. There was a photograph of one of the female presenters, modelling some outfits for a magazine, a picture of the editor himself beside a Boeing 747, a stapled booklet entitled "Aspirational Management Quotations", a recipe for guacamole, a postcard of Los Angeles' Hollywood sign.

The desk was coated in memos, more booklets, charts of viewing figures, loose leaf squared paper sprayed with numbers, budget pie charts and holiday snaps. Faxed pages of viewers' comments and presenters' silk ties drooped over one side, down onto an aluminium carpet of beer-cans. Across this map of the boss' life was a long squiggle of red wine splashed in the morning's debriefing session.

"What was I saying? Yes, there's a piece on housing, a new survey about homelessness. Usual, human-interest-y type operation. Not too taxing. Just the thing after what you've been through. Why don't you work on that for Friday morning's programme. Just a London-based thing, that should get you back into the swing of boring home news reporting. Alright?" the boss signalled with a vertical hand that the conversation was over just as his liquor-damaged phone began to squeak.

As Jonathan arose, Marsh walked in to see the boss. "I've said that you can do a quick piece on the V-Chip, if that's okay," he said, half talking to Jonathan, half talking to the boss.

"Go ahead," said the boss, "just a short piece. That'll still give you time to start the homes' thing tomorrow, that fine?"

Jonathan nodded and left the newsroom, intending to go to the coffee-bar. Instead, he began walking over to News Information, dodging a group of presenters running off to an early lunch. It seemed like a long time since he had been at TV Centre during the day and the place looked more friendly than he remembered it at night. The man in motorcycle gear had a receiver cupped to each ear when he arrived at News Information. There were groups of three or four red flashes on the telephone at his side. He made a face as if to say wait in line as Jonathan swung the doors open and saw three or four researchers, a producer and a sports' presenter in the queue, looking at their watches.

When each had been attended to and the phones had been put on hold, half an hour later, the man confided in Jonathan that he was leaving the Corporation. "This job is getting ridiculous. I've had it. How am I suppose to be providing information for the whole of the Corporation, all on my own?"

Jonathan shrugged his shoulders and began to help him hunt down the cuttings he needed on the V-Chip, an electronic device that when attached to a television-set could block out certain programmes.

The apparatus was soon going be fitted in every new American television set over thirteen inches. The aim was to transfer control over children's viewing to parents. "Don't know why smaller TVs don't need V-chips," said the News Information researcher, "my kid's got a small telly in his bedroom. Kids don't have big sets."

"Good point," said Jonathan, scribbling down a note, "I'll look into that. Oh, and good luck with whatever you do after this." The researcher glumly looked up, a fragment of thanks in his eyes.

"A bloody good idea, that V-Chip is," said the day editor, Sheila, when she saw Jonathan sit down in the newsroom with a couple of A3 sheets on the subject. "There's too much violence and something like this will stop all these kids going out and joyriding and thinking the world is one big gangster film." Others around the table murmured their agreement.

Jonathan remained silent and went about putting a package together that put the story in a very different light. Half way through his telephone call-list, Sheila said to him that the V-Chip piece would be a graphic followed by a live rather than a complete video package. Martin Mass was disturbing Jonathan's plans, from another country. He had filed an extra piece from Bosnia.

"Sorry about that, darling. I was a bit worried anyway. I mean how are you going to illustrate the kind of things children shouldn't be watching? I think the one or the six will do a package but it's a bit early for us. I mean, all the harrowing images and stuff over the nation's breakfast tables. I suppose the piece can get hairier as we pass the 9.30pm watershed."

Presenter: Right, well, aren't we watching a lot of television then, as those graphics show, I mean. So, professor, you're from America, you must have watched your average ten hours a day when growing up: it didn't affect you too much did it?

Professor: Well, I didn't really come here to discuss the effect on myself. What I came on to say was that the introduction of the V-Chip and this kind of electronic technology is deeply ironic. The news media consistently distort the news in America and I believe, here in the United Kingdom. If you look at the stories you're covering today, say the Bosnia piece, no inkling of who is supplying the arms to each side is given to your viewers. More than that, all of the coverage that the mass media has given to the war would bewilder any viewer..."

Presenter: Well, the world is quite a bewildering place isn't it?

Professor: That's not the point. Look, part of my thesis is that the role of news programmes like yours is to inculcate values, beliefs and codes of behaviour that will integrate your audience into institutional structures...

Presenter: Sorry to interrupt, er.

Professor: Look, as an eminent Nobel laureate has said, in a world of concentrated wealth and major class interest, a programme like yours is part of the systematic propaganda that...

Presenter: Sorry, to interrupt, but on the V-Chip, professor. Do you argue that empowering parents with a means of controlling their viewing is wrong then?

Professor: Look, it's already controlled. Besides, it's not a case of children seeing too much, it's a case of all of us seeing too little. Surely, the point is that today, a hundred thousand people will be murdered in Western Africa because of a legacy of colonialism, the wielding of power by transnational corporations and the vested interests. More than 15 million adults aged 20 to 64 are dying every year, just because of poverty. Look at today's news, one global proprietor is telling your Corporation it can't broadcast what it wants because he owns the satellites. Even your Corporation's transmission equipment is now privatised. How can you give impartial news when you're allied to extremist wing international news organisations?

Presenter: I'll have to stop you there, professor. Oh, sorry, we've got a little more time. So, in one sentence, to sum up, what....

Professor: As the poet, Milton, said...

Presenter: Oh, sorry, we have to move on after all. Thank you very much indeed for coming in, Professor. One thing's for sure, though, this debate is going to run and run. And for those interested in new technology, tune in later tonight at seven-thirty when Timothy Armour will be looking at the water companies and their new environmental drive to meter their customers. Over to you Sarah for the Sports...

Jonathan woke up slightly later on Friday morning because of a late night at TV Centre. He had been editing the piece about homelessness until three o'clock in the morning.

Most of his Thursday had been consumed in Cardboard City, an underground roundabout a stone's throw from the headquarters of a rival, private television station. Jonathan had been there, once.

Last time around, he had said to himself that he would never go near this place again. He had feared just crossing into the Waterloo area. But, unexpectedly, he felt pleasantly moved by the experience, sad only to see how so much of what he had known had become erased. The concrete jungle gave way to a glass terminal for trains to Europe.

The bullring was the same, though, even down to the graffiti. It was when he tried to get permission for filming that he realised how different things were now. There was no-one he knew, of course, even though he had harboured a hope of seeing some of the people from before. When he called out, someone threw a bottle at him. His cameraperson, Leonard, aimed his camera only to hear shrieks and cries. "How would you like it if someone pointed a camera around your home?" someone hollered fiercely. When he had slept there, he was never able to summon up anger.

Eventually, a man came out and appeared to want to talk.

"What are you here for?" he asked at a distance of twenty metres. "You come to do us down again?"

"No, no, we're not," Jonathan shouted back.

"Last time you came down here, you shitted on us. The police came to check on us. You going to fucking do that again? Because, we'll have you!"

The man came closer to them and Jonathan felt a shiver of recognition run up his spine. He couldn't place him. Slowly, the man came up and indicated to a group of four younger boys behind him to come out from behind a pillar.

All through the ensuing conversation, Jonathan strained to remember. The man he thought he recognised even came up to him after the dimming November light had halted filming. "I'll see you then," he said.

Jonathan looked back as he and Leonard walked up the stairs and out of the ring. He saw a bonfire of chairs and the makeshift houses, built from plastic sheeting and fruit boxes, cast wavering shadows.

The camera-person, Leonard, was a Corporation old-timer. He had worked as a sound-man in the nineteen-sixties and switched to camera-work when sound-men were no longer needed. He had been to Vietnam and Cambodia during their wars with America, the reporters he had worked with now anchormen on the main Corporation news-programmes. About fifty-seven, he looked as if he was in his forties despite his snow white short hair and the dark rings under his eyes. He had been surprised when Jonathan asked whether he wanted to go for a cup of coffee before they went to shoot the PTC.

"Thanks, that would be lovely," he said as they climbed the stairs to Hungerford Bridge. "I thought you looked rather unsteady. You alright?"

"What? Oh, yes, fine. Well, I'll have to be if I'm to cut this by tomorrow morning."

"It's just that not many producers do that anymore. Most of them are so uptight that all they want to do is race back to TV Centre and leave the night-team to get on with it. How long have you been working here?"

"Nearly a year," Jonathan replied, watching office-workers tumble down from the Strand. "I was in Bosnia."

When they reached a café, they sat down and Leonard asked about Yugoslavia. "How was that? Some of my friends say it was great, a real laugh a minute," he smiled.

"Well, there were some problems between Martin Mass and me."

"He's a right one, I worked with him in El Salvador. Completely mad, like a child with his obsession with guns and everything." Leonard gulped down his coffee.

"I'm not too happy, actually, with the whole thing."

"What do you mean?" Leonard asked, putting down the camera he had prematurely picked up off the café floor. "Oh, you mean the Corporation and all that. I'm not surprised. I'm only waiting to retire so I can get my pension, now. I don't think it's much fun any more. Everyone's too much in a rush. No-one thinks much about the actual quality of the programme. Some of these new people straight out of journalism school, they come here as producers and think they know it all when in fact they know nothing about it, I mean about production and stuff. They don't believe in quality, the quality of the shots, the lighting, the sound."

"It's not so much that. I mean, I know production values are important. It's just," Jonathan looked out at the stream of commuters, "we're not giving an accurate impression of events. Half the time, I'm not sure I have an accurate impression of events."

Leonard laughed and nodded, as if to say he couldn't care less about what they were talking about. "Come on, better get the PTC down. I want to be early enough to go to a leaving party."

"Right, let's go," Jonathan lifted up the heavy tripod and followed him out to the car. The PTC was to be outside the Houses of Parliament and he was already nervous about it.

Leonard told Jonathan not to worry and, with his calm coaxing voice, managed to get a piece outside the House of Commons which was usable. It took about twenty takes for Jonathan to sound fluent with the four sentences he had memorised.

It was only when they were on their way to TV Centre that Jonathan realised he was going to have to involve the banking system in his piece. It was private banks' economic strategy that was dictating government expenditure on house-building and Jonathan wanted it to be in his package. Leonard tuned the radio while Jonathan scribbled a script in his notepad. The traffic was bad and it was dark when they arrived back at TV Centre.

Jonathan's assigned picture editor, Harriet, had had a bad day with News Resources. When Jonathan came in with the rushes, she took them and slammed them on the counter next to her editing machines, almost in tears. But, just a couple of hours into the editing, she started to show some commitment to the piece, advising Jonathan to re-voice some parts of the package to give it extra strength. When they had made the final cut and fixed the voice-tracks, the piece stood at five minutes and library footage was piled knee-high in the editing suite.

The package Jonathan put together was filled as much with statistics as it was by the stories he had filmed. Over the previous decade and a half, 6,000 people a week had become homeless. On the day of transmission, the estimated total number of homeless was 5 million, half of them children.

It was only in the morning as Jonathan watched the Good Morning, Britain broadcast, that he realised the homelessness package had been spiked. It was about eleven when the boss rang him up.

"What the fuck do you think that piece was?" he shouted, slurring his last letter. "You're out, that's why I'm calling you. That's why." There was a pause. "I'm sorry," he said more quietly, "but we really don't have time for that kind of biased news. If you want to make ideological statements go and make documentaries or better still go and make gritty, realist films. I thought we had it straight, that you'd do a piece about the new homeless survey. Just the statistics, a bit of comment with one party saying it's terrible and one party saying it was trying to do its best. I didn't want anything about your views or the organisations you got hold of's views, none of that. It's just not for our audience. My managers would have had a fit if that piece had gone out what with it being just before the final details of our alliance with Globe Corporation are being seen to. God, if they'd seen this nonsense, I mean, you bloody mention the names of banks we're doing deals with...it's all fucking irrelevant...it's like you're just making digs at people. I thought that after Bosnia, you'd have learnt something and then you turn in an amateurish load of twaddle. You just haven't been professional. It's what Martin said, your attitude seems to be 'turn everything upside down and then you've got a good piece.' Well, we've done quite well, here, you know, doing things the way we do things. We have award-winning coverage, you know what that means? Award-winning."

Epilogue

Well, first of all I want to thank the judges. It's the third time I've won this award but that doesn't mean that I don't value it. I'd like you all to give a round of applause to the other three contenders.

(applause)

It's also a privilege to be in such company. I don't want to say too much except to thank all the backroom boys. When I say the words Martin Mass, Corporation News, Sarajevo, it's not just me. Television is about teamwork and that's why I want to thank the editors, producers, managers and cameramen, everyone, the makeup departments, even the staff at the Corporation Canteen.

(laughs)

Without them I couldn't have done what I've done in my life. The war in Yugoslavia was a hell of a place to cover, the worst conflict in Europe since the second world war. I found it tough and gruelling, and that's coming from someone who's reported from every major war-zone for the past twenty years. It was tough but it was worth it and this award is the cherry on the cake. It shows that British broadcasting is still the best in the world. When we report about home and abroad, the world listens to us, for our impartiality, our professionalism, our plain good sense. I want to just finish by saying to people tonight that we in the press have a duty to protect the freedoms and liberties that men and women in this country have fought for over centuries. If something is rotten in this country or any other country it's our duty to root it out and show it for what it is. I'm sure my colleagues would agree with me when I say that the great British public has a right to be informed about what is happening in the world. It is our duty to provide the information. And that's what we have done and will continue to do.

Only if we keep putting out programmes like the ones I and many others have worked for will the public have the continued opportunity to be informed.

We are it for most people. There's no other medium where more people get their information from. And that's why all of us here today have a heavy responsibility as we work in this wonderful industry. It is we who keep this country free of tyranny. So let us never shirk our heavy responsibility. Thank you, once again.

"It's a London I recognise."—Larry Adler
"Shows great promise."—Saul Bellow
"Uplifting, after all."—Charles Bukowski
"A dark tale from London."—Angela Carter
"A great book."—Johnny Cash
"A blistering indictment."—Spalding Gray
"An account of saddest England."—Octavio Paz
"A devastating debut."—George Plimpton
"Thatcherism dissected."—Joe Strummer

The Author

Afshin Rattansi was born in Cambridge, England in 1968. He has lived in Princeton and Los Angeles in the U.S., Vancouver in Canada, Caracas in Venezuela, Dubai in the U.A.E and Havana, Cuba as well as London in England.

After the hurricanes of the nineteen-eighties, he worked on environmental and geopolitical risk for Lloyd's of London.

He has written on literature, politics, fashion, business and current affairs for The Guardian, New Statesman and Society, Plays and Players, The Oldie, Gulf News and many other publications. Most of his life has been spent in journalism: producing programmes for Channel 4 and BBC News and BBC Radio 4's "Today" programme in the UK. More recently, he has worked on award-winning investigative programmes for the Arabic language station, Al Jazeera.

He also helped launch the world's first 24-hour, developing nation, English-language satellite television news network, based in the Middle East. He was its editor between 1999 and 2001.

In 2002, he won a Sony award for his outstanding contribution to international media and journalism.